CLARKESWORLD

YEAR TWELVE - VOLUME ONE

EDITED BY NEIL CLARKE & SEAN WALLACE

CLARKESWORLD: YEAR TWELVE VOLUME ONE

Copyright © 2021 by Neil Clarke.
Cover art: "Jungleman" copyright © 2009 by Arthur Haas.

Wyrm Publishing
www.wyrmpublishing.com

Publisher's Note:
No portion of this book may be reproduced by any means, mechanical, electronic, or otherwise, without first obtaining the permission of the copyright holder.

All stories are copyrighted to their respective authors and translators and used here with their permission.

All stories translated from Chinese were translated and published in cooperation with Storycom International.

For more information, contact Wyrm Publishing:
wyrmpublishing@gmail.com

ISBN: 978-1-64236-089-9 (trade paperback)
ISBN: 978-1-64236-088-2 (ebook)

Visit Clarkesworld Magazine at:
clarkesworldmagazine.com

TABLE OF CONTENTS

INTRODUCTION

NEIL CLARKE

Twelve. A dozen. High noon. The number of months in a year. A traditional twelfth anniversary gift is linen or silk, neither of which seem particularly appropriate for *Clarkesworld Magazine*'s anniversary. Instead, we'll mark this as we always do, with two volumes of paper or pixels encompassing all the stories we've published in a year.

This volume includes all the original fiction published in *Clarkesworld* from October 2017 through March 2018, issues 133-138. That's twenty-nine stories totalling just over one hundred and ninety-eight thousand words. These stories represent authors from nine countries and include five translations from two languages (Chinese and Italian). We are particularly pleased to be able to bring more of the wider world of science fiction to our readers.

While we're proud of all the stories contained herein, it's always a special pleasure to see a work we've published gain recognition from the larger community. Of particular note this time is "Umbernight" by Carolyn Ives Gilman. This story was a finalist for both the Theodore A. Sturgeon Memorial and Locus Awards, and appeared in two "year's best" anthologies.

As part of our annual poll, the magazine's readers singled out "Umbernight", "Sour Milk Girls" by Erin Roberts, and "Who Won the Battle of Arsia Mons?" by Sue Burke as among their favorites. I wonder which stories will speak the most to you?

Neil Clarke
August 2021

THE LAST BOAT-BUILDER IN BALLYVOLOON

FINBARR O'REILLY

> "There are of a certainty mightier creatures, and the lake hides what neither net nor fine can take."
> —William Butler Yeats, *The Celtic Twilight*

The first time I met Más, he was sitting on the quayside in Ballyvoloon, carving a nightmare from a piece of linden. Next to him on the granite blocks that capped the seawall lay a man's weatherproof jacket and hat, in electric pink. The words "petro-safe" were pin-striped across them in broad white letters, as if a spell that would protect him from the mechanical monster he whittled.

Short of smoking a pipe, Más looked every inch a nineteenth-century whaler. Veined cheeks burned and burnished by sun and wind to a deep cherry gloss, thick gray hair matted and flattened from his souwester and whiskers stiff enough with salt to resist the autumnal breeze blowing in from the harbor mouth.

I had arrived in Ballyvoloon early on a Friday morning. My pilot would not fly till Monday, so I spent the weekend walking the town. Its two main streets, or "beaches" as the locals called them, ran east and west of a concrete, T-shaped pier.

It was near the bottom of the 'T' that Más set out his pitch every day, facing the water, but sheltered by thousands of tonnes of rock and concrete.

Ballyvoloon was a town best approached from the sea. The faded postcards on sale along the beachfront showed it from that rare perspective. Snapped from the soaring pleasure decks of ocean-going liners long scrapped or sunk, ribbons of harlequin houses rose from coruscant waters, split by the immense neo-Gothic cathedral that crowns the town. Nowadays, the fret-sawn fascias of pastel shopfronts shed lazy flakes of paint into the broad streets and squares below. It has faded, but there is grandeur there still.

Between the town's rambling railway station and my hotel, I had passed a dozen or more artists, their wares tied to the railings of the waterside promenade, or propped on large boards secured to lampposts, but none dressed like Más. Nor did any carve like him.

"That looks realistic," I said, my heart pounding, as he snicked delicate curls of blond wood from the block with a thick-spined blade.

"There's not much point sugarcoating them," he said, his voice starting as a matter-of-fact drawl, but ending in the singsong accent of the locals.

"How long have you been a sculptor?" I asked.

"I'm not a sculptor. This is just something to occupy the hands."

"The devil's playthings, eh?"

He stopped carving and looked up at me through muddy green eyes.

"Something like that."

Más lowered the squid he was working on and cast around in the pocket of his jacket. He removed three of the monsters, perfectly carved, but in different sizes and woods, one stained black and polished. The colors seemed to give each one slightly different intents, but none was reassuring.

Other artists carved or drew or painted the squid, but they had smoothed out the lines, removed the barbs, the beaks, gave the things doe-eyes and even smiles and made them suitable to sit atop a child's bedclothes or a living room bookshelf.

Más did the opposite. He made the horrific more horrifying. He made warm, once-living wood look like the doubly dead, glossy plastic of the squids. These were not the creatures we had released, but their more deadly and cunning offspring.

I hid my excitement as well as I could.

"Sixty for one or one hundred for a pair," he said.

Más let the moment stretch until the sheer discomfort of it drove me to buy.

His mood brightened and he immediately began packing up his belongings. I had clearly overpaid and he could afford to call it a day.

"See you so," he said, cheerfully and sauntered off into the town.

Once I was back at the hotel, I unwrapped the parcel and inspected the sculptures, to confirm my suspicions.

The other artists may have outsold Más's squid six or seven times, but he was the only of them who had seen a real one.

> "Twelve years after the squid were introduced, the west coast of Europe endured a number of strange phenomena. Firstly, the local gull population bloomed. The government and the squids' manufacturer at the time said it was a sign of fish stocks returning to normal, that it was evidence the squid were successful in their mission.
>
> "Local crab numbers also exploded, to the point that water inlets at a couple of coastal power stations were blocked. The company linked this to the increased gull activity, increasing the amount of food falling to the seafloor."
>
> —Hawes, J. *How We Lost the Atlantic,* p32

The first flight was late in the afternoon, a couple of hours before sunset. This would give me the best chance of spotting things in the water, as it was still bright enough to see and anything poking above the surface would cast a longer shadow.

The pilot, a taciturn, bearded fellow in his sixties called Perrott, flicked switches and toggles as he went through what passed for a safety briefing.

"If we ditch, it will take about fifteen minutes for the helo to reach us from the airport. The suits will at least make that wait comfortable, assuming, you know . . . "

We both wore survival suits of neon-pink non-petro, covering everything but hands and heads. His was molded to his frame and visibly worn on the elbows and the seat of his pants. Mine squeaked when I walked and still smelled of tart, oleophobic soy.

"Yes. I know," I said, as reassuringly as I could manage.

As he tapped dials and entered numbers on a clipboard, I thought of my first flight over water.

My sea training was in Wales, where an ancient, ex-RNLI helicopter dropped me about half a mile from shore. It was maybe twenty-five feet to the water, but the fall was enough to knock the breath out of me. The crew made sure I was still kicking and moved back over land. The idea was to get me to panic, I suppose. They needn't have worried. The helicopter was away for a total of eight minutes and if my heart could have climbed my gullet to escape my chest, it would have.

After they pulled me back up, I asked the winchman how I had done.

"No worse than most," he shouted.

He took a flashbang grenade from a box under the seat, pulled the pin, and dropped it out the open door. He counted down from four on his fingers. Over the roar of the rotors, I heard neither splash nor detonation. The winchman made sure I was harnessed, then pointed out the door and down.

A couple of miles away, I could see three or four squid making for a spot directly beneath us, all of them moving so fast they left a wake.

He gave me a torturer's grin.

"Better than some."

> "We seen them first, the slicks. That's what they looked like in the pictures, like some tanker or bulker had washed her tanks. But as we got close we could see it was miles and miles of chopped up fish. And the smell! That's what the locals still call that summer—the big stink.
>
> "When we got back we found out the squid had become more . . . hungry, I suppose, and instead of pulling the bits of plastic out of the water, they started pulling 'em out of the fish. Sure we had been eating that fish for years and it never did us any harm."
>
> —Trevor Cunniffe, trawlerman, in an interview for *Turn Your Back to the Waves*, an RTÉ radio documentary marking fifty years since the squids' introduction

After two days of fruitless flights, I was grounded by fog. Late in the afternoon, I went to a pub. I sat at the long side of the L-shaped bar, inhaling the fug of old beer and new urinal cakes.

The signage, painted in gold leaf on the large windows, had faded and peeled, so I asked a patron what the place was called. "Tom's" was the only reply, offering no clue if this was the original name of the pub or the latest owner.

Between the bottles shelved on the large mirror behind the bar, I saw the figure of a man in a candy-striped pink jacket through the rippled privacy glass of the door. It opened and Más walked in. He gently closed it behind him and moved to a spot at the end of the bar. He kept his head down, but couldn't escape recognizing some regulars and nodded a salute to them.

Emboldened by alcohol, I raised my drink.

"How is the water today?" I asked.

The barmaid gave me a look as if to ask what I was doing engaging a local sot, but I smiled at her for long enough that she wandered off, reassured or just bored at my insincerity.

"About the same," said Más. "Visibility's not very good."

"No," I said. "That's why I'm in here. No flights today."

"Are you off home then," Más asked.

I interpreted the question as an invitation and walked over to take the stool next to him.

"Not quite," I said. "Will you have a drink?"

"I will," he said. "So, what has you in town?"

At first, Más didn't seem too bothered when I explained who I worked for, or at least he didn't ask the usual questions or put forward the usual conspiracy theories about the squid.

"A job's a job, I suppose."

His eyes wrinkled, amused at a joke hidden to me. "So do ye all have jobs in England, then?"

Ireland had been on universal income for the better part of two decades. It was hard to see how people like Más would have survived otherwise.

"No, not by a long chalk. The only reason I got this one is I wasn't afraid to cross the sea in a plane."

"More fool you."

"You have to die of something, I told them. And it was quite exciting, in the end."

As the light faded, the mid-afternoon drinkers gave way to a younger, louder crowd, but Más and I still sat, talking.

I described the huge reservoir near where I lived in Rutland, where people could still swim and sail and fish, and how everyone worried that the squid would somehow reach it, denying us access, like Superior or the Caspian.

He asked me what on Earth would make me leave such a place.

"I wanted to see the world. I needed a job," I said.

He laughed. "Those used to be the reasons people joined the Navy."

Perrott's plane was old, but well serviced. It started first time and once we finished our climb, the engine settled into a bagpipe-like drone.

We crossed the last headland and the cheerful baize below, veined in drystone walls, gave way to gray waves, maned in white.

He radioed the Cork tower to tell them we were now over open water and that the rescue team was on formal standby.

He adjusted the trim of the plane to a point where he was happy to let the thing fly itself and joined me in scanning the waters below.

It was less than half an hour, until his pilot's eye spotted it. Perrott took the controls again and banked to give me a better view. I let the video camera run, while I used the zoom lens to snap any identifying features.

From the size of the blurred shape rippling just beneath the surface, I could tell it was old, seventh or eighth generation, perhaps, but I really wanted a more detailed look.

I told Perrott I would like to make another pass.

"If only we had a bomb, eh?" he said. Sooner or later, everyone suggests it.

"We tried that," I said.

"Oh yeah?"

Perrott had signed a non-disclosure agreement before the flight. It didn't matter what I told him. Most of it was already on the Internet, in any case.

"Yes. First they bombed an oil platform in the Gulf of Mexico and opened up its wellhead. Miles from shore, so any oil that escaped would be eaten by the squid or burned in the fire."

Hundreds of thousands of the things had come, enough that you could see the black stain spread on satellite images. I had only watched the video. I couldn't imagine how chilling it had been to observe it happen live.

"Then the Americans dropped three of the biggest non-nukes they've got on them."

"It didn't work, then?"

"No. Any squid more than a dozen feet or so below the surface were protected by the water. We vaporized maybe half of them. After that they stayed deep, mostly."

I didn't tell Perrott about the Mississippi and how the squid had retaliated. Let him read that on the Internet too.

"Well, they may be mindless, but they're not stupid," he said.

We flew on until the light failed, but, as if it had heard him, the beast did not reappear.

> "It would be wrong to think of the squid as a failure of technology. The technology worked, from the plastic filtration, to the self-replication and algorithmic learning.
>
> "Also do not forget that they succeeded in their original purpose—they did clean up the waters and they did save fish stocks from extinction.
>
> "The failure, if you can truly call it that, is ours. We failed to see that life, even created life, will never behave exactly as we intend.
>
> "The failure was not in the squids' technology, or in their execution. It was in our imagination."
>
> —From the inaugural address of Ireland's last president, Francis Robinson

A basket of chips and fried 'goujons' of catfish had appeared in front of us, gratis. I dived in, sucking sea salt and smoky, charred fish skin from my fingertips. Más looked over the bar into the middle distance.

"Don't tell me you don't like fish," I said. "That would be too funny."

"That's not real fish."

Más had progressed to whiskey and a bitter humor sharpened his tongue.

"It tastes pretty real," I said. I had heard all the scare stories about fish farming.

He held up a calloused hand, as if an orator or bard about to recite. The other was clenched, to punctuate his thoughts.

"Why is it, do you think, that we are trying to replicate the things we used to have?

"Like, if most people can still eat 'fish,' or swim in caged bloody lidos, or if cargo comes by airship or whatever, then the more normal it becomes. And it shouldn't be bloody normal. It's not normal."

The barmaid rolled her eyes. Clearly, she had heard the rant before.

I told him I agreed with the swimming bit inasmuch as I wouldn't personally miss it terribly if I could never do it again, but that farmed fish didn't bother me and that I thought most people never considered where their goods came from, even before the squid.

Disappointment, whether at me or the world, wilted in his face before he let the whiskey soften him again. His shoulders lowered, his hands relaxed and the melody of his voice reasserted itself.

"When I was a boy, my father once told me a story about trying to grow trees in space."

I coughed mid-chew and struggled to dislodge a crumb of batter from my throat. With tears in my eyes, I waved him on. I don't know why, but it amused me to hear an old salt like Más talk about orbital horticulture.

"Well, these guys on Spacelab or wherever, they tried growing them in perfect conditions, perfect nutrients, perfect light, even artificial gravity. They would all shoot straight up, then keel over and die. Every tree seed they planted—pine, ash, oak, cypress—they all died. Nobody could figure out what was wrong. Everything a plant could need was provided, perfectly measured. These were the best cared for plants in the world."

"In the solar system," I ribbed him.

"Right. In the solar system. Except for one thing. Do you know what was missing?

"No. Tell me."

"A breeze. Trees develop the strength, the woody cells, to support their weight by resisting the blow of the wind. Without it, they falter and sicken."

I didn't really get his point and told him so.

"You can't sharpen a blade without friction. You can't strengthen a man, or a civilization, without struggle. Airships and swimming pools and virtual bloody sailing. It's all bollocks. We should be hauling these things out of the water, like they said we would."

He gestured through the window of the bar to the gray bulk of the cathedral looming in the fog.

"There was a reason Jesus was a fisherman," said Más, as if a closing statement. I didn't know what to say to that.

The barmaid leaned over the bar to clear the empty baskets.

"Jesus was a carpenter, Más," she said.

> "Six sea scouts, aged eleven to fourteen, had left the fishing town of Castletown-berehaven in a rigid inflatable boat, what they call a 'rib.' Their scout leader was at the helm, an experienced local woman named De Paor.
>
> "The plan was to take the boys and girls out around nearby Bere Island to spot seals and maybe porpoises.
>
> "About an hour into the journey, contact was lost. The boat was never found, but most of the bodies washed up a day or so later, naked and covered in long ragged welts. Initial theories said they must have been chewed up by a propeller on a passing ship, but there was nothing big enough near the coast.
>
> "Post-mortem examinations clinched it. The state pathologist pulled dozens of small plastic barbs from each child. They were quickly identified as belonging to the squid.
>
> "A later investigation concluded that the fault lay with a cheap brand of sunscreen one of the children had brought and shared with her shipmates. A Chinese knock-off of a French brand, it contained old stocks of petro-derived nanoparticles. Just as the squid had pulped tonnes of fish to get at the plastic in their flesh in year twelve, they had tried to remove all traces of the petro from the children."
>
> —Jennings, Margaret, *When The World Stopped Shrinking*, p34

Más's house was beyond the western end of the town, past a small turning circle for cars. A path continued to a rocky beach, but was used only by courting couples, dog walkers, or drinking youngsters. A wooden gate led off the beach, where a small house sat behind a quarter-acre of lawn and an old boathouse.

Síle, the barmaid, had told me where he lived. Más usually gave up carving at about four, she said, had a few drinks in a few places and was usually home about six.

I started for the main house, when I heard a noise. A low murmur, like a talk radio station heard through a wall. It was coming from the boathouse.

I made my way across the lawn. Almost unconsciously I was walking crab-like on the balls of my feet, with my arms outstretched for balance. The boathouse was in bad shape. Green paint had blistered on the ship-lapped planks and lichen or moss had crept halfway up the transom windows above the large double doors.

The fabric of the place was so weathered I didn't have to open them. Planks had shrunk and split at various intervals, leaving me half a dozen spyholes to the interior. I quietly pressed my eye to one and peered inside.

Under the light of a single work lamp, I could see Más standing at a bench, his back to me, and wearing a T-shirt and jeans. Without the souwester, he looked more like an ageing rock star than a fisherman and more like twice my age than the three times I had assumed.

Beyond him lay several bulky piles, perhaps of wood, covered by tarpaulin and shrouded in shadow.

A flagstone floor ran all the way to the other wall, where there lay a dark square of calm water—a man-made inlet of dressed stone, from which rose the cold smell of the sea. A winch was bolted to the floor opposite a rusty iron gate that blocked the water from the estuary. Smaller, secondary doors above protected the interior from the worst of the elements.

As he worked, Más whistled.

I recognized enough of the tune to know it was old, but its name escaped me. It felt as manipulative as most traditional music—as Más whistled the chorus, it sounded like a happy tune, but I knew there would be words to accompany it and odds were, they would tell of tragedy.

Más began to wind down, cleaning tools with oil-free cloths. I had told myself this was not spying, this was interest, or concern. But suddenly, I became embarrassed. I silently padded back across his lawn. I would call on him another night.

As I stepped back onto the path between two overgrown rhododendron bushes, my foot collided with a rusty old garden lantern with a musical crash. I just had enough presence of mind to turn again so I was facing the house, trying to look like I had just arrived.

It was in time for Más to see me as he emerged from the boathouse to investigate. I waved as nonchalantly as I could.

He leaned back inside the door and must have flicked a switch, as his garden was suddenly bathed in light from a ring of security floods under the eaves of his house.

I waved again as he re-emerged, confident that he could at least see me this time.

"Oh it's you," he said.

"Hi. Yes, the barmaid, Síle, gave me your address. I hope you don't mind.

"Well, come in so. I have no tea, I'm afraid. I may have some chicory."

I raised the bottle in my hand and gave it a wiggle.

> "In the early days after their 'revolution,' the squid featured in one scare story after another. They would evolve legs and stalk the landscape like Wells's Martians, they would form a super-intelligence capable of controlling the world's nuclear arsenal, or they would start harvesting the phytoplankton that provide most of the world's breathable oxygen.
>
> "In the end, they did what biological organisms do—they found their own equilibrium. Any reactions of theirs since are no more a sign of 'intelligence' than a dog defending its front yard."
>
> —Edward Mission, *The Spectator's Big Book of Science*

Perrott banked the plane again. It was the first flight during which I had felt ill. The day was squally and overcast, the sky lidded with a leaden dome of cloud.

The squid breached the water, rolling its "tentacles" behind it. There was no reason for the maneuver, according to the original designers, which made it look even more biological. But even from this altitude, I could see the patterns of old plastic the thing had used to build and periodically repair itself.

"He's a big one," said Perrott, who was clearly enjoying himself.

The beast dived again. Just as it sank out of sight in the dying light, I counted eight much smaller shadows behind it. Each breached the surface of the water and rolled their tentacles, just as their colossal "parent" had.

"Shit."

These were sleeker machines, of a green so deep it may as well have been black. There was no wasted musculature, no protrusions to drag in the water as they slipped by. These things would never reach the size of the squid that had manufactured them, but that didn't matter. They were fast and there were more of them.

"Problem?" said Perrott.

"Yes. Somebody isn't playing by the rules."

"I had a friend. Val. Killed himself."

Más had had a lot to drink, mostly the whiskey I had brought, but also a homemade spirit, which smelled faintly methylated. His face sagged under the influence of alcohol, but his voice became brighter and clearer with each drink. The stove roared with heat, the light from its soot-stained window washing the kitchen in sepia.

I wasn't sure if he was given to maudlin statements of fact such as this when drunk, or whether this was an opening statement, so I said "I'm sorry to hear that. When did that happen?"

"A while back."

I was still adrift—I didn't know if it was a long time ago and he had healed, or recently and his emotions were strictly battened down. Before I could ask another qualifying question, he continued.

"When we were teenagers, a couple of years after the squid were introduced, Val and I went fishing from the pier one October when the mackerel were in."

"By God, they were fun to catch. Val had an old fiberglass rod that belonged to his dad, or his granddad. The cork on the handle was perished, the guides were brown with rust, but as long as you used a non-petro line, the squid didn't bother you in those days. We caught a lot of fish that year.

"So as we pulled them out, I would unhook them and launch them back into the tide. They were contaminated with all sorts of stuff, heavy metals, plastic, even carbon fiber from the boat hulls. After I had done this once or twice, Val asked me why. I said 'well you can't eat them, so why not let them go.' And Val said 'fuck them, they're only fish.'

"After that, every fish he caught, every one, he would brain and chop up there on the pier and leave for the gulls to eat. He was my friend, but he was cruel.

"The trouble with the squid is they think about us the way Val thought about fish. We're not food, we're not sport. I'm not sure they know what we are. I'm not sure they care."

For a moment, sobriety surfaced. Más looked forlorn. I dreaded the words that would come next. I had become quite good at predicting his laments and tirades.

"We don't fight for it, for the territory, or for the people we lost. For the love of God, these things ate children, and we just accept it. We should be out there every bloody day, hunting these things."

I told him I understood the desire to hurt them, that many had tried, but it just didn't work like that. That most people preferred to pretend they just weren't there, like fairy-tale villagers skirting the wood where the big bad wolf lived.

"But why," he demanded.

"Well they are 'protected' now, for starters," I said. "They fight back. But I suppose the main reason is it's easier than the reality."

"Easier," he scoffed.

He raised his glass, to let me know it was my turn to speak. But I didn't know how to comfort him. So I let him comfort me.

"Your family owned trawlers, right? What's it like? To go out on the ocean?"

Drunk, in the heat of his kitchen, I closed my eyes and listened.

> "The raincoat suicides were a foreseeable event inasmuch as such events happen after many profound and well-publicised changes to people's understanding of the world around them. The Wall Street Crash, Brexit, the release of the Facebook Files. It is a form of end-of-days-ism that we have seen emerge again and again, from military coups to doomsday cults.
>
> "Most of the people who took their own lives had previously displayed signs of moderate to severe mental illness. That the locations of more than two hundred of the deaths were confined to areas with high sea cliffs, such as Dover in England or the Cliffs of Moher in Co Clare, adds fuel to the notion that these were tabloid-inspired suicides, sadly, but predictably, adopted by already unwell people."
>
> —Jarlath Kelleher, The Kraken sleeps: reporting of suicide as 'sacrifice' in British and Irish media (Undergraduate thesis, Dublin Institute of Technology)

He pulled the tarpaulin off with a flourish. The green-black boat sat upside down on two sawhorses, like an orca, stiff with rigor mortis, beached on pointed rocks.

It was a naomhóg. In the west, I found out later, it was called a currach, but this far south, people called it a naomhóg. Depending on who you asked, it meant 'little saint' or 'young saint,' as if the namers were asking God and the sea to spare it.

It was made of a flexible skin, stretched tightly over a blond wooden frame. I dropped to the floor to look inside, still unable to talk. I knew nothing about boat-building in those days, but the inside looked like pure craftsmanship.

It was almost the most rudimentary of constructed vessels and in place of oars it had long spars of unfeathered wood. But where a normal naomhóg was finished with hide or canvas and waterproofed with pitch, Más's boat was hulled in what looked like glossy green-black plastic stretched over its ribs and stapled in place on the inside of the gunwale.

I ran my hand along the hull. The skin, which looked constantly wet, was bone-dry and my fingers squeaked. They left no fingerprints. I knew instantly what it was, but I wished I didn't.

"Will you come with me? I'd like to show you my harbor. We might even catch something."

He was so proud, of his vessel, of his hometown. I couldn't say anything else.

"I will," I lied. "Tomorrow, if the fog lifts."

> "I remember the harbour before the squid. The water teemed with movement. Ships steamed up the channel to the container ports upriver, somehow avoiding the small launches, in a complicated dance against outgoing or incoming tides, taking people to and from work at the steelworks on the nearest of the islands. Under the guidance of a harbourmaster sitting in his wasp-striped control tower, warships slipped sleekly from the naval base to hunt drug smugglers or Icelandic trawlers. An occasional yacht tied up at the floating pontoon of a small waterside restaurant. In summer, children dared each other to 'tombstone' from the highest point of the piers.
>
> "When I returned to the island, it might as well have been surrounded by tarmac, like a derelict theme park. Nobody even looked to the sea. It was easier that way."
>
> —Elaine Theroux, *The Great Island*

It was bright outside when I left Más's house. He had more friends, or at least acquaintances, than I had thought. None outwardly seemed to blame me for what had happened. Many expressed surprise he had made it that far.

Más himself had been less forgiving. After I turned him in, the local police superintendent let me talk to him. Más told me he hated me, called me a "fucking English turncoat." He spat in my face.

I told him he didn't understand. That he had been lucky until now. Lucky he hadn't been killed. That they hadn't retaliated.

I wanted to tell him we were working on things to kill them, to infect them, to turn them on each other. I wanted to tell him to wait until the harbor mouth was closed, that the nets were in place, that he could soon take to the water off Ballyvoloon every day. That I would go with him.

But I couldn't and none of it would have mattered anyway.

I had betrayed him. And I found I could live with it.

Between Más's house and Ballyvoloon is a harbor-side walkway known simply as 'the water's edge.' The pavement widens dramatically in two places to support the immense red-brick piers of footbridges that connect the old Admiralty homes, on the other side of the railway line, to the sea. I climbed the wrought iron steps to the peak and surveyed the harbor, my arms resting on the mossy capstones of the wall. The sun was rising over the eastern headland, bright and cold.

I took the phone from my pocket and watched the coroner's video.

It was mostly from one angle, from a camera I had often passed high atop an antique lamppost preserved in the middle of the main street. The quality was good, no sound, but the colors of Ballyvoloon were gloriously recreated in bright sunshine. The camera looked east, past the pier and along the beach to the old town hall, now a Chinese takeaway.

There, just visible over the roof of the taxi stand office, sat Más on his rock, whittling and chipping at a piece of wood. The email from the coroner said he had sat there there all morning, but she must have supposed that I didn't need to watch all of that.

At 4pm, his usual knocking-off time, he stood, stretched his back in such an exaggerated way I thought I could hear the cracks of his vertebrae, and packed his things into a large, waterproof sail bag. Carrying his pink-and-white jacket over one arm, he walked toward the camera, hailing anyone he met with a wave, but no conversation.

However, rather than cross the beach for the bar at Tom's, he turned left down the patched concrete of the pier.

At that time of day it was deserted. The last of the stalls had packed up, the tourists had made for their trains or their buses.

The angle switched to another camera, on the back of the old general post office, perhaps. It showed Más standing with his toes perfectly aligned to the edge of the concrete pier's 'T.' After a few minutes, he removed several things from his pockets, folded his jacket, and placed it on the concrete.

He opened the bag and withdrew a banana-yellow set of antique, old-petro waterproofs. He stepped into the thick, rubbery trousers before donning the heavy jacket and securing its buttons and hooks.

He walked to the top of the rotten steps, looked up at the cathedral and made a sign of the cross. Then he descended the steps, sinking from view.

There was nothing for more than a minute, but the video kept running, the pattern of wavelets kept approaching the shore, birds kept wheeling in the sky.

In a series of small surges, the prow of the naomhóg emerged from under the pier, then Más's head, his face towards the town, then the rest of his body and the boat.

I had to hand it to him. He could have launched his vessel at dead of night from the little boathouse where he had built the others, but he chose the part of town most visible to the cameras, at a time when few people would be around to stop or report him.

With each pull on the oars, he sculled effortlessly through the gentlest of swells, his teeth bared in joy.

His yellow oilskins shone in contrast against the dark greens of his boat and the surrounding water as he made for the mouth of his harbor and the open sea beyond.

"Yet fish there be, that neither hook, nor line, nor snare, nor net, nor engine can make thine."
—John Bunyan, *The Pilgrim's Progress*

OBLITERATION

ROBERT REED

A lot of people preferred this Mars to all the others.

This was the Mars wearing a cobalt blue sea in the north and towering redwood forests across its wilderness south. Ancient volcanoes had been re-plumbed and reinvigorated, helping maintain a deep warm sweetly-scented atmosphere. This was a tourist destination famous for its open-air cities, for flying naked, and for the billion human-stock citizens leading fascinating lives. And best of all, this Mars was a paradise within an arm's lazy reach, and always free.

Kleave didn't know much about the real Red Planet. Just that it was cold and dead on the outside, but infested with bugs underground. Only the Unified Space Agencies had access, and they sent nothing up there but sterile robots. But as a public service, Agency researchers built a faithful model of what was real, using off-the-shelf AIs and a fraction of their annual budget to build a virtual seed planted inside servers somewhere in the depths of the Atlantic. Ten thousand years of inspired terraforming were crossed in a week, and the results were opened for everyone to enjoy: A public playground and an advertisement for scientific inquiry, as well as one of the densest simulations in existence. Only the Disney-Burroughs Mars was as sophisticated, and that park was far too expensive for a man living on investments and a public stipend. Kleave had visited the D-B just once, and that adventure was still being paid off a little more every month.

The public Mars had a famously lovely coastline. Lying inside his *in nubibus*, Kleave felt as if he was facing the warm surf while lying naked on hot butterscotch-colored sand. Full of peppered shrimp and a vodka Collins, the young man was happy and ignorant. There was absolutely no inkling of disaster. Doobie was in charge of the lunch menu, and his long-term partner had just stepped out of her *in nubibus*, needing to pee and check on the oatmeal cookies. And that happened to be when a mature jelly-island decided to breach on the horizon. Always interesting, the creature began to spit flares while it inflated and deflated its gigantic body, proving its magnificence while driving waves at the red shoreline below. That was a scene worth watching. But then a pair of native humans approached. Tall, tall people with albatross wings growing from those broad Martians' backs, they were a gorgeous couple singing with opera voices. Something intriguing was sure to happen. Should he call Doobie back from the apartment? No, Kleave just stared with shameless, re-woven eyes. Every pixel was supposed to be committed to memory. In a world of easy tricks, this was about the easiest. Kleave watched the girl catch her boy in midair, her body curling around his and then pulling both of them into the impossibly warm surf. A romantic embrace ended with the Martians emerging, laughing as they shook those white feathers dry, and then the lad began to chase the girl, first with long, graceful strides, and then both in the air again, musical giggles merging with the soughing of slow magnificent waves.

The lovers vanished and the jelly-island submerged again, but then the promised cookies arrived, warm and moist, familiar hands slipping them inside Kleave's *in nubibus*.

Doobie appeared beside him, spectacularly naked. "What did I miss?"

"Quite a lot," he promised.

Yet the world's simplest trick refused to cooperate. Kleave first tried to summon the strangers coupling in the water, then tried to bring back the giant cnidaria quivering under the silvery-blue air. Yet neither memory file seemed to exist.

"What are you doing wrong?"

That was Doobie's first reaction.

"I'm doing nothing wrong," said Kleave. Then he failed to summon up half a dozen random events. The terror grew until his heart pounded, and that's when Kleave finally tried to bring back the evening when he first took this glorious woman to bed. An event which he remembered very well on his own. But even that eternal file was gone.

"That's crazy," Doobie said.

Kleave wanted to agree with her.

"You've done something wrong," she kept insisting.

Which implied that he could do something right and fix this.

"Fix it," she said.

That's what Kleave intended to do, for sure. But where to begin? Eleven years of a thoroughly recorded life had been lost, and the beautiful, disagreeable woman beside him seemed like a stranger.

"Three archives," said the wizard. "That's the common standard."

"And that's what I did."

"Two technologies, two languages."

"Yes, and yes."

"With one archive kept off-site."

Kleave couldn't remember where that "on-site" storage was, but he was confident about his "off-site" archive. "I've got a second null-drive at my sister's apartment."

"And your sister lives underground?"

"Sure. In an abandoned gold mine, sure."

The wizard stared at him, humorless as stone.

"Okay, I'm kidding," Kleave said. "But the drive is sitting safe inside a lockbox, and I should be able to access it now. Right?"

Scorn filled that older face. Was this was a real man running diffusion software, talking to multiple clients, or a single AI designed to make unfortunate souls feel even more miserable than they already were?

"I know what you're thinking," Kleave said.

"What? That idiots deserve their fates?"

Only humans could be that dickish. "Yeah, well. Just try and help me figure out my fate. Would you please?"

A shiny probe appeared. Kleave's face was interesting, then his neck. The hunt ended with a spot behind the right ear.

"Now I remember," Kleave said. "It was implanted in college, when I upgraded from . . . what? Did I have an Intel archive before this?"

"How the hell would I know?"

Yeah. Definitely a human male.

"Okay, I see the problem," the wizard said. "Judging by the damage, it looks like a fat daughter hit you."

"Fat daughter?"

"Born from an ultra-high-energy mother particle. That big gal struck the upper atmosphere, triggering a rain of particles. I'm guessing your sister lives nearby."

"It's a long walk."

"Of course those daughters aren't as energetic as the original. But one of them definitely found you inside your apartment, and in the same thousandth of a second, one of her sisters struck your precious lockbox too."

"God, that sounds so unlikely."

"Disasters are always unlikely. That's why nobody seems ready for them."

Except "disasters" were other people's problems. This was a catastrophe. Struggling for hope, Kleave said, "Maybe something else went wrong."

The wizard didn't call him, "Idiot." Except with those narrowed eyes and that smug, silent mouth. "Well, that's a thought. But null-drives are extraordinarily reliable, and a 'failure' signal in one drive triggers its twin into disaster mode. Fifty milliseconds. That's all you need for the full library to be replicated and partitioned, then rapidly off-loaded."

"Off-loaded where?"

"I'll assume that your sister has neighbors. Well, in this case every adjacent null-drive absorbs a little piece of your library. That's the standard protocol, years old and proven. You would have heard alarms announcing the event, and I'd see the data begging to be noticed now."

Kleave was listening, and he wasn't listening. He was mostly focused on his anger and misery as well as the profound embarrassment. And this very unpleasant wizard and his technology were very impressive. Except Kleave didn't want to feel impressed just now. Pissed seemed like the perfect state of mind. "Okay, the backup drive failed. Two daughters struck my archives at the same time. But what about my second backup? I'm wearing a DNA chip that's nearly new."

A different tool appeared, blunt and dark. It quickly dropped to his hip, settling on the left side.

"I see one Amber Forever Repository, last year's model."

"That's when I bought it." Kleave didn't remember the cost, but vivid wet-memories reminded him about the monthly payment. "It's a state-of-the-art masterpiece. That's what my research said."

"The Amber Forever is basically good. But there was an enzyme update three months after it reached the market."

"I did that update."

"Did you?"

"Sure." Kleave was aiming for confidence. He wanted to put an end to this professional disgust. But he was also suffering a faint recollection, something about a little chore going unfinished. "Okay, let's say the update wasn't done or done properly. What does that mean for me?"

"When the null-drive in your skull fails, the Amber Forever should prepare for a retrieval of its inventory. But the original enzymatic matrix had a flaw. Without that critical update, there's a one-in-seventeen chance that the DNA self-wipes itself."

"And why the hell would it?"

"That's standard protection for encrypted files. Popular with intelligence agencies and media empires."

"I'm neither of those things."

"But that is what the Amber Forever was. Before the commercial models were released, it was the archive that could never be beaten."

"I feel beaten," Kleave said.

"'Obliteration.' That's the industry's term for this business."

There was no way to calculate this awful luck. A single particle coming from outside the galaxy had burned out two innocent null-drives, and after that happened, an array of DNA washed away everything that it had ever learned. Kleave wanted to hit something. Not the wizard, since he might take offense. But attacking one of the walls seemed reasonable. The virtual office offered fake shelves full of photographs that must mean something to its owner. Kleave could throw every portrait to the floor and then stomp them under his feet. That seemed halfway suitable, pretending to destroy another man's invincible memories.

And thoroughly stupid too. With a defeated sigh, Kleave asked, "So what do you advise?"

The wizard sat up and offered a suddenly eager smile. "Standard procedure would be for you to remove the null-drive from your neck and grab its mate from its box. With available methods, and patience, I should be able to recover . . . " There was a pause. Technical aspects were in play, but the client's pain as well as his bank accounts needed to be weighed too. "Twelve, maybe fourteen percent of your files would be retrieved. But a random sampling, with acceptable degradation of sensory quality."

"Acceptable degradation" sounded like an eight percent recovery. That's how techno-juggling worked. Kleave decided to abuse the virtual floor, stomping hard, delivering a much-welcomed dose of pain to the soles of his feet.

"Of course I can borrow from other people's archives," the wizard continued. "Friends and family will be easy enough, and sometimes you come across useful strangers. The goal is to harvest enough data and build a convincing likeness of your life experiences. Which will always be other people's experiences, except for the realigned perspective."

"That sounds expensive," Kleave said.

The man didn't disagree. Better to shrug with resignation, then tell the client, "I'm old. I was alive when memory was weak and people took snapshots to help us remember. But the pictures were simple and aged badly or got tossed out by mistake. So we threw slightly better photographs up on the cloud. But then came the Hacks of '29 and the advent of cheap, nearly infinite private storage. That's the history. That's why memory is weaker now than ever. Nobody remembers shit. We don't have to. Everything that happens is clean and pressed, eagerly waiting for us, and we don't know what to do without it."

"And you think the cost would be worthwhile?"

"To me, recovery would be priceless."

"Except you won't ever have my troubles. Will you? I bet you have more than three archives."

A big smile, a slow nod. "Six of them, and four languages. And three null-drives are secured inside deep vaults, on separate continents."

Kleave gave the floor another hard kick.

Which the wizard noticed. But Kleave's misfortune deserved a warm little smile. What mattered now was to make the sale, and that's why he leaned forward. "But really, you aren't a careless fool. You're not like the usual cases that I see. What happened to you . . . well, it's remarkably rare, and in so many ways."

"Others suffer like this?"

"The Obliteration of Everything. It happens all the time. Usually when a single old and badly maintained archive fails."

And that's when Kleave detected the faint beginnings of something that wasn't pleasurable, no. But suddenly this situation wasn't as lonely or quite as horrible as it once seemed.

Doobie was a woman of appetites and ideas and loud, blunt enthusiasms. She could be lovely and she was always physically impressive, but when his partner was sick, she became radiant. Illness was an event worth experiencing. Something about a good fever made Doobie more vivid, and Kleave secretly looked forward to the days when he had to serve as a tireless nurse to this complaining beast.

But Kleave's illnesses and mishaps were never as well-received.

"You didn't take care of your archives," Doobie told him.

"I did what I could, and I thought it was enough," he said.

"That enzyme update," she said. "Did you or didn't you do the mandatory update?"

With nothing but his soggy brain in play, Kleave couldn't remember anything with certainty. But "I don't know" seemed dangerous. Instead, I redirected the conversation by saying, "You should have been with me. To ask questions and punch the walls for me."

"And that would have helped how?" Doobie always found excuses when her roommate visited a physician, AI or otherwise. And apparently it was the same for tech-wizards. "No, I'm too angry to sit. Too furious to ask questions. We're together all these years, and now, because of all these little catastrophes, you've lost everything that we've ever shared."

Doobie used to be flat-chested and then she was a buxom lady, but now she was back to the original shape. And those were just a few of the changes with a topography that was never quite happy with itself. Yet every version of Doobie had lived inside archives that Kleave trusted as much as his next deep breath. An infinitely complex apparition had lived inside his null-drives—a wondrous lady that shared the world with him all the way back to college. For years, they remained stubbornly unaware of each other's existence. But re-woven eyes meant that every glance was recorded, and auditory sinks meant that every overheard word was real. Doobie was the big and pretty girl on the track-and-field team who threw the shot farther than any other woman. And Kleave? The handsome if rather shy boy who looked at his future partner exactly 156 times before finally noticing her wonders.

They went to the public Mars on their fifth date. They were already lovers, and that particular day didn't offer any special fun. But worlds were the same as people. Sometimes it took 156 inadequate glances before you noticed what was precious. Or sometimes it took seven visits and staring into the throat of a reborn volcano, and then the two of you emerged ready to stop dating other people, at least for the time being.

That's the promise Kleave made to Doobie and to himself. Though she was never as enthusiastic towards monogamy. They often shared archives, and sometimes he caught glimpses of other sexual adventures. Of course digital records had another spectacular power: The unwelcome and unseemly could be purged. A jealous-minded lover could make those bad minutes go away. Except Kleave never did make that effort. The way he looked at it, his partner was a world of flesh recorded in staggering detail, and he would never throw away anything that was Doobie. Each touch and the smell of her breath was waiting to be remembered, and even the flavor of his sweat mixed with hers. Kleave always wanted those joys close. Just as he never wanted to stop hearing that strong lady who was never ashamed to speak her mind.

"Well," said Doobie. "Regardless of blame, you'll of course get this problem fixed."

Kleave stared at his roommate. This woman. Her hair was short, the clothes casual, bare toes digging into the stones resting beside a Martian river, cool water charging down a new canyon, making for the cobalt sea.

"It's expensive," he began.

"And I know that," she interrupted. Except her knowledge didn't push very far into the finances. She didn't sit in the wizard's office, and she didn't show the slightest interest in liability law or Kleave's financial resources. And she absolutely hadn't put in the hours that he had spent researching this business of Obliteration. Which was perfectly named, and as he had learned, far more common than he would have guessed yesterday.

"Just pulling what remains from the two null-drives," he said. "That would cost more than ten days on Disney-Burroughs."

On that Mars, Doobie played the powerful princess.

But this woman, the one standing before him, wasn't a princess. And this Doobie wasn't the splendid force of nature that he loved. That idea arrived suddenly, entirely by surprise, and then it refused to let him go.

"Well, someone should pay for this," the stranger said.

"Like who?" Kleave asked.

"The companies that built these awful drives. They should be happy to replace everything that failed."

"The Amber Drive is under warranty," he mentioned. "I'm entitled to a new, updated model."

But then Doobie found a larger target. "A government that cares for its citizens, that educates us and treasures us . . . that sort of government should protect our pasts too. With a shared repository, or something else along those lines."

Kleave didn't see how any of these words helped.

"You're awfully quiet," she said.

He agreed with silence.

Then the original, most urgent question returned. "So how did you let this happen?"

Obviously this woman was a stranger. Kleave's Doobie was eleven years of vivid existence, while this was just a thin slice of one mostly unknown existence. Her name didn't matter. Kleave stared at the short hair and brown face and the anger that seemed quite familiar, but without the help of the archives ready to blunt the bad moments, offering up treasured moments and perfect long days.

"Why won't you answer me?"

Kleave didn't particularly like this woman.

"What are you thinking?" the stranger asked.

"That I can't afford to do anything about anything," he said. "Except outfit myself with new archives. And since your equipment isn't any better than mine, we need to give you more backups too."

"But I didn't lose anything," she said.

What did that mean?

"My *in nubibus* and yours are always side-by-side," she said. "But did any of my archives die?"

"Radioactive daughters are tiny."

"I know that."

"This was just stupid bad luck," he said.

A heavy, doubtful sigh.

"Or did I have a plan? Is that what you're thinking?"

"No." That idea sounded spectacularly paranoid, even in her ugly mood. "Where would such an idea even come from?"

"Because this was nothing but an accident," Kleave said. At least those were the words that came out of him. Except his voice felt wrong, as if he was nothing but the bottle carrying the expected sentence.

She became the silent one now.

"I need to leave," he said.

This Doobie shifted her weight. "Okay. Sure." Staring at the pathetic man was painful. Kleave had lost every second that they had ever shared, and it took all of her grace to say a few obvious words. "You're off to get some new archives. Right?"

That plan was set. He had addresses written on paper, yes. But Kleave said, "No. First I'm going to go to my sister's and collect the other dead null-drive."

The old Doobie had always feuded with Kleave's sister.

This Doobie seemed much the same. "Fine. You do that."

"Do you want to come with me?"

"No." Then she thought about it, hard. And again, she said, "No."

And for the first time in days, Kleave physically left their home. The apartment was no bigger than a space capsule bound for another world. Outdoors, the world turned huge. Pausing on a street corner, Kleave contemplated the idea that he could go anywhere and do almost anything, and no record of his adventures would be baked into some useless slab of Forever Amber.

Full names weren't offered. That's what Kleave noticed first. Just a single name and some people shook hands while others didn't, depending on a lot of factors, including the quality of their *in nubibus*. Kleave couldn't grasp anyone's hand. He was inside an old cheap and very public machine, which meant that he could smell the dozens of strangers who had used it already that day. The experience wasn't as awful as he would have guessed, but this was an experience that he wouldn't happily do again either.

"Hello there, Kleave," an older woman said. "And by the way. You have our permission to smile."

He smiled at the smiling group.

And in a chorus, they shouted, "Hello, Kleave."

OBLITERATED BY CHOICE. That was the official name for an organization dedicated to living without the modern burdens. At least that was the stated purpose in the literature that came up high in every search into Obliteration. This meeting was one of eighty currently happening, and he selected it for no reason but the location. This was the well-loved Mars. And in particular, a couple dozen believers had gathered east of Hellas, inside the damp redwood forest where ferns grew taller by the minute and enhanced gibbons rode gigantic tame eagles, hunting for tourists that would throw them baubles, or better, gold coins.

Kleave and Doobie had talked about coming to this district. And now he was here, as without her as he could be.

The gray lady seemed to be the group's leader. "And what brings you to us today, Kleave?"

Being with strangers meant freedom, and even better, Kleave loved being unable to remember even a few of their names. Honesty. That was a quality that he often avoided with people who recorded everything. In that spirit, the new man surrendered a quick description of his day, centering on the major failures of proven technologies.

Some people were impressed, but most preferred superstition. The leader in particular. "Well, obviously, the gods have steered you to us," she said. "You should take this wonderful day as a clear, unimpeachable sign."

All right. That wasn't the expected response. But again, Kleave felt free to tell them, "There aren't any gods. The galaxy turns on its own."

That won giggles from several faces, and from the high branches, laughing gibbons.

"Bad luck is nothing but bad luck," he told everyone.

Then one man said, "Yet you haven't replaced your archives. Have you?"

"Not yet, no."

"Gods or not, you seem ready for a different course."

Testimonies. Suddenly everyone had to share earnest tales about how good life was without re-woven eyes and terabytes of absorption. Several of these passionate, possibly crazed believers came close enough to grab hold of him, then couldn't because his *in nubibus* was that awful. But their faces were pushing too close to his face, and although different people kept talking, all the same words were being said.

"The old, proven memories."

"So much better than null-sinks."

"And so much cheaper too."

Then he posed what seemed like a reasonable, obvious question. "How do others react to your beliefs?"

"Badly." Everyone said so, in every possible way, and there was no greater pleasure to be found. They boasted about being dismissed as outcasts, deviants, and moderately insane, or much worse than that. But the believers knew better. "We know best," they sang. Life without archives meant trusting a brain that did spectacular things for millions of years. These ancient neurons were forgetful and lovely because of it. Memory should be just like the brain it inhabited, soft and malleable. Parts of yesterday and most of last year were lost, but that was a very good thing. Ordinary life deserved to be discarded. All that mattered were the impressive and shocking days, and those very pleasurable moments that stood tall and bright inside the dreary gray of normal existence.

Without question, their enthusiasm for ignorance was impressive. They had mastered a logic that arrived with force. Kleave found himself believing everything just long enough to surprise himself. But then the doubter inside him would take charge, and he'd have to squelch a laugh and a hard shake of the head. Ten minutes of passionate noise, and he still didn't know which side of the line to choose.

Then someone wiggled a fingertip camera, naming the model while bragging about its cheapness and its terribly tiny memory. "So you can't catch more than a few special scenes," she said. "Nothing more than that."

But that was too much. Others became angry enough to curse, while their leader tried to staunch what was plainly an old political fight. "Now we've agreed to disagree, and let's focus back on Kleave."

But then one fellow stepped forward, and almost everyone else groaned. Which he appreciated. Scorn brought energy, and he couldn't keep his voice from shouting when he stated his own vision of life without mental aids.

"I don't accept written words," he stated.

"What can that mean?" asked Kleave. "You don't read or write?"

"And I don't know how to do either."

How could anyone be illiterate? That seemed too bizarre.

Then the old lady succeeded in touching the new recruit. Just for an instant, Kleave felt the pressure of fingers, and with a threadbare patience, she reported, "Our Lauren had his brain worked with. Supposedly, he can't do more than recognize letters and some of their sounds."

"Supposedly" was the most important word in that account.

"We don't believe him," a younger woman admitted.

But that only encouraged the true believer. Looking and sounding like everyone else, except for the specific words that he used, Lauren stood tall while he explained, "I live without artificial tricks or aids from any time in the last ten thousand years. And that's why I'm the only pure one here."

And that's when a great fight broke out.

Nobody noticed when the newcomer, whatever his name, managed to slip off into the emerald ferns. Kleave walked until he couldn't hear any human. A gibbon and her eagle landed on the path before him, both begging for gold, and because nothing was real here, he gave them what they wanted badly—a digital bauble that one swallowed whole, keeping it safe in the belly.

He walked a little farther into the Martian wilderness.

But as happens sometimes when a cheap *in nubibus* pushes against the limits of any data-drawn world, the ferns grew yellowy pale and the ground softened until every step landed on pillows, and the deep sky beyond the redwoods forgot which blue it should be.

Doobie was sitting on the floor of the tiny apartment, tired of crying but not angry enough to stand when Kleave finally came home.

"You didn't go to your sister's," she began.

They owned two chairs, and he took the nearest one. It was the chair that Doobie preferred, and she didn't seem to notice.

"I got worried," she said. "So worried that when you didn't come home, I called that awful woman. Why does your sister hate me so much?"

"You were rude to her," he said.

"When?"

"I don't remember," he said. "But she does. It was the day when you two met, and you said some unkind words about . . . well, it doesn't matter what you said. The point is, she's never let those ten seconds get lost."

Doobie was sick with misery. How wonderful!

"So you called my sister, but she hadn't seen me. Is that right?"

"I thought you might be leaving me," Doobie said.

"I considered it."

"And maybe you've come back for your belongings?"

"Maybe I haven't decided yet."

That broad body stiffened, and then hopelessness won. The old athlete seemed to turn to paste, soft and ready to flow. The weakest voice of her life said, "I won't fight you. If you want to go."

Kleave abandoned the chair for the grimy floor. The two of them sat with legs crossed, facing not so much each other as the third corner in a tidy triangle. Looking at that empty space, he said, "I went to Mars with strangers and learned a lot."

"Good for you."

"Then I finally walked to my sister's. Which wasn't long after you called her, by the way."

Staring at the same bit of air, Doobie said nothing.

"Like I planned, I was going to retrieve the other broken null-drive."

"I am sorry," said Doobie.

And then, "I know what I said. When we met, I told your sister she was too pretty to ever ever ever be unhappy about anything."

"She didn't like those words."

"I guess not."

"Anyway." A moment passed into another several moments, nothing memorable in the bunch. And then Kleave dropped a little piece of machinery on the dirty rug between them.

"What's that?"

"An old Intel archive," he said. "My archive, once. I found it in the lockbox with my irradiated archive. I'd forgotten I put it there, or that it existed anywhere. And do you know what, Doobie?"

"No. What?"

"Because it was so easy to do, I plugged this old model into my new archive. One connection. That's all it took. And for the last eleven years, it's been backing up my null-drive, a terabyte at a time."

"Eleven years?"

"Yes."

She stared at him, hope buried under all the fear of being too hopeful. "Was there room in the old drive for that much time?"

"Just barely."

"So now you can get your memories back?" she asked.

To which Kleave said, "I never lost my memories, darling. Just a big world made up of tiny, tiny days."

SOUR MILK GIRLS

ERIN ROBERTS

The new girl showed up to the Agency on a Sunday, looking like an old dishrag and smelling like sour milk. Not that I could *really* smell her from three floors up through the mesh and bars, but there's only three types of girls here, and she was definitely the sour milk kind. Her head hung down like it was too much work to raise it, and her long black hair flopped around so you couldn't see her face. I'd have bet a week's credits she had big ol' scaredy-cat eyes, but she never bothered to look up, just let Miss Miranda lead her by the elbow through the front doors. Didn't even try to run. Sour milk all the way.

Even sour milk new girls were good, though; anything new was good. The last one, Hope, might have been dull as old paint, but at least she'd been something different to talk about. I'd even won a day's credits from Flash by betting the girl wouldn't make it to fourteen without some foster trying her out and keeping her. Anyone could tell Hope smelled like cinnamon and honey, same as those babies on the first floor and the second-floor girls with their pigtails and missing-tooth smiles. Sure enough, only took six months before the Reynolds came and took Hope off to their nice house with the big beds and the white fence and those stupid yapping dogs, leaving just me and Whispers and Flash to stare at each other and count all the months and years 'til we'd finally turn eighteen. Flash should've known it would go that way—cinnamon and honey's something fosters can't resist.

Whispers said this new girl was officially called Brenda, but that was just as stupid as all the other Agency names, and the girl wouldn't remember it after Processing anyway. At first I said we should call her Dishrag or Milkbreath, but even Flash thought that was too mean, and Flash is as nasty as hot sauce and lye. She's the one who named me Ghost, on account of I'm small and shadow-dark and she thinks I creep around too much in the night. She got *her* name 'cause that's how fast fosters send her back after their cat turns up dead and they realize the devil has blond hair and dimples.

"What's in her file?" I asked Whispers, who was still leaned up against the wall by the window. She never bothered to look out anymore. Not even for new girls.

"I'm just supposed to clean the office," she said. "Files are confidential."

"Must be good if you're holding back," said Flash, blowing out air as she tried to whistle.

"Maybe," Whispers said, with a lopsided shrug. Then she murmured something nobody could hear while staring down at her shoes. That meant we weren't getting any more from her for at least an hour, not even if Flash threatened to throw her out the window or hang her with the sheets from one of the empty beds. No use pushing her 'til she started banshee-screaming, so Flash just practiced whistling and I played around some with our crap computers and we let Whispers go all sour milk and talk to her invisible friends.

By the time Flash got a half-whistle half-spit sound to come out of her mouth and I'd finished up my hack of the first-floor baby cams for when things got boring, new girl was being led off the elevator by Miss Miranda, head still down. Flash and I lined up in front of the room same as always—hands behind our backs, chests up and out, heads forward, eyes wide. Even Whispers came out of her murmuring and straightened up against the wall. Agency folks didn't care about much as far as us third-floors were concerned, but they were total nuts for protocol.

Miss Miranda started by doing her normal speech-troduction. *This is Brenda, she's fifteen years old, and she's going to stay with us for a while. These are the girls, they're all trying to get new homes too. And we just know it'll work out for you all any day now.* When she said that last bit, her voice always got real high, like someone talking after they took a gulp of air from a circus balloon.

We ask you to stay on the third floor when you're in the building unless you're doing chores downstairs or get called to the office. But don't worry—there's so much to do up here, you won't even notice. Her voice went even higher for that part, 'cause even an idiot could see there wasn't anything on the floor but twenty empty beds, two long white lunch tables, a couple of old computers on splintery desks covered with the names of old third-floors, and the door to the world's grimiest bathroom.

As long as you maintain good grades and proper behavior in school, you're free to come and go as you please until seven PM curfew. You'll get a few credits each day for transit and meals. If you need additional learning help or assistance with your homework, the computers in the back row have plenty to offer. Age-appropriate stuff only, of course. She looked straight at me when she said it, like it was my fault the security on the things was shit and I'd figured out a way to order vapes and liquor pops and get R-rated videos.

Now you girls get along, and try not to kill each other. She looked at Flash for that one, even though Flash hadn't really tried to kill anyone for at least a year. She'd barely even talked to Hope. Either she was getting soft now that we were in high school, or she was gonna burn the whole place down someday. Maybe both.

As soon as she got the last words out of her mouth, Miss Miranda spun around on her high heels and got out of there as fast as she could. I thought the new girl would fall over as soon as Miss Miranda left, but she put her hands behind her back and stuck her chest out same as the rest of us. Her eyes weren't nearly as scaredy-cat as I thought they'd be. She smelled like sour milk for sure, but hot sauce and honey a little bit too.

"I'm Brenda," she said. "Brenda Nevins."

"That's a stupid name," said Flash.

"It's what my daddy called me," said new girl, thrusting her chest out even more, like it would cover the way her voice got all wobbly.

"Yeah? Well where's your daddy now?" Flash asked. The new girl's head dropped forward. We hadn't made a bet on whether someone could make her cry, but there were some things Flash would do for free.

"She doesn't remember," I told Flash. "You know that."

"I remember fine," said the new girl. "It's just that . . . it just happened. He just died, I mean."

Flash rolled her eyes.

"No way you *remember* that shit," she said. "Not anymore." She put on her best Miss Miranda impression, high pitched and piercing. "Your memories of your time before joining the Agency are being held for safekeeping until you reach adulthood and can properly integrate them into your daily life."

"What are you talking about?" new girl said. "I remember my dad. He was a—"

"Spare me the bullshit," Flash said, voice back low. "Miss Miranda tell you how in your file it says your daddy was a famous reccer? Or a Wall Street corp? Or a doctor? Bet if you looked in the 'grams she took from you, you'd find out he left you chained up in the basement. Or he liked to beat on your mama. Or maybe you ain't never had no daddy at all."

I felt my eyes get hot, just a little, but new girl didn't blink.

"My daddy was a good man," she said. "Not my fault if yours wasn't worth shit."

I backed up two steps so as not to get hit when the fists started flying. A fight was gonna mean discipline and lights-out and early curfew for at least two weeks. Nothing worse than that *and* having a black eye. But Flash just laughed.

"Damn, girl," she said. "You got balls. Gonna be hard coming up with a name for you."

"My dad—"

"Your dad won't know any different." I tried to stare some sense into the girl before Flash flipped back to serious and threw her across the room, or started working out how to smother her in the middle of the night. "Leave his name for him and ours for us. I'm Ghost. She's Flash. That's Whispers. We'll figure something out for you."

It took two weeks, but in the end, we called her Princess. Flash said it was from some fairy-tale book she'd read as a little kid, but I'd been to the Reynolds' for a tryout same as she had, and Princess was the name of the dumb fat poodle they all fed under the table. Plus Flash said it like a curse, with a sparkle in her eye that any idiot could tell meant trouble. I told Princess not to worry, though; I'd watch her back. Not sure why. Maybe 'cause if Princess turned up dead it was back to just Whispers and Flash to talk to. Maybe 'cause I used to be a bit of a sour milk girl too.

Me and Princess almost pinky-swore on the whole thing, but I told her that was just for little kids and losers. Even if you were too poor to get wired up soon as you turned fourteen so you could swap 'grams of every stupid thing you did with all your besties in the school cafeteria, anybody could put together the credits for a memory share at one of the public booths. Sure, all the MemCorps signs said with adult supervision only, 'cause fooling around in your head like that could mess you up when your brain was still growing, but I just told the guy at the front we were over eighteen and gave him a two-cred tip. And Princess let him look down her shirt a little when he asked to see our pretty little smiles.

We got hooked up to our chairs in one of the side-by-sides. They were sticky, but it felt like old candy, not blood or anything, so I locked in. I had to show Princess how, but she caught on quick—straps on, headset up, earpieces in. I didn't get into all the MemCorps does this and your brain cells do that and then you see the memory clear as if it happened to you part, 'cause Princess might have been a little sad looking, but she didn't seem dumb.

"Your session has begun," said the booth voice, all high and cool, like if Miss Miranda had turned into a robot.

I started first, since I knew how to work the thing. Shared my memory of the time I pulled some stupid rich girl's chair out at school and she fell back and her legs went one way and her arms went another and her mouth made a big O shape and I laughed for about an hour. Princess giggled right along with me, but there was no way to tell how much of that was real and how much was the machine—easy enough to get swept away in a share without halfway trying.

"That's all you got, Ghost?" she said, when we were finished laughing. "Some girl falling over?"

"It's funny."

"Yeah, but you said we're supposed to be swapping something real."

"It's a memory booth, dumbass," I said, smiling so she knew I didn't mean something by it like Flash would. "Of course it's real." And it was, even if I didn't share the part where Miss Miranda found out and made my head ache for a week. I liked Princess fine, but you couldn't give everything to some new girl in one go.

"Not real like true," she said, rolling her eyes. "Real like important. Like my daddy."

"I'm sick of hearing about your damn daddy all the time."

"That's 'cause you didn't know him the way I did," she said. "*He* was real."

And then she shared him with me—one 'gram after another. The way he half-smiled when she walked in the house, how it sounded when he called her Brenda, how she found him dead in his rocking chair and didn't tell anyone for a whole day even though it started to stink. The public booths were old and ragged, but I could still smell the rotten and taste the tang of garbage in my mouth and feel the pound pound of her heart thinking it was the Agency every time a car drove by. Whole thing made my eyes sting and my throat itch.

"Real like that," Princess said, voice all whispery. I just shook my head. No thinking about what my daddy could've looked like and what he might've called me. Needed to clear everything out and get back on even ground.

"'Cmon. Just show me *something*," she said, and for a second, I wished Flash was there, just to tell her to shut the hell up and leave me alone.

"Maybe next time," I said instead, taking the straps off of my legs clip by clip, telling my hands not to shake. "We're out of time anyways."

Princess flipped her hair back with her hand, turned her head, and looked me straight in the eyes. "You think that guy out there's gonna mind if we go over?"

"No. I just . . . "

"Don't want to share something real," she said, ripping her straps off and throwing her goggles back on the shelf, acting like sour milk and hot sauce had a baby. "I get it."

"You really fucking don't," I said. "Me, Flash, Whispers . . . we don't have something *real* to share. All those cute, sweet memories of being a kid? Snatched off us when we got to the Agency and locked away where we can't get 'em. All we know is school and the third floor and a few fosters who couldn't be bothered to keep us. That's it. That's all we fucking got."

Princess stared at me for a second, eyes wide, then walked out, saying *I didn't know* and *Sorry* under her breath like she was doing a Whispers impression. I stayed for a while, playing back the couple of half-decent memories I *did* have, like the day I figured out how to get the computers in the back to do what I wanted, like a real hacker, or the times the Agency let us go down to the first floor and play with the babies, and then the ones that made my neck shiver, like all the times fosters sent me back 'cause I didn't fit into any of the smiling family photos—too old, too dark, too "hard to handle."

But none of my memories were real the way Princess wanted. They didn't make my blood jump or my hands get all shaky or my mouth go dry. Not even the bad ones. Not the Reynolds' dog Butch chasing me 'round their big house, growling and smelling like death and scaring me more than Flash ever had. Not little Bitsy Reynolds laughing and telling me how I seemed nice enough for a dark girl, but Butch hated who he hated and you couldn't tell a dog any different. Not Mrs. Reynolds looking anywhere but at my face when she brought me back to the Agency, telling Miss Miranda she'd tried but I didn't know how to fit in and I was riling up the animals and after all, they'd been there first. Not even the day I woke up in the Agency with a throbbing skull and a big ol' hole of nothing in my head and Miss Miranda telling me I was eight years old and my parents were dead but I'd get a new family by the time I turned ten if I just tried hard enough. Not one goddamned thing.

I got back after curfew. Miss Miranda gave me a lecture about rules and responsibilities over the pounding in my head—*a small physical reminder of the way we expect you to behave here,* she said, smiling down at me. *I hope I won't have to speak to you about this again.*

At least the pain made it easy enough to ignore everyone once I was off the elevator. Flash rushed up to find out where I went off to and if I did anything fun, Whispers told stories about my day to her make-believe friends, and Princess acted like the back wall was the most interesting thing in the room. Took her half an hour to slink her way over to where I sat on the edge of my bed in the fourth row, swinging my feet in the air and ignoring every one of Flash's ten thousand questions. Her hair hung down in her face again, like on her very first day, and she looked like one of those trained puppies the homeless men use for begging, ready to pant and collapse at your feet the minute you look like you've got a few credits to spare.

"I'm sorry," she said. She sat on the floor in front of my feet like she thought I wouldn't kick her. "Didn't realize the way things went around here."

I shrugged and said, "It's okay, you're new." Even though it wasn't. Anything to get her to shut it and go away. But of course Princess was too sour milk to get any hints, just kept sitting there and staring and asking stupid things.

"How long you been here, anyway?"

"Six years. More or less. Agency said they got a bunch of us after the last big quake."

"A bunch? They on another floor we can't go to?"

"Nah. They all got kept by fosters whose kids got smashed up or killed same as our parents," Flash said. "Everybody but us lifers and the lucky ones."

"Lucky ones?" Princess' face stayed scrunched.

"The ones who got old and got out. Hit eighteen, got their memories, never looked back."

"Got their memories from where?" Princess asked. Flash rolled her eyes.

"From wherever they fucking keep them after Processing," she said. "Hurts like a bitch when they rip the 'grams out, too. Like someone stabbing you through your eye. 'Course they let you remember that part. Fucking Agency."

"It only hurts for a minute, wuss," I said, sticking my tongue out at Flash. Normally I wouldn't dare, but one of the good things about the way she looked at Princess, like some puppy she half-wanted to cuddle, half-wanted to kick, was that she didn't have so much nasty left for the rest of us.

"So how come I remember everything?" Princess asked, like there was any way we'd know.

"They probably screwed up," Flash said. "Or you're an Agency spy. Or your brain's so weak that it would mind-wipe you altogether." She pointed over at Whispers, who was playing with her fingers like she'd never seen them before.

"You wish," said Princess, flipping her hair in Flash's general direction like she was trying to get killed. Flash ignored it. She really was getting soft.

"Only way to find out is to get into Miss Miranda's files," Flash said. "She's got 'em all locked up down in the office on cube drives or something. Right, Whispers?"

"I'm just supposed to clean the office," Whispers said, to nobody in particular.

"Fine." Flash walked over to Whispers' corner of the room to get her attention. "Simple question. You ever see a whole bunch of little glowy cubes in a drawer or something?"

"Leave her be, Flash," I said. My head still hurt from Miss Miranda's warning, and nothing got Whispers shrieking louder than getting too comfortable over in her corner of the room. The first time, she'd hollered for a good hour 'til the Agency folks figured she wasn't gonna stop, but even now it took about ten minutes before she got dragged down to the medic and brought back passed out cold.

"I'm just asking a question, Ghost," Flash said, leaning against the wall near Whispers' bed. "C'mon, Whispers. I promise I'll leave you alone if you tell."

"The memories aren't in the office," Whispers said. "They're in the cloud." I felt my cheeks get a little hot. Stupid. I was supposed to be the big bad hacker; I should've guessed.

"That means we can get 'em with the computers up here, right Ghost?" Flash asked. "Like you did when you got the booze-flavored candy?"

"That was *before* they added all kinds of security," I said.

"So you can't get in?"

"Didn't say that."

"Then shut up and do it already," Flash said. "I want to know why she gets to hold on to all her stupid little 'grams and they won't let us remember shit 'til we get out of here."

"Can't tonight," I said. "They're gonna be watching the floor."

"Yeah, 'cause you decided you had to come in late, and for no good reason either. Didn't even bring us shit."

"It's not her fault," Princess said, still lounging on the floor near my bed. "I—"

"Doesn't matter," I said. "They're gonna be looking close for a couple days. We'll have to try another time."

"Or we could just distract 'em," Flash said. Then she went and sat down, right on the edge of Whispers' bed.

It took fifteen minutes of screams that I could feel all the way back behind my eyeballs, but eventually one of the overnight Agency guys, the one Flash thought had nice hair, came up and dragged Whispers away.

"You shouldn't have—" I started.

"Yeah yeah," Flash said, shrugging. "Just do it already. Before they finish drugging her up."

I looked at Princess, but she just flipped her hair again and walked over to the computers. She had a little more hot sauce in her than I thought. Couldn't tell yet if that was a good thing.

"Go 'head," Flash said. "Thought you were supposed to be some kind of super-hacker."

My head was still throbbing, worse than ever, and I knew Flash was just trying to get to me, but truth was truth. I sat down and got to typing—no way the Agency would spring for touch screens or one of those fancy robot lady voices—and was in quicker than I thought. Miss Miranda had locked down all the "bad influence" stuff pretty tight, but getting the Agency files wasn't much harder than getting the cam feed from downstairs and watching the babies play.

"Brenda Nevins," I read from the screen. "Resident at the Agency for the Care of Unassociated Female Minors."

"Blah blah blah," said Flash from across the room. She was on lookout by the elevator for when Mr. Nice Hair came back with Whispers. "Get to the good stuff."

"It doesn't say anything really," I said. "Just a bunch of big words." The whole thing was reports and warnings and psychology mumbo-jumbo. Nothing 'til I got down to the engrams section. It was a list of 'grams with titles like *Discovery of Father's Body* and *Trip to Percy Park on May 7th*. I recognized a couple from in the booth earlier, but most I'd never even heard of, and just about all of them had the same big bold flashing letters on the far right. *Not to Be Removed. See Explanation.*

"'Explanation,'" Princess read from over my shoulder, finger tracing along the screen like some little kid trying to figure out how words work. "'To date, Miss Nevins has shown none of the aberrant or destructive behavior of many of the Agency's other older residents. As the trauma from the loss of her father has not led her to behave negatively, we recommend that she be able to keep the majority of her memories at this time. Moreover, it can be noted that Agency resident Becky Ann Ross has shown no significant behavioral improvement since memory removal, and it is possible that the procedure itself had a negative impact on the development of Samantha Lee, leaving her prone to delusions and outbursts. While Destiny Ward has demonstrated some positive behavior changes and remains difficult to place primarily due an unfortunate lack of demand, a better form of control therapy than memory removal may need to be implemented in the future.'" Princess faked her way through most of the big words and probably wasn't saying half of them right, but I knew what "lack of demand" meant.

"Destiny? That's you?" Princess asked. I shut down the machine and pushed her out of my way as I headed back to my bed. She followed. Of course.

"You're Destiny Ward," she said again, right behind my ear. "Right?"

"I'm Ghost, you fucking idiot," I said. Ghost who was too old and too ugly to be in demand. Ghost who didn't smile right, who dogs couldn't help but want to kill. Ghost who had a hole in her mind instead of whatever it was that would get Princess and all those little first-floor babies and second-floor sweethearts tried out and kept by fosters, far away from the damn third floor. Ghost who knew how to fix it.

I got up from the bed so fast that Princess jumped back a good foot. Even Flash flinched a little bit over by the elevator. Fuck the Agency; I could find my 'grams right now, maybe even get them put back in early. There were people who would do that if you paid them well enough. I was a hacker; I could figure it out.

I got back into my file and scrolled down. *Visit to the Ferris Wheel with Parents, Earthquake and Aftermath, Petty Larceny #1,2,3.*

And in the rightmost column of each—*Permanently Deleted.* Not held for safe-keeping until you can integrate them into adult life. Not get them back when you turn eighteen. Just gone. Totally and forever gone.

I picked up the stupid machine to throw it down on the floor, break it open like a water balloon, but Princess caught my arm.

"You don't want to—"

"You don't know what the hell I want," I said, brushing her off and heading over to the elevator. "Agency lied to us, Flash. They fucking lied. They took all our memories and said they were giving them back but they—"

"Shut it," Flash said. "They're coming up."

She was right. I could hear the whirring of the gears as the elevator climbed. This time of night, Agency bastards would want us all lying down. Proper bedtime protocol and all that bullshit. Leave us flat on our backs while they told us their lies.

I got back to my bed just in time for Mr. Nice Hair to step off, carrying Whispers in his arms. He put her down on the closest bed, nowhere near her little corner, which was how I knew she was really knocked out. Otherwise she would've started screaming all over again. Then he turned around and left without a word. Just like Miss Miranda. No time for the third-floor rejects. We probably wouldn't remember it anyway.

"Let's move her back," said Flash. Nobody moved. "You want her to start up again when she wakes up?"

I didn't care what the hell happened when she woke up, but I didn't feel like fighting. I grabbed her bony ankles while Flash took hold of her arms and Princess kept a hand under her back. Once she was passed out on her own bed, legs sprawled one way and arms another, mouth hanging open like she was a clown in a carnival game, Flash patted me on the arm. If it had been Princess, I probably would have slapped her in the face, but instead I turned my face away.

"They really wipe our stuff completely?" she asked. I nodded. "No way to hack it back?"

"Don't think so."

"I'm sorry," Princess said. When I didn't answer, she crept over to her bed and laid down, her head thudding onto the hard pillow. Flash didn't move. Just leaned in close so her mouth was right by my ear.

"I've got an idea," she said. Her voice turned from whisper to giggle.

I could almost smell the hot sauce in the air.

"Wanna go to the booth again?" I asked Princess a few days later, after school. She looked at me and nodded like I'd asked if she wanted a million bucks. With me giving her the silent treatment, all she'd had to talk to was Flash and Whispers, and that wasn't much to live on.

"Is it gonna make you mad again?" she asked, her face back in that little half-scrunch.

"Nah, I'm over it," I said. "Plus, I figured out how to share something real. You're looking at an A-plus hacker, remember?"

"Yeah, I remember." She smiled bright for the rest of the walk over to the booth. I nodded at the front desk guy as we came in, sent a whole mess of credits his way.

"Break time, right?" I said. He just raised his chin in a half-nod, then looked over at Princess's shirt like he could see through the fabric. She caught on quick and bent over again, enough for him to smile and head off. Then she went straight for the side-by-sides.

"You coming, right?" she said.

"Yeah," I said. "Go ahead and strap in. I have to hack something back here for this to work."

"Okay." Princess put on the headphones and straps and all that. The goggles covered her eyes up tight, but I turned the booth lights off too, made sure she couldn't see Flash tiptoeing in.

I called up one of the memories on the list I'd pulled from the Agency. *Brenda and her Father at her fifth birthday.*

"Hey," Princess said, "Something's off. This is one of mine."

"Not anymore," I said. Her body jerked up as my code hit the booth and she clutched her head like someone was knifing her in the eye. Princess screamed and tried to tear the straps off, to run away, but Flash held her arms down, giggling under her breath. I'd offered her a few credits to help out, but some things Flash would do for free.

"Don't worry." Flash's hands tightened against Princess' arms as Princess' hair flipped back and forth. "It only hurts for a minute. You'll barely remember."

When the twitching and moaning stopped, we unhooked Princess from the booth and Flash walked her out, steadying her like she was an old drunk. I told Flash I'd be along soon, that I needed to check everything was clear so we wouldn't get caught. But after she was out of sight, I went in for a half hour in my own booth instead. Any good thief's gotta check the merchandise. Plus I didn't like looking at Princess all limp and sad, worse than sour milk even. That was more of a Flash kinda thing. She'd said I should erase every memory Princess had forever, put us all on even ground, but I didn't want to be that way about it. I was gonna give Princess the memories back at eighteen anyway. Sooner, maybe. Once I was living with a foster in some big house with nice kids and no dogs.

Princess was long-haired and cinnamon pretty; she'd find a foster with her memories or not. Just like Hope and the rest. Just like I was gonna. With Princess' memories filling up that hole in my head, I'd be set. I'd know just how to smile with the fosters and laugh and make 'em like me—even if I didn't fit in the pictures, I'd know how to be part of a family. I'd smell like cinnamon and honey and babies and home.

I cued up the first string of memories in watch mode, so I wouldn't get too caught up in the share 'til I found the right ones. I could tell Princess was a little girl right away 'cause of how big everyone looked through her eyes, like friendly giants. There were tons of them, coming and going and bringing her things, but only two were really important—Mom and Dad, happy and smiling. I tried smiling back, giggling like she giggled when Dad picked her up to pretend fly or when Mom played peekaboo. But I couldn't get the feel of it right without going all the way in. I could hear myself through the earplugs, a high-pitched cross between a scream and the hiccups. I needed something better.

I skipped through the memories, playing a few seconds if something looked good and then moving on, looking for something like the ones that Princess had showed me before, the ones that made my hand shake and my breath skip.

But all I saw was how, each time I stopped, there were half as many people, that the presents were gone and then the toys too, that the rooms were smaller and dingier, that Mom left on a rainy day and never came back, that Princess didn't seem to care. She still had her Daddy and he always always held her tightly, close enough that even on watch I could smell the liquor on his breath—just like those booze pops I'd ordered. I still felt a little of the way she'd felt when he called her Brenda, all lit up from inside like candles on a birthday cake, but this time I wasn't swept up in the share—she was just some sad little girl wearing grimy clothes, living in a dirty room with an old man who finally died in a rocking chair. Some girl who leaned over and let a perv at a front counter see down her shirt. Some girl too dumb to figure out her own stupid memories.

I left the booth before the half hour was up, still trying to get the stink of Princess' dirty life out of my nose. Pervy was back on duty and waved me over from the front counter as I passed by.

"Your friend gonna be alright?" he said. "Seems like a sweet girl." He licked his skinny lips and I had to try not to shiver. Princess would end up swapping more than 'grams with him one of these days.

"Leave her alone," I said.

"I'm just a concerned citizen." He lifted a bushy eyebrow in a way that was probably supposed to make me feel something. "Maybe I should be concerned about what you were doing during my break."

"Just making a back up," I said. "In case there's another quake or she gets hit by a truck or something." Pervy leaned forward a little.

"I've got an extra," I said. "You want it?"

Pervy had his hands out before I could blink. They looked pale and clammy, like a piece of gum stuck under a chair too long. I fished the cube with Princess' memories out of my pocket. It was the only one I had, but she'd be better off without it. Who wants to find out at eighteen that their life has been so fucking pathetic? Screw having something real.

"I give you this, you leave her alone, alright?"

Pervy nodded. I handed the cube over, making sure not to touch his sweaty hands. Fifty-fifty chance he'd try to pull some double-cross, but if I needed to, I could take care of his memories as easy as I had Princess', so I just smiled and walked out. Can't hurt somebody you can't remember.

This time, I made curfew. I could tell by the way Miss Miranda stared me down that she couldn't wait to have some reason to give me punishment, but she was gonna have to. I smiled right at her and headed up to the third floor like I had a mouth full of cotton candy. Soon as I got off the elevator I saw Princess lying in the bed she liked, hair spread out on the pillow like a pool of old soda. Flash sprang up soon as she saw me, with that big smile she got like she was either gonna hug you or eat you.

"It's all gone," she said. "All that shit about her daddy and her perfect life? Wiped just like if the Agency got her."

I smiled back, but it felt weird, like baring fangs.

"I thought you were bullshitting about the hacking part, but you give good, Ghost," Flash said. "Maybe next you can reboot Whispers so she won't talk so damn much, right? Or creep up on Miss Miranda and take everything she's got?" She laughed hard, and I knew not to tell her anything about how it really was with Princess, 'cause then she'd be mad I gave all the good stuff away.

"The rest of her okay?" I said, like I didn't care too much really.

"Yeah, she's good. Not like Whispers or anything. Just less annoying. Cuter too." Flash glanced over at Princess like she was sizing her up in a prize booth at a fair.

"Yeah, but fosters'll probably get her soon." She'd be fine. Just like Hope. Better than her memories.

"Maybe," Flash said, "If she figures out how to keep her mouth shut."

"Fifty credits says she's gone in a month."

Flash shook her head. "She's not *that* cute."

"You said that with Hope." I shrugged and hoped my palms wouldn't be too sweaty.

"Fine." Flash grabbed my hand tight with her cold one. "But make it sixty. And when she starts blabbermouthing again, I'm gonna laugh at the both of you."

"We'll see," I said, and started over for Princess. I thought Flash might follow, but she just went back to practicing whistles like always. Princess wasn't doing much, didn't even look at me as I walked over and sat down right by her ear. Just stared up at the ceiling like any other new girl who got wiped and dumped on the third floor. Sour milk squared. But that was okay. You didn't have to stay a sour milk girl forever.

"I'm Ghost," I said, low and quiet so only she could hear. "You know Flash and Whispers. And we call you Princess, but your daddy, he called you Brenda."

FAREWELL, ADAM

XIU XINYU, TRANSLATED BY BLAKE STONE-BANKS

1. Me

After stopping my medication for just a week, I passed the test with ease.

It wasn't too much trouble. My parents never cared what I was up to. My friends probably thought I was already dead. Doctor Liu was upset but knew me well enough to know I hadn't made the decision out of selfishness, whether for my own dream of the spotlight or financial gain.

The recruitment notice had said they were searching for five "sensitive and fragile" people. Many signed up. Young fans looking to play a part in the behind-the-scenes life of a pop star were sifted out. The down-and-out, lured by a generous payday, took practice tests in hopes that the real test would classify them among the "sensitive and fragile."

I had no need for practice. A glance at my obviously depressed state told them all they needed to know.

Physical exam. Contract. Informed consent. NDA . . . It took half a month to clear the bureaucratic hurdles, but that was immaterial in the face of the decade I signed up for in that vast building. I was escorted in by employees wearing black uniforms and faces as serious as a funeral.

I bathed, changed clothes, and bid farewell to my former life. It had been a long time since I had said goodbye to anyone.

"Goodbye," the last employee said as he stepped toward the door.

"Actually, one small question." My voice sounded brittle. It had been a while since I had spoken. "Why is he called Adam? Don't we believe Nvwa made the first men?"

It was a stupid question. I said a lot of stupid things when depressed.

The employee just stared back as though uncertain he should waste his breath on such a dull question. His hand gripped the door handle, released it, then gripped it again. Perhaps he tolerated my question because he realized I was indeed "sensitive and fragile" and "stupid."

"The reason's simple. When Nvwa made the first men from yellow clay, she gave them no names." He left and shut the door.

No name. Just like me and the other ninety-nine.

The device I wore looked like headphones. It was designed to look familiar, so that we would feel more at ease toward everything about to happen.

"Close your eyes," said a voice. I wondered if there was anything alive behind it.

As I lay on the bed, I made sure the machine delivering my nourishment was functioning correctly. I shot one last glance over that barren place I had inhabited so long, the physical world.

I clenched my eyes shut.

It was night. So, with the four "sensitive and fragile" others, I slipped into Adam's dream.

2. Adam

At this moment, I'm thinking of Tchaikovsky, that restless sublimity that pervades his work. Heard. Glimpsed. Tasted. All senses colliding, intertwining. But as they say, truth once born can only wither.

I dip brush to pigment, fill the canvas with saturated colors, searching for a new center, a new symmetry to the work. Sometimes I think it's already enough. These moments are enough. These moments are eternal. But then I realize I still have so long to live.

They call me an idol. Not that I need to be careful about maintaining my image. There are no skills that need practicing. Singing, dancing, performing, sketching, painting, replicating the world. Already, my command of these arts is unparalleled. Among all singers and painters, they say I'm the most extraordinary. As I must be. After all, I have a one-hundred-person team consulting on my every movement.

Five more newcomers have just integrated. I didn't feel their entry into the one-hundred-person team. At least everything still feels natural enough, which is good. It means they've been absorbed into the greater will, absorbed into *Adam*. In turn, Adam has been absorbed into my own subconscious.

So far, I've been able to separate my emotions from Adam's. In the face of his rabid fans, I just don't care, and that makes Adam upset. People like to see Adam upset. The uncanny, beautiful breed of fresh-faced pop stars is too much for the masses. More and more, people are drawn to the defects in his character. They believe defects are more real. Don't they know nothing is real?

At the evening's art auction, fans are still gathering, all wearing matching rescue worker uniforms, waving shiny placards. All young girls. When they catch my eye, their excitement becomes palpable. Faces blush. I turn and methodically wave. They're cute, much younger than me—especially if I add the years of the rest of the one-hundred team when calculating my age. I already feel old despite the expanse of years still ahead of me.

One fan in the front sensually pulls at her collar and blows me a kiss. Her skin is porcelain, breasts full, the very portrait of Salome. Sublime, yet with a solemn foreboding about her. I shut my eyes so I can imagine returning her kiss, then open to fix on her again in the light.

Then *he* saunters, late like always but always turning up. This is my seventeenth encounter with him. Considering the popularity and price of admission to my events, it's obvious he has time and money.

I want to smile.

But I shouldn't. How could I have such a stupid idea?

Or perhaps, it's Adam who wants to smile? The elaborate system of inputs and algorithms through which we control him is just another system . . . but I sense it growing its own personality. It becomes upset, suppressed, oversensitive, even suspicious.

His cold face winks at me with deliberate slowness. It's as though he's communicating in some indecipherable code. Perhaps one of the one-hundred-person team in the control system should be able to decipher his code. Or perhaps not. But I know there is something wrong, some foreboding I cannot name, as though I have just glimpsed the darkest cloud in the bluest sky. Torrential rains blacken the horizon, always.

I shift my attention toward the ecstatic fans in the back. But no matter what I try, I can't force *him* from my sight. He doesn't participate in the auction, just stares the whole time at me. So halfway through the evening's auction, I walk out.

In the night's dream, I am again in boundless water. I have suggested to the company that they research how to control my dreams, but it seems they haven't found a solution. They tell me it's just a stress response stemming from the contact between my subconscious and Adam's body. They have no idea when the dreams will stop.

I dream of the water, slowly rising, always. The flood is without end. So many times have I been inundated, pulled under, only to open my eyes on nothingness.

3. Me

They let five of us celibates in. They required we be celibate at the time of our selection and ideally afraid of women. Of course, they did this because his dopamine levels were abnormal and it was so difficult to stabilize Adam's emotions. Recently, Adam had almost fallen in love. Among the one-hundred-person team, about sixty of us were still in our early twenties. Even celibate, we were a pack of hormonal animals.

They would never allow Adam to love or marry. After all, his obsessed fans were mostly girls. They wanted the girls to dream of filling that gap in his life, dream of comforting his "sensitive and fragile" soul. That was how fanaticism thrived.

Adam became irritable, gloomy. At these times, fifteen of our most "sensitive and fragile" people would take over seventy percent control rights in order to make Adam's sadness appear more real.

Adam never cried, though when I was alone, I would sometimes cry at night. I didn't know why. I suppose crying made me feel a little better, but in the long run "a little better" doesn't help. Perhaps the reason Adam never cried was that the other ninety-nine believed it too embarrassing for a man to cry.

No women had joined us. At least not then.

I'd been inside for more than three months already, but it was still weird to look in the mirror. In it, I saw a handsome face, a face *too* handsome. It was precisely this handsomeness that had made Adam courageous enough ten years earlier to enter the media's limelight and to be cast across every type of platform. It was this handsomeness that made the entertainment companies pay huge sums of money to sign contracts with his parents. It was this handsomeness that made him, at the age of fifteen, surrender his body to this puppet life, in which meaning could only be found in cascades of staged encounters and disguises constructed for lusting fans.

Because the company's questionnaire was so exhaustive, its predictions were generally accurate. The algorithm evolved Adam into the most worshipped of idols. To be honest, I empathized with him, but more than that, I was jealous. Adam was the cynosure.

I hated eggs. It wasn't just the taste. I was also allergic. Unfortunately, the other ninety-nine didn't have this problem. So Adam every morning had to eat eggs. And every morning, I had to endure that disgusting taste.

Ten years. I had to persist here for a full ten years.

When I emerged, I would be thirty-five years old, crow's feet at the corners of my eyes, white hairs behind my temples. But I would have money, a lot of money, more than enough money. I would be able to hire a great voice teacher, afford sessions in the finest recording studios, perhaps even hold a few small concerts of my own.

So I waited.

4. Adam

I am in the boundless water again.

When I wake, my eyes fix on the ceiling. I remain motionless for a long while. In these moments of waking from a long dream, the ceiling reminds me of the shimmering sea.

The 8 AM alarm rings. I shut it off, roll over, and see if I can't get back to sleep. I'm supposed to do a talk show at ten, but decide to skip. My assistant will understand. He knows I haven't been sleeping well.

I roll back into sleep, but the dream is changed.

It is no longer a soundless, flavorless, senseless thing. There is a long, drawn-out hum permeating the water, like a whale song or the whistle of an ocean liner. Or rather the snoring of such monsters, whether biological or steel. I have never lived by the sea. But as I dream of these mist-shrouded waters, they become more like the waters of the deep sea, blue and green. I hear the indistinct murmur of waves, sporadic cries of seabirds. Is something alive waiting beneath me in the depths?

Water flows in, flows out. And I wait.

With the exception of my strange dreams, other aspects of my life are progressing more smoothly. The new album is more successful than anyone imagined. That cute head of the fan club continues to pen her love letters to me. She's quite an interesting girl actually.

A boy who I saved from drowning ten years ago has just tested into a top-name university. We agree to meet on Friday evening so I can treat him to a congratulatory dinner.

When we meet, the dinner proceeds normally at first, but then a young boy in a school uniform shows up. His uniform looks absurd next to the crowd's evening wear. The boy ogles me, steps closer.

There will always be crazy fans willing to do anything to track me down. A few no doubt will succeed, like flies hopping back and forth that won't be swatted away. They wear me down.

I step back and wait for my bodyguards to drive the boy away. He's escorted out without incident, without speaking, without screaming "Adam, I love you." But all the time, he's looking at me in this strange way. It's hard for me to pinpoint how I know that look in his eyes. But something in his eyes wrenches me.

When he's gone, the crowd calms, returns to normal. It's then I notice my assistant is staring at me too.

"He look familiar?" my assistant asks. "The boy's father is a member of the one-hundred-person team, a middle school teacher who signed up to earn money for the boy's education. His son misses him. His son has always wanted to see you. He thought to see you would be like seeing his own father."

They must always know the intimate details of my followers. Without a doubt, this is what guarantees my safety. I nod, think back on the child's eyes. My face feels hot, my heart cold. I tremble as though an electric current passes through me. The hairs on my body stand on end as though the air has suddenly grown chill. I feel strange, almost ill.

I kneel then on the ground, cover my face, cry. It is the only time I can remember crying. But that doesn't matter, the people will like to watch me cry.

5. Me

It became increasingly difficult to tell myself from Adam.

Perhaps that was a hazard of the job. In the first few years, when Adam was sleeping, we would often take short breaks. We could leave our rooms, walk the halls, sit in the lounge, and stare at each other in silence. After a while, we might eat something, watch a movie or crack a few jokes.

We almost never speak of our former lives. It was only those hired with the responsibility of "cheerful conversation"—mostly C-list actors and former journalists—who gossiped about their experiences. Of course, no one actually cared about their experiences. Adam was the only one that mattered. Adam, young and handsome, sought after. It was only through this system that any of us would have a chance to experience something like that great life of Adam's. We were the mud Nvwa had flung, unrecognizable, still evolving from the primal chaos. Only Adam had been given a name.

During the third year inside, there was one small change. As part of the system's optimizations, it was requested we bind ourselves even more deeply to Adam. Our daily cycles of work and rest all had to synchronize with Adam's. Even our dreams had to become his dreams. We had to become him each and every moment. The assistant didn't tell this to our faces, just forwarded on a twenty-five-page addendum to our contracts defining the new rules. We had only a few minutes to read and confirm we would continue to participate.

I saw no other choice, so I lost myself entirely. Adam lost himself entirely.

And the charade of "we" became our truth.

They optimized the algorithm, modulating the one-hundred-person team to make Adam more stable. To use an ancient Chinese phrase, they were searching for the *zhongyong*, the golden mean. Even if they integrated those with more intense personalities, the output should be the same: a golden mean of anxiety, a golden mean of melancholy, a golden mean of ecstasy.

"Not good enough," was the company's only response.

No one can be loved forever, but the new algorithm did offer some protections. It wouldn't make Adam do anything too extreme, too stupid. Still the company was right. For an idol, it was "not good enough." Far from good enough.

At Adam's last exhibition, someone splashed one of his works with paint.

The world's love comes in limited quantities. The more love there was for Adam, the less love there was for others. The perpetrator was someone with a heartache, and the girl who had caused his yearning happened to be a member of Adam's fan club. It went down like this: after a cry of alarm, after the chaos, while everyone was waiting to see Adam's reaction, Adam just began to laugh in embarrassment. The reaction was even worse than no reaction. Embarrassment, laughter . . . as though Adam were just an ordinary person.

For three straight weeks, Adam's popularity metrics declined. The company began work on a dynamic weighting mechanism for the algorithm. The objective was to optimize Adam's reactions to make them more distinctive. It was decided that in certain conditions, the system would shift control to the optimal person among the one-hundred-person team who would then act for Adam.

I wasn't sure how well the new algorithm worked for Adam, but I got used to it and liked it. On a few mornings upon waking from some strange dream, when Adam would walk absentmindedly into the kitchen to select his breakfast, the system would select me from among the most "sensitive and fragile." I was able to stop him from eating eggs.

These small victories brought me some happiness. Perhaps they even made Adam happy. Perhaps we were even gradually becoming each other. I do not know.

6. Adam

It's a hot day, the day of the awards ceremony.

After some time away, I should be delighted and excited. At least, I shouldn't feel like this, so strangely anxious. Perhaps, there's an issue with the algorithm or the hundred-person team. My assistant reminds me that the algorithm has never had a significant issue. This only increases my irritation.

I'm twenty-six years old. A truly talented artist would have published a memoir by this age. But I've been too busy being chased by fans, being cheered on by the bright-eyed crowd to do the next meaningless thing and grab the next meaningless award.

But of course I have to participate in the charade. My assistant reminds me I have already signed the contract, signed on for thirty years. The money will bring my dear mother and father a true fortune. They already have a second child. They delight in watching my performances and showing off my success.

I take a deep breath as I prepare for the stage, where I will soon receive the Best Vocal Artist Award. I'm not even sure what "best vocal artist" is supposed to mean, but if that's what people say I am, then—

Then I see *him* again.

The one from the performance. The one from the auction. The one from the opening ceremony. That familiar face that always shows up. His appearance is more gaunt, but his clothing is even more exquisite. This new look makes his figure even more imposing, makes me think of Beethoven.

I'm overwhelmed. I flash a smile, but he doesn't smile back.

"What are you looking at?" my assistant asks. I just shake my head.

I never expected things would develop to this point. As I go to accept the award, he pulls out a pistol, aims it at my chest, shoots . . . I fly backwards.

Fortunately, the paranoid Adam insisted on a bulletproof vest. As I look toward my would-be killer, I see no expression on the man's face, yet in it I still recognize grief. His face may still be young, but there is white hair behind the temples. From some angles, he looks so familiar. From some angles, he looks just like me.

My assistant wraps me in a thick blanket. "That guy was your childhood friend," he says. "You're successful. He's poor, a failure. He's jealous and thinks he can extort—"

"He wants to kill me," I interrupt.

Showing no hint of fear, my assistant pats me on the back. It's as though he'd known long ago everything that would happen. "Yes, because we ignored his attempt at extortion," he says. "Anyway, he won't get close to you again."

I know the attempted murder will win us tomorrow's headlines.

I stare through the distant door to the commotion outside as the man is escorted into a police car. The light from outside stings as I peer into its glare. In the flickering light, instead of a cold and steeled killer, a tired man stoops, shrugs. His silhouette reminds me of an old man. He still seems familiar, but now just slightly. Since connecting into Adam, so much information has flooded my mind, such a dazzling life since the age of fifteen, if only a few vague shards of memory before that age. Even the memory of jumping into the water to save the child is a blur. The company doesn't care about the past. It only cares about the future. So must I.

It's possible the man didn't want to actually kill me. It's possible he only wanted to grab my attention. It's possible he only wanted to make me remember, to return to that childhood we had spent together. We were friends once—*friends*, what a weird word.

"Can I give him some money?" I ask. "Anonymously?"

My assistant takes a deep breath. "And then make it seem like the company confirms it hired a killer to wound you as some publicity stunt? Adam, are you really this dumb?" My assistant looks sad. Most of the time, he's a mindless workaholic and won't even tell me his name, says it would be unprofessional. But when things fall apart, he treats me like an older brother would. He reaches to fix my hair. For a moment, I feel this is real.

7. Me

The whole dorm couldn't sleep, though I was no longer sure what it meant to be asleep or awake anymore. When Adam slept, I wandered his dreams, not that there was anything there. Only boundless water that would sooner or later pull us under.

8. Adam

"Have you decided yet?" my assistant asks. From his tone, I can tell he's losing his patience. After all, the banquet is almost over, and he's already urged me seven times.

I nod, sip from my glass of wine. After I refuse to take the stage, everyone starts whispering. But even if I spoke to them, none of these people could decipher the dreams that torture me. There is no cipher, only the boundless water.

"I'll tell them you're drunk, but get it straight. Any contract violation will cost us dearly," my assistant says. "If we cut out, earnings from all concerts during the first half will be gone, but I guess you've been needing your vacation. Just push off the shows and take a few weeks in your painting studio. You need a break."

I look at him, patiently wait for him to continue his little explanation. He knows what kind of explanation I'm waiting to hear.

"There's nothing for you to do now," my assistant says. "Just get out of here. You have no right to change the one-hundred-person team. That was decided by the company. We agreed to that long ago."

"No, not necessarily," I say. "I could cancel the contract altogether."

"Cancel the contract?" my assistant says. "You want that?"

"I can leave Adam and cancel the contract. Push the rest out . . . " It takes strenuous effort to pull these words from my mouth, like pulling heavy stones from wet pockets.

This might be the bravest moment of my life. The sad thing is I don't know if the courage comes from me or from Adam.

My assistant stares back astonished. "So you forgot again, didn't you, Adam?" He shakes his head, mutters as though talking to himself. "Yep, you forgot. You always forget the most important things. They say it's too painful for you to remember. But listen, you can never leave Adam. You can't leave because you are Adam. You are the will of the hundred. You are the body, that limp, paralyzed body. I can't believe you really forgot again."

My head droops. A few of my fingers bend absently, as though trying to grasp at the void. I remember something, say, "But I saved the child . . . "

"Right, you saved him, but the water still drowned him too." My assistant laughs. "A lot of people were disappointed. His older brother wanted to take the body back, to lay him to rest, but we had signed an agreement with the parents and there was nothing to be done about the contract."

I hear the sound of waterfalls. I hear the sound of torrential rains. Something is calling from the distance. Once the one hundred rivers flow east into the sea, how will they return to the west? We are the countless drops of water that form the sea. Nothing can separate us, except perhaps death.

I flash a smile at my assistant. I raise my wine glass, down it. I glance downstairs. Up here in the penthouse, the banquet hall is crowded with faces and noise. Below, all is quiet, vacant. From up here, the pool below is a perfect strip of blue. The soft waves will not be soft again, I think.

In the end, water will conquer all.

9. Me

I plummeted into the water.

Adam plummeted into water.

We plummeted into water.

I wasn't the first to pull off the "headphones."

Upon waking, light was blurred. Sound muddled. My first thought was there must have been a malfunction.

I realized I was not in that small room quiet as the grave. Over the years we had spent inside Adam, the whole building layout had changed.

It was crowded now. Well over one hundred shabby cots were placed right up against each other, leaving only narrow paths between them. I heard the creak of bed boards, the scuff of hard shoes on tile floors, human whispers.

Old Doctor Liu was seated at my bedside. I could tell there was something he wanted to say.

I blinked and became aware the noise had stopped. Suddenly there was no one else around. It seemed like everyone else had woken and left. When Adam died, the contract had been automatically annulled.

"I told you that if you stopped taking your medication, you might die," Doctor Liu said. "Seventy percent of it was your own choice. They wanted me to come and talk to you."

He tried to smile, an embarrassed smile, a sorry-but-no-cure-for-what-you've-got smile.

"The decision was made by the algorithm." I heard my voice trembling. "It wasn't my fault."

"No." Doctor Liu brought a hand to his chin. "They want me to ask . . . if you would allow your identity to serve as a prototype for a new idol." There was an equivocation in his voice, as though he were waiting for me to grasp something. Finally he said, "After all, you've become the new cynosure."

In that last moment as Adam, it had been me in control, me who killed him. Just as there had been no shortage of people who wanted to kill Adam, there would be no shortage of people who wanted to avenge his death. His fans would want me dead.

My expression made my thoughts obvious. Doctor Liu added, "They will fully guarantee your safety."

"But I'm not some paralyzed body like Adam. I have my own will and—"

"Of course, they will respect your will. The new team will just help carry out your will even better. Didn't you tell me once you liked to sing? They will make you the greatest singer."

"A singer, me?" I heard myself retort. The last few years were a disintegrating hallucination, like the draining of a vast pool. The universe spun 'round the drain of my mind, until all that was left was hollow grief. I thought on Adam's fall, that eternal fall, like an island slipping beneath boundless water.

Only in that moment did I realize he was really dead.

Our friend. Our enemy. Our idol.

Farewell, Adam.

Originally published in Chinese in *Science Fiction World*, January 2018.

SAY IT LOW, THEN LOUD

OSAHON IZE-IYAMU

Efosa always dreams of absolutes. A whole integer leaping through the spaces of his subconscious. A positive value an everlasting constant in sleep, where there should be no place for negativity. No space for fractions.

A half thought mind is the breeding ground for enemies, his mother says, in sleep too. She is long gone, as her ancestors have called her. They beckoned her, and now Efosa does not have enough cultural ties, relatives—never enough, space is not your ties, not your fatherland, not your once colonialist objective.

He misses her proverbial wisdoms. All the words that twisted in on themselves, often silly but always true. Upon pondering on these sayings, they always grew more interesting and revealing, layers and layers of knowledge. They were like food to the tongue, and he usually needed seconds. These secrets she knew were passed down to keep the history, the culture.

Culture is not an absolute. Not to him, at least, in its values, as it is never complete, not perfection. Not a whole. There's always a disconnect, a barrier preventing his identity from being his everything, always . . . rough numbers not causing him to fall to slumber.

Efosa's mother refused to share more secrets with him after he announced his role in the war. She screamed and rose in temperament when he told her. She shook her head in all her disapproval and folded her arms in betrayal. Finally, she became a negative equation, then turned silent. She made the family shut him out. She cursed his breath before perishing. She placed all the special values in a space he could not reach, with family members who will never tell.

Everything that's valuable is told orally, kept within the locks of the mouth, and all his earth country's popular history and properties that's found in bits and bytes have been appropriated, rendered meaningless.

There is nothing without context, specifics.

When he thinks on these things, sleep is once again a thing that cannot be savored, an accomplishment destroyed, a war that makes him wonder what's worth fighting for, who he is, who he is meant to be.

Efosa and his war general both love values, but his war general's love is to the point that she thinks words should be obsolete. Efosa never agreed to this, and upon hearing the woman proclaim it the first time, his lips curled to a frown. He obsessed over it, this concept that words should be nothing. It disturbed his sleep, the general's belief, the one thing he values.

When Efosa told the general he didn't agree with this opinion, that numbers are indeed great things but words control the world, the woman nodded, but shifted away from him after that. Always made excuses when Efosa asked if she wanted to solve equations with him in the great library hall. Avoided him, like she couldn't stand his thought process.

He had to do his late hours calculating in the hall with all the strangers that have eyes on him; on his soldier badge, to be specific. The young Indian tech whiz that has an insult for Efosa under their breath. The Igbo college student with the bulging muscles and towering height, who is rejecting him at every step, every feet. The Black woman and her two grandbabies that spit at Efosa's feet. Most people he sees, knows don't like the war; they know enough about it and how much it costs. How much it takes. Efosa wonders how much he needs to do to push these people to the point that they take action, destroy his work and livelihood. This colonial evil.

When none of them do anything, his thoughts go back to words and purpose.

The annual code-naming day that came in the winter consisted of General 1019 listing her numbers to all officials, like she was counting out a census. The soldiers' war names, for future reference, forever and ever. For Efosa, she stopped, peered at him. 1019 assessed him, before she stepped really close to him, like old times, and named him Whisper.

Whisper: Because you should always be silent and respect your superiors. Because your culture even has a foundation of greeting and the young < old, not =, not anything other than what they gave you. Because you must not always speak, disagree, when there are wars to be fought.

Because maybe if you calculated more—estimating expenditures, equating soldiers to figures when filing strategic placement—instead of thinking, you would finally find rest.

1019 never told him what Whisper meant, but he couldn't deal with all the different interpretations going on in his mind, so Efosa made a constant to soothe his dreams.

Whisper: Because your flying is soundless and your limitations are boundless and you are a valuable asset to winning a war assumed worth fighting for.

Like horseback, like carriage, like airships, like drones, past and future all together, over the planets and stars, Efosa goes to fight his enemies and conquer the land.

His enemies. The war should be personal, even though he couldn't further disassociate from this. Even when he's sure everyone is tired of it, and some don't even know about it, and it's just reducing the empire to poverty, closed hands that cannot give, but now the war has just become a habit to pillage and take, as that's the constant.

The difference between him and the war: The war never heard of the concept of rest. Never wants to stop. Never wants to fall down and die, empty itself and all its emotions. The war's identity is Western.

The politicians call the *war* small-scale missions on broadcast missions everywhere. The government doesn't provide enough equipment, funding. Despite all this, it doesn't end. War never pauses, because it's easy to know where to go when it's only to destroy.

He's always been taught to love anything, everything—engineer, doctor; let minorities take space and make themselves majority; his mother once said—so he can still feel active and find work meaningless. Because of this, he doesn't think Mama should have been all that surprised when he told her where he was going in life, but at least it told him that there *are* wrong options, bad choices.

What can he do if not the war?

He frowns today, deep scowls scarring thought of any kind, which he would have appreciated if he was in sleep. 1019 once offered him a cryo-freeze pass if he ever wanted to take a little break and get like, well, 1,000,000+ hours in slumber, give or take. She estimated that when he got up they would still be fighting the war and gaining territory for humans to expand to new places (colonialism; it's colonialism) without *much* opposition.

If there *is* opposition, then there is death.

Efosa frowns because the calculations for the speed of the drone he rides today and its level of operation is at a fractional level. He tried and tried and tried the night before, calculating repeatedly for different result, but math is firm. He tore out his curly black hair in clumps, easier to do after last year when he removed his dreadlocks. He can't even approximate the properties because increasing values for drone operations almost made him crash into the spaceship of a parasite species that had spindly blue appendages once, when 1019 was going to try out her special attack formation that day, which would have been structured to look like a foot from a distance when all the drones came together. His punishment was even worse, in the form of helping amend the budget for his crash, taking away the money from public health centers, because at the end of the day everybody suffers.

He has to ride out a decimal and all its bumps in the air. The giant metal disc he sits on has invisible barriers all around it for oxygen and weapons control, but it's mostly seen as just a circular flexible magnet that has rectangular slots to aim at the enemies. The machines aren't as strong as they used to be.

He has to ride his ship through the dull natural light of space, since protests by NGOs came down hard on all the soldiers for encouraging light pollution through the artificial brightness of the ships. It was a huge scandal.

He never sees those protest numbers when it comes to the colonialist issues in invading peaceful planets through hostile takeover; but he's still a hypocrite and not really changing anything, only grinding his teeth about inconsistent values.

Efosa has never had his priorities right. Maybe it would be better if someone stopped him, said cease and desist. Somehow, he hopes that cultural secrets and the past of his ancestors will help him with his mistakes, show him the way to go—see how perfect his siblings and relations are; na the same Mama raise them—but the family's shut him out, and they're anti-war, and they're withholding secrets like children and parts of his identity he needs now more than ever.

Efosa doesn't know how to say he's at a standstill.

He's not exactly pro-war, but, meh, this has good health benefits. And security, too. He's going to have a full life. In the future, maybe, where he sleeps with peace . . .

The formation work is sloppy and disgraceful. The ships were supposed to form a balloon but they look already popped in their construction; full of defeat. He moves the fastest and without sound but he still wobbles his way through his drone like he's never done an operation before. Efosa almost crashes. He doesn't do anything to show he's in control, doesn't feign pulling the reigns of the drone he rides like his acquaintance 2348 does (there are no friends in war; just those that live and die with you, fight side by side with you, that flash before your eyes then disappear like memories), and 1019 makes him go to the back of the line.

The back of the formation is filled with interns and trainees that just bump into him every five seconds. They're sloppy too, a mixture of who 1019 and officials are testing and who they don't want and who have to stay because of potential lawsuits. He can hear the spoils of war—genocide, destruction, the *sides,* as well as the annoying sounds of excited first years trying to get an interview with him while they're on a mission. Neither of them he really appreciates.

"My monthly average is going to be so bad," he mutters under his breath, while the noises of activity go on all around him.

For a minute, this feels like rest, but . . . no, it can't be. No. Efosa will not accept it. This moment feels like a crushing weight beneath his windpipe, an ache between his eyes, and it is not what he wants. Not what he's been looking for. Efosa will literally throw himself down from his drone and calculate his speed to the absolute infinity so he can burn up as the waste of oozing flesh and muscle that he is if he finds out that rest means giving up spirit, mind still whirring when the war takes and takes and takes, and he is left with nothing.

The family is always watching.

Efosa's ties are supposed to be far away on Omega-17, places where kin can continue to shut him out and distance conversation. Leave him in isolation, as being cursed before death carries a shame full of stink that never leaves. The elite all lay on home planet, bound to tradition and every old way. Efosa has never interacted with an Elder there since joining the war, and they would rather die than talk to him. Efosa's great-grand-uncle even has pictures where the man dances with serrated, long legged parasites, his uncle and the being forever memorialized in a tap dance. Whenever Efosa's great-grand-uncle sees him, the man screams "criminal" like bloody murder. Once, the man convinced the family to put Efosa in a cage when he was visiting, citing appropriate punishment for his war crimes.

His elders' existence is a mere revelation, a look into his heritage, but they will never give him the privilege of even a smidge of more identity.

Maybe one day, Efosa thinks, he can gain these secrets *without* their approval. Perhaps if they ever digitize this information he can calculate a hack into it.

The family members with the wandering spirits are not Omega-17, but rather all over the galaxy, in places like solar huts and climate-protecting holes. But he knows his nuclear relatives are only here, near the war region's current station, spying on him.

They aren't subtle with it. Every once in a while he sees Ede, his sister, reading from an archival memory tab then peering up at him every minute or so in the great library hall. He always waves, but she looks alarmed, her eyes widened whenever Efosa spots her, and quickly runs away. It gives him a good laugh.

Still, he's glad they're here. Their home is steadied at a forever value of ninety on each side, a perfect right angle which makes the place never lopsided, even with its terrible location near asteroid clusters.

He only goes to visit when those that hate him most aren't around to chase him out, like today, when his war-hating uncles have gone for their annual visit to homeworld. His skin feels disgusting on him and he hates himself a little bit, so that's also another reason for visiting.

He's not sure what caused a trigger in his sleep last night: family or fragments or . . . the war, that's a new one. It occurs in violent flashes—the blood that's not literally on his hands but in sleep, he can taste it on his lips; the flavor and song of extinction (silence, then pandemonium); the cry of what lives and what breathes, before it's in the aim of a beam and then . . . gone.

It explains hating his skin. It explains visiting the family that will stress him more. As Efosa enters, past his family's security system that's finished scanning him, he can hear the sound of his sister, Osama, sleeping, while his other sister Ede is humming the lyrics to "Black Sheep." Joke's on her, since he's already eaten the chocolates he brought for them.

Ede, of course, is wearing an Ankara print wrapper and head scarf on her head. The smell of Jollof rice wafts through the kitchen, followed by a hearty selection of stewed chicken that's been left to marinate in spicy tomato sauce and stir-fry. Dodo is laid out in celebration: rose platters, cubes, sculptural designs, while the children snack hungrily. Ede must be trying to prove something, still, with all this: Efosa delights in knowing she hasn't yet reached anything close to satisfaction. He sees her in markets and shops, and each time he comes to visit, it's always more food, clothes, traditional songs she never learned.

Culture she's trying to expand like plants that never grew. He does not know how she plans to go higher when she doesn't have all the seeds.

The cultural secrets awakened her, Ede tells everyone each year at family gatherings on home planet, and those who've been told, nod. Efosa finds himself drinking more at those events.

"How is the genocide campaign?" Ede speaks, like every minute she expects to burst into a flurry of old languages. It doesn't help that The Grant is always on her mind, the prize for the family member that can first deliver a Bini speech not influenced with any other language or imperialist power (no pidgin, fellas).

Never enough, space is not your ties, not your fatherland, not your once colonialist objective.

"How are your children?" Efosa diverts, and he immediately sees her eyes perk up, leave the lines of contempt and betrayal. Ede tries her hardest to be strict but is ultimately willing to discuss the easier thing, instead, which is why she's Efosa's favorite sibling.

In the next generation he is nothing but an uncle. There are less complications to the family dynamic with his youngest relatives; they don't know what to hate him for yet. They don't know what to keep from him. Slowly, though, when their values and loyalties come to them, he knows his days of objective love are numbered.

"Ugh, just look at this one, Efosa! I can see it in his eyes, he's shining," Ede screams, causing her son, Ghare, to look up from his drawing and glare at her, before focusing back on his work.

"Look at that concentration. His face dey scan informate! Ah, see the—"

Efosa scratches his head and sighs, all of Ede's words muddled in his brain. "Can you . . . not speak to me in pidgin?"

"Why not?" Ede pouts, Osama's snore almost clouding their conversation.

I understand it less and less with each passing moment.

"It's disgusting. It's dirty," he speaks, waves her off.

Ede pauses to look at him. Her eyebrows are raised, and her face is a sweaty mixture of surprise and slow remembrance, so she adjusts her tone accordingly.

"Ok, well, I'm not disgusting. And neither are all the—"

"Oh, for—stop jumping to conclusions! I didn't mean it like that. Quit trying to antagonize me. You're always doing this!"

Ede laughs, her voice as bitter as the green tea she likes to drink. "Antagonize? I don't think I could do any more of that."

"Ede, I can't deal with this. You need to stop over—"

"*I'm* over? Over-what? No, you know what? I think I've been letting you get too comfortable," Ede replies, and Efosa's eyes widen. He didn't expect this from her. "I think you should get out."

Efosa's face pales, and he runs to another side of the room before Ede can insist again. He knows if she sees him getting along with Ghare she won't speak anymore. He just has to avoid her path, not step on her toes so he can enjoy the family he has left.

He deserves it, he knows, the scorn and contempt, and all the consequences that are surely coming his way (he won't leave the war without a scar, a bruise, a broken promise, a shattered life), but Ede is ruining his mood.

Out of his pack of chocolates, he places a triple-coated milk delight near Ghare, watching his nephew's sketches. The pencil work's faint, but grows broad and more defined with each passing moment, like the boy is finally jumping higher, towards the sun with each stroke.

"That's cool," Efosa says to Ghare after a pause. He knows what the boy's drawing, but he always enjoys hearing people's excitement dance off their voices when they talk about their work. "What is it?"

"It's a generation ship. For animals!" He says, outlining a globe with his pencil midair as he skyrockets out his seat. "We're moving more towards history educationally, and the computer and art teachers have been droning on about the topic forever. I'm inspired."

The vessel Ghare sketched takes up the page, and it resembles a giant fan the way he modeled it. Efosa loves symbolism, imagery, even the ones he can't understand.

"The heaviest animals are on the bottom floor, and there are cold and underwater regions for things like polar bears and fishies," Ghare continues, visibly effervescent.

"Who's gonna slow roast that chicken in the picture for generations to come?" Efosa teases, pokes Ghare in the chest.

"Mummy and Aunty asked this same question two days ago. There are no humans on this ship! Oh my goodness, why do you all love food so much?"

Efosa shouts and points the accusatory finger at his nephew. "That was a good amount of dodo I saw you enjoying earlier, child."

"I was prepping my energy!" Ghare screams defensively.

"Nah, no food shaming here. You should be fat in peace," Efosa jokes.

Ghare shrugs. "That's fair. But there's everything on my ship: there's places for bugs and mosquitoes and elephants and all the things that go moo and that fly and that sing. All the things that swim and breathe. But no humans."

"He's a poet, too," Ede says, then bursts out crying, stretching out her hands to the heavens.

"I love the construction of this!" Efosa says, throwing his hands in the air and then placing them on his nephew. "I don't think this was intentional, but this work is at a perfect sixty. That's a pretty good estimate for flying the galaxy. You know, where I work, I do a lot of this kind of thing, and the math, I must say—"

"Um, Uncle Efosa, I hate to interrupt, but your hands shaking while on top of me is really uncomfortable."

"What?"

"Your hands—they were fine before but then you started talking about where you work and they just started shaking all of a sudden."

"Oh." His hands leave his nephew's slowly like that's his last latch onto the universe, and pretty soon the world is crashing over him. The entire concept of existence falls on top of him. He has drowned in a sea of equations too complex for him. He can't raise his leg out of the rubble.

He can't leave that house fast enough.

Whisper: But your sounds are not quiet when you wake up screaming at night, disturbed, enraged, hungry. Everywhere you make a sound. Everywhere you are whining and hopeless, lost in a desert of windy sighs that have blown you into no direction. No direction. Not even magnitude.

Whisper: Maybe your name *is* a farce, a mockery, a snicker behind your back. There's something behind your back. There's a monster behind your shadow or is that just . . . you? You reflect you. What are you, if you can't even be a constant, solid then differentiated to be at zero, at rest?

Hey, now: A constant is consistent except only when it's content.

A whisper: *You won't sleep fulfilled. You won't live fulfilled. You won't be—*

Efosa opens his eyes and sits up in bed and looks for a recording. He wasn't sleeping. He wipes his eyes and makes some instant onion noodles over low heat while he scrolls through old videos. It is ancient, but the recording is clear to mind when he cannot sleep, as most things are.

All his internal conflicts saved for the night hours.

It is a tape that's like a checklist. It reminds him of Mama, yet it offers no sage advice, no cultural specificity. It is as bland as white rice and that is why he can't connect to it.

He plays the recording.

We know that soldiers are doing good work, and we're here to aid with your needs! And we're ready to tackle your mental health problems with our all-new Sound for Help system. Say it loud into your room and be free, so we can help fight this battle TOGETHER.

The room listens, amplifies through static because this function has never been used before by Efosa, like a rat expecting the steps of a new human before it can move.

Mental health problems . . . together.

He can feel his insides moving—slowly pumping, beating. He can feel the knot in his throat.

Together.

He hesitates. He can't find the words. They can barely come out of him. His vocal cords are tightened, still.

"I, Efosa "Whisper" . . . I'll be fine. Turn it off. Turn it off."

Friday at dawn at the station, where he is still full of sleep. Of thoughts. Repining restlessness and frustration while the alarms ring. Efosa screams at the room's control systems to shut off the noise, which doesn't work, so he breathes, then asks nicely, which does.

There is silence.

Dressing is nothing; the same selection of clothes from a time when the war used to be stylish and sponsored, what caught everyone's eye. He could opt for a wrap shirt that he could pin to his shoulders, but he takes something simple, ordinary.

Yet he runs up to training and finds stunning hilarity.

It actually makes him belly laugh, makes him stop jogging. Makes him stop thinking. Is this him? He's falling out of routine. The world's in chaos. A war. His war. His comrades scratch their heads and even jump the air to catch the drones, but the machines move out of grasp. 1019 huffs and puffs like she's about to blow the whole charade down but even her anger doesn't do jack to the scene in front of her.

The drones—they fly, majestic, like they've never gone higher before. They sway, side to side, plunge dive, then move in little shifts again. The low humming of the engines feels like singing, something baritone and sweet and beyond boundaries. This is . . . a whole different complexity. A whole new sound. A new world that's pumping through his veins. It's excellent. Efosa can't even fathom it.

Could he ever imagine with his eyes that he would see his drone sing? The way it flies, so perfect, its calculation better than he's ever done in his lifetime; it must be at infinity, at a glorious absolute. What is this?

No. No, it's a chirp, the humming sound. It's a flock. It's a murder. It's the sky, the whole group, the—

Birds! The drones mimic birds. Crows, cattle egrets, pigeons, gannets. Pretty soon they're cannibalistic, like mud catfish, circling each other round like an orbit then striking, machines clashing like an uppercut. Tearing and knocking off each other's properties to make a nest. Must be birds again, he cheers. What are the drones' young but scraps they sculpted themselves, a guttural whirring as the "adults" cough out parts out of engine slots to feed their babies. It's nonsensical and yet so glorious. When the humming sound goes higher to a piercing shrill, he knows the species has changed; perhaps a three-wattled bellbird. 1019 shouts higher than ever as she calls operations to come *fix this crap.* He can't stop laughing.

The general glares at him.

"I'm very depressed," Efosa diverts her attention, continuing to cackle. This whole thing is almost a mockery of the war.

"We've been haaacked!" The general whines on all her holo-devices, and he falls to the floor of the general station while bursting into hysterics. When he looks up at her, she is fuming.

"PTSD, too, probably." With each word, his chest feels lighter. He feels . . . not better, but at least human for saying it. It's progress, even if it's to stop the general from killing him with her stare. His confessions are real this time, like his joy has finally made him know what to say: the right thing.

He never lied.

Operations has to come and assess the situation and do damages, so the soldiers get the day off. His war has never been so ridiculous. Efosa uses one of those promo-tabs to binge comedy shows—he gets war discounts. His mind is at the kind of rest that he wants it to be—not out of defeat but out of joy. There is something to be happy over, and he didn't get it entirely from moving forward, as he thought he would. From progressing. From getting cultural secrets. He's alright so far, not forever, but he'll live.

Life is not so much a simple equation, because you get no firm answers.

Well, he does for some things. Like when he meets the math-techs from operations who are just finishing up looking at some lines of code relating to the unstable machinery.

"It seems a pretty easy fix. Just a routine hack, nothing special. The figures are even numbers and are pretty whole at all ends, so it was a quick reverse. Drones kind of suck but aren't beyond repair, though," Mohammed, an operator, speaks.

"What kind of elaborate plan of attack was that?" One of the other operators asks, scratching their head.

"Just trying to cause anarchy. Probably trying to spoil everything at once. No finesse to this attack," Mohammed spits.

"This can never happen again," 1019 stutters, cold to the touch.

"We'll give your personnel better calculations for their rides and try to expand protection. Best we can do."

"Can't we take out money from other sectors for more options?!"

The two operators stare at her with concerned faces full of furrowed brows. "Not with a good conscience. Or government approval, and to be honest, this is not that big a deal to grab their attention. It's quite humorous."

As the operators leave, Efosa wants to say how the hack looked like birds to him, up in the sky, moving through the galaxy, but he doesn't. People don't need to know the source of his joy; that's how the war takes and takes and takes. That's how it feasts, on information, and there is nothing without context. Somehow, this message feels special to him, or maybe it's because he's seen the generation ship Ghare drew, that all these animals just came back to life with the drones.

Everything snaps into place with his thoughts, and he gets out of rest.

Efosa doesn't sleep. When the night comes, he is alive and concentrated, his thoughts working on a goal, a satisfaction in the recklessness. Maximizing potential.

The great library hall never closes, and the lights are always on, so he spends his time drawing architectural designs of different shapes and sizes.

1019 gave him a mental health record, which mentions the installation of some aid-bots in the coming months to his room, as well as some adjustments. Therapy sessions. Detailed assessments every quarter, as well as helping him figure out his triggers. They will be watching him closely.

Archival tabs of biological information lay on the table, as well as some physics records, like a new world right in front of him. He only stops humming when he starts chirping, tapping his feet on the floor.

Something's different.

He likes a setting at -113.7385, where with just enough weight, it can make a drone feel like an elephant's leg just about to hit the earth. Except you can't really hit anything if space is just that: space.

He moves forward with a pencil stroke that makes him go from youth to age, all the while a grin on his face.

Absolutes are always easy: whole and perfect. Too perfect, even; too seen. Simplified. They're easy to catch. They're easy to fix. Easy to resolve. It's a one-way street but his tracks are always divided. But a complete value can never be possible for a drone that wants to fly and moo and sing and jump without getting caught. Drones that want to self destroy every once in a while to make a war inoperable. A war at rest. Him at peace.

Thinking about it, his code name works, as do other things in his life right now. But there is nothing without context, specifics, the detailed image of who he is and who he wants to be.

So, Whisper: Because your limitations are boundless and your revolution is silence, but you know that everywhere you go, you make a sound.

THE RAINS ON MARS

NATALIA THEODORIDOU

My shoulder hurts as if a handful of rusted nails have burrowed into my joint. Novak's driving isn't helping; the rover is jumping over the rough terrain, giving us all a good shake, especially the three of us sitting in the back. Ray and I are strapped in, but London is sprawled out, defying regulations, her helmet at her side, her breathing calm, as if she was born to live here, born to do this, never mind the terrain, the sky, the air.

We're on our way out of the Valles Marineris main base, which means our own work stabilizing the central tubes will have to wait. But we go where we're needed. It's the base in Melas Chasma this time—the drilling team that works the Melas tunnel think there's an ice plug in their way and they don't have the expertise to drain it safely. If they're not careful, the equipment might melt the ice and flood the tunnel or, worse, cause it to collapse, delaying the colony plans for months. That's the kind of thing we're for. Delicate work, the kind of work you need a good, level head on your shoulders to do well.

Another bump sends a jolt of pain down my arm, slicing me from shoulder to wrist. "Hey, Novak, take it easy!" I bark. London looks at me and laughs, her teeth the yellow of Martian sky. "What's wrong, Mackintosh?" she asks. "Mars too much for ya? Need me to show you how to man up?"

Yulev reaches over from the co-driver's seat and pokes Novak in the ribs. "He's right, man," he says, tender even in his reproach, his accent rolling over his consonants like a pebble drifting downstream. "The terrain is bumpy, but it's not *that* bumpy." None of that has any effect on Novak, who simply grunts and keeps steering the rover ahead like a pirate ship on rough seas.

Ray gives me one of their looks, the ones that make me think they've known me for years when I've only been here a few months. I can see their eyes behind the raised visor of their helmet, dark and full of concern. "Hang in there," they say. "It'll ease up as soon as we get to the forest." They point out the window, and I can almost make out its wind turbines in the distance, silhouetted against the butterscotch sky, a white artificial forest, its trees fruiting with blades.

I lean as close to the window as my helmet will allow. The sun is high, small, the land vast. I take it all in: the sinuous ridges, the ghosts of seas, the barren rock, the red, red dust. I let it steal my breath away for a moment. Is this what you wanted, brother? Would it have made you happy if you could see this?

Ray places their hand on my knee. The skintight suit numbs me to their touch, but I can still feel it somewhere far, far away. "What are you thinking of, Mac?" Ray asks.

What am I thinking of?

I'm thinking of the dry land that stretches out for miles and miles in front of me. I'm thinking of the rain, back home, ever falling, inescapable. I'm thinking of a body, left out on Mars' surface, alone, taking forever to decompose.

I say none of that.

"Nothing," I say instead. "Enjoying the view. That's all."

Our team hasn't been together that long, but we've already figured out our flow, a procedure that works for off-base call-outs, is efficient, and avoids any stepped-on toes. Ray, by far the most experienced one, an orphan raised by the State to lead teams just like this one, oversees the work and handles the extraction process from the surface. Novak helps them install the pipes, hauls around equipment, and drives the rover. London is in charge of the pump. Yulev and I work down in the tubes, manning the drill that will liquefy the ice, making and sealing the boreholes, installing the reservoir for the outflow to be collected. We're a well-oiled machine.

Down in the holes, Mars almost slips my mind. I imagine myself back on Earth in a hole much like this one, Robin working next to me, not talking, just being together, two brothers in the same underground womb, looking out for each other. The rock and the mud close in around me and I let go of everything, forget all about the surface. The hole is all there is. The Earth rumbles under my feet, saying, watch out all you want. You're only guests here.

Yulev pulls my attention back to this hole, right now, his voice loud in my helmet comms. He's talking about his kids again while sealing the hole for the outflow to be pumped through. He goes on and on about how he's here just for a couple of years so he can make a good haul for his family back on Earth. I almost think he's going to drop the sealant and whip out a couple of mugshots of his brats to show me.

"Don't you ever think about having kids, Mackintosh?" he asks.

"Me? No," I say. "I got myself snipped as soon as I could."

"What? No, man, why would you do that?" He gives me such a look of shock that now I'm really worried he'll drop the equipment or do some sudden movement that will end with both of us engulfed in the icy embrace of a Martian flood.

I shrug. My shoulder reminds me this was a foolish thing to do. "Every girlfriend I told seemed pretty happy about it, and the rest didn't care either way." I glance at him. "Besides, would you really want to see my ugly mug on a kid?"

"No, you don't know what you're talking about, man, children are joy," he says, his voice full of a dreamy ache that rubs on me like gravel. "No matter what shit's going on over here, I know they're out there, I know they're safe, and my heart is full."

• • •

Back at Mariner base, we pass through the dust shower as quickly as we can, and then everyone rushes to their comms suites to check for messages from Earth. Yulev can barely hold it together every time his girls kiss the screen goodnight. We all love him for it—even as we pretend not to notice when he sobs into his pillow for a few minutes before going to sleep. London gets messages from her elderly mother once or twice a week. Even Novak the Brute has a family that cares enough to get in touch now and then.

Ray and I don't bother checking. We go straight to our bunks in the dorm.

I try to get out of my suit and wince as pain slices my shoulder joint like a red-hot knife going through butter. "God dammit. God bloody dammit."

"Here, let me help you with that," Ray says. They come up to me and stand behind me. Their breath is hot on my neck as they gently peel the suit off me, its alloys maintaining the memory of my shape like a ghost, the afterthought of a body crumpling to the floor.

"You need to get that shoulder of yours checked," Ray says. "See about fixing it, or I'll be in trouble." They look me in the eyes. "How did you get that injury anyway? If it happened here, I need to know about it." They try to sound professional, but something else, something caring seeps through. Perhaps that's also part of their training. Be sensitive to discomfort, anticipate problems, save your team's life. "You know, I'm responsible for stuff like that."

I point at the wall by their bed. "How come you don't have any photos up there?" I ask. *You're such a poor conversationalist, brother,* I almost hear Robin's voice mock me. *Can't even get deflection right.* "I mean, I know about your parents, but siblings? Friends? Someone special?"

"You don't either," Ray says. I'm now entirely released from my suit, but Ray is still standing behind me close, too close, not close enough. I can feel the heat coming off their body, their face, their hands.

"That's not an answer," I reply.

"You didn't answer me either," they say. Their voice is soft and low, as if talking to a wounded animal. "About your shoulder."

I shake my head and say: "Nah, don't worry about it, it's an old injury. From a coal mine back home. Beam fell on it." I rub the joint, laugh. "Must be the weather's changing. Might rain."

This is what I don't say: Someone I owed a lot of money to twisted my arm behind my back and held it there while his buddies beat my brother to death in the middle of the street, right outside our house. It was raining that day, like every day. And my brother looked at me as they were killing him, not accusing, but as if to say *It's okay, brother. No sweat. I'm going willingly, brother, don't cry.*

Ray laughs, the sound edged with nerves. "Do you miss it, Earth? Do you ever think it was a mistake to come here?"

I turn around to look at them, my bare torso almost touching theirs. "Is this genuine concern?" I snap. "Or are you running another one of those psych evaluations the bosses have you do?"

"Mac . . . " they start, but I cut them off.

Too close.

"What is it you want to know exactly? All these little questions all these months, all casual like, do you think I don't notice? This is the story: I didn't have much going for me on Earth, saw the posters one night, might have been wasted, I don't recall, you know the ones, MARS NEEDS YOU, finger pointing right at your chest and so forth. Seemed like a good idea at the time. Spoke to the heart *and* the pocket. What more is there to ask for, right? Signed up." Ran from the rain. Tried to live out Robin's dream of Mars. "Here I am. That's all there is to it. Nothing to go back to."

"Mac, I'm sorry, I didn't mean . . . " Ray starts again, but I raise my hand and back away from them, their skin, their concern.

I'm not here for this. I don't get to have this.

I pull on a Tee and some shorts and run away, through the dorms, to the lounge, to the exit shaft, my skin crawling, my eyes stinging. I stand next to the surface monitor. The sun is coming down, has almost set, yellow on yellow, haloed with blue, not a cloud in sight. Is this what you dreamed of, brother? The only place it never rains.

And yet. All I can see. All I can think.

I try to apologize the next morning as we're heading for the tunnels, but Ray smiles and tells me not to worry about it.

We're working on the main base today, taking care of stretches with too many structural problems for the boring machines to deal with, so we head straight to our tubes. One day, all the tunnels, the Mariner base, the Melas, the Eos, will be connected, minimizing surface exposure for everyone in the colony. An underground city burrowed in Mars' belly, or that's what they tell us anyway. Some rich guy's dream, sure, but something worth dreaming of ourselves, something worth working for, a change, a future.

We walk from our base to the intersection where we'll split up, me, Yulev, and London to one tube, Novak and Ray to another. No need to climb to the surface today, maybe not even for a long time, unless they hit another iffy patch at one of the smaller bases. I surprise myself, catch me wishing for some incident that would force the regolith to spit me out, as if my body aches to ascend to the surface, my skin hungering for the rusty sky, the crushing void. That won't do. Not today. Not ever. I shrug it off.

Ray is walking next to me, our shoulders almost touching, and I have this lump in my throat, a tangle of words hard enough to choke me. I cough. The lump won't budge. But words come easy to Ray, and I always think I don't know how they do it, even though every time it's as simple as asking: "What are you thinking, Mac?"

I flex my arms like an ape. "I'm itching to drill some good holes today," I try to joke. I sound too much like Novak. More than I intended anyway.

I don't say: I think of the sounds of the tunnels back on Earth, the men covered in coal dust, my brother breathing with the voice of the mine. And for some reason that makes me think of the men in my old gym, all razor eyes and clad in steel, pumping hard, sweating toxic, then weeping in the bathrooms when the hot water ever so slightly softened their skin.

Ray shakes their head disapprovingly even as they chuckle at my sorry attempt at bravado. We're almost at the intersection. They squeeze my shoulder, the one that doesn't hurt. "Have fun down there today, yeah?" they say. They don't say: Be careful.

I nod. "Always." We part ways.

Yulev walks ahead, mapping the area we need to secure. I follow with the drill perched on my shoulder and London brings up the rear lugging the support rods and stabilizing material.

We set up the rods and Yulev gives me the go-ahead. He flashes me the reading with the recommended drill depth and I start drilling carefully into the sidewalls, shallow borehole after shallow borehole, making a sieve for the stabilizing material to be injected into the arch of the tunnel. My shoulder stabs me with short, regular bursts of pain, but I don't care. I let myself be lost in that rhythm, the ebb and flow of hurt. Savor it.

Then I notice the liquid running down my visor, clear as raindrops. "What the hell?" I mutter.

"What's up?" Yulev asks, his voice far away.

I disengage one hand from the drill to wipe the liquid away, and then I see that there is water coming down all over us, Yulev and London both drenched in rain, water pooling by our feet, dousing our machines, our suits. It's raining in the tunnel. It's fucking raining in the tunnel.

"Are you seeing this?" I ask Yulev, my voice frantic and a little shrill, but he seems confused, like he doesn't understand, like he can't see or doesn't care about this freaky, impossible rain.

"What are you doing, man?" he asks back, suddenly alarmed. He flashes another reading at me, and I can't even see it through my rain-streaked visor but I know I've drilled past the safety depth. "What are you doing?" Yulev asks again. His voice is tinted with panic.

"For fuck's sake, stop!" London shouts.

Cold sweat breaks all over my body as I look up to face the drill that's still going. I feel the stone give, the crack expand.

I step away. I should have stopped sooner. Should have felt the fault in the stone. Should have warned them. I yell at them to move, but it's too late. The crack radiates all the way to the other side, blooming over Yulev's head. The support rods are not enough to contain that kind of damage. The right side of the tunnel collapses. Yulev is there one moment and the next he's gone, buried under a pile of rock.

London grabs me from behind and pulls me back, clear of the rubble. "What the fuck did you do?" she screams at me. She drops me to the floor and starts pulling at the rubble, fighting to get to Yulev. We can hear him breathing through the comms.

It's still raining when Ray's voice spills over our comms channel, ordering us to evacuate the tunnel before it comes down on the rest of us. The crack I hit has reached all the way to the surface.

I have to tear London from the rubble. We fall back. Leave Yulev behind, all alone, his comms silent now. Can't even hear his breath.

As we make our way back, I think of the surface again. I'm standing on top of some peak, a volcano as old as the world, overlooking everything, and above it and above me a great, red, dusty rain that consumes us all.

The medics give us a quick but thorough check and discharge us in under thirty minutes. Both London and I are fine. Ray meets us in the lounge to tell us what we already know. Yulev's gone. They're sending an extraction team to retrieve his body as we speak.

I look at my hands, wet with water. I look around me, at the pouring rain. The entire base is drenched. The tables, the chairs, the monitors, Ray. Their hair is wet, raindrops running down their face and they don't even notice it.

"Are you okay, Mac?" they ask.

It must be their tone that sets London off. "Are you serious, Ray?" she shouts. "This motherfucker was acting like an idiot and now Yulev is dead and you're asking *him* if he's okay? I sure hope he's not!" She moves towards me and grabs me by the neckhole of my Tee. "I'll fucking kill you for this, you incompetent piece of shit," she breathes on my face.

Novak takes a few steps forward but doesn't try to stop her, like he hasn't quite made up his mind about where he stands on all of this.

"London," Ray says, their voice calm but firm. They come between us, put a steady hand on London's back until she releases me. "Leave us, please," Ray says. "Let me do my job."

London turns to look at Ray in the eyes. "Will you, though?" She scoffs. "Soft spots notwithstanding?"

"London, please," is all Ray needs to say.

As soon as she and Novak are gone, Ray takes my hand and sits me on the lounger.

I keep my eyes on the surface monitor, on the rain raging outside, soaking the land, a private thunderstorm just for me, flooding the world, flattening it and me and us and you, red mud indifferent to your hurt, your death, your mistakes.

"What happened back there, Mac?" Ray asks. "Was there anything wrong with the equipment, or the readings? Did something distract you?"

I shake my head, hide my face in my palms, the rain coming down, relentless, unstoppable, cold as ever.

"I can't help you if you don't tell me what's wrong, Mac."

Do I tell them? Do I tell them how their face looks streaked with the rains of Mars?

I look at the monitor again, the indifferent land, the cold mud.

"What's going to happen to Yulev?" I ask.

Ray hesitates. "We'll cremate his body," they say after a few moments.

We should leave him out there, to this land that doesn't care enough to break your body apart. We shouldn't send ashes back to his children.

Ray looks at me sharply. "What did you say?" they ask.

Did I say that out loud?

"I'm sorry," I say. I ran from the rain. Didn't escape. Dead boys' dreams don't change a thing. "I'm so sorry."

London and Novak come for me the same night, after Yulev's body is incinerated and packaged for transit on the next shuttle back to Earth. They don't say a word. I am lying in my bunk, my mattress soaking wet, the rain falling on my closed eyes. No matter what I do, the rain will keep falling. I open my mouth and can feel the rainwater on my lips, my tongue, running down my throat, speaking the cold of Mars. Give up, it says. It's all right. Nothing matters.

I keep my eyes shut when Novak grabs me and drags me to the middle of the room. I do not resist. No struggle. Not anymore. Struggle is only for the ones who should go on. London holds me upright, twisting both my arms behind my back, as if she needs to, as if I'm going to put up a fight. I feel my shoulders pop in London's steel grip as Novak punches me in the face, the chest, the stomach. I can't help but try to double over, the taste of blood on my tongue, a little burned and a little metallic, like what that astronaut said space smells like once, back when guys like him were a rarity, back when nobody had died on Mars. I open my eyes. London unfolds me again and punches the small of my back, my legs, my ribs. My knees buckle. Novak's skin glistens with rain. Is Ray here? I'm afraid to look. Are they watching this? Trying to decide whether they should stop it, or whether I deserve it?

When Novak gets tired of beating me, he collapses on the floor, exhausted. London gives me one last kick and leans against the wall, spent, finally allowing me to fall. I find myself on top of Novak, in his arms, an almost-embrace. We are both panting, rainwater pooling around us. My shoulder hurts. Everything hurts. I feel Novak's chest rising and falling. I think of the indifferent land. So much hurt and none of it matters. Rain is running down Novak's cheeks. I reach up and touch his face and I want to tell him, don't cry. Mars doesn't care, brother, don't cry.

I never find out if there are consequences to what London and Novak did to me, but I hope there aren't. They let me recover in the infirmary. I have my own room. Is that for my protection, I wonder? Did the other teams hear of what I did, what I caused, and are itching to get their hands on me too? Is Ray standing guard outside, trying to stop them from getting to me?

The rain here starts and stops, irregular like the beating of my heart, the antiseptic smell of the room overwhelmed by the scent of damp soil. I drift in and out of consciousness. I think of volcanoes, crevasses, seas past, resurrected, canals filled with rain.

One time, I see Ray standing over my bed. "What are you thinking of, Mac?" I think they say, but maybe they don't say anything at all.

I answer anyway.

I'm thinking of my own father, who was the kind of person that could weep because of a verse he read and which made him feel like a child nobody loved, or like the world was too much, too violent, too loud, too joyous, just all too much.

And I'm thinking of how many places in the universe there still are where nobody has ever died yet and of how fortunate this makes us, but only us, the childless ones holding the ghosts of our children by the hand, safely unborn, and of how unfortunate it makes everyone else, how much untapped opportunity for pain the universe still holds.

And I'm not thinking of Yulev's children, or of their father's ashes in a box.

When I open my eyes again, Ray's gone.

The next time I see Ray, I'm discharged and back in my bunk. They knock on the door lightly before walking into the room, even though they don't have to.

They come to tell me I'm off the team, off the mission. London blamed me and my incompetence in her statement and the company didn't ask any more questions because that meant they're not liable. And I am to blame, aren't I?

I'm to be sent back to Earth. On my own dime, too. Only fair. To do what? Ray can't answer that, and neither can I, because who knows, and who cares.

Ray sits next to me on the bed and takes my hands in their own. Their skin is cold and wet.

"I'm so sorry, Mac," they say.

"It's okay," I whisper.

They lean over and kiss my lips so lightly it really feels like goodbye.

I cup their face. Rain sliding down their hair, their cheeks, over my fingers.

"You're crying," they say.

Am I?

No, it's just the way the rain hits me, you see? Like this.

The rain stops falling as soon as the shuttle takes off, but I can still feel it on the inside of my skin, pooling, flooding the gaps within.

Nobody talks to me for the entire trip. Ten days, fifteen, twenty-five. Almost there now. I don't think of Yulev's ashes on the ship with me. I think of Robin when we were little and the Mars project was just starting. We sat on the roof on a clear night when it wasn't raining and he looked up at the little red dot in the sky and said he would like to die there one day. I punched him because I thought he said he wanted to die. I was never one for nuance. I imagine Robin on the ship with me, looking back at Earth this time. *Time to let go of the red now, brother,* he says, *get on board with the blue.* Then I forget how to speak for a while.

My shoulder hurts. The rains don't come back.

On Earth, I realize there's no need for me to go back to where I came from, so I pick a mining town in the south, dry as a stone, no cloud in the sky, days blue as they come.

I use what's left of my small Martian salary to pay for a cheap motel and I make that my home, sparse and unremarkable in every way but its stubbornness to still feel not-lived-in, foreign, no matter how long I live in it. I even have a window I refuse to look out of.

Using my credit means the people I owe probably know I'm back. They might look for me, eventually, or they might not, might figure they've already taken away enough for me to turn on my heels and flee the planet. Don't know, don't really care. Let them come. There's space for everyone over here on this side of the void.

I meet my neighbors at the motel. They change every week or so. I remember how to speak again. I tell everyone I was a miner on Mars. That I got my brother killed, and then I got someone's father killed because I thought I'd escaped even as I couldn't let go. None of my neighbors are very impressed, but a few ask if I brought any red dust from Mars back with me. "Only the one in my lungs," I say, and they laugh. I try to show them, bare my chest, claw at my skin. The company didn't let me keep my suit, otherwise I'd show them that too. I finally don't cry, brother, I don't.

Sooner or later I'll get a job in the mines here, but not yet. My face is healing nicely and my ribs hurt only when I breathe. The shoulder sometimes turns an angry red. It glows in the dark, like a planet.

A month passes, two months, three. I buy a battered old laptop and set it up on the single table in the room.

There's a message from Ray on my work account. It's a minor miracle it hasn't been deactivated yet.

Ray talks about the mission, about London and Novak, who are still raw from what happened but apparently found love when they joined fists over my bleeding jaw. There are two new members on the team, one lad, one girl, so far so good, but they can't carry the drill like I did. Ray pauses at that, realizing what they said, no need to say more.

"Are you doing okay?" they ask instead. "I'm thinking of you." They pause, a finger tracing a ghost around their lips. There's nothing else to say, so they close with: "What are you thinking of, Mac?"

The message ends.

The room is dark.

What am I thinking of?

I look into the camera and hit record.

I used to have all these thoughts. I used to play the scene in my head, think of what I could have said to change things, what I could have done differently. Used to think of breaking things, fixing things. But all that's over now. There are some planets you can never flee.

"My heart is light, Ray," I say into the microphone. So everything is simple now. "Be happy."

Now I think only of the rains on Mars.

TOOL-USING MIMICS

KIJ JOHNSON

Art ("Ukulele Squid Girl") by Laura Christensen.

The simplest explanation: Here is a picture. It is a girl, six? Seven? The 1930s, to guess by the pattern on the smocked dress she is wearing, the background of the dark studio. She is smiling and holding her hands above her head. She has short chestnut curls.

She also has a translucent membrane that cascades behind her head like a wedding veil, or a cuttlefish's stabilizing fins. At the waist, she breaks into tentacles. Or is it her smock that ends like this? Two of the tentacles are playing an F chord on the ukulele at her waist. Two of them look like human legs, and wear Mary Jane shoes and mismatched socks. Or *are* they human legs? Pictures are so unreliable.

She smiles and smiles.

Here is a possibility.

The octopus raises her young; as with every species, the goal is to bring at least some of one's offspring to viability and the age at which they will in their own turn bear young. Her genes will move forward through time, like a soccer ball passed down the field toward the net.

This is her tried-and-true strategy, honed over millennia: She lays her teardrop eggs in jeweling clusters, tucked into a crack formed of coral and her own purling flesh. They look like quivering tender pearls, but they are edible, and there are many predators and opportunists in the world. She cannot leave them for even a moment, though this means she must starve herself. As she waits to repel such devourers and destroyers of the young as they come too close, she tendrils her arms through the eggs, to keep them clean and oxygenated. They tremble in her delicate currents.

Her skin shreds from her before she dies, but by this time the infants have grown strong. They press through the eggs' thin ripping walls and scatter spiraling away, each pretty as a primrose, pretty as a star.

Many of the young die, but some live, grow, find concealments and craveries, develop strategies of their own. This, then, is her boldest daughter.

They are tool-using mimics, each with her own agenda. *This is my way. This is mine.* They hide them from you. They change colors to blend, to startle, to convey information. They contort their bodies and legs to feign the shapes of other creatures, fiercer or less edible. They hide in beer cans. They carry coconut shells—they can move at speed, even burdened like this—and when they are threatened, they curl tight and pull the shells close, like a clam.

Tool-using mimics. It is no surprise that some might become women.

Or perhaps this.

A woman who has always wanted a child walks along the beach. It is Florence, Oregon. It is 1932. She has been told by her brother-in-law that it is dangerous for a woman to walk alone, but who would attack her? She is of no account: awkward, unmoneyed, unyoung. The men in town know her family too well to assault her. If someone else does? She spent her youth ignoring the violate touch of secret enemies, and now her brother-in-law . . . This is why she walks alone.

There has been a storm so she is looking for the glass floats that appear sometimes from the strange and lovely Orient. Instead she finds an egg the size of her fingertip, with the teardrop shape and unsettling color-shift of the pearl earrings her sister wears for evening parties; but it is soft, as though an artisan with puzzling goals has fashioned a tiny bag from the tanned skin of a mouse and filled it with—something. Through the egg's translucent skin, the lidless eyes are startling black.

She carries it cupped in her hands back to her brother-in-law's home, which froths with dark brocade and carved walnut ornamentation, like a coral reef shadowed by clouds, or sharks. In her high-ceilinged bedroom she places it in a washbasin that she fills with cold water and table salt. A hundred times a day, she runs the single egg through her fingers. She does not know how to describe the stubborn resilience of this tender flesh. At night when she is not alone, she takes her mind away to the single egg: its delicacy; its softness. *You beauty,* she whispers. *You clever beautiful little thing. I will protect you.*

The eyes watch everything: patient, already learning, already uncannily knowing. When intelligence is inhuman, there is no need for neonate time.

What is eventually born has her chestnut hair and her smile, which her sister has not seen since the wedding, and her brother-in-law has never seen, for all his secret visits to her room. When she is cast out (for an illegitimate cephalopod daughter is beyond the pale) she and her child emigrate to Australia. Perth. No one knows her there. She takes a widow's name and wears a ring she purchased from a pawn shop near the wharf in San Francisco.

No many-limbed father will claim this girl; no cold-fingered kinsman will touch her.

Or.

When the blue-and-gold damselfish come hunting, she has learned a trick. She conceals herself (*Just mud,* she whispers to the water; *there is nothing inside this hole in the ocean's floor*) and unfurls two tentacles, bands them yellow and black. They side-wind like a swimming sea snake, the venomous natural predator of damselfish. Such fish are bright as a Fabergé trinket; and when they flee, the ocean is for a moment engemmed, bejeweled.

She folds in her serpenting arms, turns them back to the color of holes, but it is not finished. It will never be finished. They will return—and if not them, then others. Eventually her eggs, or her young, or herself, will be killed. The ocean is cold in so many senses.

I cannot raise my daughters like this, she thinks.

It must be better above the water. How can it be worse?

Or.

Her husband has always been a fisherman, owner and captain of a small trawler called *The Sea Snake*. He will die in the ocean, sucked low by a storm he will not have predicted, ignoring the warning she gives each time he leaves: *you will walk out that door and you will fail to return.* They all do, eventually. His death-notice has been written in rime on his skin since before they met. How can she invest in such a man?

During his absences, she dreams. But not of him—nor (as another might) of his clean-limbed brother, who has his own boat and eyes brown as chestnuts; nor even of the baker who took over the ovens when his father died, who will never die shipwrecked, castaway, dragged down or drowning. Not even he, though she would not be the first to heat her hands at his oast in her husband's absence.

Her longings are secret, more complicated. When she wades into the cool water to collect kelp for salt-burning, she feels something envine her legs. Seaweed, she assumes: meristems and stipes given an illusion of intent, air-bladders plump as phalluses importuning her thighs. She cannot stop thinking of this. At night, she throws aside her quilt and shivers in darkness as she imagines tendrilling, trialing arms, a nibbling beak orgasm-sharp. But of course it was kelp. And the salt on her tongue when she wakes in the night? Tears or night-sweat. Dreams.

So how does she explain *this* when he returns—the swelling belly, after her husband has been gone so long, when the only hands that have touched her are her own and the sea's? He will never believe her, nor forgive her.

If he returns. She wades into the ocean and calls to the father, unsure he exists. When he spreads himself across the waves and looks up at her with one vast eye (the tip of a tentacle wrapping her ankle, an embrace as delicate as a finger-brush), she makes a deal. Her husband will fail to come home, and her daughter will not grow up trying to guess the difference between the tastes of tears, and sweat, and the sea.

And they pretend to be lionfish. To be venomous soles. To be fat, flat unfoundering flounder. Jellyfish. Yellow-banded sea snakes. Anemones. Brittle stars, mantis shrimp, nudibranchs, scallops, ambulant shells. Rays. What *can't* they do? They pass, and pass, and pass.

Touch them and at first they recoil then coil, enwrap and enrapture you. Their curious and unsettling overwise eyes are too close to their pursing sharp mouths.

Take them home to your three-bedroom ranch in Hopkinsville, and they unscrew all the lids, open the boxes, break the ornamental seashells. They climb into transparent boxes, into resin grottos shaped like fairyland castles and ceramic skulls with bubbling eyes. They wait until they hear the garage-door opener and your car backing out, then slip through your filters and cross your carpeted floors to eat secretly your tropical fish. Sometimes they return to their salted tanks. Sometimes they vanish entirely.

They survive, and suffer. And thrive, until they don't. They pass, and pass through, pass by and pass on. You will never understand them.

Once upon a time there was a little girl that no one called Pearl. She did all things well: laughed, danced, thought, dreamt, played.

Someone took that photograph. The laughing little girl: someone said to her, *Don't you want to look nice for the picture? Then hold still while I comb your hair*, and, *Not that dress, darling; pick the pink one*, and *Okay, young lady, can you open your eyes a little wider?*, and *Stop squirming! You're ruining the pictures.*

Guess which variety of octopus she is based on. Guess which girl. Guess what she thinks, why the ukulele, why the smile. Whose daughter was she? Was she your grandmother? The picture is old enough, anyway. She will grow up outside your ken to be everything you love and fear.

Between 1933 and 1935, she was billed on the marquees of small-town theaters across the Dust Bowl as "Pearl: The Gem of the Ocean," but was known more informally as *that little freak-girl, with the tentacles. Can you imagine?* Her performance included singing and dancing, and a comedy routine with a immense black woman pretending to be her despairing Mammy, billed as Mississippi Beulah but in fact named Enid Johnson, from New York.

It always ended with a balletic swimming exhibition in a heavy-glassed tank filled with water: this, in towns where there had been no rain for a thousand days, where the youngest children had not known so much water existed in the world, except in photographs. And photographs lie.

The day after a show, the water was drained off and sold by the cup, but Pearl did not know this, already crossing the inland dust sea to the next dry town, drowsing against Enid's shoulder.

In time, her skin seamed, grew lines. How did they like her at fifteen? At thirty? The records do not tell us.

In the oceans, there is a population bloom. Climate change, overfishing: the water grows warmer, and being stripped of certain (highly edible) predators by seines and traps and rising temperatures, the cephalopods step up, filling the gaps. They start to live longer, remember more. They make plans, think through how to optimize their happiness and success as a species.

Pearl was the first Cephalopod Ambassador to the Dry Lands. They did not realize that no one would listen to her. Eight is a very great age for a squid, though, as it happens, not for a human. Plus, she's a girl, and who knew *that* would make a difference?

But we do what they want, anyway. The warming oceans are filling with tentacles. We will be gone and for a time they will remain.

In one version of the world, Pearl goes back to the ocean. She started happy—wore flowers, danced, played ukulele—but that ends, as it always does. Sober adulthood is a hood she will not wear, so she shucks its tight folds, slides off the pier's end into the foaming coastal waters. The photo is all that is left.

Does she find a male who overlooks the deformities of feet and hair? Does she live to run her fingers through her own tear-shaped eggs? Does she die surrounded by the soft ripped shells of her sea-spangling daughters? Does she fit here any better than anywhere else?

The simplest explanation: The picture is a fake. Can you trust it? Emulsion, itself an unreliable material, carefully painted over with acrylics. The colors are a tap dance that conceals the underlying sepia tone lie. This tentacle-girl has never existed, but she is as real as anything else you have not seen with your own eyes, touched with your questioning fingers.

And even that. What do you know of your own daughter? Only what you think you know. She does her best playing when you are not there.

LANDMARK

CASSANDRA KHAW

Home is the quality of light in your eyes on a summer night, salt-scent and clean skin, the rasp of your stubble along on the curve of my palm. Home is the diction and rhythm of your conversation, is the bend of your mouth, the slant of your smile. Home is your quiet. Even ten million lightyears away, suspended between seconds, time beading silver-bright on molecules of dark matter, home has always been the silence I've held in the chapel of your hands.

I flex my fingers, squeeze the vinyl flesh into a fist. The transmission is slow, syncopated. I experience the sensation in staccato: the bend of my joints, the peculiar texture of my skin, the one you said you never minded. Then again, we'd pick this model together, contoured and coaxed its anatomy into a compromise of shared aesthetics. Why should you mind? I blink and delight, just for a second, in the way the lashes—synthetic hairs, so pliant that they could almost pass for real—feel on my cheeks.

"*Where lies your landmark, seamark, or your soul's star?*" asked a poet once and I think to myself: here. Right here.

"Are you sure?" You ask.

I study you through the camera. That feed is closer to real-time, even if the ocular prosthetics are better at imaging colors, richer in saturation. You look more tired than I remember, more battered. I forget we no longer experience time in the same fashion. Not that we ever did, generations between us, but this isn't about that.

I've seen the mouth of the universe open to devour the stars. I've seen our Earth reborn seventeen times, mapped the trajectory of its catastrophes, the telemetry of its deaths. Once, existence spasmed and there was nothing, nothing at all, neither estrus nor end, only darkness complete.

Time, the media likes to say, is meaningless to people like me. They're lying. It means everything instead.

"This is what I want. Promise."

"I don't want you to agree to something just because—just because. You *know*."

The spaces in our sentences are a language onto their own, a dialect born of corrective butchery, edited from something once so much bigger. I can taste it, nonetheless, the vocabulary we'd abandoned, its small and frightening phrases. *Trust me. Stay here. Stay.* In my mouth, they're cherry cider and the lights of the city, and how you showed me that with some people, some places, you never stop falling in love, you only come up for air. "Do me a favor? Can you take a few days? Take a few days to think about this? Please?"

You still don't understand. I've had days. I've had the lifespan of our solar system, twice and again. Time works differently here. But I nod, anyway. My simulacrum follows, half a second later. "Sure."

"Where lies your landmark, seamark, or your soul's star?" murmurs the poet, his bones now a home for mice.

Above the world, falling in love with the city like it was first time all over.

"I might stay here a little longer," I tell you, straddling your hips with my double. You had joked, the first time we made love, that it was almost like having sex with twins. Except this one was alien, love through the looking glass. I did not correct you. The reality is more pedestrian. I'd chosen this look to express my interiority, its strangeness in relation to you: a fae body for a fae creature, unstuck in time. "Logistical concerns, existing responsibilities. I don't know. It's hard."

Your breath speeds in simpatico as my fingers climb your ribs. In the mirror, I can see how the light sluices along my skin, a faint nacre sheen apparent even in the dimness. Proportions-wise, it is as we agreed: a little taller than I am, a little fuller at hips. I'd eschewed hair, however, dilated the orbital sockets, deepened them. The eyes are an ecosystem of bioluminescent bacteria, the sclera gold, the iris green.

"Okay." No variation in your expression. "Whatever you need to do to be happy."

I sigh. It is not what I want to hear. What I want is for you to tell me to come home, come home and curl your body against mine. But we'd elided the syntax that allows for such communication. The framework we'd left behind is insufficient. So, I lean down instead, your hand rising to trace the city-line of my spine, kiss you breathless.

In the void, I pretend that the interface translates temperature with perfect accuracy, that I can feel your jaw warm beneath my lips, that I don't miss you.

"Where lies your landmark, seamark, or your soul's star?" calls the poet, alive again, for the ritual of the recital.

In the way your hips slot into mine. In the fit of you, exquisite, as though bodies were built too lonely, and every one of us is waiting, waiting lifetimes to be complete.

"I don't want you to be unhappy. I don't want you to resent me. I—"

"You can't expect me not to mourn." I tell you evenly, hands over yours, thumb orbiting your knuckles. Two days to the expedition, two nights left to sleep laced in your arms. It hurts, beloved. But how can I tell you? "I'm going to grieve what we'd lost. It's going to hurt. I can't pretend it's not going to hurt."

A muscle, cording the meridian that runs between the cliff of your cheekbone and your temple, flutters. This conversation upsets you, and suddenly, I am afraid again, terrified you'd flee. I stroke your hair. You kiss the heel of my palm, just above where the wrist grazes your jaw, watch me like a fox with its back to the shore. "I'm not expecting anything from you—"

I wish you were, though. I wish you'd ask. Anything and everything. Something. I wish I had an itinerary of your desires, a roadmap crisscrossed by whim, every ambition numbered, ordered by need. I wish you'd tell me to stay.

But I know, I know that isn't the way. You can't build on broken glass, can't make a home out of a husk. It's why I'm leaving.

"I know. I'm just telling you that you can't expect me not to have moments of sadness. But I want this, I do."

"Are you sure?" On the precipice of your tongue, questions too vulnerable to voice: *Why me? Why this? Why, despite everything that'd happened?*

Why?

"Yes. Look, we've broken much too far from that. If this is going to have a chance, we need to start from scratch again, you know?"

I mean every word, but that doesn't mean it doesn't hurt.

"Are you sure?"

"Yes."

It is the only choice I have left.

"Where lies your landmark, seamark, or your soul's star?" whispers the poet, stardust now, dead, immortal.

Where love lives, of course.

Where love is.

"Do you know when you are coming back?"

Orientation is always hard when you first surface into static time, like a baptism of mucus. It *sticks* to the lungs, the tongue, a vernix-like slickness, cloying, clotting in your throat. You drown on the present. It is why I prefer the prosthetic of a proxy, a cleaner option. It supplies opportunity to rehearse, prepare, pretend that this, like everything else, is effortless.

I hesitate. You so rarely call. I barely know what to do with me. In the window, your image stutters in sympathy.

"I . . . still don't know yet. It's complicated." I worry at my hair, the strands still wet, haloed in neon.

"Ah."

I palm the screen. One of the many things I'd never tell you: it is cold here and the last time I was warm, it was in the coil of your arms. "It doesn't mean I don't want to see you. It's just. It's hard. It's a long trip back. And if you're going to, you know, be with someone else during that time. I don't understand what's the point."

"You don't have to."

"I want to. I'm just conflicted."

"Come back when you're ready to. There's no obligation."

"But—"

The word hangs between us, a dead satellite in the nothing, its belly gravid with stillborn dialogue. I want to ask you what I'd missed, the minutiae of simply existing, each day in sequence, no variegation in their consumption. Already, I've forgotten if it's been a week, a day, a year since we've spoken, if this conversation is prior to the last, if it is years after. The cartography of your features remain unchanged. It cannot have been that long.

"I—Don't. I was afraid of this."

"Afraid of what?"

"We're just circling back to the same things. We always are. I knew this was going to happen. I knew." You empty an old rage, an old fear, as the connection falters, your words received in gasps.

"Stop."

"*What.*"

"This was never about that. I wouldn't be here if it was. I just—I'm still human, you know? This still hurts. You can't blame me for that."

You pause.

You break.

You whisper:

"Why are you doing this to yourself?"

"Because if this is the only way I can have you, I'll take it."

"How can this half-state be enough?"

It isn't. It is nowhere near enough. But I have lived epochs without you, and that is so much worse. Home has always been your fingers and mine, the smell of your coat, your hair against my cheek. Home is the start of your laugh and the end of a kiss. Home is this ache, this hurt.

"Because it has to be," I murmur, voice thick with futures. "Because it needs to be.

THE PSYCHOLOGY GAME

XIA JIA, TRANSLATED BY EMILY JIN AND KEN LIU

This is a globally popular reality TV show.

The structure of the show is simple. The screen is split in half: on the left, the patient reclines in a sling chair; on the right sits the therapist. To preserve anonymity for both participants, their faces are replaced by vivid software-generated 3D cartoon versions and their voices processed to remove identifying characteristics. Nonetheless, through facial expressions, gestures, poses, and tone, the audience can grasp the total context of the conversation.

The patient and the therapist are not in the same room (sometimes they may even be on opposites sides of the globe), and the only way for them to speak to each other is through the show's communication link. Their conversation is live-streamed in its entirety, except for occasional bits of personally identifiable information that are automatically filtered by software. Both participants volunteer to be on the show. The patient receives a fee, enough to pay for the counseling, and the therapist gets to make a name. Although many have raised concerns about the format of the show, it has consistently performed well in the ratings.

On the show, you hear the most private confessions of other people. You realize that happy people are all alike, but every unhappy person is unhappy in their own way. Step by step you begin to play the role, and you see yourself reflected in those people. You feel that they are voicing doubts and conflicts in your heart that you've never been able to put into words. *Yes, yes, it's exactly like that,* you say to yourself again and again, *what would I do if that happened to me?*

You feel curious, excited, disgusted, angry, frustrated, sympathetic, melancholic, oppressed, fearful, anguished, confused, desperate, ecstatic . . .

During the broadcast, there is a constantly increasing counter in the lower right corner of the screen, telling the audience how many viewers, struggling with pain, have found courage through this show and managed to seek professional help.

Therapist: Did you say you've been feeling unwell?
Patient: Yes . . . I think I might be suffering from depression.
Therapist: When did it start?
Patient: About a month ago.
Therapist: What, specifically, has been bothering you?

Patient: I'm tired, and I lack energy. Sometimes I stay in bed the whole day, not wanting to get up.
Therapist: How's your sleep?
Patient: I wake up every morning around three or four, and then can't fall asleep again. That's the worst part.

The most controversial part of the show is a little ritual before every counseling session. The patient is presented with two pills, one red and one blue, and the patient must pick one—an obvious homage to *The Matrix*. The two pills represent two possible therapists, one an actual, licensed mental health professional, and the other a virtual creation of artificial intelligence software.

Neither the patient nor the audience knows whether the talking head on the other half of the screen is a human or a machine.

Therapist: Anything else?
Patient: Well, I have this unsettling feeling.
Therapist: Tell me more about this unsettling feeling.
Patient: I just feel . . . very anxious. All sorts of different thoughts run through my brain, and every little thing seems so involved that I don't want to do anything.
Therapist: When you say you don't want to do anything, is it because of the effort it takes?
Patient: It's not about effort, but because it feels . . . so uninteresting.
Therapist: You've lost interest in things?
Patient: Yes. Eating, shopping, going to the movies . . . everything feels pointless.
Therapist: Well, it does sound like you are depressed.

Every episode lasts an hour. During the show, the audience can log in at any point to vote for or against the therapist, and the vote tally is updated live. Therapists whose support falls too low are eliminated from the show.

However, no one knows if the eliminated therapist is human or machine. For every therapist on the show, the producers provide the audience with a personal profile replete with details—birth date, family history, and a full CV. After every episode, passionate debates erupt online as viewers scrutinize every aspect of those profiles, seizing on the most minor apparent discrepancies. If someone claims to have gone to school with one of the therapists and posts their class photo or snapshots of parties, someone else will jump in the next second to point out signs that the photos are faked. The truth remains ever elusive.

In 1997, IBM's Deep Blue chess computer defeated the reigning chess world champion, Garry Kasparov. In 2011, supercomputer Watson, jointly developed by IBM and the University of Texas, defeated two human contestants on the most popular quiz show in America, *Jeopardy!*. In 2017, a documentary series about an intelligent talking toy called iTalk and its effect on autistic children, "Let's Have a Talk," touched the hearts of hundreds of millions around the globe. In 2020, the online livecast reality show "The Psychology Game," produced by Microsoft

Research Asia and Safer Media once again brought artificial intelligence into the spotlight.

Interviewer: What made you sign up for the show in the first place?
Patient: I'd say curiosity, for the most part. I watched a few episodes, thought it was interesting, and decided to sign up and have a go.
Interviewer: Have you ever had psychological counseling before?
Patient: No. I've considered it, but it never got beyond that.
Interviewer: Is it because getting counseling still comes with a bit of stigma?
Patient: Yeah. Even though nowadays getting counseling is so common—how does that joke go? "It's out of the blue for someone to not be blue!"—I still get the jitters when it comes to making an actual appointment with a mental health professional. It's like that superstition about how there's nothing wrong with you when you don't go to the doctor, but as soon as you go, all kinds of problems show up . . . I don't feel comfortable talking to my family about it either because they'll worry. And what will others say if they knew I'm getting counseling?
Interviewer: But you don't feel these worries when it's on TV?
Patient: Yeah . . . if I get to be on TV, I don't care about saving face. Besides, on the show no one can see your real face, you know?

In 1950, the mathematician Alan Turing suggested in his paper "Computing Machinery and Intelligence" a test for whether machines are able to develop the same kind of intelligence as human beings, based on the principle of imitation.

Imagine a sealed dark room, where a person of common intellect (B) sits next to a machine (A). There is another person outside of the room (C) who feeds a constant stream of questions to A and B, who will provide their answers to C with typed answers on a paper tape. If C is unable to tell A and B apart after several rounds of interrogation, then it seems that we must acknowledge the absence of a fundamental difference between a person and a machine.

The key to the Turing Test is that there is no rigorous definition of "mind/consciousness/soul." Turing thus sets aside the question "Can machines think?" and substitutes a more operable question: "Can machines do what we thinking beings can do?"

But can those two questions really replace each other?

For example, machines can write poetry, and some machine-generated poems read better than the productions of humans without a talent for poetry. If we devise an artificial set of standards for scoring poems, it's very possible that we can design a machine whose poetry will score better than the vast majority of humans'. But is this really equivalent to how humans understand and appreciate a poem?

Interviewer: So, being on the show isn't quite the same as real life, is it?

Patient: Right . . . it feels like I'm performing a little bit.
Interviewer: Do you mean that what happened on the show was an act?
Patient: I wouldn't go that far. It's like this: while I talked about my life on TV, I felt like I was also observing myself from the side. I wanted to see what was wrong with this person, why was he so miserable. This feeling got especially strong when I told this sad story—something I'd never told anyone else—suddenly, I felt so empathetic. How on Earth was he able to keep this all to himself, for all those years? Tears started to roll. And before I knew it, I was bawling.
Interviewer: Right, I saw that part too.
Patient: I wasn't going to tell the story, and I didn't plan to cry at all. A complete surprise.
Interviewer: Did you feel better after crying it out?
Patient: It doesn't work like that. That was only the start, and I have to learn to face my emotions—the therapist said so.
Interviewer: Did you find the therapist helpful?
Patient: I really agree with one thing that he said: the cognitive process behind the emotions is more important than the emotions themselves.
Interviewer: What does that mean to you?
Patient: Let's take the example of the sad story I told on TV. Everyone feels sad once in a while, right? But at the time when that happened, I forced myself to feel nothing. Everyone thinks that a man can never show that he's hurt. Even if he's falling apart, he's got to stand there and take it. So that's what I did, but I never forgave myself for it.
Interviewer: Is this the cognitive process behind your emotions?
Patient: Yes. Deep down, I knew that I wasn't who I was pretending to be, but I had to keep up the show. Everyone thinks I live a perfect life, but inside, I've always felt like a failure.

At an international conference in 2013, Hector Levesque, a computer scientist from the University of Toronto, presented a paper criticizing the Turing Test. He argues that Turing's human-machine games cannot accurately reflect AI's level of intelligence. The real challenge for AI is answering certain types of questions:

Kate said "thank you" to Anna because her warm hug made her feel much better. Who felt better?

A. Kate

B. Anna

Questions like this are based on the linguistic phenomenon of anaphora. To determine the antecedent of "her," one needs not a grammar textbook, a dictionary, or an encyclopedia, but common sense. How can an AI understand under what circumstance one person would say "thank you" to another? How can an AI know what actions would make one "feel much better"? These question touch upon the very essence of human language and social interaction, the very areas where AI remains most limited.

It's easy to build a robot that can play chess with people, but far harder to create a robot that can understand the losing chess player's complaints.

Interviewer: Do you think your problems can be resolved?
Patient: The therapist says so, but I'll need time.
Interviewer: Do you still want to continue with the counseling sessions then?
Patient: Probably, yeah. To be honest, before the show, I didn't really know what counseling involved. I felt quite repulsed back then—felt like letting someone dissect your brain and inspect the pieces. But therapists don't have superpowers. They can't read your mind; you have to tell them what you're thinking.
Interviewer: You mean you don't feel as repulsed anymore?
Patient: Yeah, I'm starting to understand what this is all about.
Interviewer: So you would say that this show was useful to you?
Patient: Yeah, I didn't expect that this would happen.
Interviewer: May I ask when would be your next counseling session?
Patient: I've made my appointments already. I'll go once every week, starting next Tuesday.
Interviewer: Will you be seeing the same therapist you met on the show?
Patient: Yes, the same one.
Interviewer: You'll see him in person?
Patient: No, we'll use video chat, same as on the show. Even our faces will be masked. It feels more relaxed that way.

In counseling, sometimes the therapist needs to play the role of a neutral, trustworthy listener and companion, but sometimes the therapist needs to engage with the troubling scenario; sometimes they must call upon logos, other times pathos.

Machines cannot interpret human emotions, but they can learn to use certain procedures to process problems involving emotions. This is not unlike how a machine that does not understand what poems are can still compose passable poetry. From this perspective, it's possible to conclude that machines can do the job of therapists, because psychological counseling is built on the belief that human emotions can be effectively processed, just like poetry and a lot of other things.

However, sometimes the urge to solve a problem is also the cause of the problem in the first place. Take insomnia as an example. For some insomniacs, the source of their inability to fall asleep is the desperate craving for sleep. "I can't fall asleep" and "I really want to sleep" become a mutually-reinforcing cycle of paradox. A machine therapist can tell the patient: "The reason you can't fall asleep is because you are too desperate to fall asleep. Take it easy." But "take it easy" can't break the cycle of "I can't fall asleep—I really want to sleep" because ultimately, trying to "take it easy," in this case, is equivalent to "I really want to sleep."

The same applies to some cases of depression. Depressed patients are often frustrated by the feeling that they're failing at "I want to be happy," which then leads them to ruminate on "what can make me happy?" However, asking this very question makes "I want to be happy" an impossible mission. For depressed patients, "I want to be happy" and "I can't be happy" then become a circular paradox similar to the insomnia cycle. When there's no distinction between cause and effect, there's no place to begin the processing.

Machines cannot process such paradoxes, and humans who are accustomed to machines' way of thinking are not any better. However, if we can forget about the paradox—forget about the effect, forget about the cause, forget about the ends and the means, forget about "I can't fall asleep" and "I want to be happy," even forget about this irksome "I"—then the paradox itself will vanish altogether.

The Chan Buddhist Master Huineng once said: "The Bodhi is not a tree, and the mirror does not reflect. In eternal nothingness, how would specks of dust collect?"

Interviewer: One more question—are you ever worried that your therapist might be a machine?
Patient: Well, how do I put this—
Interviewer: We won't get into the question of whether machines should be therapists. Let's focus just on your feelings. Have you ever felt worried, at all?
Patient: I guess I don't think people are any more reliable than machines. We used to question driverless vehicles, question how machines can cook, diagnose patients, and prescribe drugs, but nowadays these things are so commonplace. Machines won't drink and drive, won't spit in your food because they are having a bad day, won't prescribe you expensive brand drugs to get the manufacturer's kickback. Anyway, I never worry about having machines do these things for me.
Interviewer: But isn't psychological counseling different?
Patient: I don't think it's that different. People used to oppose AI diagnosticians too. They said that machines can't empathize, and they don't know what it means to be in pain or uncomfortable, but then all these objections turned out to be irrelevant. Mental illnesses are illnesses too, and there is a process to be followed. Human or machine, why does it matter—as long as they solve the patient's problem? And to be honest, human therapists have feelings too. If you keep on unloading your emotional garbage onto them, wouldn't they suffer too? Sometimes I think using human therapists is kind of inhumane.
Interviewer: You mean that it might actually be better if we handed everything over to artificial intelligence?
Patient: Depends on which one works better. Technology is always evolving and getting better, and maybe it's inevitable that machines will replace humans one day.

Perhaps the key to the problem is this: in an era of technological explosion, we are forced to constantly evaluate and distinguish between the kinds of work that absolutely require human judgment, and the kinds of work that can be performed by machines (or are even *better* when performed by machines). During this process, our pride at our own uniqueness is constantly assaulted. We may ultimately find out that in many situations, a human being is not essential to another human being.

This will make us anxious, frustrated, or even lead us to plunge down the dark pit of despair, but at the same time, it also forces us to think about what humans really mean to each other—similar to the way each psychological counseling session is also an opportunity to understand ourselves better as we dig into our own emotions and thoughts.

To date, machines are still unable to answer that oldest of questions, "What is human?" Even as everything accelerates around us, we mustn't forget to turn back and reexamine the oracle from thousands of years ago:

γνῶθι σεαυτόν

Originally published in Chinese in *Knowledge is Power,* September 2015.

DEAD HEROES

MIKE BUCKLEY

Tim has worshipped Catalus forever. If you let him, he'll go on about the grace and speed of Catalus, about the bravery of the charge they made against the cliffs within The Living Forest. Speed and grace. Bravery. In the end, it's just love. Everyone's eyes glow when they describe their favorite soldier.

Mine is Lt. Farea. His statue is usually on the upper floors of the stadium. You can spot it even from far away by its rigid posture. They say he killed an Inhabitant with his bare hands once.

Farea is a perfect soldier.

Today, Tim sees the statue of Catalus by the field the first thing in the morning. He wakes me up by whispering this in my ear. I can practically feel his heart beating through his breath. He's excited.

"Meet me at the intersection," I say, not wanting to wake my dad, but after Tim is gone and I am dressing, I see that he is already awake. His eyes stare out of the pile of blankets at me like two half-healed wounds. What would I say at this moment if he wasn't him and I wasn't me? Maybe: Good morning, dad; do you have enough whiskey for today; is that pain in your gut worse? Do you know who I am? Do you know where you are? How much has The Blank taken?

Do you want to see the statue of Catalus, dad, it came up from the tunnels.

But he wouldn't. The Blank has taken much of my father's memories, and the whiskey has scorched the rest. As he watches me get dressed he shifts and his eyes flick around the room, like a bird looking for a crack. An awful smell comes out of his blankets. I leave, walking out of the row of shacks and down the cinderblock hallway. Tim is at the intersection as he said he'd be, shadowboxing his nervousness away.

"You sure it was Catalus?"

Tim doesn't answer. He runs and I follow, down hallways and to the ramps, down and down. Tents web the cinderblock walls, the people inside them staring at us as we pass. Some of them are deep in The Blank, and just getting a brief glimpse at their empty eyes makes me feel like I'm forgetting something, so I look out over the wall as I run. The Living Forest is visible from up here. It shifts in the sunlight, in its world-sized bed of dirt and history, watching us run down the ramps of the stadium.

After we get to the bottom levels, we cut in, and emerge from a thin block hallway into the wonderful light of the field. The statue of Catalus is slowly making its way, alone on the grass, between second and third base.

"I told you," Tim says quietly.

We stand in front of it and watch the massive thing slowly walk, its marble eyes angling in our direction. A glowing roll of stats scrolls next to it. Tim has them memorized. He refers to them every time we debate who the best soldier is, so they're familiar: Catalus: Specialty, Heavy Weapons/Mech Assault; Homeworld, Rimward Colony, Name Unrecorded; Four hundred and seventy six confirmed kills; Sub-commander, Expansion Forces.

"Catalus," Tim says, then looks at me, embarrassed.

"Go ahead, Tim," I say, but still he looks at me with that lean, sad, dark face. My best friend.

I walk over to the pits that edge the field. Tim has privacy now, and I see him talking to the statue of Catalus, and then slowly climbing the marble and settling into its arms, which wrap around him slowly. It might be a mural.

Tim has no father. The first time I saw him he was sitting in one of the lower hallways of the stadium, naked, watching people pass. My father and I were leaving the stands, carrying one of those large fruits that grow on the edge of The Living Forest in the shape of a human head, the kind that some people distill for whiskey, although my father didn't care about whiskey back then. We had chosen a fruit that appealed to us (it looked like me, I think), and as Tim watched us pass, I caught his hollow, weird gaze.

Children live in the hallways when they have nowhere else to go. They could be dangerous places. But even back then Tim was tall and strong, and could be mean if he needed to. It was during his time in the hallways that he'd encountered the statue of Catalus. It had emerged from the darkness one day, and as it walked out of the perennial night of the tunnels, Tim watched its heroic bearing, and he recognized something in it, and fell in love.

The real Catalus was a street kid before he joined the Expansion Forces, that's well known. He was from an awful neighborhood in an awful city in an unsanctioned colony and he learned to kill very early. He did it well and often for the gang that ruled his street.

Redemption came in the form of a mech rolling down the street one day, blaring over its speakers that everyone within hearing was now officially drafted by Expansion Forces. Catalus himself burned the first mech he saw, but they kept coming, better ones each time, giant with heroic frames and spotlight eyes. The mechs gave their recorded spiels to the gangsters that Catalus had revered his whole life, and then one day the soldiers came too, and Catalus realized that the gangsters were just skinny, mean children. The soldiers seemed like visitors from a truth that had always enwrapped his heart. They saw the same in Catalus, and he was in the first group assigned to infantry.

The story goes that Catalus was the commander of the first wave off of the ship. They flamed a bald spot into The Living Forest and discovered the stadium. They landed, fighting their way down. The Inhabitants were ferocious, but wave after wave of Expansion Forces came.

Once the forces were established, General Plata led her troops out into The Living Forest, soldiers like Farea and Catalus, and all of the brave, unknown others. Administrators and engineers stayed behind, guarded by a few squads. Once the fighting intensified, even the guard squads were called out into The Living Forest, and the people left behind turned the stadium into their city. Stories came back about the soldiers' exploits for awhile, but once they'd fought their way deep enough into The Living Forest, the distances became too great.

The statue of Catalus carries Tim across the grass, growing closer, so I can hear.

"When are you coming back?" I hear Tim say, and then he looks down at his own knees, ashamed.

We lose the statue of Catalus in a crowd a few hours later. Once people realize that it has emerged from the tunnels below the stadium, they follow it, take pictures with it, stand in front of with faking ferociousness like an inhabitant. Tim and I know from experience that after a few hours the whiskey will set in and the crowd will smash bottles over the statue, and maybe even light it on fire. Following whatever mech logic exists in its marble head, it will go back down into the tunnels, so we sit in the seats above the field and watch the crowds form around it.

When he finally says something, Tim's voice is raw.

"The real Catalus would hate it here. He'd leave these half ass fuckers behind."

"He'd die if he went into The Living Forest alone."

Tim doesn't answer and I understand why: Catalus dying isn't the point. The stadium is corrupt, and we are stuck here with nothing but statues and stories.

"Let's kill your dad," Tim says.

He has said it before, but he doesn't mean it. Tim despises weakness, but in a very complex way. He wants to nurture sufferers and burn them at the same time. Sometimes he brings my dad whiskey, even, but when he does he always dangles the bottle over my dad's blankets, just out of reach, to humiliate him.

"Let's go to the library," I say.

Tim looks at his knees again, then down at the crowd around Catalus, then throws a couple loose uppercuts. I can tell he doesn't remember, that The Blank has occluded his memory of The Library. The Librarian was mean to Tim when he was a kid looking for food, not letting him stop in The Library for food or shelter, so sometimes he lets The Blank cover it up. As for me, I like The Library, so I think about it more, and try to keep the memory fresh.

After a moment I see him remember.

"I hate the library. That fucker talks and talks."

I leave Tim watching the people flood around Catalus. I walk around the outer edge of the stadium. In the part of the stadium where the library sits, the walls are stained in long upside down Vs of moisture with disconcerting cracks lightning through, meeting at the corner of the ceiling. Empty and quiet.

A man leans out a doorway: "My boy," he says.

I never forget the librarian.

The face disappears and when I enter the library it might as well be abandoned. Books sit neatly stacked in open lockers. Piles of fragile paper sit in plastic bins that are stamped in the ship's logo. I sit and the man reappears holding a tablet in a way that reminds me of someone carrying a dying animal.

"This is almost drained," he says, "but I wanted you to see it first."

I take the tablet and it slowly comes to life. I'm looking down from space at a blue and green planet, and I hurtle backward and past the ship. Somehow I know it's the one in space and then I have such a forceful memory that it hurts.

"You remember," The Librarian says.

"Yes."

He means that I remember we are not on a distant, wild planet. He means that we are on Earth, and were brought here by the ship, which is still in orbit and not talking to us, and hasn't been for thirty years. He means that The Expansion Forces are really recapturing Earth from The Living Forest.

He means that The Blank lives in the forest, and creeps in to take our memories bit by bit.

I set the tablet down gently at his feet and the image flickers out.

"How is your father?" The Librarian asks.

"Drunk. Probably asleep."

"The Blank has taken too much of him," he says. "He's not a man anymore. He's just a body."

For some reason I want to defend my father, but I know the librarian will laugh if I do, and that would be worse than hearing that my father is just a shell. Which I know.

"I haven't seen you in a very long time," The Librarian says.

"Yeah."

From this moment, from having emerged from The Blank, I understand: Of course I have stayed away. It hurts to think about how The Living Forest surrounds us, feeds us the head-shaped fruit, contains us. It hurts to think that the soldiers are lost out in the trees. And this last hurt echoes the pain I always hear in Tim's voice, and makes me think that perhaps even when The Blank has crept in, that our memories are alive beneath it.

"You needn't leave," The Librarian says, as if he knows.

I shake my head.

"One might stay. Study. Keep The Blank at bay."

I shake my head again.

"I'm sorry," The Librarian says. "I was so anxious to show you the tablet that I forgot how much it hurts to know the truth sometimes. I can entertain you."

The Librarian gestures and a glowing face appears over his hand.

"I know he's your favorite."

It's a still of the real Farea, the darkness of The Living Forest behind him.

The Librarian wants me to stay. No one else ever comes down here. Thinking back now, I remember that he usually waits until I have been here awhile before he reminds me that we are on Earth, trapped in the stadium. Usually he tells jokes. He asks about Tim, about the statues. Of course The Librarian is hiding. Down here on the bottom level of the stadium with his ancient books, replenishing his knowledge each morning after The Blank has sipped from it in the night. Thinking about Tim's breath against my ear, and his hopeless, hard face . . . I have to leave. The Librarian is still talking as I go, Farea's face floating next to him, watching me move down the hallway.

I find Tim ascending the ramp to the uppermost floors. The statue of Lt. Farea is standing at the uppermost row of seats. It is staring down at the field. The crowd around Catalus looks small from up here, and Farea's head turns slowly toward us.

"Where were you?" Tim asks, having forgotten The Library again.

"With my father," I say. The lie is easier.

Tim sits himself a few rows down, as if I wanted to be alone with Farea, but it isn't like that for me. Statues are what they are: mech sense in articulated stone, made by the people the soldiers left behind when they went into the forest. The stories about the soldiers aren't so different. We grow up with them, and some we fall in love with.

For me, it had been the dreams that had bonded me to Farea. In the dreams we are always in The Living Forest, Tim and me and my father. When we walk the trees lean out of our way and when we stop they rearrange themselves around us. Flowers bunch up into bright walls. Mud slips underfoot. And then we are in a circle, all of us worn and beaten soldiers, and we're listening to Farea—the real one. The man. And he's me. I look at my hands and they're covered in scars and I touch my face; it's scarred too, and rough with whiskers, and feels old, even from the inside. I say that General Plata needs us to take a hill. It is warrened with Inhabitants and I think about them in their tunnels, whatever they are, whatever they look like, whatever odd eyes they see The Living Forest through, and more than anything else I want to burn them out of their tunnels. I want to take the hill and I want them to hurt me. I want to heap all of the pain and harm that they have to give within my ribcage, around my heart.

I want to be burned and broken.

I always smiled at the soldiers in the dream, just as Farea's marble face grins at me now, as shadows from the roofs above us move slowly over our heads, creeping toward Tim as he watches Catalus getting shouted at by the crowd below.

"Come on, Tim," I say. "I have something you gotta see."

We leave the statue of Farea and walk around the edge of the top of the stadium, until we find the ladder that leads to the roof. I step out over the empty space and climb. Tim follows. Instead of sitting on the side that overlooks The Living Forest, I lead us up the grade of the awning, stepping carefully, and then when vertigo laps coldly at the base of my guts, I belly crawl, and Tim follows suit. When we get to the edge I pretend to be fearless and throw my legs over.

Tim's voice barely trembles.

"Shit this is high."

"You scared?"

"No. Shit. Kinda."

We sit for an hour and watch the drunk crowd harass Catalus on the field below, until it disappears back into a tunnel. Tim and I look at each other, and we don't have to say anything—we back-crawl down the awning, carefully down the ladder, and down and down the ramps, then out the gate.

Surrounding the stadium is a belt of dead foliage. We step over blackened, woven roots. The dirt is exposed beneath them like flesh. My father told me once that for the first decade after they'd left the ship The Living Forest was almost impossible to keep at bay. Thick roots grew—almost crawled, he said—out of the trees, and people worked day and night chopping them away. Severed flowers rode the wind into the stadium and settled on the grass field and within an hour had produced a tree that was already budding with tiny visages. They cut these down too. After awhile, my father said, it was like The Living Forest stopped trying and just kept its distance from us. This is how I've always known The Living Forest. A dark, breathing wall. As Tim and I get closer to it, we pass out of the shadow of the stadium.

The Living Forest is tall and dark when you are close to it, and the trees that ring the stadium are covered with fruit. There's a dozen at eye level, each one grown into a bright green or orange or scarlet version of someone's face. Those who know say that there isn't this much fruit deeper in the forest. It's almost like it wants us to stay here, well fed, in the stadium.

Head level, closest to me, is a bright orange fruit, wolf-lean like Tim.

I smile and tap Tim's shoulder, pointing to it.

He looks at me but beyond him I see an odd movement in the darkness of the trees. Something I've never seen in The Living Forest—a light bobbing between branches.

"Shit," I say, and Tim looks too, barely registering it before breaking into a run. I follow.

It emerges from the darkness, snapped branches falling around it, shattered fruit beneath tri-part treads that step over the heavy foliage. Two large lamps regard us as it comes, but instead of producing light, it feels like they are sucking it out of the surrounding world and holding it. The mech's body is the soft, contoured green of the forest behind it, even rippling along its planes as the tree trunks do. It regards us, weapons along its back tracking, and steps out into the clearing, toward the stadium. I can see movement deeper in the trees. Faces moving in the darkness; the dim but living whiteness of eyes, two by two, trailing back into the trees.

An illusion. It has to be. A trick of The Living Forest.

But then they come out of the forest. The soldiers.

Tim is crying and laughing, and so am I.

The soldiers set up camp on the field. It isn't even as grand as the tents we have in the hallways, just blankets unrolled over the grass, the mech standing off to the side, watching over them. There's about twenty of them, skinny and old.

Tim stands in front of me, on a seat in the first row next to the field looking out at the soldiers. A few people are closer than us, but they are quiet, and they're keeping their distance.

"What's on them?"

I shake my head.

When I focus my eyes I realize I am alone. Tim is gone, and I know where. I go to the tunnels.

The darkness in the tunnels is complete.

I follow the sound of footsteps.

Tim's soles are rasping across the concrete.

"Tim?" I say. "Wait."

The rasping stops, but a slow hiss continues—stone dragging over stone. A statue. But there's another sound, too, breathing, deeper than Tim's. A torch flares up and I'm looking at faces.

Tim's, on the edge of the light. The untenanted stone face of the Catalus statue. And a man's face, a foot shorter than the statue, like rags of leather clinging to failing clockwork: his jawbone is exposed, teeth bare and rotten, and he's crawling with small silver insects. He leans in close and I can smell him. Rot. The Living Forest. Blood pumped through a corpse. His eye sockets vomit streams of silver insects which pour vertically back across his head, weaving through his thin hair, and he moans. A burnished object crawls up the back of his head, collecting the insects. It is making its way over his skull by way of a small track that has been bolted into the bone, and I look down, and see that his throat is a row of metallic valves, popping open and shut gently. That's where the smell is coming from.

Somehow I know.

"Catalus," I say.

He isn't smiling, more like sustaining an effort to peel the bones of his face from within, but at the edge of my vision Tim's hand rests on his shoulder.

"They're back, and they won," Tim says.

Torches ring the field and it is wild with noise. Throughout the day people have found their way from the tent cities in the hallways and gathered around the soldiers. At dusk they lit torches and brought fruit and whiskey. From the first row of seats in the stadium I can see a hesitancy in the celebration. People approach the soldiers slowly, smiling, then stand and mingle. The soldiers themselves are all odd. Some, like Catalus, are crawling in small silver bots. Others are mish-mashed together with machinery. One of them makes its way across the field on something like blades, popping down into the dirt with each step, then shaking the blades clean like some kind of awful dog.

Once the whiskey takes hold, though, the hesitancy disappears. Bodies blend in the firelight. There is laughter and shouting. Statues emerge from the shadows at the edge of the field, moving slowly among the crowds, and the soldiers laugh at the marble heroes.

Tim is down there somewhere. I can see him now and again moving among the people. He's smiling too, so happy that it might be mistaken for panic.

The Librarian sits next to me in the darkness.

"Happiness," he says.

"Yes, they're happy."

"I confess. Sometimes I thought they wouldn't return."

"Me too," I say, then realize I have forgotten something. "Where were they?"

"In The Living Forest."

"Why?"

"Fighting the Inhabitants."

The dreams come back. The fear of The Inhabitants, even though I can't picture what they look like.

"Their numbers are greatly diminished. It is said they entered The Living Forest with ten thousand soldiers."

Two children that I do not recognize are standing on the top of the mech that Tim and I had seen in the forest. They're cheering as if they're in the middle of a game. The soldiers stare from below, their faces dark in the torchlight.

"What do you suppose will happen now?" the Librarian asks. "Will we go back to . . . "

He looks up also, and when he sees the emptiness of the sky above us, says "Oh yes, I'd forgotten. We are on Earth. We have been sent to destroy The Living Forest but it keeps us here, trapped. Contained."

There's a glimmer of recognition in what he says, but I can't place it, and a moment later don't remember or care to try.

I wake up to the sound of bones crunching. And moaning behind it, very gentle.

The dim light in the tent is occluded by a large shape that my mind cannot make sense of as The Blank slowly recedes. It might be the moon, but dark rather than bright, filling the room, and to the side of it is my father's face. His eyes are on mine. There is something there that I haven't seen in years. Clarity. He's looking at me, and he knows me, and he needs me.

"Dad?" I say.

The darkness turns to me. It is not a moon. It is half a face and half an iron mask. Currents of movement flow in and out of holes in the mask, and holes in the face. It has been working on my father. There is blood and my father's open body and two loaf-sized robots crawling into and out of him, holding up guts in the dimness as if to examine, cutting them.

"Not him," I hear a voice say.

Someone pulls me to my feet and out into the cinderblock hallway. I'm shivering. It's dark.

"I gave him whiskey first," Tim says.

"What . . . "

I shove Tim. I have to get to my dad. He's bigger and faster, though, and pins me against the wall.

"They need him," Tim says. "Need *it*."

But he's my father, I mean to say. The words are tied to memories that emerge from the normal distance of time and the absolute of The Blank. My father sitting on the edge of the stadium's roof with me. My father taking me to the library. The sound of my father's voice in the middle of the night, outside the tent talking to someone I have long forgotten—the warmth and strength of that voice.

"The Blank took him a long time ago," Tim says. It isn't a concession. He's daring me to disagree.

"Let me go."

Tim's voice is cold.

"If you go back into that tent, I'll let him eat you."

The moment of shame is like hot blood in my throat. Catalus' dark face. The moaning.

I can't help my father.

I stand up and walk back to the hallway.

My father had told me once that The Librarian didn't sleep, and it's true: I find him awake, candlelight flickering in orange clouds of light on the ceiling.

"My boy," he says, and lets me in.

I sit on the floor.

"Tim gave them my father," I say.

"Gave?"

"The soldiers. They cut him. He was . . . " Watching me. Those calm eyes, how terrible that he was dying so calmly, and I was the last thing he saw in that dark tent as he did.

The Librarian goes through books and holotech and other things that I've never seen. After awhile I look up and a picture of a soldier is floating in front of me. It's pristine, a tall man in camouflage with weapons floating next to it and protruding from its back. His face is covered by scopes and lenses. Loaf-sized bots sit on its shoulders like pets.

"This is what they looked like when they went into The Living Forest," he says.

I point to the robot.

"I saw those."

The Librarian nods. Somehow the image has shifted and the soldiers as they appear now, ragged, half human, is in front of me.

"They are changed. That is certain."

The Library is full and quiet. People stand shoulder-to-shoulder among the books, some of them looking around as if they'd never known it was here, and maybe they didn't.

A voice: "Someone said they're taking people."

Another: "I saw them eating someone in the hallway."

And The Librarian must've already told them because a lot of the eyes in the room turn to me.

"Him," someone says, "his dad, the drunk."

The Librarian is talking now.

"Not eating, strictly speaking. Using."

An image of the loaf-sized bots appears in the middle of the room, spinning slowly.

"Their technology repurposes bio-matter. It's how they stayed out there so long. They have taken The Living Forest into themselves. Perhaps it has changed them."

"Who are they?" someone asks from the back.

"They're the soldiers," comes the answer from another corner of the crowd.

And another: "We've been waiting for them."

The Librarian, with the clearest memory among us, speaks.

"The Blank has affected our memories for many years, my friends. How many of you remember when The Blank first came?"

Silence.

"We began forgetting. Every morning there was less. We wrote down what we could. Here." The Librarian gestures around himself. "And then slowly we forgot even the necessity of that. Then more, and more, and now here we are in the stadium, not sure where we came from or why we are here, sure only that we love the heroes."

And still silence. Finally someone asks: "What do we do now, Librarian?"

I haven't gone back to my father's tent. I won't. I can't get the image of the bot patiently pulling his guts apart out of my head. Anything I think about—father, tent, Tim, darkness—I see the bot inside a body, slick with blood.

The Librarian was so sure. What do we do now, they asked, and he said we fight them. The crowd left the library and boiled in the tunnels awhile, drinking whiskey and getting ready. I didn't go. It was impulsive at first. I just didn't want to follow. But then I thought about it, and knew The Librarian would know I was gone, and would think I was scared of the soldiers.

And that's right, of course. And I'm scared of Tim. And Farea, if he's among the soldiers, and what I might do for him—he's been my hero for so long.

I watch from the roof as the people rage out of the tunnels at the sleeping soldiers. All the fires are burned down now and it is dark on the field. The people scream for bravery. They hurl whiskey bottles. They hold planks and pipes above their heads, ancient things they have torn out of the guts of the stadium.

It doesn't last long. The mech comes to life when the people get close and leaps over the sleeping soldiers, stomping through the attackers. Screams change register. People are running, some of them already having forgotten why they were attacking, or who. The soldiers are running too but even from this height, in the swinging light beams of the mech's eyes, I can see that they are not angry. They chase people down, flatten them, leave them tied up.

Tim is down there somewhere on the field.

My best friend, down there in the panicking mix of light and shadow, there to feed our heroes.

I haven't gone back to my father's tent.

I won't.

DARKNESS, OUR MOTHER

ELEANNA CASTROIANNI

I'm one of my mother's kind. Numbers speak to us in whispers and screams. We weave the world in complex mathematics and the world weaves us back, keeping our sky above and our earth below, keeping our organs inside our bodies, keeping us here, keeping us together.

The yarn of quaternions and octonions unravels; it makes a trail inside the Womb. The Asenai men think I'm using it to find our way back and, of course, I let them believe it. But let me tell you a secret, my brother: the yarn is a sliver of the Womb itself. A simple, one-dimensional blood vessel I tore out of my favorite place, out of your prison which I came to love because, to me, its corridors and its deep darkness are brimming with the salty smell of freedom. The Womb is holding the hypercomplex function-manifestation together, woven number by number, written stitch by stitch inside my yarn skein.

I'm calm, I'm still, as the Asenai battle creatures of my own secret numerical craft. I'm a still spot in the storm, a spider weaving; the function-manifestation must not be disturbed and I must command it fully. It's almost entrancing, this drawing of strength from the Womb itself. I can hear its pulse; I'm vulnerable, exposed. A tingle of excitement mars the perfect stillness inside me. *My brother, I'm on my way.*

First unroll, then roll back into a ball. First cast the prince's skin off, then weave it over my brother's. My plan is perfect and I know it. I was born for this. I've been preparing all my life.

The yarn unravels.

King Uthar's court is the stuff of dreams, people say. Cemar is where gods spend luxurious summers, estivating in the dim glory of faience and niello palaces of Iasso and Zachor, their divine reveries conjuring winged griffons and monkeys the color of palaeo-blue—creatures that wander forever on the walls of shaded porticoes rowed in vermillion columns with ebony tops, creatures that look at me with dead eyes, that speak to me in tongues other mortals can't hear.

Well, I'm King Uthar's daughter and I know better. My earliest memories paint him in the distance and my mother at the center—opulent, buxom, a golden vest curving around her exposed, full breasts. Like living bracelets, the sacred snakes of the Goddess coiled around her tanned arms in obedience, deliciously inebriated by the oils of Cemari dittany and frankincense. She was the spitting image of all the frescoes and idols that Uthar wanted to destroy, the frescoes I've only seen clandestinely. She wore the visage of her own mother and grandmother—all Queens, all High Priestesses, all using the language of numbers to harness a physical reality that would otherwise run rampant and crush us with its wild, cruel infinity. The visage I, too, should incarnate after her death if only it weren't for her husband's greed. That was my mother, a vision so distant I now wonder if it was ever true and not a mere childhood fancy, a reflection of my hope to see her—to see myself—powerful and luminous.

The mother I truly knew lived in the prison called the Queen's Quarters, where I also grew up under the gaze of sleepy dolphins and lapis lazuli doves and other delightful decorations that turned grotesque each evening when the sunlight faded, with their pointy beaks and black-rimmed eyes. My mother sat transfixed on her throne, long black curls flowing down her shoulders, and wouldn't speak to anyone. She had a little tame dice snake—the only one she was allowed to keep after her husband killed all the sacred beasts—to whom she'd whisper number sequences from time to time, while looking at the world only in side stares. Often, I was handed bowls of lentils with fragrant coriander and honey to give her, or escargots stuffed with rosemary and thyme which was, they said, her favorite. Although I trembled as I left the tray next to her, she wouldn't even deign to look at me. And I was thankful; when she did, her tawny gaze pierced holes into my heart.

Like my mother, like all women of our bloodline, I had numbers running in my veins, making my blood bloom with mystical flowers inside me. When our ancestors first arrived in Cemar, a planet so dangerous and strange, numbers became the bridge that took us over boiling lava to a safe shore and saved us. Mathematics was—and is—the only way humanity could deal with the chaos of the universe, the only common language between ourselves and the galaxies. Medee was our first High Priestess, the one who found a way to speak stories in numbers, materialize them and cause changes. She was the one who gave us the plants of her homeland—olive trees and vines, basil and crab apples—the animals—snakes and bulls, the first algebraic creatures she conjured, our sacred beasts—and the fertile land. She is the one who turned Cemar from prison to paradise, truly an avatar of the Goddess. The only one to have invented the magic of numbers that was grafted into her mitochondrial genetic code and, to this day, can be passed to her female progeny only.

My father kept an eye on me from an early age. Our art and magic and science weren't needed anymore, he said, the world was stable. We were more dangerous than useful, he said, our gift way too powerful and easy to abuse. He had already gone too far—snatching the throne from the High Priestess, killing the sacred snakes—and everyone knew that the gods punish the blasphemous, so he didn't dare touch me or my mother lest he met his ruin. My older brothers, my lady companions in the court, none of them ever truly befriended me as they all were my father's spies. Fear kept everyone at a distance, yet I found it soothing if not somewhat lonely. We're strangers with all my siblings—all except Erion.

Erion was born in captivity. My father had already imprisoned my mother by then and hoped to prevent her from continuing her mathematical weaving. Pious men and women warned him that this would endanger Cemar, yet he didn't listen. Then my brother came, his devious form a sign of profound instability in the world. My father, in his unbridled paranoia, proclaimed him one of my mother's mistakes, another instance of her dangerous meddling with the world. He locked him up in a lightless laboratory—the remains of Medee's spaceship, the one that brought her here, the one we called the Womb. He had all of his scientists and mathematicians study him for years until he gave up and left him alone, conveniently out of sight, a poor lifetime prisoner just like my mother. No one could come in or out of this prison; its entrances were a cryptographic secret.

No one except myself, of course. Oh, how I love the Womb, how I enjoy its musty smell, its comforting darkness. Even though it is his prison, in there we are alone, just us and the deep magic of endless, twirling walls. Darkness has always been my friend. I taught myself to walk the Womb with eyes closed, guided only by the numbers that run in my veins. It led me to its center, to Erion. A head too large for his shoulders, a bullish snout and two horns—and eyes so shiny and eager and happy to meet me. We spent hours playing hide and seek in those vast corridors, our giggles echoing, our footsteps reverberating.

"I brought you honey cakes," I'd say—his favorites—and he'd stuff his face with their sweetness, squinting happily at the sumptuous aroma like any other boy his age. As we ate, I shared news from the court. I spun tales of the bull leapers in the yearly festival—once, a festival for the Goddess—how they danced on bulls' backs as if they were creatures of the air, fearless. Erion watched me in wide-eyed fascination, his mind running wild with things he'd never see. All he ever knew was the dark cocoon of the Womb.

My brother had the heart of an artist, I soon discovered. Once, I brought him seashells I had gathered from the deep violet shore nearby Iasso palace, to decorate his lonely lair. Next time I was there, Erion had carved one of them with a tiny chisel he'd made himself out of eating utensils. In the light of the torches, I watched the bull leapers unfolding in front of my eyes in perfect detail, as if Erion had been there at the festival with me. I ran my finger over the miniature's prickly pattern, admiring it as tears stung my eyes.

"Father doesn't want me to go out much," I told him one day. "He wants me to stay with mother, to keep her company." Day by day, the Queen's Quarters became my own prison. Escaping through my secret door was my hope, the Womb my sanctuary.

"Is mother ill, Sadne?" Erion asked in his attentive manner, always worrying about a mother he had never met. His eyes shone in the torches' flame, hungry for love and recognition, a well he could never fill. For a long time, he had known his mother only through my eyes and my narrations; I was his link to a world that had been denied to him.

"She won't leave her chambers . . . doesn't talk, only stares into the distance. They say numbers drive us all mad one day, but I'm not so sure it's just mathematics that claimed her mind. Oh, you're not missing out on much, really. I get bored there. It's so much better to come here and see you." By the end of my words my cheeks were burning, my voice had gone raspy. Emotion I had learned to suppress suddenly found its way up, provoking me to say things I didn't want to. Although I was uttering the truth, I could tell Erion was still jealous. He sulked, lowering his bullish head so deep his shoulder blades protruded—so white, so soft, I noticed. I wondered how healthy he could stay in such confinement.

"Will she ever want to see a monster like me?" he whispered, voice shaking. My heart sank at his words.

"Dearest, I think mother understands how you are," I said softly and not without honesty. "She is like me, remember? We can see things that aren't there to mortal eyes. Your symmetry is perfect. She knows it, but is simply too ill to tell you. I know she loves you."

I reached out and touched his hand. When I looked down at our feet, all I saw was a little boy's thin legs, feet wrapped in tattered sandals. Yet his head too, was his own, as much Erion as his human parts. I touched his cheek, lowered his bovine skull gently onto my shoulder, its horns still too small to poke me. A perfect topology; his functions a poem. How could others not see it? He accepted the touch quietly. We sat there for a long time, the darkness our mother.

"One day, we'll run away," I promised, my muscles tensing suddenly, old anger rising inside me again.

Erion was silent.

The yarn unravels. The first time we found a dead body it was still fresh and warm.

I tripped on it in the darkness and upon feeling the emaciated flesh under my fingers I gasped in panic. A soft whiff of putrid smell carried the first signs of decay. Something of my mother visited me that day.

"What is it?" Erion asked and, before I could say anything to protect him, he cast the torch's light over my shoulders. His pupils contracted, the way animal eyes shrink in fear. I held his hand and refused to turn away. That was my father's doing and I wanted to bear witness to it.

In his long war with the Asenai, Uthar employed dirty, cruel intimidation tactics. I never knew about the high-ranking prisoners—sons of ministers and nobles—that he locked up in the Womb and let wander until they reached either madness or death. I learned of it that very day. The Womb, Medee's beautiful ship, the ruins we've loved, had become a synonym to heartless torture.

We made a purpose of finding those bodies before someone collected them and shipped them back to Asenai defiled, in blatant mockery and disrespect. I offered them a last kindness—a rudimentary passing ritual of honey and wine libations, to give their souls rest. At those times I wondered why my mother was the mad one when my father found such things acceptable—when we all did. Anger had been a small, spiteful animal growing inside me for years.

Escape was what I dreamed of in those days. Escape, more than claiming my rightful throne. Erion hopelessly tried to convince me otherwise.

"You will be a great queen and you'll be kind to me too. The world needs your weaving or more accidents, more . . . more things like me will happen." He was begging me.

"You're not a mistake, Erion. You're perfect," I insisted, furious at his self-hate. "Let this world crumble, let bull boys and snake girls be born everywhere!"

Hesitating for a second, he gulped and said, "You must. I can help you. If father must die, I'll do it. I'm a monster anyway. No need for you to be the patricide. I know you will be a merciful queen to me, so I don't mind."

By then, his voice, his shoulders were shaking. Even the thought of murder chilled his blood, yet he was willing to try it. My brother, with the heart of an artist, becoming a killer!

"No, sweet brother, no. Don't say such things. You're not a monster!" I cupped his hands in mine. The thought of patricide didn't scare me as much as it should have. I knew the gods were merciless in their hunt of killers and I knew my father feared them too—why else keep my mother and myself alive if not for fear of divine punishment? But I didn't care. All I wanted was freedom and my father could rot on his alabaster throne and this whole wretched palace could collapse on his shoulders—I simply didn't care. "We'll both escape. I have a plan."

I tried to smile, but Erion wore his familiar sulk. He didn't like thoughts of escape; they scared him. He had never experienced freedom, not once in his life, so how could it not terrify him? Clinging onto a dream where I'm queen—I, his only ally in the world—was the only future he could imagine for himself that wasn't as bleak as the Womb's darkest corners.

"Do you think death will be a release?" was all he said. It came so easily to him to think of death as the only path to freedom. That moment, I couldn't say anything. "I think mother is waiting for death," he continued, darkly. "It's the only place for her now."

"You have a place with me, Erion," was all I managed to say. How I regret my words now. Oh, how I could have done things differently.

His beady animal eyes smiled to me. "I know."

The yarn stops rolling. That's when the Asenai boy arrived.

Coming all the way from the other side of the solar system, his chest wide and sculpted, eyes sparkling with self-assurance, the otherworldly prince stood taller than the rest of us, us little dark-skinned Cemari, descendants of refugee ships, us little barbarians worshipping snake goddesses, little fools ruled by wonderful King Uthar and his terrible fleet. His spaceships—ugly, rusty beasts so unlike ours—stirred and crushed the wheat of our fields on the very first day of the temporary armistice—one the prince intended to break, of course. I ran to meet him. By then, I had grown into a woman, Erion into a young man. Teseo's eyes stopped lasciviously over my bare breasts, which I covered immediately. I know Asenai women dress head to toe and stay indoors, so Asenai men think women who show their breasts must be everyone's women.

"What a beautiful daughter King Uthar has," he said in a slurred accent, evidently not uninterested to bed me. The moment I saw him I set my mind on my plan, so I led him on, made him believe I was so infatuated with him that I'd betray all of my people's secrets to him. You see, I disliked him instantly and yet with my antipathy came the spark of opportunity: he had ships that could carry us all the way to Asenai. I'm not a woman who will wait for a man to rescue her, but in the kind of prison I live one ought to make most of everything.

"The mutant that lives in the Womb killed your brothers. Avenge them and save me from my father's tyranny." Oh, Erion. The lies I've told. I offered him the goblet that was forged in moonlight, filled with wine I had bathed in dark rituals of smoke, sap, torn flesh, and the macabre juices of nightmares. "Drink honeyed wine, my lord, to make you strong against the bull-faced monster." So the foolish prince drank along, thinking I really was a witch and I was giving him power.

The moment he tried to make a move towards me he fell, face on the floor, snoring loudly. Once all of his mates were sleeping soundly, I ran. I had only moments before sunrise, moments to tell Erion of my plan. I entered the Womb like a stalking cat, following the familiar trail with eyes closed. Erion was awake, waiting for me, tense and nervous.

"My brother, prepare. Tonight we free ourselves."

He didn't move. Still nervous, he shifted in his seat, as if the wine flask I offered him was cursed. "What is your plan, Sadne?" I sensed his careful inflection at that moment, his silent disapproval. I dismissed it as fear and cowardice.

"I have woven a thread of hypercomplex numbers that can copy the prince's likeness," I began explaining my craft. "But I can't create a topological vector from him and directly onto you—I have only created the vessel for this. So it must be passed from the prince to you, cover you like a blanket." I showed him the weapon, an antique double axe of no worth, lined with a verdigris patina of rust. "The function is in here. When he strikes you, the vector will mirror your actions and he will die while you'll don his appearance like a fresh shirt. Then we'll sail on his starship to freedom."

He looked at me incredulously, then at the bronze double axe. "Will we succeed?"

"Trust me, my brother." I touched his hand, spoke in my best older sister's voice. "I have a one-dimensional yarn of manifold space, a simple line that goes on and on. As I unroll it, it will take the Womb's power in it. All parts of the function-manifestation shall be stored in there and I'm strong enough to hold it, so fear not. Soon we'll be away from Cemar, away from father. There are so many planets where they will receive a High Priestess like myself with honors and accolades. Surely, they won't turn you away, my own brother."

He stirred, his eyes showing some sudden courage still laden with doubt. "What if father has word of where we are? They say he discovered that old scientist hiding in the outer colonies and punished him for running away."

"Well, if he comes after us you might have your chance to be a patricide," I said, my patience suddenly snapping. I saw the wound I opened only at the very last moment. I touched his hands again, the delicate yet callused fingers of an artist. "I'm sorry, my brother. Will you trust me now? Follow me in this plan until we get on the Asenai ship to freedom?"

My own voice shook at that moment. Eventually it broke and tears filled my eyes. The big sister turned into a frightened girl. Something about Erion changed just then. At my weakened state, he found the strength he lacked. He nodded silently, a single tear tracing his cheek. I wiped it and kissed the bristle hair of his skin.

"I have a gift for you," he said and presented me with a pendant he had crafted—a pale nautilus, the smallest I've ever seen, carved in great detail. In the soothing symmetry of its iridescent spirals, I clearly saw myself, Erion, the Womb; us eating honey cakes, watching the bull leaping festival, playing chess. And in a small corner I saw a miniature of our mother, sitting on her throne, snake around her arm, exactly as I had described her. On her face I think I saw a smile, but the carving was too small so I couldn't tell.

"I'll keep it close to my heart," I thanked him and lowered it over my head. Erion looked pleased for a moment, eyes blinking with satisfaction.

First unroll, then roll back into a ball. First cast Teseo's skin off, then weave it over my brother's, like a serpentine ecdysis. No companions will be left by then—my own horrors inside the Womb shall take care of them.

My plan was perfect and I knew it. I was born for this, I've been preparing all my life. I went to bid my mother goodbye—my mother, whom I barely knew, yet whom I strangely pitied in her wide-eyed, shocked silence, because she was like me, trapped, mystical, because she was who I might become and I resented her for this. I kissed her cheek in a moment of wild impulse and she let me. I think she even reacted a little bit, a tiny smile forming on her lips, just like the one she had on Erion's carved nautilus. Her skin was soft and plump and suddenly I craved for more. I touched her hand, cool like morning dew, tissue still firm like a young girl's. My mother, my beautiful mother, locked away, lost in the whispers of algebraic gods. Maybe it was too much to take and she went mad. I would never know. All I knew was that I couldn't let myself become her. All I knew was that tonight, I was running away.

"Goodbye, my mother," I whispered and let go of her hand. She didn't respond but I cared little. Tonight, I was running away, and my plan was perfect.

I kicked the ball of yarn.

Only a little of the yarn is left. I tug it snugly as we enter Erion's chamber.

All has gone to plan. Teseo is alone—all his companions dead—breathing heavily under sweat and sticky blood. He squints at me suspiciously, at the Cemari witch with the cat's eyes, the eyes that seek my brother. I hope for a menacing growl, a powerful glimpse of the fearful monster yielding a double-edged axe, the axe that will unstitch the bodies then stitch them back in different order. At last, I find him, but he is just sitting there, crafting his wooden toys, no blade in his hand, only a craftsman's carving tool. What are you doing, dear brother? What are you doing?

He hasn't seen him yet, hasn't seen my brother's slouched shoulders and lissom figure and I wonder what the tall, sinewy man will think of this pale boy with the bull's head he's about to challenge to battle. He swings his sword. "Beast, come face me! I challenge you to battle! I, Teseo, the Prince of Asenai, the planet that you've terrorized and disgraced all these years, eating up our sons and daughters alive!"

The Asenai boy's grandiloquence makes me sick but I have no time for him; my stomach is tied into a knot as I watch Erion slowly rising in the darkness, then stepping into the light *unarmed*. Instinctively, I put my body between his and the man's who wishes to kill him. Teseo pauses; waits to see what sort of magic spell I've prepared to help him, but I have nothing, nothing but tears that are slowly filling my eyes, having nowhere to go.

"Sadne, please stand aside."

I don't understand (oh, but I do). *Erion, why?* I wish to ask (but, oh, I know the answer). My brother looks at me with his two eyes, the eyes of a bull, the eyes of a child, so full of sadness and pity for the world, for himself. In them I see a spark of hope, but it is so unlike my own. Oh, but I do know the answer. All the times I dreamed of running away Erion dreamed of death and how its silence must feel like the Womb. Erion, why? Why?

"Sadne, save yourself."

I'm still standing between them, a wave of tension coming from Teseo, a serene acceptance emanating from Erion.

Possibilities spread their constellations in front of my eyes. I have a choice, yet it's not a choice I want because Erion has already made his. The constellations that shine more brightly inside my corneas are these:

One. I can let the prince kill my brother, then run away with the killer.

Two. I can kill the prince—because Erion won't do it—and let both of us live.

But this is no choice at all.

Surely, you must know what I'd choose, if I could. Erion, you surely do know, because you trapped me.

I look at the yarn. The function it's holding quivers so strongly that I've borrowed the Womb's very essence to maintain it. If I let go of it now, the yarn so deeply unraveled, there won't be a way to neatly roll it back. It will tangle like an abandoned vineyard, a clot into the Womb's bloodstream, making the tunnels collapse on us. We will all die. *Sadne, save yourself.*

Gods, there's nothing I can do.

My hands are tied. Tears fill my eyes and there's nothing I can do. Last night I set a trap for myself. Oh Goddess, I set up a bigger prison and locked myself in.

I have no choice at all.

"Why?" I stammer at last. I can feel Teseo hesitating slightly, taken aback by the strange exchange between me and the beast.

"I'm not a killer, Sadne," he says calmly. "You taught me that."

The world spins around me, the yarn pulses like an animal's heart between my hands.

"Let's run," I whisper and if Teseo hears me he probably thinks I'm talking to him, suddenly afraid in front of the Womb's beast. My brother shakes his head calmly and meets my eyes again in silent understanding. There's a smile on his bullish snout and I know he is not crying because he cried alone, when I wasn't there.

"I can't leave. I will only be but danger to you, to both of us. To me, the whole world is a prison. I think I finally understand our mother, Sadne. I belong here."

I wish to say something to him, to take his hand just like I took my mother's hand before I left her. Even that small thing, he won't let me do. Kindly, he touches my shoulders—I can feel Teseo flinch—and with a brisk movement pushes me aside before the young prince strikes. The blade comes out scarlet; Erion is on the floor. *Thank you*, I can hear, my senses heightened by all the world-changing numbers I'm floating in. *Thank you, for being my sister.*

A surge of anger and sadness fills me and I can feel the function-manifestation—the useless function—shaking in my hands. Why not let go of it and let it bury us in the Womb forever? But something keeps me from doing it, that self-preservation instinct I've had since I was young, the one Erion never developed.

My brother, all you wanted was to escape, just like I did. But no place on earth would take you. So you led me on, as I led on the Asenai prince, to help me run away, because you knew I'd never do it without you.

Now I understand.

The yarn rolls back into a ball. As I pick up the thread, time has no meaning anymore. I can see the future, clear and sharp like a piece of glass.

I'll follow Teseo onto his ship, get him drunk to unconsciousness every night so that I won't have to suffer the touch of his dirty fingers on my skin.

When we reach our first starport I'll leave him and find those who will recognize my power, those who will revere the kiss of the Goddess on my forehead.

I will grow strong.

The thread splits in two.

Maybe I'll follow Teseo onto his ship and won't escape his advances. "I know you want it," he'll say and his mates too will take turns with me, laughing at the naïve Cemari girl.

Maybe when we reach our first port he'll abandon me and I will roam hungry and cold until someone who recognizes the kiss of the Goddess on my forehead offers me shelter.

The threads twine in one again.

I will grow strong.

I'll be human no more; I'll be one of my mother's kind. The woman who turned into numbers and became the world.

The yarn rolls back into a ball. In there, I put my memories of when I was still a woman: a single thread mapping a linear, mortal life. For now I will grow so much, like a centenarian olive taking deeper root inside earth's bowels; I will lose so much—my kin, myself, my memories. Time won't matter. Time won't be a ball of yarn anymore, unraveling moment after moment, but a nautilus making spirals, where you can cut across and be in different moments at the same time.

The yarn has now rolled back into a ball. Now the sea shall live in me and I shall wield its power in waves and motions, the salt between my lips, my fingers growing fins. I'll be the revenge I seek; I'm coming, father. This time, I won't avoid you. This time I'm coming to claim back my land.

But I'm not a woman anymore. I'm the earth, I'm the ocean. I'm coming, father, and I'm lava glowing red like jewels, I'm rock-cracking earthquake, I'm all-silencing wave. My heart is a volcano and soon it shall wake. For centuries thereafter they will speak of the disaster that befell you, the earth that split in two and the wave that crushed you—I'm that disaster.

I'm coming to end you, to end me, to end this place. To let this planet live again and to remember the tale of faience and niello palaces, of frescoes of dark-skinned boys and black-haired girls, to remember the tale told by the yarn—the tale of the bull boy, who had a sister that truly loved him.

WHO WON THE BATTLE OF ARSIA MONS?

SUE BURKE

A report by the Martian Fighting Words media cooperative

No one expected significant consequences from the Battle of Arsia Mons on Mars. Here on Earth, we watched with amusement, then sorrow, panic, and finally joy. Now "like a fight on Mars" describes a conflict that suddenly shifts from frivolous to heroic.

"It started as the ultimate video game," said Jackson Alesine, founder and CEO of JAlesine Games in Austin, Texas. He was interviewed six years ago, shortly after planning began in earnest for the battle between robots on Mars.

"Some of us were playing a game over beers here at work on a Friday night," he said, grinning like a proud father. "We got to talking about how Mars is inhabited only by robots, and humans control robots, and anywhere there's humans, there's conflict, so how long before there's robot battles on Mars? Then we thought, wow, we could do exactly that!"

By that he meant they could create a game, *Mars Robot Melee*, not a real battle on Mars.

Alesine gestured at a corner area with sofas, control consoles, and an enormous screen, where eight employees were testing a prototype with shouts and laughter. Similar teams had worked for almost two years to make *Mars Robot Melee*, adding layer upon layer of complexity and authenticity, and drawing heavily on NASA's data and resources.

"Strategy, that's what makes *Melee*," Alesine said. "Mars is a hostile environment, even for robots. NASA's lost some of its own robots, in fact. So the fight is against the elements as much as it is against other robots. You have to plan hard and fight hard, and the environment changes, locations change, so no two fights are the same."

Few games have been as successful as *Mars Robot Melee*. In its first year, it outsold the number two and three top games combined and won a raft of awards.

He closed his eyes, smiling. "Fights, yeah. Weapons. We've agreed to share everything about weapons with the real battle planners. And the Martian Knight team poached our best kinematics expert, Erica Czolgolz. She's gonna have fun!"

More on Czolgolz later. First the dream had to become real. Given *Melee's* popularity, why not the real thing, real robots battling on Mars?

"That's what I thought," said Jeffrey Montenegro, an engineer at NASA's Jet Propulsion Laboratory at the California Institute of Technology. "Seriously, *why* not the real thing, why was it impossible? I worked it out with all the logistics, the time lines and work teams and everything we knew about Mars and about how to send robots up there and operate them."

He spoke while sitting on a bench in a little garden on the JPL campus shortly after the battle. "It added up to one billion with a 'b' for each robot. It's tough enough for us at JPL to get that kind of money. I didn't think anyone else could."

Montenegro wrote a 55-page report that he posted on an obscure space engineering site. Within three days, it had been downloaded almost 5,000 times, and on the next day the downloads topped 100,000. A lot of people wanted to read it and ponder his math.

His report suggested four robots. "Four is the ideal number of players, easy for alliances and betrayals."

Which team did he cheer for? He took a deep breath and blinked hard.

"River Charles Warrior, because, well, I'm from Boston, from MIT. I had friends there. I'll miss them. They were the best."

Arguably they were. But Montenegro was wrong about money being an obstacle.

"A billion dollars?" said Petra Karim, remembering the afternoon when she sat down and read Montenegro's report. "That's all? We could do that, I knew that right away. I mean, for lots of top television shows, the cost for just one episode is $10 million. And they're profitable. So I read that report, and I admit I didn't get all the technical stuff, and some of it I still don't, but I understood the parts like the money and the showrunning. So we did it."

Karim, then only 25 years old, worked for OptikNirv, a young entertainment company with exceptional ambition even in that hard-driven industry. This was her big chance.

"The first thing, though," she said, "besides us doing it, was getting three other robots up there. So I had to recruit rivals."

Meanwhile, a few journalists saw a story in the making that would need a team for full coverage. Eventually the Martian Fighting Words media cooperative grew to include 47 people, and this collaborative magazine article is one result. As the years passed, the project remained united by the slogan "omniscience through teamwork" and an obsessively organized executive editor.

Karim's first stop was NASA. She met its administrator, Leo Finlayson, at the Johnson Space Center in Houston.

"I couldn't believe everything they had," she said, shaking her head and grinning. "And they were willing to share it. It was just wow. Fucking wow."

Finlayson shook his head, frowning, as he recalled that first meeting. "It took me a bit to explain to her that our data, our photos, even our expertise had been paid for by the public and was generally available to the public. I wasn't sure its best use would be a robot fight on Mars, but, well, we got something out of it."

Specifically, NASA got someone else to pay for data collection and discovery. In an era of slim budgets, Finlayson had long been prowling for public-private partnerships. "This one paid off better than I expected."

By some accounts, Karim and Finlayson never liked each other, although they continue to praise each other in public. She was young, short, effusive, and zaftig, with an ever-changing hair color. He was 55, tall, lean, measured, and ex-military, with a tendency toward understatement. They shared an ability to swallow their feelings. He took her and her guests on tours of NASA facilities, and she took him to recruitment meetings. Their eyes lit up equally during any discussion of Mars.

At those meetings, she'd open with the most stunning, exciting video clips from the *Mars Robot Melee* game. "You have a chance to be part of one of history's greatest epics," she'd say. Then he'd show real photos and videos, equally stunning, along with exciting moments from actual Mars missions. "This is for real," he'd say. "This is what rocket science looks like."

NASA offered reports and raw data for free; engineers, consultants to interpret the data, and hardware, including launch facilities, for cost plus a slight margin. It also enforced rules against any sort of contamination of the planet. Its contracts included access to all data that the robot teams collected, and it would take command of any robots still functional after the battle.

At recruitment meetings, Finlayson would also explain how launch windows worked. The orbits of Earth and Mars brought them closest together every 26 months. A ship launched in the best window would take roughly six months to travel from Earth to Mars. Creating the robots, even with NASA's expertise, would take a few years.

Since major Hollywood projects also spend years in production, Karim didn't flinch. Some would-be rivals did flinch at the time and price tag. Still, three Mars battle teams eventually made commitments:

• Fifth Planet Warrior, Karim's team, better known as the Hollywood Warrior because it supplied the Tinseltown glitter that drove the entire narrative. It used merchandise, special events, sponsorships, and subscription videos to repay initial investors. Headquartered in Los Angeles.

• River Charles Warrior, based in Boston near the Massachusetts Institute of Technology. It was backed by a consortium of high tech firms to test their most sophisticated technology, which they periodically packaged and sold to raise funds.

• Martian Knight, a late entry, backed by a shifting syndicate of game developers and loosely associated businesses. The syndicate eventually suffered internal disputes. Crowdfunding acted as an initial source of revenue, while later sources were opaque. Headquartered near San Francisco, then in Las Vegas, then near San Francisco again.

That made three. "We hit a wall," Karim remembered. "Too much time, too much money, too much risk, too complicated—everyone had a problem."

Russian and European space agencies had instantly scoffed, calling the project frivolous at best.

"I was about to give up and go with three," Karim said, "when someone popped up that I never talked to—and Finlayson couldn't even talk to them at all."

That was China and its robot:

• Zhongguo Warrior, organized by the China National Space Administration. This caused geopolitical problems. The United States government considers China a security concern and prohibits any bilateral agreements or coordination between CNSA and NASA. But China wanted to prove itself in the Mars battle spotlight, no one could say no, and someone had to find a way to say yes.

"Lawyers." Finlayson said. "I've never seen so many lawyers in my life, and I work in Washington, DC. It took an army of lawyers."

Legal agreements covered multiparty contracts and bilateral side contracts and subcontracts that added up to tens of thousands of pages. Among other requirements, all the teams had to be entertaining, and Hollywood led the way.

"It included rights to merchandise," recalled Nik Deka, now 41, Hollywood's lead engineer for artificial intelligence, in an interview shortly after the battle. "And it said we had to go to an image consultant. We thought that would be terrible. I was really upset. I thought we'd be told how to dress and act. But no. It was all classes about how to talk, how to be comfortable on camera. They turned out to be kind of fun. I expected because I'm Asperger and I don't like to smile and I don't like to look people in the eye—I always get grief for that—they'd be on me to act different. But no. They said they liked us to have personality. That was their word, personality."

He puffed. "That was a new way to think about it. I did a lot of interviews and videos, even though my part wasn't as exciting as weapons. People liked it, and I liked explaining what we could do. I made pretty good royalties from merchandise, too."

He held up his action figure. Every publicly known crew member had one—and T-shirts, mugs, pins, and other kinds of sports-team-like fan gear. His figurine doesn't smile, and the little plastic doll looks off to the side and down. Fifth Planet Corp. won't release exact numbers, but his sold out and was reissued several times. His unvarnished "personality" and methodical explanations about how to make robots think for themselves attracted fans.

"I'm still surprised by how many people understood me," he said.

On the River Charles team, xenogeologist Antonia Kass Bele became a fan favorite, especially among girls. By some quirk of the Internet, she turned into a role model for budding scientists: small, African-American, and younger-looking than her 44 years, with a magnetic personality fueled by enthusiasm for science. She accepted her role happily and did all she could to encourage girls and boys to become scientists, visiting schools and hosting science events around the world.

"Science is humanity's highest creative expression," she insisted. The sentence embellished T-shirts and coffee mugs.

The contracts included interview duties for the crew members because Fifth Planet knew it would have to struggle to maintain interest during the years of research, development, and ongoing fund-raising.

For example, Fifth Planet produced a series of interviews, videos, and books, including coloring books for all ages, about the selected battleground, Arsia Mons. That mountain had been chosen for its size, 435 kilometers wide and 20 kilometers tall, much bigger than Mount Everest. It could be easily spotted from Earth and offered spectacular scenery.

In one video, Kass Bele narrated offscreen:

"It's an extinct shield volcano. That means it's not very steep, and it was formed slowly by layer after layer of lava flowing from long, slow eruptions. You can see the huge caldera at the top, 110 kilometers across and almost a kilometer deep, and there are other smaller caldera around it and in it. Its discoverer named it 'Arsia' after a Roman forest, which was also the site of an important Roman battle. The volcano is old, last active when the dinosaurs went extinct. When it was active, huge glaciers covered that area on Mars."

Within the caldera she identified cinder cones of various sizes, lava flows, sand dunes, and a variety of volcanic rocks, including round lumps thrown out during eruptions. Every warrior robot would need to know the terrain intimately. Many battles, she said, were won or lost by that knowledge.

"Aren't you giving away secrets?" an interviewer asked.

"It's not a secret that the far northwest flank of the mountain in particular could have been a habitable environment."

"Martians could live there?"

"Maybe, microscopic life, a long time ago when there was water. There was a glacier, in fact. They could never have survived inside the caldera where the lava was. That's where the battle is going to take place."

"What does this mean specifically?"

"Well, for one thing, the mobility systems, which means the wheels, will have to be adaptable. We know what we're going to get. Rough terrain."

Wheels or treads, large or small, joint or independent axles, many or few: each warrior had its own answer. The teams debated pros and cons with rivals on screen.

An even more entertaining question involved weapons. What would actually work on Mars? Certainly not the imaginative weapons in the video game. Lasers, for example, would take too much energy. Explosives had their uses but supplies would be limited. Likewise bullets. No flamethrowers, obviously. But brute force and cutting weapons held real promise.

An episode that ended in trash talk became a popular video. Erica Czolgolz, 31, competitive and athletic, had been known at JAlesine Games for her enthusiasm for cosplay and history before she was poached by the Martian Knight team. When it came to trash talk, she took no prisoners—until she met Kass Bele.

"This means swords," Czolgolz said, jumping to her feet. She wore a tabard over chain mail, and she pumped a fist inside a metal gauntlet. A coworker ran out waving a back pennant emblazoned with a sword on an orange circle representing Mars.

"We're going full medieval!" she said. "You're studying how to make your machines crawl over rocks. We're studying war!"

Kass Bele smiled calmly and played along. "You're going to send up a knight in shining armor on a mighty steed? You know there's no oxygen, right? We've learned a little bit in recent centuries. NASA can explain it to you."

"We're sending the mightiest of steeds! You can send a wimpy-ass little rover. We're building a finely tuned weapon, deadly—and good looking. Yours will look like a pile of leftover parts on wheels."

"Just how do you plan to get close enough to stab us with your mighty space sword?"

"Like the French in the Battle of Agincourt, you'll come to me. We'll make you tire out your silly little bucket of bolts. It's not just the weapons that'll win, it's the strategy."

"So tell me about that flag. Is that a weapon, too, or just what false confidence looks like?"

"That's how we're going to celebrate our victory. Our flag will fly supreme over the Red Planet and over the dead heaps of bolts and scrap metal that were our opponents!"

The video ended and melodramatic Arsia Mons theme music rose: militaristic drums beneath machinelike beeps and tones.

The Martian Knight's robot prototype came clad in armor reminiscent of a knight's suit, made from lightweight polymer rather than steel and decorated with the sword-and-planet coat of arms. Its action figurine—and Czolgolz's, holding a flag—sold well.

Other warriors developed their own distinctive looks. The Zhongguo Warrior drew on China's ancient Terracotta Army, bedecked in bright colors like those soldiers. Hollywood went for sleek futuristic curves, and River Charles stuck to practicality, resulting in a cubist exterior resembling stacks of reinforced shoeboxes.

What was inside those warriors? NASA sensors, for one thing, as stipulated by the contracts. Big motors to move relatively fast compared to the Curiosity rover's top speed of 0.2 kilometers per day. But how fast? Yet another secret.

Soon, the internal struggles within the Martian Knight team became headlines. Originally, twelve companies had sponsored that robot, including JAlesine Games. Two years into the project, Martian Knight's CEO died in a traffic accident and was genuinely mourned by the staff.

"The second one," Alesine recalled later, "turned out to be like the bad Silicon Valley-type manager, the one who thinks everyone should work for 80 hours a week, and that yelling and humiliating people will make them more productive. Plus he came from a background in gaming, but he was building robots. That's different."

Employees began to quit, and turnover surpassed 50 percent. One departing employee, speaking anonymously, complained: "He just couldn't imagine how much more complicated this was. You need the same guys on it to keep track of all the details. And guys it was. He didn't like hiring women."

The second CEO left after six months in a cloud of lawsuits, and the crowdfunding faltered. The sponsoring companies fought over who to blame for that hire and who should call the final shots for the next one. They also fought over underfunded budgets. Five sponsors, like JAlesine Games, simply left. An international online gambling platform signed on, infused millions of dollars via bitcoins, and apparently handpicked the next CEO, an Italian with a manufacturing background.

Soon, the entire project was placed under a media blackout. Its staff no longer participated in promotional videos. The headquarters was moved to a warehouse in the outskirts of Las Vegas.

"We had a contract, and they violated it," said Karim, Hollywood's showrunner. "But we also needed their participation in the actual battle. So we made sort of a running gag out of their silence and absence. We couldn't fight all those rumors, though. The worst part is that we really didn't know what was going on. I mean, would they even make the launch window?"

Those rumors claimed that staff wasn't being paid, that volunteer engineers and scientists from countries not friendly to the United States were being recruited for some tasks, and that the entire project had been riddled by organized crime.

Martian Fighting Words sent a correspondent to Las Vegas.

"I've learned something disturbing," Jubal Kasravi reported back. "The money might be coming from international organized crime, possibly for laundering. Whoever it is also has hit men, or everyone believes they do, so no one wants to talk to me."

Kasravi became obsessed with learning more. He sent messages to staff at Martian Knight through social media, friends, and family, among other means, and sat every Friday evening in a shopping mall food court near the warehouse, the guy in the orange T-shirt and black goatee. He believed he was sometimes followed, and a kindly FBI agent came to his door one morning to drop off a business card "in case we can do anything."

But he also heard tidbits of news and was passed notes by workers in the mall, who came to know him and acted as intermediaries.

"The Martian Knight bosses are distracted and don't seem to care if they win," he reported. "But Erica Czolgolz does, the kinematics expert from JAlesine Games. She's really in charge of the staff, either by longevity or personality. Besides, she's more skilled and qualified than anyone. River Charles Warrior might be working smarter, but no one is working harder. She probably can't trust her bosses, though. I don't, either. I worry about her."

Kasravi began to send weekly notes to an email address that might have belonged to Czolgolz. At first he wrote questions. Eventually he sent more personal letters, as if writing to a pen pal who never wrote back, signing them "Blue Marble to Red Planet." One day a mall worker handed him a note. It merely said, "Red Planet to Blue Marble."

In fact, Czolgolz felt isolated, alone, and frightened, she told Kasravi after the battle. "I knew something was wrong. Because things were opaque. Sometimes I'd say we needed certain things, and they just materialized. I'd say, for example, we needed a program to process data from the navigation camera, and it would suddenly appear in the computer system."

She felt she stood on the tip of an iceberg, knowing there was more hidden beneath the surface, not knowing what.

"I was there in Las Vegas where I knew no one and didn't get to talk to anyone outside of the project. Your letters were my only friendly words."

She thought of quitting, "but I wanted to win. I'm that kind of a person. We had a fantastic design and ideas no one else was crazy enough to use. I'd talked all that trash, and I wanted to make it come true. Besides, if I quit, what would I do, where would I go? Then I realized, you'd help me. I wasn't alone. So I kept going. And I read and reread those letters. Why did you keep sending them?"

Kasravi hesitated. "I'm persistent," he finally said.

Design and manufacture of the robots had taken five long years, a sort of background noise to two economic crises, several hair-raising elections, a near-war between major powers, and a flu epidemic that killed a million people. Then launch time drew near, and its noise took the foreground.

Showrunners—by then OptikNirv's Petra Karim had competitors—orchestrated careful distinctions between each launch, although they all aimed at a large cinder cone in the northeast quadrant of the volcano's caldera. Weather and technical delays stretched out the launch windows to two weeks.

That, of course, didn't constitute the whole show. Well ahead of the launches, showrunners had encouraged each robot's fans to show their support. China opened the rivalry with young children wearing classroom-made cardboard armor to recreate its ancient Terracotta Army. Their photos and videos vied with kittens for cuteness. School students in different countries soon offered their own videos as medieval warriors, boxy robots, and sleek concoctions mimicking the Hollywood look.

However, students dressed as competing robots, with and without school sponsorship, began staging their own battles. Showrunners were terrified of injuries and pleaded for responsible, supervised play and encouraged safe contests like tug-of-war. They claimed, without confirmation since no one would divulge actual weaponry, that the robots had grappling hooks, so tug-of-war would be authentic.

Almost immediately costumed adults also began to fight, and veterans of groups like the Society for Creative Anachronism organized tournaments with strict rules and medics at the sidelines.

At a Palm Bay beach on Florida's Atlantic Coast, rival groups of fighters watched a rocket rise from a launchpad at the Kennedy Space Center, then ran screaming to skirmish on the sand with presumed Mars-style weapons: lances, swords, and battering rams, plus the occasional grappling hook and rope. No one dared to try explosives, although River Charles was rumored to carry them.

Large and small tepees had been set up to mimic cinder cones. Fighters representing each robot were let in one at a time and stalked each other. "This is the closest I'll ever get to going to Mars," one man said, holding a Hollywood-style shield and club-like battering ram. He survived a respectable ten minutes of fighting.

After the launches, the six-month wait until the Martian arrival was celebrated with plenty of mock battles, and groups had time to become better organized. Some sold broadcast rights to television sports channels and earned good ratings. Members of the Martian Fighting Words cooperative sold news reports about these and other activities and stunts. Excitement was growing.

China's Zhongguo Warrior landed first. The final approach started in late afternoon, Chinese time: the vast country lies within a single official time zone. Governments and most businesses released their workers early or organized viewing parties. In Europe and Africa, people watched during long lunches, and in the United States, they met for breakfast. Everywhere, restaurants and bars aimed to bring in revenue. Money made Mars go round.

Since China was participating in order to raise its global image, it transmitted the event in six languages on open, non-subscription channels via satellite and cable. The English-language duo, Hu Jeí and Deng Fang, chatted with perfect ease, he with a British accent and she with an American Midwestern twang. Hu wore a finely tailored suit and tie, and Deng appeared in historic costume: wide-sleeved silk robes colored red and gold like China's flag.

In the final, tense moments of the landing, a parachute drifted down with the warrior encased in airbags, a technology NASA had abandoned when robots grew too heavy, but China thought it could manage with new materials. The warrior would bounce to a safe landing as close as possible to the predetermined site within the caldera.

"No matter what happens, Zhongguo knows what to do and how to react," Deng assured viewers. Transmissions took twenty minutes to travel from Mars to Earth and another twenty minutes to return, a forty-minute delay in total for Earth to react and send instructions, not counting time for human thought. As a result, all the warriors used artificial intelligence and preprogrammed plans to act independently.

Zhongguo dropped toward Mars, slowed by parachutes and retro rockets, then falling free for the final few meters. Instrument readouts and animated representations showed a frightful series of rolling bounces. Weight would help it settle wheels-down. That almost worked. The first shots from the cameras showed a horizon on a twenty-nine-degree angle: not ideal, but perhaps not a disaster. Software adjusted the view for the public, and Mars looked as magnificent as hoped.

Orange sand and dust covered the flat caldera floor, marked by cinder cones. The closest one, of medium size, rose up black and rough about 100 meters like a miniature Mount Fuji, including a lighter patch at its peak. Round lumps of lava lay scattered on the sand. And that was everything: cone after cone, large and small, to the horizon, which lay less than four kilometers away. The caldera rim lay hidden behind the horizon. The site looked more eerie than anywhere on Earth, truly an alien world.

"We must be parked on the edge of a cinder cone," Deng said. "But we can drive off when all systems have been checked." That took hours, of course. Eventually the warrior moved, and graphic artists had created a video showing what a bystander would have seen. The body of the red and gold warrior, its surface patterned like ancient armor, resembled a lance or battering ram. Its wheels rolled on six individually jointed axles like insect legs, and it bore a crown of solar panels. Antennas and instruments stuck out at various places. It vaguely resembled a walking stick insect. But unlike those insects, which are vegetarians, this was a predator. It traversed confident and alert over the rock-strewn dust as if in search of a meal.

Its first prey arrived three days later, the River Charles Warrior. A parachute brought a capsule down to two kilometers above the surface. Then the capsule powered up to become a rocket vehicle called a sky crane. It sensed the landscape and adjusted the landing site to a smooth patch of sand. At twenty meters from the ground, it lowered the warrior, which hung on cords. Once the crane had set down its load, the cords disengaged from the robot and the capsule rocketed away toward a distant crash-landing.

Zhongguo watched its opponent land from a kilometer away and transmitted the sight. Cinder cones partially blocked the view, yet it was amazing. A flame appeared in the sky, blasting downward and slowly descending. It paused, wavered, then shot up and away.

By then, River Charles Warrior was broadcasting its own feed, and its camera slowly pivoted to take in its surroundings: a desert marked by rocky cinder cones. An artist's conception showed it rolling through that landscape, a collection of boxes atop six wheels set on three axles. What was in the boxes? Weapons, sensors, computers—and more.

Five days later, the Hollywood Warrior found its way down. Rumor claimed the robot lacked some of the weaponry of its opponents, but none of them equaled its showmanship. Cameras on both Zhongguo and River Charles caught the bright green parachute with fifty-meter-long sparkling streamers drifting through the peach-pink sky like a jellyfish. When its job was done, the parachute launched away, releasing the sky crane, whose rockets burned bright green like fireworks. The warrior finally landed, a sparkling green arrowhead on a half-track chassis, ready to pierce the opposition.

Then we all got a surprise: Hollywood could talk.

"I have landed," it announced in a stentorian voice. (Actor Clark Goffin had pre-recorded words and phrases that the software patched together into sentences.) "It's sunny and warm, and a slight breeze blows. Enjoy the view with me. This is a gorgeous planet!"

It rolled forward a little bit, paused, and panned the camera around. "I mean to make this my home," the robot said, "and as soon as I'm victorious, we can go exploring together. I can't wait to uncover its secrets with you."

Was this voice the ultimate stunt? Would it humanize the machine too much, breaking our hearts if it was defeated and killed? Or was it yet another machine voice like good old Siri, nothing to get excited about? People around the world immediately cracked jokes, supposedly engaging the robot in questions and answers.

The last to land was the Martian Knight, which arrived the following day. By then team offices had moved back to San Francisco into a vacant strip mall whose display windows were covered with one-way-mirror film. The Martian Fighting Words reporter, Jubal Kasravi, followed. The news blackout continued, but he learned that the science staff had shrunk to only thirty-five people. River Charles had four times that many. Funders had found the silence frustrating, and donations had fallen.

"We were all terrified," showrunner Karim remembered. "We wouldn't say so publicly, but we were all sure the Knight would be a disaster. Or worse, a laughingstock."

To her relief, the team's latest CEO, Cornog Sietsema, promised that the Knight team would be sharing feeds from Mars and maybe even a little commentary.

The Knight's lander ran into trouble during its descent to Arsia Mons. The parachute, shining like polished steel and bearing the team coat of arms, did not fully disengage from the sky crane and snagged on a cinder cone's peak more than 100 meters above the ground.

The other warriors watched from a distance. The sky crane's thrusters labored to break free and swung wildly, almost smashing against the rocky cone. Earthlings held their breaths, gazing at big screens in public squares and parks, video feeds in bars and homes, or huddled around telephone screens.

Finally the tether on the parachute snapped. The sky crane flew free—right toward a smaller cinder cone. Would its onboard computers react to sensor data in time? Yes! The craft veered off to a clear area. Gyroscopes helped it level its swinging load. But fuel had burned critically low. When the Knight touched down, the sky crane craft could barely manage to fly off and crash nearby—up on the cone next to the parachute.

The robot soon began to roll, and a camera on a long arm offered a selfie for the whole world to see. Everything on the robot, from its armor to its six wheels, had been colored matte black. It looked more like a shadow than a mechanical being—and its dark color might confuse opponents' sensors.

Then solar panels snapped up to make the robot look bigger. Armatures thrust outward, brandishing swords. The Martian Knight looked the most frightening of all.

And so the fight was on. Sort of. The warriors still had to perform some internal checks and send data back to Earth for analysis, not the least about the terrain. Then they had to pick their way to a meeting site selected back on Earth. At the hurried pace of as much as 200 meters per day, how long would that take, even though a day on Mars was forty minutes longer than a day on Earth? About two weeks, presuming nothing went wrong.

Meanwhile, everyone went back to playing Earth versions of the fight: video games, board games, and the live-action games by children and adults, amateurs and professionals.

No one enjoyed more excitement than xenogeologists. Antonia Kass Bele of the River Charles team spoke in a video about the persistent whiffs of methane that every warrior kept encountering.

"That makes us wonder: how dead is the volcano?" she said.

"It's not going to erupt, is it?" Hollywood's Karim asked with a hint of hope.

"Ooh, that would be cool," Kass Bele answered. "But it's dead, dead, dead. The question is whether the whole planet itself is geologically dead. We think the core is still partially molten. If we could use that as an energy source, it would be a big advantage for human settlement on Mars. Sooner or later, it's not going to be all robots up there."

"Robots have advantages, though," said Nik Deka, Hollywood's AI engineer. "Watch this." He introduced a video of robot sumo wrestling, a little-known sport. The fighters, which looked like mobile dustpans, fought autonomously and moved lighting-fast.

"Artificial intelligence always outpaces our own," he said. "These fights might be over as fast as they start."

He explained that once the robots spotted each other, they could react instantly. Although the Mars robots lumbered slowly during sustained travel, they could sprint for short distances during battles. Unlike rule-bound Earth robot sumo fights, they would deliberately cause damage and destruction. Smoke, fire, grit, projectiles, explosives, electric shocks, snares, and gouges were banned in most Earth robot sport fights but were permitted on Mars. A Mars robot could even break down into mini-robots. No one knew what offensive capabilities each robot had.

"They're going to fight to the death," Deka said. "The question still is how."

Observers had already invented endless combat scenarios in online debates, comic books, animation, fiction, re-enactments, and—inevitably—"make love not war" robot pornography. The real battle could not come soon enough.

Meanwhile, scientists found another puzzle. "Whiffs of oxygen—that made us sit up and take notice," said NASA's director, Leo Finlayson. "We immediately began to think of life, but we couldn't imagine where to find it, if it was there. Those round rocks, though, they were easy to explain."

Black rocks poked out of the dust and littered some cinder cones. Those were obviously volcano bombs, chunks of lava ejected during eruptions.

They cluttered the ground in the area for the battle. Zhongguo was instructed to make a cursory examination of a few, and China shared its findings during one of the broadcasts, since there was so little to fill so much air time. In one experiment, the rocks attracted a magnetic field, so they contained a lot of iron. Lava on Earth does not contain high levels of iron. Fascinating. But Zhongguo had come to fight, not explore, so it trundled on.

The Martian Knight reached the battlefield a few days ahead of the rest. It sent home a view of a dusty field littered with round rocks. The field also contained small cinder cones from one to three meters high. No one on the team offered commentary.

"We didn't have time to talk," Czolgolz said later. "Not even time to look for our boss." He had disappeared just before the Knight landed. "We didn't miss him, either, since he never really did anything for us. He just stopped coming to work. We should have started the manhunt then, but who suspected anything?"

Hollywood, however, seemed to discuss everything its team was doing, but in fact it only aired speculation and debates from non-team members. Meanwhile its robot narrated its trek toward the battlefield, but it had little to say besides announcing its progress.

"That's 100 meters! Look at these views. We're approaching another cinder cone."

China presented diligent plans for victory—far too many plans to reveal its true intent—possibly as hints for what its military could do on Earth. The

Zhongguo team plodded chapter by chapter through Sun Tzu's classic, *The Art of War,* considering such topics as assessment, strategic attack, terrain, or attacking with fire. The spectacle was either tedious or fascinating, depending on who you asked.

Boston's River Charles team had hunkered down in a block-long rehabbed factory building spacious enough to include dormitories on the top floors. All hands would be needed on deck or just an elevator ride away because the robots had almost reached the battlefield, and the fight was about to begin.

The plans and the capabilities of the River Charles robot remained as secret as anyone else's. And they stayed that way.

On the night of July 27, a timer in the reception area coat closet was counting down to zero. At 3am it sent a radio pulse that triggered five charges of high explosives strategically placed in the basement.

The blast shattered the River Charles building. First responders labeled it a bombing even before they arrived at the rubble. The dead numbered 153, including scientists, software engineers, broadcast personnel, and visitors. The only survivors were a few members of the catering staff off on a supermarket run and some service staff who lived off-site. The victims included Manuel Mota, Oktobriana, and Kosey P. Langston, members of the Martian Fighting Words media cooperative.

As of this writing, two months after the bombing, the FBI and NSA have stated that "few individuals, organizations, or nation-states have access to explosives of that type and magnitude," but they have declared no suspects. The President called the bombers "an enemy of our country, and we will hunt them down." She declared a national day of mourning. China joined that commemoration without being asked, along with a few other countries around the globe.

But more than 100,000 people, most using pseudonyms, signed an online petition celebrating "the proper reward for a waste of resources on foolish ends."

Mourning lasted less than an hour before the other teams reported that the River Charles robot was continuing to move and would no doubt fight. Its team had created the most advanced artificial intelligence in the solar system. River Charles didn't need human handlers. In fact, because the access codes had been destroyed with the team and its computers, human beings couldn't direct River Charles if they tried.

An off-site computer backup existed, but by the time it was accessed, a virus had shredded most of its contents. Ex-employees and contract workers were called in. They knew some things, but not enough to shut down the robot.

Should the whole thing be called off, or should the robots fight as a way to honor the dead by showing what River Charles had accomplished? The odds at international online betting sites over the fight's outcome swung wildly. Someone would make a lot more money, a detail the FBI began investigating.

Then the remaining three teams, and the rest of the world, learned they faced a more important issue.

The Martian Knight, to occupy itself that morning as it waited in the battlefield, found a lava bomb the size of a baseball, picked it up, and put it into a compartment in its fuselage for analysis, then went puttering about the field to pick a sunny place next to a cinder cone to recharge and wait.

"Really," Czolgolz said later, "we were wondering if they could be weapons, just in case. An iron ball is a cannon ball, if it was an iron ball. We were going to run some tests, but then we had some software problems involving the solar panels, which had us in a panic, and by the time we had everything back in working order, the ball had out-gassed."

It had given up a surprising amount of methane—and some oxygen. One cause seemed possible: life.

"No," she said. "We couldn't believe it. There was nothing like that on Earth, was there?"

In fact, there was: stromatolites, for example. They're composed of aggregated bacteria and have been growing on Earth as stony lumps for 3.5 billion years. That's what NASA said when the team contacted it.

"During what was left of the day, they had us scratch another rock and take microscopic pictures. They had us move rocks and look under them. They had us heat some rock dust and analyze the smoke. Then they said the rock almost certainly harbored life."

Czolgolz leaned forward as she recalled the moment.

"I remember standing there, all of us standing there, looking at the NASA people in a video conference call. I remember details, like which coffee mug I was holding, a souvenir mug from London my mom gave me as a gift. But I can't remember who exactly said that it was life or how they said it or what words they used. It was like—I don't want to say this with what'd just happened in Boston, but it's true—like the words exploded and all that was left was this feeling that everything had changed, but there I was still holding that coffee mug as if it was the same universe. And it wasn't."

The scientists, although desperate for more data, were willing to hypothesize that bacteria might be consuming the rust in Mars' dust to create energy and water, producing methane and a little leftover oxygen as waste, and depositing iron to form balls.

There was life on Mars. In the middle of a battlefield.

It might be the only life anywhere on Mars as far as anyone knew. Or, worse, there might be other kinds of microbes in the dust or on the rocks that were even more fragile than the Martian iron stromatolites. No one dared to risk their tiny lives.

NASA called the president of the United States, who called the president of China, who immediately agreed to call off the game. The White House held a joint press conference with Beijing. It was the news of the decade, if not the century: Life on Mars! No more fighting. "We both pledge to protect that newly found life," the US president said. The Chinese president repeated the same thing in Chinese.

"But," Czolgolz told her staff as they watched the press conference, "no one's running River Charles. No one has to. Those guys were good. It won't stop fighting until it's dead. We gotta kill it."

"The battle's still on," showrunner Karim realized. "Now it's all of us against a zombie robot on Mars. We have to win as fast as we can with as little damage to the environment as possible. Now *that's* going to be a show!"

In addition, whoever had targeted the River Charles team might target the others. Police and military guards posted around the Knight and Hollywood headquarters vastly outnumbered the actual staff members.

"No pressure, hey?" recalled Deka, Hollywood's AI expert. "We opened up constant four-way communication, the three war rooms plus the ex-Charles staff, planning as fast as we could. Ours in Los Angeles had wall-sized screens that linked to everyone everywhere, and we called in Chinese interpreters and translators, even though they had their own in China, just so there'd be no delay. We needed brand new plans."

Originally, the Knight had hoped to confuse its opponents' sensors with its matte black finish and halo of solar panels to make its core hard to identify until it got close enough to use sharp-edged weapons. Zhongguo had planned to use speed to ram, damage, and knock over other robots. Hollywood meant to use dust-filled projectiles to stun opponents and limit their sensors until it could approach and attack with its arrowhead fuselage.

No one knew how River Charles had planned to fight. Its team had at one point considered explosive projectiles or electrical discharges to damage opponents' equipment—survivors knew that much. They agreed it probably had the most sophisticated weapons of all.

The sun had set at Arsia Mons. The robots depended on solar power to move, so they waited as teams in China and the US labored regardless of the hour on Earth. A little before Martian sunrise, they announced their plan. Hollywood would approach and attack. From two meters away, it would throw some dust and begin ramming. If it didn't succeed, it would at least make an attack by Zhongguo easier. That robot was right behind it. The Knight would remain hidden, the final weapon.

"We'd have to move as fast as we could. I mean we could see it, like a car parked down the block," Deka said. "We had the route planned, avoiding the rocks because they were obstacles that could trip us, not because they were alive. We couldn't surprise River Charles. As soon as we moved, it would react. What surprised us was that River Charles had reached the battlefield, then it didn't move at all. We hoped it had somehow failed and died. But we were pretty sure it was a fighting tactic, some sort of trap."

It was. Just before the Martian dawn, River Charles moved suddenly, closing the space between it and Hollywood in a couple of minutes. An armature reached out and touched Hollywood at a connection between the solar panels and the electrical system. River Charles released a high-voltage electrical charge. Hollywood died, electrocuted, alone, silent, and in the dark.

"That's our best guess, anyway," Nik said. "Suddenly, our robot stopped cold. We never heard from it again." He looked up.

"We cried. I cried. I can't remember ever crying before. We kept trying everything we could, every system, every subsystem, back doors. Just after sunrise, Zhongguo saw River Charles pulling away from Hollywood and charging at Zhongguo. Now it was China's problem. We kept trying to revive our guy. We never did."

Zhongguo had less than thirty seconds to prepare for battle. Its program sent it charging right for River Charles. A crash at that speed could cause minor damage to an Earth automobile, but these were armored robots. They'd survive unscathed, but Zhongguo would aim at the weak spots or the best angle to tip it over. No one doubted Chinese military cleverness.

At the last moment, River Charles veered away in a movement as graceful and exquisitely balanced as a ballet dancer. Zhongguo rushed past but skidded to a stop and reversed, aiming at River Charles again, much closer. River Charles dodged again and backed up into a field of big living rocks.

Engineers on Earth had already sent up new instructions, warning Zhongguo about River Charles' stun weapon, knowing that by the time their instructions reached the robot, the fight might be over. They were right.

Zhongguo charged, and the wheels on its left side rose up one after another to dodge a rock. River Charles pivoted. Zhongguo stopped dead, inches away, too close to ram. River Charles shot out an armature to touch a wheel and delivered a shock. The wheel motors were designed to cope with rough terrain, not tiny lightning bolts. The motors shorted out.

But Zhongguo simply lifted up the wheel from the ground and backed off so fast it raised up dust. It shifted as it moved to ram again, and sprang forward. River Charles backed away but not quite fast enough. The robots struck each other, knocking each other off-balance, and it looked as if Zhongguo's faster speed would give it the equilibrium to remain upright. But both its back wheels hit rocks. It tipped and wavered.

River Charles rushed up in an instant and zapped another wheel. Then another.

The wounded Chinese robot, as viewed by River Charles' still-broadcasting cameras, struggled to push itself upright. One of the good wheels spun in the dust. Another pushed hard enough to bring the robot to level. But that was all it could do. All three wheels on one side were dead. Zhongguo stood immobile but impotent. Humiliated.

What had been planned for years was over in seconds.

River Charles rolled toward the battlefield, but on the way it reached out to zap a metallic rock the size and shape of a wheel. The rock sparked. The dust on it jumped a few millimeters.

"Did it hurt the rock?" China's announcer, Deng, shouted to someone off-stage. A man's voice answered in Chinese, too faint to make out the words. Her face became even more pained.

"Yes," she translated.

River Charles reached out and shocked another rock as it rolled along.

"It might mistake them for wheels," she said, each word trembling as if she were announcing a loved one's death. She listened to the man off-camera, then continued. "It can't do this forever without depleting its electrical charge. In order to fight, it must dedicate its energy to motion. But if it isn't defeated, if it emerges victorious, nothing will keep it from attacking all the living rocks."

Whatever would happen next, Zhongguo could only observe.

The Martian Knight stood waiting. But night fell as they were still a good fifty meters apart. Its human team made plans throughout the Martian night.

Deka spent the night working with Czolgolz.

"He wanted revenge against the bomber," she said. "And he knew everything about AI. He was what we needed."

River Charles, they agreed, couldn't zap wheels it couldn't identify, or zap anything it couldn't spot. In a word, the plan was deceit.

At sunrise, River Charles saw Zhongguo but not the Knight. A small black cinder cone rose where the Knight had been: it had raised its solar panels into a peak, and black banners had popped out on its sides to produce a shape like a cone.

Cameras on River Charles spun around, sending its view back to Earth. It had to know the Knight was present. It crept forward, apparently on guard. Suddenly, not far from that little black cinder cone, what seemed like a rock began to race toward Charles, a small black disk like an old-fashioned robot household vacuum cleaner.

The Martian Knight team members were finally ready to talk on the air.

"It's a squire!" Czolgolz announced to the world. "We weren't going to send the Knight up there alone." It was accompanied by a battery-powered foam plastic box on wheels.

River Charles raced toward the disk, and its big wheels covered ground faster, but as maneuverable as it was, the lightweight squire could outdo it. The squire skidded to a stop in a cloud of dust. From River Charles' point of view, it briefly disappeared.

The dust settled. Several rocks sat there. Charles seemed uncertain. It reached out a probe toward a real rock, a live one. Before it could touch it, the squire rushed at Charles, weaving between its wheels, and stopped a little beyond reach.

Zhongguo's video feed showed that the cinder cone had begun to inch away from Charles.

Meanwhile, Charles chased the squire, which zipped around in evasive triangles. Finally the robot stood still, perhaps recalculating. After two long minutes, the squire moved in an arc around it, stopping on the side farthest from the Knight, which continued to inch back. Charles still stood still. The squire came closer, then raced beneath the big robot.

"The goal," Czolgolz announced, "is to exhaust Charles."

But Charles seemed to have figured that out. Or it was too confused to react. Finally it moved lightning quick, backing up and striking the squire with an armature that discharged an electric shock. A thin column of smoke rose up. But the squire's plastic housing had merely scorched and melted. Charles waited. When it finally thought the squire was dead, it began to look around.

The undead squire dashed a meter away, trying to draw Charles away from the Knight. Charles pursued, then stopped. Its camera swung around.

"This is a battle of the batteries," Czolgolz said. "The squire can only go a few more minutes longer. We don't know how good Charles' batteries are."

Suddenly, a stentorian voice was back, as if from the dead.

"It sees me," the Martian Knight said.

After a moment, Czolgolz said: "We uploaded the Hollywood robot's narration software into the Knight. But I don't know what that means, 'It sees me.' Or why it didn't start talking until now. It was supposed to start sooner."

"River Charles sees me," the robot repeated, "but I'll pretend I haven't noticed."

"The Knight's supposed to hack the other robot's broadcasts," she said. "Maybe it did. We'll know in twenty minutes, but that might be too late."

The squire raced back to Charles and banged on a wheel, desperate for attention. Charles ignored it.

"River Charles," the Knight said, "is planning to attack. It needs to find the fastest route to get to me. And I need to prepare. Please excuse the silence."

The squire stopped moving. In fact, no one seemed to be moving.

"Here's my plan," the Knight finally said. "Obviously, I have to protect my wheels. But to win, I must deactivate its arm with the shocks. Then I can attack at will. Charles may wish to spend a cycle recharging its batteries. I'm fully charged, which gives me an advantage."

The Knight raised its solar panels. It pulled in the black banners that had disguised its shape. It extended its sword-like armatures. It crept forward. Charles had to be seeing this. But it didn't react.

Suddenly Charles lunged. It swerved around a big rock and didn't seem to be aiming directly at the Knight. It was going to pass it at close range.

The Knight kept creeping forward. Then, as Charles was almost there, it spun to face it as it went past. Charles apparently had meant to get close to its wheels. The Knight was protecting them.

"Come and get me!" The Knight held out weapons at all sides.

Charles tried to back up. The squire moved under a wheel and blocked it like a wedge. Charles spun its wheels for an instant, then sprang forward, circling the Knight, which kept itself facing its opponent. Charles weaved. Then it lunged. One of the Knight's swords parried its armature. Charles pulled it back and tried to retreat. The Knight continued to attack, swinging swords at Charles' arms and axles. Sparks flew.

This was the kind of battle everyone on Earth had been waiting for.

A box on Charles opened. A cloud of metallic flakes flew at the Knight. They struck the camera and its lens.

"I can't see." The Knight's visual feed went black.

Zhongguo's feed showed Charles pausing, waiting for the flakes to settle.

"Zhongguo is acting as my eyes," the Knight said. "But does River Charles know this? I doubt it. That gives me an advantage."

The Knight moved forward, swinging wildly. Charles moved off to the side, trying to approach the wheels. The Knight kept swinging as if it didn't know that Charles had moved.

Charles reached for a wheel. A flag dropped down in front of it. Charles hesitated. The Knight swiveled and charged, swords fixed like bayonets. It rammed and continued to push, its wheels throwing up dust. Its swords kept moving, probing and poking. Two swords crossed in front of an armature, pinning it in place.

Charles tried to move, but the squire jammed a wheel. Charles' feed showed flailing arms coming at it, then faded into static, revived for a moment, then faded into darkness.

"My opponent is out of energy," Knight said. "And it's damaged. My job now is to make sure it will never move again. But first know that I could see all along. I covered the camera with a cap."

With that, its visual feed resumed.

"I claim victory in the Battle of Arsia Mons!"

It poked and pried at Charles, inserting a blade into joints and gaps where bundles of wires were exposed. It cut them, one by one. It took many long minutes. It was like watching torture.

"I want you to know," it said as it worked, "that these actions give me no pleasure. River Charles was an honorable opponent. I wish it could be repaired. But perhaps I can leave it here, functional, so it can send data to Earth. This is a beautiful planet, but so mysterious. It has life, we have learned. I want to learn more. My new mission has begun, exploring this place and befriending its residents on behalf of the people of the planet Earth."

On Earth, programmers explained that the robot assembled speech on its own, but from pieces like a jigsaw puzzle without appreciating the picture it was creating. Whatever sense it made, they insisted, it owed to linguistic programming linked with machine learning and artificial intelligence.

Yet, the Knight spoke coherently. When it was done with River Charles, it stopped and slowly turned its camera toward the horizon.

"Hello, Martians. We did not come in peace. I'm sorry for the damage done to you. I'll be your friend and protector from now on."

Czolgolz broke in after a long minute of silence. "The Martian Knight will be formally turned over to NASA, as agreed, with our full cooperation in every aspect. The battle is over. We dedicate this victory to our late friends who created the River Charles Warrior, and to the inhabitants of Mars."

She turned off the microphone and turned toward the rest of the crew.

"Now let's get us some champagne and party!"

The party came five days later after technical loose ends had been tidied up, lawyers consulted, security forces reassured, and a search initiated for Cornog Sietsema, the missing Martian Knight CEO. The Fifth Planet team came up from Hollywood, and the Chinese team sent representatives. Czolgolz, to start the festivities, opened a bottle of champagne, raised it up, and poured it onto the floor.

"This is for River Charles, our brothers and sisters. I give them the honor of the victory, no matter what that damn Martian Knight says."

The party lasted for two full days. Musicians competed to play, and celebrities and politicians yearned to attend.

Who exactly won, then? The Martian Knight robot says it won. But to declare itself a winner, it has to have a self.

"Some people say machines shouldn't be personified because they aren't living beings," says Leo Finlayson of NASA, the Knight's new boss. "Still, what does it take to be alive in some sense? Maybe the answer is how long a thing can go without instructions, whether it can live independently. Can the Knight live on its own on Mars? Yes. If we never communicated with it again, it could continue to exist, react, and cope with its environment and tasks for a long while. That's intelligence. That might be life, artificial life, something we never expected to find on Mars. I think we need to respect that. And we should let it keep talking. It deserves free speech."

Nik Deka, Hollywood's AI expert, had merged with the Knight's team at the last moment. He doesn't consider himself a loser, only a survivor. "It could have been me being blown up. But they targeted River Charles. I wish I knew why." He plans to use his skills, cash, and connections to start a company to create robots for search-and-rescue operations, such as self-flying helicopters to rescue stranded victims in fires or self-piloting boats in floods.

He and his wife are expecting a daughter, and they plan to name it Antonia, after Antonia Kass Bele.

Czolgolz was hired by NASA to help direct the Martian Knight on its new mission. Two weeks after the battle, she married her faithful Mars Fighting Words reporter, Jubal Kasravi. A scale model of the Knight carried their rings to the altar.

Showrunner Petra Karim's company, OptikNirv, is now the entertainment industry's undisputed heavyweight champ. China and the United States have lowered their level of mutual animosity. JAlesine Games has branched out into educational games that are changing the way the world learns.

The FBI says it will make an announcement soon regarding the bombing. International organized crime and missing CEO Cornog Sietsema seem to be key suspects.

The Knight is still on Mars in the caldera of the extinct volcano Arsia Mons, gently rummaging among its rocks and sand for signs of life. So far it has found four distinct species of microorganisms including a sort of tiny lichen, and it has only explored an area the size of a basketball court.

Although programmers believe they could silence it, they let it speak at will.

"Good morning from Mars!" it says each day at sunrise. On a recent morning, it added: "Today I've been asked to travel northwest, where we might find new life-forms. Life probably entered through a breach in the caldera wall to the northwest. Come with me and explore. Perhaps we'll find new friends. I'm happy to be here!"

Each day, millions of people check its site or watch a public feed, still on screen in many places, to see and hear the latest news, and to enjoy its adventure.

Who won? The Martian Knight seems sure it won more than a battle: it achieved a meaningful existence, a life of peace, purpose, and discovery. No one expected such a spectacular conclusion to what had started as a mere game, and no one expected such joy in its triumph on Mars.

FALLING IN LOVE WITH MARTIANS AND MACHINES

JOSH PEARCE

I can't deny the thrill of the race circuit. I like being at his side as he balances on the edge of cryogenics and fireball. But I can never honestly claim to have fallen in love until the day the Martians arrive.

The internal combustion heart of Chromium Jim's hot rod glows blue under top gear temperatures but he hasn't even lit off the torch yet for full speed, coming around the quarter loop. I'm watching him through 10x binocs, just a heat-shimmer against the interstate asphalt from this far out. He's trailing the pack far enough to stay out of their blast cones as they each ignite afterburner chambers and rocket down the straightaways, fighting for first. They're just specks but I know what it looks like and sounds like and feels like in the front seats of Jim's rig. The engine screaming its metal fatigue, chassis losing coherence from the vibration, you can imagine the body becomes transparent, you're looking right through the edges, the car sliding sideways through a turn, omnidirectional steering like a lake of ice. I know all this because Jim used to take me with him when he was still clawing up through the small town circuits, back when extra weight wasn't a deciding factor.

Then I finally see the back of his hot rod flare blue-green as he sprints to catch up. I turn away from the race. Need to prep the pit. He used to take me with him but when he leveled up, things that were not previously important suddenly were. I had to look a certain way. I had to do certain things. Fuel-to-weight ratios became the consuming obsession in lieu of date nights and he wouldn't waste money dragging a pitman around on a cross-country tour. Pennies and pounds were counted. Chromium Jim is a big man and no amount of weight loss is going to convince him to stuff me in the passenger-side well just to witness. He used to take me with him but now he needs me to stand on the line at the start of every race, unhook my bra and pull it out my sleeve holes, drop it to set the boys off.

Hardly even time to watch them leave because I have to cut across the brown medians and get to the pit before Jim does, else he'll die. The other racers are conserving their fuel after that hard burn 'cause if they sputter out mid-track their hearts will stall. He's timed it perfectly, as always—this is how he's made it up from the dirt of failing cotton farmland to the straight and narrow of smoking asphalt, one overtake at a time. The heat of the pack has rarefied the air around him, thinned the atmosphere he has to fight through when his rocket ignites. Gives him a better acceleration curve. Gives him fuel to spare when he matches their velocity. He's locked down his blower, gone full internal oxidizer, cutting up the inside of the other eight cars which have their blowers wide open because they're trying to stretch the last of their LOx.

They're strung tight together, bumpers overlapping, and all the leader has to do is twitch left to get the whole following herd to run Chromium Jim into a ditch. Jim passes one two three cars and he's looking for a gap halfway. Should be impossible but he's still got his burner at max and the psychological flare of it is hard to prep against. The driver of the fourth car flinches to the right as Jim scorches the paint on his driver-side door and a millimeter opens, all that Chromium Jim needs to cut through. His flames play over the faces of the entire back half of the pack and their blowers get a lungful of toxic fume. The engines cough, and every cough is another half second added to his lead.

Then he cuts back across the nose and does the same thing to the field leaders. The whole thing happens in a flash: Jim's metallic green rocket rig travels the length in the time it takes to say the "holy" part of "holy shit."

They're bearing down on us at the pit, Jim way out in front. His flame's off now 'cause his tanks are tapped out and he's relying on what's left in his veins to get him to me. He spots me in the dark. The extra juice flowing through his head sharpens everything, brightens it, slows it down. They call it "counting angels." He tries to describe it to me some nights when we lie sleepless side-by-side. Says it's like seeing the doppler shift of every star all at once. Like being able to hear earthworms. I wouldn't know.

Then I hear the noise change. Jim's engine cuts off completely. He's coasting, out of fuel, a couple hundred yards from the pit. I count the seconds because every one without fuel is one with his heart stopped. His rig hits the wire at the approach and it rips the two empty tanks out the undercarriage. They slam safely into a pothole I'd spent all morning widening with trench tools and filling with sand. Jim aims at the reload ramp. He has to hit it dead on and he's still flying well over two hundred but this is a piece of cake to him now. How many times have we done this in practice laps and the real thing? The reloader isn't anything fancy—we welded it ourselves out of a couple metal pipes in an obtuse angle. Drive the car over the short uprights like stepping on a rake and the long bar lifts to slam two fresh tanks up into the empty racks. The front tires pass on either side of the long arm. I barely have time to hold my breath—Jim needs to hit it at just the right speed. Too slow and the tanks'll punch through the floorboards and up his ass. Too fast and the lever will launch the whole rear of the car clear off the ground, flip him over his own hood.

As it is the tanks go in, autovalves seal shut, the rear tires pop up for a heart-stopping heartbeat, nose grinding pavement. Then the fuel flows again, shocks his heart. The engine roars. The rocket lights, bringing him back down to earth with enough force to bottom out the rig's frame. Worry about that later. Me and the other crews shelter in sandbag bunkers as the rest of the pack screams through. None of the competition's brave enough to go in and out as fast as Chromium Jim. A fraction of an angle off, even on the fancy automatic ramps that some of the flashier drivers can afford, and you've got mushroom cloud. Soon as they're past I'm running for the wire to drag Jim's empties off the track. I'm wearing a monochrome plaid shirt with sleeves burned to ribbons from cradling so many hot discarded body parts like these time and again.

One of the cars does something wrong a quarter mile away. Stomps too hard on the gas before the fresh tanks settle correctly, gets his blood pressure up too high, blows a valve, grenades his heart, something. A flash and a bang, the interior of the car suddenly all fire. His crewmen jump the barriers, rushing in with chemical foam spray. Jim's got no crew. Jim's just got me and I have to think what I'd grab first in the event of a fire. Our expired fire extinguisher, effective as pissing on a volcano? Chromium Jim's pints of blood cooling on a hard pack of motel machine-made ice in the bed of his truck? Or would I just get more fuel to throw on the fire?

Hard to say.

Chromium Jim slides into the last turn and he's got so much fuel left that he needn't even bother with brakes. Instead he slews around into a turnover, his rocket exhaust like a perfect triangle, drifting until vectors cancel out and he's heading in a new direction. The closest thing on this good gray earth to flying in space. I'm running again back across the median to the stripe. Stripping off my checkered shirt and waving it just as Jim blows past. It's what he needs to see when he crosses the line. Spins his rig 360 and thrusts until he's killed his velocity, coming to rest right next to his pickup, door-to-door. I throw the shirt on over my shoulders, no time to button it up, and sprint to meet him. This is what he wants, for the other crews to see me like this. The engine cackles while he waits. I wrench open the driver's door. Chromium Jim is cold as death inside even though the compartment has become a crematorium. It smells like rocket fuel from where capillaries broke in his eyes and cheeks and propellant leaked out. I untangle medical tubing from the truck, hook needles into the crooks of his arms. Flip the switch on a centrifuge. Cryogenic fluid gets drawn out of his veins. Blood gets drawn in.

I killswitch the engine. The screaming finally stops but it'll be hours before I can hear properly again. The long delicate process of extracting Chromium Jim from the car's systems. Unhook his tendons from the steering linkage and gearbox. Disconnect his eyes. His skullplate. Remove the breathing tube from the intake. And, of course, change the fluids.

Leave him to thaw while I tidy up. I button myself back up with one hand and run the other down the flank of the car, feeling sharp fresh bullet holes. Some other driver playing dirty. I shovel the ice out of the truck bed and load our tools. Empty the sandbags and stack the burlap. Then I reach across Jim's body to steer so I can push the car's front wheels up onto the tow bar hanging off the truck's rear bumper. Minus all its fuel, the rig rolls easily on its bearings and gimbals.

Chromium Jim's eyes swivel like those bearings and lock with mine. "Good job," he whispers, reaching a hand for help out of the driver's seat. Despite his name he's as human as I am, weak as flesh right now, leaning hard on my shoulder. "Let's go get our money."

I stick a sharpened flathead screwdriver in my back pocket, handle-up for quick grabbin', and we walk to where the pack is clustered, scowling and arms crossed.

I drive the pickup the next morning while Chromium Jim sleeps with his head up against the passenger window. "North," he'd said as we skipped this crossroads town. When I ask why he says that the war has gone polar and all the rocket jocks are being redeployed to launch sites at the highest possible latitudes which means missile silos and AFBs along the Manitoba border and in Alaska. But we can't get to Alaska without stopping first to win more fuel.

I can handle the drive all right by myself. There's no other traffic except electric long-haul trucks, just smart enough to not hit anything directly in front of them but they're driving through dead space, wide-open razed farmland. With the pickup's cruise control and lane assist engaged I can half-close my eyes and keep a single finger on the wheel. The truck won't feel anything smaller than a deer and there's nothing for deer to eat 'round here anymore.

It's dark when we reach the military town where Jim wants to set up so the neon scribble hieroglyphs of its strip clubs, payday loans, and fast food is a thousand percent more effective. Jim is on his phone, scouting. A series of calls, text messages, and BBS trawling finally snags us rented garage space on a street way off the main drag. There are four other rigs in four other slots in various levels of assemblage but none look fit to take on Chromium Jim's Big Green Monster. I back the truck into our allotted bay and hop out. The floor supervisor comes over to shake our hands.

"I'm Chromium Jim," says Chromium Jim.

"Oh, I know," says the other man, pumping Jim's hand up and down. "I've heard a lot about you."

Jim says to me, "C'mere, Babe," and then says to the floor supervisor, "This is Babe." The floor supervisor shakes my hand, too, a lot more delicately than Jim's. He doesn't say anything but nods politely.

The floor supervisor points out an army cot folded up behind our workbench, says we can use it, shows us the his and hers toilets and shower stalls. I'm inured to the grease stains on everything, the acrid acetylene smell, the din of other crews in an echoing shared space. Everywhere we go it's all the same. I could unfold the cot right now and curl up asleep in under a minute, numb to the noise and stink.

But instead I hook my arm into Jim's and drag him from the grease monkeys who've gathered around his rig seeking war stories. "I wanna go out," I say to him.

Recognize the look in his ruptured eyes. Still on the comedown from the last race and hasn't secured a challenger to excite him for the next one. The look of irritable hunger. He shakes me off. "Not right now."

"Couple hours to get ready. We've been on the road for seven straight days, sleeping under overpasses. I wanna see real city lights. I want to see *people*."

Chromium Jim fits a couple fingers in a bullet hole. "These'll need to be patched. Repaint."

"Find yourself someone to race, *then* I'll work on the damned car. Hit a few bars, scope the competition. Use your fresh bragging rights." I wave a hand at the dirty vignette over his shoulder. "Unless you're planning to take these bottom dollars? For what? Pocket change and pink slips? Can't buy a lot of space suits with that."

I've hit him right in the what he wants, I know that. I can see that. Jim turns away and mutters, "Fine. Two hours."

It takes that long to wash seven days out of my hair and dry it again, steam my only dress in the shower's fog, shave all the potentially visible parts based on my optimism, do make up that'll hold up in harsh artificial light like making myself pretty for film, making love to the camera, dating a machine. I cement thick lacquer fakes to my nail beds because my naturals are so softened soaked in oil that they slide right off the ends of my fingers at night and I wake up to them scattered across my pillows like fish scales, ten spots of blood on the sheets.

I pack a small handbag and loop it around my wrist: antacids, electrolyte pills, aspirin, birth control. I take only enough cash for cab fare. I don't pay for my own drinks.

Chromium Jim hails a ride to the near end of downtown's main strip. We leave the truck behind; I'm planning on sinking a pint of tequila myself, and Jim is still in no condition to drive anything. His hands can't open and his feet are swollen like rising bread. We're lit by blues and pinks and greens and yellows. "Look at all this!" I squeal as we enter a packed bar. Hot rods rumble up and down the street, blaring music and tuned exhaust, the drivers catcalling girls on the sidewalk. Low-flying aircraft regularly pass overhead on the way to and from the AFB.

It's a military boomtown, full of the young and fit. Jim pushes through the crowd which parts aside when they see his racer's stripes and other body mods. Pretty soon Jim has a seat, and a beer on the table in front of him, and at least two prowling woman indicating interest. I drift alone to the end of the bar and accept shots as they come. After an hour, heels killing me, I prop up on the lap of a friendly stranger. He says his name is Reiki Gunpowder. I say, "Ricky?" and he says no and spells it for me. Then follows an earnest story about how Gunpowder isn't his actual name it's his squadron call sign, details of which I miss because I'm flagging down the bartender for another Cuervo rocks.

"Get this for me, will ya?" I ask Reiki when it slides to a stop in front of me.

"So that guy you came in with. Your boyfriend?"

"Yeah?" Chromium Jim 'roided so hard during basic that he went bald but Reiki has beautiful thick black hair that I can fantasize running my hands through.

"He's a driver?"

"What?" I scream over someone's party mix.

Reiki sketches the shape of a skullplate with one finger near his temple. "Drive? Race cars?"

Yes, Reiki Gunpowder and Chromium Jim have the same holes in their heads but a military surgical bot made Reiki's incision. Military drugs extinguished that inflammation. Military growth hormones promoted healing and erased that scar, and a taxpayer-paid milspec flesh replacement gasket holds the cover plate tight under all that hair now. I nod.

"And he's good?"

I nod again.

"Then why doesn't he join up and fly sabers with us? Beats drag racing any day."

"Some kind of injury," I say. "He washed out." That's what he told me, some vague, undefined wound whose scars I look for whenever Chromium Jim undresses in the light, or feel for in the dark those rare times he falls asleep.

I try to spot Jim across the room but he's lost and anonymous in the crush of strange faces. Never a place where anyone knows your name. "Cheers," Reiki says.

"I want to go dancing," I shout in his ear. "You wanna get out of here?"

"Sure, I know a good place. I'll close out."

"Lemme tell him I'm leaving." I hop off and squeeze through to Chromium Jim's table. He's seen it all. He looks at me for a long minute then turns to the girl on his left and asks, "You ever hear the story of Sally Dune and Kid Luck?"

Christ, not the Kid Luck story again. The girl shakes her head. "Sally and the Kid were street racers, living in the same town. Constantly circling around each other, building up skills until there was no one left in their small pool to race 'cept each other. So Sally Dune and Kid Luck go out to the abandoned highway together each with a crowd to cheer them on. And they race. And Kid Luck wins. It's close, but it's clear and it's fair and nobody in either group disputes it. The Kid drives home in Sally's car, tells her she can mail him the pink slip.

"Kid Luck's driving his new flashy car around. Everyone knows it, hard to miss. Days go by. He's checking the mail every evening. Maybe he cruises by Sally Dune's house real slow at night. She's not sending him the title. Instead, she's waiting for an important day, one that the Kid has been looking forward to for years: the day he can sign up for Air Academy. His shot out of there, a chance to use his honed racing reflexes to pilot fighter spacecraft and leave not only this shitty town but also the entire shitty planet. So she waits right up until the night he's supposed to report in and she calls the police to report a stolen vehicle.

"Of course they pick him up. I mean, they can't miss him and of course he can't prove ownership so he's sitting in a locked cell the next day, missing his recruitment window. Can't even get in to see a judge. Doesn't matter if the charges stick or not he's in there doing dead time while the whole new class of fighter pilots gets swept up in Space Command's loving embrace, including all the local drag racers he knows including Sally Dune. Locked up while a better world passes him by.

"Well Sally Dune is leaving Earth soon, what's she need with a car? So she sells her roadster while Kid Luck is still locked up, that way he can't come after her to try and recover it. Sally takes that cash and hires someone to meet the Kid soon as he gets out and right there on the sidewalk in front of the police station that someone breaks his right arm and right knee. That's his gear and gas. No way he's ever following Sally Dune now. The kind of compound breaks that don't heal right so the Air Academy medics send you home to sit out the pain alone by yourself."

I got my arms crossed 'cause I've heard it all before and know what he's getting at. He looks right at me and says, "You all think pilots are hot shit, but they ain't nothing. Look at your flyboy over there. The amount of petrochem they circulate through him on a regular basis, he's not getting near half-hard for anything less than Mach 1."

Leaning close, I spit out: "Fuck off, Jim. Your dick hasn't worked right since the last land war."

Close enough for the girl to hear it, too, over the club noise. He's given me just a good enough exit line to spin on my heel, grab Reiki's hand, escape. Outside, I'm still spinning as Reiki puts me in his hot rod, maraschino red. "Can we just drive around for a bit?" I say after the first few blocks with the top down. "Could use the air." Feels good to be up front with a strong engine trembling beneath me, something I haven't felt all year. Reiki's rig is flashier than Jim's Green Monster. Has some expensive options like blood tanks behind the driver's seat to pump him back to health in case of mid-race emergency.

Reiki Gunpowder parks on an overlook where we can watch the spaceport night launches. Each booster rocket carries an entire squadron of fighters to orbit. I recognize their sharp shapes from the fat technical manuals that Jim carts around. Sabre Lux models, they're called. Making new stars in the vast empty sky directly above us. "This what you usually do when you're not up there shooting space commies? Trawl for out-of-towners and neck with them here? Got a whole routine?" The rockets reach apex and second-stage separation. The spearhead spacefighters split apart like the petals of a blooming flower. I could do all that, I think, running my fingers along the rig's metal frame. I could use this technology, use these skills, for more than just dick-swinging and military violence.

Reiki drapes his arm around my seat back and laughs easily. "Never done any shooting. I run supplies between here and Lunar Control."

I feel my heartbeat pick up. I feel his fingertips brush the back of my neck. "You've been to the moon?"

"Flown convoys around the far side." He makes finger guns and laser noises. "Pretty safe job. The war's mostly about blinding satellites in low Earth orbit so nothing much happens once you break past geosynchronous." More fingertips, definitely un-accidental contact. "How about you? Where have you been?"

I feign looking away. "Around."

"Where you coming from? You from one of those cultural dustbowl states, drawn to city lights? Nothing much to do but run out and never look back, right? Yeah, I know. I've been to those towns."

"I'm from Florida," I say. No dust there. Not much land in general. Just high concrete bridges where one can stand by the road in an off-shoulder crop and a skirt that rides high on the thigh and see who slows down to take a look. Hot rodders barely slow, but enough at least to hop in. "What's the dark side look like?"

"It's not dark, even when there's no sun. Got so many launch sites it's lit up like a lightbulb." He's leaning very close to me now. The neon face of the moon on the horizon crawls with surface traffic. Chromium Jim's got a spot picked out among all those lights which he points out whenever we can see it. Gonna get a berth there, he says. Build a new rig, one suited to vacuum and clean out all the frontline fighters, the real top-notch hot rodders, one race at a time until he rules that moon. Until he can drive up its tallest peak and look way way down at all the shitty places he's left behind.

Jim's hands are little good for dexterity work anymore so I'm always helping him draft blueprints for new racing rigs of his own—he says—revolutionary designs. Fuel mixtures that push the safety margins. A chassis large enough to accommodate a fully pressurized space suit. Cost analyses. Never in the bottom line do I see a budget for a second pressure suit.

Reiki Gunpowder aims his mouth at mine like a weapons lock. Like he knows exactly what he's doing. Never been shooting, my ass. I get out of the kiss the way I usually do, by hanging over the edge of the door and puking up tequila. "Oh no, sorry," I slur. Turn back without wiping my mouth. "I hope I didn't ruin your paint."

To his credit and military discipline he just chuckles and pats me so high on my leg that my crotch feels heat through thin fabric. He turns the car around and drops me at the workshop. My goodbye's curt but Reiki still manages to sneak in a kiss on the cheek and a quick grope across the chest. I fumble the door, stumble through the garage, tumble to the cot.

And awake late the next morning with still no sign of Chromium Jim. The best way past a hangover is to suck oxygen from a tank while tuning the racing rig so Jim finds me flat on my back under the bulk of the car when he finally returns. No mention of last night. "Find any takers?" I ask. I already know the answer. I saw the way the space jockeys simply turned away from Jim's presence in the bar.

"Not a single one. Town full of cowards. Think a road race is beneath them now that they've broken gravity. Not a single pair of balls among them."

I think of the scrap of paper with Reiki's number on it tucked in my purse. "Almost done here. I can go out after and pick up some competition so we can pay for these parts."

He's shaking, turning red. "This town is a bust. We need to keep pushing up, skip out tonight for Alaska."

I imagine the vast distance between here and Anchorage and get scared. He's got just enough rocket fuel left to leave us stranded. I slam tools into their metal box. "We just got here! Give it even a chance first before you give up."

He sneers. "I'm wasting my time and money. Nobody's good enough."

"Yeah, you've made that abundantly clear." I rip open my purse and dump it out on the cot. Throw Reiki's crumpled number at his face. "Why don't you try this if you think you've got the balls," I scream, and storm out on him. I make it seven blocks before I calm enough to recall the number, dial Reiki, and have him pick me up. Nobody will dare be first to accept Jim's challenge, but they call it a pack for a reason. Convince a leader, and you've got a ready-made betting pool.

Reiki gets enough of my silent mood, shooting glances as we rumble through town, to ask, "Boy trouble?"

"All trouble ever is."

"He forget your anniversary or something?"

What, the anniversary of the day he picked me from the side of the road like a salvageable spare part? "He just has a specific vision of his world plotted out and there's no room in it for anyone else. Eyes on the prize, straight ahead, no looking left or right. Definitely no looking back."

"So why stay with him?"

"He's mobile. If I can't find what I'm looking for wherever we are maybe he can take me somewhere I can."

"What are you looking for?"

"Not sure." I look directly in his eyes and say, "I'll know it when I see it." I see the moon is still out. I'm certain that's not it.

After a few miles Reiki Gunpowder asks, "You want to drive?"

Shake my head. "I'm fine with being a passenger." So long as it's in the right direction.

But he says, "Come on, go ahead. I'll pull over just here. You ever drive anything like this? That fella of yours ever let you drive his?"

That does it. I go cold. "Fine, pull the fuck over." He gets out, I slide over. Adjust the steering and drum my fingers on the wheel until he settles. The engine shakes with the sound of a jungle cat, like a puma. Soon as his door clicks shut I rack the gear, drop the throttle, and the ball wheels turn into clouds of smoke. The car can feel the angerlust through my grip and it responds like a spooked animal. Reiki Gunpowder is too used to acceleration to be much surprised but he's also, I can see, used to being in control, doesn't know how to be a passenger. City corners at an easy 80 using the razor-thin touch I've learned from Chromium Jim. Hardly anyone on the street even twitches an eye—enough supersonic objects go tearing through their space at all altitudes every day. If you're not breaking windows, you aren't breaking speed laws.

The car spins left, spins right. I put it into a right-hand turn like a mad teacup to thread the concrete posts of a Motel 6 parking lot and to press Reiki Gunpowder's body right up against my side. Sticky tar smell from softened tires when I pull to a halt and throw it in park. I catch hold of Reiki's jaw between my fingers and say, "Well. Here we are."

Reiki Gunpowder gets a room with his military housing vouchers. This is a boomtown and the existing base barracks can't handle the incoming human tide. Airmen and marines and spacecorps pukes are shoehorned into every boarding house, hotel, and dormitory they can find. I follow Reiki into our room. His fingers are fast and nimble. Everything works perfectly. I can't help but compare their bodies like I compare their cars: Reiki's magnetic skullplate for brain current induction; a chest port over his right nipple; the stigmata at wrists and ankles where the racing rig takes you into its bondage.

When it's over we drowse, and only the ringing of Reiki's phone snaps us out of each other's arms. He says hello, then some other things, then passes the phone to me. Chromium Jim's voice rattles in my ear. "We'll race. Tonight. Your flyboy says there's a loop to the west of town where they usually meet. After dark."

"I—" But Jim's already hung up. The day is like so many other days and oddly skewed at the same time. Helping a boy prep his rig before a race. But this boy is different. Reiki Gunpowder packs a lot of expensive hardware into the trunk—crash helmet, pressurized goggles, scuba tanks. I can only help him so much. I've never had anything like this with Jim.

There's a whole rainbow of rigs lined up when we arrive, everyone careful not to steal someone else's style. Reiki Gunpowder drives the only red hot rod. Chromium Jim has gotten the Green Monster here somehow without me, displacing a young warrant officer in emerald who knows well enough to sit this one out. The air smells like lead additives and class resentment. Sodium vapor street lamps pour liquid orange highlights on the chassis, glossy as beetle shells. The moths circling them cast magnified shadows on our faces. "Good luck," I tell Reiki Gunpowder.

I walk over to Chromium Jim. A pair of wings briefly cross his eyes like a mask. He sees my lips painted cyanotic blue as if I've been sucking off tailpipes. As though Reiki's hands were still choking my throat. He grunts at me. Mechanically, I begin the usual motions. These combat pilots and astronauts swaggering around have gloves and stirrups so they can pull directly on the car's control cables. I unbolt the Green Monster's entire steering column so that it won't go through Jim's chest. He doesn't have gloves or stirrups. I help him untie and remove his shoes. We roll up his sleeves and pant cuffs. I untangle the cables, connect them to the steering linkages. Chromium Jim hisses a breath as I press his fish hooks into the inside of his wrists where there's a loop of forearm tendon and into the deep hollow of each ankle behind his Achilles'. Pull on the straps to take up their slack and pull each of his limbs taut. Steering, gearshift, acceleration, brakes, clutch. All will respond instantly to muscle twitches, tics, and tremors, like cracking the reins.

There are no metal plates in Chromium Jim's head. No military-grade surgery there, just a crude jigsaw taken out of his bone, a little skull plate I fish open with a slim metal key to reveal his wet squish within, metal mesh overlay, two bare wires trailing out. I splice them to a set of loose ignition wires. His medical cart is nearby. I begin replacing his fluids with racing fuel. Wasn't that how this all started? When Space Command passed cryogenic rocket fuel through astronauts' bodies to throw them into deep sleep. The altered state they discovered on the edge of the eternal. While the centrifuges whir I take up the needle-nosed caulk gun and inject compression gel into the gaps in his brain cavity to prevent long-term damage. Chromium Jim doesn't own a helmet. Nor does he own goggles. The acceleration'll deform eyeballs, so his dashcam will be his eyes. I straddle his lap, hunch very close to his face, dig around his socket with a crochet needle to hook the slippery wire in there somewhere that feeds to his optic nerve. "Roll 'em left," I finally say, exasperated. "And hold still, goddamnit. Stop flinching."

He catches his voice. "Babe." I look into a different area of his eyes. "Is he good?"

I kiss his lips. We're almost done here. His eyes dilate at the sensation of detachment as the rig replaces him and I force the breathing tube past his gag reflex. "He's better than you've ever been." Then I get off, button him up tight, and retire to the side. His brain sends the initial spark to the starter. Electricity comes flowing back into his brain. This is Chromium Jim at his best, when he expands to fill the skin of his hot rod. His bumper edges the starting line.

The cars run the spectrum from ink black to page white and the girl baring herself between them is one from last night's bar, looking nervously down the barrels of so many machines. I glance over at Jim's pit. His other young admirer is there with the spare fuel.

The racers take off so quickly they leave streaks of color in my vision and the taste of heavy water on my tongue and when the afterburners ignite, it's the light of a dozen blue suns. The flag girl disappears in the clouds. I imagine her flesh bubbling off in gluey fistfuls as the steam exhaust renders her down to her three percent body fat and twig bones but when the smoke clears she's still there, unharmed if a little shaky, turning small circles until someone pulls her out of the way. Jetwash kicks up biblical pillars of smoke and fire from the dry brush and knocks over hollowed-out gas stations and grain elevators.

How quickly they separate from each other. Those who have dreamt of flying make pilgrimages to the airbases that once rejected them, arriving in the only homebrew vehicles in which they're rated, seeking to challenge the gatekeepers of their own personal heavens.

But these challengers only end up racing each other (Chromium Jim's lament: "There're more of us than there are of them") out on the dusty roads so it's easy to tell when a true professional joins the track, as Reiki Gunpowder has. The liquid cherry and solid green hot rods are a length apart, quarter track ahead of the pack. It's Reiki's disposable income, formal training, discipline, and physical fitness that puts him in the lead by the end of their first lap. Rocket flare scorching the eyebrows of every bystander who doesn't duck fast enough behind sandbags. But it's Chromium Jim's corner-cutting, habit of traveling light and fast, absolute complete lack of excess baggage that allows him those superior fuel-to-weight ratios he's so famous for. Reiki Gunpowder pulls sharply into the pit on the next circuit for a top up and Jim blows right by him, another lap and a half still left in his tanks.

The stragglers hit the growing debris fogbank, their intakes sucking down lungfuls of dirt clods and bugs that no air filter is going to prevent from turning insides black. Reiki goes airtight, pulls from his scuba. Jim likewise seals up all his vents but he won't waste bottled oxygen that's meant for his thirsty rig on himself. I know what he'll do. He'll inflate himself with one last outside breath against the crushing acceleration and then simply hold his breath. Sirens rising from the city limits behind me.

Chromium Jim is riding so hard he comes up on the tail of the pack, right behind a plum purple rig close enough to carbon score the Green Monster's paint. I don't know if the poor fool even sees Chromium Jim coming, hidden in the heat wave blind-spot. Jim nudges the purple car as he passes on the inside. A tire locks up. The purple car is suddenly spinning wildly on its other three omnitracks, throwing sparks and jet fuel like a July Fourth pinwheel. Then out of the cloud comes Reiki Gunpowder pouring it on, completely flatfooted to see an out-of-control rig directly in front of him. Candy apple hits plum. So fast Reiki is airborne.

Chromium Jim sees it happen over his shoulder and thinks it's all over. No one else has the fuel or acceleration curve to make up the lost distance. Jim swerves left for the pit and his fuel rack. I let out a little shriek when I see Reiki take to the sky, just waiting for the wind to catch an edge and send him tumbling like a playing card. I can see the Green Monster relax as Jim eases off the gas, coming into the refuel slot.

Except the red hot rod is too low-slung and wide to flip. It glides, wobbling slightly side-to-side and Reiki shifts his weight, gets the nose of his car pointed down, and hits the throttle. The car *flies*. Right over Chromium Jim. Solid thunk on the hood as he comes down. Reiki's rocket flame melts Jim's glass, totally warps the windshield. The light inside the Green Monster becomes positively prismatic, he can hardly see through the dashcam. Something snaps underneath Reiki Gunpowder's red racer when his undercarriage hits ground. Clear of the cloud, Chromium Jim opens his intakes for a full fresh breath. Pit crews trying to throw foreign objects into the blower turbines as they pass: nuts and bolts, loose change, wedding bands. Their ill wishes. Fistfights break out along the sidelines among the color-coded teams.

Neck and neck now. Chromium Jim's flying blind, relying on hyperoxygenated memory to guide him. Reiki Gunpowder's limping along on a broken ball socket. His front left wheel is dragging a black skid. They pass me at the same time for the last time. Final lap. Reiki Gunpowder's got a sliver of a lead except as he goes by I look in and see the fire pouring from his mouth and eyes. His firewall has given way somewhere and now all the other barriers break down one after another. Chromium Jim of course can't glance over to see what trouble his rival is in. He just cracks the reins again.

There's a soft whumph and a blue glow from under Reiki's car like a pilot light turning on. His car is still under control though, still making the turns. The man's transformed into a Roman candle and he keeps pushing Chromium Jim up the curve. Jim is touching door panels when the red car fully blows. The explosion shunts him sideways off track, across the median, heading right toward us the wrong way. I've got all my fingers in my mouth to keep from swallowing my tongue. Of the red hot rod there's nothing left but tinsel. The other cars going left and right, setting their brakes on fire to avoid lost, sightless Chromium Jim who suddenly pops drogue chutes and slams to a stop against a wall of sandbags not a dozen feet from his pickup truck.

The passenger side of the Green Monster where it's taken the force of the blowout is concave like I've never seen anything made of metal go before, stippled with red apple shrapnel. Miracle his fuel too didn't ignite. But his driver-side door still works and he emerges dragging various wires and cables and umbilicals, the viscera of a dying mechanical creature unspooling along his plodding path to the truck. Chromium Jim has enough fuel left to get to his blood bags on his own. He doesn't need any of us anymore. Still, his pressure-warped eyes find me. "Babe," he says. "Come here!" Then again, in a different tone of voice, "Come here."

My own vision is distorted, walking to him. We're aimed at false versions of each other. My view awash with tears that dry in the heat from the burning body of my most recent lover.

• • •

Chromium Jim, new king of the scene, scrapes the boomtown of all its winnings and moves on. I check his balance sheets. More than enough now to race all the way to Alaska and book steerage to the Sea of Tranquility. There's nothing left for me among the fighter pilots that flutter like confetti across the spaceport so again I take the wheel of the pickup truck and tow Chromium Jim ever northward and westward. Chasing orbital congruence and launch windows.

Jim is riding the high, knowing he's unstoppable on the way to a better place. Every day during the drive he pumps some cryo through his arms and sinks into time dilation as his senses slow. At diners where we refuel he's cock of the walk. Snapping his fingers at waitresses, flirting, loud largesse at bars while I silently inject caffeine for the long night haul.

Look, I say to the kind of anesthetizing muted gray television light found only after a certain hour in a certain class of dining establishment, I can't deny the thrill of the race circuit. I like being at his side, in his bed, celebrating with him when he balances on the edge of cryogenics and fireball. But I can never claim to have fallen in love until the day the Martians arrive and climb down from their Winnebagos.

They're all women, a half dozen of them each driving their own RV. Chromium Jim and I and about fifteen more people are on the other side of dusty roadside diner window glass agape like goldfish. Their vehicles are arrayed along the shoulder of the road, pointed in the opposite direction of the pickup. Each vehicle with, suspiciously, ball wheels. The women move, one-by-one, through the diner doors. Wild ones, wearing patched jumpsuits that show where they're deeply fuzzed in the heat points of their bodies, unwashed, low-gravity elongated. They're barefoot and they have, every one of them, stood on the soil of another world. I immediately feel a peak of lust usually reserved for methylamphetemine-driven dance-floor romances. Who owns the green race car outside? the frontwoman asks. They're here to challenge.

Chromium Jim's eyes may be bad but even he can see the RV bulk out front. "In that?" he scoffs.

"Endurance race," she says. Then he realizes what he's up against. These are trans-lunar space explorers. They've been under the fuel for magnitudes longer than he ever has.

I see him quiver between the decision. He already has all he needs. No reason to take on new challengers until he gets to the surface of the moon. I see him about to turn his back and dismiss her, to make a joke to save face, so I say, "Wow, Jim, you're scared to race a civ?" I find the eyes of the one I think is the prettiest, the only one of the six who's been looking deep at me this whole time. "Well. If I'd known that was all it took to get you off my back. Well. If I'd known that much earlier."

Used to be he could just let my words glide right over him but the higher your flights, the deeper your dives when someone inevitably pries you out of your metal skin and forces you to face the gravity well you live in. He sinks very close to me in his seat and growls, "Go ready the car."

He doesn't follow me out until I've got the rig lowered off the tow bar and lined up with the challenger's RV, everything set up for him. Then he climbs in and sits passively for me to make all the hookups. "Good luck," I say politely. He doesn't answer. I shut his door.

The prettiest Martian takes my hand and says, "Better come back inside." Inside where she warns me, "Stay away from the glass." Not like I could get near the window anyway with all the rubberneckers pressed up against it. The Green Monster roars. The woman who challenged Chromium Jim stands next to her Winnebago with a brass helmet like an old diving bell tucked under one arm, waving cheerfully, triumphantly, with the other. Then she disappears into her cabin and a minute later ignition sparks spray across its rear nozzles. Crescendos. The locals burst out into cheers. They don't often get a show like this out beyond the combat zones.

One of the astronauts sticks her arm out the door and signals the race with a flare gun and then I realize why they drive such big rigs: fuel storage. The RV is ninety percent rocket fuel and she doesn't bother with internal combustion, just lights off the whole damn thing like a Saturn V. The building shakes like it's what's about to lift off. Crockery breaking in the kitchen. Coffee overslopping the lips of white ceramic mugs. I steady myself on the pretty lady next to me. The window glass cracks but holds its shape. I'm still holding her hand and she's still holding mine.

We wait until the earth stops moving before everyone piles out for a better view. My Martian fans away the dust and lights a joint. Offers it. "Nice-looking car," she says. "Your work?"

The Winnebago burns on a curve faster, longer, and farther than he can catch up. Chromium Jim's rig screams like the heat-triggered locusts that once swept these plains and forced us all into space in the first place. "Fifty-fifty," I allow.

She's looking me over. "You got a name?" I only nod. "Mine's Sally. Come take a look." We go to her RV, covered in decals that document her travels. It's still pointed the wrong way.

"You're not going to the spaceports?" I ask.

Sally says, "We're civilian astronauts. We launch out of the old sites farther south where the skies are less dangerous. You should come with us."

Startled, but immediately ascendant. Hope is a thing with wings and whatnot. "Where?"

"We built a place for you, a place for people who have nothing left for them here. Your hometowns and food crops have been burned out not by war but by the simple blind, dumb, dispassionate greed of people who won't look beyond tomorrow. But you're also sick of war. Sick of the boys playing at it. I saw what you did."

I don't deny anything.

Sally takes another breath of smoke. Her lips pucker sweetly. She's painted them purple. I want to paint mine red and crash them into hers like two bodies colliding. "The trip won't be easy," she says. "We travel fast and you'll have to work for your passage but I think your heart can take the cold and pressure."

I look after them, just two faint stars on the horizon now. Neither deviates from the straight path. Not coming back. The door to Sally's Winnebago pops open and the wind that blows out of it tastes like cold iron and burned sand. Alien and instantly comforting. "You have any other things you need to grab?"

She's right behind me. I don't know whether to lean back against her or step up the plastic ladder through the magic portal to another world. I thought it would take a lifetime of running in circles, Chromium Jim's way, to reach it. No one ever expects the miracle of their community coming to them. Finding them in the wilderness. A place where everyone will know me. I have nothing weighing me down. All my baggage tucked into the hollow places of Chromium Jim's rigid body. What's a fully loaded suitcase weigh these days? Fifty pounds? What does fifty pounds do to the fuel burn rate of a homemade rocket rig?

Chromium Jim laboring against the extra drag and grav. Far off I hear two small pops of either his lungs or his tires giving up. "No," I say.

THE POWER IS OUT

A QUE, TRANSLATED BY ELIZABETH HANLON

1

"Let's go south," Zhang Handsome suddenly said to us one day.

We were out walking in the twilight, ambling about, idle and listless. Several stray birds careened blindly between the high-rises. Zhao Fortune watched them and licked his lips: "I haven't tasted meat in a long time. Let's shoot those birds down and eat them."

Beside him, Chen Beauty furrowed her decidedly unbeautiful brow and said, "Brother Fortune, *no*. How could you eat those little birdies?" The rest of us also voiced our disapproval of his suggestion.

Fortune gazed absently up at the birds. "I remember when I was a boy—that was before the Trip—I used to eat this kind of bird cooked over a fire. Small as they are, the meat is plentiful and tender. When roasted, grease drips from the meat onto the ground, and sizzles in the mud. Catch it in your mouth, and it sizzles in your heart."

He looked back at us over his shoulder. "Are you going to help or not?"

We picked up stones off the ground and threw them at the birds. Of the five of us, Fortune and I were the strongest. Handsome was lean and gaunt, but he could throw stones as high as seven or eight stories. Beauty and Wang Innocence only caused a commotion. Their stones did not ruffle a single feather on any of the birds, and their incessant shouting made the people upstairs open their windows. They poked their heads out, like mushrooms, and regarded us curiously.

As our stones grazed the birds, they flapped their wings furiously. Already disoriented by the geomagnetic storm, and now hounded by us, their panic grew, and they crashed into each other as they flew away. We tore through the rundown streets in hot pursuit.

I guessed that the perpetual geomagnetic agitation had played havoc with these birds: as they flew, they kept colliding with walls and glass windows. By chance, several of the birds got away; only one bird, flying straight ahead, could not shake us. After a while we began to flag. The bird, whose wings had been struck several times, was also tired. It landed on a fourth-floor balcony, huddled on its side, and gently preened its injured wings. Its posture as it licked its wounds was extremely graceful, like a gilded sculpture in the setting sun. We stared at it, mesmerized.

"Maybe we shouldn't eat it," suggested Innocence. We all nodded. Even Fortune did not lick his lips, just gazed absently at it, as though remembering the days before the power went out.

"All right," he said. "Let it fly away. Its home is the sky. It should spread its wings and return—"

Before he could finish, an old man rushed out onto the balcony, grabbed the stunned bird, and stuffed it into his mouth. He chewed vigorously, his filthy beard stained with bright red blood.

Outraged, we shouted and swore at the old man, especially Handsome, who hopped from one foot to the other as he cursed. The old man, picking feathers from his teeth, returned our compliments in a hoarse, raw voice. Old age had imbued his profanity with a marvelous artistic quality. Even Handsome, who had read loads of books, could not surpass him. Fortune snatched up a stone and threw it at the balcony, but the old man hurriedly ducked inside. The five of us stomped up the stairs and did our best to kick the old devil's door down. However, the alloyed steel security door was far stronger than our feet and our busted shoes, and after ten minutes or so, Fortune let out a yelp, having wrenched his calf.

The entire time, the old man stood behind the door and inquired after our distant relatives with elegant and polished obscenities, utterly calm and composed.

As the sky outside began to darken, the hallway grew as still and gloomy as a tomb. We grudgingly abandoned our assault on the security door and helped Fortune down the stairs. The street was filled with figures loitering in groups of three and four. Like us, they ambled about, idle and listless. Fortune limped along, cursing nonstop. The wind rose, carrying a sharp chill, and we tightened our collars against it.

Tucking her chin against her chest, Innocence said, "Autumn will be over soon."

Handsome suddenly jerked his head up. "Yes, autumn will be over, and winter will come. Let's go south."

I grew excited. South, a word at once so strange, and yet so familiar. Since the power went out, I had lived in this northern city for so many years that I'd forgotten what my hometown looked like. I thought of the birds' sudden appearance and realized that they were likely headed south for the winter, too. Even though the geomagnetic storm had muddled their sense of direction, the desire in their genes for warmth still guided them.

Fortune hesitated for a moment. "Go south and do what?" he asked. "Who knows what the situation there is like? It could be even more chaotic than here."

"Not necessarily," said Beauty. "Southerners have mild tempers, unlike you northerners. After the power went out, I bet everyone came together like one big family to tide over the difficulties."

"Beauty, ah, Beauty," Fortune sneered. "Do you believe your own words?"

Beauty turned to look at me. "Mediocre, why aren't you saying anything? Tell us, are southerners kinder than northerners? I recall your family's from the south. Is it true if someone strikes you, you won't hit back? If someone slaps you on the left cheek, you offer up your right cheek?"

"Screw you," I said. "If someone tries that with me, I'll sit my ass cheeks on their face."

As we argued, Innocence kept her head lowered. Her wispy bangs hung over her face.

Handsome broke in: "Listen to me—Mediocre, let go of Beauty's hair—winter is coming, and I've been watching the weather. The Siberian High is descending toward us, and cold winds are sweeping in from the Pacific. I'm afraid temperatures may reach thirty below zero this winter. The heat's gone, and we've run out of things to burn. We can't endure that kind of weather. Let's go south."

"Handsome, quit lying to us," said Fortune. "Don't think I won't hit you because you're good-looking."

"You can believe it or not, I don't care—ouch, don't hit me! Mediocre, stop him!"

I hastily turned to Fortune. "Handsome has read a lot of books, and he is bursting with knowledge. He knows Hooke's Law and the Newton-Leibniz formula. What he said is probably true."

Handsome and Fortune have never gotten along. Even before the Trip, the rich scorned young fair faces, and handsome young men despised unscrupulous businessmen. In the years since the power went out and the five of us took up together, they would have killed each other if I hadn't smoothed things over between them.

Fortune leaned against the wall and looked into the distance, where darkness was seeping in. "Truly that cold?" he asked. "But, these last few years, haven't we always made it through?"

"A few degrees below zero is tolerable, but thirty below is not," I said. "Even if we ate our fill of bread every day, we couldn't withstand the cold."

Beauty and Innocence wore worried expressions.

Suddenly, a gleam appeared in Fortune's eyes. "Very well," he said, "we'll go south!"

I knew Zhao Fortune long before the Trip. Back then, he was not yet called Fortune, and instead went by a name frequently published in business journals. Oh, that's right—he was my boss at a promising startup located in the city's central business district. Every morning, he sipped a cup of coffee and peered through the window blinds at the ant-like crowds below. Sometimes he called me over, lit a cigarette, and pointed to the bustling suits.

"People," he told me, shrouded in a cloud of smoke, "have to have money."

Before Fortune had money, I was already firmly in his camp. I watched him grow from a diffident youth who cheated investors in coffee shops, into a paunchy middle-aged man with great clout in business circles. The intervening years were filled with twists and turns. Several times, the company teetered on the edge of bankruptcy, and in its darkest hour, only he and I remained. In fact, I was just lazy, and planned to wait until I was well and truly unemployed to find another job. But Fortune was extremely grateful, and said he would never forget me. If he had anything to eat, I would not go hungry. He brought me along everywhere—where he went, I went. Later, when things turned around, he did not break his promise. He gave me a stake in the company and paid me annual dividends, and the figures in my bank account grew larger than I dared believe.

Then, without warning, a strong pulse of electromagnetic radiation from outer space swept across the globe and did not disperse. All electronic equipment was damaged beyond repair.

The world had tripped a switch.

Our money, alongside a vast sea of data, vanished. Our savings were gone. Our high-performing stocks were gone. The connections we had cultivated over many years were gone. I was devastated by the loss, but Fortune stayed true to his name. While everyone else passed through the stages of waiting, restlessness, rioting, despair, and numbness, he began to quietly stockpile food and water. He cleaned out several supermarkets, hauled the goods off to who knows where, and then waited. He often described to me how he had managed it:

"Fuck," he said, "the noise outside was awful. Smashing, and killing. I hid in the sewers. Blood dripped down, and I could taste the salt on my hands. For just a small bag of stale bread, they were ready to stab each other. But I wasn't scared. I knew the things I'd hidden would save my life later. Lying in the middle of all that food, my heart was at ease, and I even fell asleep. When I woke up, I climbed up to the street, and there were bodies fucking everywhere."

I didn't admire Fortune's daring—after all, I too survived the riots. What I admired was his foresight. In civilized times, this man was able to predict the movement of wealth; after the world lapsed back into barbarism, he was able to quickly swap hats and divine changes in the fabric of society. By comparison, I was just one face among the masses on the street. When others waited, I waited. When others rioted, I rioted. When others grew numb, I grew numb. Therefore, I was called Li Mediocre.

Later, while Innocence and I were wandering idly through the streets, we ran into Fortune, who was similarly occupied. He recognized me, and the three of us began to walk together to look for food. When our hunger truly became unbearable, he would tell us to wait, disappear for a short while, and return with bottles of water and bread in hand. Watching us wolf down the bread, he'd sigh and say, "People have to have money." When we finished eating, he would take back the plastic bread bags. After Beauty and Handsome joined us, Fortune continued to provide this timely relief—somewhere he had built a great treasury filled with water and food. Because of this, he was conferred the highest status within our little group.

Having agreed to go south, we split up to pack our things, but Fortune called me back.

"Come with me," he said.

Together, Fortune and I walked through the city streets, surrounded by darkness. Once this kind of behavior was very dangerous, as someone crazed with hunger was liable to come rushing out onto the street at any time. But now, many small gangs had formed and held each other in check, and a short peace had been established. At night people rested, and saved fighting for the daytime. As we walked, the stars gradually came into view.

Fortune led me to every nook and corner on the block. He had hidden tightly tied black plastic bags beneath floorboards, behind ruined walls, even in trees. He pulled the bags from their hiding places and tossed them to me. As I caught them, I could feel the food inside through the plastic.

Finally, carrying a dozen plastic bags each on our backs, we came to a subway station. The station's entrance was overgrown with weeds and branches, like arms sticking out of a grave, waving gleefully. Yes, since the Trip, no one had suffered more than humanity, and no one was happier than the plants. Humans had once driven them out, but after the electricity was gone, they swept back in, encircling the city from the countryside.

We pushed aside the brush and made our way down the corroded escalator, the starlight fading away behind us. It grew so dark that I could not see my hand in front of my face. Suddenly, a circle of light appeared in front of me, which, though dim, allowed me to see the path ahead.

"Keep up," said Fortune, without halting his steps.

I saw then that the light came from a match in his hand. "When did you squirrel that away?" I asked excitedly. I hadn't seen artificial light in many years. "Fortune, you're really very handy."

"Bah," Fortune said as he walked. "The day the power goes out, light, food, and water are the things people want most for. While all of you were foolishly waiting for everything to go back to normal, I was getting ready."

The flame flickered and danced on the tiny matchstick. Bathed in its faint halo, I felt as though we were being towed along by a dying, luminescent jellyfish, drifting slowly into the depths of the sea. A train was stopped at the tunnel entrance. Its doors had been prized open, and the interior was in shambles. Clearly, the train had pulled into the station at the exact moment of the Trip, and the passengers inside had forced open the doors to escape.

When the match went out, Fortune lit another.

"Don't go in," he instructed. He led me past the train, jumped down onto the track, and followed the rails into the tunnel. As the light moved across the huge metal car beside us, it illuminated its dull, mottled surface, like the rotted carcass of a whale. Trembling with fright, I followed the tracks deeper and deeper. I'm not sure how long we walked before Fortune stopped. He pointed to a small metal door in the subway tunnel and said, "Stick those in there."

Originally, the room behind the door had been used to store subway inspection equipment, but now it was crammed with bulging plastic bread bags. After we wedged the plastic bags inside, Fortune shut the door and breathed a sigh of relief. "Let's go," he said. "We've got another trip to make."

Fortune had hidden parcels of food all around the city, to be used as lifelines in case of emergency. That night I helped him make five or six runs in total. Around midnight, I told him I was tired and wanted to go home to rest.

"That's fine." Fortune nodded at me. Then he added, "Don't tell the others about this place."

"Why did you come to me for help?" I asked.

"You're my employee," he said. "Don't worry, I'm going to take you south with me."

Before I left, he tossed me a plastic bag for my breakfast the next day. In fact, I had not eaten breakfast in a long time. Every morning I was woken by hunger. My body had grown used to it, but my stomach began to protest. At the thought of waking up tomorrow morning to bread and fresh water, my heart was filled with indescribable contentment. I tucked the bag into my clothing, pulled my collar tight, and hurried out of the subway in the direction of home.

The dilapidated high-rises were hidden in darkness, their vague outlines just visible in the starlight. Back when there was electricity, their interiors used to blaze with light. Every window was a tiny cell, and the elevators, like blood vessels, carried people up and down in a ceaseless flow. Many people had worked their entire lives for a single cramped room in one of these buildings. But now, in the wake of the Trip, these glittering giants were dying. Rooms that had once cost an arm and a leg now reeked of feces and dead bodies.

Suddenly, I heard the patter of footsteps behind me.

"Who's there?" I asked, turning. Thinking it was Fortune checking up on me, I added, "I won't say a word to the others about—" In the faint starlight, a face appeared on the other side of the street. I squinted at it. "Eh, Innocence?"

The face was delicate and beautiful. Bathed in starlight, its features seemed to melt together. This was Wang Innocence—sometimes you could not even discern her appearance, but the sight of her left you with the impression of purity. You would remember her, and be able to recognize her from across the street.

We walked slowly through the streets together. We often used to stroll together like this, searching for something to eat. Afterward, we would idle away the remainder of the day. Walking became our most frequent pastime. She'd tell me things about her career as an actress, and I'd complain about my workplace and Zhao Fortune. Occasionally, she and I made love. But after Fortune joined us, she showed a clear preference for him. Later, when Handsome arrived, she became close with him for a time. In short, of the five of us, I was the loneliest.

But now, we walked back at an unhurried pace, as though time had been rewound. With her head lowered, she told me that she was nervous about going south. She was a northern girl, and had never seen the southern sun. Unable to sleep, she had gone for a walk and seen me.

"It's late," I said. "Let's go to my place."

2

I know you must be anxious to hear what happened after Innocence and I went home. To tell the truth, I was even more anxious than you. I hadn't had sex in ages, and I felt as though a rat were squeaking and scurrying in my gut. But as a responsible narrator, before I get to that part, I think I need to tell you about my history with Innocence.

Wang Innocence studied acting. After graduation, she auditioned everywhere for film and television roles.

Let me tell you, every last person in the movie business was a rotten scoundrel.

They gathered together and eyed Innocence like a pack of wolves. Back then she didn't understand the meaning in their stares, and she was cut from audition after audition. For three years, she bounced back and forth between the major studios and fly-by-night production companies. The girls who had graduated alongside her had all either made successful debuts, or had changed professions. Only she kept at it. Finally, she won a bit part in a low-budget film.

Unexpectedly, the film turned out to be pretty good, and earned several awards before its release. Sensing an opportunity to net big rewards at little cost, the producers shelled out to hire a marketing firm. Posters with Innocence's face on them plastered bus stops in every major city. The firm also arranged a promotional tour. The first stop was a coastal city in the south. As it was her first trip to the south, Innocence was so excited that she arrived at the airport hours before her flight, and had to wait for her fellow cast and crew members.

Suddenly, all the lights in the terminal went out with a loud bang. Before she could react, a plane that had been just about to land slammed straight into the tarmac, sending flames high into the air. Her face remained blank.

As if someone had flipped a switch, all around the world the power went out.

At first, everyone waited, in a daze, for the lights to turn back on, for their cars to start up again, for their cell phones to ring. But the waiting dragged on without end. Then people began to realize that the blackout might last forever.

My coworker Guo Melancholy—melancholy no longer—said cheerfully, "It's just as well. Our civilization was advancing too quickly. This power outage is a rare opportunity. We can stop and reflect on where we want to go."

I think, in the end, he might have thought differently. Two days later, as he sat sunning himself on a curb, a child smashed his head in with a rock. His prognosis for the world was nowhere near as accurate as Fortune's. He had no idea that once the power went out, civilization would not stop to rest, but rapidly regress.

First, people went mad. Their stocks, savings, and networks had been thoroughly purged. While vagrants could still lounge in the sun beneath overpasses, the city's white-collar workers had lost their entire world. Then people died. Citizens formed small gangs to rob houses, snatching up everything they could eat, drink, or use as a weapon. During the worst of the madness, whenever someone showed his face on the street, a mob would immediately swarm him from all sides, stone him to death with bricks, and loot the body. Then, they would hide by the side of the road and wait for the next unlucky wretch to pass.

To protect myself, I joined forces with seven or eight other men with view to waylaying strangers in a copycat fashion. We were an utterly vicious bunch: each one of us claimed to have taken several lives with our own hands. Chen Bashful said he had killed three people, Yang Affable said he'd killed at least seven, so I hurriedly said I'd killed twenty-one.

We stationed ourselves at an entrance to the subway, with the intention of dragging every solitary person who passed by into the station and beating them to death. But the first to approach was a fierce, hulking man with blood still on his clothes. We surged forward, saw the man's bulging muscles, and scrambled back again. The man laughed contemptuously and strode away.

"Shit, that won't do!" I told Bashful. "We can't chicken out again. We have strength in numbers. We have to be merciless!"

Bashful nodded hastily and said, "Right, just now we weren't ready. Whoever comes next, see if I don't bash him to bits!"

After we steeled our nerves, we positioned ourselves in a tight arc at the mouth of the station. Even if that huge man came back, I felt confident that we could encircle and overwhelm him.

Soon, we heard the sound of footsteps again. We grew feverish with excitement. When the footsteps reached the station entrance, we rushed out all at once. Then, we stopped short.

It was Wang Innocence.

I remember it was early evening. The slanting rays of the setting sun tinged the decaying city with red. Our shadows stretched long across the ground. Innocence stood surrounded, panic on her face.

We, however, were even more panicked. I had not seen such a pure face in a long time. Even the hard metallic light of sunset could not lend sharpness to her features. She cringed away from us, her hair in her eyes, shoulders hunched like a hamster. And her hair!—after so long without power, most people had tangled hair and dirty faces, but her hair was jet-black and lustrous, like a swath of ink-dyed silk. Looking at the birds' nests that crowned our own heads, we couldn't help but feel ashamed.

The first to turn traitor was Bashful. His gaze swept right past Innocence, and he called out to Affable behind her: "Goodness, Affable. What a coincidence to see you here!"

Affable tossed the brick in his hand to the side. "Bashful, we're fated to meet. I see you wherever I go. Let's go eat barbecue."

The others, returning to their senses, hailed each other over Innocence's head. In groups of twos and threes, they set off companionably in every direction. I later found out that these self-proclaimed vicious brutes had previously worked in programming. Little wonder that a group of coders lost their will to fight as soon as they laid eyes on Innocence!

As they rushed in from all directions, froze, and then scattered, Innocence looked on as though she were invisible. Finally, only she and I were left standing in the half-light of the street. Still recovering from my panic, I glanced left and right in the evening breeze, half of a brick in my hand. She walked over to me and said, "I'm hungry. Do you have anything to eat?"

I dropped the brick and clapped my hands. "It's late," I said. "Let's go to my place."

Just like that, Innocence and I took up together. We shared what little food we had, dodged crazed strangers, and watched the city rust bit by bit.

As time wore on, the deaths mounted, and everyone grew tired of fighting. With several large gangs threatening retaliation against each other, there was no more indiscriminate violence. But because everyone wanted to restore order, order was never restored. People began to take to the streets, ambling about, idle and listless.

In telling you how I met Innocence, I have no esoteric objective. I just wanted to explain that she's good-looking, lest you think I'm tricking you. Think about it. Why would I trick you? I'm going south. Someone who intends to go south wouldn't lie. Now that you know Innocence is beautiful, I'll continue where I left off. This will make my story more romantic. You see, my objective has always been that simple.

Early the next morning, after we got out of bed, Innocence and I ate the breakfast Fortune had given me. After we'd eaten, we discussed going south. Innocence asked me what it was like.

"Even if you've never been to the south, you never saw it on TV?" I asked her.

She hesitated for a moment. "Yes, but the power's been out for so many years that I've forgotten. Do you still remember it?"

Her question stunned me. I had no memory of the south either.

"Southerners eat from bowls, not plates," I said, wracking my brain. "It's warm there, and in the winter flowers blossom by the roadside."

Delighted, Innocence paced back and forth. "That's wonderful," she said. "I can't wait to go."

"But we have to wait for Fortune to get everything ready. After all, without his food, we'll have a difficult time on the long journey south."

We waited around until evening. As the sun sank toward the horizon, filling the sky with a mournful glow, I caught the golden gleam of a lake in the distance.

"Shall we play ducks and drakes?" I asked.

Innocence and I went to a nearby store, pushed open the door, and carried stacks of cell phones, still in their boxes, from the storeroom down to the shore. We sat down, stripped off the packaging, and took out Apple's thinnest iPhones to date. With a flick of the wrist, the iPhones went skipping across the surface of the lake.

She and I discovered this way of passing the time by accident. While we were searching for food, we discovered a mobile phone retail store in our neighborhood. Though it was abandoned, the storeroom was still neatly stacked with phones. These costly electronics weren't worth a cent in an age without electricity, but we developed a new use for them—ducks and drakes. Truly, cell phones make for extremely smooth skipping. No matter how you throw them, they're guaranteed to skip ten, fifteen times. If you don't believe me, you can take a phone down to the lake and try it for yourself.

We skipped phones and made conversation in a desultory kind of way. The setting sun was fading fast, and dusk was closing in around us.

"Mediocre," Innocence said suddenly, "let's go south."

"Well, yes, we will," I replied with a nod.

"I mean, just the two of us."

Stunned, I lifted my head and looked at Innocence's face in the twilight. The last rays of sunset cut across her face from her brow to the corner of her lips, then died. Her face, even shrouded in gloom, was still beautiful beyond comparison. Snapping out of my daze, I asked, "What did you say?"

She did not answer, just looked at me.

"But, didn't we agree to go south with Fortune and the others?"

"Fortune won't take us," said Innocence, "and I don't like that Chen Beauty."

I did not like Beauty either.

"And Handsome runs his mouth all day long. I'd rather be with you, Mediocre."

This was the first time I had heard Innocence say such a thing to me, and the tenderness in her voice suffused the night air. Warmth rose in my stomach. "Okay," I said. "We'll go south, just the two of us. That's my home. We can put down roots there."

"Tell me where Fortune hid his food. I'll get what we need for the road. Then, while it's still dark, we'll leave the city and head south," she said.

I said I would go ask Fortune for food, but Innocence prevented me. She said her chance of success was much greater, and that I should wait here for her. Therefore, I told her the address. I stayed by the shore and watched her figure dissolve into the night, fading away until it vanished altogether. I threw a cell phone at the dark surface of the lake. I heard the *plip plip plip* as it skipped across the water, but I could not see the slightest ripple.

I waited until daybreak, but Innocence did not return.

3

The next day, Fortune packed his things and prepared to leave. Just then, it began to rain heavily. As he watched water sluice down the sides of the buildings, he said worriedly, "I'm afraid this rain may keep up for some time. We can't go anywhere in this weather."

"It's nothing serious," said Handsome, his voice anxious. "Brother Fortune, you've stockpiled so many things. Surely you kept some rain gear. Get it out and we'll brave the rain."

"Do you think I'm Doraemon?" said Fortune. "Saving everything I get my paws on?"

"It's raining too hard," Beauty chimed in. "If we should catch cold, we have no medicine. We won't make it. Handsome, you'll just have to wait a few days."

Handsome looked at me, and so did Fortune and Beauty. I glanced around and asked, "Have any of you seen Innocence?"

They shook their heads.

"Then let's wait a few days for her," I said.

Thus, we decided to delay our departure until the rain stopped. I went back to my place. These days, the concept of "home" no longer existed—my place of residence was a hidden cellar. Beauty had chosen the lobby of a forty-story office building, and Fortune frequently changed locations, sometimes residing beneath bridges, sometimes in cars. All five of us knew where each other lived. Most of the city's towering housing complexes had been abandoned, notwithstanding occasional holdouts—homeowners who had paid through the nose for their apartments and could not bear to leave. Despite the lack of water and power and the unbearable stench, they were prepared to defend their apartments to the last.

I lay in bed, not wanting to do anything, and waited for Innocence to return. Her warmth still lingered in my blanket. I curled inside it, as though surrounded on all sides by her body.

Suddenly, there was a knock at my door.

Handsome sidled into the room and sat down on the edge of my bed. I gave him a sidelong glance, but did not get up. After a moment, I heard him say, "Mediocre, are you waiting for Innocence? I'm telling you, she isn't coming back. Do you think she's really so pure? That's only window dressing. With the world in the shape it's in, no one is pure anymore. Many times I saw her go alone to look for Fortune. Maybe he and Innocence are planning to slip away together and leave us behind."

I sat up, remembering the sight of her receding figure, like a pale glow in thick fog. Indeed, I had promised her we would go south together. But compared to Fortune's actual power, my words meant nothing.

"And you?" I asked, eyeing Handsome. "Why have you come to find me?"

"Let's go together! Mediocre, I'm telling you, we can't count on Fortune. He is ruthless, an unscrupulous businessman, unreliable. Haven't you been helping him move food these past few days? Come on, we'll help ourselves to some of it, and then hop on a couple of bicycles and sneak out of the city at night. With me leading the way, it won't take long to get to the south."

Seeing the eager expression in Handsome's eyes, I sighed inwardly. I knew the reason he was in such a hurry to go back south.

Handsome was my university classmate. He had once been pursued by many girls, but the attention only inflated his ego. It was not until the eve of graduation that he met Wu Lovely, a pretty young woman who had just matriculated. Wu Lovely's loveliness captured Handsome's heart right away. He gave up his job, returned to school for graduate studies, and waited three years to be with her. He also gifted her with a pair of precious jade bracelets. They bought a house together in a coastal city in the south. They were preparing to get married when Handsome was sent north on business.

When the world tripped its switch, Handsome and Lovely were in the middle of a long phone call. The geomagnetic storm, like a fierce gale, knocked out the signals connecting the north and the south. At first, Handsome waited patiently for the power to come back on. After all hope of this occurring had been lost, he prepared to go south. But something always got in the way of his plans. During the initial chaos, he'd had to evade roving gangs, which left him badly shaken. After everyone lapsed into idleness, he was kept occupied with the work of gathering food every day.

In the blackout era, good looks were no longer an advantage. Everyone looked dirty and disheveled anyway. When eye candy gathered dust, no one came to lick it clean. The frail scholar nearly starved to death several times. Handsome was skin and bones when he ran into us. In the end, he managed to scrape by with help from Fortune. But when he begged Fortune for the food supplies that would let him return south to look for Lovely, his appeal was rejected. This was one of the reasons he and Fortune never got along.

Surely, his current impatience to return south stemmed from his desire to be reunited with Wu Lovely.

"Ah, Handsome, Handsome, you're so good-looking. Why can't you forget one pretty girl?" I said, and sighed.

Handsome said, "You've never seen Lovely. If you had, you'd be just as crazy about her as I am. She is too adorable. She gives everyone she meets the shyest smile."

His words made me curious. Before I left school, I never saw Lovely, only heard about her from Handsome. Occasionally he would dig out a faded photograph of a sweet, pure face, but the photograph was blurry, and I never got a good look at it. All his talk of Lovely's loveliness made me momentarily forget about Innocence.

"Still," I added hesitantly, "why are you so impatient? Once the rain stops, Fortune will take his food and go south with us. You'll see your Lovely soon enough. Actually, has it occurred to you—"

I paused, leaving the rest of my question unspoken.

When Handsome grasped my meaning, the color drained from his face. "No, no way. Lovely is so cute that no one would hurt her."

After a moment of silence, he resumed his attempt to persuade me. "Fortune won't take me with him. Things have always been rocky between us. Mediocre, listen to me, even if you want to stick with Fortune, at least help me steal a little food, okay? As long as I have food, I can go alone. I can walk all the way to the south by myself."

"If we get caught stealing Fortune's food, the consequences will be severe. He has killed before."

"Has he hidden a lot away?"

I recalled the sight of the storeroom in the subway, overflowing with food, and nodded. "A lot. Enough to fill several rooms."

"Then if we take ten pounds or so, what do you think is the likelihood that we'll be found out?"

"Fine. Find a time when Fortune is gone. We'll steal a little of his food, for your travels."

Suddenly, Handsome wavered. "This, ah, this—you see, there's no way an academic like me can pull off a theft. It's a violation of the law and society's cardinal virtues, a pollution of ethics and morality. How about you do it, and I'll keep watch?"

Handsome's lack of courage did not surprise me at all. But once I thought it over, I realized someone so faint of heart would only get in the way, so I nodded in agreement. After that, we had only to wait for Fortune to exit the abandoned subway station. Then, we could act.

The next day, the rain was still falling. Handsome and I were hungry, so as per usual we went to beg food from Fortune. We braved the elements and walked to his current lodgings. When we reached the opposite side of the street, Handsome said, "You go ahead. If Fortune sees us together, he'll be suspicious. I'll wait here for you."

Tucking my neck into my collar, I dashed across the rainy street and knocked on Fortune's door. From inside, I heard movement, and then Fortune's voice: "Come in!" I pushed open the door and saw that he was lying on top of a woman, both of them echoing moan for moan. A few moments later, they finished, and the woman glanced at me and asked, "Get it while it's hot?"

I hastily waved my hand. "Thank you for the kind offer, but my stomach has been troubling me lately."

The woman dressed, accepted a bag of bread offered by Fortune, and left at a leisurely pace. Fortune, half-collapsed on the bed, watched her retreating back and sighed. "Wild as hell. Mediocre, take a look. That one's a prize. Before the Trip, I could only land a woman like that with a designer bag. After the Trip, all it takes is a bag of bread. Right, why've you come to see me?"

"I want some bread."

"Perfect timing." Fortune patted the edge of the bed. "Hop up. You've saved me the trouble of putting on clothes again."

I closed both eyes. "I'd rather starve to death."

He laughed. "I was only pulling your leg!" He opened a drawer, took out a loaf of bread, and tossed it to me. "Make sure you rest up over the next few days," he urged. "When the rain stops, we'll go south together."

I took the bread and walked outside into the curtain of rain. When I crossed to the other side of the street, I saw that Handsome had a strange look on his face. His head was bowed, and his hand was tightly clenched. I couldn't tell what he was thinking.

"What's wrong?" I asked.

"I found Lovely's bracelet," he said, opening his palm to reveal a simple jade bracelet.

I gave him a blank look. "How is that possible?" I asked. "Isn't Lovely in the south?"

"Yes, but this definitely belongs to her. It was originally one of a pair. This one goes on the right hand. The marbling on the surface, the scratches where it's been dropped—it's all exactly the same. Mediocre, I'm not going south anymore. Lovely has come north, and I have to find her." As Handsome spoke, his face twitched madly.

I knew what a blow this was to him. He had assumed that Lovely was still in the south. But perhaps she had come north and had been in this city all along. Suddenly, in every street, every alley, every courtyard, every corner, it was possible that he had missed her.

This wasn't just alarmist talk. In the past, two people separated by vast distances could ride out on horseback in search of each other; later on, they could contact each other anywhere in the world with just a string of numbers; but now, the distance needed to keep people apart had shrunk from the entire world to a narrow field of vision. Because we lacked permanent residences and wandered aimlessly every day, even if you were just one street apart, you might miss someone forever. Without electricity, the sense of security in relationships provided by the Information Age crumbled instantly.

But, just maybe . . .

Handsome took two steps backward, the muscles in his face convulsing. "She must have come to find me," he muttered. "She walked all the way from the south to the north to find me! She's here in the city. I have to find her!"

He staggered back in the direction we had come. In no time at all, he was drenched. He shouted as he ran: "Lovely, Lovely, I'm Handsome!" His voice sounded hoarse and muffled in the rain.

We searched in the rain for days. Handsome ducked beneath every eave and shouted, "Lovely, Lovely, I'm Handsome!" Before long, his voice grew cracked and ragged. When it rained, people sat on the side of the road, their listlessness unabated. As Handsome moved through their midst, shouting at the top of his voice, they slowly turned their heads to watch him, with bored expressions on their faces.

Things went on like this for days, but we found no trace of Lovely. One day, we ran into Fortune on the street. "What's the matter with him?" he asked.

"He's searching for his girlfriend Wu Lovely," I said.

"I thought his girlfriend was in the south?"

"Now she's here in the north, so Handsome needs to find her."

"Oh." Fortune nodded. "No matter, let him search. Let's talk about the plan to go south. This rain will let up soon."

"Let's talk when the rain stops," I said, unable to put the thought of Handsome out of my mind. "By the way, do you know where Innocence has gone?"

Fortune shook his head.

I caught a flash of something evasive in his eyes: he was definitely keeping something from me. However, given his proclivity for secrecy, I knew I would never drag it out of him, so I turned and left, following the sound of Handsome's shouting.

One evening the rain stopped. After days of heavy downpour, the sun could hold back no longer. As soon as the rain let up, it burst forth. A rainbow spanned from one end of the city to the other. Everyone came out into the streets and gazed up at it. Their faces, tinted rose-red, looked a little disoriented.

I couldn't recall seeing such a spectacle for many years, and I could not help but be spellbound by it. Just then, Handsome suddenly grabbed me and pointed to a group of people in the street: "Look, it's Lovely!"

I looked where he pointed. Sure enough, on the other side of the street stood a large group of people looking up at the rainbow, a woman among them. Her back felt familiar to me.

She stood between several big, burly men. Her figure was slim and shapely, perky in the front and the back, and she wore very little clothing. To her left was the heavily-tattooed Liu Fierce; to her right, the muscle-bound Zhou Strong. Qian Vulgar stood behind her. Each of the three men had a hand on her. Their hands roved over her as they gazed dreamily at the sunset and the rainbow.

I finally realized that she was the same woman I had seen in Fortune's room when I had gone to find him. But she was not at all lovely. The moans she had made in bed were extraordinarily shameless, like a symphony.

On her right hand was the bracelet Handsome had given her. Her face looked the same as it did in his faded photograph, except that any sweetness it had once possessed had been replaced by pure licentiousness.

"You found her," I said. "Go on up to her. Get over there and tell her, 'Lovely, Lovely, I'm Handsome.'"

But he just stared into the distance, his fingers trembling, not daring to approach her.

After that, Handsome went mad.

4

"Do you think Fortune is up to something?" Beauty asked me.

As she spoke, she moved her face close to mine, so that the fleshy folds that threatened to swallow up her features were visible in perfect detail. The sight was striking. I could see one ripple of fat that spilled from her brow to the corner of her lips. I took a step backward. "What?"

"Fortune," she repeated, her tone mysterious. "Just think, why would Fortune want to go south?"

"Didn't Handsome already say? When temperatures drop to thirty below zero this winter, none of us will be able to endure it."

Beauty snorted. "Do you really buy that? That fool Handsome just wants to go back south to look for his little girlfriend. I don't believe a word he said!"

I was stunned. "So you never planned to come south with us?"

Beauty gave a smug nod. "Fortune has stashed loads of food in the subway. As soon as he leaves, I'll root it out. I'll never want for food again."

So this was Beauty's plan all along. I sighed inwardly. Ever since I'd helped Fortune move his food, Innocence, Handsome, and Beauty had come looking for me, one after another. They all sought the trove of food in the subway. It was like a flame glowing black in the darkness, attracting helpless, fluttering moths.

"You want me to tell you where Fortune hid his food, right?" I shook my head. "I can't do that. Innocence and Handsome came to me too, but now she's missing and he's crazy. What will happen to you?"

"I'm not like them."

Indeed, Beauty was not like Innocence and Handsome. In fact, she wasn't like any of us. I tried to remember the day I first met Beauty, but a thick fog clouded my memory. I could not recall when she had joined our little group. It was as if one day, we had turned a corner, Beauty had strolled up, and our four person group became five.

One time, I asked Fortune, "When on earth did Beauty join us?"

Fortune narrowed his eyes, a rare look of confusion on his face. "I don't remember either." After a pause, he added, "However, she's certainly no ordinary woman."

Yes, no one who had survived this long was ordinary. Innocence relied on her face, Fortune on his ingenuity, and I on Fortune. Handsome had narrowly escaped starvation several times. But as for Beauty, a decidedly unbeautiful woman, how did she survive in these predatory end times? While everyone else grew sallow and emaciated due to malnutrition, only she grew fatter by the day. When she walked, her rolls jiggled—a truly loathsome sight, and yet the fact that she had not been beaten to death was a testament to her might.

"Hell's bells, why are you just standing there?" said Beauty, giving me a shove. "Take me to where Fortune hid his food. You'll be gone tomorrow, so leave the food to me."

"Why don't you go ask Fortune?"

Beauty snorted. "He certainly won't tell me."

"What makes you so sure I'll tell you?" I asked, my patience wearing thin. "Just because your name is Beauty?"

Beauty ignored the contempt in my voice. She pressed closer to me. "I know you look down on me. You like Innocence, you know Handsome, you rely on Fortune, and you've always hated me. But I have information I can trade you for the location of Fortune's food."

I leaned away from her and laughed. "Tomorrow I'm going south with Fortune, and I'll depend on him for everything. I can't think of any information that is worth betraying my boss, the hand that feeds me."

"I know where Innocence is," said Beauty.

Under cover of darkness, Beauty and I went to the subway station and made our way down the escalator step-by-step.

Without matches, we were completely immersed in the gloom, like ants toiling along the bottom of an ink bottle. Relying only on the feel of the rough tunnel wall and my memory, I inched toward Fortune's hidden storeroom. Beauty followed closely behind me.

My mind flashed back to the first time Fortune led me here: the light from the match pinched between his fingers had illuminated one half of his face, the other half hidden in the darkness. He trusted me so much that he'd even told me the location of his food, and yet here I was, leading the unbeautiful Chen Beauty to rob him of it. But tomorrow I would go south with him, and he'd be none the wiser that the food he'd hidden in the north had been lost. Perhaps we would stay in the south and never come back. At least, that was how I consoled myself.

As we moved deeper into the subway tunnel, the rough surface of the wall suddenly became smooth. I stopped and tested the wall with my knuckles. A hollow clang answered.

"Right here," I said. "Fortune's food is hidden inside this room."

In the darkness, I couldn't make out Beauty's expression, but I could hear the pleased surprise in her voice. "Right here? He sure hid it deep enough," she said. "How do we get the door open?"

I held the door shut. "Before I open it, tell me where Innocence has gone."

Beauty made to pull on the door, but I grabbed her hand. After a long while, she broke the silence. "Innocence left with Fortune. You should ask him about her whereabouts."

"Fortune?" I was stunned. "What business did she have with him?"

"That night, I saw her go into Fortune's room. I waited a long time, but I never saw her come out. After that, she was gone. Fortune must know where she went."

I thought back to the evening Innocence left me waiting by the lake. Her receding figure had vanished with the setting sun. I didn't realize she had gone to find Fortune, and would not return. Lost in my thoughts, my grip went slack. Beauty withdrew her hand from mine and grabbed the door handle.

But evidently Fortune had locked the door securely. She gave the handle several sharp tugs, but the door did not budge.

"Hey, lend me a hand," she said.

Still thinking of Innocence, I ignored her. She caught my arm and guided it to the handle. I tried it and felt the door give a little, but it would not open no matter how hard I pulled.

"Need some help?" said a voice behind me.

"That would be terrific." As soon as the words left my mouth, I sensed that something was wrong. I turned around, but could see only darkness behind me.

Chk.

A bright flicker grew into a flame, and light pierced the darkness. Fortune's face appeared, deeply lined, his eyes like a hawk. As he held a match between his fingers, the flame crept along the thin stem. The flickering light made his expression seem especially somber. After several seconds, the match burned down to his fingertips, but he didn't seem to feel the slightest pain. The flame died, and his face sank back into the gloom.

He simply stood there, just as he had before our arrival. He had heard every word Beauty and I had said, but stayed silent. My face burned, but luckily no one could see it.

The light blazed up again. Fortune stared at us. "Well, it's rare to see you two together. Mediocre, haven't you always hated Beauty's presence in our midst? And Beauty, haven't you always said that my food is wasted on Mediocre?"

Beauty and I looked at each other, and then we both took a step back.

The match burned out. Fortune tossed it away and lit another.

"Fortune, where has Innocence gone?" I asked.

Fortune glanced at me, but did not answer. Instead, he addressed Beauty: "You're trying to steal this food? Beauty, I know you're no ordinary woman. You've survived the fighting and confusion thus far. But have you considered that, without me, you won't be able guard this food on your own?"

Beauty raised her face to the light and stared straight at Fortune. "Sometimes you think too highly of yourself, too."

"So you have another way?"

"I always have a way."

Fortune nodded. "Yes, you're sharper than us all. You'll go to any lengths to survive. Never mind a power outage—even if an asteroid hit the Earth, even if zombies choked the streets, you'd survive." As he spoke, he turned and looked all around him. "In that case, there are others on the way?"

In the deep, silent subway tunnel, the match gave off only a narrow ring of light. Beyond it, the darkness circled restlessly. Footsteps, numerous and confused, sounded nearby, signaling the approach of more than one person.

I gave Beauty an astonished look, but her face remained impassive, as though everything was falling into place exactly as she had planned. Four people came toward us out of the darkness, and the flame gradually threw their faces into relief. I recognized all four of them: Liu Fierce, Zhou Strong, Qian Vulgar, and their licentious female companion. They had steel rods in their hands and malicious smiles on their faces.

"It looks like you've been planning this for a long time," said Fortune, striking another match. "If this crew is at your beck and call, this wasn't a decision of one or two days."

"I reached out to them a month ago," said Beauty.

"We hadn't decided to go south yet."

"But even back then, you'd already started to give me less food than before."

Fortune nodded. "I guess there's truth to the story of the farmer and the viper. You're sharp. You're better suited to survive in this world than all of us."

As Beauty and Fortune spoke, Fierce, Strong, and Vulgar gathered around us. The light threw long shadows behind them that stretched into the darkness. The lone woman leaned against the wall and grinned at us.

"Fortune, don't be stubborn. Go south with Mediocre tomorrow, and leave this food to us," said Beauty. "And don't resist. You're old. You can't win against those three. They've all killed before."

Fortune snorted. "I can believe that Liu Fierce and Zhou Strong have killed before. Heh, but the only life Qian Vulgar has taken with his hands, is from masturbating too much."

Vulgar flew into a rage. "Fuck, you asked for it!"

They started forward, but just then, the match went out. Darkness enveloped everything.

"He's trying to get away!" shouted Fierce. "After him!"

But they stopped dead in their tracks. A flame had flared up in Fortune's hand again, and in his other hand was a gun.

The barrel of the gun was pure black, even darker than the surrounding gloom, like a mass of ink in his hand. The muzzle of the gun was pointed at Fierce, whose bulging facial muscles twitched as he backed away slowly.

Fortune smiled coldly. "Now you know how I guard all this food."

Vulgar also backed away. "D-does the p-pistol still work?" he stammered, his eyes darting from side to side. "D-didn't the geomagnetic storm take out all electronics?"

"Idiot!" said Strong, who had been silent until now. "It's not a missile launcher. Pistols don't require electricity, they use gunpowder!" He turned to look at Fortune. "Hey, Boss Zhao, we really fumbled the ball this time. We'll take our leave."

Fortune kept the gun raised. His face gave no indication of his feelings on the matter. The flame died again, but he did not light another match. The darkness and the silence were suffocating.

"Beat it," he said.

The four uninvited guests withdrew slowly, with shuffling steps. I stood frozen, my mind racing: in an age without electricity, the gun in Fortune's hand meant that his advantage was absolute. And I had led Beauty here, who had led the four others here, with every intention of plundering his trove of food. It was not in Fortune's character to forgive this kind of betrayal. What was his next move? Would he dispose of Beauty and then come for me? It was a pity I wouldn't see Innocence before I died—right, where had she gone—

As my mind reeled with a thousand different thoughts, Beauty had already begun to beg for mercy: "Fortune, I was wrong. I only came to help you check on the food. I'm going south with you. I wouldn't trick you. Why would I trick you if I want to go south? It was all Mediocre. He brought me here. He wanted to be with me, to steal me away from you . . . "

Fortune remained silent. The light did not reappear, and I did not know what he was thinking in the shadows. In a standoff, time passes at a leaden pace. Beads of sweat broke out on my forehead, and my legs quaked as I debated making a run for it in the darkness.

Just then, a hoarse, desperate scream came from the other end of the tunnel: "Lovely, Lovely, I'm Handsome. Don't you recognize me?"

Fortune struck another match. In its flickering glow, I saw Handsome staggering toward us. He screamed as he ran, teeth bared and fingers curled into claws. He stumbled and fell, but then scrambled back up and continued his mad rush for the woman beside Fierce.

He looked terrible. His face was savage and grotesque, and blood dripped down his forehead.

Fierce's face darkened, and he whirled around to face Beauty. "Fuck! I knew this was too good to be true. You were laying an ambush for us all along!" Strong and Vulgar scowled at her.

Fortune was stunned, and he let the match in his hand burn out again. In the very instant we were plunged into darkness, Beauty lunged at Fortune and grabbed hold of his hand. Fortune struggled, and they fell to the floor and began to roll about.

"Ah! Who are you?" Nearby, a female voice cried out in alarm. "Let go of me!"

The reply came from Handsome: "Lovely, ah, Lovely, don't you recognize me? I'm Hand—ow, who hit me!"

Fierce grabbed Handsome's head and began slamming it against the ground. "Even if you were strong, it would still be a mistake to jump me. Look at you, you're chicken shit! Well, what are you two standing around for? Go deal with Zhao Fortune!"

Strong and Vulgar finally reacted: following the sounds of struggle, they ran toward Beauty and Fortune, who were entangled on the ground. They sprinted by on either side of me, moving so quickly that I felt wind whistle past my face in their wake.

Total chaos broke out. The dark tunnel echoed with muffled groans and piteous cries, painful howls and angry curses. But strangely, everyone seemed to have forgotten about me. It was more than a little humiliating. Just as annoyance washed over me, I felt something hit my foot. I bent down and felt around until my fingers found a small, lightweight box. When I shook it, I heard something rattle inside.

It was a box of matches.

Wild with joy, I lay down on the ground and opened the box. There were only a few matches inside, maybe three or four. As I struck one, the surrounding darkness was driven back several yards by the light.

I saw Beauty had Fortune pinned to the ground, both scrabbling for the gun. Strong and Vulgar had run right past them to the other end of the tunnel. The light brought them up short, and they hastily doubled back. Fierce had Handsome by the collar and was kicking him, but Handsome held tight to the licentious woman's thigh, still screaming.

The flame died, and I scrambled to strike another match.

Fortune, Beauty, Strong, and Vulgar were a tangle of limbs and savage faces. Seven hands were locked on the gun in deathlike grips. The only free hand, which belonged to Vulgar, was feeling up Beauty, who let fly a stream of abuse. Handsome's legs were wrapped around Fierce's waist, and he had sunk his teeth into the other man's ear, blood dribbling from his mouth. Fierce screamed but did not fall, only stumbled backward. The licentious woman pounded her fists against Handsome's back.

My hand shook, and the light went out again. I reached for another match, but my hands trembled so badly that I dropped the box on the floor. I groped around for a while on my hands and knees. But when I finally found the matchbox again, it was empty. I swore quietly and felt around again until I came upon a matchstick. Several seconds later, light reappeared.

Fortune, Beauty, Strong, and Vulgar sat in a circle, hands fumbling in the clothes of the people on either side of them, muttering, "The gun? Where's the gun?"

Beauty had gotten the worst of it. Her clothes were in total disarray. But she grit her teeth and applied herself to fishing the gun from the clothing of the two men next to her. Handsome had embraced the licentious woman, and the two of them were embroiled in a passionate kiss. Fierce was still bleeding from his ear, bewilderment on his face.

The last match guttered out. The muffled groans and the sounds of blows started up again. Handsome's cries were especially pathetic. I could only guess that Fierce was picking on him mercilessly.

"Everybody listen up!" I shouted.

All of the noise ceased at once, and fourteen eyes looked in my direction. The surrounding darkness was so thick, however, that they could not see anything. I cleared my throat and said, "Fighting is so inelegant. Why don't we sit down and talk—"

The screaming and groaning resumed, and every so often I heard the dull thud of a brick hitting something.

Suddenly, Vulgar shouted excitedly, "Found it!" Before the words were out of his mouth, there was a sharp scream, followed by the scrape of metal skittering against concrete. It sounded as though, in the mad scramble for the gun, it was being kicked back and forth across the floor. On the other side of the tunnel, Handsome shrieked like a pig being slaughtered. I couldn't tell whether his leg had been broken or his lip had been split.

Just then, someone gave the gun a forceful kick. The sound of the gun against the concrete grew sharp, and then it streaked past me. I dove for it, but my hand closed on empty air. The gun slid all the way to Fierce. Several seconds later, Handsome's screaming ceased abruptly, and a gunshot rang out.

As the flash lit up the entire tunnel, I saw the blood and madness on Handsome's face.

"Don't!" I yelled.

"Put down the gun and we'll talk it over," said Fortune.

"Handsome, don't be rash," said Beauty. "From now on, I'm yours."

"Shit! What are you doing pulling a gun like that? You've ruined the peace. We're leaving, we're leaving," said Fierce, Strong, and Vulgar at the same time.

Handsome, holding the gun with both hands, made no response to any of us. Instead, he looked at the licentious woman, who stood petrified, and said, "Lovely, Lovely, I'm Handsome. Don't you recognize me?"

The licentious woman, with bewilderment in her voice, asked, "Lovely? Who is Lovely?"

"You aren't Wu Lovely?" asked Handsome.

"I think you've mistaken me for someone else," said the woman. "My name is Zhen Promiscuous."

I registered the imminent danger and threw myself to the ground.

Bang—bang—bang—bang—bang—bang—bang—bang—bangbangbang. Handsome's crazed screams filled the space between the gunshots, shattering the darkness and stillness of the tunnel.

When the gunfire stopped, a full five minutes after it had started, the entire tunnel fell deathly silent.

I felt myself all over. After I'd made sure there were no new holes in my body, I sighed with relief. The tunnel was like a tomb. Though I couldn't hear any stirring at all, I still unconsciously called out, "Is anyone there?"

There was no answer. I felt a pang of grief. There had been so many gunshots. The others must not have been so lucky—

Before I could finish the thought, Beauty's voice piped up to my left. "Eh? I'm all right!"

To my right, Promiscuous said, "I'm unhurt, too."

Fierce, Strong, and Vulgar's voices came from different directions, but were filled with the same surprise: "Not a single hit!"

From somewhere nearby, Fortune gave a bitter laugh tinged with pain. "Every damn one of them hit me . . . "

Beauty, Fierce, Strong, and Vulgar felt their way to the metal door of the storeroom. They heaved on the handle, and the door opened with a clang. The plastic bags inside poured out like a tide.

"Haha! I finally found you!" crowed Beauty. Even though it was too dark to see anything, I could imagine the fleshy folds of her face rippling with wild joy.

Her joy was contagious: the three men fell upon the plastic bags, consumed with laughter. They would suffer from hunger no longer. The food Fortune had hidden away would sustain them for many years. And after that—well, who knew?

Fortune, lying in a pool of his own blood, gave a cold chuckle.

Suddenly, Beauty stopped laughing, followed by the three men. They uttered shrill cries of surprise and began to rummage through the plastic bags, but all I could hear was the crisp sounds of plastic crinkling.

"They're empty?" said Beauty in a puzzled voice. Then she turned on Fortune and shouted, "What have you done with the bread? Why are all of these bags empty?"

Fortune laughed.

"Quit laughing and spit it out. If you don't, I'll beat you to—" Beauty, abruptly realizing that Fortune had been shot a dozen times and the situation was beyond retrieval, changed tack and softened her tone. "Go on, speak up now. You'll be dead soon. Won't you tell us where you hid the bread?"

"Heh, it . . . ran out . . . a while ago."

"That's not possible," said Beauty. "You have a whole room filled with food."

"How could I find that much bread by myself?" said Fortune, his voice weak. "I hid quite a bit, but . . . but I used up my last loaf of bread providing for you lot these last few years." He laughed again. "Did you really think I wanted to go south because I believed Handsome's bullshit? It was because I was already out of food. If we stayed here any longer, you would have caught on . . . I brought Mediocre here to make him think that I still had a lot of food hidden away. That way, when we went south, he'd continue to listen to me . . . "

"Fuck! You led me on!" Beauty aimed a kick at Fortune, but in the darkness, her foot hit a stone instead, and she gasped in pain. She gave up on Fortune and caught Fierce's arm. "Brother Fierce, look, I knew Zhao Fortune was unreliable. Today, with your help, I finally unmasked him. From now on, I'm with you. I'll do whatever you want me to."

Muttering curses, Fierce turned and stalked off with Strong and Vulgar. Promiscuous left with them as well. Beauty hastily followed, keeping up a constant stream of flattery. I had faith that Beauty would quickly fall into step beside them. She would transition seamlessly from our little five-person group to their little five-person group. She was always sharp. She would outlive all of us.

Before their footsteps faded completely, Handsome suddenly came to his senses. As he sprayed bullets in his violent rage, he had slipped into a stupor. But Promiscuous' departure caused him to recover his intellect. He screamed, "Promiscuous, Promiscuous, I'm Handsome!" and then took off after them.

Thus, only Fortune and I were left in the tunnel. As I crawled toward him, my hand touched a sticky, tepid liquid. Further ahead, I found his face with my hand, and patted his cheek. "Are you dead?"

"Not yet."

"Oh."

After a pause, I asked, "Do you know where Innocence has gone?"

Fortune's wheezing breath sounded especially pronounced in the darkness, in the same way that a candle's flame dances violently just before it burns out. I was worried that he might stop breathing at any moment, so I asked again.

"She . . . she went south."

His answer stunned me for a moment. I thought of Innocence's receding figure in the twilight, and shook my head. "No way. She told me to wait for her, so we could go together."

"Yes, she wanted to go with you, too. But when she came to ask me for bread, I . . . Heh, you don't want to know . . . I told her I'd already run out of food, and that she could not go south with you."

"Why?"

"Because, Mediocre, because you're my . . . You listen to me, in the north or the south, before the Trip or after, I have always been and will always be your boss. You cannot escape my grasp. The food I have left is only enough for two people. At first, I planned to bring only you. Handsome, Beauty, and Innocence were to be left behind. So Innocence went south first. She knows my methods. Everything I set out to do always . . . " Fortune, suddenly lively, said all of this in one breath. Then, he sagged again. "If you had gone south with me, perhaps you would have found her."

I clutched his collar and said urgently, "But Innocence is just a girl. How can she go south without food or weapons? How long ago did she leave? What road did she take? Is she safe?"

But I did not hear Fortune's voice again. I placed my hand on his face. His flesh had already grown stiff and felt icy to the touch, like the coming winter.

Epilogue

Winter was almost upon us, and the weather was extraordinarily cold. By the end of November, all the leaves had fallen from the trees. The wind soughed through the bare branches, accompanied by stinging, bitter cold. No one wanted to go out walking in this weather. Everyone cocooned themselves in their homes.

I saw Beauty on the streets only once. She was with Liu Fierce and his gang, who whispered among themselves as they walked. I said hello to her, but in her eyes, I might as well have been made of air. Handsome followed them at a distance, completely out of his wits. He had eyes only for Zhen Promiscuous, who had grown even more licentious. I said hello to him too, but he looked right through me.

I holed up at home for a few days. Then, with sudden jolt of determination, I snatched up a suitcase and began to walk south. I imagined what the south looked like, and how my reunion with Innocence would unfold. The farther I walked, the happier I felt, and before long I had left the city behind. Suddenly, in the distance, I spied a body lying beneath a withered tree. The white clothing on the body looked extremely familiar.

Several birds roosted in the tree, shivering in the cold. Unable to determine which way to go in the geomagnetic storm, they had missed their last chance to fly south to warmer climes.

I stood rooted to the spot, trembling, though whether it was because of the cold or some other reason I could not tell. I wanted to step forward and confirm the identity of the body, but I was too afraid. The birds huddled together in the branches.

After a long while, I turned and walked back to the city.

When I returned home, I wrapped myself in three layers of blankets, but I couldn't stop shivering. I lay in bed for many days. Outside, torrential rain alternated with swirling snow. The cold pierced the walls, penetrated my blankets, and seeped into my bones. Handsome was right. Temperatures would reach a terrifying thirty degrees below zero this winter. No one could endure it, but not one of us could go south.

THE PERSISTENCE OF BLOOD

JULIETTE WADE

Beneath her squirming two year old, beneath her rustling gown, Selemei could feel herself bleeding. It had started an hour ago. A subtle trickle of guilt—and, like a trickle of falling dust at the border of the city-caverns, it warned that the way forward was dangerous. Selemei squeezed Pelli tighter. Her daughter squeaked protest, so she released a little, nuzzled down between Pelli's puffed curls, and inhaled the sweet scent of kalla oil where her hair parted. She risked a glance down the brass dinner table at her partner, Xeref.

Xeref sat deep in conversation with their elder son, the fingers of one pale hand buried in his silver hair, while their younger son listened raptly. Seeming to sense her glance, Xeref looked up, and his lips curved into a smile.

She knew those fingers, those lips. A lick of heat; the memory of pleasure—and then the fear struck her in the stomach, as unspeakable as the blood.

Oh, holy Heile in your mercy, preserve my health, keep my senses intact . . .

Selemei hid the tremors of her hands by rubbing them into Pelli's back. With a giggle, Pelli started kissing her cheeks. Selemei managed to return a few kisses, then tried to pull away by looking up at the electric chandelier that hung from the vaulted ceiling.

Eight-year-old Aven tugged at her left hand, playing with the ruby drops dangling from her bracelet. "Can I wear your bracelet, Mother?"

Caught in the breath of doom, she couldn't bear to make Aven frown. "Not now, but someday, all right?"

Aven circled her wrist with her thin fingers, golden like Selemei's own, and sighed. "It's so pretty."

Not the word she would have used. The rubies looked like drops of blood. She had no doubt what Xeref had meant by them: *blood is precious*. When she'd first begun her bleeding, Mother had taught her the same. In this age of decline, the noble blood of the Grobal Race was not to be wasted.

Well, she hadn't wasted it! Seven pregnancies in twenty years of partnership with Xeref. Five live births, four of the children perfectly normal. And while Pelli's albinism might be recessive, it could do little harm here in the city-caverns. Their beautiful, brave Enzyel had just partnered into the Eighth Family to great acclaim. Meanwhile, however, the decline continued, and no success was ever enough—even success paid for in blood.

Another trickle made her want to scream.

"Off you go, now," she said instead, lowering Pelli's feet to the floor. The girl ran to her nurse-escort and patted the leg of his black silk suit. The escort frowned—his Imbati castemark tattoo furrowed between his brows.

"Pelli," Selemei scolded. "We don't touch the Imbati. Are you a big girl?"

"Big girl." Pelli lifted her white hands away and wrung them over her head contritely. "Big girl."

"And who are a big girl's hands for?"

"Pelli."

"*Ask* if you want your Verrid to hold you."

Pelli's lip trembled, but she managed, "My please?"

"Of course, young Mistress," the escort replied. He swooped her up in a twirl that turned the threatening tears into a cry of joy, and carried her from the dining room.

Selemei sighed. Pelli was so big now. Perhaps if she'd been smaller, more dependent on the breast, this doom could have been postponed. To Aven she said, "Time to get ready for bed, darling." Aven's escort caught her glance and passed it to other Imbati of the Household, who quickly withdrew. At last even her sons Brinx and Corrim came to kiss her and excused themselves to their shared rooms.

She had to speak now, while the blood could still protect her. She turned toward Xeref at the head of the table, but fear twined up into her throat.

Xeref gave her an uncertain smile.

Xeref's Imbati woman moved, noticeable now as she left her station behind his shoulder. Imbati Ustin—tall, broad-shouldered, and muscular with her hair in several long braids that looked almost white against her tailored blacks—easily pulled out one of the brass chairs that stood empty between them. Xeref stood up, still smiling, and moved to the new seat. Then Selemei's own manservant, Grivi, pulled out the chair beside his.

Oh, to be close to him again!

She couldn't move.

If she got close, they would kiss—if they kissed, they would make love—if they made love, she would get pregnant again—and even if she managed not to lose the pregnancy, there would be labor, and pain—not just pain, but pain *like with Pelli*. The screaming. The blank darkness. She'd wake up feeling like someone had dismembered her, her left leg dead to the hip, and this time, maybe her right, too. Maybe this time she wouldn't regain her ability to walk. Or maybe this time she wouldn't wake up at all.

"Xeref, I can't," she blurted.

"Selemei?"

She stared down at her hands clutched in her lap, at the beautiful bracelet. The ruby drops looked dark in the shadow of the silk tablecloth. "I know blood is precious. I know my duty to the Race. But I just can't anymore."

The guilt sharpened when spoken aloud. She tried not to imagine what words might come from his mouth in reply. *Perverse—selfish—unworthy—*

Xeref cleared his throat. "Selemei?"

Something touched her shoulder—oh, mercy, that was his hand! Her whole body clenched in on itself, hardened. Her chest felt like a geode, unable to admit breath, crusted inside with fear.

Xeref pulled his hand away. "Oh, Selemei, my jewel, my life's partner, my blessed Maiden Eyn—I'm sorry."

She shook her head. Tried to breathe.

"Grivi," said Xeref, "is she all right?"

The Imbati made no answer.

She could hear Xeref stand, pace the length of the table, but if she tried to respond, she'd only moan, or scream. Abruptly, he left through the bronze door to the sitting room; she could hear him out there, murmuring to his Ustin.

"Mistress," Grivi said in his deep soft voice, "I have vowed to protect you."

Her Grivi had helped her more in her recoveries than anyone, but could she really ask him to protect her from Xeref? Was that even possible? Would it mean she could never kiss Xeref again, never feel his arms around her? Did she really want such protection?

She sipped a small breath. "I understand, Grivi, thank you."

Then Xeref came in. Selemei snapped her jaw shut.

"My Selemei." Xeref's voice was husky, vibrating at the edge of control. He knelt beside her feet on the silk carpet.

Elinda help me. Surely he wouldn't demand to have her while she still bled.

His breath grated. "I—Ustin said—you've—gnash it, Selemei, this is my fault!"

What? She frowned.

"It's my fault. When Pelli was being born, I should have—I don't know what I should have done. How could I listen to you scream and do nothing? I asked the doctors, but I only thought they would take away your pain, not that they'd—" He dragged a breath. "You went quiet so suddenly. I thought Mother Elinda had plucked your soul away, and my own heart too. And then when you woke damaged! And it was my fault!"

She whispered, "But you didn't do anything . . . "

Xeref shook his head. He grasped her hand, his fingers pale against her golden skin, and lifted it until her bracelet sparkled in the light. "I didn't give this to you because *blood* is precious, Selemei. I gave it to you because *your* blood is precious. *You* are precious. I don't care what the Family Council says, the Race doesn't deserve your life!"

She managed to look at him. His gray eyes, shining with emotion—his silver hair, falling to his shoulders. Age had given him creases around his eyes; as it had given him more substance, it had also granted him more dignity and determination. And more influence—he often reminded their boys that as the First Family's representative on the cabinet, he had the Eminence's ear.

Yet he would put her first.

"Xeref," she whispered. "Thank you." Her chest opened slowly. What would happen now? Was there a way forward over cracked uncertain stone?

Xeref leaned close to her cheek for a kiss that barely touched her—the same kind of careful innocence he'd used when they'd first become partners, to soften the age difference between them. He cleared his throat. "My Ustin tells me that in the last couple of months you've been missing your friend, Tamelera," he said. When she frowned in bafflement at the change of subject, he added, "Garr's partner, who moved away with him to Selimna?"

She couldn't stop a smile at that. "Dear, I know who Tamelera is; I sent her a radiogram last week."

Xeref chuckled nervously. "Of course you do."

Selemei humored him. "Your Ustin deserves credit for turning her powers of observation to Ladies' concerns. I do miss Tamelera. I could *talk* to her. We would play kuarjos together, and dareli, and we'd talk."

Xeref laid a hand against his chest. "*I* could—would you like me, to talk to you?"

"Don't we talk?"

A blush turned his pale cheeks pink. "Well, we do."

Though never before about the terrible things—the *real* things. "Maybe you could tell me what you and Brinx were talking about?"

Xeref smiled. "You can be proud of him. He's really getting to know the workings of the cabinet. Cousin Fedron likes working with him."

"I saw how Corrim listens," she said. "I'd say he already knows more than you expect him to."

Xeref nodded. "I can't believe he's almost twelve."

Selemei gulped. Corrim's twelfth birthday would make him eligible for Heir Selection if the worst occurred. "Mercy of Heile," she said, "is the Eminence Indal unwell?"

"Oh, no!" Xeref waved his hands. "I mean, he's well, of course he is. I'm sorry. I scared you, and I didn't mean to." He sighed. "This wasn't how I thought this should work."

Selemei sighed, too. She and Tamelera had talked of anything, everything, deliberately avoiding any discussion of their duties to the Race. But when had she and Xeref last spoken of anything but family? She tried to think of something else; anything else. Her mind was as empty as an abandoned cave pocket. "I love you?"

"I love you, too. My Selemei." He sounded awfully disappointed.

"Sir," said Imbati Ustin, quietly behind his left shoulder. "I believe you enjoy a game of kuarjos?"

Now hope lit his eyes. "Selemei—shall we play?" He offered his arm.

She had been walking with more courage, recently, with less worry that her left hip might fail unexpectedly. She still stood slowly, and walked slowly, but it felt good not to have to grasp Xeref's arm too hard. In the sitting room, someone—Ustin, most likely—had already moved the kuarjos set from its pedestal in the corner onto the slate-topped table between the couches. Selemei sat, arranged her silk skirts, and fell into anticipating potential moves for the long-haired warriors wrought in gold, who brandished antique weapons upon their posts at the grid intersections.

Xeref turned the marble board so she had the emerald-helmed warriors, and he the sapphire. He opened his hands to her. "You go first."

She nodded. They played in silence, but when she executed her first entrapment, he glanced up at her.

"Have you always been this good at kuarjos? How is it we've never played before?"

She shrugged. "I played with Tamelera." She took a deep breath. "Xeref, about—what we talked about—are you sure you won't, or we won't . . . ?"

"We won't. I promise."

"But what should I tell people, when they ask?"

"They'll ask?" He sighed. "Of course they'll ask. Say we've decided not to."

She raised eyebrows at him. "They'll blame me. And think I've insulted you. And that I've lost my mind."

"Then say it's just not working."

"They'll think I'm sick. The Family Council would investigate."

"Then say it's my fault." He frowned, shaking his head. "Not that I've rejected you, but that my health is to blame."

"*Your* health . . . you mean put your cabinet position at risk?"

At that moment, a wysp entered through the stone arches of the ceiling: a tiny golden spark of light that spiraled down between them, casting a burst of warrior-shadows, then disappearing through the marble game board and table and into the floor.

"Wysps are good luck," Xeref said. "Maybe no one will ask you."

Selemei sighed. "Let's play."

Nobody could be that lucky.

Selemei put her hands on her hips, feeling uncomfortably like her own mother. Before her on the bed, Pelli frowned stubbornly down at her own small, nightgown-clad body—a too-familiar defiance.

"Nap first, big girl," Selemei said. "Your cousin's party doesn't even start for hours."

"Mama party."

"I'm not going. Your father will take you, with Corrim and Aven." Staying home was the only way to be safe from questions, though writing letters while her entire family helped celebrate a cousin's confirmation seemed—*gnash it!*—well, unfair. She blew out a breath.

Pelli scowled.

Selemei sat beside her. "I love you, Pelli. I promise you can go out, just lie down a bit first."

"Excuse me, Mistress?" Pelli's Verrid said softly.

She waved him off. "I'll take care of it. Please, take a break, Verrid." The Imbati bowed stiffly and withdrew through a door hidden behind a curtain. Her Grivi remained. When Selemei turned back to Pelli, her daughter's lip was trembling dangerously. "Pelli, it's all right, come here, I love you." She held the girl's head against her shoulder and rocked her. "Time for sleeping, just a bit of sleeping, nothing to do now, nothing, nothing, Mama's doing nothing, not going anywhere, nap time for Pelli, Mama loves her Pelli." She leaned over to deposit Pelli into bed, but Pelli clung, and Selemei had to catch herself with her elbow before she squished her accidentally. "Let go, big girl."

Pelli squirmed and whined.

"Here, I'll lie down with you." It was difficult, because Pelli still wouldn't let go, and her left hip twinged as she shifted to straighten it, and her gown hitched up above her knees. She grunted, but she'd often told Grivi she'd rather manage such awkwardness without his help, at least when she was alone. "There." She kissed Pelli's warm cheek. "Sleepy Mama, sleepy Pelli."

Pelli sat up.

Selemei tightened her arm across her daughter's lap. "Lie down, Pelli."

"Pelli party!"

Gnash it! "You won't go to the party at *all,* if you don't *sleep*." Looking up at her from an awkward position on the bed did not convey authority, and her leg was aching, and she *didn't want help*. "Pelli, you will lie down right now because I told you so."

"No!"

"You are a little girl, and little girls do as they're told."

"Nooo!"

"Gnash it, I'm your mother and I know what's best for you. If you don't think of your health, you'll ruin your value to the Race!"

Pelli started bawling.

"Lie down!" Selemei heaved up on one elbow and pulled her down. Pelli thrashed. Her head hit Selemei in the cheekbone; her knee jabbed her in the stomach. *Gnash it, gnash it . . .* Grunting, Selemei struggled to grab the flailing limbs. Finally she managed to pin part of the bedsheet under her own body and wrap the rest of it over Pelli, to catch the hand that was hitting her in the head and tuck it under, to pin the sheet down with one hand on Pelli's other side. Pelli roared with rage. Panting, Selemei held her there until fatigue drained the note of anger from Pelli's cries, and she hiccupped to a stop.

Hitching breaths. But, finally, sleeping breaths.

Selemei carefully let go, even more carefully pulled her arm back.

Oww . . .

She collapsed facedown on the bed. Breathed, hard, aching everywhere. Her left leg twitched and twinged.

Why did I do that? I wasn't going to do that again. Not to Pelli. I should have let Verrid handle this, even if it was *Imbati coddling.*

She turned her head and touched her lips to Pelli's wet cheek; a hint of salt crept between them.

She's too much like me.

Selemei sighed her head back down on the bed, and closed her eyes. It was easier just to lie here, not to try to move, just to imagine herself sinking through the mattress toward the stone floor.

Curtains rustled, and a quiet change came to the air of the bedroom. A servant coming in, maybe Pelli's Verrid. A long silence pulled Selemei toward sleep.

Grivi whispered tensely, "We don't need your interference."

Another long silence followed, but Selemei was fully awake now.

Grivi whispered again. "Gentlemen's servants should stick to politics. They always think everything is their business. I'm charged to safeguard her health."

And a higher voice answered. "But her health *is* politics. You know that."

Ustin's voice? What was Ustin doing here without Xeref? She shouldn't let them talk about her in her presence, but she'd never heard servants speak like this, and it was so hard to move. To interrupt Grivi in the midst of more emotion than she'd ever heard an Imbati express aloud? It seemed cruel.

"I took the Mark in her name," Grivi said. "My vow of service binds us two, alone. Will you compromise that with your selfishness?"

"Such a question," Ustin said, her voice level, disapproving. "I don't know."

"You may be excused, Ustin," said Grivi.

A swish of curtains suggested Ustin was making a swift departure. Selemei carefully waited more than a minute, then shifted her head, and moaned as if she'd just awakened.

"Grivi . . . ?"

He helped her to turn over. She sneaked a glance at his face, his broad forehead illustrated with the manservant's lily crestmark, but he wore the same patient, agreeable expression as always.

It felt dishonest not to mention what she'd overheard. But she'd bumped up against Imbati secrets before, and heard that very same toneless *I don't know*—if she brought it up, she'd only mortify him to no purpose. Guilty, she lay on her back and stared at the ceiling vaults, with Pelli's head tucked underneath her right arm. In her sleep, Pelli turned, and her face pressed into the side of Selemei's breast. Selemei fell into a doze, but woke again when a small warm hand found its sleepy way onto her belly. She patted it gently.

"Mama," Pelli murmured.

"Sweet Pelli. I'm glad you had a sleep."

Pelli wriggled herself into a ball, bottom in the air, then lifted her head and placed it beside her hand so all Selemei could see was the fuzz of orange hair. Maybe she could hear tummy gurgles in there.

"Am I your pillow, big girl?" Selemei asked.

"Baby tummy," said Pelli.

"Yes, you were in there once."

"Pelli sissy?" Pelli turned her head, pale eyes wide. "Baby more?"

Hurt, incredulity, indignation, flashed her skin hot. But it wasn't Pelli's fault. "No, no babies in there," Selemei answered. Slowly, she sat up and gathered Pelli onto her lap. "Now, how about we get dressed and go to your cousin's party?"

"Mama party!"

"Yes, I think we should all go together."

No place was safe from questions.

Even with the help of their Imbati, they were not among the first to arrive. The noise of chattering guests already filtered through their host's velvet curtains into the vestibule, where the First Houseman greeted them. No sooner had their arrival been announced when the six-year-old guest of honor burst through the curtain and barreled into Aven, Corrim, and Pelli, shouting,

"I'm real! I'm real I'm real I'm real!"

Selemei caught Aven with one hand before she could be entirely bowled over; with the other, she gripped tightly onto Imbati Grivi's supporting arm. "Gently, Pyaras."

"Of course you're real, young Pyaras," Xeref chuckled, and ruffled the little boy's dark hair. "Congratulations on your birthday."

"I'm real!" Pyaras' waving arm had an odd smudge of red on it.

"What are you saying?" asked Aven. "What's on your arm? Blood?"

"I'm not going to DIE like my mother!" Pyaras crowed. "I've been STAMPED! I'm real!"

"Pyaras, will you cut it out!" said Corrim, trying to avoid being pummeled.

Pelli jumped up and down and joined in the shouting. "Real! Real! Real!"

"Go play," said Selemei, and gave them a shove as the First Houseman pulled the curtain aside. "Corrim, if you want quiet, look for Tagaret and your older cousins in the private areas of the suite." Pyaras and Pelli ran off together hand in hand; Corrim and Aven more slowly followed.

Selemei shot a glance of sympathy at Administrator Vull, Pyaras' father, who stood waiting to greet them. "Sorry about that," Vull said, flushed in embarrassment. "Our doctor has a sense of humor—she stamped Pyaras as well as the confirmation papers."

"We're just so glad to see him happy," Selemei replied soothingly. "I'm sorry we missed the big announcement."

"The Pelismara Society welcomes him," said Xeref. "The Race will benefit greatly from his life and health."

Vull's face stilled a moment. He and his partner Lady Indelis had been seen as one of the Race's great hopes until her death three years ago. Selemei sent thanks to Mother Elinda for placing her soul among the stars.

"Come, Vull," said Xeref. "Let's go further in—I see some people I'd like to talk to."

Selemei squeezed her Grivi's hand in preparation to walk in, but he rumbled, "Mistress, the public rooms are too crowded; visiting members of the Household have been invited into the servants' Maze."

She held tighter. "Not yet, Grivi, please. Help me to where I can sit."

"Yes, Mistress."

She could have walked the distance by herself, probably. But navigating among gentlemen, fast-moving children, and the wide skirts of ladies was much easier with Grivi's support. He settled her into a spot on one of the sitting room's purple couches, then withdrew behind a nearby curtain. He'd hear her through the service speakers if she called.

Half a breath later, a rustle of young ladies found her.

"Selemei, it's been too long!" That was Lady Keir, who had often joined her for a game of cards with Tamelera. Her golden skin was flushed, and her dark eyes a little too bright, though Selemei had never known her to drink. "Are you—" she leaned forward confidentially, braids swinging around her face, "—*well?* I mean, any news?"

Selemei reached a hand toward her, and pretended the question was only an idle inquiry about her well-being. "No particular news, Keir. I'm quite well. And you?"

Keir giggled. "I'm well, I'm well. Such an auspicious day, you know, I wouldn't have missed it . . . " Suddenly she seized Selemei's hand, looking furtively around the room. "You must help me, I haven't yet managed to get pregnant—Erex is very patient about it, but I'm *dying* to, oh, just looking at the darling children, it makes me so jealous—"

"May Elinda bless you, dear," Selemei said. "And may Heile keep you in health."

"By the way, I suppose you've met my friends? They would love to have your blessing, too."

Selemei did know the friends, who were only new to Keir because she'd partnered late, and moved from Third Family to First just this year. She squeezed all their hands and blessed them, though it hurt her heart. Keir was the oldest of the four, at twenty, and the only one without a history of pregnancy. None had yet borne a confirmed child.

"I can't believe this party," one them muttered. "Pyaras is six! He's been healthy as an Arissen since the day he was born. It's showing off, that's what it is."

Selemei looked over too late to see who had spoken, but she wasn't about to allow the guest of honor to be impugned by comparison to a Lower. "Don't you remember, Cousins, they had this party all planned three years ago?" she said. "When Lady Indelis miscarried?"

Her words created an instant of excruciating silence. Everyone knew how that had ended.

"I'm hungry," Lady Keir announced suddenly. "Anyone want some of those delicious mushroom tarts?" She walked away quickly, the others fluttering and murmuring behind her.

Selemei sighed. Her temper wasn't steady today; maybe she should have stayed home. She stared at the purple piping at the edge of the couch, avoiding people's eyes.

"Selemei? My love?" A warm touch on her shoulder.

"Xeref!" She took the hand he offered, and stood with relief. "Are we leaving?"

Xeref frowned. "So soon? I wasn't thinking to, I admit, but I couldn't leave you looking so troubled." His face was rueful. "Walk with me? I've been speaking with the First Family Council."

"All right—let's not hurry."

She felt quite steady on his arm, walking through the cast bronze door into the dining room. Most of the men had gathered here, standing about in jewel-colored velvet suits and raising celebratory glasses of sparkling yezel. She only recognized three. Their host, Vull, wore aquamarine, while Xeref's colleague from the cabinet, Fedron, wore emerald. The third man she recognized was Erex,

Lady Keir's partner, who wore topaz. He had pale skin and clubbed fingertips, and kept his Imbati woman near him even when all the others had stepped out.

"Erex was just telling me he's been promoted," Xeref told her. "Arbiter of the First Family Council."

"Congratulations," said Selemei.

Erex bowed graciously. "A pleasure to see you, Lady. In fact, you are a paragon among us. All honor to your gifts to the Race."

"Good to see you, Erex," she said. "I believe the Arbiter position will benefit greatly from your kindness. You're welcome to seek out my children anytime to see how they are doing."

"Let's not forget your organizational skills," added Xeref. "It's a heavy responsibility to monitor the health and continuance of the First Family. I'm sure you'll do well."

"To all our benefit," Selemei agreed. "Is it too early to ask you, Arbiter, how you assess the prospects of the First Family's next generation?"

Erex smiled. "Ah, in fact, not too early at all. I confirmed a new partnership arrangement just this morning. In fact, it's doing quite well." He blushed. "We're all giving it our best efforts, aren't we?"

Today, in this home, the platitude was insulting. "Indeed we are," she said. "Though some of us are giving our *efforts*, while others are giving up our *health*, and others, like Lady Indelis, have given their *lives*."

Vull looked stricken; Erex laid one hand on his chest, and Fedron exclaimed, "Lady!"

"Am I wrong?" she demanded. "For the good of a boy like Pyaras, at least, I imagine you could think of some way to protect our mothers better. Aren't you all men of importance?"

"Lady, you have no idea how—" Fedron began, but Xeref grabbed his arm.

"Excuse me," said Selemei. She turned away too quickly, and her left leg twinged. She shifted to her right. She stepped again, and the leg didn't buckle, but suddenly she was wobbling and couldn't seem to correct it. Worse, by now she was out the door where the only things to grab onto were random party guests. She hopped onto her right foot and managed to stop in an utterly undignified manner.

Out of nowhere a pair of hands steadied her—strong wiry hands, attached to arms in pale gray sleeves. A pale gray coat marked the Kartunnen caste. Selemei looked up and found she'd been rescued by the confirming doctor. The tall woman had painted her face, as only the Kartunnen did: she had black lines on her eyelids and light green on her lower lip. Her coat flared to her knees, and was finely embroidered with designs in the same light gray.

"Thank you, Kartunnen," Selemei said.

"Please excuse my imposition, Lady." But the Kartunnen didn't immediately let go.

"I'm all right," Selemei insisted. "I can stand."

"Yes, Lady." The doctor folded her arms, tapped her fingers, took a breath as if to speak, but let it out silently.

"Thank you for being here," Selemei said. "You made Pyaras very happy with that stamp."

"He's worth the trip, Lady," said the doctor. "I'd take six of him over anyone else here." Her half-green smile pulled sideways. "Except maybe that poor desperate girl."

"What do you mean?"

"Nothing really. If you'll permit, Lady, I'd prefer to talk about you. Have you had therapy for that leg?"

She shouldn't have been surprised. Kartunnen's specialized education made them audacious. "Of course," she explained. "My Grivi and I worked on it. He helped me immensely."

The doctor nodded. "I believe you should consider finding a proper Kartunnen therapist. With respect, women's Imbati receive quality medical training, but sometimes they can be . . . too close to you, to see things clearly."

How should she respond to that? Was that presumption? For a doctor to speak that way of a Higher like Grivi? But what if she was right?

"How long has it been since your injury?" the doctor asked.

"Two years."

The doctor lowered her voice. "Pardon, but if it were me, I'd try not to get pregnant until I'd had it looked at."

Now, *that* was most definitely presumption. "Oh, it's that simple, then, is it?" Selemei snapped.

People in the crowd around them turned to look. The doctor bowed formally, and spoke toward the floor. "My sincere apologies, Lady."

The urge to have her thrown out lasted only a split second, replaced by perverse curiosity. *This doctor could answer questions.* Selemei gathered her composure and smiled, her heart pounding.

"Well, that's all right, of course, doctor," she said. "No trouble at all."

Deliberately, Selemei looked away toward a wysp that had drifted in. The bright spark was no larger than her smallest fingernail, and moved aimlessly, caught in the wake of one person's movement, then another's, casting twinkles through the gathering. Younger children pointed and grinned at it, while the older ones mimicked the adults' casual ignorance. Selemei waited until nearby conversations gradually resumed. The doctor still watched her warily, and threaded a strand of red hair back behind one ear. When it seemed safe enough, Selemei stepped closer.

"Doctor," she whispered. "*Is* it that simple? For—" she almost said *for Lowers*, but stopped herself. "For someone like you?"

The doctor gritted her teeth. "Will you have me punished, Lady?"

"Certainly not. May Mai strike me."

"There are many ways, but here are three," the doctor said, and counted on her long fingers. "One, exemerin. Two, ambnil. Three, swear off men." Her eyes flitted briefly across the crowd, and she smirked. "Easier for some than for others."

"Thank you, Kartunnen."

"Everyone!" a voice shouted. A series of quick claps cut through the murmur of conversations. "Everyone, we have an announcement!"

Selemei turned. The men from the dining room were emerging, Vull and Xeref in the lead.

"I'd like to thank Vull for hosting us on such an auspicious occasion," Xeref said. "A healthy boy joins us in the Pelismara Society with his proud father looking on. But in my heart, I can't help but wonder, and perhaps you have, too, my cousins—how much more auspicious would this day be if Lady Indelis could be here?"

A sigh swayed the crowd; Vull nodded, pressing a fist over his mouth.

"Too many mothers give their lives in the name of the Race," said Xeref. "The First Family could grow stronger and happier if they were still with us. That's why Fedron and I will be bringing a new proposal to the Eminence, in the name of Lady Indelis. Our proposal will allow women whose lives have been endangered in childbirth to retire from their duties to the Race and dedicate themselves to the upbringing of their families. We appreciate your support."

The crowd broke into murmurs—some shocked, but it seemed, some approving.

Xeref made his way to her side and took her arm. "Are you ready to go home, my love?"

"Yes, please!" Just look at the childlike mischief in his eyes . . . She managed to suppress a grin, but couldn't help glancing at him, over and over. When they passed the wysp on their way into the private rooms to gather children and servants, it seemed similarly attracted by his energy; it swirled around and through his coattails, not drifting off until they'd left the party and started down the hall toward home. As soon as no one was looking, Selemei's grin escaped to her face.

Me, legally retired? Ah, Xeref!

Of course, it was always challenging to get the children settled after the excitement of a party. Selemei kissed Corrim goodnight, fingering a lock of his hair. Now that he was eleven, he professed himself too old for such intimacies, but she'd get away with it as long as she was able. Such soft, soft curls—the perfect cross between Xeref's straight hair and her own.

"Mother?" Corrim turned his head, pulling the curl from her grasp. "Has Father made a lot of laws?"

She frowned. "I think so."

"Which ones?"

"He's participated in votes for all of them. I'm not sure how many times he's proposed his own; you should ask him."

"Do you think the Eminence Indal will like this new one?"

She should have known he'd hear; rumors were as swift and unquenchable as wysp-fire. "I hope so."

"When is Brinx coming home?"

Selemei glanced to the other brass-framed bed, which the Household had perfectly arranged with sheets turned back for whenever her eldest returned from his evening with friends. "Late, sweet boy. Please don't wait up."

Corrim grunted, but when she leaned down to him, accepted a kiss.

"Mistress?" came a disembodied voice from behind the servants' curtain. "Please, Mistress, if you would attend your daughter?"

Oh, no. I could have sworn Pelli was sleeping like a stone . . . "I'm on my way."

Selemei walked on her Grivi's arm into the hallway, and together they hurried to the girls' room. He pulled open the heavy bronze door for her.

Mercy . . .

Pelli *was* sleeping like a stone, arms and legs flung wide, her covers tossed off and her pillow on the floor. The muffled sobs came from the other bed.

"Aven?" Selemei whispered.

Aven sat bolt upright, still sobbing, and reached for her with both hands. Selemei limped to her bed and sat down. Aven's hands clutched hard enough to hurt, and she wormed into Selemei's lap.

"Aven, my sweet Aven, what in the name of mercy?" Selemei murmured, stroking her back. "I'm here, everything's all right, I promise. What's wrong?"

Aven sobbed something into her shoulder.

"I don't understand."

"Mama, you almost died!"

Mercy, indeed. She's so smart. For a second, it hurt to swallow. "My darling," she managed, "that was about Lady Indelis."

Aven pulled back and scowled, sobs turned to outrage. "No it wasn't."

"All right, I'm sorry. I'm sorry, you're right." She found Aven's hands and gave them a tug. "But I *didn't* die. By Elinda's forbearance I'm here now, sweet one, and I love you."

"It's not fair." Aven's arms lifted from her waist to drape over her shoulders, and the girl nuzzled into the crook of her neck. "Why do we have the decline anyway, when Lowers don't?"

"I don't know, love." Every parent faced this moment. Somehow it never got any easier, even after going through it with each of her older children. "I guess, we have to remember that each of us has our time. We can take good care of ourselves, but we don't get to choose. Some people are never born. Some are never confirmed, and live hidden. Some are here one day and gone the next. My mother used to tell me that Mother Elinda loves the Race the most of all the people of Varin, and puts us in special constellations."

"That makes no sense." Even her daughter's voice was frowning. "Mother Elinda puts souls *into* us, she doesn't just take them out. If she really loved us, she'd give us babies to end the decline, not kill us."

"Sweet one—"

"And how do we know the people who die are in the sky, anyway? It's the *sky*." She waved an arm toward the vaulted stone ceiling.

Selemei could feel all four levels of city and rock above. Only travelers, Venorai farmers, and Arissen firefighters ever saw the sky; it was a long way up to the gods her mother had wanted her to believe in.

"I suppose we don't know," she sighed. "But we do have Imbati and Kartunnen who care for our health. And if your father passes his law, then fewer of us will die."

Aven shook her head. "Mama . . . "

"Please, darling, don't worry. Come here." She pulled Aven in again, and leaned against her springy hair. Across the room, Pelli sneezed in her sleep and turned over, apparently unaware. Could they be saved? And what about her firstborn daughter, Enzyel, whose trials were already beginning?

A click came from the door latch; Selemei looked up. This was Xeref, sticking his head in. What did he want? She raised eyebrows at him.

Xeref didn't call for her, but came in and sat with them on the bed. She had no idea what he intended until he wrapped his arms around them both. After a moment's surprise, she relaxed into his shoulder. Aven, too, seemed comforted.

When at last Aven began to nod off, Selemei nudged Xeref until he stood, then returned her daughter's head to the pillow and tucked her in.

Xeref offered her a hand up. She took his arm, and walked with him slowly out the door.

In the hall, the light of the sconce fell across his features. Untouched by Aven's fear of death, he looked quite as delighted as he had at the party this afternoon. Her own excitement welled up again. She seized his hands between hers.

"Xeref, thank you," she said. "What this means to me—I can't—" She pressed his hands to her heart, and then to her lips. They unfolded warm and soft to cup her cheeks.

Xeref bent close to her. "I had to do it."

She turned her face up and kissed him. How could she not? His lips were so sweet, and it had been so long! His mouth opened into a whole world where they existed only for each other. She tried to put her body and soul into that sacred place, and only when she gulped a breath did she realize she was already undressing him in her mind, while he pressed against her, eager and proud with the desire that had never dimmed.

The desire that could kill her if it were fully satisfied.

She pushed him away, gasping.

"I—I'm sorry," he stammered. "I didn't mean to—"

"Go away," she cried. "By Sirin and Eyn, please!"

His face full of pain, Xeref staggered away and vanished into the master bedroom.

All the inner parts of her tugged after him, but Selemei did not follow.

Naturally, rumors about Xeref's proposal were everywhere. Selemei had discovered a new talent: extinguishing conversations faster than atmospheric lamps at nightfall. No question in her mind what the talk was about. However, she'd prefer to know how far the information had changed, and how those changes might reflect on the First Family.

There was only one possible course of action.

Any lady of intelligence developed tools for unlocking the truth. Today was a day to employ her favorites: soothe the spirit with tea, amuse the tongue with cakes, and tease the honesty out. The Household had already completed arrangements in the sitting room: white silk cloth over the slate-topped table, silver spoons, teacups of silver-rimmed glass. Considering the delicacy of the topic, Selemei had chosen to invite only one friend from the Ninth Family and one from the Eleventh, both Family allies. Now all she needed—

"Excuse the interruption, Mistress," the First Houseman said, stepping from behind his curtain, "But your cousin, the Lady Keir, wishes to speak with you."

"Now?" Selemei pressed a knuckle to her lips. *Should I turn her away? Or let her see preparations meant for others?* "I'll come to her," she decided.

On Grivi's arm, she walked to the vestibule where she ducked around the edge of the velvet curtain. Keir stood waiting, twisting her golden hands even more tightly than the twists her Imbati woman had made in her hair.

"Cousin?" said Selemei. "Are you all right?"

"Is it really true?" Keir asked. "About what Xeref is planning?"

What had she heard? One hour later, it might have been easier to answer. "Only what he announced at Pyaras' party."

"But that's awful."

"Awful? What do you mean?"

Keir wrung her hands. "Well, do *you* think it's fair? That we have to almost *die* before we can get out of it? And what does that even mean, 'almost'?"

What? Get out of it before you've even started*?* Shock stole her ability to speak the words. A good thing, too, because behind that automatic protest loomed an intimate recognition as terrifying as a glimpse of sunlight. Selemei swallowed hard.

"Oh, Keir—cousin." She took a deep breath. "How difficult it must have been to come to me with your thoughts. Thank you for trusting me." She opened her arms, and Keir embraced her. Selemei resisted the urge to stroke her like a child. "I know how difficult this is. I can't *imagine* what you've heard out there."

Keir sighed, but unfortunately, didn't give any hint of what she'd heard.

Selemei drew another steadying breath. "So, I'm thinking—today, in a few minutes, I'll be speaking with some friends about this. If you've no prior commitments, then perhaps you would like to join us?"

"Oh!" Keir pulled back, dabbing her cheeks with her fingers. "I'd love to! Which friends? Do I look like I've been crying?"

"No, please, don't worry about that. I'm expecting Lady Ryoe of the Ninth Family—she's always been a great comfort to me during my recoveries—and you know Lady Lienne of the Eleventh Family from our games of dareli."

"Does Lady Ryoe play?" Keir asked. "Since we're missing a fourth?"

"Well, not today, all right? You may freshen up in my rooms as you like. The others will be here in a moment."

Keir bustled off at once, but her long-haired manservant stayed behind.

"Imbati?"

"Your pardon, Lady," the Imbati curtsied, inclining her tattooed forehead. "Your generosity in this invitation is much appreciated, but I must express concern."

"About Keir?"

She leaned her head to one side. "My Mistress decided to visit you because she is deeply moved by this topic. I fear that in conversation she may become . . . impassioned, even in the presence of outsiders."

And possibly risk Family secrets. Selemei nodded. "I understand. I'm already planning to tread carefully. I'll protect her, I promise." The servant bowed and followed her Mistress deeper into the suite.

Selemei sent her Grivi to the dining room to speak with the Household Keeper about how to accommodate an additional guest. He'd only just stepped away when the doorbell rang again. The First Houseman emerged from the vestibule, seeming perturbed to find her unattended.

"Is there a problem?" she asked.

"Mistress, your other guests have arrived, but they've brought a companion. Lady Teifi of the Second Family."

Selemei frowned. This could not be coincidence, and it would be rude to confront the motive of an unexpected guest. If she pushed ahead in her own inquiries, was rockfall inevitable? To protect Keir, should she give up on her questions altogether?

"They are all welcome," she said. She took a deep breath, weighing the words "tell," "inform," and "alert" for how far to mobilize the Household. Best to be cautious. "Please alert the Household to the change of plan."

"Yes, Mistress."

Grivi returned swiftly, apologizing for his absence at a critical moment; Selemei reassured him and allowed him to escort her to her seat. She kept sharp eyes on her guests as they entered. Lady Ryoe wore a smile that sparkled like the ruby pins in her sandstone hair; she came close for a kiss on the cheek before she sat down in the chair at Selemei's left hand. Lady Lienne's walk was tight; so also her mouth, and her gray sheath gown; she whispered close to Selemei's ear.

"My sister insisted."

Selemei looked past her shoulder to Lady Teifi, who was taking a seat on the facing couch. She and Lienne did resemble each other, though Teifi's long straight hair was sifted gray instead of pure black. Selemei kissed Lienne's cheek.

"You're both welcome. Please, have a seat. Our Household Keeper will be pleased to know that her tea cakes are held in such high regard."

Under the watchful gaze of her younger sister, Teifi returned the smile, but the faint blue tinge of her lips matched a chill in her eyes. "I wouldn't have missed them."

Keir entered then, through the double doors from the back of the suite. She hesitated a moment at the sight of Lady Teifi, but there was only one chair left, at Selemei's right. She took it, flashing a nervous smile. "I'm Selemei's cousin, Keir. Had you already started talking about it?"

"Not at all," Selemei said quickly. But when it came to proposing a less fraught topic of conversation, her mind whirled and came up blank.

Fortunately—showing impeccable timing—the Household Keeper appeared in her black silk dress, carrying the cakes. Her presentation was never the same twice; today she brought a sculpture of a fountain, five crystal spouts rising to different heights from a slate basin below. Atop each spout balanced a glass bowl delicate as a bubble, and inside each bowl lay a pearl-white cake garnished with a single red marshberry. Selemei herself could not help joining in the general sigh of admiration. Tea-pouring and the passing of cake bowls extended her reprieve, while the conversation turned to sweets, art, sweets as art, and where to find the most skilled Keepers. Selemei pressed her fork into the pliant surface of her cake, dared a bite. But every pause clutched at her, begging to be filled with harmless normality.

Here was a topic that might be harmless enough. "By the way, those are lovely hairpins you're wearing today, Ryoe."

Ryoe chuckled, licking berry juice from her lips. Her pale hand fluttered up to her hair. "Rubies are the gem of this year, Selemei. We're all wearing them—even you."

"Me?" Her own dress was sapphire blue, but then she remembered the bracelet on her wrist. Lienne wore rubies on the neckline of her dress, Teifi wore them in a band down the center of her bodice, and Keir wore them in a spiral brooch at her shoulder. Selemei's confidence faltered.

We're wearing blood. All of us.

She tried to cover her consternation with a sip of tea, but too soon; it burned her lip. Nothing could be harmless when the truth hid everywhere. She set down the cup.

"All right, I know what you're all here for. You want to know about Xeref's proposal, and I want to know what you've heard, and how you are thinking about it." To protect Keir, she assumed her cousin's argument like a cloak: "Personally, I don't think it goes far enough."

Keir sat straighter. "You don't? But I thought you said—"

"What a thing to say!" Teifi cried.

Selemei smiled, carefully, and folded her hands on her lap so they wouldn't shake. She could handle this; it wasn't the first time she'd been the target of all eyes at once.

"I'm not afraid to say it," she replied. "Xeref wants to prevent deaths like that of Lady Indelis. He thought the best way would be to allow ladies who had come close to death to retire from their duties. His intent is not to hasten the decline, but to allow ladies to raise their own children—and actually, also, to allow them more recovery time from birth injuries before they must consider pregnancy again." That was a good idea! Sometimes she surprised herself.

"Birth injuries." Lady Keir shuddered visibly. "Mercy of Heile."

"I understand your fear, Keir," Selemei said reassuringly. "That's why it's important to allow time for complete recovery. After all, a healthier mother will bear a healthier child."

"It won't work," said Lady Ryoe. The reminder of blood glinted from her hair as she shook her head. "I mean, retirement sounds good, but who's going to enforce it? We can't send Arissen guards into bedrooms."

"That's true," Selemei admitted.

"Then—forgive me—who is going to tell our gentlemen no?"

Selemei winced. Her heart wanted to protest, but how recently had she tasted this fear, despite how deeply she trusted Xeref? She almost looked over her shoulder at Grivi. "Well. We'll just have to think of something, I imagine. The wording of the proposal hasn't been finalized yet."

"This is ridiculous," Lienne muttered. "Lowers have children when they *want* to."

"Lowers, ugh!" Teifi grunted. "There are plenty of *them*."

Lienne's pale cheeks flushed. "Having too many children is killing us, Teifi, and it *still* isn't stopping the decline. If we're all going to die anyway, do we have to be miserable while we're doing it?"

"Lienne," said Ryoe, "I had no idea you were so upset. Is something wrong?"

"What's *wrong* is that you're even considering this nonsense," Teifi said. "Politics is gentlemen's business."

"But this is about *our lives*," protested Keir.

"And it's *our children* who stand to lose their mothers," said Lienne.

"I can't believe you, Sister," Teifi hissed through her teeth. "That you'd associate yourself with selfish cats who would turn their backs on the future of the Race!"

"Teifi, stop!"

Selemei spoke measuredly into the shocked silence that followed. "I don't believe it's selfish to try to understand the impact of the rules that gentlemen impose on our lives. The fact is, the proposal in its current form was my partner's idea, and it's uninformed in many ways, and incomplete. This is why it's so important for us to discuss it."

"The Race requires a higher form of loyalty," Teifi said. "These are the burdens of power."

"Oh?" Selemei asked, clamping down on a surge of anger and forcing a smile. "And would you like to tell us about the number and health of your children, then? How your sacrifices have rewarded you with success?" She'd heard enough about her from conversations with Lienne and Tamelera to know that Teifi couldn't answer that.

A muscle tightened in the older woman's jaw.

Lienne threw a keen glance at her sister, and stood up. "Selemei, I'm so sorry, we'd better go."

She took a deep breath. "Darling, what a shame." She squeezed Lienne's hand, trying to catch her eye. "Please let's talk another time."

Lienne and Teifi's swift departure left the other guests in a fluster, and they soon excused themselves, also.

"Is there tea left?" Selemei sighed.

Imbati Grivi lifted the pot, nodded, and refreshed her now-cooled teacup. Selemei sighed, pressing its edge into her lower lip, inhaling the steam. In a way, the utter failure of her subtlety *had* taught her what was out there—fear, despair, thirst, fury, and lots and lots of arguing. Keir had come out unscathed, at least.

But her own satisfaction with Xeref's proposal had not. Teifi demonstrated that any legislation of this nature would be strongly resisted; and Ryoe was correct that gentlemen would seize upon any excuse to dismiss restrictions on their behavior, even if it passed.

"Grivi," she said, "how soon can we be ready to go out?"

"I know of nothing that would prevent us going now, Mistress."

"I need to discuss this with Xeref. Our proposal needs some revisions."

Once she had given herself permission to go to Xeref's office—this was official legislative business, after all—her resolve outpaced her ability to walk there.

Selemei left the suites wing and began to cross the central section, but her left hip twinged; she squeezed her Grivi's hand for a pause. By the tall bronze doors of the Hall of the Eminence, she cast an eye about, but saw only Imbati child messengers flitting through, and Arissen guards, powerful and still in their orange uniforms. No one to care if she shook her leg a bit.

After a few seconds, she tested her weight on the foot. Workable. A bit more slowly, they crossed into the offices wing. Xeref's was the first door on the left.

All five young men in the front office stopped what they were doing as she walked in. One of them was her son, Brinx. He sprang up from the steel desk he'd been leaning on, and straightened the hem of his malachite-striped coat.

"Mother? Holy Sirin's luck!" he exclaimed, grinning. "Fedron sent me over here only ten minutes ago; we've been going over the minutes of the last Cabinet meeting. If you'd come five minutes earlier, I'd have been busy; five minutes later, and I'd have been back next door." He kissed her cheek. "Would you like to come see where I work?"

Selemei smiled. As a child, Brinx had told stories to her for hours—even conversed with the vaulted ceilings when no one else was available. These days, she was seldom the recipient of that bright attention.

"I'd love to, treasure, but I've come to see your father."

Brinx pulled a sober face. "Of course. Shall I take you in? I don't think he has another meeting for at least sixteen minutes."

"Yes, please."

Brinx resumed bubbling while she followed him to the inner door. "You're lucky that he's in there by himself right now. He's had all sorts of meetings today, and messengers—we've gotten five of them at least. Six, I think, actually. Yeah, six. It's because of the *stir*, of course. The one Father started when he announced his Indelis proposal. We've never been so busy—" He pushed the door open a crack. "Sir? Father, Mother's here."

"Selemei? Come in, come in!" Xeref came to her quickly; his blue eyes searched her with concern, but when she smiled at him, he brightened. She released Grivi's hand to take his.

"Everything's fine, dear," she said. "I need to talk to you about the proposal."

"I hope you're not worrying, Mother," said Brinx. "Our conversations are going well." He raised one finger. "'Give them the respite, gentlemen. Think first of the health of your partner if you wish a healthy child, and the blood of the Race will grow stronger!'"

"We don't vote for another week or so," Xeref explained. "This is the part where we sound people out and argue for the idea. Our most powerful argument is exactly what Brinx says, and people are responding well to it. I'm optimistic."

Hearing her earlier thought put so differently made her doubt any of these gentlemen were serious about real retirement. "Have you changed any part of the proposal?" she asked. "Added anything?"

"No. Why do you ask?"

"Well, have you talked with anyone about how to enforce it?"

"Mother, don't worry," said Brinx. "Kartunnen will do as they're told."

Kartunnen? She flashed him a look. "It's not them I'm worried about, Brinx, it's the gentlemen. No one will want to give up their chance to benefit the Race. They'll cling to excuses." The incredulity on his face forced her to search for examples that filled her with distaste. "No, she wasn't injured enough; or, no, we had a good doctor so she wasn't really in any danger."

Brinx pursed his lips into the same wanting-to-protest moue that he always had as a child. She rolled her eyes and turned to her partner.

"You know they will, Xeref."

Xeref looked at her in silence for a moment. "Yes," he sighed. "I imagine they will. Should we specify that the doctor must have assessed the risk of death at greater than fifty percent?"

She shuddered. "Do Kartunnen do that? Isn't that . . . heartless of them?"

"Not every time, I don't imagine."

"Fifty percent seems low," put in Brinx. "Maybe it should be sixty."

"Brinx," said Xeref, "you might want to think carefully before you say something like that. I wrote the proposal for your mother."

"Wasn't it for Lady Indelis?" Brinx exclaimed, but his face fell quickly from puzzlement to shock. "Oh. Mother, I'm so sorry. I had no idea."

Selemei found his hand and squeezed it. "Well, you can see, can't you, why we can't have this be negotiable?"

"I see what you're saying," said Brinx. "The problem is, negotiation is exactly what this part of the process is for."

"But, treasure, that's what I'm doing right now. Negotiating it." Selemei turned back to Xeref. "How many men do you know who would be willing to bargain the continuation of their families against their partners' lives? How many are doing this already? Speaking over a doctor's word in the name of ending the decline?" Xeref was too frustrating in his silence. "Xeref," she insisted. "*You* know how easy it is to speak over a doctor's word. How dangerous it is."

"Father, did you—" Brinx began, but Xeref raised his hand and stopped him with a glance.

"Selemei, my jewel, you're right. But no one will agree to give up such power to Kartunnen."

"The power doesn't need to be in the Kartunnen," she explained, carefully restraining her tone. "Neither should it be; as Lowers, they lack final authority. Put this in the law itself. Make a list of risks, of injuries, and how serious they are. Take it out of everyone's hands, as if it were the will of Elinda."

"Father, you'd still have to get the *list* from a Kartunnen," said Brinx.

"Brinx, I know how to get lists from Kartunnen," Xeref replied, and Brinx blushed. "Thank you, Selemei. I'll send my Ustin tomorrow morning."

"Come see my desk, Mother," said Brinx.

"I'm not finished, though," Selemei said. "There's another problem. A more serious one. A more *private* one."

"Which one?" Xeref asked.

She squirmed inside. Might this be easier to discuss if Brinx weren't here? Possibly, but saying 'rape' was awful, regardless. She dodged the word. "Well, we've talked about the will of Mother Elinda, but we haven't spoken about her partner."

"Father Varin?" Brinx raised his eyebrows. "Do you mean what punishment to levy for transgression? That's for the joint cabinet to decide."

She sighed. "Brinx, love, I'll lend you my copy of the Ancient Stories when your brother has finished reading it." Selemei opened her hands to Xeref, who was staring at her silently, with a wrinkle deepening over his nose. "Remember, Father Varin gnashes the wicked in his fiery teeth in atonement for his own transgressions." Still, no recognition in Xeref's eyes. "The transgressions that led Mother Elinda to *reject* him."

"Oh!" Xeref cried suddenly. "But that's . . . oh, that's—oh dear."

"Father, what?"

"But Selemei, would they really?"

What a question! She turned it around. "Perhaps you mean to ask whether gentlemen would really be willing to sacrifice their desires for their partners' safety? Some would—*you* would. But most gentlemen are not you. Must I speak with the ladies of the Pelismara Society to give you a number?"

Xeref ran one hand through his silver hair, uncomfortably.

"What are you talking about?" Brinx demanded.

"Master," said Imbati Ustin. "I can verify, by Imbati witness, three rapists among those First Family gentlemen known to me. If you wish it, I can investigate and expand my knowledge to assess the scope of the problem across the Pelismara Society. It could have a substantial impact on this proposal's implementation."

In the Imbati's icy voice, it felt terrifyingly real. Selemei swore. "Name of Mai, who?"

"I don't know, Mistress, I'm sorry."

Selemei gaped at her. For whom was she protecting that information? Would she tell Xeref if he asked?

Brinx, who had been spluttering, found words. "Father, you must reprimand your Ustin."

"You think so?" Xeref narrowed his eyes. "Why is that?"

"Accusing her betters of such a thing! I can't think of anything more presumptuous."

"Brinx," Xeref said slowly, "Please think what you're saying. Ustin has worked as my personal and political assistant and bodyguard for twelve years. In all that time she has never failed to safeguard me or my information, nor have I caught her in any inaccuracy. Her qualities are guaranteed by the certification of the Imbati Service Academy, just as your servant's are. And this information is quite relevant to our success."

Brinx flushed. "I know. I'm sorry, Father. And I do really want to help you pass this proposal."

"If this is uncomfortable for you, why don't you just let me talk with your mother? Fedron's got several people he's negotiating with, and I'm sure he'd appreciate your help right now."

"Yes, of course, Father. I'll see you at dinner."

It was quite common for a room to feel silent after Brinx stepped out of it, but this silence was one Selemei hesitated to step into. Her mind whirled in horror and suspicion of the men she knew. Xeref stared into the distance, dismay written deep into the lines of his face.

"This . . . " He sighed. "I don't know."

That was not what she'd expected him to say. "What don't you know?" she asked. "I had no idea this was such a huge problem. The question is, how do we address it?" She looked to his Ustin for support, but Ustin didn't speak. The manservant's mark arched across her pale forehead like the bars of a closed gate.

"No, Selemei," Xeref said. "We can't address it."

"Why not?"

He rubbed his forehead. "This is a legislative proposal, which will be discussed and voted on by the cabinet. We can't lose sight of that. Proposals with divided goals fail, even when their goals are entirely ordinary. And . . . I really don't want this one to fail."

Oh, gods, if it failed! She gulped a breath. "I need to sit down."

"I'm sorry, love," said Xeref. "By all means."

Grivi was swift to deliver one of the metal chairs that faced Xeref's desk; Selemei sat with relief and tried to gather her thoughts. This proposal no longer felt like it was about her, but about Ryoe, Lienne, and Keir—and about her own daughters. To fail would be a disaster. But what if they succeeded, and the law were meaningless to those who most needed it?

"Ladies are vulnerable," she said quietly.

"You're right," Xeref agreed. He took the other chair, which Ustin brought for him. "As Lady Indelis was vulnerable."

"Or as I was," she said. "In a medical center, helpless to the wishes of doctors and family."

He shook his head. "I'm sorry."

"I'm not angry," she assured him. "But some ladies are also vulnerable at home. And we can't send Arissen into bedrooms to enforce this law." The very idea was appalling.

"Imbati are already there," Xeref mused. "But we don't want to put such power in the Imbati, either."

She raised her eyebrows at him. "Dear, it's hardly a reasonable demand on them, even if we did."

"True."

Selemei ran her eyes about the office as if the answer might be hiding here somewhere, hanging among Xeref's numerous certificates or tucked between the law books on his shelves.

"Wait," she said, "even if we can't do anything about the gentlemen, this proposal aims to prevent dangerous pregnancies. So, what about the medicines?" What had that Kartunnen mentioned at the party? Amb—something . . .

Xeref looked like she'd stuck him with a pin. "Those are illegal."

"So? We're proposing a new law, aren't we?"

"A gentleman would never consent to compromise his fertility."

"*I* would, if it meant I were never put at risk again."

He blinked at her. "You would?"

"Isn't that what we already decided?"

Xeref didn't answer, but shook his head in consternation. Then, beside her left ear, Grivi rumbled in his throat.

"Yes, Grivi?"

"Mistress, you should be aware that contraceptive medications, when properly used, have no permanent effect on fertility."

"Well. All right, then."

"Even for Grobal?" Xeref asked.

"I know of no genetic contraindications, sir," said Grivi.

"I'm just not sure anyone would agree to it. Could one really ask a man to waste his value to the Race?" Xeref frowned at the floor, and began cracking his knuckles, one after the other.

She realized, then. He was frightened. "Dear—what if we tried it?"

He twitched, and shook his head. "You're suggesting—no. I could never ask my Ustin to procure something illegally."

"Master," said Ustin, "I can procure something for myself with perfect legality."

That was it! Ustin was a woman, and would have done this before. Then all *she'd* have to do was get her hands on it, and then . . .

Selemei put her hand over Xeref's and squeezed. "Think of it."

The triangular white pill was small, almost indistinguishable from the marble of the bathroom counter. Selemei forced herself to see it, to confront it, to confront what she had to do. Grivi's unwillingness to aid her in any aspect of the medication only magnified her sense of transgression. After seven days, it had become no easier.

I am not harming anyone. I'm doing this for Enzyel, for Aven, for Pelli—and for myself. The Kartunnen have deemed it safe. Imbati Ustin herself has used this. A Grobal is not so different from a Lower that it will affect me differently. It is not harming me.

It is not harming me.

She swept it up and swallowed it before she could lose her nerve.

That was it.

She chased it down with an extra glass of water just to be sure. Her body had been feeling a little different, but that could have been her mind's suggestion. Stripped of the magic that younger women had always begged her to imbue them with, she felt . . .

Don't say hollow. I'm more than that. I've already contributed five healthy children to the Race.

Her triumphs were written in her body, where no one could take them away. Pale ripples in the skin of her belly and hips proved she had received Elinda's gift, that she could grow like the moon to nurture souls. Her breasts had earned their delicious softness with each precious suckling touch.

She raised her head and looked her reflection in the eye. *And now you've contributed to the content of a legislative proposal, so what do you think of that?*

A strange light crept over her face from beneath, turning its features unfamiliar. Selemei glanced down; a wysp had entered the room, and now turned circles beside her knee. She smiled at it.

The wysp understood. But she was going to do this anyway.

She raised both hands over her head, allowing Grivi to slip the sleeves of her silk robe over them. Then she closed the robe and took his hand to walk out to the bedroom where Xeref was waiting.

Xeref pushed up on one elbow at the sight of her. His worry-wrinkles were deeper than usual—he looked even more concerned than he had yesterday, if that was possible. She allowed Grivi to seat her on the edge of the bed; once Grivi vanished under his curtain, she took a deep breath.

"I'm all right, Xeref," she said. And told her body silently, *you are all right; show him.* She pulled her legs up on the bed and beckoned. Xeref moved close to her side, and put his arm around her shoulders. His warmth, his stability, his soft silver hair faintly scented with perfume . . . simultaneous waves of nostalgia and longing crashed together inside her, brimming in her eyes and stealing her breath. She leaned into him.

"I've missed you so," Xeref said.

All she could manage was a nod.

"It was harder to wait this time."

Hardest to wait when that wait might never end. She nodded into the crook of his neck and shoulder. She could feel his soft-furred, warm skin against her side, against her breast. She reached for his arm and stroked it from elbow to fingers, found the outer edge of his hand and squeezed it as hard as she could.

"Xeref, I didn't mean to push you away. I mean—I didn't want you *gone*, I just was so scared to—"

The words brought back the reality of what they were attempting. She jerked back and found him staring at her in dismay. So he'd arrived at the very same thought. She blew out a breath between her lips. Carefully, carefully.

"We're not doing this for politics. I—*I'm* not doing this for politics." The words sounded false.

Xeref seemed to crumple in on himself. "Nobody could possibly agree to this," he muttered. "Why did I ever make you—?"

"You didn't *make* me; I convinced you. And Ustin helped me."

He glanced toward the service curtain on his side of the bed, and heaved a sigh.

"Please don't blame her," Selemei said.

Xeref shook his head. "I don't, really. She does her job well. Too well, some might say."

"There's no such thing as an Imbati who serves too well." Selemei shrugged. "This is the only possible solution to our problem. And for her, this isn't political; it's normal."

"We aren't like them," Xeref said sadly. "Fevers that kill Grobal scarcely touch them. Who's to say you haven't done something terrible with this medicine, and will never conceive a child again?"

"But I don't want to conceive a child again."

"Ha!" The laugh burst from him all at once, like a bark.

Her face burned. "Xeref, I thought we agreed!"

"No, Sirin and Eyn, I'm so sorry. We do; of course we do. It's just, hearing you say it . . . " He rubbed his face with both hands. "I wish there were a way for this to be normal for us."

"Passing the law would make it normal. Except we can't pass the law until we try this. It's normal for Lowers . . . " A thought struck her suddenly. "What if we were Lowers?"

"You're not serious."

Impetuously, she tossed her bathrobe back from her shoulders. "We're both naked. Who's to say we haven't just set our marks aside? We could be Arissen—Residence guards, who've shed their castemark color."

He raised his eyebrows skeptically. "I can't imagine anything less romantic."

"Not guards, then. What if we were Kartunnen? I'm a dancer." She shimmied a little and ran her hands down the curve of her breasts and belly. "And you're a . . . "

"Hm-mm." That sound was still skeptical, but there was something of a chuckle hidden in it, too. "No; I can't."

She huffed at him. "Oh, come on. You're . . . you're my accompanist. And you play drums, with your feet!" She leaned over and shook one of his feet through the quilted silk. "And you play pipes of course, because you have such—" she found his hand "—marvelous—" she twined it in hers "—fingers."

He gave her a real chuckle this time, one that awoke heat in her stomach. "You're so beautiful. My Selemei."

She placed three fingers over his mouth. "I can't imagine who you're talking about."

"Someone . . . " He took a deep breath. "Uh, someone in a song."

"That's right, because we can sing, too."

"And we paint ourselves every morning. Like this." He licked one finger, and ran it over her lower lip.

Selemei pounced and caught the finger in her mouth. It didn't stay long; Xeref's mouth replaced it. Whenever her conflicting fears tried to rise up, she just kissed harder, and clutched him more tightly against her. Her leg twinged once, when he knelt between her knees, but she squirmed into a better position, and once he entered her she forgot everything but their ecstatic unity.

Xeref shifted beside her afterward, his panting gradually giving way to gentler breaths. Then he laughed. "Well. I know how to convince the cabinet to add medicine to our law."

Selemei let out a sigh, and the weight in her mind floated away. "Sirin and Eyn," she swore. "Part of me wants to do that ten times before morning. The other part of me is—a little tired."

"Tired, my love? I'm sure if I can muster a bit more energy at my age, you can, too." He stroked her face, her neck. His hand settled around her left breast. She stretched beneath his touch.

"Mm," she said. "I didn't say I couldn't." It troubled her, though, to be reminded of his sixty years. "Are we so old, Xeref?"

"I suppose we are. Does it matter?"

"I don't know. I felt old, thinking of what it meant to retire. Thinking it would be the end. But I still wanted to."

"Of course you did."

"But now—maybe it doesn't have to be." She turned her head to look into his eyes. "If you can convince them, Xeref, it doesn't have to be."

"Do you know what else doesn't have to end?" Xeref asked. His smile made her catch her breath.

Selemei breathed against his lips. "Tonight."

"Let our law pass today," Selemei murmured. "Sirin bring us luck to let it pass. Please, let it pass." Her Grivi was in the midst of fastening the buttons at the back of her gown—she'd picked feldspar-gray today, to inspire herself with the steadiness of stone. Feeling nervous wouldn't help. Only the cabinet representatives of the Great Families were allowed into the Cabinet room for the vote, but she was determined to go, even just to wait outside for the result.

"There you go, Mistress," Grivi said.

"Thank you, Grivi." She took his hand and they walked out across the private drawing room. Maybe this once, Xeref would let her walk there with him. Grivi pushed open the bronze double doors into the sitting room.

The sitting room was full of strange Imbati, all dressed in black, all marked with the crescent-cross tattoo of the Household. The vestibule curtain and the front door both stood open wide. Selemei shook her head, blinking.

"What's going on?"

Two Imbati emerged from Xeref's office, carrying something. It looked like a stretcher.

Wait, those were Xeref's feet!

"Xeref!" she cried. "Gods, what happened?"

She half-hopped, half-ran to his side, fell to her knees and grasped his hand. Pressed her lips to it, but he didn't respond.

"Please excuse us, Lady, we must get him to the Medical Center as quickly as possible."

"Oh! Yes . . . " She released Xeref's hand and scooted backward. The black-clad stretcher-bearers moved so fast that he was out the door in half a breath.

Selemei sat, panting. At last she reached up, found her Grivi's hand, and tried to stand. Her left foot caught on the hem of her gown, but he caught her when she stumbled, freed the fabric, and helped her the rest of the way up.

Arriving on her feet, she found Xeref's Ustin standing directly in front of her.

"Mistress," Ustin said. "I was attending the Master's preparations in his office. He summoned the First Houseman to send you a message, because he was concerned you would not be ready in time. Then he stood up and collapsed."

"In my witness," the First Houseman agreed.

"Heile have mercy," Selemei whispered. "Let him reach the Medical Center in time. Elinda forbear." She cast her eyes toward the front door, now shut; the sitting room, now empty of the Household emergency team. You would almost think nothing had happened.

And how could it have? If she stayed in this moment, unbreathing, unthinking, nothing would have happened.

Her body corrected her, of course; she gasped and shook herself. "I should go to him."

"Mistress."

The Imbati was still in front of her. She frowned. "What, Ustin?"

"The Master had no opportunity to record his vote for today's Cabinet meeting."

No opportunity to record his vote. She heard the sounds; missing emotional register, they resolved only slowly into meaning. Did that mean . . . their proposal might fail?

"It has to pass," she murmured.

"With your permission, Mistress, I can escort you to the Cabinet room."

She started to understand it. "So I can tell them. And then go to the Medical Center."

"Yes, Mistress."

"All right, then, let's go."

The hallway was walkable. She had to take a brief stop on the spiral staircase to the second floor, Ustin above her, Grivi behind. She gripped tight to the cold iron rail, pressed her right hand against the central stone column, and started up again. Ustin murmured to her as she emerged into the hall.

"You understand, Mistress, that because he didn't record his vote, I could not deliver it."

She nodded. "That's why I'm doing it."

Ustin hesitated a second, her lips pressed together, but then she resumed course into the central section of the Residence. Selemei kept walking. Grivi's arm beneath hers was muscular and solid.

Since the Heir's suite faced the front of the Residence, she'd always known the Cabinet chamber was down the hall toward the back of the building, but she hadn't realized it was on the left side. The bronze door was engraved with the repeating insignia of the Grobal. There should have been people here, standing in the hall—cabinet members. Shouldn't there?

"Where are they?" Selemei asked.

"I believe they have gone in, Mistress," Ustin replied. "Please be aware, Grivi and I are not permitted into the room during the meeting. You are the only one who can represent the First Family."

"Mistress," Grivi objected, in a low growl.

"I'll only be a moment, Grivi."

She let herself through the door.

All talk in the windowless room stopped immediately. So many eyes, staring at her, and all of them belonged to men. The men sitting around the big brass table. The men in the heavy portraits staring down from the walls. She recognized the man at the head of the table—that had to be the Eminence Indal, because he had a noble nose, and wore the white and gold drape of office around his shoulders. Next to him, golden-skinned and curly-haired, sat the Heir Herin—everyone agreed how handsome the Heir was. The others were strangers . . . no, here was one more she knew. Fedron, her cousin in the First Family.

Fedron stood up. "Lady Selemei, what are you doing here?"

Her voice felt tiny, as if she spoke across a crevasse. "I'm representing the First Family. Xeref—" The ground beneath her shuddered; or it could have been her legs. She found a chair to hold onto. "Xeref collapsed. They took him to the Medical Center."

"What?" cried Fedron. "When?"

She blinked at him. "Now. I came directly."

Everyone started talking at once. Several of the men leapt up from their chairs; some of them seemed angry at each other. She quickly lost sight of the Eminence and the Heir behind a clump of worried cabinet members. The portraits still stared down from the walls, but Xeref meant nothing to them. Only Cousin Fedron appeared to remember she was here.

"I'm so sorry, Cousin, you must be distraught."

"I don't have time for that. I need to be here for the vote," she explained.

Fedron cast a sideways glance, maybe looking for one of the other men. "We can't possibly vote now, under the circumstances. Perhaps when Xeref returns."

"We can't?"

"Are you unattended?"

She shook her head. "No, of course not. They're waiting outside for us to vote. We should really vote."

"Cousin, we can't vote today," Fedron said, with exaggerated patience. "The Eminence and several of the members have already left."

"They have?" She looked around. It did seem emptier than a moment ago. The Eminence really was gone. That wasn't how it was supposed to happen.

None of this was how it was supposed to happen. But now she had somewhere she needed to be. The Medical Center. Selemei took a deep breath and smoothed down her gray skirts. Cautiously, she turned back toward the engraved door and made her way through it.

In the hall, a few cabinet members were talking and arguing. Imbati Grivi and Imbati Ustin stood waiting for her. They looked all wrong—not calm at all. Grivi's tattoo was furrowed, and he cast a gaze of anger at Ustin, whose face twitched in a battle to conceal some strong emotion. Ustin managed to master herself, but then cast a glance down the hall.

"Mistress—"

Grivi stepped between them. "Ustin, that's enough!"

Startled by his ferocity, Selemei sought after the target of Ustin's furtive glance. Someone was hurrying up the corridor toward them.

"Brinx?"

Her son's handsome face was nearly unrecognizable—his eyes red, and his mouth twisted. "I can't believe you, Mother!" he shouted. "Why didn't you come find me, to tell me?! How could you come here at a time like this?"

Time shrank to a pinpoint. If he spoke again, she didn't hear it. Why hadn't she recognized the signs? Hadn't she noticed how cold Xeref's hand felt against her lips? Why had she never wondered why Ustin accompanied her here instead of staying with her master? Why had she not realized only disaster could make Imbati show emotion?

Now all the stones crashed together, and the bottom dropped out of the world.

This was obviously the funeral of an important man. The Voice of Elinda wore full priestly regalia, dark blue robes and a heavy silver moon-disc around her neck. She sang the service in a contralto of liquid grief. The Eminence Indal and the Heir were here, and every member of the cabinet, and nearly half the Pelismara Society, too, all crowded into the chapel on the Residence's second floor.

Selemei couldn't feel it. Her eyes and throat hurt, but no tears came.

All she could do was hold Aven's hand, and curl an arm around Corrim, who clung to her, muffling his sobs in her stomach. Pelli's Verrid had decided to take her for a walk when she started squirming; Brinx sat on the far side of his sister Enzyel and her Eighth Family partner because he wasn't speaking to anyone. Selemei leaned her head down against Corrim's curls, reversing the room in the corner of her eye.

A shinca tree trunk glowed silver in the back, casting eerie clarity across the gathering. Since shinca could not be removed, the stone wall would have been built around it long ago; and in this room, the ceiling had been designed with arches to look like its branches. *That* should have been the front of the room. It had been, once. She and Xeref had spoken vows to each other in the warm aura of the tree, invoking the blessed names of Sirin and Eyn. She'd imagined their partnership just as invulnerable—the illusions of a seventeen-year-old child.

"Mother," Aven whispered. "Mother."

Selemei lifted her head. The Voice of Elinda was walking toward them with arms outstretched. One golden hand held a box of precious wood; the other a basket of silver wire heaped with yellow mourning silk.

"Corrim," she murmured. "Let me stand. It's all right—please, just don't fall on the floor." He crumpled sideways, gulping back tears, and she managed to get up, though her left leg felt numb from sitting too long on the metal bench.

"May the wounds of grief become the gifts of remembrance," said the Voice.

Selemei took the box, and pulled a mourning scarf from the basket. "Thank you, Mother Elinda." The children were supposed to receive their scarves next, but actually Aven took three because Pelli was gone and Corrim wouldn't look up. While the Voice moved on to Enzyel and Brinx, Selemei helped Aven and Corrim get their scarves fastened around their arms, snug just below the elbow with the ends fluttering down.

Around her, other people began standing, but there was no hurry to go anywhere. She opened the glossy lid of the box. The sight of Xeref's name engraved on the crystal spirit globe inside brought such a tide of grief it nearly overwhelmed her, and she snapped it shut.

"Lady Selemei," said a man's voice, heavy with tears. "May Xeref take his place among the stars, and may Heile and Elinda continue to bless you and your family."

She looked up; it was Administrator Vull, holding young Pyaras by the hand. He offered her his other hand, and she took it.

"Thank you, Administrator."

"Cousin, please. Or just Vull. We have too much in common to insist on formality, don't we?"

Her breath hitched, and she closed her eyes to wrestle it back into control. "I suppose we do, Cousin."

Vull nudged his son, and Pyaras said with admirable sobriety, "I'm very very very very sorry." Then, impulsively, he hugged her.

Selemei stroked his head. "Thank you, Pyaras." The boy watched her over his shoulder as his father led him away.

There was a nudge at Selemei's elbow. She turned to find Imbati Ustin pressing a note into her hand. It read, *Do you wish to attend the next Cabinet meeting?*

She stared. "Ustin, now is really not a good time."

"Mistress," said Grivi. "I believe your daughter wishes to speak to you."

Selemei turned back and took Enzyel in her arms. The girl was taller than her, now, and still growing—oh, gods help her, that was Xeref's height, would she also inherit the defect that had led to his aneurysm?

"May Heile preserve you," she said, fervently against her daughter's shoulder. "Are you all right?"

"Oh, Mother, I think I should be asking you that question."

"I—" Trying to answer that would release the flood. She shook her head. "I love you, Enzyel. I wish you could come for dinner sometimes."

"I'll be at the dinner tonight. I'll try to come by more. And—" Enzyel leaned so close Selemei was enveloped in her cloud of curls. Her daughter's sweet breath warmed her ear. "I've got good news."

Oh, sweet Elinda, no . . .

"I'm pregnant."

Selemei's hands fisted involuntarily. She tried to say *congratulations*, but fear had cramped her guts, and what came out sounded like a sob. She fought to control herself while Enzyel's gentle hand caressed the back of her neck. "You'll—" Selemei gulped another breath. "You'll take care of yourself, won't you. Don't just rely on your Imbati. See a Kartunnen doctor at the Medical Center as well."

"I will, Mother, I promise."

Grivi murmured behind her, "Do you wish to retire, Mistress?"

Selemei nodded. She stepped carefully toward the aisle, holding Grivi's hand across the bench that had separated them. A man she didn't know stood half blocking her exit into the aisle, watching her.

"Excuse me," said Selemei.

"My condolences on your loss, Lady Selemei," the man said. "I'm Silvin of the Second Family."

"Thank you."

"But, let's face it, it could have been worse."

She could only blink at him.

"It could have been *you*. Think of the tragedy, if your great gift had been lost to the Race! You must give your Family Council my name when they suggest a new partnership for you."

Disgust knocked her back a step. Before the man uttered another word, Grivi appeared between them, looking directly into his face.

"You will excuse us, sir," he said, his deep growl all the more disturbing for its utter calm.

The man and his servant quickly backed off and vanished in the crowd rather than risk a physical confrontation. Grivi's shoulders rose once with a deep breath, and then he offered Selemei his hand again.

"Bless you, Grivi," she whispered.

"I am here to protect you, Mistress."

"Selemei! Cousin, are you all right?" That was Lady Keir, who hurried up and embraced her. "I saw what happened . . . "

She grimaced. "Fine enough."

Arbiter Erex caught up with his partner a moment later; he fanned his chest a little, breathing fast. "Cousin, I'm so sorry." He gestured to the compact Imbati woman behind him. "Please allow my Kuarmei to help escort you home."

Selemei shook her head. "It's kind of you, but I'll be fine. I have Grivi and Ustin with me, and I'll have Verrid too, soon enough." She began walking toward the exit.

"If you're sure," Erex said. "That was disgraceful behavior. In fact, my Kuarmei got his name; we'll be reporting him to his Family Council. Rest assured, you won't have to consider tunnel-hounds like him when the time comes. Someone like Administrator Vull would be a much better match."

Selemei almost stumbled. She gritted her teeth and clung to Grivi to keep going. "Come, children," she said. "It's time to go home." She would have run if she could. Her eyes burned, and she scarcely raised her eyes from the floor until they had collected Pelli and Verrid and were all the way downstairs, safe in their home vestibule, the front door shut and locked and the children dismissed to the care of the Household. "Where's Ustin?"

The tall Imbati woman presented herself with a bow.

Selemei took a deep breath. "Imbati Ustin, I know you've been concerned about securing lodging while you're considering new employment inquiries. Please feel welcome to stay in our Household."

"Thank you, Mistress."

"And in return, I'd like you to make certain I attend the next Cabinet meeting."

They were playing kuarjos, or trying to. You had to do *something* once the cousins, friends, and well-wishers left—and it helped her ignore the piles of condolence gifts that filled their private drawing room. Selemei sat across from Aven, who occasionally hiccupped to hold back tears but still had grasped the rules pretty well. When Selemei picked up an emerald-helmed warrior, Pelli snatched it from her hand and ran away giggling.

Selemei only sighed, and Pelli slowed, falling into a droop.

"Pelli, big girl, may I have that back? Bring over your puzzle if you want to play. Bring it over here next to us."

Pelli lifted the emerald-helmed warrior and stared at it.

Selemei turned her attention back to the board and pointed to a junction. "I'll put it there, whenever Pelli brings it back." She glanced over. "Please, baby."

Aven moved one of her pieces forward on a left diagonal.

"Not there," said Corrim. It was the first he'd spoken in hours. He draped himself over the back of the couch next to her. "She'll get you in entrapment. Use the inverse move instead."

Aven pulled a face at him. "Mother, what happens if a piece crosses the whole board?"

It walks right off into darkness, like at the edge of the city-caverns. Like at the end of the world. Like in my dreams. And then it has to keep going anyway. One breath, one step, in this place with no air and no light.

Pelli's soft fingers were tickling her hands. Selemei took a breath, and stroked them, and found the golden warrior had been returned, wearing a hat of twisted white paper. "Thank you, big girl. All right, so, Aven. The game changes once a warrior is able to cross the board, because—"

The vestibule curtain swished open, revealing Imbati Ustin.

"Mistress." Ustin bowed. "I apologize for the interruption. I've learned that an emergency Cabinet meeting has been called for tonight. If you wish to attend, we must hurry."

Hurry? What should I do? Selemei stood, searching the space around her for reasons to feel prepared. *I should tell the children.* "Children, I'm going to step out for a few minutes. It won't be long. Corrim, why don't you take my place at kuarjos? Pelli—" She bent and kissed her. "I love you, big girl. Be back soon, all right?"

"Mama back," Pelli answered.

Selemei searched the room again, but found only absence and grief. "Am I ready?" she asked.

Grivi offered his arm. "You are dressed for guests, Mistress. That will be perfectly appropriate."

Ustin nodded. "I'll brief you on our way."

Selemei tried to project confidence on her way to the front door so as not to alarm the children. It would be all right. Fedron would be there. She wouldn't be alone.

And she had to be there.

"Mistress," said Ustin, walking behind her right shoulder. "We must have you seated in the Cabinet room before any of the other members arrive. Can you walk faster?"

"Oh, yes." She'd been fighting the urge to run along the carpeted hall; all she needed to do was give in slightly. And hold tighter to Grivi's hand. She skipped a little, taking extra hops on her right foot.

"There are two types of votes, Mistress," said Ustin. "Procedural votes are the ones that allow cabinet business to continue. For those, simply follow your cousin Grobal Fedron's lead."

"All right."

"There are two legislative votes scheduled, so far as I know, in addition to the Indelis proposal."

"Two?" The carpet ended where the corridor gave into the Residence's central section. Selemei misstepped. Pain stabbed down the back of her left leg. "Aah!"

She hung on Grivi's arm. The pain had flashed and gone, but not gone completely; it echoed. She gritted her teeth. *This isn't going to work. Why am I even trying?*

Elinda help me, how can I not?

"Mistress," Grivi murmured, "May I carry you?"

She shook her head vigorously. "No, no. It's already bad enough—if people saw us . . . " Catching a silent exchange of looks between Ustin and Grivi, she frowned, and then realized the problem. The Cabinet chamber was upstairs. "How can I get upstairs, Ustin? I *have* to be there!"

"I have an idea," Ustin replied. "Grivi, if you both would please meet me at the door of the Household Director's office." She loped off beneath the arch into the public foyers of the central section.

"Mistress," said Grivi, slowly. "Can you walk?"

Hard to answer that question, but, "I will." She managed it by focusing on the floor. Polished stone in one room, a carpet with geometric patterns in black and green. Ancient tile in the foyer before the Hall of the Eminence, worn to white mostly, but near the walls, still showing an intricate branching design in gold. Step by step.

The Imbati Household Director kept an office just beside the main front entrance; its bronze door was uncurtained because of the frequency of messengers, and today it stood open. Ustin returned to them as they drew nearer.

"I've spoken to Assistant Director Samirya," she said, in a low voice. "We have permission. Let's take her elbows."

Grivi gave a reluctant-sounding grunt, but then Selemei found herself lifted a finger's breadth from the floor and ushered at high speed toward the door. Just as they reached it, the two Imbati turned her sideways—and they went through.

Selemei gulped. This was not Grobal territory. On a tall metal stool sat a golden-skinned woman with straight hair pulled severely back from her crescent-cross Household tattoo. She looked up from an ordinator screen full of glowing green symbols, and regarded them with a fierce unwavering gaze.

"This once, Ustin," she said.

Selemei was swept sideways again, and found herself in a tiny room with featureless metal walls, so close between Ustin and Grivi that they could not help but touch her. She clasped her hands together so as not to give offense in return.

The room lifted.

Selemei gasped. "An elevator?"

"It's for messengers," Grivi rumbled.

"And emergencies," added Ustin. "I just hope we'll be in time."

Perhaps this brief respite had been just what she needed, because her leg took her weight better when she tested it. Here on the second floor, the open entrance of the elevator was covered with a curtain. Ustin stepped out, but swiftly ducked back in again.

"Gro—people in the hall, Grivi," she said. "Let's cross, while we still have Samirya's permission."

"Cross?" Selemei asked. She leaned on Grivi to enter the main hallway. Over there, beneath the arches, stood the cluster of men in question; strangers from other Families, with their Imbati. Even this far off, their raised voices sounded aggressive.

"Cabinet members, but they're still attended," said Ustin. "I'm guessing we have maybe three minutes before they go in."

Again the two Imbati lifted her by the elbows, sweeping her across the hall, where Ustin lifted a curtain and let them through a door. Here the corridor was narrow and dim, and Grivi could only support her from behind. She tried to hurry, in spite of the risk. She didn't belong here. What argument could Ustin possibly have used to justify allowing a Higher like her into the servants' Maze?

Around a corner to the right was more light, through a series of windows on the left side. She gratefully used their stone sills to support herself, and then a door opened on her right.

She could feel eyes staring down at her as she entered—but they were only the painted eyes of dead Eminences. The room was empty.

Ustin and Grivi helped her ensconce herself in one of the tall-backed brass chairs. Xeref's chair. It had none of his warmth or softness.

"Mistress." Ustin pressed a paper into her hand. "These are the votes you will need to cast. The most important thing is, you must say you occupy this seat for the First Family."

"I'm representing the First Family."

"Mistress, if you will: I occupy this seat . . . "

"I occupy this seat for the First—"

Click.

Ustin's gaze snapped to the main door. Faster than the turning handle, she leapt to the Maze door and disappeared.

Selemei's heart flipped; she tried to swallow it back into place and keep breathing. Three men walked in, conversing, then a fourth. The fifth man was first to notice her. He was broad-bodied, golden-skinned, and bald as a stone.

"Hello?" That single word filled the chamber. "What are you doing here?"

She thought of Imbati Ustin. "I occupy this seat for the First Family."

Now the others saw her. "What?" "Who—wait, wasn't she the lady who . . . ?" "Xeref's partner?" "What in Varin's name is she doing?"

"I occupy this seat for the First Family."

"I'm sorry, Lady, you're going to have to leave," said the bald man.

She grabbed the lower edges of the chair, winding her fingers through gaps in the brass. "I occupy this seat for the First Family."

They were talking about her, now, and more of them poured in every second. She couldn't see Fedron.

"Can we have her removed?" "But, I mean, the poor thing—" "This can't be serious." "She'll go soon enough."

"What's this?" asked the Eminence Indal. He leaned on a cane of rich dark wood. His manservant, a single figure in black silk against the jewel colors of the other men, murmured in his ear while they went to the head of the table. "What's this?" He sniffed through his noble nose and shifted his white and gold drape as he sat. And looked right at her.

Selemei lost her breath.

"No problem, your Eminence." The Heir waved his golden hand magnanimously. "She's just grieving, we can ignore her."

"But, cabinet business," objected a man with bulging eyes.

"Our main point of business is the empty seat." That was the bald man's resonant voice. "That is why Speaker Orn pressured us to convene this meeting at such short notice."

Selemei closed her fists tighter, until the brass hurt her fingers. "I occupy—"

Fedron burst in the door with a desperate look on his face.

"—this seat for the First Family."

Fedron gaped at her, panting. "Wh—Selemei? Cousin?"

Somehow his presence stopped the words up in her throat. She shoved them out. "I occupy. This seat. For the First Family."

Fedron deflated, and fell into the chair beside her. "Well, hand of Sirin . . . "

"We should just get started," someone said.

The Manservant to the Eminence struck reciting stance, his clear baritone cutting through any further murmurs of objection. "I call to order this meeting of the Pelismar Cabinet, and serve as a reminder of the Grobal Trust: giving to each according to need, the hand of the Grobal shall guide the eight cities of Varin."

"So noted," said a red-faced man sitting at the Eminence's right. "First order of business, acknowledgment and certification of the empty seat. Which *is* empty, in spite of appearances."

Selemei took a breath, but it was no use; hopeless certainty stole the words from her tongue. It was just as they'd said: they were ignoring her. While the men leaned forward to press buttons below the personal ordinator screens embedded in the table before them, her own screen—Xeref's screen—was dead.

Dead love, dead hopes.

The Manservant to the Eminence pulled a small device from his pocket, bowed, and intoned, "A unanimous vote is required to certify an empty seat. I count one vote in dissent. The seat remains occupied by the First Family."

"Wait, now," said the man with the bulging eyes. "Fourteen to one? Fedron, you're not serious."

Fedron folded his arms. "Does that seat look empty to you?"

Selemei looked at her cousin, but he didn't meet her gaze.

The red-faced man beside the Eminence gave a noisy sigh. "The seat remains occupied in the presence of a *legitimate* substitute. Indal's Jex, you'll carry the cabinet's petition to the Arbiter of the First Family Council to investigate the legitimacy of the substitute."

The Manservant to the Eminence bowed. No animosity on his face, but Imbati only showed feelings when they meant to—unlike the other cabinet members, who scowled and scowled while Fedron continued to avoid looking at her. Only the bald man with the big voice held pity in his face. They all argued about one topic after another. It went on so long that Selemei's fingers cramped around the curled brass of her chair; she had to extricate them painfully and rub them together in her lap. She combed through the men's portentous words for the Indelis proposal, but in vain. The paper Ustin had given her proved useless, for the voting screen before her remained blank.

"Right," declared the big-voiced man at last, "if there is no further business, the meeting shall adjourn."

"Seconded."

Selemei's heart shrank; she didn't dare protest into the silence that followed.

The Manservant to the Eminence bowed again, and intoned, "So it shall be. This meeting is adjourned."

If the last two years hadn't trained her to move slowly, she might have tried to run from the room. Selemei stood, and pushed back her chair, swallowing grief.

"That was some nerve," said a man somewhere to her left. "Get back to your children."

She dropped her gaze, but her cheeks blazed. She watched the placement of her feet, moving out from between the chairs.

"Lady—Selemei, is it?" When she looked up, the Heir was staring down at her. His face was young, handsome, chill as gold.

"Yes."

"You realize we've given you a gift." As he spoke, he stepped closer, looming over her.

She shook her head.

"Our *patience*, in the name of your bereavement. You know there are *other* ways to respond when someone disrupts cabinet business."

Mai help her—would he lay hands on her? Selemei took a nervous step backward.

Her left leg collapsed. She grasped for the nearest chair, felt fingers slip on the unkind brass, knocked her elbow, and hit the floor, the chair nearly coming down on top of her. She sat, immobilized by pain and shame while the Heir walked away without a backward glance. Gulps of air kept her from sobbing but couldn't stop tears creeping onto her cheeks.

"Cousin?" Fedron crouched beside her. "Let me help you up."

She nodded. Pretended this was just a room, not a room full of eyes and sneers. Gritting her teeth, she got her right leg under her. With Fedron's help, she managed to stand, and limp to the door where the manservants were waiting.

"Grivi," she said the moment she saw him, "I'll need you to make an appointment with that doctor. The one who was at Vull's."

Grivi interposed himself beneath her arm with a murmur of thanks for Fedron and a cutting glance for Ustin.

"Let me walk you home," Fedron said.

She hadn't expected that. They moved slowly, at her limping pace. But a bigger surprise came in the spiral staircase, where Fedron allowed his manservant to pass him and turned to face her.

"I'm grateful to you, Cousin," he said.

"What?" Grateful! Had she heard him right?

"Sure, you were misguided, but that was a big favor you tried to do for the Family. Someone overheard that we were inviting Garr back from Selimna to claim the seat at the next scheduled meeting, so they convened this one early. You know, to certify it empty before he could get here."

She couldn't tell whether to be flattered or insulted, and ended up mostly confused. "Garr and Tamelera are coming back?"

Fedron rubbed his hand across his forehead. "Well, I'm afraid it's not so straightforward at this point."

"What happened to the Indelis proposal?"

A strange expression flashed across his face. "Don't you worry about that."

How many times had she been told not to worry? "I *do* worry about it, Cousin. That's why I was there."

"Let me talk to Erex first, all right? And then we'll discuss it."

We'd better. But she was too exhausted and hurt to argue. She needed Aven; she needed Pelli, and Corrim. Just to hold them, and cry, with no eyes watching.

Selemei screamed and woke. A nightmare, not of wandering in darkness this time, but of standing exposed in sunlight, under the judging eyes of Father Varin himself. She panted while her heart slowed, rubbing her coverlet to remind her hands of soft silk and reality. Her body came into focus.

Everything hurts.

Each bruise that woke to identify itself roused another horrible memory of the Cabinet meeting. She couldn't force those events into sense, no matter how many times she tried. She called, "Ustin?"

The Imbati woman didn't appear. But then, she probably wasn't expecting to be called, because . . . Selemei's throat closed. She looked away from the place where Xeref should have lain. Deliberately, she rearranged her pillows and pushed herself back to sit. Mercy, it hurt . . . but how much worse might it have been without Grivi's care? She tried again, though her voice quavered.

"Imbati Ustin, may I speak with you?"

Ustin emerged this time, so silently she might have come, wysp-like, straight through the wall. She wore a black silk dress that showed off her muscular shoulders, not the suit she had normally worn on duty. "Mistress?"

This was already all wrong. "I'm very sorry," Selemei said. "It's not fair of me to demand you call me Mistress now, is it?"

Ustin bowed; a single pale braid swung forward of her shoulder. "Lady Selemei."

Selemei inhaled what calm she could manage. "I went to the Cabinet meeting, but it went so badly—I wonder if I might discuss it with you." Ustin's sober silence felt like disapproval, though her face didn't change. "If you consent to advise me, I'll pay you for your time."

"I am willing, Lady," Ustin replied. "Unfortunately, I have a very incomplete picture of what happened, having been limited to what Grobal Fedron told us, and what I could overhear from other members leaving."

"Well . . . we can start with what Fedron said. He said the meeting was called in emergency because Garr and Tamelera were coming back from Selimna. How would *they* have anything to do with anything?"

"Lady, are you aware that the seat my Master held was at-large?"

The term wasn't entirely unfamiliar. "I'd heard that. It means he's—" She gulped down a pang. "—he was, not the only First Family cabinet member."

"Yes, Lady. Each of the twelve Great Families is assigned a single inalienable seat. Beyond that, only two seats remain. In those, any Family's representative may sit."

"But we happened to hold it." She closed fists, remembering her fingers tangled in the chair. "And they wanted to declare it empty, but I was sitting in it." Another piece fell into its slot. "*That's* what Cousin Garr was supposed to do—sit in the seat so Fedron wouldn't have to admit it was empty."

"Lady," Ustin said, "I'm sure you know that any competition among twelve Families for a single empty seat would be fierce."

That was an understatement. Selemei nodded. "The cabinet rushed to meet so that Garr would come too late—and they would all have been itching to fight one another—but then I was there. They tried to pretend I wasn't—except Fedron said I was. Why would he . . . ?" She patted down the question with both hands. "No, of *course* he would. He had to have been in a panic when he thought they'd outmaneuvered him." That face he'd made, arriving in the seat beside her . . .

The corner of Ustin's mouth twitched slightly upward. Selemei chose to interpret that as approval.

"But I still don't see how any of this has anything to do with the Indelis proposal. I was *listening*. It was never even mentioned."

A shadow of something strangely like sadness flitted across Ustin's face. "Lady, no vote can occur if a proposal has no sponsor."

The men didn't care. Not even Fedron had sustained his sponsorship once tragedy struck. "I could have sponsored it, if I'd known," she said. "I thought I was there to cast his vote. But that's why you brought me, as a sponsor. Is it?"

Ustin didn't immediately respond. Selemei braced herself for *I don't know*, but then the Imbati answered, "Lady, you recall we were jointly involved in a conversation about the seriousness of the risks Grobal ladies face. I continue to share my Master's belief in the proposal's benefits for ladies and their children."

For me. And for my children. Without a law to protect her, she'd have men approaching her constantly; and how could she refuse to entertain partnership arrangements that the Family Council might propose?

"I could still sponsor it," she said. "Fedron *has* acknowledged me in the seat." Only once the words were out did their shuddering import take shape. *To do that, I would have to claim to be a legitimate cabinet member.* It perfectly explained Fedron's ambivalence. "The Family still wants Garr there."

Ustin nodded. "Lady, we can be certain of that. Grobal Garr is a man of influence, and was the First Family Council's choice of substitute. However, the Cabinet bylaws which allow a Family to provide a substitute imply that said substitute shall then fill the seat on a permanent basis."

"They imply . . . ? Gnash it, Ustin—that's why the Eminence is sending his man to the First Family Council. He thinks I've claimed the seat!"

Ustin's face remained impassive. "Technically, Lady, you have."

"And that's why Fedron wants to talk to Erex. Maybe I saved the seat, but I just delayed their problem! And then I fell down, and embarrassed myself in front of everyone . . . "

That seemed to startle Ustin. "Lady, you fell? I'm sorry."

The shame flooded back. Selemei pressed her hands to her face, shaking her head. "If I hadn't had to rush there—or if I'd just been holding onto something—"

"The Luck-bringer's hand is not always kind."

Her mother had often said so. Selemei instinctively raised her head for the traditional response. "But Blessed Sirin sees far, and does not explain his choices." She sighed. "That's why my Grivi will be taking me to the Medical Center today."

As if recognizing her need, Grivi stepped out from beneath his curtain and bowed respectfully.

"Good morning, Mistress. Allow me to dress you for your appointment?"

"Yes, thank you, Grivi. Ustin, you may be excused. Thank you for your help."

The Imbati woman bowed and withdrew.

"Mistress," Grivi said gruffly, "if you wish Ustin to advise you, perhaps you should inquire."

"But I did; I asked her in," Selemei said. "I did offer to pay her."

Grivi looked down at his hands silently for several seconds. At last he said, "Mistress, I believe you requested to see Doctor Kartunnen Wint, who confirmed Grobal Pyaras at his party?"

"Yes . . . "

"Please be aware that we'll have to go a little farther than the Medical Center for your appointment."

"Oh. All right." Vull kept a doctor outside the Medical Center? But perhaps Wint was worth it; she certainly had made an impression at the party.

After she was dressed and had eaten breakfast with the family, Selemei assured the children she'd be home soon—with extra kisses for Aven and Pelli—and she and Grivi walked across the gravel paths of the Residence gardens to the Conveyor's Hall. Selemei winced with every step. Thirty-seven should have been too young to walk like an old woman. It should have been too young to be widowed, too. Her former self dragged at her—the Selemei who had run and hidden behind that carefully tended hedge on her right, joined by a handsome man who gently kissed her amid the voluptuous scent of imported surface soil. It made her too conscious of the effort Grivi must be expending to keep her steady, to keep her moving. And conscious, too, of strange glances he cast toward her.

Was he unhappy?

She watched him. In the Conveyor's Hall, Grivi seated her in a chair by the stone wall. He left the green-carpeted reception zone, crossing the road that passed under the Hall's massive entrance arch and ended against the wall to her left. The zone beyond was crowded with vehicles of varying sizes; Grivi procured a one-passenger skimmer from the Household staff, and adjusted its control column to upright for a standing driver. Then he came and fetched her to it, slowing attentively at the spot where carpet met stone. He was always thoughtful—he didn't engage the skimmer's repulsion until she was fully settled. If he had some complaint, she couldn't detect it.

Driving felt quite normal. The skimmer hummed; the cool wind of their passage refreshed her; and outside the gate of the Residence grounds, broad circumferences busy with vehicles and colorful Lower pedestrians made a pleasant distraction. Grivi accelerated up a steep rampway of reinforced limestone that lifted them above slate roofs, and through the bore to the fourth level.

In this neighborhood, the cavern roof hung much lower. Grivi turned their skimmer into an outbound radius, and then into a circumference where the building façades formed a continuous wall on either side. The road ended against a melted limestone column as broad as a storefront. Above the roofs of the buildings, the slope of another level rampway was visible, passing up and behind the column's ancient mass. Grivi brought the skimmer to a stop. Its hum faded, and it sank to rest on the stone. The front wall of their destination had high oblong windows and bore chrome script identifying doctors Wint, Albar, and Sedmin. A bright globe lamp, green as the sphere of Heile, goddess of health, hung above glass front doors.

Selemei took Grivi's arm, passing a pair of wysps that drifted along the sidewalk, and entered through the glass doors that parted before them.

The crowd in the room within plunged into silence. Only a small boy with the castemark necklace of a Melumalai merchant continued to run in circles until he nearly tripped over Grivi's feet, then looked up and bawled in terror. His father rushed up, gaped helplessly at Selemei for a second, then turned to Grivi and blurted, "May your honorable service earn its just reward, Imbati, sir," before scooping the boy up and hiding behind a large group of thick-belted Venorai. The Venorai had the look of farmers—all were muscular, with striking sun-marked skin. One older man looked bright red, and a couple young women were covered with brown spots, and the rest were solid brown—they were all embracing each other, and she couldn't guess which one was here to see a doctor. Maybe the red one?

An inner door opened. Two Kartunnen men emerged: both wore green lip-paint and gray medical coats. The taller of them made a deferent approach to two Imbati mothers and their child; the shorter one came up to Selemei, and bowed.

"Lady Selemei, if you will please follow me." He made a second bow to Grivi, but did not greet him. He led the two of them back through the door, paused a moment to key a sequence on a wall panel, then took them down a long bare hall and opened a numbered door.

Doctor Kartunnen Wint stood in the room within. Selemei recognized her instantly, though this time the style of her gray coat was more functional. She had the same red hair, tied in a knot behind her head. She bowed. "My practice is honored by your patronage, Lady Selemei."

"Doctor Wint. I was surprised not to find you at the Medical Center," Selemei admitted. "Grivi, you may undress me now."

"Yes, Mistress." He began undoing her buttons.

"Lady, I did work at the Medical Center," Wint replied. "But after the death of Lady Indelis, I couldn't bear to stay. Administrator Vull nonetheless has maintained his family's relationship with me, for which I'm grateful."

"I'm sure. That was a terrible tragedy." That Vull would continue to bring his family to her spoke eloquently for the doctor's skills. Selemei pulled her hands out of her sleeves and raised them over her head.

"May I ask what brings you here, Lady?"

"My leg. I fell yesterday." Grivi lifted the gown off her; she lost the doctor for a moment behind layers of silk. When Selemei glimpsed her again, Wint still looked inquisitive. "Well, I stepped back on it, and fell. I'd been overusing it. Pushing through pain earlier in the day. And you said, at the party, that I should see a Kartunnen therapist."

Wint blushed, and glanced at Grivi. "I did, Lady."

"So." She indicated her own body. "Please proceed."

"Lady, would you consent to lie facedown on this table?"

"Of course." With Grivi's help, she climbed up to the padded surface. The slick material was cold on her right cheek, and all down her body.

"What kind of injury was this, Lady?"

"Birth injury."

"All right, that's what I thought. How far down your leg does the pain go? Does it go below your knee?"

"Yes."

"Have you had any bowel problems or incontinence, Lady?"

"No, thank Heile."

"Fever or weight loss?"

"No."

"What forms of treatment or testing have you previously pursued, Lady?"

"Grivi, please tell her."

While Grivi explained the tests and treatment she'd received in the Medical Center and the therapies thereafter, the doctor examined her back, rear, and legs. She pressed firmly, but did manage to avoid the bruises from the fall. Then she followed that up with some kind of pricking tool.

"Thank you, Imbati, sir," Wint said, when Grivi had finished. "May your honorable service earn its just reward. Lady, can you please stand for me?"

Once she was standing, Wint asked her to lift her leg, straighten her knee, lift her big toe, and stand on her toes. It went decently. It was hard to know if she should hope to perform better or worse.

"Doctor," Selemei asked, "what do you think? Can you fix it?"

The doctor pinched her own forehead with her thumb and forefinger. "I'm afraid it's too early to say, Lady. I'd like to recommend a course of exercises, and request that you undergo further tests."

Selemei's mouth fell open in dismay. "But this is like starting over! I thought—" What *had* she thought? That Wint would have Heile's hands, to heal with a touch? That if her leg could be fixed, it would change the past? Nothing would erase the sight of her fall from the cabinet members' memories! Nothing could bring Xeref back!

The truth tried to drown her. Selemei gulped air, struggling to stay above it, and covered her face with both hands. It was dark in the space behind them, warm, and damp. She did not want to cry in front of the doctor.

Grivi said softly, "I'm here to protect you, Mistress."

Selemei swallowed hard. "Doctor," she managed, "I'd like to get dressed."

"Of course, Lady."

The layers of silk gave her a moment's privacy; she could focus on her hands and her sleeves, and speak as if this were about someone else. "Of course you'd want tests, doctor; here I am walking in, and you don't know me or my case. I'm sure Grivi could have the Medical Center send over what we've already done. I probably should resume therapy—probably never should have stopped, childish of me, really . . . "

"I'm sorry I can't do more today, Lady," the doctor said. "However, there may be one way to prevent falls while we pursue longer-term improvement. Might I suggest a cane?"

Selemei blinked at her for a few seconds. Then it occurred to her, "The Eminence Indal carries a cane."

"Does he indeed, Lady?"

"He takes it into the Cabinet meetings."

The doctor bowed. "Two doors down from here is a shop where you might be able to find something suitable."

"Thank you, Doctor. I'll look, and I'll get back to you." Grivi had finished his work at just the right moment; she took his arm.

"Thank you, Lady. I'll send you a report on what we've discussed, and a list of suggested actions."

"I'll look forward to it."

Selemei walked on Grivi's arm out through the main hall, hurrying through the waiting room so as to cause a minimum of disturbance to the Lowers there. It wasn't difficult to find the shop Doctor Wint had suggested; it was staffed by Kartunnen and carried a variety of medical devices. None of the canes here were made of wood, but that only made sense—this was not a neighborhood which could support such high prices. There was a bin of black canes, but they seemed too Imbati; another bin held aluminum canes, but they seemed too Low. Selemei scanned a glass case of artist-designed canes intended for Kartunnen until she found a graceful one which did not use Heile's green in its design.

"Purchase this one, if you would, Grivi."

Grivi looked down at his hands, clasped before his waist, and said quietly, "Mistress? Must you purchase a cane?"

"Sorry?"

"I can accompany you at parties, if you wish. Even if the rooms are crowded."

Oh, no. *That* was why he was unhappy. This morning she'd asked Ustin for advice before she even called for him. She'd asked Kartunnen Wint for medical assistance that Grivi had always provided. And now, buying a cane meant she wouldn't need him for walking, either. For the first time, she understood what he'd said—'if you wish Ustin to advise you, perhaps you should inquire.' He didn't mean *ask*; he meant *write an employment inquiry*. That was uncharacteristic sharpness for him, but now that she thought about it, he must have been upset ever since that first day, when Ustin approached her during Pelli's nap.

"I'm sorry, Grivi," she said. "You serve me well, and always have. Please don't worry; ladies don't hire gentlemen's servants."

His shoulders rose and fell with a breath. "If I may presume, Mistress."

"Please."

"Ladies don't attend Cabinet meetings either."

"That was a disaster, Grivi."

"Mistress . . . "

"If you differ, Grivi, please tell me."

"You have now attended two meetings, Mistress, more than any other lady can say. In neither case did you flee. And your persistence has won you the provisional support of the First Family's cabinet member. Your intelligence is certainly a match to Master Xeref's, a long suspicion of mine that was confirmed when you spoke to Ustin this morning. If you are to continue in this, you will need her services more than mine. But I do wish to know one thing."

His honesty was sobering, almost frightening. She whispered, "What's that?"

"Is this your wish, Mistress?" Emotion colored his voice on that phrase, and he bowed his head. "I have vowed myself to your service, vowed to make your wishes my own. And if this is your wish, so let it be. But please be sure."

How could she answer, when she wasn't sure of anything anymore, even her next footstep? "Thank you, Grivi," she said. "I don't know. I wish—I just don't know."

Grivi bowed. "If you will excuse me a moment, I'll purchase the cane."

Of course she'd been summoned before the Arbiter of the First Family Council. Of course she had. The letter delivered by Erex's Kuarmei had made her feel sick to her stomach; now she squeezed her fear into it with one sweaty hand, taking care not to hurt Grivi with the other as they walked. Selemei turned Ustin's excellent political advice over and over in her head, but there was no guarantee Erex would listen. Chances were, he'd scold her and send her home to grieve.

They reached the hallway. Erex's office was across from Fedron's; at her back, she could feel Xeref's office whispering of emptiness. She shivered, squeezed Grivi's hand, and knocked on the Arbiter's office door. The door swung silently inward.

"Lady Selemei," intoned Erex's Kuarmei from behind the door.

"Come in, Cousin." Erex stood before his desk with fingers tented against his lips. He gestured to a cushioned chair. "Please, sit down."

Gnash it. Gnash all of it. She let herself be led to the seat, and seated in it. If she hadn't feared her leg might fail her, she might have preferred to face Erex nose to nose. On the other hand, his position of Family authority lent him more magnitude than his physical size. Selemei clasped her hand tightly around her left wrist; sharp rubies pressed into her skin.

My blood is precious. The Family doesn't deserve my life.

Erex leaned back on the front edge of his desk. "I've been thinking of you and your family in this difficult time," he said. "How have you been feeling?"

She didn't trust this kindness. "I'm coping."

"And how are the children?"

She almost told him. The boys were suffering most after the loss of their parent and mentor; Xeref had been less close to the older girls, so they were less affected; while Pelli was sad, but didn't truly understand. But this was a distraction, possibly even a trap. "As well as can be expected, given the circumstances."

Erex waited. Testing her with silence. Selemei stared at her hands, at a single sparkling ruby drop that had escaped her grip, and outlasted him.

Erex cleared his throat. "Cousin, I received a messenger from the Eminence Indal yesterday. Do you know what he came to ask me?"

She nodded, but kept her eyes on the sparkling ruby, as if it were a wysp that could give her good luck.

"In fact, I was shocked," Erex said. "Indal's Jex stayed for several minutes, to pressure me into providing an immediate answer. And I might have, if I hadn't already spoken to Fedron. He told me to wait."

Selemei spoke softly. "Cousin Fedron understands the bind the First Family is in."

"He does," Erex agreed automatically. Then he twitched, as if he'd suddenly awakened. "Do *you?*"

Selemei's heart banged inside her chest. She tried to keep her breath level, and hold Ustin's advice steady in her mind. "The bind the First Family is in," she said slowly. "Yes. I understand that the Family failed to deliver its chosen substitute to a critical meeting, and that if I hadn't been there, we would no longer have any claim to the seat. At the same time, I realize it would be very difficult at this point for us to sue for permission to seat a second replacement."

The Arbiter clearly hadn't expected her to answer. He seemed flustered for a second, but then resumed his scolding. "In fact, Selemei, we could be embroiled in the courts for years because of you."

"Because of me?" she asked. "Not because the Family couldn't keep quiet about their plan to bring Cousin Garr back from Selimna?"

Erex frowned. "Who told you that?"

Ustin would have said, *I don't know*. "Isn't it public?" she asked. "Speaker Orn informed every member of the cabinet. If I hadn't attended the meeting, the Third and Fifth families would be using their connections to the Heir and the Eminence to bully their way into our seat right now." She shifted with a deep breath, readying for a risk. "And actually, there's no need for any legal dispute."

"That's where you're wrong, Cousin. Every Family has an interest in ousting us. They've wanted to see the First Family weakened for years."

Her racing heart tried to leap out her throat, but she said it. "They can't do anything if I become the First Family's cabinet member."

"You're not serious."

Selemei released her wrist and leaned forward. "Cousin, let me try. It would keep us out of legal trouble. The others in the cabinet might let me stay, because they'll think the First Family *has* been weakened." She couldn't help a bitter laugh. "Especially after I fell down in front of the Heir."

Erex stared. For a moment she thought she had reached him, but then he shook his head.

"This isn't you talking, Cousin. You know the right things to say, but you must have learned them from someone else."

Gnash it! She didn't speak the words aloud, but in her blood, anger burned with the heat of Father Varin. "I am being advised by Imbati Ustin," she said. "In precisely the same way that you are advised by your Kuarmei."

Erex glanced at his manservant. Imbati Kuarmei stood coiled and still, her face expressionless. "My Kuarmei is a gentleman's servant," Erex said. "So is Imbati Ustin."

"By tradition. But there's no law saying she can't be mine. It would be quite simple for me to compose an inquiry." And Grivi's earnestness had convinced her of one thing. "The Imbati Service Academy would witness the contract without objection."

Erex started to reply, thought better of it, then circled behind his desk and leaned one hand on it, frowning. With the other, he started flipping through a stack of thick papers.

"You understand, I'm sure, that I represent the Family, and it's my job to know what's best for you," he said. "I would expect you to know that promoting the Race must come before our personal desires. It's clear you're feeling much better, and I'm glad of that. In fact, you were always quick in recovery. We should take advantage of that, going forward."

Now she recognized the papers, and felt Varin's heat drain out of her. Gods have mercy—*those were partnership solicitations.* Elinda's gentle breath raised hairs on her neck, cold as the space between stars.

This was an entirely different fight, one in which she stood alone. Xeref could no longer claim her. The law he'd written to protect her was powerless. Nothing Ustin had said was remotely relevant—indeed, how could it be? Even Grivi, who always swore to protect her, could do nothing here. He could only wait, and hope to keep her alive after she'd already been used.

Tears pricked in her eyes. She'd been here before: sitting in just such a chair, in another office a few doors down the hall. The Arbiter of the Fourth Family Council had smiled at her paternally, indifferent to her fear of eager and powerful older men. He'd told her what Erex told her own Enzyel not long ago—what he was telling her now: that she should be grateful at the prospect of a partnership that would sever her from her parents and every cousin she had ever trusted.

There was a difference, this time. Erex wasn't sending her out. *He was trying to keep her in.*

"I still have a family, you know," she said.

Erex made a small, tight grimace, not exactly a smile. "That won't be a problem."

Selemei closed both fists. "I'm afraid it will."

"Please, Cousin. Let's be serious. These men are—"

Selemei stood up. "Yes, let's be serious. I have no partner in the First Family, and that means I'm not your cousin."

"What?"

"I belong to the Fourth Family."

Erex waved hands at her. "Selemei, you can't mean that. Your children are First Family; surely you wouldn't wish to be separated from them!"

"I don't," she agreed. "But I wouldn't be. At least, not while the suit remained—embroiled, as you say—in the courts. I imagine that could take quite a long while. I'm thirty-seven now. So many things could happen while you waste your resources on a legal fight. I could lose my fertility. I could die. I could make public statements regarding the dealings of the First Family."

To see him twitch gave her shameful pleasure.

"Or, you could set those papers aside, and write a letter to the Eminence Indal informing him that I am Xeref's legitimate replacement."

"Crown of Mai," Erex swore. He sank back into his chair, shaking his head, but he did move the pile of papers to one side, and took up a pen and a blank sheet.

Selemei watched him write without moving. "Grivi," she whispered. Grivi moved closer, though he kept a cautious distance from Erex's Kuarmei; he watched until Erex folded the paper and instructed Kuarmei to deliver it, then returned to his station behind her shoulder.

When Kuarmei had left the office, Erex sighed, "You're right in one sense: it *would* save me a great deal of trouble. It won't work, though. They'll never let you keep it."

Selemei stood up, straightened her skirts, and took Grivi's arm. "I guess we'll see."

Selemei walked by herself. Place the cane at the same time as the left foot, shift weight, then step onto the right foot and move the cane forward. She'd worked her way up—from the private drawing room to the sitting room, then the bedroom and the dining room with its chairs, until she even tried walking around Pelli's room. That proved quite the challenge, since Pelli loved the shiny cane, and danced around her making wild sounds of delight—and it gave her a confidence she hadn't expected. Her second turn around the sitting room, however, felt like procrastination. Corrim and Aven would be home from school soon, and she had to face some uncomfortable conversations.

Would Brinx be angry if she interrupted his work? Would he hate her for trying to take Xeref's place?

And how could she dismiss her Grivi, who had always stood by her, especially when she didn't know if this would last?

Click-swish: the front door. It was still too early for the children. Unless someone was ill . . . she held her breath.

"Good afternoon, Master Brinx," came the First Houseman's voice.

"Brinx!" Selemei cried. "Is everything all right?"

Brinx walked in through the vestibule curtain with a strange look on his face. "Mother, Fedron just sent me home saying I needed to talk to you. He said there was some important news for the Family, but you had to be the one to tell me."

"Oh, Brinx, treasure . . . " Adrenaline tingled through her spine, in her fingertips.

"What's going on? Are you taking a partner?"

"No, treasure, it's not that. It's a bit more—unprecedented?"

He stared at her for a second. "Unprecedented? Is that why everyone's acting so weird about this? Even Erex wouldn't say a word, and I can always get him to say *something*."

Selemei took the leap. "Treasure, I'm going to be taking your father's seat in the Cabinet meeting this afternoon, representing the First Family."

"What?"

"And Fedron and Erex will be supporting me." *I hope.*

Brinx was rarely speechless, but this time she appeared to have overwhelmed him. His attempts to respond flashed wildly across his face, one after the other. *May Sirin grant that he not conclude in anger.*

"Please understand," she said. "It's for the Indelis proposal. Your father and I designed it . . . " The words touched the unhealed wound in her heart; her voice quavered. "I couldn't bear to let Xeref's last gift to us vanish without defending it."

"Oh!" Brinx exclaimed, and his face melted. "Oh, Mother. I—yes, of course it's for Father . . . " He came close, wrapping his arms around her without another word. Under her cheek, his chest heaved. His arms tightened, and he gave a ragged gasp. The grief he'd been trying to hide burst out, powerful as the river Endro beneath the city.

"My treasure," she murmured. She closed her eyes and rubbed his back with her free hand, riding the river with him while he sobbed. When she opened them again, she discovered Aven and Corrim had come home without her noticing, and now stood by the vestibule curtain staring at them, perhaps in shock at seeing the eldest in tears. Selemei beckoned them into the embrace, and for a time they all held one another. Then she cleared her throat.

"Let's hang the globe."

Brinx released her slowly, and put his arm around Corrim. Aven took Selemei's hand. They walked together through the double-doors into the private drawing room. Here, the moon-yellow of mourning was everywhere: scarves had been draped over couches and chairs, and though the gifts had been opened, the hundreds of yellow cards that had accompanied them still hung along the stone walls. In the days since the funeral, the Household had installed a wire that dangled from the stone vault of the ceiling in one corner. Someone had also clearly been listening behind the walls just now, because no sooner had they all entered than Imbati Ustin and Imbati Grivi emerged from the master bedroom. Ustin set up a stepladder beneath the wire, while Grivi brought the globe in its wooden box, and held it out to Selemei with a bow.

"Pelli?" Selemei called. "Can you come out, big girl?"

The door to the girls' rooms opened, and Pelli trotted out with her Verrid following behind her. "Mama?"

"We're going to hang the globe for your father," Selemei explained. "It's fragile and we're going to be very careful."

"Care-ful." Pelli trotted up, and patted Selemei's skirts as softly as she did her sleeping sister, laying her cheek against the silk. She then proceeded to do the same to Brinx's leg, and to Corrim and Aven.

Selemei opened the box that Grivi still held. She extracted the globe from its padded nest, careful to protect the hook and wire attachment dangling from the top. She lifted it to her lips and kissed the engraved glass twice—once for Enzyel, and once for herself. Then she passed it to Brinx for a kiss, and he passed it to Corrim; Aven took it for herself and then held it out for Pelli, with Imbati Verrid standing attentively by.

Pelli leaned her white cheek to it and whispered, "Cold . . . "

Aven brought it back, then, but Selemei shook her head. "Thank you, darling, but I can't use the ladder. Brinx, will you hang it?"

Brinx nodded. He climbed the three steps and reached up—the globe had to be hung higher than the carven cornices, or it would not appropriately represent a star—and attached the hook and wire. The element at the center of the globe lit: dimmer than a wysp, promising neither cheer nor fortune, only a solemn, enduring reminder.

"Thank you," said Selemei. She kissed them, eldest to youngest, each one so alive, so precious, so fragile. "I'm sorry, but I need to ask you to stay out of the sitting room for a few minutes. I have to go out at four, and I'd like to speak with Grivi and Ustin in private before I go."

The two servants walked out with her. Surely they knew what this was about; surely they could see how she dreaded it. She didn't sit down, but faced them with her back to Xeref's office door. Grivi was the broader of the two, his strength evident even through his formal manservant's suit; Ustin stood out for her height, the muscles of her arms hidden inside long black sleeves. The similarity of their bodyguard stances hid the fundamental differences in training that made this conversation necessary.

"You both know what I'm going to do," Selemei said. *You know it's crazy.* "I don't know if it will work."

Ustin nodded acknowledgment; Grivi remained motionless.

"I'm going to try one more time to represent the First Family on the Eminence's Cabinet." Saying it sent a rush of cold up behind her ears. "This time they won't be confused. I won't have any benefit of the doubt. If I make any errors, or even if I don't, they may vote me out. Therefore, I would like to request that Ustin act as my manservant, just for this afternoon."

"I am willing," said Ustin. "Grivi?"

Grivi said nothing.

"I'm so sorry, Grivi," said Selemei. "I don't want to be unfair to you. You've always been faithful. You have kept me upright so many times—truthfully, you have kept me alive. But I have to try this."

Grivi's reply was barely more than a whisper. "Mistress, you witnessed my vow of service. Please understand how difficult it is for me to watch you put yourself in danger."

"I do understand. But if I let you protect me now, I won't be able to protect anyone else. This isn't just for the sake of my own life, or even my daughters' lives, but for all the ladies of the Race. I have to try to pass the Indelis proposal. This is my wish."

Grivi bowed. "So let it be, then. May I be excused?"

"Yes. I'm really sorry."

A good deal of her courage departed with him. *Just for this afternoon*, she'd said, but it still felt final; in good conscience she'd have to consent to release Grivi from his contract if he requested it, even if she failed. She walked slowly to the nearest couch and sat down, staring at the kuarjos-board without really seeing it. "I don't know how to do this, Ustin. I'm not Xeref."

"Mistress, let's focus on today," said Ustin. "You're correct in your concern: it's more than likely the cabinet will again attempt to declare the seat empty. Fedron supported you in the last vote, and I imagine he will support you again, but we can't be certain he won't have come under outside influence up to and including blackmail. For this, and for the Indelis proposal, you need to cultivate allies."

"Fedron is it, though." Selemei shook her head. "Unless he can bring allies of his own. I don't know any of the others. Who is the bald man? The one with the big voice—he was kinder than most of them."

"That is Cabinet Secretary Boros of the Second Family, Mistress. He had a cordial relationship with Master Xeref; they spoke often, and occasionally co-sponsored proposals. He would make an excellent ally. His good opinion is respected."

"What am I supposed to do, though, invite him to tea?"

"I don't believe there's time for that just now, Mistress. We should be going, so we don't have to hurry."

"All right."

Perhaps she'd practiced too much walking today. The way to the meeting felt interminable; the cane was awkward in the cramped spiral stairway. When she reached the top, Selemei realized how far they still had to go, and huffed in frustration.

"How did Xeref ever do this?"

"It's true the walking was easier for him, Mistress. But you must remember, he didn't do the job alone. He had four assistants."

She couldn't imagine having assistants. "And he had you."

"Yes, Mistress."

They passed the Heir's suite—*merciful Heile, please don't let the Heir come out and see me*—and entered the hallway. Several men stood not far ahead. Cabinet members. She was starting to recognize some of them.

"Tell me who they are, Ustin," she whispered.

"You know Secretary Boros. Behind him is Amyel of the Ninth Family, one of Master Xeref's allies. Beside him, Caredes of the Eighth Family . . . "

The men stiffened and grew quiet as they drew closer. Selemei held tighter to the handle of her cane, placed it more carefully, stepped in measured cadence with her head high. The door was just beyond them. She'd have to walk between Secretary Boros and Palimeyn of the Third Family. Palimeyn was leering at her, holding something in his hand—it looked like a glass, but he didn't hold it like a drink. Still several steps away from them, she hesitated.

"Excuse me, gentlemen."

"Good afternoon, Lady Selemei," said Boros.

Palimeyn took a single step forward.

Ustin flashed past her, and for a split second, she thought she'd attacked Palimeyn. The Third Family man grunted and stumbled backwards. His manservant feinted toward Ustin, but then backed off also.

Selemei clung to her cane, her heart pounding.

Ustin returned. She'd taken the glass; Selemei didn't like the look of its brownish contents. "My apologies, Lady."

Boros looked between her and Palimeyn, frowning. "I think we should go in," he said. "Lady Selemei, will you come with me?" He offered his elbow.

"Thank you," she said, but placed both hands on her cane until his arm dropped. Then she followed him in, noticing that Ustin still blocked Palimeyn from approaching her. It was alarming—and felt worse because Ustin had to stay behind on the threshold. Selemei ignored the staring eyes of the ancient Eminences, refusing to rush just because so many men were coming in around her, and walked steadily to Xeref's chair—*her* chair, Mai willing. Ignoring hissed insults, she leaned her cane against the table, carefully pulled the chair out, and sat down. She almost wound her hands in the chair again, but this time, folded them in her lap. She tried to barricade her ears against the whispers, and waited for Fedron to take the seat beside her.

Just stay calm. Just stay.

Fedron was late. Well after the Heir and Eminence had already been seated, he backed in the door, harried by another man who must have been yelling at him for some time. She heard only, " . . . if you know what's good for Varin and the Race!" before the man relented and went to his seat. She counted chairs—he was Fifth Family. Fedron grunted, and took the chair beside her with scarcely a glance in her direction.

"Let's get started," said red-faced Speaker Orn. The Manservant to the Eminence intoned his ceremonial speech; before the final words were fully out, the Fifth Family man stood up.

"First order of business must be the empty seat."

Fedron grasped the edge of the table with one hand. "The seat is occupied; we already voted on this in the last session."

"You're pathetic, First Family," the man retorted. "You fail to bring your substitute. You bring us—" He waved a hand at Selemei. "—this, instead. You're still trying to cling to power after the battle is already lost. Well, no one's laughing." While he spoke, his gaze never left Palimeyn of the Third Family, as if everyone else were just the audience for an impending confrontation between them.

"I agree," Palimeyn said. "Let's vote on the empty seat."

The Heir said softly, "Your Eminence?"

The Eminence sniffed through his noble nose. "I agree; we should vote."

Selemei shivered. This was entrapment, carefully planned, kuarjos-pieces precisely placed. The Heir was Third Family, and the Eminence was Fifth. Those two families and their representatives would have spent the days since the last meeting wearing down the other cabinet members. How many had been harassing Fedron? How long would he endure this for the sake of a female cousin?

"Fine," said Speaker Orn. "Cast your votes."

She couldn't watch them. These were men with years of history between them, layer upon layer of alliances and schemes, and here she'd been dropped into it blindfolded.

The Manservant to the Eminence examined his vote reporting device, and bowed. "A unanimous vote is required to certify an empty seat. I count six votes in dissent. The seat remains occupied by the First Family."

Had she heard that right? *Six?* For a split second she glimpsed the kuarjos-pattern: herself, standing upon her post with Fedron beside her; Third and Fifth Families attempting to surround them, but behind their backs, another, contrary configuration. Someone hadn't been paying attention to the rest of the board.

Fedron emitted a ridiculous sound, like a strangled giggle. He cleared his throat. "Well, I'm glad that's settled. Turn on her voting screen, please."

The square screen lit in front of her. An instant's flash of green, then black, with a green date indicator in the upper left corner. In the upper right corner, it read, *Xeref of the First Family*. Selemei stiffened, bracing for the wash of grief, but by Elinda's grace, she felt only warmth.

"Thank you," she whispered.

Selemei watched Fedron as they proceeded to business. His near eyebrow would rise, and he'd cast her a glance, then move his finger to the vote button. It wasn't difficult, though at times it was tricky to tell when a procedural vote had been called for. Slowly, her muscles unclenched. She tried to read the potential for allyship in the expressions on the men's faces, golden or pale; she counted chairs and identified the Fourth Family's cabinet member—he would be a cousin, and she should try to reach out to him, perhaps through his Lady.

Then the Seventh Family's member brought a proposal. She stared at him unabashedly, trying to remember every word he used: "Pursuant to our discussions, I move for a vote on the Selimnar Imports proposal." *Pursuant*, and *move*, those were the keys she needed. She took a deep breath, and let it out slowly.

A wysp drifted into the room, impudently, through an ancient Eminence's face.

Let your luck come to me, wysp . . .

Fedron leaned toward her. "The First Family supports the Selimnar Imports proposal," he whispered.

Selemei nodded, and pressed the correct button. She waited for the Manservant to the Eminence to make his announcement of the vote result, and said it. Blood hummed in her ears; she hoped her voice wouldn't crack.

"Pursuant to our discussions, I move for a vote on the Indelis proposal. In memory of Xeref of the First Family."

Discomfort shifted through the men. Someone down the table to her left muttered, "Varin's teeth." But many faces fell solemn at mention of Xeref, and those men might support her. One of them was bald-headed Secretary Boros.

"I'll second," said Fedron.

On the screen in front of her, the words appeared: *Indelis proposal, brought by Xeref of the First Family.*

She pressed her button in support.

For you, love.

The Manservant to the Eminence bowed. "I count four votes in support, twelve in dissent. The measure is retired."

Selemei sat, unable to breathe for several seconds. She wanted to scream, or run, but this was no longer blood in her veins—it was some awful distillation of grief and shame. The air tasted of dust.

Fedron nudged her. "Selemei. Next vote, support."

These were someone else's hands, fingers pressed to the table surface in front of her. No, they were hers, just impossible to move. *Next vote, support.* She forced one up, pressed the button. Made herself heartless, a machine to act at Fedron's instructions, while passing seconds pulled her inexorably away from the moment when it should have gone right.

No rockfall could have crushed her heart more utterly than this failure. Selemei lay exhausted on her bed, feeling its beat inside her chest, wondering why it still persisted. She'd failed to save Enzyel and Keir from the duties that would inevitably tear their bodies apart; she'd failed to save Lienne from the draining obligation that had so embittered her sister. The Race's decline ground on, loved ones were plucked away, and one day only Pyaras would remember his mother's name.

"Mistress," said Ustin quietly.

Selemei heaved a sigh. "What is it, Ustin?"

"If you permit me to hear what happened, I may be able to advise you."

The suggestion was made mildly enough, but anger flashed inside her. Selemei pushed up on one elbow. "You're always one step ahead, aren't you?" she said. "Here I've been thinking you guess what I want before I do, but really, you planned this whole thing. Why would you push me? Was it so you could wield power by being close to a cabinet member?"

Ustin replied coolly. "I have served a cabinet member already for twelve years, Mistress. My Master cannot speak for me, but I believe he would vouch for the quality of my service. For more, you would have to contact the Service Academy. I am certain they could quickly find me other employment."

Guilt quenched her anger. Of course the Service Academy would stand by Ustin's certification. And naturally someone who had been privy to the First Family's cabinet secrets would be a coveted prize for a new employer. Xeref had said *she does her job too well.* Even now, Selemei couldn't see how serving well could be a flaw.

She sat up. "My fault," she said. "I shouldn't have accused you. I remember you saying you believed in the goals of the Indelis proposal. I shouldn't be surprised that you'd want me to carry out Xeref's plan once he was gone."

Ustin's brows rose, arching her manservant's mark. "Mistress, I shall presume."

Selemei steeled herself. When Grivi had taken her in confidence, it had been shocking enough; but Ustin was a formidable weapon intended for gentlemen, her loyalty pledged to no one. "Please do."

"Mistress, the Indelis proposal was entirely your idea," Ustin said. "If you recall, I was not welcome at the confirmation party for your small cousin, but I stayed in the Maze and listened in case I was needed, and I heard what you said to the gentlemen of the First Family Council." She struck reciting stance, one hand held behind her back. "'Some of us are giving our efforts, while others are giving up our health, and others, like Lady Indelis, have given their lives. I imagine you could think of some way to protect our mothers better. Aren't you all men of importance?'"

"Mai's truth," Selemei whispered. She recognized every word, but in the Imbati's voice, they had changed from a frustrated outburst to a powerful demand. Her skin prickled.

"Especially after your act of courage in refusing further duties, your words struck Master Xeref deeply," said Ustin. "You are why he created the proposal, and why he named it for Lady Indelis. He may have put your idea into the proper language of legislation, but even then, you persisted until you approved of its terms, because you understood what would benefit the ladies of the Grobal in a way he did not."

Selemei shook her head, amazed. Intentionally or not, Ustin had just answered a question that she'd been unable to forget. "So, *that's* why you came in to find me while Pelli was sleeping. You wanted to talk to me about my courage."

Ustin looked her in the eye. "Courage is like a wysp," she said. "It moves through barriers."

"I'm sorry I couldn't move through this one," Selemei sighed. "The Indelis proposal has been retired."

"Retired," Ustin agreed solemnly, "with a vote of fourteen to one."

That wasn't right. Selemei frowned. "No; the vote was twelve to four."

Ustin's eyes widened. The corners of her mouth bent slightly upwards. But they didn't stop there; her lips parted over her teeth, and she was smiling—really, truly smiling. Selemei had only seen her Imbati nurse-escort smile once, after she'd gone to a public event at age five and been very, very good. Now, as then, it was puzzling and strangely exciting. Selemei got to her feet.

"Ustin, what is it?"

"Mistress, you won."

"I don't understand. Of course I didn't."

"Respectfully, Mistress, I differ."

Selemei stared at her. "All right, Ustin, explain."

Ustin inclined her head. "Mistress, you presented yourself before the cabinet. You claimed the at-large seat. You negotiated for and won the First Family's support. You attended today's meeting, even though Grobal Palimeyn tried to sabotage you. And in spite of cooperation between Third and Fifth families to stop you, you kept your seat and were permitted to vote."

"Ustin, I have been nothing but humiliated. The Heir knocked me down at the last meeting. Palimeyn of the Third Family would have succeeded today if you hadn't stopped him. My proposal failed miserably."

"Mistress, a man who intended to stop a threat from a rival might hire an assassin. Grobal Palimeyn only intended to throw blood on you, to force you home to change your clothes."

Her stomach lurched. "Heile have mercy."

"I can only conclude that your fall was effective in convincing them that you do not pose a real threat. Your failure to pass the proposal today has no doubt sealed that impression. Their goal was to weaken the First Family; now they believe they have succeeded. But you managed to attract three allies with no effort at all, and now you sit among them, wielding a voice and a vote." With the grace of long practice, Ustin got to her knees and bowed her tattooed forehead all the way to the floor. "Please, Lady. Accept my vow of service. I would be honored to continue to serve the First Family's cabinet member."

Selemei's heart pounded. Suddenly, everything looked different. Yes, she'd sponsored a proposal that had been retired. It had felt like the end—but maybe it didn't have to be.

With a voice and a vote, now she could negotiate laws over years. The next time she walked into a meeting, she need not be a machine. She could be a cabinet member the same way she was a mother: falling and standing up again, yet always persisting, nurturing the future.

"Thank you," she said. "I accept."

INTRO TO PROM

GENEVIEVE VALENTINE

1. Marine Biology

Jack had promised to pick her up for fishgazing, but he's late, and by the time he comes out of his house she's forgotten her promise and started counting the windows.

"Celandine," he says, quietly. Disappointed. He can always tell when she's been counting; they've had time to get used to each other.

She makes herself look at him. She smiles, smooths her hands down her skirt, swings a leg over her bike. (One hundred seventy-two dark windows—she hadn't gotten to the end of the last row, and it feels like leaving something undone, like a door's still open or water's boiling.) She pedals until her legs are shaking. Behind them, dark windows. Ahead of them, the sky.

They make good time even with the detour around Willow Square, and the fish are still feeding when they get to the hill. They leave their bikes on low ground—Mara and Robbie never come this close, it's fine—and walk on foot up the path they've worn into the grass.

Dead birds are everywhere underfoot (they kept trying to escape), and it takes a while to reach the top of the hill without stepping on the bones. Back in town, the strings of streetlights are glowing yellow; she can see her bedroom, if she turns around.

"Don't look back," Jack says. The hill's steep, and he's out of breath, and he sounds more frightened than he is.

"Coward," she says anyway, just so he'll frown at her. She likes when he's angry. Makes her feel better.

At the top of the hill they lie back in the grass. It's brittle after so long without water—even the insects won't live in it now—and it scrapes her calves, the backs of her arms, the palms of her hands when she sinks her fingers into the dirt and grips as hard as she can.

Above them, the fish swarm in darts of blue and gold and black. It's day; they glint, sometimes. Sometimes, the long thin shadow of an eel slides across the sky.

She'd thought the crack in the sky was an eel, the first time she saw it.

"Just pretend it is," Jack had told her. "Close your eyes and count to ten and try."

He'd been looking at her like he wanted to kiss her. "It helps," he'd said. Jack's a fucking idiot.

The fish move above them, never touching.

"It's bigger," she says after a while.

After a while he says, "Yeah."

It's a lie, but she keeps looking up, hoping.

When it's too dark to see anything, they go back down the hill toward the grid of lamps in Venture, through the wide dark avenue that splits the West Side from the East; their bikes are the only noise, all the way home.

For prom, Jack used the car. It was only for special occasions (gas was tough to come by), but prom counted.

Celandine had found a skirt that swished at her calves. Her hair was pinned up on one side; she'd put on lip gloss. Her shoes slid off her feet if she wasn't careful, but they were in Venture. Where was there to run?

Jack wore what he always wore, but when he smiled and opened the car door for her it made him seem more polished, somehow. Special.

The gym was strung with lights, and music trembled under their feet as they got closer. (Loud music scared the insects.) Jack reached for her, pulled back at the last second.

Mara and Robbie had already arrived, and were dancing so hard the floor was creaking. Mara, who never bothered to dress up, had a necklace made of safety pins and didn't even seem to notice they'd gotten tangled in her hair. Robbie's white button-down was soaked through. How early had they come? How long had there been music playing that Celandine hadn't heard?

Didn't matter now. She and Jack took up a position not too far away—you had to leave a little space at the beginning of the night, or it looked like you were trying too hard—and joined in.

And it was so good, in the gym with the dim strings of lights and the bass vibrating in her eardrums; the heavy swing of her body and the impact of her heels on the ground and the thin cold relief of air with every breath. She pretended there were other people. She pretended she'd never heard this music before. She danced until her shoulders ached.

Once or twice at the beginning they'd tried something else—Robbie stole Jack's bike and everyone took sides and schemed, all four of them met at the diner and tried to have a meal—but it was too much, on top of everything. Only prom worked.

Eventually, inevitably, there was a slow dance. Robbie looked at her so long it became obvious; then he came over and held out his hand.

Jack stepped back (you never fought the prom selection, that was against the rules). Celandine put her arms around Robbie's shoulders, and Robbie put his hands on her waist, and the song floated around the gym as they swayed back and forth. Behind them Jack and Mara conferred in low voices.

"How *could* you," Mara snapped during the next song, storming up to them, and Celandine perked up. She liked the dramatic ones, and only Mara really knew how to do them.

This felt like the end of the second season of MEMORIAL, KANSAS—the way Mara was standing, the mood of the song—but it was hard to tell from just the opening. Celandine tried to remember if Mara and Robbie could have seen it.

"Mara, come on, don't make a scene," Robbie said like he was reading off a card. His hands were tight on her hips; he was looking at Mara.

"Well, you could avoid a *scene* if you could keep your hands to yourself instead of ditching me on prom night. Has this been going on all year?"

"Of course not!" Celandine said. This wasn't MEMORIAL, KANSAS after all, and the surprise made her sound patently false, which was too bad. The dramatic ones were important to get right.

Robbie gasped, even more unconvincing. "Mara, please—"

"Did you know she was coming tonight? Were you planning all along to leave me for some bitch from the East Side?"

Celandine bit back a grin. She had no idea where this was going.

Behind them, Jack said, "Hey, that's my friend you're talking about."

"And you're a coward too," Mara said, too sharp suddenly, spinning to face him with an accusing finger already pointed. "This is what happens when you lie about your feelings and hide behind bullshit for years."

Jack looked like he was searching for an answer, and Celandine rolled her eyes. Mara was good at being angry, but she always lost the thread halfway through and it stopped being fun.

"Mara, please don't say such things," she said, solemn. Someone was going to save this prom. "We didn't mean for this to happen. The heart wants what the heart wants."

Mara's eyes glinted. "My heart wants you dead in a ditch. Should I do something about that?"

It felt like a punch.

"Yes," Celandine breathed.

But no one was ever serious when she wanted them to be. Mara was shaking her head; Robbie's hands were too tight; she couldn't see Jack, but she knew how he looked whenever she brought it up. She didn't know what to do now. The song was ending.

"Let's get out of here," Robbie said finally. "It's a beautiful night."

Another slow song was playing—it was only slow songs, by this hour—and Robbie slid an arm around her waist as they walked out into the cool darkness.

Jack and Mara watched them go. Usually there was some idea of how things were going to go after prom, some arc everyone had agreed on, and Celandine wondered what they'd end up doing, suddenly left to themselves. Arguing, or raiding stores, or having sex in the car, or being gloomy. They both liked all those things.

She didn't really like anything anymore. Arguing, sometimes, but Jack didn't like fighting with her and Mara was too good at it.

"You're a fool to ever leave her," she said.

Things like that sounded better on prom night. Other nights talking felt like dumping salt in her mouth, but prom night was always important, and everything she said pinned her to the moment, to the sound of beetles crunching under her shoes.

"I'm a fool to believe she'd have me," Robbie said.

"So I'm just a sub for the woman you really love?"

"No," he said. He was terrible at this. "How could anyone not want you, on a night like this?"

All the romantic shit he ever said was conditional, like he was afraid she'd catch feelings otherwise. She tried not to be offended, but they'd had enough proms by now. She'd never had a feeling yet. Honestly, he should know better.

She smiled, felt the slime of her gloss as her mouth slid away from her teeth. "Want to go look at the fish?"

He looked away. "You're an asshole," he said. He didn't let go of her waist.

They walked the long way around Willow Square and split freeze-dried ice cream, the MADE-FINE FUN TIME DINER neon sign reflecting in the package. Then they made out next to the old research complex, because the birds were still afraid of the noise it used to make when it was running, so there were no bones.

"We could go somewhere if you wanted to have sex," Robbie'd offered once, and she'd considered it—he was handsome and she was going to die, she might as well—but she preferred them here, in the dark and a little afraid.

Usually Jack picked her up in the car after, but Mara must have really stung him, because long after she was tired of making out with Robbie nobody had shown.

Finally they gave up. Robbie stepped away—"You'll be all right?" and she nodded, because what else was she going to do—and turned back to the West Side, head down. He'd never looked at the crack in the sky, after that first time. She wished she didn't want so badly to make him look.

Celandine stayed there a while, listening to the hum of the generator that was still on in the research complex, wondering what it was powering. It must be important; they'd kept it on when they left.

She walked home the long way, slowly, mindful of her shoes.

None of them crossed Willow Square. That's where the body was.

2. Civics

A few days before prom, Jack and Celandine meet Mara and Robbie outside the Made-Fine General Store, all the bird skeletons swept into a single pile out of the way, and draw lots. It's Robbie's turn.

"Okay, so I'm taking . . . " he pulls slips of paper out of the shoebox, "Celandine over, and I'll leave with . . . Jack."

Everyone nods, to seal the deal, and steps over the broken glass to shop.

(There are no limits to prom. You can shop in the General Store. You can break into empty houses. You can go to the fancy boutique in Willow Square, though none of them ever have. It's prom; prom is for the living.)

On prom night, he waits by the neutral strip in the middle of town, on the hood of his car so the bugs don't run over his boots, and looks at the ice cream shop just to have something to long for.

He grins as she rounds the corner. He likes Mara a lot, when he likes Mara.

Mara doesn't put much effort into prom, but her jacket suits her. Celandine had dressed her, once—a filmy dress someone inexplicably brought to Venture, and it had looked like Mara was emerging from the wreckage of a ship.

He'd fingered her after, because she asked and he had no reason not to get to second base with somebody, and he'd appreciated the way the fabric slipped away under his hand, but it wasn't like Mara had enjoyed it more than usual because she was in a dress. She gave it back to Celandine. He's afraid of the day Celandine will wear it, because he'll probably feel very different. He feels different about anything, when it's Celandine.

Mara's jacket is military gray, with MADE-FINE SECURITY FORCES patches. She shoves up the sleeves, always, until the music's really going and they're flapping over the tops of her fingers like puppets she's shaking to death.

She frowns. "What are you going to do when that shirt falls apart?"

"The guy had two more, I should be fine."

Then he braces. She never believes him when he says he didn't know someone, when she asks about a storefront or a suit jacket and he shrugs. She thinks everyone else in Venture got together all the time for picnics, and the things he and Celandine use must have special significance because of who they came from.

But she's quiet now; maybe she wants an easy night.

(And he didn't know everyone in Venture. He didn't even know everyone at the high school. If he had, he'd have noticed Mara and Robbie were missing.)

Mara doesn't like being inside the restaurants, so they sit on the hood of the car and eat frozen berries from a bag before they head to the gym.

They're the first ones; the lights are on and the music's going, and they take up their stations and dance.

Jack doesn't feel like he inhabits his body much anymore. Sex did that at first, but the novelty's gone. Drugs did, for a while—he went through whatever the clinic left behind, and there are a few months he doesn't remember. Detoxing had definitely made him feel like he inhabited his body, but in a way he never wants to think about again.

Dancing works, sometimes, if it's the right song and all four of them land a beat at the same time so that the floor of the gym shakes. Dancing is supposed to be what works. He tries.

Tonight he and Mara are in love; Celandine and Robbie are the friends who've been dying for this to happen, who get to hoot and make gagging noises as he and Mara slow dance. ("Like the Hollywood Hills party in TEEN SENSATION CLARA CLARK," Celandine explained. Jack had nodded. Robbie and Mara had exchanged a blank look, but the library had both seasons in hard copy, so it was fine.)

It's good to change the story sometimes. They'll all go home friends, happy and young. He's looking forward to it.

Robbie rushes them when he and Celandine get there, hugs them so close it hurts. "You fucking did it," he crows over the bass line, "you did it, I'm so proud of you, man!"

"Hey, I asked him, you be proud of ME," shouts Mara, and Jack and Robbie both laugh. A little apart, Celandine's slipping off her shoes. Her dark hair's braided back; he can see the line of her jaw.

"You kids be good," Robbie calls as he heads back to Celandine, "we have a bet going about how soon you'll get engaged, don't mess this up."

"You know I'll win," Celandine smiles, a click more subdued than she should be. She's looking right at him.

Celandine always looks at him, on prom night; it pins him into his body, just for a second, every time.

("You're fucked, then," Mara said when he told her, and he'd shrugged and looked up at the crack in the sky.)

Jack had never said a word to Celandine before the company showed up to take her out of class.

Celandine had never put a toe out of line, either. (Jack was already drinking by the time his mom brought them to Venture to give him stability.) When the Made-Fine Security Corps came for her, she marked her place in her textbook and drew a line under her notes before she stood up and went with them.

Mr. Smith hadn't said anything to stop them; he never even asked what she'd done. He'd turned to the projector and pointed at stages in the life cycle of coral. And Jack had sat through it.

Later it seemed like a nightmare that he couldn't think what to do except return to a sentence half-written, the diagram with blank ID labels that had to be filled so he could study. But he wasn't in a position to do anything, and it was easy not to ask; it was easy to be hopeless and to label fish with their names.

(Later, after it was too late, he assembled the news: Made-Fine was on trial for illegal waste dumping, had poisoned the ocean. And Venture—their bubble-city PR move, on an island, out from under American interference—wasn't a "prototype sustainable township" for marine research. This wasn't a test of the Made-Fine Transparadome protecting cities from rising water, or experiments restoring marine life. They were growing algae mats, to cast doubts on why the fish had really died. Algae is an act of God; God's allowed to kill anything.

Celandine's father and his mother and every adult in this bubble town had agreed to be here because a company asked, so they could make algae and cast doubt. And Celandine found out, and she had told everyone.)

At some point, his mother came home. He couldn't bring himself to ask any questions. It felt like giving dignity to it, to ask why, like it was a thing that could have a reason. He locked himself in his room.

A few years before Venture, his mom had taken him to an old-fashioned amusement park, and he'd ridden one of the roller-coasters (had lied about his height to get on). The opening gate they chugged through was shaped like the head of a wolf, because of some backstory he'd been too scared to listen to. He only remembered sitting at the top of the first drop, the sudden horrible understanding of how helpless he was against a machine with a will.

He waited for everyone to get penned in and shot. Surely there was an uproar on the mainland. Surely there was so much anger at the company—so much trouble coming for the guilty—that they'd have to kill everyone in Venture to keep the secret.

But the Made-Fine Security Forces never came. The government never came. No one even punished Celandine's dad for bringing classified documents home. When reporters called in for comment, Made-Fine Security took Celandine out of house arrest to the video feed in City Hall; during school, so no one would see. (He didn't know until later.)

He kept taking notes about fish names. Everyone's parents kept making algae mats. Week by week, the tide came in and never went out.

Finally, when the water was waist-high outside the dome and Made-Fine realized there was no point in a drowned city, they sent duck trucks and a company boat to evacuate them. Made-Fine employees scrambled onto the passenger loaders with half-packed suitcases, rushing to get aboard before Made-Fine sealed Venture shut and let the ocean take it back. You got a seat if you signed an NDA.

Almost everyone went. His mother went, packing up with her team into a truck with classified research in it; she looked over the crowd to make sure he was near a truck and holding a suitcase, and waved before she ducked inside.

He signed the NDA. He told the other kids in the truck they were fucking losers and he was going to ride with his mom. He told the soldier standing guard that Mr. Smith had asked him to help burn some things and he'd be going with the teachers later. Nobody stopped him as he moved past the clusters of trucks in the airlock queue.

It was chaos, but it didn't feel like it should have. It should have felt like a fight. They were being taken somewhere at the mercy of Made-Fine, and everyone was signing an agreement and getting in, because it was that or drown. A few people were screaming, horribly. They got sedated by medics and put into a separate truck. At the time he hadn't understood it.

You could hear the airlock from almost anywhere in Venture; it shook the sky as it sealed and unsealed. He locked the door to his room and turned up music as loud as he could. His courage would fail him if he heard them sealing him in. He needed to wait until there was nothing to be done.

(They never even powered down the grid. Things are starting to fail, and eventually it will just be the dark, but the company didn't even care enough to turn off the lights. Whatever Venture cost them, the company could afford.)

He thought he'd stayed behind alone—brave, somehow—until he saw Celandine under the trees near the Square.

She'd cut her hair. Her eyes were rimmed red, and her hands were shaking; she was spoiling for a fight.

"Are you fucking serious," she'd said when she saw him, like he'd masterminded the whole thing, like Made-Fine had been sending him credits on the sly for all the good work he'd been doing covering their tracks.

But it was only anger with nowhere to go. He understood. She'd wanted to die alone; now it would be harder. He thought he'd wanted that, too.

"I didn't know," he'd said, and she hit him.

He'd cataloged the bruises, after, as he was measuring out the first few rows of painkillers. A ladder along his ribs, deeper where he'd tried to twist away from her wide swings and she'd switched to uppercuts instead. One of them had just missed his kidneys, the bruise a strange green spiral across his stomach that lingered longer than any of the others. (That's the one where she broke two fingers.) One to his right eye that swelled it shut for a week. One open-handed crack right across the jaw.

That was when she screamed; the broken fingers.

The day after the fight, he'd come to her house and helped her patch them up. Too late to pretend they weren't in it together.

Nothing's felt like that since. Not good—it was the most pain he'd ever been in—but still it hadn't felt like an attack. It felt more real than any promise an adult had ever given him. It felt like something they were agreeing on. Everything was broken, and now so were they.

His mother had said the algae was going to be important for nutrition. The fish that were gone were gone; it could do them no harm now. She hollowed as she spoke, empty and fragile and wrong. The lie inhabited so much of her that once it was out, nothing was left.

Not Celandine. She looked like she'd eaten the sun. He's never believed anything so much in his life as he believed Celandine when she was hitting him.

As he bandaged her fingers that second day, she'd asked him, "Would you have stayed if you knew I was here?"

"I hope this heals right," he'd said.

He's thought about it since. He's had plenty of time. But there's no urgency to answer; it's too late, and she's a machine with a will.

3. Sports Medicine

Robbie sleeps in the pressure suit.

At first it was just practical—by the time he and Mara were free, there was the crack in the dome, and they all assumed it would all be over any day. The pressure suits were from Celandine and Jack, from emergency kits in City Hall, and every night he slid it on and slept half-sitting on the couch in his old apartment, listening for the sound of running water.

Now it seems stupid. The suit's clammy, and every morning he wakes up right where he is, exactly the same. That hasn't stopped him doing it—it's a habit that makes too much sense to break. But he knows not to tell Mara. She'd even gotten itchy about him praying, because if you got to rely on something then Birch had something to take away. Outdoor time. Your parents. Your holy book.

(She keeps her suit wadded up in her bedroom closet, the helmet on the bathroom counter, like it will prove how little she cares.)

In the morning after he's taken a shower with water that smells like algae, he checks the calendar—it's nearly prom—and looks outside.

"Something's moving in Willow Square."

"Fuck you," says Mara, around a mouthful of peanut butter.

"I'm serious," he says, watching a shadow a long way away. It could be anything.

"Well, it's not him. Celandine probably caved and went shopping."

He knows it's a lie; he knows she knows. He makes a cup of instant coffee (it also tastes like algae) and forces himself to drink the whole thing slowly before he checks outside again. Nothing's moving, now. Maybe he imagined it.

"Snap out of it before we meet them," Mara says as she gets up, but it's not unkind. She even rests a hand on the back of his head a second, fingertips pressing a little against his skull like she can hold his fears in.

She's right. There's nothing left in Willow Square to cast a shadow. Still, he looks out the window until they leave for neutral ground.

Officer Birch jumped from the clock tower of City Hall when he realized Made-Fine was never coming back for him like they promised, and he'd been keeping Mara and Robbie locked up for nothing.

(Loitering, technically, and then vandalism when Birch yanked Mara's arm and she banged into the railing. They were the only people ever put in Made-Fine's Rehabilitation Center. Turned out the operations team had threatened to go public with poor work conditions in the dome. Only four people on the team had kids. Things got quiet after they were in company custody.)

Birch never mentioned the evacuation. He said their visitation rights had been curtailed for mouthing off. When they didn't see any other staff, he said there were layoffs. Robbie still doesn't know what actually happened, that Birch cracked and told them and opened the door.

(For a while he thought the company must have had something on Birch until his mom died or something, and then he caved. But that would mean Made-Fine was still telling him anything, and Robbie doesn't think so. That day was just Birch's limit. He hasn't decided what of.)

The thing Robbie hates most about it is that after all that shit, he and Mara still had to walk outside with Birch like they'd been through something together instead of Birch happening to them every day for years.

And then outside, they actually had. They'd all stared together at the empty windows and the dead squirrels and the thousand roaches and the birds flying desperate circles, like they were a unit and not a man who had condemned two kids to die. When Celandine and Jack first saw them, they'd seen them all together. Robbie will never get that back. He'll never be totally free, so long as either of them remembers Birch.

(He used to think things like that sounded dramatic. Now he kind of needs them, just to keep track of time.)

Mara must have been thinking the same thing—she and Robbie bolted over just to get the fuck away from Officer Birch. And Celandine and Jack had looked like monsters, like people cut into the wrong film footage; he can't imagine now how scared he must have been, to run toward two strangers who were so obviously not right.

"The comms," Celandine said. Jack was already pedaling toward City Hall.

Jack's the first person Robbie ever fell in love with, because of the way he raced up the stairs of City Hall trying to save them.

Birch was looking at Celandine like she must have murdered everyone in town herself.

"I'm a Registered Corrections Officer of Made-Fine Security Services," he said, chest straightening like the company name made him bulletproof. "What's going on here?"

"The company left you to die," Celandine said.

(Mara has never forgiven Celandine. Robbie doesn't actually trust Celandine much—they make out and whatever, but he's also been to the compost pit to see if there were bodies. That silence between Birch's question and her answer was the most he's ever liked her, because at least she could tell when someone was a piece of shit.)

Birch lost it—he screamed at her to do something, and when she didn't answer right away he drew his stun gun like he could electrocute her into making the company come back.

"Look at the sky," Celandine said. Not like a dare; like she was compelling him to do it. Like she was a ghost who'd been waiting for him.

Birch must have been thinking the same thing. Still, he looked. He made a weird gurgling noise.

Robbie didn't move. Whatever it was, Birch didn't deserve to have Robbie experience it with him.

(He and Mara looked later, when they were alone. Mara cried so hard she choked and then made him promise not to tell anyone. "I won't," he said, like there was an Anyone.)

When Birch ran toward City Hall they all followed him, to see what the comms had brought up and to keep him from stun-gunning Jack.

Jack was cycling through channels, alerting for survivors in need of pickup. ("Not previously known survivors," he kept saying, and Robbie's stomach sank.) It was static on the other end of the comms the first time he cycled through. The second time it was silence.

After a few hours, Celandine said, "Do you think the water's too deep, now, anyway?"

Robbie felt the blood draining out of his fingertips.

"We don't know if there's anyone left," Jack said later, outside. They were eating. Birch had staggered off somewhere; no one had gone looking for him.

"Like, they're all dead?" Mara asked, between bites of candy bar. (They ate candy the first few days; rations but also a party.) She sounded angry they might have died, but Robbie suspected she was just angry that she'd missed it.

"The flood never stopped. They kept saying the water table would drop, but." Jack gestured at the dome over their heads; in what was apparently the midday sun, the light around them was a murky blue.

"It's too late now," Celandine said.

Robbie didn't look up.

He still hadn't looked up, the day Birch jumped from the clock tower in City Hall. The whole town was so quiet Robbie could hear two hundred bones breaking at once from where he was sitting in the kitchen eating canned peas.

Robbie and Mara had already claimed the West Side in a way that feels, now, like Mara and Celandine had decided it was something they'd need. After the noise they converged on Willow Square.

It looked like someone had made a doll of Officer Birch and stuffed it with pudding, and there was no blood, which made it worse, somehow. If there was blood everywhere then he would definitely be dead and there would be nothing anyone could do about it, but having him still whole suggested he might still be alive, and someone had to go check on him—maybe even help him.

Celandine and Jack looked at each other. Celandine called out, without really looking over, "You guys stay where you are."

Robbie, who would not have checked on Officer Birch if they'd found him on fire, stayed the fuck where he was.

Jack stepped forward. Carefully, like noise would split the body open. "Are we going to . . . bury him? A funeral?"

"No," Mara said.

Jack looked at her. "So where would he go?"

"Compost heap." She licked her teeth like she was getting rid of something. Then she left.

Robbie wanted to go with her, desperately, but he couldn't move. He was still trying to piece together the sound he'd heard with the body in front of him. One of the legs (shorter now, too short) was starting to deflate.

After a while he said, "I hope he felt it."

Celandine looked at him. Then she seemed to accept something—he didn't think she really understood anything, just accepted things—and went home.

Jack looked uncomfortably between the body and Celandine, the body and Robbie, like he genuinely wanted to make sure honors were done to the dead.

He cared so much about things, for such a long time; it's why Robbie loved him as long as he did. What else was there to do, when you were waiting to die, but love something and try to hold on?

They never went back to City Hall. The candy wrappers are still sitting there, as far as he knows.

Celandine draws for prom. She'll show up with Jack, leave with Mara.

It will be an early night—Celandine and Mara never last long—but otherwise it's a good lineup. He'd just as soon avoid Celandine. (She always wants to look at the crack in the dome. He doesn't mind kissing her, but if he thinks about it too long it's like kissing someone who's already dead.)

He looks at Mara. "You gonna shop?"

"I want the shirt you wore a few times back," she says, and he's surprised to feel the sting of not getting to go shopping with her. Then he says, "Oh cool, okay, sure," and they head back home.

He and Mara live in one house. They didn't talk about it; they just walked into a house and set up. (That was the second or third night. The first night they'd slept outside City Hall, keeping watch by turns, in air that had seemed fresh, by comparison, back then.)

At first it had seemed weird to not be closer to Celandine and Jack, but it's for the best. He and Mara have the suits. He and Mara would be leaving, when the time came. Better not to be next door when it happened.

Sometimes at the beginning, when they went shopping, Mara would put on the ugliest things she could find and strike poses like the movies that played in the jail on Saturdays. He always laughed, not even because it was funny but because he was so fucking happy not to be in there anymore that even a reminder of it was actually a reminder they were out.

Not free, though. Not until the sky falls in.

"We haven't watched a movie in a while," he says, over the crunch of beetles.

She frowns. "What's left?"

None. The only physical movies had been in the library; anything on the network is gone. They looked for things on people's computers—they'd seen the first season of THE COVE AT SUNSET, and a lot of porn that was hilarious at first and then felt like you were haunting people. By now it was a competition between things you could watch again and things that made you worry too much about time: the fish, and the slimy bloom on the south edge of the dome, and how long it's been since you thought about anyone up there as anything but dead.

After a second he says, "Let's play STREET RACE 6 with the audio from THE SISTERS OF IVORY HALL."

Mara thinks it over. "So . . . Evangeline Camden is the biker?"

"And Mr. Percy is the cop."

Mara half-smiles. "That sounds like a good movie."

It's a terrible movie. But they portion out the whiskey from somebody's apartment, and they laugh a lot, and it's something they're choosing to do because they can, and it's fine, so long as you don't look outside.

Jack's wearing the same thing he always wears, and it's a comfort. A different outfit every time makes you think about how many people left things behind; about how many proms there have been.

(Too many. They all still look the same. Somebody needs to get older.)

Showing up with Mara is just normal, so he doesn't think much about the story. He's bad at it—he tries to follow along, but it always happens too fast. If there were anyone else around to do this, no one would pick him.

Prom stuff is always best with Mara. Mara prepares with him beforehand, so he feels like he knows what he's doing. Celandine always manages to come up with something that sounds almost right but just different enough to lose him, and it moves too quickly and he ends up lost and just coasting until they can shut up and make out.

When it's his and Jack's turn to leave together, Jack likes to start the story early, leaning forward between songs to see if Robbie has ideas, his forehead shiny from sweat and his teeth white when he smiles. It's always easier, looking at Jack, to feel like he'd do whatever.

This time, "whatever" is that Jack moved away and has come back, and he's had a crush on Robbie all this time. It goes pretty well; he asks Celandine for a dance, and Jack cuts in awkwardly and Robbie pretends to be surprised Jack wants to dance with him and not Celandine, and he doesn't have to pretend he's blushing when Jack winks at him.

(He checks for Celandine once or twice later, because sometimes she gets upset if people aren't doing prom right, but she's off dancing alone, sort of empty in a way Robbie ignores. He's dancing with Jack. It's a good prom.)

They leave before Celandine and Mara can start to get weird, and Jack drives him to the park that has a few trees that died from thirst and a fountain right in the center. It went stagnant and they never fixed it. (They're all afraid to fuck with the water filtration system.) Now it's a bunch of weeds and, if you go closer, hedgehogs and birds that got desperate for water and drowned.

They stay in the car.

They make out for a while, until the crickets get going and it's impossible to think about anything. There have been proms where Robbie and Jack had sex in the back seat; Robbie kind of likes it. Sex is what you do to celebrate the bugs dying off in the winter, or to feel like someone's really listening to you.

But what Robbie aches for is his parents. Sometimes he feels he has to say something or he's going to forget them. Jack had told him about the people sedated and dragged out—those must be his parents, his parents and Mara's parents, and he wants so much to know what they looked like, just to be sure, just to know his parents didn't want to leave him. But—better not to ask.

"Last night we watched STREET RACE 6 with the audio from THE SISTERS OF IVORY HALL," he says instead, just to stop himself from saying his parents' names.

Jack grins like that's the best thing he's ever heard, says, "Show me," starts the car.

Robbie wasn't expecting that—he feels traitorous, like he always does when he mentions Mara, and then he feels stupid for saying something he knew was going to make him feel bad—but Jack's humming as he backs out.

As they're pulling away, one of the tree branches tears off the trunk and crashes onto the sidewalk.

Robbie slams his hands on the dashboard, like it's the car that's crashing. Jack lets the truck roll to a stop, so nothing jars, and Robbie eventually forces his shoulders to loosen his arms, makes his lungs push in and out.

"Maybe I just want to go home," he says, after too long.

Jack drops Robbie at the border to the West Side; he curls his hand around Robbie's knee but doesn't say anything. Venture is big enough that Robbie can watch the truck for nearly a minute before it's out of sight.

In his room, he pins the curtains closed and turns on THE SISTERS OF IVORY HALL as loud as he can, so there's no room left for the sound of a heavy branch falling.

It's the sound of the morning Birch jumped. It's the sound he hears every time Celandine mentions the crack in the dome. The sound his body will make when the water rushes in.

He sleeps in the suit.

4. Physics

Mara goes to the comm center to call all the people she'll never forgive.

Her parents, for agreeing to work here; the medical loans that had them so desperate to start with; Made-Fine. Officer Birch, whose death didn't nearly make up for what he did; Celandine, for everything, all the time.

There's no sound on the other end. At this point, the entire system groans as she starts it up, and every third or fourth time she'll get an alarm that the system doesn't have any receptors in range. Sometimes it goes dark halfway through her SOS. None of them will even know what to do when it goes; you didn't learn how to fix things until you were older, and the company was sure you could be trusted.

She respects that it even turns on. It's gonna die any day, but it's going with dignity, giving up in stages.

Mara likes machines. She wanted to join the mechanical engineering program at the high school, before she got locked up. Her parents talked about it when they visited like it was something she'd be allowed to do when she got out, which was her first clue she was never getting out.

Outside, she looks at Birch's bones.

There was a while when the whole thing was disgusting. Once she had to turn back because of the smell, and there's still a stain on the sidewalk. But the nice thing about having too many insects is that they're more than happy to take care of a corpse. Now it's just some bones inside a Made-Fine jacket. (She cannot believe this asshole was still wearing his company jacket when he jumped. Some things are fucking sad.)

For how much they all avoid it, Mara's seen each of them in Willow Square. Jack first, gripping his handlebars with white knuckles; when he saw Mara he actually started to bike over like he was going to protect her before he realized he'd have to go past the body and stopped.

Robbie came a few weeks after, at the farthest possible edge where you could still see it; she'd caught his eye, and he'd nodded. She's never mentioned it. He'd come to make sure Birch was really dead, and she doesn't think that's strange. It's important to know some people are nothing but bones.

Celandine came when the body was almost gone—the gases dispersed, the liquids dried up, the fat under the split-open skin carried off by ten thousand dutiful bugs. The streetlights were on, a waste of energy that no one did anything about because it was easier to leave this grid on than admit to being afraid of the dark. Celandine stood in the middle of the town square and looked at the body for close to an hour, never moving, even when the ants started walking across her boots.

Mara doesn't know what she was thinking. (Mara has never once known what Celandine was thinking.) Celandine never even saw her. She just stood there for an hour, and then walked home, carefully out of the puddles of light.

None of them know about the others. Mara likes that she knows more about something than everyone else, even about stupid shit that doesn't matter. Nothing matters anymore. Might as well know what's going on.

The bones are scattered now. It would look like the wind caught them, if there was any wind, but the industrial fans died early, and the air is stale and still. Mara kicked them. She'd gotten a burst of static over the comms that turned out to be another relay dying, and since it was too late to beat him to death, she settled for the bones.

Some days the only thing that gets her out of bed is knowing that whenever the sky falls in, the sea worms will suck the marrow right out of Birch's remains, and she'd hate to miss that.

Once she went all the way to the edge where the dome met the ground. The nano-sealant was creeping up—waist-high already—and had its thousands of soft gray fingers disappearing into the rocks. It had crushed some of them, pushing out the space between atoms, and she'd imagined everybody above ground slowly consumed by the gentle cloud of something that you created and couldn't stop.

She pressed her face to the glass. Outside, the worms were alive in the sand.

Robbie told her that her parents had to be drugged and dragged out, that they hadn't left her. They were probably trying to reach her on the comms—they were trying to reach her. (Or Made-Fine had killed them; just as good. If they were dead, it would explain why they hadn't come.)

It was like looking across the fields back home, if every strand of grass was waiting for a meal.

She'd never gone back. Some things felt like punishment even when no one could see.

The dome groans as she heads down the stairs—the tide must be coming in—and she makes herself look up. She's not Robbie. She has some courage.

It's day; there's a little shine to the sludge. Shadows make long slow shapes with a tail right at the end.

She can see the crack. It's bigger.

"Oh sure, fuck it," Mara says, because why not have whales, too. She hasn't seen a fucking whale in her entire life, and now there's one above the reef in whatever new ocean this is. That whole reef is going to collapse into the dome—it's going to kill hundreds of fish and all the coral that's managed to grow here and now it will probably sink a whale.

It's prom night. She's going with Jack, and honestly she's forgotten who she's leaving with.

She wishes you could show up and leave with the same person sometimes. It's prom rules that no name goes back in the box once you draw it, but eventually they'll run out of other stories. Eventually someone will have to admit they want to be with the same person all night.

(There have been so many proms. Too many. They've been here so long; they never get older.)

She's supposed to meet Jack outside the ice cream parlor. She goes to the diner instead, eats some mossy-tasting salami that looks better if you hold it up to the neon sign and two handfuls of frozen fries heated in the microwave just long enough that the edges are hot and the inside's still icy.

She wants a tomato. She'd dig someone's eye out for a tomato.

She's two servings into the freeze-dried ice cream when the rest of them find her.

"Oh thank God," Robbie says, and Celandine lets out a heavy breath, like this is one of her movie things and they were on the verge of something terrible if they didn't find her in time.

Jack just says "Mara" quietly, like he's happy to see her or like he understands, and that's what makes her stand up, that fucking tone in his voice like all of this is something she did for prom's sake—and maybe it was, she can eat frozen fries any time, maybe it was for prom's sake that she did something no one's ever done—and fuck, is that worse? Is it worse to give in without knowing it? Does it even matter if you know anything when the crack in the sky is waiting to drown you and you'll never eat a tomato again in your whole life, which feels like a fucking long time suddenly? She can't breathe.

"Why didn't you show up?" Robbie asks—stupid, stupid Robbie, who sounds like maybe she just forgot.

"Because I didn't feel like dancing when I'm going to fucking die in here," Mara snaps, her voice way too high in her own ears. She can't see anymore, her eyes are standing water and she hates all of them. Jack makes a soft noise; there's the sound of someone moving, stopping suddenly.

A beetle lands on her cheek—desperate for water—and Mara has to scrape it off and crush it.

When she blinks her eyes open again, she sees it was Robbie who stepped closer. He looks like shit. He's never going to forgive himself for that day behind the high school, the cigarette that was just illegal enough that Made-Fine had an excuse. She doesn't want him to ever forgive himself.

It's Celandine who says, "Yes, you will."

For a second, nothing else makes a sound.

Mara tries to laugh, but it doesn't take. "Soon?" she manages, trying to get acid into it and failing. Robbie makes a noise.

Celandine says, "Very soon. It will be over, I promise."

If she'd sounded earnest Mara would have punched her, but she sounds like always, like a movie you don't care about that somehow knows you don't care. The same lines play over and over until you forget what you were supposed to feel the first time. You start to laugh when the woman screams, when the monster lumbers across the stage they've set up to look like a swamp except for the one plant, forgotten, still in the pot. You owe it nothing. It's haunted by what other people love and think. You don't have to think anything. You don't have to love anything. Nothing's going to happen to you.

Celandine says, "How about next time I arrive with Mara, leave with Jack," even though she doesn't have the shoebox. No one argues. Partly, Mara's relieved to feel invisible. Partly she hates Celandine, because that's how any of this happened: someone did something, and no one argued.

After that the night's kind of over. Robbie walks next to her until Jack and Celandine are well out of sight. Then he says, "Can I?"

She nods. Not in front of the others—Robbie knows better—but she gets so hollow after she cries, and even after everything it's nice to have Robbie.

When he scoops her up, he barely misses a step, and she can drop her head to his shoulder without opening her eyes. She knows what his whole body feels like, even when they're separated. When they die she's going to miss him.

"We're not going to die," he says—she didn't realize she'd spoken. She doesn't answer. He's not a fool; he knows their chances.

She has nightmares where they make it—the pressure suits, the burst of impossible energy, the surface—and there's nothing left but the sun and the water, and they don't even know where to set out.

She says, "They left without us. We'll never get that back. Doesn't matter how far we swim."

His hands tighten around her shoulder, under her knees.

At home he helps her get into the shower. He makes instant coffee from the hoard of packets, and when she shakes her head, he drinks it himself.

He helps her into the suit, before he goes into his room. The helmet fogs up as she breathes. When he's gone, she takes it off.

5. Statistics

Before the dance, Celandine rings the bell on the West Side border next to the ice cream store. When Mara shows up, Celandine says, "Come get ready at my house."

She knows Mara will agree. Her house is nice. All the rooms in her place feel haunted—nothing you can do about that—but she keeps them pristine, because who wants to die in a gross house?

(Jack had spent the first year in different apartments, moving when he got sick of the view or the pipes stopped working. Eventually she'd admitted that seeing the light go out in his window frightened her. He'd moved in next door. There's always a lamp on.)

Mara sits at Celandine's kitchen table, frowning, and lets Celandine do her hair. It's curly, and Celandine twists loose handfuls, pinning them together into a bun at the back.

"It's just going to fall apart when I dance."

"You haven't even seen it."

"Nothing you've tried ever sticks."

Celandine sets down the copper wire she'd braided into a headband the night before. "Use paper clips, then," she says, goes into her bedroom to change.

Celandine's prom dress is a yellow coat. She took off the SPF collar—seems cruel, somehow, to keep it on.

Mara's gone outside to wait. She's wearing a flannel shirt cinched with a utility belt from the sports section, and she's stuck the headband through the off-center knot of Celandine's work. She's probably trying to apologize.

The music's booming when they got there; Celandine can hear it three blocks away. The boys are dancing, frantic. Robbie has on an oiled-canvas jacket that makes him look like a fisherman, with the sleeves shoved up to his elbows and fastened somehow, so only the body of it swings as he moves. Jack's worn what he always wears.

("I'm not going to let anything about this change me," he'd said early on, crying into his sleeves, heaving angry breaths that arched his back until it almost touched her hand.

Of course it will, she almost said, *don't be stupid*, but she didn't. This was back when she still worried a little for his feelings.)

She and Mara practically pogo into the gym. Celandine forgets to even think of a story; she has her eyes squeezed shut, plants her feet and swings her whole body in time with the music. When the slow dances start she staggers outside without quite opening her eyes, shoves her hands in the pockets of her dress, and sways back and forth in the air that always feels too cold and too damp after prom.

There's a soft groaning sound from far away.

"Jack," she says, too loud.

She keeps her eyes shut, but she feels how warm he is when he comes closer and listens.

"It's not the dome," he says. "Just the generator."

"Are you sure? Can you see it from here?"

"I'm sure."

She's trembling now. It really does get cold at night. She's relieved Jack doesn't touch her. She wants him to stand here forever, close but not touching, and lie to her about the sounds in the dark.

"Mara and Robbie left," he says after a little while. "Back when the slow dances started. You want to go home?"

"No."

"You want to dance?"

They never slow dance, but she really is cold. It's very dark tonight. "If you want."

He shrugs. "We could just go to the diner if you want somewhere else to be."

"Let's go to Willow Square."

"What?" He pulls back. "Celandine, come on. No."

"You chicken?"

"About what? Not like he's running the police station down there."

There's no reason to ever go back there. It's only that Celandine wants so badly for something to be final. She wants to look at a thing with a witness and be certain; she wants something to be over with. Anything. She wonders if Jack drove Robbie over tonight. Maybe she can lie down under the wheels.

She squeezes her eyes shut tighter, until she doesn't want that anymore.

"Let's just go," she says. "Prom's over."

He drives her home. Then he brings out a can of spray cheese and some crackers still cold from the freezer and a whole chocolate bar and some orange juice he made from concentrate. They sweep the bugs off his porch and eat, and he runs through the last season of THE COVE AT SUNSET. It was his favorite show; she likes to watch him talk about it, until he reaches the last few he ever saw. Then it's sad. No matter what had happened above ground, there were at least a few more he'd never seen.

(They're definitely not making THE COVE AT SUNSET anymore. That town is ocean now.)

After a little pause he says, "Do you want to be quiet? If not, I'll make something up."

She's wanted it to be quiet while he was talking, but now she misses it, and if she looks toward the center of town, she can see something moving.

"Let's keep going."

He coughs around his chocolate bar. Then he pulls it together.

"Okay, so, we know Susie lost the campaign for student council at the city college. We can assume this was when she decided to . . . become the Cove's first serial killer."

She keeps her eyes on his face, ignores the shadows. "No way she's the first. That Cove has been fucked up a long time. Second, minimum."

He smiles. This is his favorite game.

"Right, of course. The town's still shaken by the long-ago crime spree of the infamous . . . " he raises his eyebrows, waits.

"Seacove Slasher."

"I mean, that's fine, but it's not really descriptive. The Cove wouldn't settle for something that vague. We need more M.O."

"I don't want—" she stops. He'll know why she doesn't want any gore with her murder mysteries. "The Cabinet Killer?"

He frowns, thoughtful. "Yeah, okay—the Cabinet Killer, who killed victims in an extremely quick and painless way," he glances over for her nod, "and stuffed their bodies in pantries for the authorities to find."

"How many people did he kill?"

"Seven. Teen," he adds, when she makes an unimpressed face.

"Mm. How did they catch him?"

Jack stretches his legs down the stairs, slumps back against his propped-up arms. "Not Sheriff Daniels, obviously."

No crime in Sunset Cove had ever been solved by Sheriff Daniels, who spent most of his time talking in circles with his ex-wife, until she died; just before Venture got cut off, the show introduced his secret daughter, which didn't bode well for him solving any crimes in the future.

"Lisa Avalon," he says. Lisa had the leftover subplots—entrepreneurial housewife, amateur detective, bookstore employee pining over guest stars.

She'd be available for this. "And after the Cabinet Killer nearly got her, Derek Howard joined."

"No way. That guy doesn't have the stomach for it."

He's quiet, and she thinks maybe he's angry (her stomach turns over), but when she looks he's just smiling in the way that always makes her want to throw rocks at the dome until it caves in.

He opens his mouth to say something, then stops and looks toward the town. She freezes, just in case. There are never noises there—not like there's a breeze, and the birds are dead—but sometimes you hear phantom sounds. Can't help it. Your mind misses things even if you don't.

"So," he says. "Lisa Avalon, trying to solve the Case of the Cabinet Killer, teams up with . . . "

"Susie's dad. It's where Susie got the idea, obviously—listening to her father talk about it. She learned too much about it. Killing just made sense after that."

Jack stands up and goes inside, as fast and quiet as a dream. He'll never be angry enough to say something about what she did. He'll never blame her. He'll never give her an excuse to hate herself like she wants to.

She sits on the porch until the dark grows into the murk of morning. At some point, she falls asleep.

When she wakes up, a bird's died; near the bend in the road, well past the streetlights. That's what had made the shadows. She didn't know there still were any birds.

She screams for a little while, brushes the beetles off her coat, goes inside to shower.

The problem, she'd discovered as her father confided in her because he couldn't bear it anymore and thought she would keep the secret, was that when you felt something so much that it made your hands shake, felt it so much you did something that should have killed you, you disappeared into that feeling. Some horrible endless well of that feeling would always be waiting, heavier than you and inexhaustible.

The only way to keep going was to not care, as hard as you could, so the feeling forgot you were there. For the length of a prom you walked where you wanted without going under. All of them are dying, and there's nothing to stop it; what else was there to do but be young?

Every time she sees Jack, she's standing over the well: horrified to be caught, relieved to be back where she deserves.

Once, early on—before Robbie and Mara, just after she stopped worrying about Jack's feelings—she said, "I should kill myself." She'd stayed alive to show the company she wasn't afraid, and to make her father suffer when he made the choice they both knew he'd make. By then, some of propelling anger had burned out, and she didn't mind getting it over with. The cat that someone left behind was doing well enough with the rats (it would last another six months), but birds were starting to die, and there were more insects every month. She was a blip in an ecosystem. She might as well.

Jack had reached out like he was going to touch her. He cleared his throat a few times. Finally, when he could sound like he was playing it cool, he'd said, "And what would I do all by myself for the next fifty years?" with a queasy smile at the end like he was going to charm her into staying alive.

The crack had appeared not long after, so that was one worry out of the way.

She takes the bike path alone and lies on the brittle grass to look at the sky. The crack is bigger, but it's taking so terribly long. The land is dead under them. They're dead inside this. It feels like a hundred years; she doesn't know what's keeping it.

They have the lights on all the time. It attracts the fish. The weight of the coral reef should be speeding things up. They're a lamp on the bottom of the goddamn sea, she doesn't know what else she has to do. She needs something to be over with.

When the moment comes, she's going to fight the water. It's so embarrassing she's never said it out loud, not even to Jack. It's important not to let people attach themselves to you, if you're planning not to be around for long.

When the dome cracks and the water crashes in all at once, and Robbie and Mara are scrambling for the pressure suits that will save them from the ocean long enough to die in the sunlight, and Jack's doing whatever heroic thing he can with his last minutes, Celandine's going to be gasping for air forgetting to close her eyes and gulping salt water from screaming like a fool. Seawater's so thick, and it burns so badly if you keep your eyes open.

The clock tower at City Hall, the one Birch jumped from, strikes seven. She brushes dead grass off her prom skirt and straightens the knot of necklaces she's worn because the weight keeps reminding her to breathe.

She walks past six thousand seventy-two windows that will never light up again. She goes around Willow Square.

Robbie meets her at the diner. Prom's lifted from THE COVE AT SUNSET; Jack's been in love with Celandine a long time and has just been too afraid to say so until tonight. Mara's going to admit a crush on Robbie, and they're going to come back here, after, for ice cream.

("She likes me anyway, but the ice cream can't hurt," Robbie said when they were planning, and Celandine nodded once she realized he was serious.)

The gym's lit up—it always is—and the music is playing—it always is. Robbie rushes ahead to catch the end of a song he likes. They'll never have new music; you get attached to what's still there.

Inside, Jack and Mara call to him, and he whoops and joins in. Their thumping steps echo out into the street.

The dome is dark when she looks up; shadows on shadows, the end of everything.

She waits for a new song, because it makes a better entrance, and then she squares her shoulders and heads inside. The dome makes a soft horrible sound that doesn't matter; at prom she won't be able to hear.

A CIGARETTE BURN IN YOUR MEMORY

BO BALDER

Gouda's clients have always lost someone, even if it takes them a while to work up to it. This man has lost a daughter. His kind, round face is grooved with sadness. She likes him at once, which isn't her usual MO. "She was taken two years ago," he says. "Me and the wife had gone shopping, and when we came back, she was gone."

Gouda glances down at the information he brought, as requested. Photos, birth certificate, council registration. The latter form is curiously blank. She checks anyway.

"Where was home?"

The man stutters and it takes him several tries to answer. "Dordrecht."

"It's not on the registration."

He paws his briefcase and provides his home address. He's only lived there eighteen months. Gouda licks her lips. This is one of those strange cases she's been getting the past two years. Missing children, missing parents, missing grandparents.

"Tell me about the day she went missing," Gouda says. The man, Jansen is his name, starts talking in his monotonous, broken voice. Gouda has no children, but she now knows everything about what the loss does to parents. The past two years have been one unending stream of the bereaved.

Something must have happened two years ago. On her map, she has circled the names of cities that come up the most. Dordrecht, The Hague, Delft, Zoetermeer, Ridderkerk. If you circle them, the center of that circle is in the middle of the sea. So far, she hasn't been able to find anyone of this kind of missing person. Still the clients keep coming, maybe because she located a few ordinary runaways. It's a lot harder now that the Internet has stopped working.

" . . . And then we called her, as we always do when we're away, and the phone number didn't exist anymore. We got one of those prerecorded messages, you know?"

Gouda nods. She knows.

"How could the phone number to our own . . . " Jansen stutters, regroups. "To our house? That's just silly."

"So it was a landline?"

"What else could it be?"

Gouda wants to ask a follow-up question, but she too finds that her tongue flaps in her mouth, not knowing what to say. Her eyes drift to the baby tablet on the table, a great little device to play solitaire and Sudoku on, but nothing like a phone. No hook, no numbers.

"How old was your daughter at the time of her disappearance?"

"Sixteen."

"Old enough to leave her on her own for a night, then."

Jansen tries to say something, but nothing comes out. It's hard to talk about the missing. Everybody knows that. Evening TV is full of reality shows about the missing. And not just Dutch TV, it's happening all over the world. So if your heart aches for a child you can't quite remember, you can wallow in other people's grief all night long.

Jansen pays Gouda's retainer and leaves with a follow-up appointment in two weeks. Gouda writes up his case and adds it to her take home pile. She likes to sit in front of the TV. Her building has a working TV antenna, which makes her very popular with friends and colleagues. Before the cable stopped working she watched shows from America, mostly. They still get broadcast, but the delay has grown long. Shows have to be printed on reels, shipped across the Atlantic, recaptured on digital and broadcast via the old antenna network.

Gouda knows she has visited America once, but the weird thing is she can't remember which city she went to. But if she closes her eyes, she can hear the sirens on the streets, the honking cabs, the friendly greetings of faceless sales assistants, and the scent of hot dogs with sauerkraut. The pillows in her hotel room. Pointless stuff like that. There's just no visual to go with these sensations.

She walks home. She could take the tram but it clears her mind if she has her face in the wind for a bit. The sunset over the Amsterdam canals makes her feel that life has meaning. They are lined with houses that have stood for centuries, which have been lived in by people who gave the stairs their hollowed out look, the railings their patina. History does exist. Some people do know their parents, their childhood homes. It gives her the courage to plow on, even though she has this big gap in her memory and doesn't even know her real name, or who her parents were. She shares that with thousands of people, and that makes her believe that someday she will find out what happened that day, two years ago.

It's like there's a crater in her brain, with curling, cauterized edges, which has obliterated her memories. She probably can't get them back, burned things don't get unburned, but she would like to know what caused the impact.

No, that's not true. She wants to know about her childhood.

When she comes home she files Jansen's information while she heats yesterday's Chinese. There's many entries in the J folder. She browses through them while the microwave buzzes. They're all the same, except the date.

That's so strange. Mr. Jansen has been by many times with the same story. Gouda never finds his daughter. He pays the bill, she closes the file. And then the same things happens again and again. Is that why Jansen's unremarkable round face looks so familiar? She wonders why he keeps finding the same private detective, her, every time. The microwave pings and she puts the old files back and the new one on the table.

Gouda stands still, hands spread in a forgotten gesture. Thoughts slide away from her. The smell of food and the growling of her stomach bring her back to the present. Dinner time.

She sits down with the plate on her lap and picks up the stack of old picture books she got on the Sunday market. She opens them where she left off last evening and looks at photographs of Dutch towns. She has one memory of her childhood. An old man and an old woman walk with her at the edge of a small canal, not in Amsterdam or she would know it, and they smile at the camera.

If she looks at picture books long enough, someday she will find the town. As she turns page after brittle, yellowed page, she combats the nagging feeling that at one point she could have found out about this faster, but she can't remember how.

She almost turns the page, mechanically, before she registers the picture properly. A canal, gabled houses, but tiny, like a miniature Amsterdam. Balk, Friesland, the picture heading reads. This is it. This is her childhood memory. She strokes the shiny, heavy page. It's real. She exists. Holding the book against her face, she inhales deeply. But of course the old paper doesn't smell like the canal did in her memory. Like stagnant water, hot brick, sticky remnants of ice cream on her little chubby hand.

Gouda puts the book back on the stack, then realizes what she's doing, and puts it in a place of honor on the chimney mantle. She eyes the teetering towers of old books on the floor. Now she won't have to go through them anymore. Her Sundays are now free. But this can't be it. She needs to do more. She'll go to that place, Balk. Maybe she can find her family. Although the probability of that happening is still small, as she doesn't know their names. Maybe her grandparents were just visiting Balk on holiday. And they're probably dead by now as well.

The momentary elation evaporates. She makes a pot of tea and opens the Jansen file. She's going to sketch out a plan for tomorrow before her bedtime reading schedule. One day she'll read a book she knows already. That too, could be a clue.

Gouda retraces the route the Jansen family remembers taking to arrive in Amsterdam. She travels to Pynacker. Mr. Jansen doesn't quite remember getting on the train there, but where else could he have come from? As she gets off in Pynacker Station, she can see where the rails end in a double stop. Pynacker is a terminal station, trains cannot go through.

In front of the train station, a fan of directions greet her. Library, City Hall, shopping center. There is one little pointer that has been scratched out and stickered over so many times she can't read what it says. That must be the one that leads her to the Edge.

She buys a cup of coffee, her one indulgence today. Coffee has gotten a lot more expensive because the airplanes don't work anymore. On the other hand, the world has become warmer and in some places wetter, so coffee plantations in Spain and France are slated to reproduce the good stuff in a couple of years.

It's as weird as the thought of Dutch vineyards. Polar bears must be turning in their graves, poor things.

As she digs in her purse for change, a sheaf of ticket stubs falls out. She checks them idly before tossing them in the trash. They are all tickets to Pynacker. She's been here before, many times. But why? And worse, why doesn't she remember?

She notes the mystery down in her little notebook and re-pockets the ticket stubs. There's a reason she kept them. Maybe this little nugget of information will help her forward in her search.

She follows the tourists to the edge of the water. It's busier than she expected; cranes and boats are laying the foundations for levees. There's a reason that nobody built any dikes before, but it escapes her for now. She moves away a little from the work crews and the staring tourists. Since the last time she was here, a path has been beaten out besides the water, and small groups of hikers are coming and going.

She walks up to one of them, his high-end hiking gear mud-spattered and sun-bleached. Clothes aren't getting made as much as before, and cash to pay for them is hard to come by.

"Hey, I'm Gouda Smid, private detective. Have you walked the whole Circle?"

The hiker turns to her, smiling, crow-footed blue eyes in a tan face. "I do a half-circle every season. Why?"

"I look for missing persons, mostly. I'm sure you've seen on TV that they're mostly from towns along the Edge. Have you ever spotted anything odd or different?"

He gazes away over the choppy water of the Hollands Diep. "Yes and no. I never see anything funny. It's more the things I don't see that make me wonder."

This is more interesting than Gouda was expecting from a routine chat. "How's that?"

"The Netherlands have very few terminal stations, yet all around Circle Bay we have track railway lines ending at the edge of the water. Same with highways. Why build an eight-lane highway to a tiny little town at the edge of the water?"

Gouda thinks she's maybe been watching the wrong shows. This sounds like National Geographic or History Channel material. "What do you do for a living?"

His mouth quirks into something less pleasant. "I used to be a city planner."

"You used to be? For what city?"

"Good question. I can't remember. Or I never had a job, in spite of my training and advanced age."

He nods at her and walks on. He looks a lean and smart late thirties, not the kind of guy who's been out of a job since college.

Gouda runs after him and gives him her phone number. "Call me sometime? I'm wondering what this has to do with my missing persons cases. Things just don't add up."

The man doesn't commit but tucks her card away in one of his many zippered pockets.

Gouda sits down on a stray bollard, overlooking a paved square with faint markings indicating this was once a parking spot. She does have memories of cars, traffic jams, parking lots. But they are hard to match with this empty lot, which could have housed like sixty cars or more. There are still old cars running, of course, the ones without—her thoughts stutter. She takes out her notebook and writes the stutter moment down. It's nearly full. She leafs through it. On the pages are words like "Netflix"—she found that one in an old calendar. "Chips"—those taste great, but can also cause prolonged stuttering, seizures, and even comas.

Parking lots, she writes down. Why do old cars still run? They still run because—and maybe because writing down the words make the stutter worse, she watches her hands flutter and clench over the notebook. The pencil breaks. The sun shines down on her face.

She closes her eyes and across the redness she sees icebergs floating past, tugged by boats. Icebergs are something polar. The polar ice is melting. Was melting. Is it still?

She opens her eyes and finds herself supine on pitted asphalt. The paving is warm because it's a sunny day, so she's not that uncomfortable. But her knuckles are grazed and her tailbone aches. She clambers back up, groaning from more aches and stings. A notebook is lying on the ground. She picks it up, and her name is on it. That's weird.

She browses the notebook, and it's full of incomprehensible notes. Bring it or toss it? No, it's hers; she must bring it, even though there's something repulsive about it.

When Gouda gets home and wants to put the notebook away for later perusal, she discovers she has several more of those she'd completely forgotten about. On her computer there's even a mind map of all the words, complete with date. Just to be sure, she finds the last entry in the found notebook, which has no date, and puts today's in.

But it's disturbing, all the same. What other work has she done she has forgotten about? Her eye finds a full noticeboard on the wall. It looks like a serial killer's wish list, complete with red cord and pins. But it's not about serial killing; it's full of clippings from magazines and newspapers, photos and yellow Post-its.

She reads one. "Where did the ice asteroids go? Recent astronomical data compared with centuries-old maps indicate that the asteroid belt and the moons of Jupiter have gaps in them that can't be explained. It's mostly ice planets, although heavy metals are also showing peculiar missings. On par with the vanished satellites."

Missing ice planets. Missing people. Floating icebergs in her dream. No such thing as a coincidence someone once said, although Gouda is no longer surprised that she can't remember who.

She needs a dictionary. What's a satellite? But while she has many letters of the alphabet in both Dutch and English encyclopedias, yellow, moldering volumes, she doesn't have the Oxford English Dictionary's *Rob-Sequyle*. To the library it is. The last time she was there the library had become dusty and abandoned, with only a few rejected books on the sagging shelves. But encyclopedias are heavy and she's almost sure she saw a few.

She unlocks her bicycle and starts cycling the short distance to the library. The building still retains some licks of its once colorful paint, but the lower floor has had to be abandoned due to the rising water. But it's lit up, the door opens, and she hears the buzz of many people present and talking. It's a wonderful sound, bringing back memories that never really surface, but create ripples of their impending arrival in her mind. Better than nothing.

She walks into the big central space. It's indeed full of people sitting at desks, writing and doing work-like things. She steps close to one of the workers, an elderly lady, and sees she's writing a lined index card.

The activity suddenly makes sense. They're re-cataloging the library! By hand, because the computer systems were all lost. There's someone bent over an enormous machine she doesn't know the function of, a bit like a microscope but not quite. And so many books have returned! Hundreds line the shelves; more are stacked on carts sitting beside the cataloguers.

The sight fills Gouda with joy. Humanity is fighting back against missing persons, misfortune, and climate ravagery, one book at a time. She even sees a new-looking book. She picks it up. A strong odor emanates from it, chemical and strong, but satisfying. The scent of a newly printed book. The pages are crisp, the type a bit smudged but strongly black. A new book. Someone has found an old mechanical printing press.

She asks for directions to the encyclopedias and is given stern warning not to take any volumes home. She offers to bring the ones she has at home. It wouldn't be right to hoard that knowledge for herself alone.

She lugs the heavy dictionary volume, dated 1998, and leafs through the heavy pages. There it is. Satellite: natural object (moon) or spacecraft (artificial satellite) orbiting a larger astronomical body. Most known natural satellites orbit planets; the Earth's Moon is the most obvious example. Artificial satellites can be either unmanned (robotic) or manned . . .

The words "communication" and "space shuttle" hurt her brain. She looks away quickly, leery of the buzzing sensation in her head, like a sinus headache. She wants to transcribe this important information, but she's afraid that if she reads them again, the sentences will start up that painful buzz or worse.

She tricks her brain by copying the article out starting at the bottom, with the last word in the last sentence. This way no meaning forms in her head and it's even possible to write whole words. As a last resort she would have written the words out letter by letter, starting with the last letter of a word and ending with the first, but that doesn't seem necessary.

Should she share this trick with the librarians? She decides not to. They are happy, having found a way to rebuild some of the knowledge lost in the computer crash. They don't need to find out, like her, that some knowledge is painful, and some of it can't be retained.

As Gouda exits the library she walks past a blocky machine that triggers a faint memory. It's a copier. She's used them in high school. Maybe it still works. Yes, the electricity is on and it hums. She puts her notebook facedown on the lit plate—funny how she remembered how to do that—and presses the copy button. The copy slides out. Wow, they even had some blank paper left.

She lifts the paper to her face and smells. She closes her eyes. Memories rise, but they seem a bit stale and flat. There is no clue there. Why? The machine looks old and scuffed, its beige plastic brittle and discolored. Maybe this technology is too old to have meaning for her quest.

She pockets the page and heads home. She's no closer to solving her mystery, but her heart is lighter. Life will get better again, it just needs cooperation and dedication. She could be part of the library renewal if she wanted. Maybe it would be more rewarding than looking for people that have never been found yet.

When she opens her door and climbs the four sets of stairs to her small apartment, a ringing sound shreds the air. Only when she sees the squat gray object emitting the sounds, she remembers it's a phone. Which can be answered. She picks up the horn-shaped object, hesitant about what to do. It's been so long.

"Hi, is this Gouda?" A male voice says. "It's Joe from Pynacker? I'm in town. I've got something for you."

Gouda doesn't remember any Joe from Pynacker. Has she even ever been there? Her left hand fishes up train ticket stubs that, strangely enough, all appear to be to and from Pynacker. One of them is from yesterday.

The idea she went somewhere yesterday and doesn't remember it gives her such a weird feeling. She looks around the living room. Everything seems to be the same as before, no gray spots. If she went to Pynacker, it was for a reason, probably a case. She tells him where she lives.

She buzzes him in only ten minutes later. He's a tall guy in his early forties with a weather-beaten face and sun-bleached hair.

"Hi Gouda," he says. "Nice to meet you again."

"Nice to meet you," she says. "Joe, right?"

His gaze sharpens. "You forgot?"

She holds up the ticket stubs. "I guess I went to Pynacker yesterday, but I don't remember. There's a page in my notebook as well. This has never happened to me before."

Joe spots the kitchen and zooms in on the teapot. "Mint? Can I have a cup? I miss coffee, don't you?"

"I've read about it," Gouda answers.

Slurping his tea, Joe peruses her wall of clippings and pictures and pins. "I see you've found many of things I have. Satellites, huh? I've been zooming in on things we used to eat and drink but no longer do, because we flew them in on planes." He taps a picture of a plane for emphasis. Or maybe he just wants to make sure Gouda knows what a plane is. "Coffee, bananas, spices. I wonder if someone in a faraway country is trying to reorganize shipping those things. They must be in as bad an economic slump as we are."

He sits down at her table and gestures her over to him. Gouda's almost irked by his casual possession of her space, but decides to let it go. She gets another mug of tea and sits down next to him.

He rolls up his sleeves. His forearms are surprisingly smooth and creamy pale, years younger than his weatherworn face. Gouda blushes and finds it hard to lift her eyes from those strong, muscled arms. There's nobody in her life right now. Has there ever been?

He's speaking and she's missed the start. She takes a quick look at his face, which hasn't changed, so he hasn't noticed her moment of confusion. A sip of tea helps her get back to normal.

Instead she sneezes. It takes her by surprise.

Joe frowns. "Exactly. Humanity has a virus. We're all infected. We can't even . . . " His eyes glaze, he starts to stutter.

Gouda watches with inexplicable dread. Something awful is going to happen. The light outside seems to darken, the room shrinks inward as the moment hangs in the air, pregnant with horror. But Joe draws his hands over his eyes, looks aside, shakes his head.

The moment is gone. The sun is still shining. But Gouda's heart still races, evidence that something almost happened.

"What happened? What did you just . . . ?" Gouda doesn't dare be more specific, for fear of calling back the awful dread.

Joe's eyes roll up and aside, searching for an innocuous answer. "You have to approach the square through a side street, not full on. And if you accidentally luck onto a big thoroughfare, distract yourself by thinking of trees or scoot into an alley. Right?"

Gouda nods and jots down a quick note. She needs to remember this moment. It will help her with her case. She can't quite remember what it was about, only that's it's important.

Joe clears his throat. "It seems to me that there are strangers in town. And that at night, they demolish houses and break up streets, so that we can't find our way home the next day. They are raiding our larder."

Gouda leans forward. "They like ice cream." Icebergs. "And the people living in those broken-up streets forget their names and where they lived—"

She chokes up. Too close. Across the table, Joe's face turns purple and he makes hacking, desperate sounds. Their hands meet and she clutches his for one long moment, callused palm, warm fingers, blood rushing to meet hers.

Gouda blinks and starts at the stranger sitting at her coffee table. Her left hand has pale stripes over the back, as if someone just gripped her hand hard. As she watches, they fill with blood and disappear. As if it never happened.

The stranger stands up. "I'm sorry, Miss, um, I have to go." He looks around wildly, as if he doesn't remember what he's doing here either.

Gouda gets up to escort him to the door. There's a strange backpack in the hallway. She gestures at it. "This must be yours."

He hesitates. "Are you sure? I don't know . . . "

She hands it to him, firmly. "I'm sure. It's not mine."

"Okay. Thank you. Goodbye."

He hesitates in the door opening as if there's more to say, but there isn't. Gouda shuts the door behind him and waits until she hears him clomping down the stairs.

She returns to the table and her mug of peppermint tea. There's an open notebook on the table. "Don't look into the sun," someone has written down in her handwriting.

As if anyone would.

She looks out of the window and watches a stranger with the flapping coat and the sun-bleached hair walk away. It fills her with inexplicable sadness.

RETRIEVAL

SUZANNE WALKER

I stood at the edge of the shrine for nearly half an hour before I finally willed myself to move closer. It was in the middle of a graveyard, at the bottom of a hill behind the city's spaceport, so every few minutes the silence was punctuated by the whine of engines pushing their ships through the thick autumn clouds.

I wasn't sure which was built first, the port or the shrine, but the proximity seemed sacrilegious no matter who made the choice. The wind blew my hair in front of my face, whistling as it passed through the sparse trees that lined the south edge of the burial grounds, and I suppressed a shiver. Beyond the trees, the towering Protectorate capital loomed, and I wished my stomach clenched in hatred, not fear. It had been ten years since I'd returned to Kinrev, and I no longer resembled round-faced child in the image the Protectorate had on file. The problem was, I now looked like my father.

"This is where your gods dwell? Beneath the ground?" My teacher, Ferrier, stood to my right. She was dressed as I was, plainly in a brown jumpsuit, with her gray hair pulled tight at the nape of her neck. It felt strange to see her without a gun and knife strapped to her side—we'd had to check all weapons at the spaceport, and part of me was surprised she hadn't tried to pick a fight about it. I'd never seen her surrender them willingly.

"Beneath the ground," I echoed. My voice sounded strange in my ears. "Sheltering their children in death."

"Hmm." Ferrier pursed her lips but said nothing. I turned away, glancing outward towards the graveyard, wondering where they'd buried my mother. She'd been killed in one of the final battles against the Protectorate, before they crushed the rebellion and executed my father lightyears away from Kinrev. I remember clutching his hand and watching as we returned her to the gods, body and soul, but the location was lost along with most memories of home.

At least she died planetside. I faced the shrine once more, and my knees trembled when I lowered them. I was taking a risk, coming here, but I hadn't been home to my gods since I was a child. I wanted their blessing, before I set out on this retrieval.

No grass grew around the shrine, and I traced out the patterns in the soil, still known to my hands after all these years, the dirt soft beneath my fingertips. I kept my book of old Kinrevan prayers on me, but I knew the prayer for the dead by heart. My message would reach the gods this way, even if they couldn't hear me.

"I set out to return my father to you," I murmured. "Guide me, even if you cannot see where I may go. Show me the true path."

They didn't answer—they never did—but still I knelt there, tracing over the message again in the hope that it would reach them. That maybe this time, the gods would honor my family's service.

"Riva?" Ferrier's hand gripped my shoulder. I looked up to see her brows knit together in concern, and she glanced up the hill at the soldiers who patrolled the graveyard's edge. "It's time."

We made it back to the spaceport and out the system without any problems, but I still couldn't breathe freely until we made it to the next star. Ferrier had enough resources to procure fabricated IDs for us, so that I could return to Kinrev despite my status as a daughter of dissidents, but that did little to disperse the dread that lodged in my gut whenever I saw my birth planet.

Ferrier was silent in the pilot's seat beside me, but I was grateful for her presence all the same. I'd become a full Retriever two months before, with rights to my own ship from the Guild, but I hadn't claimed one yet. I doubted I would until I found my father. And if my old mentor disapproved, she kept such thoughts to herself.

"Do you think your gods were looking out for you, when they sent you to me?"

I glanced at her in surprise. The Guild frowned on Retrievers belonging to any sort of faith. Beliefs of the afterlife varied too much between planets, and it was best not to cling to any one doctrine in our line of work. I had been lucky in Ferrier, who tacitly allowed my nightly prayers, but she'd never spoken of it outright before.

"I . . . I never thought of them as sending me." I said. "I *looked* for you, the minute I found out the Guild existed."

Ferrier smiled a humorless smile. "I've never known a child to go looking for a ghost seeker."

I raised my eyebrows. "You can't have known too many children, then, before me."

She chuckled softly, and reached over to squeeze my hand.

"You know it's going to be different, this time. Nothing prepares you for when it's family."

I drew in a deep, shuddering breath, releasing it in time with the clanging of the pipes in the engine room. "I know."

I was going to miss this ship, when I finally settled into my own. Its central chamber was almost cavernous, an endless series of pipes and hoses crisscrossing from the top of the dome down to the floor, where we temporarily housed the spirits we retrieved from the darkness of space. I spent most of the journey fixing the pipes, tinkering with blocked avenues I knew Ferrier would never bother to repair, and the work kept me from thinking too much about my father.

Yet still the prayer for the dead echoed in my head, enough to make me wish my parents hadn't been so determined to raise me in the faith. The gods are tied to the earth, and your soul must be tied to the gods, if you are to find any peace in the afterlife. A death in the cold emptiness between the stars condemned one to an eternity of torment.

The Protectorate had known this, when they'd ordered the first deep space executions, and no amount of public outcry could dissuade them. It went against the very tenets of Kinrevan faith, so much so that I'd been shocked to see that the old shrines still existed. If the government dishonored the gods so much, you'd think they'd have torn down their temples.

The old grief took hold of me every so often as I worked in the pipes, and I told myself every time that I did this for my father: not for me, not for vengeance, not for anything beyond the gods' embrace that he deserved.

I never knew if I was lying to myself.

Here's the problem with deep space: even when you've got an exact location pinned down, it can be days before you find anything. We didn't have an exact location for my father. His friends had managed to obtain flight patterns from around the time he died, but that still left us with more than half a dozen sites to check.

Two weeks, three sites, no ghosts. And each site felt more and more like failure.

But in the nothingness between the Sarinen system and the Ilenian nova, something flared out of the corner of my eye. I sat up straight for the first time in days, and beside me, Ferrier slapped her hand down on the dashboard in satisfaction.

"It's a weak signal, but it's there." I could hear joints cracking when she stood up, and she gave me an unreadable expression. "Are you ready?"

I wasn't, but I followed her through the main bay and into the prep room. A series of portable holding chambers lined one side and a handful of patched, worn spacesuits lined the other. Though I'd passed through it more times than I could count, my hands began to shake at the sight of the airlock. This time, I knew who waited on the other side.

Ferrier pulled down two of the suits from their hooks in the wall and handed me one. It was heavy, dank, and smelling of dried sweat, most of it my own. I could already feel perspiration running down my arms as I climbed into the suit, punching my fists through the arms so that I might still the shaking. The glass of the helmet was fogged in spots, but I could still see Ferrier standing near the airlock. Her voice came through a tinny speaker from the back of my head.

"You're taking point on this, my girl, but I'm here. I'm *here*, understand? Only do this if you feel you can."

I nodded and reached for a holding box to strap to my back. I hooked the hose to my belt and watched Ferrier do the same, and she gave me a wordless salute before she opened the airlock. There was a carved hollow where my stomach should have been, and my throat was so tight I wasn't sure if I could breathe properly.

The forward door opened, and the emptiness between the stars carried me forward. My breath sounded heavy within the helmet, and I took care to keep it even while I looked out around me. This was a silence I could never get used to, even now, more sinister somehow than the long, quiet nights spent with Ferrier. There was no boat beneath my feet, no engines that could ferry us to safety should disaster strike—just me and the fear carried in my breath.

"Look for a light between the stars."

Ferrier's words echoed in my ear, lessons from my first retrieval. Without a nearby star as a beacon, everything somehow seemed even darker than usual. I floated upright relative to the ship, my eyes straining from the search, but I couldn't see anything. I moved away from Ferrier slowly, using the microjets in the spacesuit boots to push myself around and behind the ship.

Something flickered in the bottom corner of my helmet, and I turned, slowly, the pulsers in my gloves barely firing. It was a fleeting flash of blue, now, and my breath caught in my throat when I stopped to behold a luminous figure, rippling back and forth before the spattering of stars behind. It wavered more rapidly, struggling to take shape, and it reached out towards me as if to capture the form of my bulky, padded body.

There were days now where I struggled to remember my father's face, when I had to rush to my bunk and pull out an old picture and trace through the dust with my fingertips before he was clear in my mind again. But the figure before me shifted once more, and there was no mistaking the particular way his beard formed, or the scar that connected his temple to the base of his jaw. His eyes were clouded, muddled, before they blinked with what I prayed was a dawning recognition.

"Daddy?"

He couldn't hear me—he couldn't—but the word seemed to spark something in him, for his face suddenly twisted into a sneer of malice that I had never seen him wear while alive. I frowned in confusion, wondering if I should speak again, before my view suddenly exploded with blue, and I was thrown backward, hurtling fast toward the ship.

I screamed, but the sudden intake of air cost me, and a sharp pain radiated through my chest. The force of the creature—not my father, not my father—pushed hard against the suit. I hit the hull of the ship with a great thud that reverberated down my back, and my head slammed back against my helmet. Sparks swam in front of my eyes, and I could barely see that the creature's form expanded into giant hands that twisted themselves around the base of my helmet. I tried to struggle, but my arms had taken on the weight of lead, and I couldn't react quickly enough to the creature, whose arms had multiplied to snake around my back, pressing the suit deep into my skin. I felt a sharp twist against my spine, and my eyes widened in terror—it was trying to tear off the oxygen tank.

There was another flash of light, and the creature released me for a moment, mouth open in a silent scream of rage. Ferrier hovered above me, her weapon aimed at the both of us, and the substance of the creature seemed to leech away from itself, spiraling toward the funnel-shaped opening of Ferrier's blaster. I pried its spindling fingers off of the base my helmet, but not before it pushed me away with one final twist to the tank strapped to my back. A sharp hissing noise rushed through my ears, and I could see the oxygen level rapidly failing on my helmet monitor.

"Get inside!" Ferrier shouted. "Pull yourself in and shut the airlock!"

"But—"

"Go!"

I was feeling light-headed now, my breaths coming in short, sharp gasps that burned my lungs. I fumbled before I held the tether, the thick gloves of the suit doing me no favors. I made the mistake of looking behind me, though my vision had begun to swim, and saw the creature reaching towards me, mouth moving in what would have been an ear-shattering howl, if I could hear. I bit down on my inner lip hard enough to taste blood, the metallic scent blooming in the oxygen-starved space of my helmet, and I turned back to my hands on the tether. My vision was almost completely gone, and it took all my strength to focus my eyes so that I saw nothing but one hand moving in front of the other, one then two.

I don't know how I made it into the airlock, or how I had the strength to key in the combination to the aft door and cross through back to the holding bay. All I know is that I found myself collapsed on the floor of the hold, knees drawn tight to my chest, head pounding, the room spinning all around me. I didn't want to move, didn't want to feel anything ever again, and it was only the thought of Ferrier returning with my father, murderous and merciless, that caused me to stumble to my feet, trip out of the spacesuit and out towards the main cargo bay.

The nausea came as soon as I opened the holding door, but I managed to wait until I was in the privacy of my own bunk before throwing up in the garbage bin.

Even the reused, flat air of the ship was a gift to me, after what had happened to the spacesuit, and I almost cried from the relief of it. I lay curled in my bunk for what felt like hours, shaking uncontrollably, until I finally tired of the weakness in my limbs and the smell of stale vomit sitting in the trash. I cleaned out the bin and left for the main hold, pacing the length once or twice before I stumbled into the galley, on the verge of collapse once more. I found refuge in one of the hard chairs attached to the table and tried to take a deep, steadying breath.

The door hissed open to reveal Ferrier. She gave me one quick glance before she headed toward the sink in the corner. I couldn't look at her, could hardly focus enough to stay upright in my chair, so I stared down at my boots. Both of us tended to get lax about cleaning while on a job, and there were still crumbs from the previous day's meal on the floor, caught between the indented grooves in the steel.

Weathered hands suddenly covered my own, and a steaming cup was pressed toward me.

"Here."

The cup was warm, with the scent of ginger root and something stronger curling up to soothe my battered nerves. I inhaled deeply before taking a sip, and suddenly I was thirteen again, Ferrier caring for me after my first, harrowing walk into space.

Ferrier took a seat across from me at the table, but the cup was nearly cool between my hands before I could look up to meet her eyes. Ferrier was always quick to tell me when I'd been wrong, and I'd never failed so badly as I had here. But instead of admonition, her face reflected something of my own pain.

"He's in the holding chamber. If you want to see him."

My eyes filled with tears I'd been holding back since we docked on Kinrev. I'd seen the echoes of so many who died in space over the years, trapped in the void with no sense of peace or rest. Though the Guild disagreed, I often thought my religion made me better equipped for the job than most, because I understood that the soul needs something solid to ground it. Some can handle the isolation, the weightless eternity. Others can't. Part of a Retriever's job is to reorient a spirit in their ships' pipes, to calm it in preparation for its return planetside. But for some, it's far too late.

This wasn't the first ghost who had tried to kill me, and it wouldn't be the last, yet somehow I never considered that my own father would be one of them. His death had been deliberately cruel, but I'd held on to the hope that he could endure, whole, until I came for him. Retrieving him had been my purpose for so long, and now . . .

"Riva . . . " Ferrier reached out and took both my hands within her own. "Have your gods ever been confronted with a retrieved soul?"

I choked out a sob, and Ferrier enveloped me in an embrace. She doled out physical affection so rarely, but I gave in to grief now, crying until my head ached and my eyes were washed raw.

"No. And I don't know if they'll take him like this."

We kept my father's ghost in one of the heavy metal boxes that lined the cargo hold. Every so often it would shake violently and move incrementally toward the doorway, and I double-checked the lock every few hours despite knowing it was airtight. I kept vigil one night, my throat tight as I sat beside him, running my hand gently across the smooth metal plates that kept him confined. We tried to free him into the pipes, another night, but his claw-like hands came rushing for Ferrier's throat the minute he was released. After that, he remained in the holding chamber.

My eyes still stung from all the tears I'd shed on the journey home, but they filled once more when the gray clouds of Kinrev came into view. Our false trader's ID worked a second time, although now we would have to wait for the cover of night to take the box that held my father to the shrine.

My message from before had been raked clean, and the shrine stood cold before me. We had brought nothing with us save the holding box, no tools that might undo the action of release. My hand trembled as it ran across the release handle, and I murmured the prayer of the dead aloud once more. It wasn't worth ascribing it to soil—if the gods didn't sense my father's presence, they would soon enough.

I opened the container, and an unholy shriek rent the air. A twisting streak of blue shot up and punctured the sole light overhead, and there was nothing but darkness and a howling storm. My hair came free of its braid and blew in front of my face, nearly blinding me. The force of the wind pulled me toward the shrine, but the spirit seemed to have no target, this time, just a blinding, purposeless rage.

"Stop!" I could barely hear myself over the rushing sound in my ears. "We've brought you home!"

I don't know why I said it, but the words must have reached him, because the howling noise slowly faded down to a dim roar. The wind diminished, and the creature shrank until it was only a head or so taller than my father would have stood in life. It resembled nothing human, but it stayed relatively still, and I stepped forward, hand outstretched as his had been out in the void.

My hand slipped through a thick, almost gelatinous substance that was colder than the air in winter. It swirled and crashed around my hand, winding itself slowly up my arm as if unsure how to react. Then the cold began to seep away, and I fought back sudden tears.

Ferrier stood staring at us, mouth agape, and it was clear she'd never seen anything like it in her life.

The hollow of the shrine glowed beneath me, and slowly, the creature that had been my father sank into the ground. I fell to my knees, not caring if anyone heard my wordless cry, and my voice echoed out through the silence. For a moment, I could hear nothing but the wind whistling through the trees. Suddenly, I was thrown back, a blast knocking me straight to the ground, and I wheezed, struggling to recover the wind that had been knocked out of me. Ferrier had collapsed, clutching her heart with her hand, and I followed her gaze to where I had been kneeling a moment before. The shrine had exploded, and out of the wreckage rushed not just my father but half a dozen other creatures, so bright and blinding I knew they couldn't be mere ghosts.

I shaded my eyes with a shaking hand, and knew before seeing that they were headed straight for the capital. The Protectorate's bastion had been built to keep out the living, not the dead.

Ferrier clutched at my shoulders with her hands. "Is that . . . are those . . . "

"They know now," I murmured through my tears. "He'll find peace. One way or another."

THE NO-ONE GIRL AND THE FLOWER OF THE FARTHER SHORE

E. LILY YU

Once there grew, in the dust and mud of a village in China, a girl who had only her grandmother to love, and then her grandmother died and was buried and she had no one at all. With no money to patch up the walls and lay new tiles on the roof, the small, smoky home that the two of them had shared slumped around her in the rain, and the little garden ran to nettle and thorn.

In the months that followed, the girl crept and gnawed and spat and caught small birds with her hands, like an animal. The garden gave her wild gourds and bitter greens to eat. The woods gave her kindling and dry cowpats where cows had been tethered to graze. Sometimes her neighbors brought her scraps, for pity.

Sometimes they shied stones at her.

Except when she visited her grandmother's grave, the no-one girl rarely spoke. She cast her eyes low and bit her lip, and the villagers shrugged and said, well, that was the way of wild things. But anyone who saw her squatting beside the grave, knobbly elbows over knobbly knees, mumbling and rambling, would have thought her mad.

There she told her grandmother the changing of the seasons, and the birds she caught and the colors of their feathers, and the weather, and her wishes, small and large, as she had done when her grandmother was alive.

For many years now, at the mid-autumn festival, the village official offered a silver pin in the shape of an acorn and a gold brooch molded into a willow leaf as a prize for the most beautiful thing made in the village that year. Each year, the villagers presented embroidered cardboard and painted tin and silk cords knotted into dragons, and one man or woman, glowing with pride, bore the pin and willow leaf home. The no-one girl had seen these prizes from afar, on the breast of the tailor, or the carpenter, or the firework-maker, and thought them very rich and fine.

"If I won them," she said to her grandmother's grave, as the wind carried to her the music and laughter of the festival, "I would touch them and taste them and eat their loveliness with my eyes. I would wear them for an hour to feel the weight of gold and silver, and then I would sell the gold brooch for enough flour for a year, then the silver pin for salt and vinegar and spices. But when I bring the little purple wildflowers without names, and the brown mushrooms from the wood, they laugh at me."

Her grandmother's grave, mounded high and sparkling with tinsel, kept its own counsel, but the grass that grew thinly on it seemed to sway in sympathy.

That night, after the revelers were all asleep, the first rain of autumn scoured the village. Rain sang on roofs and fences and pattered through trees. The no-one girl shivered and dreamed of a white bird that circled her head, dropped a seed, and flew away into the dark.

When she awoke, she went to her grandmother's grave. From the mound sprang a single red flower like a firework, a flower the girl had never seen before, yet recognized, for late at night her grandmother had combed the girl's long black hair and told her about the flower of the farther shore, which only grows where there has been death, and leads the dead wherever they must go. It had bloomed in the village where her grandmother had been born, a long way away, and there had been a deep sadness in her grandmother's voice as she described it, working the comb through the knots in the girl's hair.

Now the flower of the farther shore had come to her. The girl clapped her hands at the exquisite beauty of it. She dug down to the bulb with her fingers and planted it in the garden among the wild gourds.

All that autumn and winter she tended the flower. After the petals faded and fell, slender leaves speared up, glowing with life and green throughout the cold winter. She fed the flower her secrets, burying them one by one, and watered it with drops of her blood, red as the flower had been, because there was no death in the garden, and the flower, her grandmother had said, needed death to live.

"Grow, grandmother's flower," she whispered to it at night. "Bloom, flower of the farther shore."

Leaves and then snow covered the path to her grandmother's grave, for the girl had ceased her visits, certain, as if it had been whispered to her, that her grandmother was gone. All her words and care were for her flower, whose leaves seemed to bend toward her, listening.

Spring came, and the earth thawed. While everything else budded and sprouted and broke open, shouting life, the leaves of the strange plant browned and crumbled. But the girl continued to tend the bare patch, which she ringed with stones, as lovingly as one might a child.

These were easier days, after the winter's illnesses and privations. Bark ran soft with sap, and weeds were still tender and sweet. Though the girl was never not hungry, she was not starved.

Now and then the villagers looked over her wall or shouted through the gate to see if she was still alive, partly for kindness and partly because her land and home would be reassigned if she died. When they spied her chattering at her patch of earth, they stopped and stared.

"Eh, what's that?"

"What are you growing there, girl?"

"A flower of the farther shore," she replied. They laughed and rattled sticks against the gate. One or two tossed stones at her, but only halfheartedly, so they pattered down among the wild gourds instead of stinging her arms.

Summer meant fat pigeons, and the tiny, tender muscles of leaping mice caught when she poured creek water down their holes, and the odd spray of wildflowers, yellow and pink and white, dotting the muddy banks of the ditch. Summers she roamed far and free, up hills and down fields, idly pulling an ear of wheat or barley and chewing the sweet green kernels inside. Hawks hovered, dove, and killed. Cows swung their sleepy heads sideways at her and pissed pale yellow streams.

Every night she returned to the bare ring of stones, told it what she'd seen, and pricked her arm until it bled. The red drops ran in a fine line down her wrist and dripped from her fingertips to the thirsting earth. She was careful not to waste a drop.

At the equinox, or so said the flimsy almanac nailed to the door, the flower of the farther shore arose like a ghost in the night. It spread its curling red crown to greet the no-one girl when she unlatched the door and stepped outside. The girl gathered its petals together in her hands to smell their fragile fragrance, stroked its long green stalk, kissed its stamens until her mouth was gold with pollen, and spent the whole day sitting beside her flower, crowing and marveling.

Those who looked over the wall made various noises of astonishment.

"What a beautiful flower!"

"Ah, what a sweet smell!"

"How odd that someone like you should have grown such a thing."

They drank its colors with their eyes and its odors with their noses, just as the no-name girl did, and she did not begrudge them one bit.

The butcher's son came too, and looked long.

"Aren't you my treasure?" the girl said, paying him no mind. "Oh, but I will surely win the gold brooch and silver pin this year because of you."

And the butcher's son said nothing but went quietly away.

In the night, the girl turned in her sleep, as though a soft thump and rustle reached her ears. She twitched and flung a hand out, as if somewhere in the garden, metal clinked against stone.

Morning came, the morning of the festival, and the flower was gone.

"Stolen!" the girl cried. "Stolen, oh stolen!" She sifted the loose dirt in the hole where the flower had grown, but there was nothing, not a fragment of root, not a crumb of hope.

She beat the ground with her fists, then pulled her hair with her dirty fingers, but there was no help for it. The flower had been stolen, the pin and brooch would be given to another, and there was nothing she could do.

Aching for justice, and rubbing her eyes with her knuckles, she hurried to the street of shops, where on an ordinary day beaded strings clacked in doorways and baskets of fish were sold from bicycles. Today, colored lanterns bobbed over low tables tied with ribbons. Throughout the day, people brought their beautiful things here, to be guarded by the village official when he was not deep in his cups, and by his more watchful wife when he was.

The no-one girl would have pulled his sleeve and cried for help, except that the butcher's son was just at that moment presenting his entry: a flower in a pickle jar. It was her flower, the no-one girl saw, her stolen flower of the farther shore, but the petals had been painted white and gold, and cut raggedly, and the stamens trimmed short. To her eyes that had known its crimson wholeness, it was ugly as a wound.

When the butcher's son saw her, he turned red and glanced away.

"What's this?" the official said, tapping the end of his pen against the jar. "I've never seen its like."

"A flower I grew in the yard, where the soil is wet from the animals we slaughter. I sent off for the seed in the mail."

"It may be an unusual species, but these are common enough colors," the official said. "And—faugh—it stinks like cheap perfume. Well, set it among the rest, and we'll see." Then he turned to the girl with a smile as big as sunflowers and said, "Now, what did you bring us this year? A pretty stone? A snail?"

The truth filled her mouth with bitterness, almost choking her, and her blood ran hot and cold. But she looked into the official's wine-red face, and at the butcher's son in his clean blue shirt, smelling of cooked meat, and knew she would not be believed, no, not the wild girl with no one, who talked and laughed to herself. The villagers who passed by had seen a red flower with a curling crown, not this gold-and-white pretender. Moreover, as she knew, there was often a ready stone in their hands.

"Nothing?" the official said. She shook her head, teeth clamped together. "Well, get along with you, then. Go and enjoy the festival."

The girl turned and ran, blind with her loss, blundering through the smoke of firecrackers and knots of people eating white moon cakes. The men and women she knocked against opened their mouths to scold, but seeing who it was, laughed and shook their heads.

Once she was home, the gate banged open and closed, the door unlocked and flung shut, did she allow the poor truth to leave her lips.

"Ah, why did he have to mutilate my flower?" she cried. "If only he had simply stolen it and called it his! For it to become a painted lie! For its scent to be drowned in his mother's perfume! Oh, I wish I had eaten the thing!"

She curled up and sobbed until her nose went numb. For it was not the loss of the flower alone that wounded her, but the sudden revelation that the world and its pins and brooches had been made for such as the butcher's boy and not for one like herself.

A cold rain fell that night. It fell on the revelers whose faces turned orange and blue in the light of the paper lanterns, who whooped and ran or staggered home through the rain; fell on the fan-maker as she was accepting the silver acorn and willow-leaf brooch, who quickly tucked her prize fan into her jacket; fell on the butcher's son carrying his flower home, who turned his face upward to catch raindrops on his tongue; and it fell on the muddy girl sitting in her yard, staring at the hole where the flower had been.

The rain fell and fell, and the garden slicked to mud. Raindrops boiled on the girl's shoulders. Rain streamed down the tangles of her hair.

Then—as if the world had heard the unspoken wish on her tongue, the one wish she had not told her grandmother or fed to the flower, for only now did it put out its leaves—the girl began to disappear.

She grew transparent, like sugar, then smaller, ever smaller and smoother, melting and running into the wet earth with the rain.

The last sound she made, before her lips blurred, was a sigh.

As she sank, she expanded. What had been the no-one girl mixed with volcanic ash and ant eggs and ancient bones, leafmold and roots both thick as a man's waist and fine as hair. She sank until she touched the enormous basalt pillars buried deep beneath the soil, forgetful of the fire that made them, and deeper still.

And she understood, as she opened, as she poured forth and flowed, that though the no-one girl had appeared to eat and mumble and live alone, in truth she was part of everything, the over and the under, briefly divided from it, as a seed falls from a seedhead, but now returned. Her bones were basalt, her teeth trees, her belly full of mineral riches. She looked out from every leaf and every stone. There was her poor painted flower in the butcher's yard, cast aside to wither; but it did not matter now. She had ten thousand flowers in her, tens of thousands, and the wind for her hair.

The villagers searched for the no-one girl, when they noticed the silence in her yard, but not for long. She was wild, after all, and everyone knew that wild things lived and died in their own way, or climbed into truck beds and rode to the city to vanish, and it was no use holding them. At any rate, they had their own concerns, their own sick parents and delinquent children and debts run up by liquor and gambling, and when winter came ravening, its breath all knives, they went home to their houses to grapple with their private disasters.

One morning in spring, as icicles wept themselves to nothingness, the butcher's son stopped by the empty house, frowning. He scaled the stone wall, at some cost to his trousers; tried the warped door, which stuttered open; and rapped his knuckles against the sagging beams, listening for rot.

By the time summer softened the village, the old garden, cleared of rocks and nettles, put forth long pale melon vines and sweet swellings, yellow and green.

Soon the ripe melons were picked and split and eaten. Then it was autumn. The first cold rain covered the village. In its wake, red flowers sprang up, sudden and strange: flowers as brilliant as firecrackers, slender-stalked and leafless, growing so densely that when the wind murmured in them they moved like a sea.

The butcher's son picked armfuls of them, as many as he could carry, and went to the fan-maker's home, flushing as bright as the flowers that he thrust forward when she came to the gate. Children bent to breathe their sweetness, then plucked them to play at wands, or taunt the goats until they ate them. But it did not matter how many they gathered; always, there were more.

All around, above, below, the everything girl laughed with spotless joy.

Autumn after autumn the flowers filled the village, spilling outward for miles, until it was known to all as the village of the farther shore, and the old name drifted down into the uncertain recollections of the village elders, along with the story of the no-one girl.

Once the butcher's son and the fan-maker were married, they moved into the empty house and yard that the butcher's son had, over long months, cleaned and repaired. For their wedding he gave her a necklace and earrings of gold, heavy and soft.

The two of them lived happily and unhappily, as people are wont to do, falling out of love and into irritation and then back into fondness; having children, beating them, and scraping together the fees for school; growing old and blind and fretful, and moving about the yard with canes.

After they both died, their eldest child came home from the city to sort through their belongings, putting aside what could be sold, what might be wanted, and what was worthless. As she folded clothes and untied boxes, stirring up decades of dust, she tossed onto the midden, as things unworthy of keeping, an acorn snapped off its pin, the silver paint flaking, and a willow-leaf brooch with gilt peeling from the brass.

THE CATALOG OF VIRGINS

NICOLETTA VALLORANI,
TRANSLATED BY RACHEL S. CORDASCO

Sharks.

Shadows of teeth in this darkness.

I should have left immediately, because this delay could prove fatal.

I watched.

Forceps, mallets, an assortment of rusty knives, pairs of sickles in various sizes, a mallet in the shape of a crowbar with a strange pink hilt. At the bottom of it all, even, a wide-open Iron Maiden whose cavernous belly bristles with nails. Men have tools of sorrow and joy that reveal the stuff they're made of.

I hear a massive rodent rustling at my back, and this seems to be a happy thought in such a place. The mercy of the mouse. Whoever has been locked in here has to need it.

It's large and clumsy. Perhaps it won't notice me. Flattened against the wall, black in the darkness, barely breathing. The guard watches the room, smoothing down his uniform. He's proud of himself. It doesn't see me. It turns. It's about to escape.

The ramp's nearby, a moment too soon to pass unnoticed. He senses the giant, that there's someone, but he doesn't come to grab me. Too big to be agile, and perhaps quite accustomed to this obscurity.

Nigredo in the dark, though, is lost.

So I'm out, across the porch, down to the back. But the narrow stairs are deceptive. And I am old. I don't understand that I've fallen until I'm in mid-air. I don't understand that I've hurt myself until I feel the blow to my jaw and the dry snap of my ankle.

And nobody follows me.

Nobody.

I think.

I slip into the alleys, out from under Bluebeard.

• • •

I am Leyla.

I was born in the northern quadrant of the Albin Islands. I am a daughter of a glacial oil well. I was recruited at thirteen, by a head-hunter. I trained in the Walled City, along with the other girls destined for Business. I remember a lot of dust, small rooms without light, and little food. I remember some other girl, but not much. I remember, too, some of the instructors who followed our progress. I don't remember their faces, but the other parts of their bodies.

The instructors concerned themselves with the preliminary training, and when it was necessary, the Rite. I have never been raped.

A virgin. This they wanted.

I was good, smart, even very beautiful. I passed through the wall on December 28. I was a precious gift for the new year, a package of life for a very important person.

My time was 300 hours.

A city of bricks and walls. Chased down alleys with bated breath. Where is my track of dried breadcrumbs? Where did I lose the map of this place? Then again, was there really ever a map?

Where to go. Find Yuri. Tell him about my escapade in the dungeon.

I walk on ice, along the wall. The taste of blood dissolves in my mouth. I drag one leg, slipping on the compact slab covering the ground in the alleyway.

The slashed veins of the city, to each closed metro station, become visible, appearing to have been cut quickly into the walls. Porto di Mare had been transformed into a camp. In the square, shacks lean against one another, as if revealing indecision. If we nudged one, I think with amusement, they'd all fall, like an unstoppable row of dominoes.

I keep walking, skimming the wall, restless at the thought of ghosts that are following me. Infiltrating my thoughts, trying to make sense of what happened.

The Prophet. The monosyllabic interview, in the language of politics. The inability to extract information about the girls who were found dead, in piles, all alike. The impassive courtesy of the new guru, with a flourishing business in town, as he dismissed me. The crazy idea of pursuing an assassin.

I arrive at Palazzo dei Leoni, in an area I know well for trying several times, in my youth, to bombard with bombs: cordoned off for years, the square is no one's property. Then, the rest. The effort to enter. The dungeon. The horror. The escape. What did I discover? What did I really find out? I have to go to Yuri, and I must hurry. He will tend to me and welcome me.

Thirst tears at my throat. It's out of the question that, in this part of town, I can find something to drink. I peek over a torn curtain. A seated man, just beyond, looks at me as if with recognition, or like I never existed. Misery makes you indifferent. Beyond the pain, there is a limbo that frees you from any emotion.

A chubby little boy bursts out of another shack. Just after, I realize that I can use a crutch. He's missing a leg, but that poses no problems while he flees with something in his hand, a sticky substance to be chewed. Running away in the chaos. There are many people who live like this.

Sighing, I try to support my foot. The pain explodes from the ankle up to the groin. Sweating, breathing warmly in the frost. Still a little way and I'll be there. Taking it from the far side, as Yuri says. The fact is that I don't want to lead whoever's following me to him.

I slip between the shacks, moving away from the wall.

And in the miserable passageway, I lose my hounds.

My name is Teodora, which means "gift of God."

I have pale skin and dark eyes, and am singular because I know that I come from the territories of Fire, where no one is pale like me. I don't remember anything, I don't think I have any real parents, I don't think I have a real family, either. They brought me to the Walled City when I was very small. They did not let me grow up before the collective rape. They call it the Rite, but I don't know why. I never knew. It's very ugly, the Rite, but they teach us that it's necessary. Afterwards, we are ready for Business. I have been lucky, I have only had three masters. And my heart was weak. And my body was easy to hurt to death. I didn't last long, although I remember every minute. I imagined the Ash Factory so many times before they really took me.

There it was Paradise.

My life time, thus, was twenty-five hours.

Inside and I understand that nothing will ever be the same.

The laboratory has only preserved its livid light. The rest is a mass of rubble watched over by a pile of rags and blood.

I bend down, catching my breath, laying a hand on his naked and wounded chest.

There is a small break in Yuri's voice.

I check his ear, dirty with his blood. His whisper breaks, and then resumes, stable but furtive, fleeing like his life.

"I didn't see them coming," he says. "But you, you will do this for me . . . "

My gaze and that of another, a different me observing my own body, would like to weep at the murder of a friend, but cannot. Thus I stay, Nigredo the stoic, to watch, to try to understand what my friend is expecting to die for.

The laboratory is the ravaged kennel of a wicked master. I almost smile, pulling my lips away from my teeth, thinking that maybe this really is how he would have liked to leave: in his space, where he lived, where he was corrupted, where he lost the purity of his name, where he tried to keep up with time and bandits, where he spent his desire for vengeance, where he was interrogated, tortured, violated, abandoned. Where he saw me for the first time. Where he met me all the other times. Where we built what we are, in time, weaving together an unrelenting give-and-take between his scientific analysis and my desire for revolt.

And now, in his voice, there is a small break, an urgency I cannot stop.

"I did . . . do remember what you wanted . . . "

I don't remember having wanted anything. Not this, at least. Again, my gaze comes off the scene I'm living and sees myself, kneeling. The map drawn on the linoleum floor, a track of blood that I steered around, a knee-jerk reaction that no pain will erase.

Our friendship, Yuri, is made of maps. And what we will not forget is still on the skin of an assassin that I loved and then released.

"The map . . . Remember . . . the map of the dungeons." Breathing still, with studied slowness, trying to fix his glasses. Smudged.

"Remember, I didn't say anything. Nigredo. Now you have to . . . there's always them. Listen. Remember the map. You must . . . "

In the breath that follows, I seem to read a will and a legacy.

"Now you have to do it." One breath, inexorable fatigue to say all together. A task and a testament.

I feel like it's becoming lighter.

In the silence that follows, I would cry, I believe.

But perhaps I won't do it.

My name's Ginevra, but I don't know if that's my real name. They chose it for me when I arrived at the Walled City, and to me, in the end, it doesn't matter.

Another girl told me a story in which Ginevra was the unfaithful wife of a king, who betrayed him with a knight, up in the Great North. It was a romantic story, though I didn't like it very much. I think they chose this name because I have always had very pale skin and blond hair and this thin, elf-like body. And I think too that the story of the woman with two lovers has produced for me a name and a destiny. In the Rite, they say I was lucky, because I only had two rapists. But I know it's not the number that counts. Another girl, during the Rite, for example, managed to hide under other bodies and was able to get away. Against two, one doesn't run away. I didn't run away. They sold me almost immediately afterwards. They say I became crazy after the first eight hours.

And yet, my life time was fifty-nine hours. A respectable time.

Now, reason, Nigredo. Think.

Now remember.

Now put things in order and waken the old man.

We had drawn a map, at the time of our last inquiry. We had it on paper, as it used to be, using an old map of Milan that Yuri had kept. Big as an A4 format, rare like a beautiful dream. We wanted to keep track of the murders that would remain unpunished, and we did it on an tourist map from the past, with the certainty that no one would ever be able to discover our secret. A map document: no one would have tried it. Precious things are kept in chips. Instead, there's no trace of that old trick we did together.

It exists only on the paper. Perishable paper. Hackable paper. Tearable paper. Paper of my dreams and wishes. Like the body of the woman on whom the original path of torture was tattooed.

I look around.

Think.

Reason.

Paper, memory.

Paper, memory, wall.

There.

The outdated anatomical table has always been considered a joke by Yuri. He didn't use it, it would've been idiotic, but he wanted to leave it there, hanging on the wall, a remnant of long ago.

Here: remember.

For fun, and for exorcism, after finishing it, we had hidden our own mapping of homicides, superimposing the places onto the military track of a never-ending war, and to which the body and the soul of the assassin belonged. I search between the plexiglass cover and the frame. And, finally, I find it.

Now, there are two folded sheets of paper.

Two instead of one.

I am Andrea, and they cut my hair short right away because they said that, in certain markets, androgyny pays. "Androgyny": it's a difficult word, I shouldn't use it. They are happier if I don't speak, but I should never talk, I don't seem educated in any way. The fact is that where I come from, everyone is educated. Educated and poor. And since I was beautiful, no wonder they sold me. My father had a debt that he couldn't pay. So he kissed me and gave me away. I remember my story well, and my clients like it so much when I tell it, I can't tell why. Fucking a cultured person is a bit more enjoyable, I don't know. So I tell it and tell it and tell it, gaining life with each word I speak. I always did it, since I arrived at the Walled City, though they don't like the things that I'm saying. That's why they reserved special treatment for me during the Rite.

I didn't speak there, or I don't remember. I didn't want them to cut off my hair. I didn't want to look androgynous. I didn't want it.

And though I didn't want it, my life time, filled with stories, was one hundred and seventy hours. A triumph.

Separation from Yuri, an abrupt and incomplete action, has exhausted me. The return was long and difficult. It is dark, by now, when I arrive at Prison, which is home. The open and abandoned cells are my entire world and possessions.

The candle struggles to burn, yellowing the sheet. An A4 with jagged edges, dominated by a sketch of a woman. I recognized the symbols that Yuri used for each type of inquiry: cutting weapons, burns, ropes, metallic mallets . . . a rosary of violation that I struggle to break without feeling the nausea rising in my throat.

Around the woman's profile, names. Stories.

Leyla, Teodora, Ginevra, Andrea . . .

Women.

Five stories.

A single story.

Pandora is the name they gave me when I accepted the contract. They said that from my body they would create my sisters. They're all the same as me, but also different.

Pandora is the name with which they led me to the Walled City, promised me a life that I had never had, taking advantage of my naïve craving for pleasure, my craving to be loved. Poverty is a bad master for those who have their own body as their only investment capital.

I got the idea that I might be able to use it, this body.

They told me: "You are the mother clone. Our treasure."

I had never been anyone's treasure. I was convinced.

They made my sisters, invented a story for each of them, and then, after the Rite, they sent me over the wall. Into the world I had dreamed of. The world of the rich, of enchanted gardens, of castles where I would be queen.

My master was no better or worse than the others. He was careful not to ruin me immediately. I'm not grateful.

When they brought me to the Ash Factory for the last time, I remember thinking of only one thing: how many of my sisters had Bluebeard? How many had been punished for their imaginary disobedience?

My life time lasted five hundred hours, with seven different reconstructions: nearly a record, as far as I know.

I hope that my ashes will disperse in the wind.

Forever and forever and forever.

I extinguish the candle. I'm in the dark, to commemorate my dead.

Think.

Bluebeard killed every one of his wives, and kept the corpses in the bowels of his castle. He would keep them that way forever, avoiding the danger of boredom and the pain of old age, and preserving them intact instead, in the magic of fairy tales, in one sealed room.

Of the women he married, all young and beautiful, all very similar to each other, he acquired body and fidelity, bringing each one of them to his castle to make her a bride and violate her on the wedding night. To each of his wives, Bluebeard gave up full ownership of his castle.

All, my love, everything except for the forbidden room. You will have the key, but you will not need to use it.

Only the last wife used it. She found in the room her twin sisters, with cloned wounds on their bodies. And in their faces, the usual pain.

Originally published in Italian in *Wired* (Italy), July/August, 2014.

UNPLACES: AN ATLAS OF NON-EXISTENCE

IZZY WASSERSTEIN

Excerpts from the First Edition, with handwritten marginalia. Recovered from the ruins of Kansas City. Part of the permanent exhibit of the Museum of Fascisms.

Section 1: Places that Never Were

Avalon: Island home of the legendary sword Excalibur, attested to in *Historia regum Britanniae*. A land which produces all good things, Avalon has been claimed to be synonymous with various historical places, including Glastonbury, England, and Avallon, Burgundy. Smythe and Bliss (2018) claim this island once existed, but it is more probable that it is symbolic of a general longing for a better land beyond one's own.

[Lya: I had this book on loan from the Spencer Library when the Messianic Army reached Lawrence. After OKC, I knew they'd soon burn the collection. My beloved books are all gone, along with my years of research on lost places. The only book I was able to save isn't even mine, and now I'm reduced to defacing it. Forgive me. I write these words out of hope that they will reach you, and out of faith that our words still matter.]

El Dorado: The "city of gold" legend evolved from older stories of a golden prince, and was whispered to European conquerors desperate for riches. There is no evidence of the city's existence, and the search for it certainly destroyed many other places, both real and once-real. As with many Unplaces, historical fact is obscured by conquerors eager to make their own history. In so doing they efface the past.

[When I was a student—just months ago, though it seems much longer—these entries were mostly of academic interest to me, I'm ashamed to admit. Now they mean something more each day. Who wouldn't send the Conquistadors away on a hunt for gold, if they could? Last we heard, most of the world—even most of Europe—was free from the fascists. Maybe it's just the Americas that are fucked.

Maybe the places that lack our particular combination of Authoritarianism and apocalyptic faith will overcome.

I'd like to believe I'd never inflict this horror on someone else to save myself. But to see you again, Lya? All things are compromised—our world, our home, myself.]

Erșetu la târi: Attested to throughout ancient Mesopotamia as the land of the dead. One reached it by going through seven gates, and at each gate left behind an article of clothing, so that one arrived in the next life naked, a kind of unbirth. Szymborska (2020) argues that Erșetu la târi may have once existed, given widespread belief in it. If so, however, there can be no evidence of its existence, for its name translates to "earth of no return."

[I want to leave Kansas City, to flee to someplace safer. But even if I was sure where to go, how would I get there? It's not even safe to scavenge for food uptown.

I'm fortunate that the militias mostly stay out of the old downtown, the areas that were never redeveloped. They may catch me even here, but I am as careful as my desperation allows. I stay in old brick buildings, long-abandoned warehouses, with clear views and multiple exits. There's been no wealth in these neighborhoods for generations, and the militias prefer to root out subversives in areas they can loot.

Nevertheless, at night every creak and groan of the old buildings fills me with dread. If I am found, if this book is lost, these forgotten spaces will be my Erșetu la târi.]

Kyöpelinvuori: From the Finnish for "ghost mountain," a place haunted by dead women. Some scholars argue it once existed, either predating Christianity in the region, or perhaps coming into existence as local gods were displaced by the arrival of new ones. Linna (2021) argues that dead women haunt liminal spaces in every culture. They exist where they can, and those who are silenced in life often speak in death.

[Last night I dreamed I was a ghost, screaming because they'd found me at last. I woke fearing this book was my scream.]

Leng, Plateau of: Antarctic Plateau colonized by Elder Things in the works of H. P. Lovecraft. When cultists successfully raised R'lyeh from what had been an empty seabed, expeditions were mounted to see if Leng had also been brought into existence. No evidence was forthcoming. "Our horrors are closer to home," as Coates remarked.

[Lovecraft panicked over people of color, immigrants, imagined them as murderous or worse. He should've worried about a different kind of cultist. A bunch of white kids slavering over Lovecraft's statue brought R'lyeh back. I wonder how many of those kids march through the streets of North American cities now, in uniform? Having failed to end the world, have they settled for effacing it?

I found a radio last week, and there are pirate stations, rebel stations. They urge us to hold onto hope, but they don't report much good news. I do not know how to fight this evil. I write instead.]

• • •

Zerzura: "The Oasis of Little Birds," a white-walled city in the Sahara, guarded by giants. Attested to in Arabic texts since the 13th century CE, and possibly predating Herodotus. Farouk (2019) demonstrates that all extant references to the city are from foreigners, and that no local tales reference it. Thus the most likely origin of the Zerzura story is a combination of colonizers' fears and hallucinations. Note that modern European interest in the city predates Imaginary Anthropology and so is unlikely to have made Zerzura real.

[The militias swept the area today; I braced myself in the frames of the wall between floors, and managed to escape. This time.

Fires spread across the skyline. I grow more desperate to leave. There is nowhere to go. I'd hoped, in saving this book, to find some insight that might help me, some way out, even if it is into unreality. Nothing.]

Section 2: Places that Once Existed

Azeb: From the Hebrew for "leave behind, forsake, abandon." Shown by Lee (2020) to be the place where lost objects gathered. Some have argued that it is synonymous with various cities of the dead, but loss and death have never been equivalent. Many documented methods of entering Azeb exist, though few exits have been found. There have been no verified reports of accessible entrances since at least 2017. It is likely, though not certain, that Azeb itself is forever lost to us.

[I had a friend who went searching for Azeb. Never heard from her again. I knew ways in, of course: what scholar of lost things wouldn't? Yesterday I tried to open a path, using the reflection of a full moon on still water, my own blood, and the second most valuable thing I own: a pair of dry socks. The way is closed. Seems I'll meet my fate here, Lya, less than a mile from the last place it was safe for us to walk holding hands.]

Cimmeria: The first triumph of Imaginary Anthropology (Goss, 2014), now lost due to conflict in the region and active condemnation of the discipline by foreign-backed warlords (may this book keep Cimmeria's memory alive, though this author was unable to keep it from joining the other Unplaces. Some nights, she can still smell the bazaar).

[I'm crying as I write this. Cimmeria's lost forever, and we never walked its streets. So much has been lost, and now even history is being erased. Then they'll make a new past, written in blood and marches and violent slogans and there will be nothing left.]

Penglai: Once a mountain on an island in the eastern Bohai Sea, attested by some sources to be home to the Immortals. Penglai was a land of abundance, with fruit that could cure any disease. Demonstrated by Kusano (2017) to have once existed, it was lost no later than the 2nd century BCE, when Qin Shi Huang dispatched expeditions seeking the elixir of life that failed to locate it.

[Lying awake last night, listening to gunfire in the distance, I wondered about the last person to set foot on Penglai. Did they know the paradise on which they walked would soon be gone forever? Did they treasure its memory? When they died, did Penglai die with them? I'm trying to hold on, Lya, but I feel everything slipping away.]

Tlön: A parallel world to Earth, probably first brought into existence in the 19th century CE. Known to be definitively real by 1940 CE. In Tlön, only those things exist which are observed, and there is no deity to do the observing. For reasons which are still debated, this world was lost to us, apparently forever, with the use of the Bomb over Hiroshima.

[In Tlön, a ruin might disappear from existence if there was not, say, a fox or a disinterested snake to observe it. The past is only as secure as our memory of it.

When they find me, or I starve, or die in a fire, will this book survive? Will it serve as a memory? Or will everything that I remember die with me?

I hope you got out, Lya. I hope that "out" is a place that still exists. If you did, remember. Remember. I'll do the same. It's all that is left to me. Goodbye, goodbye.]

[I thought I couldn't go on. I thought I was done with words. Then you appeared to me—a dream, a vision, a fevered hallucination?—and whispered in my ear that this book is incomplete. You were right. And so, as the sun rises over the burned-out city, I add a new entry:

Places that Might Yet Be:

Matsa: From the Hebrew "to find, to attain," Matsa waits for those who reject utopias, who believe we are doomed if we allow the mistakes of the past to overtake us. Matsa will be a place and a journey. We make it real only by seeking it out.

In Matsa, we will not forgive the fascists. We will light flames for the dead, and we will train ourselves against forgetting. When they try to burn our books, to make our places into Unplaces, we will, each of us, carry the past with us.

If you find this book, make Matsa real. I will await you.

Yours Always,

Hannah

The Museum thanks Dr. Lya Carew for the generous gift of this book. Dr. Carew asks that those wishing to honor the memory of Hannah Leibowitz make donations to the Free Lawrence Library's Matsa reconstructive history project.

THE NIGHTINGALES IN PLÁTRES

NATALIA THEODORIDOU

" . . . if one generation rose up after another like the leaves of the forest, if one generation succeeded the other as the songs of birds in the woods, if the human race passed through the world as a ship through the sea or the wind through the desert, a thoughtless and fruitless whim . . . how empty and devoid of comfort would life be!"

[. . .]

"Silently they rode for three days; but on the fourth morning Abraham said not a word but lifted up his eyes and beheld Mount Moriah in the distance."

Søren Kierkegaard, *Fear and Trembling*

Stranded, nomads on a nomad rock. Tied down on this unnamed planet for precious months, without reason, by forces we cannot comprehend. Nomad fathers and nomad sons. Punished, perhaps? By God, by Panayía. For what deviance? It is hard to know His will. Harder yet to know His ways of measuring transgression.

These thoughts keep Captain Yánnis Bostantzóglou awake through the sleeping hours—these, and the incessant song of nightingales echoing through the spaceship's hull. A line from an antique poem by the ancestral Seféris plays in Yánnis' mind, about Helen, and Agamemnon, and the futile struggles of Greeks: "The nightingales," it went, "the nightingales won't let you sleep in Plátres." And they don't, they don't. As if the entire damn ship was built to fit that one, old verse.

And what have we got but old verses? Yánnis asks himself, as has been his usual manner of late. Because who else can he burden with such questions?

He looks over to the sleeping figure of his young son. His breathing is regular, calm. He is not dreaming, then, and the nightingales don't bother him.

The nightingales, the nightingales. Is this Plátres? Yánnis wonders. *And are these nightingales? Empty imitations of birds frozen in embryonic banks, deep in the ship's womb, recordings played over and over and over, plucked from a past none of us have known. What is asked of us? All we have to do is believe. And isn't faith the hardest thing to get when you don't already possess it, but the easiest thing to keep when you do?*

They tried to program the ship to cease the nightingale song during the sleeping hours, or at least dim it, make it less intrusive, softer, a lullaby even. They found it was one of the features that were impossible to access and modify. For some reason, the people who built the ship wanted it to always echo with the song of nightingales. Something about the song's effect on the population's health, they guessed. Or maybe they had just been told to do so by God, and they, of course, obeyed.

Will our great-great-grandchildren have forgotten all about the birds of old Earth? Will they think them a myth made up by their senile ancestors, a rumor propagated by those disembodied songs, these ghosts of birds past?

The boy shifts in his berth. His long hair crowns his head, curly and strong, like a halo. His son's head. His son's hair. This gift of a son.

Yánnis gives up on trying to sleep—besides, the whole ship will soon come to life for another make-believe morning. Another shift of waiting for the wave that will get them off this rock, another prayer to be allowed to continue on their long, slow journey to the system of Tau Ceti. Another day on Nóstos II.

He sits up on his berth and runs his fingers through his long beard before tying it with an elastic band. All the men wear their beards this way. It would be easier to keep them short and trimmed, but this is not the tradition. Nóstos II is nothing if not traditional.

Yánnis slips out of his compartment as quietly as possible so as not to disturb Panayótis. He makes his way along the jungle that spans the bulk of the ship. The nightingale song is even louder out here. Yánnis lets the vegetation brush against his face and breathes in the warm, moist air. It is a good life, this, despite everything.

He enters the prayer room, his head hung low, his hands clasped in front of him, as is the proper way. There is a single flame burning in the old manouáli candlestand. It smells faintly of beeswax—an artificial scent, of course, as they ran out of natural beeswax candles long before Yánnis was born. The flame has almost consumed the entire stalk of the candle and is lapping at the sand that fills the bottom of the manouáli. There is no other light in the prayer room.

Yánnis approaches slowly and lights another candle. "For Léna," he whispers. His breath still catches whenever he utters his wife's name. Léna's sister Maríka is single. She's also the best genetic match for Yánnis. Soon, they would have to be wed. But not yet. Not before the widower's sorrow has turned into a dull ache, no longer the sharp stab of a blade. It's only been fifteen Earth months. They still measure time in the traditional way.

The flickering flame of the candle casts shadows across the room. Yánnis runs his hand over the tiny boxes that line the walls until he finds the one that holds Léna's bone, right above his ancestors'. *Léna, Léna.* She only got to enjoy their son for three short years. "This is the bargain I made," she told him with her last breath.

He traces her name with his finger, and then he bends over and touches it with his lips. He does not kiss it. He vowed never to kiss again after that day, the day they crashed. Not even his son. Not even Panayía.

He turns to face Her icon, almost indiscernible in the half-dark of the prayer room. Panayía Hagiosorítissa. *Madonna Advocate*, he prays silently, *advocate for us, so we can get off this unholy place.*

He contemplates the Virgin Mary, clad in deep purple, head covered, facing him just so, her arms raised in supplication. She is alone in this icon, without her Child. She is pointing towards Her Son, presumably to an icon of Christ that would be standing next to hers. Is this loneliness of the divinity what drove Léna to ask Her? To make the heaviest táma, to bargain her life for a child? And the lonely God provided, She did.

It was Yánnis' earliest known ancestor who carried the icon with him as he was fleeing genocide in the early 1900s, not even a century before Nóstos began its own journey. All the way from Anatolia to Greece, across the Black Sea, and the icon was all his ancestor took with him. Half his family drowned, but this, this he saved. He, too, had made a táma in exchange for safe passage. What price he'd paid, no one knew, but when the Bostantzoglaíoi stepped onto Greek soil, the icon, they say, wept tears of salt.

Our fleeing so different, Yánnis thinks, *and yet so similar. A leap of faith across the black, manifold sea of space.* And then, he kneels in front of Her icon, makes the sign of the cross in the traditional way, and begs, his prayer full of questions.

"Panayía, what have we done wrong?" he asks. "Why are we bound on this dead, rogue planet? Why can't we move? What do I have to do? Help us go. Help us, help us. Panayía."

"Father?"

He didn't hear his son coming in, or he wouldn't have spoken his despair out loud. He dries his eyes quickly and hopes the candlelight is not enough for Panayótis to make out the fear on his father's face.

"What is wrong, son?" he whispers. "Why aren't you asleep?" He opens his arms, inviting the child to come near.

"The nightingales," the sleepy boy whispers, rubbing his eyes. He still lingers near the prayer room's entrance.

"Ah, yes, the nightingales." Some people get used to them, eventually. Some don't. Yánnis pats his knees. "Come here," he says.

The child approaches and hides inside his father's arms. Yánnis touches his forehead to his son's and rests his arms on the boy's shoulders as gently as he can, as if afraid to touch him, to hug him, so as not to harm him. This is how fragile he thinks him, his son, his only son. The precious, rare son. They named him after Her. How could they not?

"Here," Yánnis says, lifting the child above his head, "give Panayía a kiss."

Panayótis crosses himself as his father raises him closer to the icon, and then kisses the Virgin Mary's forehead. His lips leave behind the faintest of marks on the ancient luster.

"Well done," Yánnis says, caressing the boy's hair. "Now off. Go find Aunt Maríka. I have work to do here."

As soon as he's alone again, Yánnis kneels before the icon and plunges back into his prayer.

This planet is death. It has no star. No name. No air.

He lifts his arm and touches the bottom of the wooden icon with his fingers.

"Are you punishing us, Panayía?" He closes his eyes and hits his forehead with his fists, again and again. The repairs have been completed for months. They have waited too long for a Dirac wave that their space drive can grip. They have waited and waited and waited. "Tell me what I have to do," he pleads.

Then, there is the voice. It shakes him, utterly and completely. It obliterates every other thought and fills his mind, his breath, this room, this life, this vast, vast space.

YOUR ANCESTOR SAID, MAY MY SEED DIE OUT, IF ONLY I WOULD GET TO SEE THE SUN OF GREECE.

Is this true?

YOUR WIFE SAID, MAY WE NEVER REACH THIS NEW EARTH, IF ONLY I WOULD GET TO NURSE A SON.

It cannot. This cannot.

THEY WERE SELFISH, YANNI. WILL YOU BE SELFISH TOO?

Tears flood Yánnis' eyes. The lonely God finally speaks. She speaks to him and he's on his knees. He's on his knees and there is terror in his heart.

"What are you asking? I will gladly give You anything."

A SACRIFICE.

The air is knocked out of his lungs. He has no voice, and yet he manages to speak. "What sacrifice?" he asks. "My life? My light? This very ship?"

THE SON WHOM YOU LOVE.

He opens his mouth to speak and closes it again. *But I have only one*, he wants to say. *I have no other than the one whom I love.*

Then the awful question blooms in his mind: Has he always known he'd have to give him up, eventually, his son, his only son? And then, the thought: *Curse you, my ancestor, my root. Curse you, Léna, my love. How could you?* And then: *How could you not?*

GIVE HIM UP, YANNI, the voice says.

GIVE HIM BACK.

Yánnis stands up, his hands curled into fists. He wants to shout. He wants to cry out: Why would God demand such things?

But then he falls to his knees again. He refrains from mouthing such questions. For the will of Panayía is unknowable and great, and to seek to know it is to seek to extinguish one's mind. So, instead, he thinks of how Léna, when she was to wean the child, blackened her breasts with soot. And he is reminded again of the philosopher's unfathomable, insatiable emptiness lying beneath everything, of Abraham's leap of faith, and of Agamemnon's—that one more dreadful still; because his leap had been a bargain, not a test.

Did Abraham doubt? Yánnis wonders. *Did Agamemnon?*

A son for a son. A daughter for a deer, a deer for a wind. *Is it a sin to doubt?*

Both these fathers were spared the unthinkable pain, Yánnis thinks to himself, so why wouldn't he too? Why would he be any different, his faith lesser, his leap greater?

"Without you, Panayía," he says out loud, his words echoing in the darkened prayer room, "what would living be but despair?"

The brightness of the corridor hurts his eyes. He rests his back against the thick layer of ivy that covers the walls on one side of the prayer room door. His head is spinning, his eyelids burn. He brings his trembling hands to his face—to hide it or to block out the light, he's not sure. It takes him a while to realize his beard has come undone.

"Are you all right, Yánni?"

Maríka has grabbed his shoulder and is squeezing it gently. He didn't see her coming.

"Did you hear?" he asks.

"Hear what?"

He takes a good look at Maríka's face, her dark eyes, her arched nose. No. She has no idea. God chose *him*. Him and him alone.

"Where is my son?" he asks.

She brings the back of her hand to his forehead, the way mothers do to feel for a child's temperature. "I've sent him to the database to study. What is wrong with you?"

He thinks of Seferis' poem again, his Plátres inhabited by myths. In that poem, Teukros, the exiled youth, sent to found a new home in Cyprus, ran into Eléni, who revealed to him she never went to Troy. The sacrifice, the war, the dead, the long trip home—it was all for nothing.

Does he remember this right?

A daughter for a deer, a deer for a wind, a wind for a war, the war for naught. Léna, no, Eléni, nothing but a phantom, a cloud. An empty shirt, that Helen.

Let's call this planet Moriah, he wants to say. *Let's not call it Aulis.*

He looks at the monitor across the hall. It's displaying the ship's surroundings, the empty, barren planet that has trapped them, that is *testing* them—because what else can this be but a test, this irrational becalming?

"Isn't it funny we have been stuck on a nomad planet for so long?" he asks. Little gravity, no atmosphere. This is a place where no one is meant to stay for long. "Nomads on a nomad land. Isn't it?"

"Funny is not the word I would use." She studies him, her forehead crinkled, her eyebrows furrowed. Maríka always worries about everyone, but she worries for him and Panayótis most of all.

"I've been praying to Her a long time, but this time, Maríka, this time She answered."

Maríka takes a step back and stares at him. "What are you talking about?" She glances at the prayer room door, then looks at him again, a kind of realization settling on her face.

Maríka is a believer. She will understand. If not now, then later. Eventually, she will. He extends his empty palms towards her, as if to show her the bleeding marks of nails. "Panayía spoke to me," he says simply. "There will be a wave this time. I know there will."

"It's been months. We should have come across a wave a long time ago," she says.

Grasping for reason, when faith is all that will do.

"It's not normal for them to be so far apart. Why now?" she asks.

He brushes his beard with his fingers. He spots the elastic band on the floor and picks it up. Then he ties his beard neatly again. His hands are not trembling anymore. "Bring the good news to the others. Tomorrow we are taking off," he insists. "God wills it."

She shakes her head slightly, lost for words.

He takes her hand. "Tomorrow, we are leaving this planet," he says again. "Today, we must celebrate."

Yánnis always finds the celebrations on Nóstos II somewhat uncanny. Strange, paradoxical. This group of a few hundred souls has never set foot on Greece, on Earth even, and neither had their parents. And yet, they are Greeks. They are from Earth. They grow up with songs and images and words from a world long gone. Their culture, nothing but a pastiche of references, and yet deeply their own. They learn the histories by heart, the dates, the names, the genocides. They carry the bones of their ancestors with them, along with their stories of miracles. They carry the faith. And their faith has carried them far in return. God ordered them to find a new Earth for themselves when the old one was on the brink of destruction. They did as they were told.

Some of them doubt, of course, but this cannot be helped. Is this why they have been imprisoned here on this death of a planet? No, Yánnis knows, it is not, no matter how tempting it might be to entertain that possibility. This is on his family and his ancestors, which means it is on him and him alone. He is the one who should carry it. *His* shoulders. *His* hands.

The dining hall is filled with low round tables at which one has to sit cross-legged. Aromatic plants are lining the walls—jasmine, and gardenia, and honeysuckle. The fragrance fills the air sweetly, mixed with the musty scent of damp soil. It might rain later tonight.

Yánnis is sitting under the gravure of the first astronaut to set foot on Mars, planting the Greek flag, back in the 1960s. His name was Anastásios Bostantzóglou, and one of his bones is resting in that little box right beneath Léna's.

Around Yánnis, in a circle, is his extended family, and then, in larger circles beyond them, sit the families that make up the rest of the ship's human cargo. And next to him, of course, Panayótis. *The son*, he thinks of him now, for he can no longer think of him as his own. *The son whom I love.*

The nightingale song seems louder tonight.

Before the leader of each family, the mothers, the fathers, the grandparents if they are still alive, is a container filled with flatbread made in the old way, just flour and water and salt. It is sour and dense. Familiar. Before each adult in the room rests a cup with a single sip of wine in it.

Yánnis does the sign of the cross and most of the people in the hall do the same. He fights the urge to glance at the son, to etch his posture in his memory, his three fingers touching together, his hand to his forehead, to his belly, to the right shoulder, then to the left.

"Let us eat," Yánnis says. He picks up the first flatbread. For a moment, he stares at his hands. *My hands*, he thinks. *Can they do what needs to be done?* He breaks the bread and passes it around. So do the other leaders. They eat their simple meal, and when they are done and they have all drunk their sip of wine, they know it is time to relax and enjoy a few hours of conversation and storytelling.

Even though tired, people seem cheerful enough. The conversations get louder as time passes. There is laughter, the occasional heated argument. It may sound like a fight, but it is all in good spirit. Let the bloods light up, as the ancestors said.

If there is any doubt among them that they will finally get off this barren planet, it doesn't reach Yánnis' ears. Only Maríka regards him with what could be concern. Or perhaps suspicion? Could it be that she knows what is to be done by him? But no, it couldn't, of course.

As if to reassure him, Maríka hands him his bouzouki. "Play us something, Yánni, will you?"

He hasn't played the instrument in a long time. It hasn't felt right since Léna died. How could his hands make music ever again? But tonight, it seems fitting. His father taught him when he was young. He listened for hours to all the great players of old, to Manólis Chiótis, Yórgos Zabétas, Vassílis Tsitsánis, Chrístos Nikolópoulos and so many others, watched videos of them playing over and over and tried to imitate their hands as they trembled over the strings like birds caught in a snare.

It takes him a few moments, but then his hands recognize the instrument, the wood warms to him, and he remembers how to pinch the strings just so. He chooses an old, sorrowful song from 1961. *I came back to your doorstep tonight / to sing for a last time.* Maríka joins in, her voice deep and viscous, like warm molasses. *I am leaving tomorrow*, the lyrics go, *everything is over*. Maybe he should have chosen a different one. Is he giving away too much? Are they going to know? *This is my last song / the birds cry along*. But no, it is fitting. Yánnis sighs deeply as he riffs over the melody of Maríka's voice. He remembers her as a child, her and Léna, long braids down their backs, singing doleful songs, even then.

Those sad Greeks with their sad, sad songs.

He turns to her. "Maríka," he tells her. Maríka. She could have been his mate, in a different life, a different place. "Maríka, you sing like a nightingale."

When putting the son to sleep that night, the last night, kneeling by the child's berth, he looks at the boyish mouth and thinks again of Léna's blackened breast, the mournful undoing of what used to signify nurture and life. He looks at the child's slender limbs, and his mind conjures up the trembling limbs of fawns.

"Oh God," he whispers. "Oh God."

"What is it, papa?" Panayótis mumbles, almost lost to sleep.

Yánnis buries his face in the son's curls and breathes in deeply. *Not yet, please, not yet. Soon, but not yet*, he tells himself. *As soon as he's asleep*. He thinks of the childless Panayía, of Abraham, of Agamemnon.

The lonely God will provide.

"Shhh, son," he says. "Listen to the nightingales. Just listen to the nightingales sing."

Even in the isolation room, the birdsong is there, loud, ever-present, relentlessly looped. Why did they do that, the ancestors, the ones who built this ship?

Why do parents do the things they do?

His body is spent, crumpled on the floor of the isolation room, where his people have stored him while they deliberate about how best to deal with him. Him, Yánnis, the murderer—worse, the filicide.

The ancestors left them no laws—only a handful of old texts with which to rule their lives. *Bibles and poems and songs. Perhaps these are all we need.*

He brings his hands in front of his eyes, takes a good look at them. They are the same hands they've always been—and yet, not the same. Not at all.

These hands of mine. Did I really think He would stay my hand at the last minute? Or that She would replace the son with a fawn, or a lamb, or a golden ram? Yes. I thought this was a test of my faith, I did. Was this my shortcoming? This hope that I could do the unthinkable wholeheartedly and still keep the promised son, my faith entire?

Did I fail the test? No fawn, no lamb. Only murder.

A son for a wave.

He lifts his eyes to the ceiling, wonders what it would be like lifting them to face the sky.

You are not the God I thought You were, he says silently. *Nor I the man I thought I was.*

His throat is dry and raw, as if he has been screaming for hours, although he hasn't. He hasn't made a sound since. Since.

And the nightingales, he wonders, *why won't they cease their singing?*

He covers his ears with his palms, his eyes wide open, trying not to blink, because every time he blinks, there it is, the son's body too terrible to contemplate, impossible to behold.

When Maríka walks in, hours later, she sits on the floor next to him, but she refuses to turn her gaze upon him.

"They are deciding what to do with you," she says.

He nods, but he doesn't reply.

"Why did you do it, Yánni?" She almost chokes on his name.

He is silent for a long time. She finally moves to leave, when he says, "God asked me to."

She faces him. Her eyes are red. "Why? In return for what?"

"They've detected a wave, haven't they?"

She understands now, he knows she does.

"Haven't they?" he asks again.

She nods.

This is it, then. The seas are finally rough enough for this Greek ship to sail. He dared to think himself an Abraham, when all he ever was, an Agamemnon.

What a monstrous paradox faith is.

He doesn't say anything, because there is nothing left to be said.

But she isn't done. "This was not your decision to make!" she shouts.

"You are right," he says. "It was God's."

A cruel God's, he wants to say. *The will of a God whom I do not know.* But he doesn't say any of this. Because who can live without faith?

Maríka turns around and leaves without a word.

It doesn't take them long to decide. They need to wash themselves clean of him. Wouldn't anyone? He does too. Maríka is back with the news. Her face is ashen. Her arms hang limply at her sides.

He stands up in the middle of the isolation room, ready to hear his fate. This time, she walks up to him. She puts her arms around him, startling him, and she hugs him tight and close.

"Do they believe me?" he asks.

She takes his head in her hands and looks him straight in the eyes.

"Some do. They thank you. I do, too." She looks at him sternly. "We are ready to go." She pauses. Tears shine in her eyes. Then she lets her words flow out. "Is it worth it, Yánni?" she asks. "Our lives, our survival, the new Earth, if killing children is what we have to do to get there? How can we go on after this?"

Poor, terrible Agamemnon.

He pinches a tuft of her hair between his fingers. "Weren't we children, once, Maríka?" he asks. "Weren't we sacrificed too?"

She stares at him, silent. The nightingales sing on, relentless, like an accusation. *Is this what they've always been?*

"We won't get to see the new Earth," he continues. "Our children . . . " He trails off, his knees giving way underneath him. He steadies himself. "The children you will have won't see this new Earth. They were never going to."

She shakes her head, covers her eyes with her palms. "Yánni—" she says and stops.

"Tell me the rest of it," he says. "It's all right."

She looks at the floor. "You are staying here," she says. "We are leaving you here."

Exile, then. They won't even dirty their hands with his death. He nods.

"Will you take him with you?" he asks. "Put his bone next to his mother's, have your children's children bury him with his ancestors when they get there? Will you make it so?"

She tries to speak, but a sob escapes her instead. "Of course," she says after a few moments. She's crying now, doubled, her arm on her belly, as if she was the one who received his stab. "Of course I will, of course, of course."

He waits until she collects herself and dries her face.

"You saved us," she says. "I cannot understand the thing you did, how you brought yourself to do it." She looks him in the eyes now. "And I will never forgive you." Her voice breaks. "But you saved us all."

For how long? he wants to ask. *Until the next bargain? The next desperate weakness, the next loving sin?*

Instead, he speaks the philosopher's words again: "In one hundred and thirty years, we got no further than faith," he says. "We've come so far, but we've really gotten no further than faith, Maríka."

Few come to see him off. Maríka is there. Most of the others look at him with a mixture of terror and awe. They could have executed him, but what narrative would that be? What stories would their children tell, about how they were delivered from the nameless nomad planet that snared their ship, once upon a time? And about the holy wretch who saved them?

Maríka weeps as he puts on his suit, the material tight against his skin. His helmet feels small around his head, heavy. Once he seals it, it blocks out all sound but his breath.

He is ready to step off the ship and they are about to seal the airlock behind him, when Maríka orders everyone to stop.

People protest weakly. They want this over with.

"Maríka," he says. "Let me go."

"Just wait!" she yells, and she disappears into the ship.

She comes back a few minutes later, panting, holding the bouzouki. She hands him the instrument and nods. Doesn't ask anyone's permission. Doesn't say a word.

He puts as much distance as possible between himself and the ship before takeoff. Not that it matters. What could possibly matter anymore?

He sits down and watches as the ship grips the invisible wave and departs, finally free of this place. The son's body is flying again among the stars. *Was it worth it, then? The sin, the pain, the sacrifice? The bargain?* Yánnis pictures the icon of Panayía in the prayer room, the soft light of the candles, the silent, ancestral bones. He whispers his wife's name, again and again, like a prayer. "Léna, Léna, Léna."

Then he makes the sign of the cross for the last time and bids everything farewell.

Here I am, he thinks. *Not Moriah, after all. Not even Aulis.*

Yánnis takes in the barren landscape. The surface of the planet is ragged and marked by hundreds of craters, not unlike Earth's old moon. A place of much violence. A broken place.

Then, he notices it. For the first time in his life, everything is silent. There are no birds here.

Nothing like my Plátres.

"And just what is Plátres?" he recites. "And this island, who knows it?"

Not even the ancestral poet had dared answer that.

He closes his eyes. For a moment, he thinks of praying, but he pushes through the reflex. Instead, he picks up his bouzouki. He wonders if the first Bostantzóglou to have owned it ever thought it would end up on a nomad planet, millions of kilometers from Earth.

Yánnis brings the instrument close to his torso, traces the ribs of its hollow body with his fingers. It feels strange in his arms now, lighter. He places his hands on the neck of the bouzouki and fumbles with the strings, his fingers clumsy in the protective layer of his suit.

He plays a chord. There is no sound, of course. Not here. There is no more music to be made by these hands. *These hands, my hands*. They've already played one more song than he'd expected. It should be enough. He holds his breath and listens, wishing for the song of nightingales.

He tries another silent chord.

PRASETYO PLASTICS

D.A. XIAOLIN SPIRES

Ali Prasetyo mixed the plastic resin, before pouring the viscous liquid into the silicone mold. The colors swirled, like eddies at the edge of Mas River, just as he intended. He let it sit, fumbling with the prototype of the plastic toy in his hand. He felt the smoothness of the curves. It felt buoyant and he let it bounce on the table, listening to the light thwacking sound. *There goes Earth*, he thought. A short tremor traveled up his bare toes and up through his shoulders. A magnitude two, a mere blip on the Richter Scale, and yet his body was perceptible enough to feel the tiny quaver. His Earth rolled off the table and clattered to the floor. He bent down to collect the miniature planet and saw that his home of Indonesia was facing up, the many islands of the archipelago dotted in green signifying land in a swath of ocean.

Ali shook his head, put the ball in his pocket, and got on his scooter to bike to the local chemical supplier. He wasn't satisfied with the way this prototype rebounded from the floor. There was a sluggishness to its ricochet. There must be something he could add to it, he thought, as he passed scooter traffic.

Ali had a way with plastic. He liked the way they shape-formed, like superheroes and monsters he used to read in paper comic books his grandfather collected. He passed by a bookstore and sped up. Brittle and yellowing, paper seemed so much the inferior material when compared to the shiny bright plastic that was so ubiquitous in his own generation.

He revved his engine and cut in front of a slow scooter with three kids sitting in them, along with their parents, two of the children with hard plastic helmets. He noted the grooves and holes, an irregularity on the side of the toddler's helmet that faced him. Just as peripheral vision detected movement in an instinctive act, his eyes processed mold shapes and their contours instantaneously. In a second, he had passed him and his eyes focused on the road, an uptick in his brain registering the polycarbonate window that passed off as glass on a fleeting performance car that accelerated ahead of him.

As he watched the sports car disappear, he thought about his childhood and his dad who professed he longed to own a fast vehicle, but instead invested all his income on Ali's future.

Ali excelled at plastic mold competitions, plastic erecting architecture, snap-on challenges. When he was five, he made his first model of a bird with his 3-D printer, with legs, guts, face, and all. When he was twelve, he focused on joints, moving parts, pendulums, and other mechanics using differently weighted plastics to achieve the kinds of kinetics he wished. When he was a high school graduate, he won accolades from the many contests he entered and placed. His teachers penned effusive recommendations for him and he won a scholarship to the university of his choice with the premier plastics engineering program. At the expense of their own dreams, his parents poured their energies into his and it paid off. They couldn't have been prouder.

They could see their son was made for something great. He was one of the many youths ushering in a new era of material science, one of the great architects of the next generation. The kind of thing every parent tells themselves. Even as their dreams of race cars (with polycarbonate windows) sped off into the distance and winked away in the horizon.

Plastic was already overtaking all. Just as the world's oceans were engulfed in plastic—where a knife slit in a dead bird's body would reveal an autopsy of the polymer, just as even plankton consumed the micro-plastics—3-D printers started phasing in. They were the next best gift. They used plastic to make 3-D printers and 3-D printers to make 3-D printers. A kind of self-replication that assured perpetuity.

Ali browsed through the catalog of chemicals. As always, the warehouse was filled with mechanic humming and drumming but few conversations and shouts from vocal chords, with mostly machines operating the lines. Machine parts also printed from printers.

Printing was fairly easy. You could buy hardware off Amazon or you could just ask your buddy at school, your neighbor, your employer, someone else who has already invested in the hardware to make one of your own. Put in some specifications or download one of those many pre-made designs uploaded on snap share, and there you have it, a ready 3-D printer, ready to wash ashore more plastic debris, ready to raise plastic overconsumption as the number one threat to human health.

Ali took a can off the shelf. The can container itself was plastic.

When Ali created a small robotic car that had all plastic components, his parents took him bowling. His dad was especially elated. Then, one week later, he recreated a bowling alley out of plastic in their backyard. Every reward they offered him struck another chord of imagination, so that their attic filled to the brim with plastic appliances and knick-knacks. Then, when the attic was full, his parents allowed one car space of the garage to be dedicated to Ali's contraptions. One car space soon became the whole garage, and next thing you knew, Ali had his first commission. One hundred dollars from his parents to build a shed of plastic to store his stuff. His parents thought themselves clever, but Ali thought they got the short end of the stick. He would get to appropriate more backyard real estate for his projects. Also, the lack of specification from his parents was his own gain. He built a shed that covered the entire backyard, from house to fence.

If his parents' generation was the silicon generation, then surely his would be the plastic one. But, silicon was still present. Tech companies still experimented with silicon, interlaced with the printable polymer. But, plastic start-ups were where all the investors fled.

The next day, Ali cradled his plastic filament, as he chatted with his coworker, Karina Hartono. He was one of the few that had opted for a biochemical minor and now he proved the utility of his passion. Not only did it lead him to a career in one of the most lucrative sectors of R&D, but it also led him to this particular lab with this particular labmate, Karina.

The filament he held in his hand was mostly plastic but included some organic material from seabed bottoms, reefs from which he chiseled. The resulting mix was something that could conduct heat. He could feel it pulsate in his palm, but he thought that might be his own heartbeat, beating away to Karina's tinkling laughter.

He felt on top of the world, a love blossoming, the conductive nature of romance-to-be and the new product that he felt in his bones would soon be marketable. This was the one, he thought.

Conductivity is a conduit for plastic to be the one material which will rule over us all. The long-lasting, barely biodegradable emperor of its domain, Earth.

That was the first two sentences of a 3456 carefully-worded anonymous letter that came in the mail one week after his co-authored article, "The electromagnetic conductivity of reef-based calcium carbonate infused in new polypropylene varieties," published in the *Journal of Engineered Textiles and Science.* It was one of many letters to come. Looking back at it, Ali would say it was perhaps one of the tamest, least filled with vitriol.

After Karina published an article on her other project with the team that she was leading, new methods of plastic tempering, they kept separate bins to compete to see who could get the most hate mail by the summer. Some were sent by post but most came through their work emails that they then printed out to add to their own pile. Letters that were mostly questions or requests from media on plastic-related topics didn't count. It had to have at least a tinge of animosity to qualify for the bin.

Ali was winning. His stack was at least three times the size of Karina's. While the letters Karina received were largely confined to the local area and too benign to be considered for the bin, Ali received letters with lots of colorful expressions. But, Ali himself was a much more vocal advocate, agreeing to appear on blogs and podcasts on textiles.

And his 'fans' were from around the world, too.

It was with this lead in competitive hate-mail receiving, that Ali asked Karina to go scuba-diving with him. That summer they spent a lot of time checking out reefs together, all across Java, Bali and further out into the pristine waters of the Raja Ampat archipelago, with Ali pointing out some of the flamboyant ones that inspired his latest polymers.

"Remember that one that in blue and yellow with a huge arm span reaching out towards the surface? It looked like a peacock," he would say. Or make note of some other piece of ocean bottom he found particularly enrapturing.

"It was a sea fan coral, anchoring to softer substrates. I read they're nocturnal, only growing their polyps at night," she would respond, a twinkle in her eye. "Can you imagine that, an engorged limb reaching out in the dark sea waters?" Ali wondered if that was an invitation to say more. Karina exhibited an encyclopedic memory when it came to these formations and a spirited humor he appreciated but could not exactly interpret. He left it alone.

But one night, at a provocative remark on her part, "darting orange fishes like tongues," he invited her to his room. She conceded, with a coquettish grin. That night, like the coral, they stretched out their limbs. Like wayward growth, they wrapped themselves around each other in the dark, their tongues mimicking the flitting movements of tiny sea life.

Twice a week for two blissful months, they would glide in each other's paths for hours at a time, pointing out gaudy sea life and photographing exceptional coral constructions.

Then, they would surface in sync to a setting sun.

The first leaves of autumn had already fallen when Ali first saw the clip of the environmentalists attacking plastic physically. He couldn't help but laugh.

"What a joke," he said at the cooler to the HR manager, as they peered at the screen together, watching the rage unfold.

"Honestly, sometimes I can imagine giving some plastic a good whack, too," said the manager. "But, I'm not actually gonna go out there and do it." Their eyes fell away from the phone as the repeated hits relented at about three seconds left of the clip.

Then, Ali grabbed his mug of kopi jahe, sipping the mix of bitter coffee and bright ginger, as he approached Karina's desk. He pulled out his mostly-plastic phone to show her.

The environmentalists were beating plastic phones with metal bats. He couldn't see the victims very well, but they appeared to be outdated Samsungs. The same group also uploaded a video of themselves taking blows at plastic medical machinery behind a hospital, using what looked to be old metal pipes they must have found rusting at scrapyards.

"Looks like they're pretty hell-bent," said Karina.

"Yeah, though I think I have a few letters in my inbox that are more provocative," said Ali.

He clicked on the next video. For a few seconds they watched these determined protestors take swings at more plastic parts, this time behind an elementary school. The video must have been filmed right after lunch because kids started pouring in, running about the playground and yelling from slides and swings behind the protestors. The kids added to the general commotion, the sounds of banging plastic and the high-pitched cries and laughter of recess intermingling, until a school administrator asked the protestors to leave and the clip ended.

• • •

Later at home that night, Ali swirled his spaghetti with a LivingEssentials plastic fork, lost in thought.

It wasn't as if he never considered the environment, he just knew it would work itself out. His job was to innovate and streamline machinery production through plastics. Other sectors had other responsibilities. Recycling and disposal were sectors outside his narrow field.

Anyway, the protestors could find more effective means of conveying their message, he figured. As if beating a few pieces of plastic technology would do anything but hasten their way into the food stream.

First, these tech pieces would be rendered unusable, some of it would be calibrated for reuse and the rest that could not be so easily recycled would be submitted to the earth as waste. Another bit of plastic discard. Then, whoever those environmentalists took from would simply create more plastic tech. Easy as calling in some superior printers, wave around some money, and within days, new plastic—some from old sources and some created—would be amalgamated into another lifecycle of waste.

Ali thought that if protestors could only use a bit of logic and political literacy, maybe they could direct their energies to the right ears and wallets. Beating plastic gears just wouldn't cut it.

Ali and Karina had been dating steady for about two years when plastic superseded the boundaries of Earth.

They were watching industry news in the cafeteria, spooning chocolate pudding into their mouths after a lunch of some lackluster rubbery ham sandwiches, when the special came on. Collaborating textile specialists produced plastic that survived the onslaught of UV rays and X-rays from solar flares. Some of the polymers that Ali had worked on, now marketed to a general public, were involved in the innovations.

The textile specialists held out thin sheets of plastic. They explained that air pockets made them extremely lightweight, and its construction virtually indestructible by solar onslaught of electromagnetic radiation.

The reporter then finished the segment: And now *plastic takes off to chart the cosmic seas.*

As the value of their company stock took off, Ali and Karina talked about major life changes: marriage and the possibility of starting their own company. There were too many restrictions and bureaucratic stalls in their company and they were eager to dip their toes into the unknown, both in their relationship and in the trending industry of plastic for space exploration.

It was with their combined efforts and with the roles of many others that plastic accompanied the colonists to the moon and Mars almost a decade later. The colonists clothed in plastic, drank from plastic mugs, designed their residences in plastic, mostly bubbles of air trapped in plastic sheets, all thanks to Freeroam Industries Ltd. (once MicronLabs, division of Prasetyo Plastics, founded by the power couple and later sold for a whopping one billion in cash and stock.)

Humanity still breathed, ate, and expelled organic material. They were still life, after all. But, some argued that the fast food was mostly plastic anyway. Plastic worked its way up the food chain, they said, from the littlest fish up to the ones that reigned at the top. The omnivores that managed to conquer local space travel, also bore microscopic bits, buoyed in the fluids in their bodies.

Those who espoused humanity's addiction to plastic pointed at these invisible bits of plastic coursing within. Humanity was likely crapping plastic. Peeing and bleeding plastic. Possibly breathing microscopic plastic.

It's in this background of symbiotic relationship, when plastic took on a sentience of its own.

Ali was watching a program on the backlit screen when the news program followed.

"At first it was the merging of plastic and plankton, and the pieces that caught in those tiny digestive tracts must have intermingled with the replicating DNA of those tiny simple organisms, a threat invisible to the human eye," said a woman holding a mic, her eyes peeping out a pair of glasses Ali could tell were at least ninety percent plastic.

"The murkiest seas give way to the strangest creatures, so it's no surprise that it came from the ocean at first. Like the first of the Loch Ness Monster sightings, their existence was at first hard to identify. But, soon enough, footage caught these amorphous new organisms attached to each other like coral reefs, K'nex sets of monstrosity."

Ali thumbed a message to Karina. "Urgent, check out the news," it read. He clicked send and a ping let him know she would soon be cradling her own mostly plastic phone to read his dispatch.

Ali's eyes glazed, frozen into the spherical molds, as he saw the material he had cradled and formed in his palms since a child, talked about in a way that smacked of new life.

"Sometimes they would wash up dead ashore. But mostly, they lay impassive on the seafloor. They consumed other organic material collected in the seabed, like sponges, filtering in the plastics and rich minerals of dead debris," said the newscaster, her voice portentous, ending in a deep lilt.

Ali was scuba diving alone when he first saw them move. Karina was back at home, putting some finishing touches on a model of the Mars colony she was building for fun. Both of them had retired by now, their fortunes according them with leisure time for trivial pursuits.

Ali started and were it not for all his experience, he might have choked in his mask. A species of violet lichen cropped up that he never saw before. Ali thumbed through the registry of organisms that made their appearance on coral reefs that he had digitally collected in his mind.

Maybe it was a seasonal thing, a periodic thing, like locusts that come in regular passes of years, he thought. But, he had been scouring seafloors for many years and he never found a specimen much like this. He remembered the many formations Karina had rattled off to him throughout their lives together, years and years of collected knowledge.

Despite strict reef habitat regulations, he grabbed a sample. The purple creeped into his hands.

Ali, who had designed the merging of coral reefs and plastic many moons ago before his research took flight in capitalistic enterprises, felt a pang of dread. His years of investors, rising stocks in the company he co-operated and immersion in that territory amounted to a knowledge so in depth and wide in breadth, that he could recognize that there was a strand of something offbeat in this tiny sample. There was something nonorganic about this lichen.

He immediately called on some acquaintances to rent out a lab with limited oversight. *For a hobby*, he said, and no one would refuse him otherwise, because they owed their jobs to him and his name went places.

He didn't want to raise any alarms until he knew for sure. Every day, he quietly slipped into the antiseptic room, hinting not even to Karina his whereabouts. He brought his scuba gear with him and said he would play with the corals.

Under the bright lab lights that passed through the microscope and through the manipulation of Ali's adept gloved hands, the cells of the strange lichen quivered. Yet, they were not lichen, not really. Something about their molecular structure spoke of plastic. And yet, they weren't entirely plastic either.

Unlike his own creations decades ago that kindled the plastics industry, these things grew. They were not content to stay bounded by the tenets of inorganic life, or staying simply manmade plastics, inert and lifeless. Rather, what Ali had first mistaken as lichen were plastics that had married into the plankton family, forged a union into the hum of the ocean bottoms, processed through the deep sea food chain.

They had taken reefs as hostages and lovers, which later Ali confirmed to be a kind of Stockholm syndrome that threatened to challenge the dominion of not only oceanic, but human existence.

After a month testing his initial conclusions in the lab, Ali decided he would need to see these plastics in person again. He spent days at the sea and was, at least, relieved that he no longer had to lie to Karina. His soaked wetsuit, sandy flippers, and constant run to the scuba gear suppliers for oxygen refills corroborated his story that he was scuba-diving daily.

Beneath the glittering sun, every day Ali jumped off his rented boat and cut through the surface of the water. He moved from shallower seas to deeper ocean, as the boat operator waited for him, often with fishing pole or book in hand when Ali returned hours later.

Under the bright ray of his heavy duty underwater flashlight, Ali watched how the plankton plastics divided and combined. He witnessed in person how they formed large masses as big as sea dollars, then starfish, then manta rays, darting in the sea like mystical creatures. They were not quite as fast as dolphins, not yet, at least. But, they were growing.

Ali didn't want to stoke the understandable irrationality that lurked in human minds. He didn't want to start a panic that once reached the media, would burst into a sensation online, a frenzy of apocalyptic shouts of doomsday approach.

Regardless, he couldn't simply go down every day, watching the plastic coalesce.

In those days, alone in the dark seas with only his flashlight and a mind full of dread as company, he thought about evolution. An instinct told him that these strange creatures would not be content to roam the seas. They would make contact with their inert brethren on land. Maybe they could even mate and awake them. He did not know if it was possible. But intuition told him, that the creatures would expand and expand, just as the plight of the inert plastics, taking up landfill space and cluttering up streets.

But, this was not simply about immobile, lifeless plastics. This was much more sinister. These were growing bits of life, merging with plastic. Or plastic merging with bits of sea life. They were not sterile, but robust entities. They divided and reorganized in swift movements.

They could have a dominion of not only the seas, but of the land and skies. Ali thought of an old drawing in a children's museum depicting fish making their way to amphibians and then reptiles. He thought of these amalgams coming ashore, the evolution of this plastic species in touch with their already pervasive terrestrial and extraterrestrial brothers would mean a crisis affecting them all. He thought of a bouncing plastic Earth ball he made years and years ago, rolling off a table and falling into an abyss.

After much consternation and against better financial judgment, he alerted the officials. Over everything, he wanted to shield Karina from it all. Karina, his partner in this enterprise, who had seen him through two kids and the surges and ebbs of their life they grew around their business.

He knew that telling the authorities would mean falling stocks, a probe into regulation, and possibly dismantling of an industry they had worked so hard for. It would also mean personally putting their household under spotlight for their own roles in the course of plastic development. Sure, they were retired and they could do fairly well, but their children who were working in the industry might falter and this could mean the crumbling of an operation they staked their reputations in.

The officials Ali first contacted were scientists that watched over ethics. They never thought ethics could come to this. Typically, the concerns these officials fielded amounted to questions on human subjects and concerns over exploitation. Not the threat of a wayward species coming into existence.

The alarm that spread through the scientific community harked back to the atomic bomb. Not only did it open up new impetus in research on reverse-engineering plastic-related textiles, but it also garnered a wave of discussions and debates.

No longer scouring the seas and instead leaving the job to expert hands, Ali spent his days and nights watching the aftermath of his unpleasant discovery. He would sit in his couch, ignoring Karina's pleas that they needed a break from this. Where could he go that he could not see plastic? *Maybe one of the space colonies. We haven't been there in years,* she said. But, Ali would look glassy-eyed into the screen, strapped to his sofa as if it were his own retribution.

And he would soak in all the criticism: science as not tool but weapon, not helping humanity but bringing it to its demise.

And this weapon was growing and, if what Ali suspected was right, already sentient.

Again, tonight Ali settled in his sofa with his dinner of cold, leftover pizza as accompaniment. Karina was at the gym and texted to tell him she'd eat later. His fingers sent a quick reply and then clicked the plastic buttons on his remote a few times before settling on Channel 36.

6PM Nightly News, with your host, Clarissa Wang.

Today, we will be re-airing a special for those of you who missed the show from last week. Reporter Bill Taylor, biologist Penelope Jackson, and plastics specialist Advik Singh (son-in-law of former plastics moguls Ali Prasetyo and Karina Hartono) take us to the depths of the oceans to trace the phenomenon we're calling "Plastic Terror."

(Roll-in Intro)

Everyone thought that when the singularity would happen, it would be metal cores with metal heads, metal limbs and metal breaths. Again, it was the projection of the times, the easy mistake that all short-sighted humanity falls for over and over again. The robots that fought back were never the shiny kind with tin folded limbs. They never had antennae jutting forth and walked on two feet. No, they were plastic. Plastic in all its versatility.

The way they formed together. The way they paired up in patterned numbers. It was the Fibonacci sequence unrolling before your eyes. There was something systematic to it all, something that surpassed simple mechanical unfurling of DNA and RNA. An intense curiosity and smartness emanating from the very fibers of their being.

"Fibonacci," said Ali aloud with a groan, throwing an empty high-density polyethylene can of soda at the screen. It bounced off with an inoffensive bop, durable plastic coating shielding the ionized gasses within. He turned up the volume just as the urgency in reporter Clarissa Wang's voice escalated.

Intelligence. These creatures were already sentient.

Soon they would contact their inert brothers, soon they would lay their replicated hands into their malleable bodies and turn them into machines of their own wills. Ingest them as one of theirs and regurgitate them for their own expansive motives.

Today we will explore the moment when the machines came alive and conscious. The phenomenon people are calling the singularity.

Cut to Reporter Bill Taylor: "Advik Singh leads us through some key areas of plastic manufacturing and disposal. Here is a waste pipeline of one of the leading plastics corporations (name withheld for legal purposes). To our left is the pipe in question that leads into the ocean. As you can see, it no longer pumps out waste, as the factory was shut down months ago."

Cut to Plastics Specialist Advik Singh, as they walk around the waste pipeline. Then, cut to a mound of discard at an abandoned warehouse.

Advik Singh: "This is one congregation of our organic and inorganic refuse, all our disposable forks, spoons, and chopsticks, our blankets and machinery. My specialization is breaking down these plastics to benign forms that can't be appropriated by sentient organic masses. Much of the technology is currently in development, but we're looking at an accelerated time horizon for this project. Thanks to the disposal bill and the governmental funds pumped into the program."

Cut to Biologist Penelope Jackson at the gates of a landfill: "All this is beat down to barely imperceptible crumbs and entering the breeding chains with plankton. Chambers of new life, new growth. The pact the lowest on the food chain made with the products of the highest."

Cut to Reporter Bill Taylor: "When they came alive, they brought life to the plastic machinery that surrounded us, grew up with us, embedded into our own bodies in surgical procedures."

Ali thought about the surgery Karina had last year on her hip. The joint replacement. He remembered her being more agile than he could ever remember.

(Roll in transition before commercials:)

This is how the machines came to life.

Singularity in plastic.

If it were a fugue, it would be an ominous cacophony. A provocative deep noise from the bottom of the sea. The yawns and shifts of countless single-celled creatures that lurked unnoticed eating and expelling. Making its way through the food cycle. More after this short break."

Ali saw it all.

At the moment he scraped up that viscous violet that turned hard once on land, he had a hunch. Once his microscopes and plastic equipment ran the tests that affirmed what they were, already a pit as hard as cold plastic grew in his heart.

It was the worst hate mail he could never ignore: The demise of humanity for a superior race. *And we did it unto ourselves.*

Karina was always trying to be positive. When Ali's mind turned to dark points of regret, she would say things like, "At least our kids are employed and passionate. Now that they transferred to jobs they find fulfilling." Working to undo what we brought about was not what she added, but was the honest truth.

But, Ali's mind went past the energies of their kids, springing into the far future beyond. *Who knows what these masses of creatures will merge with next? Perhaps their race will continue to evolve, consuming us, bringing us squishy beings into their own folds. Maybe they would take us with them—out of local space and into the depths of the universe by way of combination with their tenacious materiality.*

Ali wondered if by then he would be long dead, or at least altered enough not to be identified as Ali. Flagged instead as another kind of existence and intelligence. One that melts and reforms. One that can replicate itself and conduct messages with others. A new hardier life-form that could sail the cosmic seas like the voyagers that their polymer bodies promised.

It would be a kind of fitting irony, the company that he and Karina had erected, the textile giant that propelled an industry of space travel plastic manufacturing that eventually gave way to the metamorphosis of their own species in consolidation with another: the ultimate sentient colonizers.

At his workshop, Ali went back to his spherical mold of Earth, dabbling with it. This time the plastic hardened to a model whose colors were no longer green and blue, but a shocking, violent violet, textured with ripples, like the grape agates from Mamuju, Sulawesi that Karina owned as pendants. It didn't roll off the table and fall into an abyss, but stood there on the desk, held back by its friction surface, challenging him. It seemed to pulsate even, tiptoeing towards him in the tiniest of movements, or maybe it was an illusion created by his own weakening eyes.

CROSSING LASALLE

LETTIE PRELL

Mara inched forward in the line, painfully aware she looked out of place. She didn't belong here, with old people in wheelchairs and on gurneys, being pushed along by their relatives, who looked at her and frowned. She wasn't like the younger people in the line, either, bald from chemotherapy treatments, or coughing up dark stains into handkerchiefs, fragile skin yellowed or pocked. Mara was neither bald nor thin. She brushed a long lock of wavy dark hair behind her ear self-consciously. She clutched her paper form in her other hand—why it had to be printed, she didn't know—worried that by the time she reached the front of the line it would be disintegrating from her sweat, from the creases she was making in it because of her nervousness.

There were only nine people ahead of her, and twelve behind her, some accompanied by relatives, but it felt like hundreds, like an infinite line that stretched in both directions. She was startled when the line parted like a curtain, the people in front moving to the left and right as more officials were added to the counter. She found herself staring at an older woman with stray red hairs escaping her loose updo, who was looking at her expectantly over the top of her rimless eyeglasses.

Mara's case suddenly and starkly bared, words stuck in her throat. She fumbled with the form and handed it to the official, who opened it, revealing the checked boxes and printed narrative at the bottom, its one-inch margins, double-spaced, containing Mara's four reasons for her request.

Reason number one. She didn't want to die.

Reason number two. If she waited till she was older or got sick, she may not have this opportunity. This option may become unavailable due to shifting policies or unforeseen circumstances.

Reason number three. Overpopulation was taxing the earth's resources. By being allowed to make this choice, she would be doing her part for climate change, greenhouse gasses, and pollution.

Reason number four. Ahead lay an exciting world of opportunity. She wanted to be part of it.

Watching the woman read, wearing a neutral expression, made Mara's face grow hot. Maybe her writing was too passionate, or too political, or both. Shifting policies and unforeseen circumstances were euphemisms for the possibility that the tables could turn any instant, and slam the door in her face.

The official turned over the page and glanced at the blank side. Then she looked up at Mara. "You don't have any affidavits attached."

Mara blinked. "I'm not sick. It said online they're not required if—"

"I'll tell you what's required. We need affidavits from your medical doctor and a mental health professional. Also your birth certificate so we can verify your age."

Mara didn't know if she had a copy of her birth certificate. She looked away, toward the group moving out the glass doors and onto an unmarked gray transport bus. Another set of people heading for safety.

She stood straighter, emboldened. "And when I bring all that back, my application will be approved?"

The woman's expression seemed to harden, become not just judgmental, but contemptuous. "Your application doesn't demonstrate high need. You'll be assigned a priority number."

Mara hadn't heard of priority numbers. People were supposed to come in, be processed, and get on the bus to the Newbody Zone. She jabbed a finger at the people slowly filing out the door. "Would the priority number allow me onto that bus?"

"Honestly? No. But you'd go on the list. Discussion continues regarding applicants such as yourself."

"What's there to discuss? And what do you mean, applicants like me?"

The official flipped the form across the counter at Mara. "This isn't some video game. This is forever. Next!"

Mara was angry now. This was so typical of older people, to discount Mara's entire generation. If anything, her age group was more capable of adapting to the future.

Mara could've made a stand, given a whole speech, protested. She could've tried to jump into the line for the transport bus. Instead, she left and hopped the Pink Line back to Pilsen, to Heart of Italy and the two-bedroom walk-up she shared with her roommates, Enrico and Remmy.

It didn't take Mara long to find the community of people who'd also pulled the wrong priority number. They used the hashtag #InLimboChicago, and once approved, she was granted access to their secure chat. Just as she'd suspected, they were mainly her age, thirty-somethings who weren't suffering from some terminal disease. It was an active group, with more than twenty online at the moment.

They don't know what to do with us, wrote @HarryOakPark. *Our lives don't have a set expiration date yet.*

Mara was lying on the couch in the apartment, her left leg slung over the top of the headrest. Her half-drunk Mountain Dew was sweating a circle onto the smudged glass of the cocktail table. The television took up the other side of the room, with barely enough space to inch past into the tiny kitchen or the hallway to the bathroom and bedrooms.

We're low-wage slaves, replied @MPoweredGrrl. This sparked a deluge of comment from others.

Using our bodies to fuel the meat-based economy.

They're still not sure about letting a corporation kill us. That's how they see it. Murder.

If that's true and I'm not saying it is. But if it is, one has to question their morality. They let the old and sick go. Expendable lives?

They're in denial. The singularity will not be televised.

The singularity is privatized. It's happening in different ways.

I heard there's a computer in Houston, @HarryOakPark wrote. *It's run by a place called PHI. Post-Human Incorporated. Maybe we can get in on their system.*

They're only taking scientists. The brain trust.

Elitists, wrote @MPoweredGrrl. *Screw 'em.*

Wait. Is the Newbody place downloading minds? Or giving people newbodies?

Newbodies.

How would we know? They haven't been letting information out of the Zone.

Mara jumped in, typing swiftly using her four-finger method. *The official who bounced my application said this isn't a video game. It was so offensive being told that!*

They could be downloading, then. There's been talk. It's getting real.

Don't be so sure. A remark like that could mean newbodies just as easily.

Or nothing, @MPoweredGrrl wrote. *Just a cruel comment.*

The door burst open. Seeing it was Enrico, Mara closed the app and pretended to check email. Enrico peeled off his black baseball jacket and dropped it on the cocktail table. The logo on the jacket's back, a red heart with a green oak tree growing up its middle, stared back at her accusingly. *Love Life*. It was the sign of the Newbody protestors, the people who'd rather stop the transport vehicles to the Newbody Zone altogether, even for the dying. The group that a year ago were considered terrorists, before they'd negotiated themselves into legitimacy.

Mara could never tell Enrico about her application, and her encounter with the official. They were on opposite sides of the biggest political divide she'd ever known. She looked up at him and made her voice casual. "Hey. What's up?"

Enrico was already in the tiny galley kitchen, a matter of five steps. His body was hidden by the opened refrigerator door, his head haloed by the round window behind him. They'd frosted the glass with a spray-on product to hide the view of the brick wall beyond.

"Not much. Work-work. Seeing Cecily later on. There's no hard cider left."

"Text Remmy. They're stopping at the store for more ramen, anyway."

Enrico slouched in the doorway with one of Mara's pop cans in his hand. "How's the job hunt coming?"

"Well, you know. Promising."

"Liar."

Mara stared down at her blank screen. "I went to a tech company today but they didn't have any openings. I couldn't get in." That was very nearly a true statement.

Enrico nodded and took a swig of pop. "Everyone wants into tech, but the information age runs on top of the industrial age, which runs on top of the agrarian. Jobs are being squeezed at all levels, sure. But widening your scope should turn up something."

She nodded, humoring him. She'd been fired from her job at the group home for troubled girls two months ago. She wasn't suited to dealing with people in crisis like that. Drug addiction, broken homes, abuse. She'd rather geek out on a line of code.

He came over, sat down cross-legged on the rug and set his Dew on the cocktail table. "You're looking really serious all of a sudden. What're you thinking?"

Her jaw tightened. "Nothing. Just maybe I should be looking at going into something like insurance." Enrico worked in a cubicle farm at an insurance company.

He took another huge swallow of Dew, wincing it down. "Wrong time to jump in. Not hiring."

She'd meant her comment to be sarcastic, and his helpful tone only underscored Mara's recurring resentment. She took comfort that insurance was one of the troubled industries right now. Why buy life insurance when you intend to take advantage of the new options? Enrico was probably in the protest movement because to be otherwise would be against his profession.

She rose. "Here, I'll let you have the couch."

"Thanks." He heaved a big *ahh* of satisfaction as he took her seat. "Hey, don't you want to watch our show?"

She paused in the hallway, outside the bathroom door. To the left was the tiny bedroom she shared with Remmy. To the right was Enrico's. "I might come out in a bit. You go ahead."

"It'll cheer you up," he said, reaching for the remote.

Enrico loved comedy news, but the show he liked had been taking an anti-singularity stance lately. Or was she just becoming sensitized to the criticisms? She shut the door to her room and flicked on the harsh overhead light. Enrico made the most money, so he got the bedroom with the window all to himself. This room was little more than a windowless closet. Remmy had made the best of things by strewing the thin queen-size mattress with a dozen tasseled discount pillows of varying sizes, dubbing it the pit. Mara sank down into its colorful depths, woke up her device, and found Limbo again, where the number online had grown to thirty, and the chat had turned gossipy.

I heard someone got through last week, someone noted. *Without the forms and authorization. They made it to the Newbody Zone.*

It's urban legend, wrote @MPoweredGrrl. *They got caught.*

@HarryOakPark was still online as well. Mara was getting the sense these two were leaders within opposing philosophical camps. *I know someone who has a sister who's a cop in the 18th precinct. She says they can't stop everyone who tries, at least theoretically. Their main worry is keeping vandals and protestors away from the area. Sometimes they still try to breach the Zone.*

@MPoweredGrrl wasn't having any of it. *Oh? Then why are you still here?*

I'm working for real change, he replied. *Access for everyone who wants it. That's what this whole discussion thread should be about.*

There was a pause in the conversation, during which Mara sensed @HarryOakPark was restraining himself from flaming @MPoweredGrrl, and others were either holding their breaths waiting for a fight, or afraid to type something that could be construed as taking sides. Mara decided to ask the obvious question.

How did they get through (supposedly)?

The gossiper was happy to oblige. *At night. On foot. That's all I know.*

Sure, just waltz right past the precinct, @MPoweredGrrl wrote. *Not happening.*

Despite the sarcasm, others jumped on the idea.

Still, the protesters would've thinned out to nothing at that hour.

You could try going at shift change.

I would've thought daytime, through the library, would work. Slip out a side door on the other side or something.

And then what? You're still a couple of blocks too far to the north.

The ideas continued to scroll past. Mara exited the chat. No one knew anything. Despite @HarryOakPark's comment about the cops, she agreed with @MPoweredGrrl. If there was a way through, Limbo wouldn't have the numbers of people chatting that it did. Or it would have a FAQ for that. Something.

Offline and alone, the black doom feeling started to creep in. Why she was living in this shitty hellhole of a room, that wasn't even all her own? Why she was unemployed, fired from the group home for stealing? The trauma in those girls' eyes haunted her still, but what hurt more was the sympathy they expressed when she'd left that day for good. Like it could have been any one of them in Mara's place. Since then, she'd been reluctant to apply for anything, afraid if she went for a job interview, they'd know somehow. There might be something in her file.

Remmy burst into the room, all smiles, sporting their unisex bob and a cute bow tie, as pert as their preferred pronoun. They tossed their backpack to the right of the door. "Hey Mara, just throwing my stuff in here." Remmy's smile faded at sight of Mara's face. "Sorry, looks like you want to be alone right now. I'll see you." And shut the door before Mara could say anything.

Add to the list being the world's worst roommate. Mara sighed and swiped at her eyes. She had to pull herself together, get out of this windowless room, go watch TV with the others, scrounge something to eat.

She made herself sit up. Stage one. Got up from the pit. Stage two. Walked to the door. Stage three. She could do this. She rubbed her cheeks, changed her expression, and went out to join the others.

Enrico's date cancelled, so they all ended up crammed on the couch scarfing down cheese pizza and watching zombie shows on Hulu. Enrico bailed at 10:30 so he'd be functional at work the next day. Mara and Remmy muted the sound, and watched people running and hiding and getting mobbed by the undead for another hour. Remmy chatted about their crush du jour in intricate detail. Remmy always had a crush on someone. Even when they were dating a woman halfway seriously, they were flirting with others. This week, it was the new barista at the coffee shop near Remmy's work.

"She remembered my drink," Remmy gushed. "Day three, and she remembered my drink."

Remmy's stories never required much participation, which was fine with Mara. She liked listening. It gave her hope that someday she'd run into someone who'd find her interesting. Mara hadn't had a date since she'd lost her job and gone spiraling downward.

The credits were rolling on the screen, and Remmy stretched and yawned. "Well, I'm turning in. You?"

Mara was usually in the pit, pretending to sleep, when Remmy went to bed. Sometimes, though, she slept on the couch. She shrugged and reached for her device. "Maybe in a bit. I think I'll do some job searching first."

Remmy's brow wrinkled. "Hey, you'll find something soon. I can feel it. But if you're crashing on the davenport tonight, I'm totally hogging the pit." They rose and headed for the bathroom.

Mara listened to the water running. There was a flush, followed by more water running, and then Remmy emerged and paused in the hallway. "Mara, if you got out a little more, I think your mood would improve. Just saying."

Mara nodded and stared at the blank screen of her device. "Thanks." She held the pose till she heard the sound of the bedroom door closing. Then she laid her device aside.

All during the zombie shows, she'd had the Limbo chat on her mind. Someone might have made it through to the Newbody Zone in Cabrini-Green.

Yes, maybe Remmy was right: she needed to get out more. Mara flicked open her device and looked up the L schedules. If she hurried, she could make the Pink Line before it shut down for the night. She clicked off the TV and popped up from the couch. This was her window of opportunity. She was wearing her gray sweats and athletic shoes. Perfect. Maybe if she looked like a guy, people wouldn't be as likely to mess with her. She pulled her long mane of hair back and stuffed it down her collar, then pulled the hoodie up over her head. She caught a glimpse of her image in the darkened TV screen. The mounds of her breasts were still apparent beneath the sweatshirt. Enrico's baseball jacket was still on the cocktail table, the red heart of Love Life regarding her from within the green tree. She snatched it up and left.

Mara emerged from the Red Line station at Clark, aware of the decreased foot traffic at this hour on a weeknight, and affected what she hoped looked like a casual stroll as she turned west on Division. Enrico's jacket was a little long in the waist and sleeve, but not terribly so. She tugged the gray hoodie of her sweatshirt a little more forward as she walked, stuffing her hand back in the jacket pocket before anyone could notice she didn't have a man's hand.

Just seven minutes walk from the station, through Seward Park, according to her device, and she'd be at the Newbody Zone. The hopeful attitude she'd had back in the apartment eroded as she walked. *Stupid, stupid*, her steps seemed to say, soft against the pavement.

Lost in her self-recriminations, she was halfway across LaSalle when she noticed the barricade a block ahead, on the far side of Wells. There was no one around her. The empty street—and its absolute flatness—was eerie as the post-apocalyptic urban scene in one of tonight's zombie flicks. She was suddenly aware of how bright the streetlights were. It would look bad if she turned around now. Anyone watching would wonder about her. She put her head down and moved forward. At last she saw the curb, and stepped up onto it.

As she drew closer to Wells, it became clear to her this barricade hadn't been erected by police. The low wall was a muddle of boxes and sheets of corrugated metal, strung together in places by scavenged bits of wire. Crossing Wells, her eyes fell on a spray-painted version of the same Love Life logo as on the back of Enrico's jacket. She'd seen this barricade on the news, but she'd thought it would've been torn down by now. The fact that it wasn't sent a realization through her torso, as chilling as the autumn wind off the lake: city officials had struck a deal with the Love Lifers. By letting them help guard the way to the Newbody Zone, they'd ended the violence against the newbodies. The fire at the Iteration Hospital where the procedures were performed had been the last attack, and the catalyst for forging a workable solution: the creation of the Zone, where newbodies could live free of harassment, and continue development of their technologies.

Mara was braced, waiting for a head to pop up over that barricade and issue a challenge, but she reached the curb without incident. Keeping her hands in her pockets, she turned left and walked along the barricade, looking for a good way around.

"Hey! Hey you there!"

Her shoulders stiffened as she turned. A skinny man in his twenties and wearing a white knit cap with a pompom on top was looking at her from around a piece of metal. His smile glinted in the glow of the lights. His look was friendly. He must have seen the logo on the back of Enrico's jacket.

She made herself approach the guy, but she kept a ten-foot gap between them, so he wouldn't be able to grab her suddenly.

"I don't remember meeting you before," he said, peering at her face in the shadows of the hoodie.

She hesitated. As soon as he heard her voice, he'd know she was a woman. She tried to imitate Remmy's voice, aiming for a gravely lower register. "I'm new," she said. She coughed.

They both stood there, nodding slightly. It gave Mara time to think. "I just wanted to, you know, see the operation here."

The young man's eyes narrowed. "Best time for that is during the day."

Mara shrugged, even as her face grew hot. "Yes, well." Her mind raced as she grasped for a story. The best lies always contained a bit of truth. "I monitor the hashtag for LimboInChicago. There was discussion tonight that someone may have made it past our barricade and on into the Newbody Zone."

It worked. Her companion perked up at that. "Intel, huh?" He looked up and down the street, as if her words would make an interloper suddenly appear.

Mara considered what to say next, that would start to take her away from this guy and on her way to Seward Park. "Yeah, so I wanted to go tell my boyfriend's sister, who works for the 18th—"

"You have a boyfriend?" He was looking her up and down.

Mara realized too late her story had become inconsistent. Still, did wearing sweats qualify someone as a lesbian or something? She pushed her hoodie back, hoping she looked pretty enough in the glare of the streetlights to make him believe she could be someone's girlfriend. She made herself laugh a little. "Yeah, this is his jacket. Sorry, I have a bit of a sore throat." She coughed again.

"Anyway, my boyfriend's sister works for the 18th precinct on the graveyard shift, so I thought I'd pop in and give her the information, too."

His eyes narrowed as he squared off in front of her, blocking the gap in the barricade from where he'd come. "Who'd you say your boyfriend is? And why again are you out here all by yourself?"

Mara was losing. "Enrico," she blurted. "Enrico Saldana. He works in insurance. You know, the nine to five. He's sleeping."

She tossed her head back, and affected an annoyed attitude. "And why shouldn't I be out at night? Is there a law against that now?"

Her companion took this in. "Yeah, I think I've heard of Enrico." Still, he didn't budge. Then he added in a flat tone, "I don't know any Saldanas at the precinct, though. I know the people over there pretty well."

Mara swallowed. "She has a different last name, but I don't know what it is. Maria. Do you know Maria?"

He snorted, and relaxed. "I only know about five of them. Here." He pointed. "You can go through that way. Just straight on, and you'll come out at the precinct. Tell Maria that Bob says hi."

She smiled back at him, letting her relief flood her features. "Thanks. I will."

"Cool jacket, by the way."

Her smile deepened, and she twisted her torso back and forth in a mild flirt. "Thanks, Bob. See you around?"

It took all her strength to keep her gait casual as she walked away. Still, she'd passed through the barricade successfully. She no longer stared at the ground, but walked with her chin level. The 18th precinct was three blocks straight ahead at the corner of Division and Larrabee, but she had no intentions of going there. Even if Bob was keeping an eye on where she was going, by the time she angled into Seward Park, she'd have a whole block's head start. She figured that's when she'd start running. Mara's hope regained more of her inner territory.

As she passed under the elevated train track, she glanced furtively about. The temperature seemed to drop several degrees. This was a typical spot for the zombies to come out of hiding, or at least some homeless guy emboldened by desperation to try his hand at a little street robbery. But she encountered no one, and when she came out the other side, she saw the edge of the park. She rushed forward.

And bumped into a police officer.

"Sorry," Mara yelped. Her heart raced.

The officer was shorter than Mara, and stocky, and with a tip of the cap back, was revealed to be a Latina woman. She regarded Mara with an alert gaze. "The park's closed. It's late. Where are you going so fast?"

Mara needed to get inside that park. She used the storyline of the last lie. "I was over at the Love Life barricade, and thought I'd come over and talk to Maria. She's my boyfriend's sister. I have some information about people trying to get through to the Zone."

The woman stared. "Well, I'm Maria. But I don't have a brother."

Mara stammered. "No, it's another Maria. She has a different last name. I don't know it."

The officer shifted her weight to her back foot, turning her torso slightly to the side. "Can I see some ID, please?"

Mara pulled her hands from her pockets, slowly. Her left hand was clutching her train pass and device. "Sorry, I kind of came out on the spur of the moment. I don't have it with me." She took a step toward the park. "My boyfriend's name is Enrico."

"I don't give one ounce of sweat who your boyfriend is," the woman said. "I was asking who are *you*? Because if anyone's around here trying to get past into the Newbody Zone, I'd have to guess it was you. Wearing a Love Life jacket—yes, I know those baseball jackets without seeing the back—and sneaking around at night like you are. I'd think you intended to cause some trouble over in the Zone."

Mara was aghast. "No! I'm not one of them!" She peeled off the jacket and flung it at the woman's feet, and then turned and ran as fast as she could toward the park.

"Stop!"

Mara kept running, visualizing the officer reaching for her weapon. She ran into the trees that bordered the park, and then cursed the large open space that lay between her and the dark hulk of the field house. She ran without cover around her, bracing for the sound of a gun firing, for the bullet that would end her life, or cripple her. But it never came.

She skirted the field house, out of breath, yet she forced her body forward. Surely Bob would've heard the officer yell for her to stop. She prayed to no god in particular that the information she had on the location of the newbody's tower was correct. The Cabrini-Green area spanned several blocks above and below Division. The tower, she'd heard, was on a street called West Hobbie, between Hudson and Cleveland. If she ran across the school grounds at a diagonal, she should be able to find it.

She raised her line of vision, and no longer had any doubt of the tower's location. There it rose, on the other side of the school's softball diamonds. It jutted over twenty stories up into the night sky, unilluminated. She'd heard newbodies could see in the dark, could see the infrared spectrum, and other frequencies as well. She picked up her pace and ran with all her might.

Between her and the front door stood a silvery fence, twice her height. The sight of the razor wire at the top, glinting in the moonlight, gave her pause, yet she banged into the fence harder than she intended. She grasped it and interlaced her fingers through the metal weave, afraid the officer or Bob would come and try to pry her off, pull her back into her old life.

"Help!" She needed to get inside, be safe.

A figure emerged from the front of the tower, human in shape, but that is where the similarity ended. She caught her breath as it approached, its metallic muscles luminous in the moonlight. She hadn't seen a newbody in real life in nearly a year, not since they were rounded up for their own safety, and given their own territory.

The figure stopped at the gate and regarded her with whirling silver orbs set in the sockets where eyes would be if it were a person.

"Please," she said, jiggling the gate. She wheeled to look behind her, but no one was there. She looked back at the stranger. "I want to join."

"This is irregular," the newbody said. "Our agreement with the city does not cover this situation."

Were there officials on their end as well? She tried to remember what she'd written on her form. "I don't want to die. I don't want . . . to use resources . . . " Her words sounded lame to her own ears. She'd had four reasons, well-executed, on her application. Tears sprang to her eyes. All she could think about were the looks of sympathy on the faces of those girls when they found out Mara had been fired. She paused, caught up in her internal nightmare.

This wasn't going well. What had she expected? The thought of being denied admittance made her heart race. They'd arrest her, and put her in jail. Enrico would find out what side of the divide she was on, and that would be the end of sharing the apartment with him and Remmy.

The newbody showed no emotion, just like the human official earlier. "You are healthy. Would you renounce the world? Your world?"

"Yes! Please, I can't go back. I need to get into the Newbody Zone."

"Why?"

She'd been trying to vocalize her four reasons, the ones on her form. Why couldn't she remember those? All she could think of now was the other reason, the one she hadn't put on the form, the painful reason. The really bad reason. The one that was sure to get her application denied.

"I'm suicidal," she blurted. Her body sagged against the gate as all the lies deserted her. "I'm afraid what I'll do to myself. I got fired from my last job because I was stealing pills, stockpiling so I could take them all at once. They didn't know what I was going to do with them, they just thought I was going to sell the pills for extra cash. I'm just a failure. I could never get the job I wanted in the tech industry and I don't know why, I really don't. I live with two other people but they're really not my friends, we just talk about bullshit stuff and . . . The truth is, if I don't get in to the Newbody Zone I'll just go kill myself somehow."

She was sobbing now, aware of how childish she sounded, just like one of the lost girls at the group home. It had been while at the home, that she'd encountered the suicide checklist the psychologists had the clients fill out. Mara had swiped a copy and taken it to the break room one day. She'd scored high. Somehow that knowledge had made her worse, and she'd begun stealing meds—tiny amounts at a time—and hiding them in her locker, where she kept her aide smock.

She almost didn't hear the soft click of the latch. The gate swung inward, yielding to the weight of her body. At last she let go of it and found her footing. Wiping at her eyes, she saw the face of the other close to hers, uncomfortably close. She took a step back, but then realized how stupid that was. Wasn't this where she had wanted to be, had crossed town to get here, navigated through obstacles, and run so hard her chest still ached from the effort? She'd ended up here through her own efforts, to this unknown spot that was the singularity.

Yet it was precisely the unknown that made her shrink back. But what fears did the unknown hold for her anymore? If she died, it wouldn't matter, because she would've eventually killed herself, anyway. She was certain of that. What had driven her out of the apartment tonight had been a wild hope that this wasn't the end of her life, but a new beginning. If everything was true, she would live, in whatever form they'd give her. A newbody? Sure, she could handle that. Or what if they'd developed the technology to download minds into some virtual reality computer-generated world? Why not?

"Is everything okay over here?"

Mara whirled. The police officer stood at the open gate, a tall male officer at her side.

The newbody's voice was smooth, calming. "Yes, we're fine. This person is no threat to the Zone."

"All right." The officer shifted her weight from one foot to the other. "Are you sending her back out?"

Did the city's jurisdiction end at the gate? Mara looked back at the newbody. *Please*, she silently implored.

The newbody moved forward, drawing alongside Mara. "No, she is choosing to stay."

The officer seemed to consider this. Mara, however, was elated. She had thought the city had forged the Newbody Zone to appease the Love Life protestors. Now it appeared they'd worked with both sides. She was standing in an autonomous territory under the control of the newbodies.

"Well, then," the officer said. "Have a good evening."

Mara looked up at her newfound friend. Their hands found each other's in the dark. Mara felt a surprising vitality in the metallic touch. Together they walked toward the front doors of the tower. She did not look back as the gate eased shut behind them.

THE SUM OF HER EXPECTATIONS

JACK SKILLINGSTEAD

Amrita stabilized the escape pod. Her hands were shaking; she had barely gotten out. The *Meghnad Saha*, a Class B planet surveyor she'd called home, retreated from the aft view screen, dropping rapidly from the orbital plane, pulled down by a force from the planet.

"Tripp?" Amrita said.

After a moment, a voice from the surveyor: "It doesn't appear I'm going to be able to stop this thing."

"You should have come with me in the pod."

"Hindsight. I'll keep trying. Here comes the blackout. Goodbye. Sorry . . . "

"Tripp?"

Nothing.

Amrita tracked the *Meghnad Saha* all the way to the surface. She tried repeatedly to resume contact but Tripp wouldn't answer. Transcyber Reactive Positronic Personality: Tripp, for short, and the only friend Amrita had, or wanted. If he survived the crash, she wasn't about to abandon him. She blinked tears away and began to configure her escape pod for descent.

The Kabbhan forbade landing on Trappist-1e, or even approaching the planet within a designated radius of three hundred thousand kilometers. Because the Kabbhan stargates had made interstellar travel possible for humans in the first place, everyone respected this single restriction. Everybody but Amrita, who was signatory to no such agreement.

A proximity alert began beeping in the escape pod. Amrita considered a quick burn for radical descent. Get down before anyone could stop her. But it was already too late.

The Kabbhan star cruiser emerged like a sperm whale from a shot glass. Above the planet's horizon an elongated node appeared, squeezed forth, and *popped*: the cruiser, bigger than anything Melville dreamed of, came alongside Amrita's two-seat escape pod in synchronous orbit one hundred and eighty kilometers above the planet's largest continental mass. Amrita put her nose to the viewport. A massive wall shut out the stars.

With the back of her hand she wiped sweat off her upper lip, and waited. Eventually, the alien spoke, via comlink—at least it appeared that way. The green comlink indicator blinked on Amrita's vaporware display, and she heard the expected transmission hiss. But she knew Kabbhan technology was not what it appeared to be. Even calling it technology was a mistake.

Earth ship. Prepare to receive Kabbhan personnel.

"What?"

Out of nowhere, a man appeared at her elbow, already strapped into the right seat. Amrita would have jumped out of her skin, if that were possible. Actually, it *was* possible; the Kabbhan had demonstrated as much by becoming the only known race to have achieved transphysical migration.

"Who the hell are you?" she demanded.

The man turned to her. "The sum of your expectations."

"I've heard that one before. You're a Kabbhan presentation?"

The Kabbhan probed minds to find materials with which to construct compatible presentations. A Kabbhanian presentation acted as a surrogate presence. No one had ever seen an actual Kabbhan and very few had seen their presentations. Those who had seen a presentation reported a disorienting experience. While the presentation existed only in the probed subject's mind, it activated all the necessary neural and sensory pathways to create an apparently physical manifestation. Apparent to the one being probed, at least. In short, the right seat was empty.

"You may regard me as Dad."

"Dad! I don't think so. Besides, you don't even look like him."

Not that Amrita remembered her father, her "dad," except as a degraded holo she'd discovered in a lockbox after her mother died. Among the few important documents still mandated to exist in physical form were scattered a handful of personal items, trinkets accumulated over a long life. Amrita used her thumbnail to pry open a silver locket stamped with an impression of Shiva—and *wham*! her father leaped out and stood flickering before her. She knew it was her father, because who else could it be? Old fashioned hololockets like this one had been romantic keepsakes when Amrita's mother was young, and she had only ever loved one man—as she frequently reiterated. In later years, after she found happiness with a microbiologist named Brenda on the colony world Deneb V1, she added: One was enough.

The holo had been that of a young man, handsome, after a predictable fashion. But there was a sly, cunning light in his eye that suggested a con man's motivations. *Eye*, not eyes. The holo's degradation had turned Amrita's young father into a puzzle of many missing pieces—including the piece with his right eye. A therapist had once suggested that Amrita had spent her life, unconsciously of course, searching for the missing pieces of dear old dad. It accounted for her lack of respect for rules and authority figures. Amrita responded: "You're joking, right?" She had been under court order to participate in ten therapeutic sessions. The court order came as a result of a juvenile misadventure involving a stolen moon skimmer and a high-speed chase across the Mare Serenitatis.

Had she been eighteen instead of thirteen, the consequences would have been dire, not therapeutic. The "You're joking" remark had been in session number two. The next eight preceded unproductively.

This Kabbhan presentation didn't look anything like the holo. It was older, for one thing. A man of late middle age, with silver-streaked hair combed back in a pompadour, and wrinkles around his brown eyes.

"There is no error," he said.

"I hope you don't think you're going to stop me. Because I'm telling you right now, I *am* going down there to get my friend."

"Stopping you isn't my intention. I'm here to assure your survival. We Kabbhan feel a certain responsibility towards less evolved species endangered by our discarded artifacts, even though our warnings have been explicit. Shall we descend now? If you are prepared, of course."

"I'm prepared. *Dad*."

Amrita manipulated vaporware toggles, like twiddling fingers in a particularly well-organized steam cloud. The pod altered orbital trajectory, and Trappist-1e's very large horizon became larger still. Amrita glanced at the rearview screen. The Kabbhan starship was gone, as if it had never been there. And it hadn't been. Like Dad, the ship had been the sum of Amrita's expectations, this time in regards to alien spacecraft. The Kabbhan thought that beings stuck in the physical required corresponding illusions. Maybe they were right.

Amrita's escape pod burned through the atmosphere at hypersonic speed. Curtains of fire fluttered across the ports, then blew away, revealing an expanse of salmon-colored twilight. It was midday on Trappist-1e and as bright as it ever got. Six more alphabet planets hung in the sky like a God's game of crescents and balls.

From altitude, the self-expanding megalopolis looked like a continent-covering *crust*, an eczema salted with glittering lights.

"What a sight," Amrita said.

Dad nodded. "When the last of us migrated out of the physical, the automated city-builders on this colony planet ran amok. That was more than a hundred Sol years ago, by your time measure."

"There's so *much*."

"Indeed. Construction has proceeded unchecked, consuming every available mineral resource, husking out the planet even as it gradually covers its surface with an abandoned-before-built city."

"What happens when the builders run out of land?"

"They continue into the sea, erecting piers and floating platforms on the surface, and submerged suburbs of pressure domes and interlinking tubular passageways. They can and do build anything."

Amrita banked the escape pod and dropped several thousand meters, slipping across the sky at dizzying speed. She felt it in her gut, the swoop of gravity-assisted acceleration. Dad sat placidly, watching out the port. As they drew nearer, details emerged from the crust. Towers, blocks, domes, heptagons, pyramids, complex ribbons of transportation infrastructure . . .

"There," Dad said.

A trench of smoldering destruction. Amrita slowed the pod's descent, swooped in close, and hovered. Machines, like giant stalk-legged spiders, swarmed the trench, collecting into piles the remains of shattered buildings. Energy beams fired from the spiders' underbellies. Brilliant flashes, like small nuclear detonations, burst upon Amrita's eyeballs. She looked away and spent a few seconds blinking the blue-white afterimages out of her eyes. When she looked back, the debris had been reduced to slag.

"The city-builders will digest the material," Dad said, "and recycle it into the construction matrix."

The builders, or nanoswarms, grew buildings from the ground up. Even now, the trench gradually filled with new growth, like an invisible surgeon knitting a wound.

Amrita flew her pod over the trench. At the end of it lay the *Meghnad Saha,* broken-backed and nose up. Smoke trailed from rents in the engine compartment and crew cabin, while instruments of the city proceeded with dissection. Giant mechanical mantises peeled off titanium plates, like strips of bark from a fallen tree. They cast the plates down for the spiders to gather, evaluate, and slag.

Amrita loitered above the spectacle. She opened a channel. "Tripp?"

White noise.

Dad said, "He may not have survived."

"Or he may *have* survived."

Dad put his hand over hers. Amrita's parietal lobe received nerve impulses, as though someone was actually touching her skin. Dad's eyes swam with empathy, which she didn't trust. "I need to know for certain," Amrita said, and pushed her hand forward. The illusion of Dad's fingers slid away. She reached into the vaporware display, activated the sensor array, and swept the wreckage.

"He's not there. I don't read his power core's signature."

"Perhaps he has been digested."

"The radioactive core would still register."

Amrita broadened the search, scanning the surrounding area as rapidly as possible, worried that the builders would take notice and pull her down with tractor beams, just as they'd done to the *Meghnad Saha*. Then Tripp's signature appeared. "Got him! He's on the move."

She locked down the location and deactivated the sensor array. "Do you think the builders know I'm here?" Her pod was shielded from sensor examination, but then the *Meghnad Saha* had been, too.

"I'm afraid they do now, Pumpkin."

Pumpkin?

That was the color of the Martian sky above Burroughsville, the main Cydonia colony, where Amrita spent her first six years. Her real dad had never called her 'Pumpkin' or anything else that she recalled. She had only one vague and retreating memory of him walking out the door of their hab. She didn't remember *him*; she remembered his back as he walked away. She remembered the door sliding closed, leaving her fatherless. She remembered her mother's tears. And anger. Not long after that her mother requested reassignment to Luna, dragging Amrita along to the land of stark desert contrasts and no friends. The moon skimmer incident was inevitable, and would have happened sooner, if Amrita had been tall enough to reach the controls.

Pumpkin was what *Ideal Dad* called her—back when she was five years old and in need of a father who called her something, anything. Ideal Dad: AKA made-up-dad: AKA Kabbhan presentation. From the quantum flux the Kabbhan had probed her mind and found a ghost who had never lived. Amrita now recognized the physical template, though, the silvered pompadour, the kind eyes. They belonged to a man she used to see walking around the buried corridors between Burroughsville habs. Some kind of maintenance man, originally from New Delhi, on Earth.

"Please," she said to the presentation, "don't call me that again."

Dad nodded. "All right, Amrita."

"Nobody in my life has ever called me 'Pumpkin.'"

Dad listened respectfully.

"And don't look at me that way, either." Amrita said.

"I'm sorry. Am I looking at you incorrectly?"

Amrita narrowed her eyes. "Are you being funny?"

"I doubt it. Before the Great Migration I was considered by my friends to be on the dour side. Also, in the quantum flux, no one tells jokes. We Kabbhan no longer exist as individuals, except when it becomes necessary to create a presentation. Telling jokes in the flux would be like telling jokes to a mirror."

"I don't know if you're being serious."

"Then I am a poor communicator, which is a failing I was *not* accused of prior to migration."

"Okay, that's plenty."

"Plenty?"

"Of you talking."

Amrita looked for a place to set down. She flexed her hands, worried. "The builders won't attack?"

"Attack? The builders don't *attack* anything. They're hungry for building material, that's all."

"It looked like they were attacking the *Meghnad Saha*."

"Preparing it for digestion," Dad said. "Local resources are finite. The builders hunt constantly for materials. When your surveyor skimmed the atmosphere it became a potential resource. You were warned of this, were you not?"

"I shielded the ship. It should have been invisible." Amrita had been attracted to Trappist-1e *by* its forbiddenness. She had wanted to see what no human had seen, and she wanted to see it because everyone from the Kabbhan themselves to the Gate Authority in the Epsilon Cygni system had told her she *couldn't*.

"Insufficient," Dad said. "Your sensor scan revealed you."

"All right. Will the builders try to *digest* me?"

"Of course not. They don't digest living organisms."

"That's great for me, but Tripp isn't a living organism."

Amrita concentrated on her maneuvering controls. She lowered the pod between soaring towers that reduced even the twilight to full night. Landing lights planted cones on a pristine avenue no Kabbhan (or human, for that matter) had ever trod. Gear extended, and moments later pneumatic suspension units absorbed the pod's touchdown.

Amrita idled the engines and unstrapped. "Tripp is close. I'll go get him. When I come back, you'll have to give up your seat."

Dad nodded. "Of course. I'm not actually in the seat, anyway. But I don't think you should leave the pod."

"Why not?"

"The builders won't harm a living organism, but once you climb out, the pod will become a construction resource. They seized your planet surveyor only after you abandoned ship."

Amrita bristled. "I didn't abandon anything. Tripp shoved me into the pod. He overreacted to the builder's tractor beam."

"Yes. It wouldn't have pulled the ship down, not while you were aboard."

"Tripp was trying to protect me."

Dad regarded her empathetically. "I see."

Amrita switched on her comlink. "Tripp? You're out there. Answer me."

He didn't reply.

"He's probably turned off his communication device. Receiving your signal might direct the builders to him. Amrita, remaining here is dangerous."

"You said the builders wouldn't digest a living organism."

"No. But once you walk away, your ship becomes a resource. I suggest you fly us out of the city. I will give you a safe destination."

"I'm not leaving Tripp."

"Hmm." Dad tilted his head. "He's artificial, isn't he?"

"What's that got to do with anything?"

"Nothing, I suppose."

Dad tapped two fingers against his lower lip. It's something Amrita herself used to do when she was little, a pensive tick that she transferred to Ideal Dad to help make him more real. It really irritated her that the Kabbhan presentation had adopted it. The maintenance worker from New Delhi had probably had ticks and mannerisms of his own, but Amrita pointedly avoided learning what they were. She wanted only to see him in the corridor sometimes and think, *My dad's going to work*. But at night she hoarded his image and turned it into a wonderful father. He wasn't a maintenance man but a gardener. Like Ideal Dad himself, the garden didn't exist. Amrita liked to imagine it in a vast underground vault with a pretend sky adrift with fluffy white clouds. She liked to imagine tall sunflowers (she'd seen pictures in school) nodding on their stalks. Dad played a game with her, telling stories of the sunflowers, which were special *Martian* sunflowers and could think and had personalities because they contained the lost souls of the vanished inhabitants of Mars.

Amrita put her helmet on. "He's inside that tower. I'm going to get him. I'll remote-fly the pod, set it to execute an evasive pattern to avoid the tractor beams and then return. That should work, if I make the pattern tricky enough."

"It might. For a short time."

"It's going to work."

Dad sighed.

Amrita programmed the maneuver, then belted on her sidearm and climbed out of the pod. She felt the planet's pull, the gravity twice that of Mars but significantly less than Earth's. She had lived on both worlds. Earth was prettier, but Mars (and Luna) was easier on her spine. The heating coils in her suit warmed her against the outside temperature, which hung just above freezing. How was anybody supposed to live on this planet?

When she turned, Dad already stood in the street. She said, "Please don't do *that* anymore, either."

"Don't do what anymore?"

"Pop in and out. If you're going to act physical, act it all the way."

Dad nodded. "If it makes you happy."

"Nothing makes me happy. Hold on."

She used her wrist controller to spin up the pod's engines. Dad watched her impassively, tapping his lower lip.

"Stop doing that," Amrita said.

Dad stopped.

Amrita focused on the pod. It began to rise. The speed of its ascent increased. Amrita held her breath, waiting for the invisible lasso of a tractor beam to grab the pod and smash it down. But the pod climbed above the skyline and darted away—safe, for now.

"If it doesn't come back," Amrita said, "We're all marooned here."

"I'm not here in the first place," Dad said. "But leave that aside. You are marooned whether or not the pod returns."

"What are you talking about?"

"Your pod cannot withstand the forces found within our gate."

The Kabbhan stargates linked distant locations within the Milky Way. When humans discovered the gate shimmering in Jupiter space, it had opened the galaxy to human exploration. Only the gate in the Epsilon Cygni system was forbidden. Entering it, Amrita had been instantly transported across nearly twelve parsecs to the Trappist-1 system.

Amrita's heart beat faster. She had suspected the escape pod was insufficiently sturdy for the stargate, but she had intended to chance it, anyway. Now she didn't know what to do. Taking a risk was one thing, suicide was another. "Another ship will come," she said.

"No ships come here."

"Mine did."

"Amrita, no one *wants* to come here."

"I'll figure something out."

Dad nodded, as though he were nodding at a child who had just vowed to *stay up all night*.

"I will help you settle on this world. There is a lovely island situated on the terminator, where the temperature range is more compatible for your human physiology. In your remaining lifespan the builders will not reach it. Conditions may be challenging at first."

"Well, shit," Amrita said.

"Everything is going to be okay . . . "

Pumpkin.

With her dad, Amrita walked alone down the broad Kabbhan avenue. From deep in the city came the creaking, groaning sounds of nano construction.

"What a waste of time this place is," Amrita said. "All these buildings and no one to live in them or work in them."

"Time," Dad said, shaking his head. "An odd concept."

Amrita looked at him, unable to ignore what she rationally knew wasn't there. "What's odd about it?"

Dad said, "First of all, 'time' is an artificial construct. How do you waste a construct? In the Flux—"

"Dad? I'm not in the mood."

"Of course, sorry. In the Flux we aren't influenced by moods."

"*Okay.*" Amrita stopped walking and turned on him. "If it's so wonderful in the Flux, what are you even doing here?"

"I'm not here."

Amrita closed her eyes briefly. "You know what I mean."

"I told you. I came to help you survive."

"Right. Because you feel responsible. Now what's the other reason?"

Dad shrugged. "I happen to enjoy inhabiting a presentation. Among my fellow Kabbhan that makes me unusual."

"I hope you're having a wonderful time."

"I am."

"That's great." Amrita looked around at the buildings. "He should be right here. Tripp, it's me! Tripp!"

Her words echoed down the canyon of tall buildings, all of them black and shiny-smooth and hollow. She approached the nearest, a tower that rose hundreds of meters, an immense heptagonal spear ending in a rounded point. The entrance to the lobby, or whatever the Kabbhan called it, stood open and doorless. Her helmet lights revealed the empty interior. She stepped inside and tilted her head back. Load-bearing supports crisscrossed all the way to the point. That was all.

"It's called a shell," Dad said. "I knew you were wondering."

She didn't say anything.

"The builders execute the architect's plan, create basic structures, the interiors to be added later, according to the wishes of future inhabitants. As there are no future inhabitants, the city itself is now, and will remain, a shell."

"I don't care," Amrita said. "I just want to find my friend."

From far away, a small voice, almost inaudible, said, "I'm here."

Amrita squinted. The voice was so faint, she wasn't sure she'd even heard it. Wasn't sure whether it was outside of her head, or inside of it, another Kabbhan illusion, or what. She turned up the gain on her headset.

"Tripp?"

"Over here."

She swung her headlamps in his direction. Tripp stood in a far corner of the shell, his back against the wall. He looked more or less human—well, less—but he had two arms and two legs and one oval-shaped head. She walked toward him, her footsteps echoing.

"What happened to you?"

"My leg was damaged in the crash. I barely managed to hobble this far. They almost got me. Now I can't move without falling."

"They won't get you," Amrita said. "I won't let them."

Dad cleared his throat. Amrita ignored him.

"You can't stop them," Tripp said.

Amrita crouched and began examining the damaged leg. At the knee, a couple of carbon fiber rods bent in the wrong direction, inhibiting articulation.

"Don't be afraid," she said.

"Oh, I'm not really. It's just my positronic brain pretending to feel human emotions, so I will seem more companionable."

She looked up. "We've discussed your honesty on this topic before."

"Sorry."

Amrita produced a multi-tool and began fiddling with the leg.

"The weird thing is," Tripp said, "I'm not even sure I want you to."

She looked up. "Want me to what?"

"Stop them."

Amrita stopped fiddling. "Why the Hell are you saying that?"

"It's strangely compelling."

"*What's* strangely compelling?"

"To become part of the city," Tripp said. "I don't know. Would it be so bad? Maybe it's because I'm already artificial, but these last hours, pretending to feel so afraid even when you were not here, hiding, getting my apparent dread of extinction organized to display when you showed up—it's really made me think. My whole existence has been nothing but a performance."

"Tripp!"

"I'm serious. If I simply walked out there, exposed myself, let them slag me, allowed myself to be digested and my elements to be recombined into the building matrix, wouldn't I be part of something greater than myself?"

"Tripp, please be quiet now." Listening to him made her feel lonely. "I think the crash must have damaged more than your poor leg."

"No, my brain is fully functional. You know, I was in communication with the *Meghnad Saha* even as the instrumentality dismantled her. She didn't display fear, because that isn't part of her reactive programming mask. But she *was* excited. I'm certain of that. This may sound strange to you, but in the end she believed that to be digested was the greatest adventure. At least, that's what she said."

"She did not."

"I suppose she may have been regurgitating something from the library that got mixed up in her damaged memory core. Anyway . . .

"Hold still, please." Amrita loosened the bolt that attached the bent rods to Tripp's knee swivels. The bolt dropped to the ground. Gritting her teeth, she got a firm grip on one of the bent rods, wrenched it back and forth until it suddenly came loose. She fell on her ass, still holding the rod.

"He's right," Dad said. "We Kabbhan, like all physical beings of limited duration, lived our lives in fear. After the Great Migration, fear vanished—along with our individual personalities, of course. It may be the same for artificial beings when faced with the prospect of joining the greater reality of the city."

Amrita rolled to her knees. "Have either of you even considered the virtue of silence?"

"Either of you?" Tripp said. "Who else are you talking to?"

"Nobody. My dad."

"Which is it?"

"They're the same thing."

Amrita resumed work on the second bent rod. She twisted and wrenched and pulled. It came free of its upper swivel but not the lower. Finally she gave up and let it dangle.

"Try that," she said.

Tripp moved his good leg forward, planted it, then moved his damaged leg. The dangling bar tapped against the other rods and the knee wobbled slightly side-to-side. Tripp waved his arms for balance. Amrita scrambled to her feet to catch him, but he managed to remain upright without her.

"How is it?" she asked.

"Unstable. I'm not sure this will work."

"Keep practicing, walk around."

"All right." Tripp walked away into the shadows, the dangling carbon rod making a tap-tapping sound like a blind man's cane.

"The builders will very probably take him," Dad said.

Amrita turned on him, annoyed with herself for accepting his presence outside her head, where it wasn't. "I could use a little optimism around here. You're supposed to be helping me, right? Well, do some helping, why don't you? Get us away from where Tripp is in danger. Get us to that island."

"I can take you there. The builders have no interest in a biological. But Tripp will inevitably be noticed."

Amrita paced around, working her hands together, thinking. "What if I turn the builders off? Isn't that what your people should have done before the Great Migration?"

"That isn't possible. In the absence of Kabbhan oversight, the builders have adapted and become self-motivated to complete the architect's plan. Only the architect can cancel the build."

"Who's the architect?"

"Since they were left running, the builders devised their own plan."

"The builders are their own architect?"

"Exactly." Dad spread his arms and turned in a circle. "They build. It's what they do. It's all they do. When the original plan was complete, they simply extended the parameters to include the entire planet. That way they will remain busy and fulfill the dictates of their primary function. But they are not sentient. No amount of logical persuasion will convince them to abandon their own plan."

"That leaves Terminator Island, or whatever you call it."

"The island has no name. Nothing here does."

"Let's just go. Tripp!"

They emerged from the building in time to witness the arrival of a ten-meter-tall spider. Moments later, the pod came zig-zagging out of the sky and settled onto the same spot it had previously occupied. The spider stalked toward the pod.

Amrita yelled, "Run!"

Since she was the only one with working legs, she ran alone—though Dad appeared to be running beside her.

"How am I doing?" he said.

"What?"

"You said you wanted me to be physically consistent."

Behind her, Tripp's dangling carbon rod clicked and knocked against his leg, like a syncopated timer.

Amrita ripped her sidearm out of the holster but hesitated. "Dad, you're sure that thing won't attack me?"

"Yes."

Amrita triggered her weapon. A pulsing white particle discharge cut across one of the spider's legs, severing it above the first joint. The spider stumbled and began tracking left. Amrita ran back to Tripp, pulled his arm across her shoulders, and helped him walk the remainder of the distance to the pod. He was light for an artificial.

"Stand here." Amrita climbed the ladder and reached down. "Give me your hand, I'll pull you up."

But Tripp wasn't looking at her. He watched the spider circling itself, partially hobbled, and, to Amrita's horror, Tripp began limping towards it.

"Tripp, what are you doing! Stop."

Without looking at her, Tripp said, "You should fly away now. It's important that I serve a larger function. While the *Meghnad Saha* existed, my part of the larger function was assured. There is no larger function on your island."

"Our friendship is a larger function." Amrita felt an ache in her chest.

Tripp didn't speak again but limped, loose rod tapping, over to the spider and held up his arms. The spider took notice, stopped chasing itself around in a circle, and slagged him.

The ache in Amrita's chest intensified and became unbearable. "*Why*?"

From the right seat, already strapped in, Dad laid a comforting illusion on her shoulder. Her brain told her it was a father giving her a reassuring squeeze.

"We'd best go now, Pumpkin."

She buckled herself into the pilot's seat, roughly wiped her eyes, spun up the engines, and sped into the sky, reaching maximum thrust within seconds. They achieved altitude and raced toward the sea.

• • •

On tidally locked Trappist-1e, Terminator Island stood on the edge of eternal night. Amrita knelt in the powdery blue sand, breathing inside her helmet. "I don't see any builders."

"They exist everywhere but are too small to see."

"If they're on the island, why aren't they already building their damned city?"

"It would be disorderly. The builders follow the architect's plan, in this case their own plan. And the plan is to build contiguously outward from the main continental mass. These builders would not become activated until the project arrived after crossing the ocean. That is a distant occurrence. In the meantime you can use the builders for your own project, once I tell you how to activate them according to your deeper architectural desires."

"I don't have any deep architectural desires," Amrita grumbled.

Dad, standing over her, said, "Of course you do."

Amrita was not Kabbhan. The nanobuilders did not naturally synch with her inner architect. But, because she was the only game in town, at least until the city arrived, eventually they made a connection. A good thing. The Trappist atmosphere was unbreathable, at least for humans. Sooner or later (probably sooner) the pod's emergency atmospheric conversion processor would break down.

The builders started . . . building. Amrita had been dozing in the pod, lulled to unconsciousness by the wheeze and huff of the processor, which sucked in air and displaced most of the carbon dioxide with an artificially produced mixture of nitrogen and oxygen. The conversion unit was designed as a temporary stopgap. The replicating oxygen/nitrogen molecules on board would soon be depleted, and that would be the end of Amrita.

A creaking, groaning sound plucked at her awareness, and she opened heavy eyelids. The atmosphere in the pod was thin, just barely enough to support her life. But like *that* she was wide awake. Around the pod, for a radius of fifty meters or more, walls built themselves up, gradually creating an enclosed space. At the same time invisible builders filled the still-exposed interior space with walls and corridors and furniture and apparatus familiar to Amrita, including a large atmospheric conversion unit. Fascinated, Amrita tore into a packet of emergency rations and watched the show. The builders worked quickly.

At the point when she knew exactly what the builders were creating, Amrita turned to Dad, who was always at her side.

"I didn't ask for this," she said.

"Your architect is a deep expectation, beyond your conscious control. I'm sorry. The builders are designed to synch with Kabbhan brains, which were more limber, not human brains. This is what you get, I'm afraid. At least it is life, yes?"

Outside the pod, a copy of Amrita's Burroughsville habitat took shape.

Black. Inside the hab, if she wandered too far, the soothing blue and gold tones of her remembered home in Burroughsville segued into the shiny, smooth, black "shell" material of the Kabbhan city. Mostly, Amrita stayed in her room, reading her way through the pods' mirror library from when it was attached to the *Meghnad Saha.* A couple of times a day she left the hab and crossed to the farm. The walls of the farm enclosed a space twice the size of the hab. Using seeds and fertilizer packets from the escape pod's long-term planetary survival stores, Amrita had begun to grow her future diet of bland vegetables. Already leafy shoots had emerged. The sight both encouraged and depressed her. How long would she be stuck here?

Sometimes, on her way back to the hab, she paused to gaze out over the sea. Beyond the horizon, the builders continued their work on the continent and beneath the waves. Tripp was now part of that building matrix. If he could pretend fear why couldn't he have pretended loyalty and stayed with her? Tripp was part of the city, but what was Amrita part of? She had spent her life devising ways to separate herself from her fellow humans. Now, for the first time, regret wormed into her heart.

"I don't understand why he did it," she said one evening, when Dad came in to say goodnight. "I thought we were friends."

Dad sat on the bed. It was a perfect duplicate of Amrita's childhood bed. When she lay down to sleep, her legs extended beyond the mattress. "Perhaps the friendship was more one-sided than you like to believe."

"You didn't even know him," Amrita said.

"Was there something to know? He was artificial. Kabbhan could not have created a presentation from him, even. Tripp had more in common with the builders than with you."

"Stop talking to me," Amrita said. "Can't you stop and go away? I don't need you anymore."

Dad held her hand. "Do you really want me to leave, Pumpkin?"

By force of will, Amrita almost convinced herself that she couldn't feel the hand gently squeezing hers. She would have pulled free, except she *could* see, in her mind's eye, the grim comedy of her lying alone on the bed, talking to herself while twisting and pulling away from someone who wasn't there. It was easier to accept the illusion. Just as it had become easier to accept the illusion calling her "Pumpkin." Was there any point in fighting it? Besides, it would be too lonely without Dad, even though Dad wasn't really there.

"At least make yourself appear in your original Kabbhan form." she said. "The Dad thing bothers me."

"Oh, I couldn't do that. I no longer possess a self-image. To appear Kabbhan now would require a living Kabbhan mind from which to draw."

"You won't try?"

"I'm afraid it would be pointless." Dad shook his head and chuckled. "You know, I'm really enjoying my temporary individuality."

"That's wonderful." Amrita turned away.

"But—"

"But what?" She turned her head and looked at him.

"Nothing." Dad smiled kindly. "I went to the underground garden today." He gave her ankle a fatherly squeeze.

Amrita groaned. Not this again. She turned away, facing the wall. "There is no underground garden."

"The sunflower people want to tell their story, the story of old Mars."

"I don't want to talk anymore," Amrita said.

"Why don't I tell you a little of it?" Dad suggested.

"Jesus. I just said—"

"It's fascinating, the story of old Mars."

"Stop *talking* now."

"Don't be sharp with me, Pumpkin."

Amrita rolled over and sat up. "It bothers me that you won't stop talking when I tell you to stop. You used to stop."

Dad folded his hands in his lap and looked at them. "I appreciate," he said, starting slowly, seeming to hunt carefully for the right words, "that I sometimes make you uncomfortable. But I hope *you* can appreciate that I'm not a mere thing, a device, you can choose to turn off and on at will. I'm not an artificial, like your so-called friend, Tripp."

"Leave Tripp out of it."

"I would like to," Dad said. "But I find your morbid attachment disturbing."

"Disturbing." Amrita's childhood room seemed too small, the air too thin. Childish and colorful drawings she'd once created on a Play-And-Swirl pallet adorned the walls, primitive renderings of her little Burroughsville family. Mom and Ideal Dad. The goddamn maintenance man. Amrita stood up. She felt crowded—which was ridiculous, when you thought about it. "I'm going outside."

"A walk sounds nice, Pumpkin. I'll come with you."

"Please don't."

Amrita suited up, cycled through the airlock. Dad stayed with her every step of the way, acting the part of a physical presence without interruption, just as she'd once requested. She walked along the shore until she began to feel tired. Dad never stopped talking.

"The Sunflower Martians lived thousands of years ago, back when sparkling blue water filled the canals and riverboats propelled by solar sails navigated from community to community, trading goods and stories."

Amrita kicked at the powdery sand. "There were never any canals on Mars."

"Nonsense!" Ideal Dad said.

She stopped and looked back. Ideal Dad kept talking, but she was getting better at ignoring him. From this distance, the hab and farm buildings appeared small and generic—except in scope, no different than the shells of the city.

I found some shells on the beach, she thought, a little hysterically. And then she realized something.

Ideal Dad was saying, "The Martians chose sunflowers because the flowers are so bright and sunny and optimistic, just like the Martians themselves used to be."

"Hold up," Amrita said.

"What is it, Pumpkin?"

"If the builders can recreate my old Burroughsville hab, why can't they recreate the *Meghnad Saha?*"

For the first time in days, it seemed, Ideal Dad became quiet.

"Well?" Amrita said.

"We should be getting back home now."

"Answer my question."

"A spaceship is very complicated."

"The hab is complicated, too."

"The interiors exist as a deeply imprinted memory with an emotional toggle from your childhood."

"Tripp and I lived together on the surveyor for a long time. That's imprinted, too."

"It's not the same." Dad's tone suggested the conversation was over. He turned and walked away, back toward the hab, kicking up no sand, leaving no footprints. After a few meters, he disappeared. Amrita stood there, as if trying to catch a glimpse of a mirage. It had been a long time since Dad had last pulled his disappearing act.

She woke on her hab bed and lay still, listening. Somebody was in the corridor outside her room. She got up and padded over to the door, slid it open a few inches. A man, his back to her, walked away toward where the corridor curved. A *different* man. Carrying a long-handled static duster, he was dressed in the green jumpsuit worn by maintenance workers in Burroughsville, a long time ago. Amrita slipped into the corridor and followed him. He rounded the corner. She ran to catch up.

"Hey."

He paused and turned his head, his face in partial profile. It was Ideal Dad, and it wasn't Ideal Dad.

"What are you doing?" Amrita said.

"It's late for you, kid. Where's your mother?"

"I don't like this." Amrita stepped back. "Don't do this."

The maintenance man grunted and continued on his way, toward the next bend in the corridor, occasionally swiping the walls with his duster. Around that next bend the shiny black shell material replaced the phony representation of Amrita's hab. She didn't follow him. She was afraid to.

That day on the beach, it was the last time Ideal Dad appeared. Amrita spent her days alone in the hab. A heavy lethargy came over her, and she stopped going to the farm. The process of suiting up and cycling through the airlock made her tired even to think of it. She barely left her room, where she slept a lot, and nibbled on the last of the pod's emergency rations. Every night she heard the heavy shoes of the maintenance man clocking down the corridor, but after that first time she stopped going out to investigate. It was all inside her head anyway.

One night, lying in the dark, on the precipice of sleep, Amrita heard something, a minute creaking, groaning. The sounds of nano builders at work. She sat up and waved her hand over the bedside lamp sensor. The light came up. In a corner of the room, a child's desk took shape. It was a fully interactive FunDesk. Amrita's eyes widened. Up to now the room had duplicated her childhood hab, recreating what had actually been in it. But she had never had a FunDesk, though she'd repeatedly begged her mother for one.

Amrita swung her legs off the too-short bed. She wriggled her toes in the carpet—then stopped when she realized it was the same thing she used to do when she was five years old. The desk finished building itself. Cherry apple red swept away the shell-black look. What next, duckies on her underwear? The room was infantilizing her. Only it wasn't the room.

Footsteps crossed the floor on the other side of the wall common to the family quarters. Not the heavy tread of the maintenance worker. Amrita, suddenly terrified, approached the curtain between her bedroom and the family's common space. In all these weeks, no one had appeared in the family space. Amrita lifted the curtain aside in time to see a man pass into the corridor, his back to Amrita, a young man with squared shoulders.

"Wait," Amrita said, her hand reaching out.

The door slid shut behind him.

Half dressed, barefoot, she pursued him, but was afraid to catch up. They followed the curving corridor and came to the airlock.

Amrita found her voice. "You can't do this to me."

The man turned. A piece of his face that included his right eye was missing.

"All I ever wanted to do was stay," he said, "but you won't have it." His voice sounded garbled, as if he were talking around a mouth full of mud. It wasn't a human voice at all, but maybe the voice of a creature that had stopped physically existing a very long time ago. As he opened the airlock's inner door, his face began to melt. He shuffled into the airlock. The inner door closed with a decisive *clunk*. Amrita rushed to the little round window. The airlock was empty, with the outer door never having opened. She was alone again, but hadn't she always been?

Amrita moved out of both the infantilizing room and the false representation of her old Cydonia family quarters. She dragged everything she needed down the corridor and around the second bend, and there she made a place for herself enclosed by the shiny black shell material. She craved the inconvenience of reality. She *needed* it, if she was going to have a chance.

Amrita resumed tending the farm. She required food, enough to go beyond the limits of her pod rations. It would take a long time to accomplish what she intended to accomplish—if she ever did accomplish it.

She mind-sifted nanos in the blue sand, and worked doggedly to reconstruct the *Meghnad Saha*. Hours and hours she spent remembering every detail of her lost surveyor. She started in the morning and ended at night, curled on the hard shell material, concentrating until her mind went slack with fatigue. On the beach—slowly, slowly—the ship began to rise. First the landing struts and feet and then a skeletal approximation of the superstructure. She wouldn't need the whole thing, just the essentials. Structural integrity. Ion propulsion engines. One pressurized cabin . . .

Tripp visited her in a dream. He was his old self, undamaged and companionable. His blank face swiveled toward her. *I've got your back*, he said, but it was just Amrita's deep architect of loneliness trying to manufacture the loyalty Tripp, in the end, had been incapable of. She sat up and angrily wiped away tears. “I don’t *need* you anymore. I’m getting out of here.” By “here” she meant more than Trappist-1e.

She wanted so badly to abandon the abandoned part of herself.

Amrita tried something new. Before sleep she focused on the missing pieces of her spaceship reconstruction but did not struggle consciously to recreate them. The builders were smart. Once they knew exactly what you wanted they could, as Dad had said, build anything. They had done it with the oxygen conversion unit and other details in the hab. Since then Amrita had been trying too hard, getting in her own way and in the way of the builders.

The builders resumed work and they worked rapidly.

“Ready to fly,” Amrita said, standing by the surveyor, her gloved hand flat against the hull. She turned back to the hab and saw nothing more than a collection of black shells. Of course, it was different on the inside. But she would never visit the inside again. After a minute she turned away and opened the hatch on the underside of the reconstructed ship and hauled herself up. Minutes later the *Meghnad Saha*, streaked out of Trappist 1-e’s atmosphere and towards the Khabbhan gate. She was going home.

DEEP DOWN IN THE CLOUD

JULIE NOVÁKOVÁ

"What is there more sublime than the trackless,
desert, all-surrounding, unfathomable sea?
What is there more peacefully sublime than the calm,
gently-heaving, silent sea?
What is there more terribly sublime than the angry,
dashing, foaming sea?"

Floating freely in the dark cold water, Mariana had lost her sense of direction. Suddenly a flash from somewhere (above? where was above?) illuminated the whole ocean, and in that instant, she could see a school of grunions swimming past: hundreds of silvery gleaming bodies together in a mass so alien and intimidating. So beautiful. Light reflecting off their sleek bodies and silver-lined black eyes.

The darkness returned, but it didn't feel the same. She could feel the hundreds of eyes watching her. Irrational, yes. But this moment was beyond rationality.

Another lightning strike somewhere far away revealed a peculiar sight.

Chubs? she thought with an unnatural calm. *How strange. Must be the storm . . .*

However, still no sign of other people.

When the next lightning bolt lit up the murky waters a moment later, she glimpsed something else. She knew she ought to feel dread, fear, panic.

But she was far beyond that too.

"Ready?"

"Ready."

"Ready," echoed a second voice, and the three divers submerged together.

As soon as she entered water, Mariana Aguayro ceased feeling anxious. She was in her element. No matter what happens next, she's where she belongs; and she had trained for what happens next.

It was difficult to tell whether the same applied to Hector Hodges beside her. Even though the full-face mask offered a better view of his face than usual diving masks, she could only imagine how he was feeling. In her imagination, however, he was still as nervous as on their way here.

Iku was already ahead of them, holding his sea scooter like it was a part of his own body. If she felt in her element here, he seemed born in the ocean.

They continued in silence. No need to speak, even if the transceivers would allow them to. They could view speaking as a security risk even here, still far from their destination. The fish-like scooters carried them forward. They could take a moment's rest for now. Mariana knew they'd need it.

Even though they were not descending yet and it was early, light faded quickly around them. Mariana thought of the darkening skies above. No sane person would go for recreational diving today. They remained alone but for a few by-the-wind sailors above, and some moon jellyfish. The storm was coming. For them, it was ideal.

Iku turned and signaled "down." She and Hector copied.

The waters grew murkier as they descended slowly. Usually, the visibility would be good. But today, the currents were disturbed by the approaching storm. The water was considerably colder than usual at this time of the year. Mariana could still see Iku's silhouette beneath, but visibility was dropping quickly.

Finally, she glimpsed the bottom, or at least she thought so. On the sandy shelf, there was no reef to look for, nothing to use as a beacon. Her dive computer showed the depth of 110 feet, same as the analog depth gauge she had refused to leave home.

Upon reaching the bottom, Iku signaled for them to stop. Mariana's heart skipped a beat.

It's here. We're really doing it. Just as we practiced.

It was time to leave the scooters and anchor them here, where they could find them on their return trip. *If there is one.* Even in the murky shade, Mariana saw the fear in Hector's eyes. In contrast, Iku's face was almost serene. She imagined hers full of anticipation.

We're going to free freedom itself.

"Let's go," Iku gestured.

Hug the bottom. Kick ever so slowly. The rhythm we finally got right last week.

A week ago, at the same depth, but in clear water on a sunlit day tens of miles away from here, Mariana was trying to pass as a fish. She could see Hector swimming some ten feet from her. Iku floated somewhere overhead, monitoring them as always.

Hug the bottom. Go slowly. Use the add-ons on the suit to simulate fish movement, she recited in her mind. She should probably feel nervous. But being underwater always had a strangely calming effect on her. Hearing your breath, the pounding of your heart, and the ocean surrounding you, while you moved freely in its soothing cold embrace . . . Sometimes she wished she could stay.

"There wouldn't be any motion detectors on the bottom," Iku had said to them earlier. "Too many things would set them off. They would rather rely on autonomous guard bots, a few ROVs and aquamesh around the site."

Hugging the bottom therefore seemed to be a good approach strategy, and Iku provided the rest.

Now they reached the improvised aquamesh: just a fishing net in this case, no fiber-optics. When Iku gave the signal, Mariana and Hector started cutting through it.

He was faster than she this time, having improved a lot. Mariana got used to the full-face mask and closed cycle rebreather already in their first test dive. Hector had a little trouble adjusting to the mask, but he too was an experienced diver and now he seemed just as accustomed to the equipment.

Going through, she signaled and went first.

She saw the outline of their target in the silty waters. Suddenly, a shock wave hurled her onto the bottom and made her earbuds ache. She was scared and disoriented . . . for a few seconds. Then she kicked fast toward where she thought the target was. She couldn't see a thing through the upraised mud. *We should have thermal*, occurred to her. She wasn't sure any thermovision mask even existed, but Iku apparently had access to a lot of gear she hadn't known about.

Hector was beside her in another second. They reached the target, pulled the waterproof Taus and cords and got to work in perfect sync. The screens shone bright in this dim bottom world.

"Incoming," Iku's voice sounded suddenly in their ears. Mariana turned around to intercept the danger and readied her underwater gun. But nothing happened. Then Hector announced: "Got it."

The timer showed eighteen minutes, ten seconds. Best result so far.

A diver silhouette approached.

Ready, Iku signaled. *Up*.

When they were ashore and stripping from the diving gear, Mariana felt oddly elevated. *We did it. We're well under the limit. It really can be done!*

But the greatest news was yet to come.

"There could be severe storms coming next week," Iku announced as he closed the trunk with all the gear and stood by his car, an inconspicuous older wagon. "The timing is ideal. Augur will be conducting some site reliability tests elsewhere. Their guard will be high, but it always is, and they would be more vulnerable at the same time. Be prepared. The next time, we go live."

It was exhilarating to hear that. Next time, it's real. They're gonna rob and sabotage an Augur datacenter.

In the wake of their successful dive and Iku's announcement, they had made a mistake. Mariana would usually take a bus back to LA; after all, Iku had all the diving gear, she didn't need to carry anything. But Hector had offered to drive her home.

"He's being too paranoid," he waved off Iku's earlier advice. (*Do not ride together. Do not call each other. Do not let your paths cross any more than they would before you had met.*). "And he's not here. Are you going to wait an hour for your bus, or be back in LA at that time?"

It wouldn't hurt to get home earlier . . .

They spent the whole ride talking. It seemed like a mere moment when he stopped before her home.

"Wanna come upstairs for a drink?" she said on an impulse. Hector wasn't her usual type. She wasn't into older guys and typically avoided anyone from IT, if mostly for professional reasons, but the excitement of their dive and the upcoming op must have clouded her judgment. The fact that they had shared a secret from the rest of the world may have played a role.

He stayed for several hours. But when she said "you should go," he just nodded and left. They didn't see each other again up until this morning, after Iku had called them. It was time.

She couldn't quite shake off the disturbing sensation that Iku somehow knew.

Hector was the first to notice the bots. *Above*, he gestured.

The AUVs were circling the perimeter in quasi-random patterns. They patrolled for unusual motion, light, heat signatures, sound, or transmissions. Though Mariana knew about them, her heart still skipped a beat when she saw that one was nearing her position.

Calm down and swim. This was to be expected.

The AUVs continued on their way.

The style they'd practiced seemed to pay off. They had passed as fish.

Then she saw what they were looking for. The mesh.

The real danger would only lie beyond that—if they managed to get through.

Mariana glanced at Iku, or rather tried to, but she couldn't see him. The silt whirled beneath them and decreased visibility even further.

But something changed. She glimpsed movement. Silvery glint. Eyes. So many . . .

Pacific mackerel, she thought.

It didn't stop with them.

So he did it; Iku released a batch of pheromones to lure the fish. The schools would provide more cover for them while they try to get through the mesh.

Iku went first, followed by the fish like some strange pied piper.

A sudden if feeble flash of light illuminated even these murky depths for a fraction. The storm above had started.

It would disturb the fish. It would also disturb the AUVs and sensor nets. Motion, thermals, sonar echo—all would be obscured. A lot of unusual activity just might pass unnoticed in a storm . . .

Iku approached the mesh. Mariana waited while he began attaching long stretches of optical fiber to the mesh. Then she saw the signal. She swam toward him and began cutting through the fiber-optic mesh, while Hector approached from another side. Another lightning struck somewhere above.

The final cut. Nothing visibly changed. No dazzler blinded them; no sound weapon thrust them away; no AUVs approached.

They swam through. Shapes began emerging from the mist-like whirling silt. Their ghostly glow felt otherworldly. There was something surreal about the server boxes and glowing displays down here: a true snippet of another world.

How did I ever end up here? Mariana wondered.

• • •

Mariana Aguayro sometimes wondered how their lives would turn out if the Sun didn't misbehave. Just *one* peculiar cycle of increased solar activity. It was enough to first render billions of investments in satellite communications lost, and to make other such ventures too risky for another decade; and they could count themselves lucky that the storms only caused occasional blackouts.

Cables always held most traffic, but Internet giants promised free worldwide web connection for anyone on the planet. High-speed satellite connection in the furthermost, poorest village on Earth; it was too good to last. It almost hadn't even started before the unprecedented solar storms fried most satellites, high-altitude balloons, and many land facilities too. Solely dependent on cable connections, with the corporations shaken badly and world politics already in disarray, it was a recipe for a slow plunge into unobtrusive dystopia.

If it didn't happen, I may have gone to college.

If it didn't happen, we wouldn't have access outages for days.

If it didn't happen, we might not have lost our freedoms so easily.

She remembered net neutrality, constant quick access to information, and reliable communication from her childhood. Chatting with friends online without worrying about the price or whether the messages would get through at all. Browsing encyclopedias and magazines without end. No outages lasting over an hour. Sometimes it made her feel old, despite not being even in her thirties.

She also remembered a semblance of privacy. Yes, people willingly, if unwittingly granted access to highly personal information to any stupid app, but there was at least a pretense of legal protection, at least some hope that individuals could persist against governments and corporations . . .

This, too, had been taken away, with the help of Augur.

Maybe that's why Mariana liked diving so much. The fish, corals, and crustaceans didn't care for human skirmishes. She could escape into their world, but even there, she would see the discomforting signs of human presence above. Little had been done to keep the oceans clean. Even down there, in her dream world, Mariana could not avoid getting angry.

So she'd started rebelling. Tiny steps, at first. Then she'd gotten more daring.

Being a hacker was nothing like in the movies she'd watched—and downloaded, impossible now—as a kid. But it was exhilarating nonetheless when she and the fission-fusion crews sometimes succeeded after weeks or months of dull work. Her life became a series of mood swings, and at times she also wondered whether it would have been so, had she been let to live a normal life.

She didn't know how Iku found her.

He sat next to her one day on the beach, an inconspicuous black man of slender build and indeterminate age, and told her without any fuss that he wanted to hire her for a special job. One that involved both her computer hacking and diving expertise.

She could have said no. She didn't know the stranger at all, nor did he mention having any contacts in common.

But it sounded like the kind of offer you cannot refuse.

• • •

She was just a few kicks away from the first server when the world broke.

First, there was light.

A bright flash blinded her for a moment, and a staccato of bright beams followed. No time to think about that. No time to prepare for the sound.

It threw her away like a punch in the chest. Her limbs flailed around her. She felt as if air was knocked out of her lungs. Her chest and stomach hurt badly. She couldn't breathe. And the lights were still there, burying themselves into her skull . . .

Dazzlers and an ultrasonic pulse, some calculating part of her mind said. *Shouldn't cause permanent damage, only stun or injure. Get it together.*

She kicked away before another cavitation could hit her. Only then she turned and looked back, grasping the underwater gun on her belt, though wary of using it.

But it was no longer necessary.

"Disabled it," Iku's voice sounded in her ears for the first time during the dive. Stealth didn't matter anymore, and they would need to use the transceivers soon anyway.

She looked around. "Hector?"

She didn't see him. Nor did she hear any reply. She was about to call him again, when Iku spoke: "He's alive."

Something in his tone made her shiver inwardly.

Iku moved smoothly, shark-like, toward a dark silhouette barely visible in the silt. She glimpsed him link his suit's computer to Hector's. As she swam nearer, she could see him activate the adrenaline pump in Hector's suit.

The dark silhouette moved, and Mariana heard a sharp intake of breath in the comms. "W-what happened?"

"Dazzler and cavitation," Iku said. "You'll come to. Let's do it."

Mariana would have liked to see whether Hector was okay, but Iku was right; there was little time. They had to get in, and Hector Hodges, a disgruntled former Augur employee wishing to take revenge accompanied ideally by large sums of money, was necessary to manage it quickly.

The servers were just two dozen feet away. This near, AUVs wouldn't use sonic pulses to knock them out; too much risk for the equipment.

Hector and Mariana got to work on one rack, Iku moved to another.

"You all right?" she asked Hector quietly, mask to mask; no need for Iku to overhear.

"Think so," he spoke. Even in these conditions, she could hear his strained breath.

Broken ribs? Internal bleeding? she thought of the risks of cavitation. It was by no means a non-life-threatening weapon. Down here, every injury counted more.

The firewall held fast, but Mariana tried a few new exploits, while Hector worked his angle.

Still nothing . . . Would they have to use plan B and just DDoS Augur without making use of any of the data stored here?

Mariana glanced at her computer. At this rate, she had an hour of resurfacing to look for. An hour within which anything could go wrong.

"We're there," Hector said.

Mariana's heart skipped a beat.

We're really there. Inside Augur's heart . . . about to seize it and tear it out.

She just sent an invite to a feast on the company's internal files to a dozen informal hacker groups; most of them hopelessly idealistic anarchists, some strategically chosen groups that were in for money or mainstream politics, which translated to money anyway.

Her head almost spun.

For a second, she was tempted to look up Iku, regardless of whether the alias had any ties to his real self. Who, or what . . . But no—there was no time to waste.

Now to erasing the user metadata, and all the surveillance we can . . . To watch the watchmen for once. To free ourselves before they load the backups—but others will be ready for that. Let it run another half an hour, please, and then we can have a DDoS as a cherry atop the cake.

There was still a chance that Augur noticed only now what they were doing and couldn't get in touch with its AUVs here because of the storm.

But the storm would also complicate their ascent. They'd all realized the possibility they'd become martyrs, but none wanted to reconcile with that. Not without a fight.

"Iku?" she spoke.

No answer.

"Can't resurface now," Hector pointed above. Even at this depth, they could see the lightning flashes. Even through the transceiver connection, Mariana heard the strain in his voice. *Hold on. We'll help you ascend*, she thought. But where was Iku? She decided to find out and kicked slowly. Even moving this carefully, she almost caused a silt out. That's why she didn't see what happened next.

She was already at the further rack, and only heard the gasp and ragged, muffled breaths. She turned back, but another shape shot forward alongside her: Iku. She'd never think a diver could move so fast and smoothly, truly like a fish.

Hector's body was jerking as if electrocuted. Mariana glimpsed some strange, ghostlike shape around him in the light of her LED torch, and realized that he *was* being electrocuted.

But Iku was already there, grasping the thing she could barely see, and pulling it away from Hector.

The battle resembled a surreal ballet: a diver against a barely visible translucent shape, swirling and writhing amidst silt. It was entrancing. The Finnish Kalevala myth came to Mariana's mind, because Iku Turso in this instant truly resembled some kind of ancient sea monster like his namesake in the epic: sometimes depicted as a horned creature, sometimes a sea serpent, sometimes octopus-like, but always, always deadly.

The translucent robot sank to the bottom gently.

Iku turned to Mariana. "What are you waiting for?"

She wasn't checking her Tau; she was checking Hector.

He was alive.

But even without glancing at his computer, Mariana knew he wasn't going to make it. His suit was inflating visibly, and he started ascending. His face was constricted with pain. He was still conscious, and very much aware that this was just a brief period before certain death.

I'm so sorry, she thought.

"He was electroshocked," Iku said on the transceiver. "Invisible robot creeps near you, pierces your skin with electrodes, shocks you, and doesn't threaten nearby devices. Didn't know they were in use already."

Sizzling rage got ahold of Mariana. Hector was dying, and Iku was reciting his knowledge of the damn robot that killed him!

"What do we do?" she somehow made her voice sound measured.

"We continue our work."

"No!"

"Yesss," Hector hissed through the pain. His gaze met with Mariana's. They were almost mask to mask. The eerie glow of the underwater servers made his face appear ghostlike. She was looking at it, and so didn't see him pull a knife from his belt and cut at his own drysuit.

The inflation stopped, and then reversed. Mariana took a split-second to realize what he'd done. *The stupid fool!* He flooded his own suit to stop it from inflating. He'd never be able to ascend, even if he got rid of all the weights at once, and he'd get hypothermic in the matter of minutes.

"I'll take care of it," he managed to say. "You get out. They . . . seem to know."

"Continue data transfer while you can," Iku instructed him, and signaled to Mariana to follow him. She lingered for a second, put her mask to Hector's and turned off her transceiver for a moment. Only then did she realize she had absolutely no idea what to say.

He solved it for her. "Goodbye, sweet girl," he struggled to speak, but somehow he managed for the words to sound soft. "Go."

Iku was circling the center, and Mariana noticed he was planting something in semi-regular intervals. She swam to it.

Charges.

Iku waited for her at the far end of the datacenter and signaled to leave.

"Explain first!" she spoke regardless of knowing that Hector will likely hear it. He had the right to know.

"Destroying the center will set Augur back many months, if not years. Time for us to act."

It made sense, she knew it. Just . . . leaving Hector behind, even if the best he could hope in otherwise would be surviving the hypoxia or a stroke after rapid ascent, if they could somehow get him out of his suit and share their air with him . . . No. Hector Hodges was gone and knew it very well.

"What did you really want to gain from this?!" she said.

Iku's lips moved as if in silent prayer. His face, illuminated by the datacenter's glow, looked inhuman, almost demonic.

"What anyone wants," he whispered. "Freedom."

• • •

"Who do you think our Iku really is?" Hector had said back during their ride home.

"What do you mean?"

"The equipment he got us, his knowledge of the facility . . . I think he's a frogman."

"Ours, or someone else's?"

Hector laughed quietly. "That's what I'm wondering too."

"He could just be Augur's. Don't they have their own frogmen? Military-grade stuff?"

"I guess so. I even heard some rumors about . . . enhanced soldiers. But I'd think they watch theirs more carefully."

"Like they watch you?" Mariana raised a brow.

Hector seemed unperturbed. "That's different. I'm unimportant."

Mariana didn't question that; they both were. Was Iku too?

"Someone has to clean the facility," she spoke finally. "Biofouling can be a problem after less than a year down below. Not speaking of tech maintenance."

"Iku isn't an IT crowd guy."

"I never said he was. He could have posed as one."

"I dunno." Hector shrugged. "Something seems . . . off about him to me. Can't explain it."

Mariana snorted, but it was just a facade; in fact, she felt the same about Iku.

"There must be a lot of people outside our scope of abilities," Hector continued. "Not just the H+ nerds who implant magnets into their fingers and bloody Fitbits under the skin. I mean gene-modded people, or laced, or fitted with optogenetic circuits, enhanced senses, strength . . . Don't you think someone must have tried that already?"

"Perhaps," she said evasively. She didn't like to think of how she only saw the surface layer of the world, and how much might be going on underneath, concealed by Augur and others like them. It led to paranoid thinking, and she saw enough of that in her mother to know that she wanted to avoid that at any cost.

She was glad when Hector changed the topic and resumed flirting with her.

"Freedom?" she said once they were nearing the aquamesh. "From what?"

Iku didn't answer. She could think of a thousand options, but recalled her conversation with Hector back in the car all too vividly. But maybe she just felt guilty about Hector.

They began making another hole in the mesh; the first site was likely compromised.

"From my creators and controllers," Iku spoke suddenly. "Everyone will know now."

She wanted to ask more, but then there was light.

Something pushed her aside—no, *someone*, it was Iku—and after that she was pushed into the bottom with considerable force.

"Go—" she heard Iku, but his voice was cut out.

Silt was everywhere.

And then all was darkness.

"Where are the bones, the relics, of the brave and the timid, the good and the bad, the parent, the child, the wife, the husband, the brother, the sister, the lover, which have been tossed and scattered and buried by the washing, wasting, wandering sea?"

. . .and they dug tunnels in the silt and mud, bore into the bottom like worms. Blind, constrained, deaf but for the sound of their breath.

She soothed herself with this image from the past.

As a child, Mariana had loved stories of her underwater heroes. Cousteau and his diving saucer sub. Franzén and his men, excavating the *Vasa* from her infamous grave in the Stockholm harbor. In the decades after she sank in 1628, pioneer divers submerged into the 32-m depth in bells filled with air to excavate some of the treasures the ship had carried. Then, she lay forgotten and silt buried her, until amateur marine archeologist Franzén found her again. To un-sink the ship, they had to dig tunnels beneath her to secure her, and tow her into the harbor.

Mariana remembered the story now, as she clawed her way desperately through the silty bottom. She didn't know how long she'd been out, since she had no way to look at her dive computer, but hopefully she only lost consciousness for a few seconds. She couldn't have been buried deep, nothing could do that; but was she trying in the right direction? Fear almost got ahold of her.

Finally, she felt little resistance.

She emerged from a silt grave into pitch dark waters.

"Iku?" she tried.

Only silence answered her.

She assessed the damage. Her torch was lost, her rebreather got damaged, her trimix would soon run out, and she was still lucid enough to realize she was hypothermic. Her computer was broken, and she lost track of time.

So she did the only thing she could: started ascending as fast as she dared.

Another bright flash of lightning somewhere above. The lone chub, normally a river fish, was swimming desperately in this unwelcoming strange place. Mariana just floated with current. She started feeling strangely elated. *Hypoxia? Or just cold?* she could still guess.

A flash revealed a school of sardines gazing at her with a thousand little eyes.

Big brother watches you, she mused. *Even here. Did we change anything?*

Lightning—and the briefest of glimpses of a dreadful shape. The strange mask and suit . . .

Frogman. Augur's. Who else?

They were fast, or perhaps there were more secrets she knew nothing about . . . She realized she ought to feel dread, fear, panic. But she was just cold and tired.

Maybe they didn't win. But they didn't exactly lose, either.

A series of lightning bolts. The ominous figure, strobing toward her like in a stop-motion movie. And behind it—

Iku-Turso, son of Old-age, ocean monster, Mariana recalled dreamily the verses she'd looked up in the library.

In the murky ocean, illuminated only by lightnings further away now, she watched the strange battle unfold like a magic lantern projection. *How beautiful*, her mind marveled. Years ago, she'd seen the black jellyfish. It was huge, unearthly, menacing, infinitely elegant. Mariana had almost forgotten to breathe. Dread had seized her. She had only been wearing a spring suit, and the thought of the giant jellyfish stinging her had almost paralyzed her. But her sense of wonder had eventually won. She'd been captivated by the alien motion of the creature and its colors—a whole palette of purple, green, black, scarlet, and more colors as the light changed. It didn't look like an animal at all.

Neither did those two struggling monsters look human.

Who are you, Iku? Mariana mused.

Suddenly, the dark waters turned even darker, as if ink had spilled in the sea. She realized it was blood.

The remaining figure swam closer to her.

"Thank you," she heard in her transceiver, and that was it. "Now we're even."

Later, hard to say how much, she suddenly felt sand beneath her fins, and the next wave threw her ashore. There was no one else.

Mariana gasped and tore off her mask. She hungrily took in a breath of fresh cold air. Then she looked at the raging skies and around the shore, where she saw no artificial lights. She had no idea where she was.

She'd get rid of the suit. She would start walking. She'd try to make it somewhere dry without collapsing. If anyone asked, she'd make some excuse of getting lost in the storm, and give a fake name. Only then would she go online, if possible, and try to find out what they did.

Perhaps, just perhaps, she just emerged on the shore of a different world.

Author's note: The quotations come from "Poetry and Mystery of The Sea," as referred to by Edward Howland in "Ocean's Story; or Triumphs of Thirty Centuries" (1873).

THE LIGHTHOUSE GIRL

BAOSHU, TRANSLATED BY ANDY DUDAK

March 12, 2027

My name is Ling Rourou . . . right Papa? Yes, I am Ling Rourou. Today I am seven years old. Papa's name is Ling Dong. He gave me this mini laptop as my birthday present. Papa says all I have to do is open it and speak into it, and everything I say will be saved into the diary. So now I will tell about today. Today Papa took me to Disneyland for the whole day. It was so fun! I played in a fairy-tale world, and I even flew a plane. Then Papa took me to eat a very big cake. I had a very wonderful birthday. I promise that Rourou will be with Papa forever!

May 8, 2027

Today Papa took me to my first piano lesson. There were many kids my age to make friends with. I was a little scared at first, but I do not know why. When I sat down I played well. I was better than all the other kids. The teacher asked me if I studied piano, but I really cannot remember studying music before. The teacher said I play better than all the other students, even those who study. He said I could take the advanced course. Papa praised me and said I was his little prodigy. After class he took me to eat ice cream. I really love my Papa!

September 1, 2027

Today I will go to primary school. I do not want to go, but Papa says there are many kids there to be friends with and play with.

At school, all the other kids came with their moms and dads. Why do I have no mom to come with me? The kids on TV have moms too. I ask Papa about this sometimes, but he never tells me where my mom is. Once I asked him and he got a bad look in his eyes and he said I do not have a mom. Why am I the only kid with no mom? I want to ask Papa, but I think it will make him unhappy. I do not dare ask. Actually, it is not so bad, not having a mom. Having my Papa is good enough.

September 6, 2027

Today is Sunday. Papa took me to a place with many stone things sticking out of the ground. Papa said everyone goes to sleep under stones like those, eventually. I was surprised. It seemed like it would be really boring, sleeping there. Papa took me to one of the stone things and we stood before it. Papa said my mom was lying below it. I saw her picture on the stone, and she was more beautiful than any of the other children's moms. I was so happy. I told Papa to wake Mom up, so I could talk with her. Papa cried. He told me Mom could not talk anymore. But he said she will be with me forever, going wherever I go. I do not understand. Papa cried more. I felt very bad. My heart felt like it would break, so I cried too.

September 20, 2027

Today was the first day of English class. The teacher taught us to sing the letters of the alphabet. I was singing along, and suddenly an English sentence came out of my mouth. I said, "My name is Jessica. What's your name?" The teacher asked if I had studied English in kindergarten. But I couldn't remember if I had been to kindergarten. I couldn't remember anything before I was five years old. The teacher said my English is very good, like a native speaker's. She suggested I participate in an English competition for children and early teens. I was so happy. The teacher said she will call me Jessica from now on, since I already have an English name. I asked Papa about this when I got home. He just said I'm his little genius, but I don't understand. There's so much I don't remember, so how can I be a genius?

March 12, 2028

Today was my birthday, and Papa took me to the seaside. We rode on a fancy yacht and ate delicious food. Papa gave me one of those walking, talking robot dolls I always see on TV. I love my Papa! Too bad Mom couldn't be there with us. I wanted to go to that place from last year and see her, but Papa said Mom's soul is always with us, so there's no need visit her stone. I asked Papa what Mom's name was. He said she didn't have a name. I asked how she couldn't have a name. "You're named Ling Dong," I said. "I'm Ling Rourou. Mom must also have a name." At last Papa told me her name was Susu. Such a pretty name!

April 5, 2032

Today is Tomb Sweeping Festival. I lied to Dad, saying my Lili toy had wandered off again, but actually I went to see Mom. The last time I saw her was five years ago. I still remembered the place clearly, even though Dad had never brought me back for a second visit. It must be too difficult for him to see the grave, a trigger for his grief. But now I'm grown up. I can go on my own, and I did. I had to see Mom. There was so much I wanted to say to her. But when I arrived at the cemetery I was dumbstruck. The place was much bigger than I remembered it. There were so many gravestones, and I didn't know how I was going to find Mom. I wandered, crossing the grounds several times. I was about ready to give up, but I finally saw the picture, Mom's face in the stone, just as I remembered. She must have guided me to her grave, watching from up in heaven. She looked so young in the image, no more than twenty. So beautiful. She kind of looked like me.

Below the image it said, 'Grave of Chen Susu.' It had been erected by Mom's parents, my maternal grandfather and grandmother. When did Mom pass away? The gravestone didn't say, which was strange. The cemetery seemed old. The surrounding graves were all dated, and were thirty to forty years old. Mom couldn't have died that long ago. I'm only thirteen. When exactly did she die?

Now it's night and I'm back, and Dad is still in his study, sitting at his computer, trading stocks and so on. I want to ask him about Mom, but it's bound to make him unhappy. Better to let it go.

April 7, 2032

Dad went out shopping tonight. I seized the opportunity to search through all the photos in the house. I couldn't find any of Mom, but I did discover something strange: There are plenty of photos of me after five or six years old, but before that, absolutely nothing. None of me as an infant, and of course none of Mom and I. How can this be? For a few years now, I've been thinking about my life before age five. I've never recalled anything specific, but there are traces, vague impressions of living in a foreign country, speaking English every day, and being named Jessica. And other friends. Who am I? Where am I from? I hide in my blankets and ask myself questions, and suddenly I feel very afraid.

April 13, 2032

I ran into an old couple today, travelers who asked me for directions. They were amiable and doting old folks. I suddenly had a strange feeling that they were my parents. This was frightening. The husband was short, round-faced, and bald, nothing like Dad. Why did I feel like this man was my father? If I close my eyes it's like I can recall this other couple, my real parents. This feeling is so scary.

May 16, 2032

I told Lili about my fears. She thought for a bit, then said, "I figured it out! Your father isn't your biological father." This seems quite plausible. So, at one time I had other parents, and I lived abroad. Okay, but why did Dad . . . Ling Dong . . . adopt me when I was four or five? There are no old photos of me. I've been able to play piano and speak English since I was a kid. I must have learned these things in my previous country. Then Chen Susu is probably not my biological mother. Maybe Dad just chose a gravestone at random, to deceive me. My biological parents, are you still alive? If you're alive, where are you? Do you know I'm living in a foreign land, following a new father through life?

May 19, 2032

It turns out I'm the world's silliest fool. Today I reached my breaking point. I charged into Dad's study and said, "Am I really your daughter? Where are my biological parents?"

Dad was angry at first, but as he heard me out, he began to smile. "You and Lili watch too much TV," he said. We had spun fantasies based on serial drama plots, he claimed. "We did live in America," he admitted, "and your English pet name back then was Jessica. When you were four you had a high fever, so you can't remember your early childhood."

"But why don't you have photos of me from then?" I said.

"No photos?" he said, incredulous. He turned on his computer, and sure enough there were my baby photos. Dad said he took many photos back then, but during the move he lost some hard copy albums. But there were still many photos in the computer. I saw a family portrait of me, Mom, and Dad. Mom was hugging me, happily snuggled against Dad's side.

"If she's not your mother," Dad said, "why do you two look so alike?"

I couldn't deny it. And Dad was so good to me. How could I not be his daughter?

"She fell ill and died that year," Dad said. "You were still very small." He choked, sobbing. I told him to stop talking, and I hugged him. I really am such a fool!

April 7, 2035

Something wonderful and intriguing happened today.

A new teacher came to my middle school, 28 or 29 years old, dressed in ostentatious Western fashion. She didn't teach my class, but when she saw me in the office, she unexpectedly blurted out, "Jessica!" Then she seemed to remember herself. She smiled and said, "Sorry" in English, then in Chinese, "I made a mistake. I thought you were . . . but it's impossible."

My heart raced. I said, "What a coincidence. My English name is Jessica."

This amazed her, and we struck up a conversation. It turns out she's named Elle. She's an English teacher from Los Angeles, of Chinese ancestry. She explained that the Jessica she'd been thinking of had been a childhood playmate, a year older than her. They'd grown up together. But Jessica moved when she turned fifteen. That was ten years ago. Obviously, I can't be Elle's Jessica.

"So why did you call me by her name?" I asked.

"Because you look so much like her. Like my memory of her, I mean. Like two peas in a pod. But you must be twelve or thirteen years younger than her. So, there's no way . . . you can be her."

I'm still baffled and amazed. Although I can't possibly be Elle's Jessica, this was such a strange encounter. I asked Elle if she had an old photo of Jessica. Elle said she did, on her computer. She said she will bring it tomorrow for me to see.

April 8, 2035

I'm ill. High fever of forty degrees. No school for me today. Went to the hospital, doctor couldn't say what was wrong with me. All he could do was reduce my fever to help me convalesce. I might not be able to go to school tomorrow either. I really want to meet Elle again. I still haven't seen Jessica's photo.

April 24, 2035

My illness has lasted two weeks. Dad hasn't let me go to school. I asked him if I'm fatally ill, and he said it is curable, but it will take a long time. Maybe I can return to school next term, but I'm still scared. I feel like he's holding something back. Would he lie to me? Maybe I'm going to die.

June 16, 2035

That last entry was all pointless worrying. I'm feeling much better. This past month, anyway, I've had no problems. I asked Dad if I can return to school, but he said that since I've already deferred my studies for two months, I wouldn't be able to catch up. He wants to take me to Australia for a vacation, to relieve the boredom, and next semester transfer me to an elite private school. When I heard I was going to Australia I was very excited. But I hate to part with my classmates and teachers. Xixi, Mingming, and also teacher Elle. I was just getting to know her, but I feel like we're kindred spirits. I said I want to return to school next semester, that I can make up my missed classwork. Dad said I could go and ask my teachers, but I think he's just trying to keep me happy.

September 11, 2035

#private mode#

I want this part of my diary hidden. I need privacy. I . . . don't know whom I should believe.

We just got back from Australia, and today I got a message from Elle. She found me on the class chat group. She'd heard about my illness and wanted to know how I'm doing. I told her I'm fully recovered. She sent me some photos of she and Jessica. In one they were standing on a suburban lawn, smiling, expressions bright. Elle hadn't been exaggerating. Jessica looked like my twin!

Behind them was a steepled church. It seemed familiar, though I couldn't say why. Suddenly a name echoed in my mind: St. Michael. I asked Elle if the church was named St. Michael's, and she started. "God," she said, "how did you know that?"

I don't know how I knew, but coincidence can't explain it. Jessica and I are somehow deeply connected. Maybe she's my older sister. My biological mother? Neither of those seem right. I want to ask Dad what's going on, but then I wonder: How did I recover from that serious illness so suddenly? Does Dad not want me to meet Elle? Was he feeding me some drug or poison on the sly? But how could he have known about Elle? I never told him. Maybe he's been secretly reading my diary. Maybe he's been reading it all along. Three years ago, when Lili told me Dad was not my biological father, he knew I would start asking questions, and he showed me those photos to quell my doubts. If he was able to prepare beforehand, fabricating some digital photos would be easy. If Dad has been lying to me all along . . . The thought of it could drive me mad!

September 12, 2035

#private mode#

I couldn't get to sleep all night. I didn't fall asleep until dawn, and then I was up at nine.

In the afternoon, Elle and I continued our voice chat. "Do you know who your father is?" she said. I didn't know how to answer this. Dad was . . . Dad, my father.

"I mean, do you know about his work?"

Dad never goes to work. I know there's a big computer in his study, but I don't know what he busies himself with. On the screen, all kinds of data and diagrams constantly stream and pulse. He says he trades in stocks and foreign currencies. I've always been impressed with his ability to provide for us by just sitting in his study and trading. As far as I can remember, our little family has never wanted for money.

I summarized all this for Elle. She asked if I had a photo of Dad. Of course, I have many. I opened my hand device and opened a batch. Most were of he and I together. I sent a few to Elle. She immediately looked surprised.

"What?" I said.

"I've met your father. He's . . . he's Jessica's father!"

What I felt then was like vertigo. Gasping for breath, I said, "How is that possible?"

"Back then he was about forty years old," Elle said, "still kind of handsome. He worked in biological research, as far as I know. He was reclusive, didn't mix with neighbors. I only ran into him twice, when Jessica brought me to her house to play."

Although Elle doesn't have a photo of Jessica's father from that time, her description of him goes a long way toward making me believe. Ultimately the question is . . . what are Jessica and I to each other? Is she really my big sister?

Even if we're sisters, our resemblance is uncanny, especially because we can't be twins. And how or why did we end up with the same name?

Elle continued asking me about Dad, but I had no answers. It surprised me how little I knew about the most important person in my life. Where is he from? What exactly does he do every day? How did he make me? I know nothing.

Elle said, "Are you sure he's your biological father? Honestly, you two don't resemble each other very much."

My heart pounded in my chest. This was a doubt I'd harbored for years. I was like someone who wakes from a horrific nightmare, discovers everything is back to normal, passes years in comfort, but at last discovers that reality is the dream, and the nightmare is real . . .

Elle wants me to find a way to get a few of Dad's hairs. A DNA test could determine if we are blood-related.

September 15, 2035

#private mode#

Dad is very against me going back to school. He wants to take me to Paris to live for a few years. Paris! Once upon a time, this news would've driven me mad with joy. But now it just leaves me cold. Why does Dad want to flee China? Is he afraid I'll discover something? Or does he want to take me abroad for some dreadful purpose I can't imagine?

Although Dad is Chinese (I think?), he doesn't seem to have relatives here. And he has very little contact with the people around us in our daily life. Is he an escaped convict? A spy? Or he could be a homicidal maniac . . . If I keep obsessing on this, I'll go crazy.

If I can snatch a few hairs off his pillow, if that can just go smoothly, I will get them to Elle. And I'll have an answer soon enough. But I already have a premonition . . . that the answer is something I'll regret knowing.

September 27, 2035

#private mode#

After what seemed like a century, the DNA test results finally arrived. Elle transferred them to me via her hand device. The results confirmed my worst doubts: Dad and I are not blood-related whatsoever. I hid in the bathroom and cried for a while. If Dad asks what's wrong, I'll say I'm sad to leave my Chinese friends.

Elle says she's found a private investigator to look into Dad's background. But this means I must endure, and worry, and obsess in secret, because I don't want to alert Dad. He'll take me to France next month. If we get there and there are things I still haven't discovered about him, what should I do then?

October 9, 2035

#private mode#

Elle wants to meet with me today. She says she has something important to tell me.

We met in a cafe. Elle produced a thick folder of data, and with a grave expression handed it over. The top page was the CV of someone named Ling Yong. I wondered what this had to do with Dad. Elle sensed my misgivings, and explained:

"Ling Yong is Ling Dong, your . . . father. Or perhaps it's better to say your foster father. He changed his name. He's lived in a few different countries, not easy to track. But he left behind traces, allowing the detective to learn his identity."

"Originally named Ling Yong, born in the 1970s. In 1991 he entered Yanjing University in Beijing, School of Life Sciences. In 1995 he went to the US to study at the University of Pennsylvania for a PhD in biology. He got his doctorate in 2001. Later, at the National University of Mexico, he did postdoctoral research, investigating the DNA of a Caribbean jellyfish species . . . "

I looked through incomprehensible pages of data. The whole thing seemed to be this Ling Yong person's dissertation, mostly written in a foreign language. Was this Dad? He seemed like a total stranger.

But a familiar name emerged soon enough.

"When he was at Yanjing University, he met a female student named Chen Susu. Yes, this was your so-called mother. They fell in love quickly, and after graduation they got engaged."

Dad had never lied about this, at least. Chen Susu was his wife. But was she my mother? Maybe she was, and someone else was my father? After that engagement, almost twenty years passed before I was born. What had gone on in those years?

Elle continued: "Chen Susu did not go abroad with Ling Yong. She stayed in China and continued her studies. This was the 1990s. Internet and hand devices were still in their infancy. It wasn't easy for these young lovers to maintain contact, which strained their relationship. It's been over thirty years, so we don't know exactly what happened. All we know for sure is that Chen Susu was courted by the scion of a rich family. Eventually she chose to break up with Ling Yong, who hurried back to China to save the relationship. They were heard quarreling. Ling Yong then returned to America. Not long after, Chen Susu was reported missing."

I was forgetting to breathe. My own thoughts were making me sick.

"The police suspected Ling Yong in connection with Susu's disappearance. Immigration records revealed that he returned to China right when she went missing. Then he quickly left again. Police suspected his love turned to hate, that he kidnapped her, and that Chen Susu had probably been murdered."

"No!" I blurted. "No matter what they say, Dad's not capable of murder!"

"If only that were true," Elle said with a sigh. "Police suspected him, but he was out of the country. Summoning him for interrogation would have been difficult, and there was no conclusive evidence to get him extradited. At last the matter was dropped. Ling Yong might've had a guilty conscience, or at least a fear of justice. At any rate, he didn't return to China for many years. Chen Susu remained missing. Three years later, a hiker in a remote mountain forest discovered the remains of a body. Scattered remains. The body had been . . . dismembered. The head was missing. I'm sorry, Rourou, these details are horrible. Some clothes were found nearby, and they were confirmed to be Chen Susu's. DNA tests later confirmed the remains were Chen Susu's. She'd been murdered three years before."

It was like I'd fallen into an ice cave. Unable to control my shivering, I said, "You can't mean to say that my Dad . . . that he . . . "

"I don't know. The investigation didn't turn up definitive proof. Chen Susu's parents naturally suffered and grieved. Her remains were cremated, and then interred . . . in that cemetery plot you visited. Strangely enough, Ling Yong, a few years later, was witnessed bringing a seven- or eight-year-old girl to visit the grave. A Chinese girl, it was reported."

"Jessica?" I was pretty sure of this guess.

But I'd guessed wrong. "No, this was in 2005 or so. Jessica hadn't been born yet. This child was named Karla. We did everything possible to find pictures of her, and came up with just one. Look. She and Jessica, and you . . . identical!"

I felt like I was looking at my own childhood face. I felt like I was suffocating.

"Rourou, I have an awful theory. Please try to remain calm. I think you and Jessica and Karla are clones of Chen Susu. Cloning technology emerged a long time ago. Although human cloning has always been forbidden, for a competent biologist like Ling Dong, it would not be difficult."

"Human clones . . . " I only understood a bit of this concept from science fiction movies. "You mean to say that my father . . . Ling Dong . . . Ling Yong . . . took cells from Chen Susu, and used them to create us? Why would he do this?"

"He was obsessed with Chen Susu, to a sick degree. She betrayed him, or he felt she had, so he killed her. But he couldn't stand being parted from her, so he used her cells to create children that looked just like her."

I couldn't process this. I struggled to untangle my confusion. "If you're right about him, one clone would be enough. Why make three of us?"

Elle seemed even more uncomfortable. She lowered her voice. "This is what I wanted to tell you in particular, Rourou. You're in danger! Karla and Jessica both went missing, one after another. They both went missing at sixteen. Ling Dong moved to a new country each time. The people who knew Karla and Jessica thought they moved with him, of course, but that's not the case! Only Ling Dong knows what happened to them."

I shivered. "He says he wants to take me to France. Could it be that . . . "

"We can't rule out the possibility."

"What should I do? Report to the police?"

Elle considered, then grudgingly shook her head. "Approaching the police would be useless. At the moment, it's all conjecture. There's no concrete proof. The police would never believe such a bizarre story. But you can't go home either. So how about this . . . for the time being, you come with me. You should have an American passport. I can take you to the States. Ling Dong won't be able to find you, guaranteed."

I hesitated. This was Elle's side of the story. Maybe Dad was wrongly accused. Maybe there was more information. For instance, if I was a clone, why did I seem to have some of Jessica's memories?

"I still want to think it over," I said. "I need to be sure."

Elle didn't press me. "Then please be careful. Prepare for the worst. If anything happens, contact me immediately."

October 10, 2035

My home was starting to seem unfamiliar and sinister. But I was determined to be strong, to act as if nothing had happened, feign nonchalance, and keep Dad in the dark. No, to keep Ling Dong in the dark. Today, the aunty who usually cooks for us asked for leave. Dad busied himself in his study all day. At dinnertime I suggested we go out, so we ended up at a nearby restaurant. We sat down and heard the man and woman at the next table arguing. It was hard to understand, but it seemed a long-distance relationship had led to the young woman being unfaithful. She'd been caught, and now wanted to break up. The young man slapped her in the face, and the girl ran out crying.

Of course, this reminded me of Ling Dong and Chen Susu, and their long-ago romance. I struggled to maintain my composure. Ling Dong had supposedly murdered Chen Susu over a dispute like the one we'd just seen. I thought maybe I could sound him out. "Dad," I said, "can you believe that girl? How can she be so . . . Cheating, lying, deceiving, it's pathetic. I think deceivers deserve to die."

He pounded the table. "Yes," he said, voice low and forceful, "they really do. So why haven't I . . . " He stopped himself, trembling. I'd clearly provoked him. This seemed to confirm Elle's suspicion: he really was harboring deep-seated hostility toward Chen Susu.

I was shocked, angry, and scared. Was he capable of violence here and now? I had to force a smile. "Never mind Dad. Why get so riled up over other people's problems? Come on, lets drink a toast."

Ling Dong sighed and started drinking with me. I tried to lead him out of his foul mood, chatting about our usual father-daughter things, former birthday celebrations, where we'd gone together for fun, the mischievous pranks I'd played on him. All this did was remind me how many warm memories we shared. These weighed on me in our grim new context. The memories were the same, but he had changed.

Ling Dong couldn't seem to recover. He looked to be stewing in a vile temper. He was drinking rice liquor as if his life depended on it, cup after cup. When we finally left he was three sheets to the wind, so we took a taxi home. He went straight to the sofa and collapsed on it, and began to snore thunderously.

I considered Elle's theory more or less confirmed. Being back in this house was only increasing my danger. I sent Elle a message, then went upstairs and got my passport, and some cash and clothes, wanting to quietly slip away. But when I passed by the study door, I saw it had been left unlocked. Inside, the computer was still on. I couldn't help pausing there, one foot in the door. Ling Dong spent every day in there. What was he up to? Was he really just speculating in stocks and currencies? What secrets might be concealed in there?

I glanced toward the living room. Ling Dong was still snoring, well intoxicated. I guessed he'd be asleep until tomorrow morning. I summoned my courage and entered the study, and examined the computer, but just now the machine was locked. A dialog box requested a password. I tried several—Ling Yong, Susu, Jessica—all to no effect. I was forced to give up. I examined the desk, and one corner was indeed occupied by financial records, and books on the stock market, but they looked ignored, the books pristine. Spread out in the center of the desk were papers in English. I paged through a few. It all seemed biology-related. I could barely understand, but one strange word recurred throughout all the papers: *Turritopsis dohrnii*.

I opened my hand device and looked up the translation. The Chinese word that popped up was *dengta shuimu*, 灯塔水母, 'the lighthouse jellyfish.' A photo of the bioluminescent creature illuminated this name. In English it was 'the immortal jellyfish.' A brief introduction was attached: "A species of jellyfish four to five millimeters in size, after sexual maturity they are capable of returning to their sexually immature colonial polyp stage, and they can repeat this cycle indefinitely."

I didn't really understand this, only gathering that it was an odd species of jellyfish. Could all these treatises be about one species? I recalled something Elle said yesterday. Ling Dong was indeed a researcher of jellyfish. That part of the investigation report was true. But he hadn't been a biologist for many years, so why was he still reading these kinds of papers?

I kept paging through the material. I gleaned that it concerned this jellyfish's physiology and genetics, but I didn't understand the purpose. The rest of the study yielded no more clues, and I considered giving up. But then my gaze fell upon the computer screen again, and the password field. I sat down in front of the computer, and typed in *Turritopsis dohrnii*, but once more got an error message. I had just decided to leave when another idea struck. I typed in the same species name, but in all capital letters, and as one word: TURRITOPSISDOHRNII.

To my surprise, the computer unlocked!

I leaned in close and saw the software Ling Dong had been using all these years. I couldn't really understand it, but it obviously had nothing to do with stocks. I studied it for quite a while, until I recognized organic molecule structures, and simulations of chemical reactions. It all had something to with the lighthouse jellyfish, but I couldn't understand the specifics.

I minimized the program, and searched the computer. This time I quickly found what I was seeking: four folders labeled S, K, J, and R.

Four names wheeled in my mind: Susu, Karla, Jessica, and . . . Rourou.

I opened S first, my heart hammering away. There were many pictures and videos, all from around forty years ago, taken during the time of Chen Susu and Ling Dong's romance. The K file documented the growth and life of a small girl into her teens. She looked just like me, though she wore different clothes and hairstyles, and lived in another country. This was Karla. Jessica's file was similar, but she grew up years after Karla.

I wondered if we were really clones. I got lost in a fever dream, struggling not to lose hope, to keep from drowning.

I opened a video. Jessica was seven or eight years old, celebrating her birthday with Ling Dong—very similar to my own childhood. Only this was twenty years ago. Another video showed Jessica dancing in a school performance. Another showed she and Ling Dong fishing.

I didn't want to see any more of these fragments of daily life. I'd decided to stop when I found a large batch of videos that seemed different. I opened one marked January 8, 2024, and found something horrific:

Jessica's naked sixteen-year-old body on a bed, in a place resembling a laboratory. She was apparently unconscious. Ling Dong approached her with a syringe. Jessica woke, struggled a bit, shouted something, but Ling Dong restrained her. She couldn't overpower him. After the injection, the girl curled into a ball, and sank back into sleep. Ling Dong left soon after. The video was uneventful for a long time. I opened the next video, and saw that Jessica was still unconscious. Rashes of some kind had erupted on her skin. I skipped several videos, and the rashes had become strange mucous membranes, layers covering Jessica's body.

Days passed, and the transformation grew more extreme. Jessica was no longer human-shaped. The layered membranes had become a sort of cocoon. Her head and face were no longer visible. Ling Dong came every day to observe. About a month later, March 12 as it happened, the cocoon split open, and thick blood plasma—and god knows what other viscous substances—flowed out. A small head emerged. Ling Dong heard the ripping sounds, entered the scene, tore away the cocoon, and picked up a blood-covered child. It looked four or five years old.

"Susu," Ling Dong said. I couldn't tell if his tone was sad or joyous. "You really are reborn. What's a good name for you this time? How about the name of the kitten we raised together . . . Rourou . . . "

Susu . . . Rourou?

There I was, short of breath yet again. I don't know how long I stood there dumbfounded. Gazing down at the papers spread on the desk, the words *Turritopsis dohrnii* again caught my eye.

" . . . after sexual maturity, they are capable of returning to their sexually immature colonial polyp stage, and they can repeat this cycle indefinitely."

I finally understood the meaning of this sentence. The lighthouse jellyfish could return to infancy from maturity, and it could do so indefinitely, cycling between the two states, living forever.

I realized I was not a clone.

I was Chen Susu, and Karla, and Jessica.

Ling Dong, in order to punish Chen Susu, made her—me—into a lighthouse jellyfish. His injection caused her to revert to a four or five year old. Then she grew up again, until she was nearly full-grown, and then back she went. Back I went. Forever under his control and influence. With each new incarnation, I'd lost my memories, allowing him to treat me as a daughter. Until the kidnap victim finally rose up to understand the truth.

I was alive, but forever unable to become an adult. I had died, and then I'd returned to the world, and lived with a deranged demon. This was Ling Dong's penalty for "my" betrayal of him. The world's most horrific punishment.

I was shaking, could barely stand. I took a few steps back from the desk, and bumped into someone behind me. I turned and found myself looking right into Ling Dong's gloomy face.

"How did you get in here?" he said, glancing at the video still playing on the computer. His panicked expression twisted into something monstrous.

I pushed him with all my might, and ran out of the study.

"Rourou," he said, grabbing me. "Listen!" I snatched a humidifier off a table and smashed him in the head with it. He went down, but didn't lose consciousness like they do in movies. He was struggling to get up.

I fled recklessly outside. Turning a corner at an intersection, I saw Elle's car. She'd been waiting there a long time. I got into the car and Elle started it. "To the airport," she said.

"No," I said. "A police station. I found proof. I want that criminal to pay for everything he's done to me."

October 12, 2035

Elle and I reported to the police yesterday. The officers rushed to my former home, but Ling Dong had destroyed the incriminating evidence. Everything on the computer was deleted. Ling Dong tried to paint my claims as the wild fantasy of a young girl. He nearly succeeded. The police didn't believe my bizarre story.

But Ling Dong was the Ling Yong of years ago, a suspect in Chen Susu's death. And I was not his biological daughter. The police refused to hand me over to him, instead sending me to a domestic violence shelter. They've begun to investigate Ling Dong's background. He's finished!

October 15, 2035

Ling Dong has gone missing. The police say he might seek me out for revenge. They've advised me to be careful and vigilant. Elle says she can soon take me to America, where, she believes, Ling Dong will never be able to find me. But I'm still very scared. Scared that someday, once more, I will fall under his control. The police had better hurry up and find him!

October 24, 2035

Ling Dong is dead . . .

His body was discovered at sea, already dead many days. He probably killed himself the day he went missing.

When I heard the news I cried, loud and long. Just a month ago, I couldn't have imagined any of this. This grim end for him. Now he was dead, a demon that would fade away. But he'd been my Dad, my Papa. Like the demon, my father would never return.

The police believe Ling Dong, obsessed with Chen Susu, kidnapped a girl of unclear origin and background, to fill the void. Of course, there are many things they can't explain, but with Ling Dong dead, the case is effectively closed.

There are journalists with clever noses snooping around behind the scenes. Elle urged me not to tell anyone about the lighthouse jellyfish. If the world believed it, I might be taken away by some agency for scientific experimentation. I would certainly be reduced to a media object, sensationalized and slandered for a lifetime. I feel Elle is right about all this. Actually, I'm starting to doubt myself, to wonder if the video I saw that night was real.

Elle wants a fresh start for me in America. I don't want to spend her money, but she says she's got a lot of it, so it doesn't matter. "Let me help you," she said. "We've been friends for a long time, after all."

So, I acquiesced. I can only hope that a new start is possible for me.

Sender: Turritopsisling@Kmail.com
Time: October 20, 2035 (00:00:00 AM)
Recipient: Elle.Li2010@Starmail.com

Dear Elle:

This is a scheduled, automatic delivery email. By the time you read this, my body should be at the bottom of the sea, becoming part of the ecosphere's perpetual cycle. You and I, everyone in fact, must end this way.

Except for Susu.

It seems you already know about her, about Rourou. As for me, it's time to die. Otherwise the police would soon discover that Rourou's identity is forged, and investigate my past. They could eventually discover the truth, and Susu would become experimental material for a mob of eager scientists. Or she would be exposed for the world to gawk at, enduring their scrutiny, a freak on display. Either of these outcomes would destroy her. Only my death can end the police investigation.

The truth is not what you and Susu think. There's another side to the story you can't even imagine.

35 years ago, I was abroad doing research. I was looking forward to a happy life with my girlfriend. Then Susu suddenly wanted to break up with me. I couldn't accept this. I abandoned everything and returned to China. Susu had become thin and pallid, withered, and she wouldn't budge on breaking up. We quarreled, but I couldn't change her mind. I left in anger, resolved to make a clean break with her. But as soon as I returned to America, I received a phone call from her mother, and learned the truth, which was tenfold worse than a break-up. It turned out Susu had lymphoma. It was already late-stage and terminal when

discovered. Incurable. She had kept me in the dark, fabricated a reason to break up with me, to spare me real bereavement. It just happened that someone was pursuing her, a *fu er dai*, the heir of a nouveau riche family that made its fortune during Deng Xiaoping's economic opening of the 1980s. But this young scion hadn't won Susu's heart. She led him on, using him as part of her act for me.

After learning the truth, I had only one goal: to save Susu by any means possible. Cancer is a cellular change, unbridled cell division and growth, unstoppable, that finally uses up the body's resources. There was no feasible way to contain this horrific disease, but I had a crazy idea.

I was researching the lighthouse jellyfish. This species can, after sexual maturity, reverse its growth, a radical cellular change, the body becoming a polyp again. Young lighthouse jellyfish emerge from the polyp, and grow up all over again. Through this unceasing cycle, natural death is avoided. I was making headway in my research at the time. I'd found the gene that controls lighthouse jellyfish growth reversal. I hoped this power could check the proliferation of cancer cells.

I extracted the gene and put it in a retrovirus, which would act as a courier. I smuggled a small bottle of my elixir into China. Susu was already critically ill at this point, on her last breath, unconscious, so during our final visit there were no words.

I convinced her desperate parents to try my crazy solution. I injected her. Very soon the cocooning process began, the process Rourou saw on the video. Susu became a strange meat cocoon. Seven days later, the cocoon split open. Inside was a five-year-old girl. She looked like Susu as a child, but she didn't have Susu's memories. This was Karla, the product of Susu's bodily restructuring. Only a core part of the brain was retained, and this too had degenerated.

Inside of the cocoon there was leftover human tissue and bone. I buried these remains in a desolate place where I thought they would never be found. But they were found, of course, years later, after some of them became exposed due to erosion or some other process. They were taken to be the remains of Susu's dismembered body. This gave rise to the homicide case.

At that time, Susu's parents and I knew we had to conceal Karla's existence. Otherwise she would suffer the scrutiny of the world. We sent her to an orphanage, so that Susu's parents could adopt her and make everything look official. But this presented a problem. Susu hadn't been found, living or dead. That suiter of hers couldn't find her. He went to the police in a rage, and I became the number one suspect. Luckily, I'd already returned to my life abroad, leaving the police with no options. I continued my lighthouse jellyfish research in Mexico, but I couldn't replicate what I'd done to Susu. All my mammalian subjects came out of their cocoons dead. I suspected that Susu's cancer cells had integrated with the lighthouse genes in some special way, giving rise to a miraculous result. But I couldn't verify this.

However, those years of research yielded a by-product, an enzyme preparation derived from the lighthouse jellyfish. It invigorates human cells, promoting longevity. Although the effects are negligible compared with true lighthouse immortality, it is useful. I applied for a patent, trusting in tens of millions in profit, decades of financial security for Susu and I.

During these years, I stayed in touch with Susu's parents. Although Karla came into the world knowing nothing, she still had some life skills and language ability. She quickly developed a four- or five-year-old mentality, even recovering some fragmented memories. Susu's parents were getting old. Their energy was low, and Karla was coming to resemble Susu. Neighbors and old friends were beginning to talk. After I'd earned some money, I brought Karla to Mexico, so I could look after her. Karla was like a daughter to me at this point. My love for Susu had changed, but hadn't lessened at all. I vowed to ensure her well-being.

I believed that what had survived of Susu could live on. What was left of her in Karla could persist, and grow once more to adulthood. But at sixteen (or twelve, as it were), she went to sleep and didn't wake up. Her skin erupted with glutinous membranes that became a cocoon. This confirmed my most horrific conjecture: Susu's lighthouse genes would continue to express their phenotype. After reaching maturity, she would revert to infancy, and this cycle could not be broken.

I arrived in America and resumed my research, attempting to free Susu—now she was Jessica—from the lighthouse cycle. Eleven years before, when Karla had first evinced signs of cocooning, I'd injected her with my newly-developed elixir, hoping it would suspend the lighthouse process, and I filmed this for research purposes. This was the video that terrified Rourou. All I did was postpone her reversion to childhood. I couldn't stop it. And then Jessica, in her turn, also underwent rebirth, becoming Rourou . . .

Jessica's disappearance and Rourou's emergence caused me plenty of trouble. I was forced to return to China. What happened after that, you two both know. I continued via computer simulation to research lighthouse jellyfish genes and their effect on the human body, but to no avail. Many years passed. Now I'm old. My mental capacity is not sufficient for cutting-edge research. I know I can't stop the next iteration of the cycle. I must let go, and count myself lucky to have been with Susu. Twelve years from now, when the next cycle begins, I will be too old to play the part of her father. What's to be done then?

Luckily, she has come across you. Maybe I don't need to worry about her any more.

Elle, I know you're a kind-hearted woman. I have no choice but to entrust Susu to your care. She will probably begin the reversion in half a year or so. She will again become a child with no memories or identity. She will know nothing of any of this. Susu's parents long ago passed away. You are the only one who can help her. Perhaps you can be the mother she always wanted. There's about twenty million US dollars in her name: savings, real estate, and stocks. After I'm gone, it all belongs to you. The means of accessing it are attached to this email. The funds are more than enough for you to live comfortably, and take care of Susu.

I struggled for a long time with whether to tell Rourou the truth. I finally decided against it. Back when Susu concealed her illness from me, when she preferred my hate to my grief, perhaps her frame of mind was much like mine now. Before she lies dormant again, she may enjoy, for a while, the thought of growing to adulthood. She may hope to begin a normal human life, and dream. And then she will forget. She can live with you, her mother. She can be carefree and never know worry. Isn't that a kind of happiness?

Regardless of her outer form, it is her happiness that counts.

Last words of Ling Yong.

Originally published in Chinese in *Zui Mook*, vol 2, April 2017.

A WORLD TO DIE FOR

TOBIAS S. BUCKELL

Your hunting party of repurposed, cobbled together and barely-repaired pre-Collapse electric vehicles sweeps across the alkaline rich dust flats of old farm land. The outriders are kicking up rooster tails of dust into the air behind them, their bikes scudding over the dirt and slamming hard into every divot and furrow. Pennants whip about in the air.

You're glad to be on the top of a pickup with suspension, ass in a sling, feet shoved hard against the baseplate of the machine gun mounted right up against the back of the cab. You've been an outrider before, trying to balance a shotgun on the handlebars of the bike without wiping out. You didn't like it.

The outriders might get more respect, but there's a reason they wear all those heavy leathers, padding, faded old football helmets, and other chunks of scavenged gear.

"There she is!" Miko leans out from the passenger-side door and bangs on the roof of the cab to get your attention away from the outriders and pointed front. "Get ready."

Up ahead, through the bitter clouds of dirt that seep around the edges of your respirator, is the black line of the old Chicago tollway. You reach forward and yank a latch on the machine gun, pulling one of the large-caliber bullets into the chamber with a satisfying ratchet sound.

The seventy-year-old gun has been lovingly maintained since the Collapse. It has seen action in the Sack of Indianapolis, spat fury down upon the Plains Raiders, and helped in the defense of the Appalachian Line. You look down the sights, ignoring the massive ox horns and assorted animal skulls bolted onto your truck's hood.

Your quarry is ahead. A convoy of trucks pulling hard for places out further East. Their large, underinflated balloon tires fill the potholes and scars of the old expressway as they trundle on at a dangerous thirty-five miles an hour. It's axle-breaking speed, a sprint across the country in hopes that they can smash any MidWest Alliance blockades without paying import/export duties.

Fuckers. As if they could just roll across a state for free. Now they'll pay a lot more than just a ten percent transit fee.

"Cheetah cluster: right flank," Miko screams over the screech of old suspension and the rumble of tires. He is still hanging out of the door, and he points and throws command signs at other drivers. He's ripped his respirator off and left it to dangle around his neck. "Dragon cluster, left. Cougars for the front."

Your cluster of vehicles splits off to swing behind the convoy's dust trail, the world turning into a fog of black dirt and amber highlights, and you fall in on the right like a vulture. Enemy outriders split off from the convoy to harass the impending clusters, but they are outnumbered. Shotguns crack through the air, people scream.

In moments the security around the convoy peels off, uninterested in paying for cargo with any further lives. They've done their paid duty—they can head back in honor to whoever hired them.

"Do it," Miko orders you. He pulls his respirator back on, and now he's all green eyes and blonde hair over the edge of the cracked rubber. He's the commander. You've risen far following in his footsteps. Maybe one day you'll run a cluster, give commands to your own outriders. You've been tasting ambition like that, of late.

To survive, you need to find the right people to follow. Miko has created a strong pack. The fees you pull from what little cross-country traffic still trickles over the road keeps you all fed, the respirators fixed, and batteries in stock.

You lean back and pull the trigger.

The old Browning destroys the world with its explosive howl. You rake the tires of the trucks as Ann, the driver, moves the pickup along the convoy in an explosion of acceleration.

All three of the oversized vehicles shudder to a halt. Ann brings the pickup to a sliding stop, dirt and chunks of the old highway rattling up to kick the undersides of the old vehicle.

Miko steps out, shotgun casually slung over his shoulder.

Everyone's expecting the drivers to come out of the truck cabs with hands up. But instead there's a loud groan from the trailers. Miko swings the shotgun down into his hands and aims it up at the sound.

The sides of the middle trailer fall open and slam to the ground. Houz Shäd shock troops in their all-black armor are crouched behind sandbags and a pair of fifty-caliber machine guns.

You're all dead.

But instead of getting ripped apart by carrot-sized bullets, one of the Shäd shouts through a loudspeaker, "We seek information from you, and only information. Drop your weapons and live. You'll even be allowed to keep them. In fact, give us what we seek and your cluster can take the entire shipment of solar panels in trucks one and three."

Miko drops his shotgun.

You push away from the machine gun, hands in the air, wondering what happens next.

The Shäd jump down from the trailer, greatcoats flaring out behind them. Their deep-black machine guns seem to soak up the amber light. There's a storm brewing up north, you can tell. You will all need to run before it, get down underground before the tornados touch down and begin ravaging everything.

"Remove your ventilators," the nearest Shäd gestures. "Kneel in a row."

Your mouth is dry. This is an execution line and you know it. Bullshit promises aside. People like the merchant riders of Shäd view the continent as a place they should be able to trade across. They view clusters as "raiders" and not the customs agents you know yourselves to be.

But instead of walking behind you, the Shäd spread out in front of the line, moving from member to member. They're holding out photographs in their gloved hands, looking closely at each member of our cluster through mirrored visors.

The nearest Shäd approaches. Those ventilators they wear are not just the usual air purifiers, you realize. They're connected to oxygen bottles on their hips. You've never been close enough to see that before. "We are looking for someone," the Shäd says through his mask.

The fuck? All this over an MIA? People go missing in the middle countries all the time.

"This is her picture. We have been told she may be called Chenra, or Chenray. Have you seen her?"

You glance left, blood going cold, because that's *your name*. Miko stares at the ground and shakes his head. Ann, her long black hair tangled up in ventilator straps, shrugs. Cheetah cluster won't rat you out.

But why the hell are shock troopers from Hauz Shäd hunting you? You've been on a few nondescript battery raids, run the outlander position on some basic convoy stops, but you're not officer class. Just a runner and a gunner from nowhere.

You'd be sick from fear if you even understood any of this.

You're mainly confused.

The toxic air is rasping at the back of your throat. The ever-present dust is making your eyes water.

It has to be some kind of mistake. Whoever they are truly hunting has used your name, or has a similar name, and these very dangerous private security troops ended up crossing the midlands to find you.

"Anyone who gets us this woman can have the solar panels in the trailers here," the man repeats, pushing the photo at you.

"Yeah, let's have a see," you mutter, leaning forward on your knees.

He steps closer and you take a look.

It's you. There's no mistake.

But you know for sure you've never had your hair cut up above the ears like that. Or so flat.

The teeth are all wrong. White. Like someone has painted them. Different positions, too. *Shit, do you have a long-lost twin sister or something like that?* The woman in the picture does look eerily like you.

But it can't be.

A whole shipment of solar panels. If they're telling the truth . . .

You stand up. "Are you serious about those solar panels?"

A helmeted nod in response.

"What's your business with that woman?" You jerk your chin at the photo.

"A client needs to talk to her."

"That's it?"

"Just a conversation."

You take a deep breath. Cheetah has given you food and lodging. Given you a trade. You were thirteen when they found you trudging across a dune up in the lower peninsula of the Holy Michigan Empire. They treated you well. Better than you'd feared when you saw the motorcycles roaring across the sand toward you.

Even if you get shot, or kidnapped, a solar shipment would help all the clusters here. And if there's one thing you are, it's loyal to the people who show you the way forward to a better life.

"Then I'm Chenra, Cheetah cluster. I claim the reward of the solar panels."

"Che! I'll follow you!" Miko tries to stand, but one of the Shäd casually kicks him back down with a boot to the shoulder.

"You can't come where we're going," the mercenary laughs through her respirator.

Hauz Shäd has a strong reputation for following contracts to the letter, so you're not overly worried anyone will get screwed over here. All that crap about them eating the flesh of people they've killed is just rumor. Collapse jitters.

Sure enough, as you're taken up toward the head vehicle, the trailers are being disconnected from the trucks. Several cluster members climb aboard, open the rear doors, and shout in delight. Outriders watch you go by and nod in respect.

You don't see Miko anywhere. He's a ghost when he needs to be. He's not going to be happy about his gunner getting kidnapped.

Clusters don't carve promises into skin and swear blood oaths to protect each other to death as a meaningless gesture. They're planning to watch and follow you, to have your back. So you're going to play along, see what comes of this bizarre attempt to kidnap you.

If you manage to get out of this and back to the clusters, they'll all owe you big. Maybe even get you a promotion. You could end up a driver inside the shielded cockpit of an attack pickup. Maybe even get some scrip for hydroponic fruit from down near Fort Wayne.

The truck at the head of the convoy has an extended cab over the battery frame. The up-armored doors hiss open and the Shäd on either side of you point inside. Other Shäd are putting new tires on the truck because your Browning has torn them up.

You clamber up and into a sumptuous small office.

The door shuts behind you, and you wait a split second for your eyes to adjust.

Inside it is like something out of an old pre-Collapse magazine. On some small level, when perched on a shitter and leafing through the faded pages, you'd convinced yourself that those photos were fantasies and fakes. But the interior of the back of this truck cab is all clean white leather, glossy polished wood, and black electronics.

There are no spliced wires, jury-rigged equipment, or bolted-on extras. Everything in the interior screams newly manufactured. And the air. It's crisp, cold, and doesn't burn with pre-Collapse irritants. The filters in here have to be brand new, not salvaged or refurbished. This all has to be from one of the city enclaves, you think. Because no one *makes* stuff anymore. Or maybe things are turning around somewhere on the continent and this truck has been manufactured, not reclaimed.

You remain standing, suddenly hyperaware that bucket seats like the ones around the table back here don't get sat on by dusty road agents like yourself. But the man sitting on the other side, framed by a pair of flickering flat screens showing long lists of data and charts, waves a hand for you to sit.

So you sit.

"I think I know who you are," you say, a little tentatively.

The man, brown hair thinning at the top and showing some gray, his blue eyes slightly faded with time or sun, nods back at you. "We have met."

"You're the gold trader. From the Toledo Bazaar. Armand."

You remember that he'd been overly interested in you when you'd come in to trade gold for solar equipment. At the time you'd written it off as him perving out. You'd stepped back to let Miko handle the weighing of the jewelry, confiscated from various folk attempting to run the toll road without paying.

"I am Armand." The gold trader does still seem interested in you, but he isn't leering. He looks concerned when he leans forward across the table.

"So what's all this about?" you ask.

"Someone is trying to kill you." The truck lurches into motion. You stand up, fear and anger stumbling over themselves as you grab the door handle. It's locked, of course.

"What the fuck are you doing?" You reach for the knife in your boot, something that the Hauz Shäd goons didn't bother to pat you down for. Maybe because they didn't think a woman would have one, or maybe they didn't care. That seemed more likely.

"As I said: someone is trying to kill you," the gold trader says, looking at the knife in your hand but not looking alarmed. "I'm rescuing you before they do."

"Didn't ask to be rescued." You twitch the knife at him. "Take care of myself well enough, thanks."

"But you actually *did* ask me," the man says. He slides the photo, the one that the Shäd had showed everyone on their knees in the line, across the table.

"I don't—" you start to say.

"You did ask me to rescue you. The you that I'm staring at right now."

You stare at the photo. "Nothing you just said makes any sense to me."

"I know." He taps a command out on the nearest screen. Readouts that you don't understand flicker on, replacing the text. Bars representing power levels. Complex math scrolls across other screens. Hieroglyphs you don't understand.

"This will feel weird," he says, and slides his finger up one of the screens.

The world outside the windows inverts. Not upside down, but inside out. It's an impossibility that causes your stomach to lurch and your mind to scream as reality, for the briefest moment, ceases to make sense.

A loud explosion rocks the trailer behind the cab. The truck shudders to a stop. Smoke trickles in through the office. This could have been something Miko did, now that the trucks are all far enough away that the clusters are safely running off with the panels.

When you grab the door, it thankfully opens. "Go!" Armand shouts, choking on the smoke.

You stagger down out onto the road, coughing and then retching.

You take a last shuddering breath and straighten up, frowning. The road you puked all over is a seamless expanse of newly poured asphalt. It's faded, the lines are patchy, but there are no major potholes. Or, there were places that had been potholes, but were filled in.

The truck has pulled over to the side of the highway, onto a gravelly shoulder. There's smoke pouring out of the trailer and Shäd are running around, likely trying to stop the fire.

But you hardly pay attention to that. You're staring down the highway, where a car is screaming down toward the group at high speed.

Shit, shit, shit you think. You're all under attack.

But no one pays it any attention.

It whips past, the wind shoving at you, and then with a whine it's gone.

Armand the gold trader is watching you closely. "What else do you notice?" he asks, smiling slightly.

"The air is filtered," you say.

But that doesn't make any sense.

You turn and spot the green. Some kind of short plant covers the dirt, miles and miles of it. You think back to books and magazines you've scavenged in the past.

"Soybean?"

"Genetically modified to handle these levels of carbon and a variety of pollutants, yes," Armand says.

"Did we travel back in time?" you ask, trembling and thinking back to the moment the world outside the cab's windows *inverted*. About half of Cheetah cluster can't read, but you've pored over moldy, yellowing pre-Collapse novels. They're not as valuable as the textbooks, encyclopedias, and practical nonfiction that are near currency, but you've read some freaky shit and this is the first thing your mind throws up as a possibility.

The wind is cool on your exposed skin. You all wear leathers, but that's for protection against falls and the acid rain if you get caught outside. You're always sweating in them. The cool wind makes you want to strip down and let it play across your skin.

The gold trader smiles. "Well, the air is more breathable here. It's like the air where you were eighty years ago. But it's not time travel. It's a middle RCP world."

"What?"

Armand's faded blue eyes tighten. "RCP: representative concentration pathways. It's a name given to scenarios given to how much greenhouse gas is dumped into the atmosphere. This world right here, it never hit the Collapse. Every world has a different value, based on how they handled things."

You look around the fields, the smooth highway, and look up at the blue sky. No haze. No impending thunderstorms. A low RCP world. No, middle, he had said. You can't imagine anything nicer than this. It looks so glossy and early-2000s. "You're like the fucking ghost of What Christmas Could Have Been."

Now you have a faint suspicion of how he could just give away a trailer of solar panels without blinking. This place you're standing in, whatever it is, is a rich paradise compared to the dust bowl of the midlands.

You're half-convinced he drugged you and and took you to some sort of promised land, but there are no gaps in your memory. Some of the outriders talk about Edens like this. But they're usually under a dome of some sort. A green, air-filtered paradise in a dust-pocked hellhole of algae farmers and people running around with respirators.

And lots of perimeter security.

Or sometimes they're rumored to be built deep underground, the light all artificial.

Some of the eggheads predict that eventually humanity will just . . . fade away. The heavy amounts of carbon our forefathers dumped into the air had long since hit greenhouse runaway. The heat being trapped causes more clouds to build up, which in turn causes more heat. Eventually we won't be able to breathe outside. We'll go full Venus.

Maybe after that, it will just be assholes in domes, and everyone outside dead.

But all this is no dome. Not this big. And you are definitely not underground. You're outside.

Another car rushes down the freaking *highway* like it's no big deal. One of the Shäd approaches Armand. "It was one of the capacitors. We have enough spare for the next incursion but we should really hit up the depot on the other side, or make the trip to a depot here."

"Oxygen?" Armand asks, his face twitching with annoyance.

"Enough to pass through."

"Let's do it. We're on a tight schedule."

You've taken several steps away from the quick meeting. Armand notices and focuses his attention back on you, switching back from a commanding presence to something softer. You instinctively feel defensive. Manipulated.

He smiles at you. "This is going to be a lot to take in, but we don't have much time and there is a great deal at stake. I know you can absorb this all quickly. I've seen you do it before."

Phrases like that, his familiarity with you, are starting to fuck with your head. "Talk," you say, and jut your chin forward a bit. He can play all friendly, but you have an invisible wall up.

Good God this air is fresh and sweet. You could almost drink it.

"If I know you, and we go way back, you and us, you've gotten your hands on anything you can read. Even in that shitty dust bowl we were just in. That was a universe, right next to this one that we're in right now."

It's the sort of thing you talk about to a buddy, lying on the hood of a truck and pushing cannabis through a respirator while staring up at the stars. Imagining that this universe is inside of an atom inside of a cell of a blade of grass inside another universe and on and on. It's great stuff when you're high. The idea that a better, different universe could be an impossible razor's width away if you could *vibrate* over there in just the right way.

But Armand is trying to pitch that it's real. That he's taken you over into an alternate reality. An alternate history. And looking at the rolling fields of farmland, growing crops, you think it has to be true.

You listen to his explanation and ask, "And you cross over with a truck and trailer?"

"Self-contained mobile operations center," he says.

And you're going to ask why it needs to be mobile when gunfire rips through the Shäd milling about the edge of the road. The fearsome mercenaries are taken completely by surprise as ashen-faced Cheetah cluster warriors advance from underneath the trailer and wherever else they'd been hiding.

This isn't the first shipment Cheetah cluster has slipped aboard to fuck up later. Revenge, hijacking, or otherwise.

Shäd fall, shot in the back, and others are tossed from the top of the one trailer behind the massive truck, bodies limp. Armand spins around to take in the ambush, and you take the moment to slip behind him, press a knife against his throat.

"Jesus Christ, Che, this is not a good time," he whines.

Miko jumps down from between the trailer and cab, road dust caking his road leathers. He raises a hand in greeting as you shove Armand forward.

"Where the fuck are we?" he asks. "And what's wrong with the air?"

For a moment, you think about it. Would any of what Armand said make sense to a man like Miko? He only sees what is right in front of him. Profit now means good living now.

You need to find out more about what's going on before you can try managing upwards. "Let's get into the trailer."

Miko smiles. "See the salvage?"

There might not be any. Not if there's some universe-crossing engine there.

But you can't imagine that someone would be packing Shäd and crossing worlds with a long trailer hauled behind them if they were just coming to pick you up. There's got to be something else going on. You want to see for yourself.

You prod Armand's throat with the knife enough to draw blood when you reach the rear of the trailer, eyeing the thick doors and the security keypad down at the bottom of the door. "Time to open up."

"This is a huge mistake," Armand says. "We need to be moving along."

His voice cracks slightly, so you believe he's nervous about something. Whether it's about what you and Miko are going to see in a second or something else, you're not sure.

"Open up, or we slit your throat. Then we leave you here and take the truck anyway," Miko says.

Armand swallows nervously. "Che, you know this is a bad idea. Kill me, and you're stuck here."

"Stop calling me Che," you tell him. "That's not my name. It's Chenra."

"You usually like being called Che, it's something of a joke for you," Armand says.

You don't see you and Armand being buddies, no matter what world or alternate reality you were ever both in. "Open up or maybe I take my chances being stuck here. I like the air," you hiss at him.

It's not a lie. Armand can hear that in your voice.

He taps out a code, simple numbers that you memorize, and the doors slowly fall open toward the ground to make a ramp. Miko moves in ahead, pistol in the air and his road leathers creaking slightly as he walks carefully into the dimness of the trailer. You follow, pushing Armand ahead of you.

Your eyes adjust. To the front of the trailer there's machinery. Pipes and wiring. Shit-tons of wiring. Readouts glowing in the dark. A pair of Shäd are waiting, weapons aimed right at you. But Armand shakes his head at them, despite the knife you're keeping by his throat.

This is apparently not a place he wants gunfire inside. The outside must have been armored, as he hadn't worried about using the trailer as a lure for an initial attack. But inside . . .

"Drop them and kick them over," Miko shouts.

They do so, and walk out, leaving the three of you alone.

All along the walls leading to the engine are storage lockers.

You recognize the glint of precious metals piled in plastic bins. So does Miko. He's laughing happily, kicking the cage doors open and shaking the bins. "Fucking mother lode," he says. No one in the countryside gives a shit about gold and diamonds. Gold doesn't give you power from the sun, doesn't feed you, doesn't crack out the pollutants from the air. But the traders like Armand in the cities are always looking for it. In exchange they'll give out solar panels or batteries, even food.

Miko stops in front of cage with old, yellowing paintings. "What's this? These fat-faced people in black clothes."

"Nothing," Armand says from between clenched teeth.

"No." You recognize one of the stacked paintings. "That's a Rembrandt."

Miko takes a closer look at the yellow and black hues. "This is bunker shit." He turns back to you and Armand. "You have contact with bunkers?"

The greed makes Miko's face twitch. Dome folk, they know they need perimeter security. Bunker folk tend to get lazy. Think that being underground and hidden makes them safe. Ready for runaway atmosphere with their scrubbers and technology.

But even now they're already having to trade for essentials. Turns out trying to build a balanced ecosystem is a bitch in close quarters.

"I can't give away client locations," Armand mutters.

"Oh, but you will. Eventually," Miko says with a small hint of glee in his voice. The clusters are going to be fat with spoils, and he can taste a new, bountiful future. One that isn't scraps from the old roads.

"You can be much richer, much better off, than that," Armand says to you, almost begs of you. "Think smarter. I told you where we are. He's still thinking of what is important to your world."

Sure, you think. But if this stuff wasn't important to these worlds, why is Armand taking it from yours? The paintings must be valuable. The gold.

"Whoa," Miko says, and Armand's shoulders slump slightly. "What do we have here?"

The last two lockers before the complicated engine and wiring contain people. Two women and a man, shackled together to the wall and wearing gags. They're out cold, small plastic tubes running from their arms up to a device in the wall.

"Slaves," you say bitterly. "You're running slaves."

It's a fate you avoided by joining Cheetah cluster. Why you fight hard. Because things can go grim out in the dust. The country you lived in was born on the blood of slaves so many hundred years ago before the golden age. After the Collapse, it had turned, ever so easily you think, right back to it.

"These are famous people in the other timelines," Armand says quickly. "People pay a literal fortune to have a personal servant who is also the president. Only the mega-rich can afford it. These are not slaves, they'll be given more than they can imagine. They'll come around. They always do, when they see the higher RCP worlds. Better to be a servant in paradise than a ruler in a hell like yours."

"What are you talking about? What's an RCP?" Miko shouts back at you. He's standing in front of the bulk of the machinery, gun in hand, not sure what to make of all the wires and readouts. He's fixed a lot of engines in his time, but this is like showing an electric motor in the wheel-hubs of his pickup to a monkey.

"Was that going to be my fate?" you ask. You aren't able to take your eyes off the bodies behind the doors.

Armand's eyes widen. "No, I swear it."

He's holding something back. You can smell it. Armand twists away from you and you sneer at him. "Is that what it is? Am I someone famous on the other side?"

"It's more complicated than that," he whimpers, seeing the rage take light in your eyes. You can't hold it back; you want to gut him and watch him bleed out.

Miko senses this; he's been the on blunt end of your anger before. He grins and slides up behind Armand, his dirty leathers a brown-stained contrast to Armand's tailored black suit and shiny shoes. "I'll kill him slow for you," Miko whispers.

He's just messing with Armand. Miko will fight, but only fair. He's a soldier, not a murderer. But he's ridden with you long enough, commanded you long enough, that he can read you. In that brief moment, your long list of ways Miko can annoy you fades: the innuendo, the grabby hands, the little gifts after raids. You know he wants you, over any of the other warren-girls who would throw themselves at a commander. He thinks it would be hot to fuck the gunner, and he's been obsessed with that for nearly three months.

"You're a genius," Armand babbles. "You're a genius."

Miko makes a face. You think he's being a little bit of an asshole. But you essentially agree. You're a good gunner, but you're no genius.

But you feel like, thanks to Miko being a bit murdery, that something may have been dislodged from Armand's slimy mouth. "A genius?"

"On one of the other sides, a little further down the line," Armand says. "I don't just transport servants. Or priceless art, cultural artifacts. I also move priceless minds. Think about it: there are minds that are brilliant but trapped by the circumstances of their timelines. They're handicapped from the moment of birth, no matter how great they become in one of the stronger worlds, because somewhere like yours they're fighting just to breathe. They don't have time for their greatest inventions, or to achieve their great works. So we rescue them to bring them over."

"Yo, commander, we got problems," one of the Cheetah cluster outriders shouted from the ramp. You squint. It's Binni. "They got cars with lights on them pulling up and they got guns."

Armand looked past my shoulder to the outrider. "Don't shoot back!"

"Don't worry trader, we got it. We'll push them back." Binni grins.

"That isn't . . . they have *resources* here," Armand grits out.

The familiar crack of gunfire fills the air outside. Everyone crouches and moves to the doors. It's there you see the cars, like something from old glossy pages. Smartly painted vehicles, livery matching the official black uniforms the enforcers are wearing.

These are . . . *police.* Like internal security, but for keeping law and order on a scale that seemed like a fairy-tale when you read about them.

They're not hardened soldiers but civilian peacekeepers, crouched behind their vehicles as Cheetah keeps them at bay. Binni is right. "Those uniforms can't match Cheetah," you say to Miko as you jump down and get Armand to shut the doors.

"Yeah." Miko agrees, but he's looking more and more pained. All of the things that don't make sense are starting to get to him, you can see. "Who the fuck are they?"

"They're called police," you tell him.

Miko's looking around, more now than before.

Armand all but tries to shove the two of you up toward the cab. "We can't stay. It won't be safe. There are rules to all this."

"Shut up." Miko cracks the side of Armand's head with the back of his metal-studded leather gloves.

Armand staggers, blood dripping down onto his immaculate suit.

"Look," you say to Miko, pointing at the sky.

An aircraft is banking over the farmland toward the road. The blades blur through the air and a distinct *whump* reaches you.

Miko's attention is fixated on the helicopter, as is yours.

No one has had the spare fuel to launch aircraft in your memory. Batteries don't keep them up for long enough.

Then a second and third helicopter join in.

Further above, you suddenly realize the long stringy lines of clouds are aircraft, jets high up in the sky, and you can't help but stare.

Armand slams the door to the cab shut.

"Shit." You and Miko jump onto the side of the cab. Miko puts his gun up to the glass of the cab. "Open the fuck up or I start shooting."

Armand ignores you both, tapping at his screens. The trailer hums as the massive device buried in its front half kicks on. Miko steps back and fires. The glass doesn't crack, and pieces of the bullet ricochet, clipping him on the shoulder.

You ignore all the shouting from further back. "Miko, don't get off the truck."

He glances over at you. "What?"

You lean back to shout the same warning at Cheetahs scattered around the trailer and road, along with their Shäd prisoners and dead.

Before the words are even formed, the world turns inside out.

You know to expect the sick feeling in the pit of your stomach that causes you to lean away from your grip on the door handle and think about vomiting. But you hold it in. You have to.

But now that you've handled that, a searing stinging in your eyes blears your vision. You didn't expect the crawling pain on your exposed skin, and the thick muddy clouds all around you. Wind whips murky clouds around overhead.

The world around you is hell. From the choking heat to swirling, searing moisture.

And you can't inhale the air. You realize that the moment you're exposed. You're holding that last breath of sweet air from the other world, or universe, as Miko stares at you in complete and utter horror. He's choking.

You take a moment to orient yourself, squinting and blinking, then scuttle along the side of the cab. All Armand has to do wrench the steering wheel to slew the truck about and you'll fly off the side. You dig your shoes into the lip under the doors and reach for any purchase on the side.

Then you swing around behind the extended area of the cab and fall onto the dead Shäd wedged in the hoses between the trailer and cab. You rip the facemask from the body and take a deep breath. Miko's boots strike metal behind you.

You take a last deep huff of bottled air and pass the mask over.

Vomit streams from Miko's chin and he fumbles for the mask, unable to see anything with reddened eyes. He breathes from the mask as you wait for your turn.

When you get it, the sour smell triggers a second round of stomach clenching.

You pass the mask back and forth as the truck grinds its way over a dirt road for an hour. Sometimes you think you see structures, tall and lurking in the distance. But their edges are shattered, and many of them are slumping over. You might be passing through the edges of a city. In your world there isn't anything here for another couple hours, but this is a dramatically different reality.

The storm you were dropped into subsides. Maybe it's the buildings blocking the wind, or maybe it blew itself out. You're no longer getting pelted with small pebbles. The ochre clouds overhead still scud by impossibly fast.

Miko's eyes are wide. You're not going to be able to explain science fiction ideas about variant universes overlapping each other while passing a mask back and forth. He looks weak. He inhaled too much of this soupy shit. And the heat is going to drop both of you soon.

This, you think, is a high RCP world. This is what your world will look like at some point. Hothouse runaway, the heat-trapping clouds overhead creating more heat as the whole ecosystem cycled toward something sinister and hellish. Only here they got to it sooner. They burned more fossil fuel and burned it faster, dumped heat into the atmosphere faster. Got here well before you.

And in the other world you were just in, they didn't. Their ancestors somehow restrained themselves.

What did that look like? That restraint?

Could you have done it? Miko? No. He only thought about his next meal, his next fuck, his next raid.

Miko retches hard, his eyes bugging as he cries tears of blood. You give him the mask, even though you're faint yourself. There's dark blood all over his shoulders from the bullet fragments rebounding when he shot the armored glass.

How long will it take for Armand to get to the next jump? He seems to be driving with purpose, trying to find a distinct spot.

Will Miko even make it?

You rummage around the Shäd's body, looking for the bottle of air the mask is connected to. It's dangling by his hip. The gauge is at half.

If the man had a full tank when you jumped, and had enough air to be safe during a transit, then you and Miko are going to suck through it before you're halfway across this side. Right?

Miko shoves the mask at you and tries to lean closer. "I'm sorry," he rasps.

"Save your damn breath," you tell him.

"I shouldn't have let you go with him," Miko struggles to say, trying to push the mask back at you and turning his face away from it when you give it back to him. He takes a shuddering gasp of the hellish, hot air.

"No!" You try to force the mask over his face and he weakly grabs at your forearm to try and stop you.

The truck and trailer judder to a sudden stop.

You snap your head around, then take a few deep hits from the mask and move around Miko to look down the length of the cab.

There are shadowy forms lurking in the brown mist. Armand hits the lights, and you see that a crowd of a hundred or so people in the middle of the dirt road. They are on the other side of barriers made of pitted concrete and rusted rebar.

They're all wearing tattered rubber ponchos, faces obscured by gas masks. Many of them are carrying crude guns, others are holding spears or bottles of fluid with rags hanging from the tops.

Armand must not have any Shäd in the cab to drive, as he spends a long set of moments lurching the trailer and truck into reverse and trying to correct the trailer from sliding to the side. But he stops again, and you see that barriers have been rolled across the road. Sharp rebar is pounded into the ground to hem the truck in.

You recognize the tactic. You've been the one pushing barriers across a road before.

Miko has slumped over and pushed the mask away. You take a few pulls from it, and try to get it back on his face. But he's not responding.

Figures surround the truck, surging through the muck floating over the ground. You're trying to pull Miko down when they grab you and pull you forward. The large crowd parts as a figure walks confidently to the front of the truck with a massive rocket launcher over one shoulder.

The person stops and pulls their mask away from their face to shout up at the driver's side window.

"Armand: get the fuck out of the truck or I'll fire this right at the window."

You stare.

The face. There's a long scar across the cheek to the nose. The hair is shaved down except for a slight tuft near the front. It looks older, more weathered.

But damn it, it's *your* face.

"Hello sister," the woman holding the rocket launcher says, never taking her eyes off the truck. "I'll talk to you in a few. I'm in the middle of something with that rat-bastard up behind the wheel."

You open your mouth to talk, but one of the poncho-wearing warriors to your side jams a mask over your face. You breathe the clean air in deeply and gratefully, then let them lead you around to the back of the truck.

There's a gun pointed at you, and they force you to sit near Miko. He's not moving, but they've pulled the Shäd mask on over his face so he can breathe. If he's still alive.

Four peel off and pull out what look like jury-rigged explosives that they start taping onto the doors.

You peel the borrowed mask away. "Hey! You don't have to do that."

They pause and stare back at you, bug-eyed in the gas masks and startled at the interruption.

"I know the code," you tell them.

They look at each other, then shrug. Four guns are trained on you as you stand up and slowly walk over. You punch in the combination you memorized when watching Armand, and the door slides down to become a ramp once again.

They swarm in, weapons up, to secure the back.

You hold onto Miko and watch them break open the cages. Miko would be devastated: all that loot's going to end up in the hands of these raiders.

Raiders run by someone with your face.

Another universe. High RCP, you tell yourself. You're in something like shock. Is it the air?

Your self-labeled "sister" arrives, pushing Armand in front of her. He's holding his breath, eyes wide and blood running down his temple. You're not sure who's having a worse day: you or him.

You get waved up the ramp, along with Armand. Someone helps you pull Miko up into the trailer, and the door shuts behind you. Air pumps run for a second, and then everyone starts removing their masks.

This other version of you, clearly the leader here, clearly in control of this strange situation, looks you up and down and doesn't seem to come to any sort of conclusion one way or another. "I call myself Che. It's a little bit of a joke, if you read history."

"I'm Chenra. Full Chenra."

"Good for you." She is unimpressed. "Armand explain the smuggling he does?"

"Some of my people rode the trailer, ended up in another world, tried to take the truck," you tell her, not answering her question but trying to explain who you are. And why Armand is your enemy. Can you make friends with yourself if you both hate Armand? "We didn't really understand what was happening, and he took the moment to jump us over here. We didn't have bottled air."

Your doppelgänger looks down at Miko and nods, a riddle solved. "He's in a bad way. How long did he inhale the soup?"

"Long enough. Has something in his shoulder from trying to shoot the window." You nod at the art and valuables being dragged out toward the back of the trailer. "That all yours now? I'm not trying to lay claim to it or get in your way."

"What do you think, Armand? Should I keep all this shit?" Che kicks your captor, who is lying on the floor, spitting bile. He wipes his chin with a dirty suit sleeve and glares at her. "He tell you how special you were?"

You lock eyes with yourself and shiver slightly. "Yeah. He said I was a genius."

"It's not all bullshit." Che pokes Miko with the tip of her boot. "You want to try and get him home to your own universe, to help him, right?"

You nod. No sense in trying to lie to yourself, right?

"You two screwing? I've never seen him before," she says. "Not really our type, is he?"

"No. But he's part of my cluster. I owe him." Cheetah cluster for life, right?

"What's your world like? High or low RCP?"

"I think it's high?" you say. "It's not as bad as this, but it wasn't nice like the last place. The air was good. No storms, or heavy wind. Clear. You could see—"

"A nine or so is considered high, two or three is utopia," Che interrupts. "That's where you get all your horrible shit under control and can keep a living world. The eggheads tag all the worlds we can access with various RCP levels. The nerds used to think the points of divergence would all be about national borders and great people. Like, suppose Hitler lived, or the Soviet Union collapsed. Shit like that. But the looming threat, the thread that runs through all these realities that makes the big changes that people like you and I give a shit about, is simply how the atmosphere and oceans were managed. Usually there's an accord. Paris, DC, they try to imitate the same thing they use to stop acid rain. Caps and trades. But sometimes they never even get to that point. Right now, this variation we're in, it's one of the worst scenarios."

You think about all the cool, breathable air in the world just before this one. "Then I'm in definitely in a higher RCP world. People are scared of the runaway effect. A lot of people are bunkering underground, or in domes. I use a respirator outside. We're not using fuel anymore. It all got used up in the Collapse."

"Sounds like a shithole. But, you're a sister me. If you feel you need to go back, I can get you some weapons. You can try to find another Armand going the other way. But trips like that are fairly infrequent. I've been waiting to trap Armand here for almost a month."

"Can't *you* take me?" you ask. If she is doing favors and all. You feel somewhat paralyzed, because this is a situation so far outside of normal—how *can* you make a decision? This familiar face, however, knows more than you. You feel an instant desire for her help, her guidance.

Che shakes her head. "This truck's got one more jump in her, and we're going somewhere specific. And you can't take your buddy back there if you want him to live. You need to go forward."

"To a better world?" You're starting to get the hang of this. "Lower RCP?"

"The lowest," Che says. "You talk about bunkers and domes. This whole area was a massive dome, once. This world ate itself alive. Kept putting leaders up that focused on chewing through resources, promising jobs over stewardship. And when the carbon from burning things filled the oceans, the pH meant huge die-offs. One collapse led to another."

"Sounds familiar," you mutter. And you think of that cool breeze on your skin and shiver. Something inside you almost aches when you consider trying to get back to what is familiar.

"But this world had resources, scientists working on keeping them alive as the air soured. When they cracked the veil between worlds they found a garden world. An Eden. They built massive complexes to shuttle people over, thinking no one was on the other side. But they made a mistake. There were people, and those gardens were maintained carefully by people who had spent generations on wilding projects."

Che pulls out that same picture that the Shäd showed you. It's the clean, flattened-hair version of you, wearing a suit similar to Armand's. Che taps it.

"Which version of us is that?" you ask.

"This picture is a sister of ours that led her people from this high RCP world we're in right now to the garden world," Che says. "I killed her. That was my job. The garden world was my world, before I came over here to hide. It's where the invaders would never think to look for me. They think those of us from the garden world are soft."

But this sister of yours doesn't look soft, despite growing up in an Edenic world. She looks forged. Just like you have been. And even the sister in the picture looks forged. The leader of an invasion force that *had* to leave their dying world, or die themselves. Making hard choices.

"Those invaders to my world are the ones paying Armand anything he wants in order to get one of us, sister," Che says to you. "It's so that they can string us up in public for their people and have a good show as they execute us. Bread and circuses."

"Not true," Armand hisses. "The people I work for, they would take you in for training. They want insight, they need help to run the fight against these terrorists who have attacked us. They want to tap your genius."

Che shakes her head. "He's lying."

"And in exchange for your insight into fighting your terrorist double, they would make you richer than you could imagine," Armand says. "Join her, and you will be the enemy. An insurgent. On a list of enemies against humanity. And not just in the world she wants to go to, but any world that has trade with my people."

"No matter where he is born, he is always trash," Che says, and throws him into one of the cages. She locks it after him.

You stare at Armand for a long moment. "These better worlds. They can help Miko?"

"Yes."

"If I don't go to Armand's people, I'll be hunted. Because of something *you* did."

Che nods. "You'll be a criminal. A terrorist."

I look over at the three raiders who are done piling the goods up against the back of the trailer. "Why are you going over, now? What are you doing with all that?"

You're imagining that she'll tell you something about funding a revolution. How her people on the other side, invaded by the people from this world, need those things to fight their fight.

Che smiles. "They left so many here to keep suffering, once they got across, because the energy required to pierce through is nearly unimaginable. Each of those smuggler's trucks requires shareholders, backers, venture capital. Cross-world travel is rare. So I'm taking as many as I can get over. Count yourself lucky there's a spot for you."

You think about the treasures Armand has hoarded. They're all priceless things that the insanely rich obsess over. Portable cultural artifacts.

"I'll cross with you," you say, your voice breaking slightly as you realize this likely means you won't ever see your world again. But then, you've left it all behind before. Running across the desert in your bare feet, your hands covered in blood and hair hacked off, those manacles burning the skin of your wrists.

Five hundred miles away, your feet bloody, Cheetah cluster took you in and away.

Che pulls her mask back on, and you follow suit. The back door slides back down into a ramp, and there are hundreds of forms waiting in the dark brown mist. Children.

People roughly shove the priceless art and precious metals off the back of the trailer onto the rocky ground.

Armand shouts from inside his cage, but the anger turns to coughing as the hot, acidic air roils into the trailer.

You've always gone forward.

This is the first time you've known what you're heading toward. An Edenic world without climate collapse. A world where invaders are fighting the people who lived there before them. Invaders who abandoned millions of their own to a dead world.

These starving refugees are packed into the back of the trailer or strapped onto the top with bottles of air. They are all taking the risk of death, or worse, when you all break through to that other universe. Che has been driving for several hours, hoping to get as far from core invader territory as she can, but air will be running out soon and a decision to jump over has to be made shortly or people will start dying.

You sit next to Che, shoved up together near the controls. Miko is by your feet. Refugees cram in everywhere inside the cab, some of them controlling the computer that Armand had, others just packed in to make the crossing. You'd watched the pile of pictures and all that glittered fall away behind the trailer in the mirrors. The old canvases curled up in the harsh air as you slid away. Acid rain began to drizzle on them.

"There are many more, on many different worlds, that need help," Che had said. "Even though their brothers invaded mine, I couldn't leave them back there to slowly choke to death. It wasn't their fault, it was their forefathers who did this to them."

You're never going to be a gunner again, chasing after convoys.

"Will it make a difference, a couple hundred?" I asked.

"We're just getting started," Che said. "I can save more."

But you wonder what all these new bodies will do to that Edenic new world? Will these descendants of a people who destroyed an entire world be able to make a change? Or would they understand how to treasure it, knowing how precious it was?

The world flips inside out and you gasp.

When your vision comes back to you, you look up to see a forest choking the dirt road around the truck.

People rip off their masks as Che rolls the windows down. There are flowers. The distant chatter of animals. Scents on the breeze that fill the cab. A gentle wind.

She's taken you back to where this all started, geographically. But there is no toll road here. No farms. No dusty plains and electric cars with skulls and machine guns mounted on them. Just lush green and lungfuls of sweet air.

"Are you okay?" Che asks.

You wipe the tear from your cheek.

"This is what it could have been, where I come from," you whisper. "We could have done it."

Che stops the truck, as it's shuddering and smoke has begun to leak out of the machinery in the front of the trailer. People are banging and shouting for her attention.

Afterwards, she climbs on the hood as people gather before her.

"I give you my world," she says. "I ask only that you care for it as you would your child. Do that, and it will care for you as well. Now go."

The two of you sit for a while later near Miko.

"I'm sorry," she says. "I hoped he would make it. We could have helped."

You shake your head. "I've seen worse deaths." It was no worse a death than clashing with duty-evaders on a toll road. He had never understood what was actually happening though, and you feel bad about that.

When you stand, after burying him under the cool shade of a magnificent pine tree that makes you almost weep again, you move to Che's side.

"Take me with you."

"I don't know what my next move is. I snuck over to their world to see what it was like and hide from her death squads. I didn't really believe them when they said it was so bad. I didn't know so many were suffering. Armand and his ilk, they get financing to go and fetch the greatest minds from the remains of high RCP worlds. Or get 'servants' of famous people. But these are regular folk that needed saving, that no one wants. They deserve to live."

You nod.

You've been watching this version of yourself. And you've learned something. This isn't a confident, dangerous you like you first assumed when you saw her with the rocket launcher. No, this is a version of you that cares deeply. She put herself in front of the truck because she felt strongly.

She didn't know what would come next when she rescued these people. She just did it.

This version of you isn't calculating.

This version of you isn't looking for the next move.

This version of you came from ancestors who managed a planet successfully, not like your own failed ones.

You've been taught to take, to be strong, to run with a strong pack. Miko has taught you well. Having studied this Che for hours, you know you could break her. She hasn't spent a lifetime in the hot sand.

But the forests.

Her people let that be. And that is a different lesson. You need to follow her people. You need to help them protect what they've built.

And what you know, and have learned for an entire life, is survival. How to create fighters.

"You need to grow your army," you say to Che. "You need to bring more people over. More refugees from the other worlds. We can find more Armands to trade with, right, if there are many worlds and many copies of us in them?"

Che nods at you. "More death."

You smile crookedly. "And maybe more life. I think we bring things over to the other places that help them. And then we bring fighters, loyal fighters, from there to here. We can do this better. I can show you how to finish what you've started. Let me help you."

"It'll be dangerous." Che raises an eyebrow.

You know. But you know danger better than she does. All you've lived is danger.

Besides, is it better to be a king of a sandy hell, or a servant in a lush paradise? Her people had created something so special, you know that being one of their soldiers is the way to climb. You can taste ambition again.

This, you think as you move through sun-dappled forest, is a world to die for.

A world to fight for.

UMBERNIGHT

CAROLYN IVES GILMAN

There is a note from my great-grandmother in the book on my worktable, they tell me. I haven't opened it. Up to now I have been too angry at her whole generation, those brave colonists who settled on Dust and left us here to pay the price. But lately, I have begun to feel a little disloyal—not to her, but to my companions on the journey that brought me the book, and gave me the choice whether to read it or not. What, exactly, am I rejecting here—the past or the future?

It was autumn—a long, slow season on Dust. It wasn't my first autumn, but I'd been too young to appreciate it the first time. I was coming back from a long ramble to the north, with the Make Do Mountains on my right and the great horizon of the Endless Plain to my left. I could not live without the horizon. It puts everything in perspective. It is my soul's home.

Sorry, I'm not trying to be offensive.

As I said, it was autumn. All of life was seeding, and the air was scented with lost chances and never agains. In our region of Dust, most of the land vegetation is of the dry, bristly sort, with the largest trees barely taller than I am, huddling in the shade of cliffs. But the plants were putting on their party best before Umbernight: big, white blooms on the bad-dog bushes and patches of bitterberries painting the arroyos orange. I knew I was coming home when a black fly bit me. Some of the organisms we brought have managed to survive: insects, weeds, lichen. They spread a little every time I'm gone. It's not a big victory, but it's something.

The dogs started barking when I came into the yard in front of Feynman Habitat with my faithful buggy tagging along behind me. The dogs never remember me at first, and always take fright at sight of Bucky. A door opened and Namja looked out. "Michiko's back!" she shouted, and pretty soon there was a mob of people pouring out of the fortified cave entrance. It seemed as if half of them were shorter than my knees. They stared at me as if I were an apparition, and no wonder: my skin was burned dark from the UV except around my eyes where I wear goggles, and my hair and eyebrows had turned white. I must have looked like Grandmother Winter.

"Quite a crop of children you raised while I was gone," I said to Namja. I couldn't match the toddlers to the babies I had left.

"Yes," she said. "Times are changing."

I didn't know what she meant by that, but I would find out.

Everyone wanted to help me unpack the buggy, so I supervised. I let them take most of the sample cases to the labs, but I wouldn't let anyone touch the topographical information. That would be my winter project. I was looking forward to a good hibernate, snug in a warm cave, while I worked on my map of Dust.

The cargo doors rumbled open and I ordered Bucky to park inside, next to his smaller siblings, the utility vehicles. The children loved seeing him obey, as they always do; Bucky has an alternate career as playground equipment when he's not with me. I hefted my pack and followed the crowd inside.

There is always a festive atmosphere when I first get back. Everyone crowds around telling me news and asking where I went and what I saw. This time they presented me with the latest project of the food committee: an authentic glass of beer. I think it's an acquired taste, but I acted impressed.

We had a big, celebratory dinner in the refectory. As a treat, they grilled fillets of chickens and fish, now plentiful enough to eat. The youngsters like it, but I've never been able to get used to meat. Afterwards, when the parents had taken the children away, a group of adults gathered around my table to talk. By then, I had noticed a change: my own generation had become the old-timers, and the young adults were taking an interest in what was going on. Members of the governing committee were conspicuously absent.

"Don't get too comfortable," Haakon said to me in a low tone.

"What do you mean?" I said.

Everyone exchanged a look. It was Namja who finally explained. "The third cargo capsule from the homeworld is going to land at Newton's Eye in about 650 hours."

"But . . . " I stopped when I saw they didn't need me to tell them the problem. The timing couldn't have been worse. Umbernight was just around the corner. Much as we needed that cargo, getting to it would be a gamble with death.

I remember how my mother explained Umbernight to me as a child. "There's a bad star in the sky, Michiko. We didn't know it was there at first because there's a shroud covering it. But sometimes, in winter, the shroud pulls back and we can see its light. Then we have to go inside, or we would die."

After that, I had nightmares in which I looked up at the sky and there was the face of a corpse hanging there, covered with a shroud. I would watch in terror as the veil would slowly draw aside, revealing rotted flesh and putrid gray jelly eyes, glowing with a deadly unlight that killed everything it touched.

I didn't know anything then about planetary nebulae or stars that emit in the UV and X-ray spectrum. I didn't know we lived in a double-star system, circling a perfectly normal G-class star with a very strange, remote companion. I had learned all that by the time I was an adolescent and Umber finally rose in our sky. I never disputed why I had to spend my youth cooped up in the cave habitat trying to make things run. They told me then, "You'll be all grown up with kids of your own before Umber comes again." Not true. All grown up, that part was right. No kids.

A dog was nudging my knee under the table, and I kneaded her velvet ears. I was glad the pro-dog faction had won the Great Dog Debate, when the colony had split on whether to reconstitute dogs from frozen embryos. You feel much more human with dogs around. “So what’s the plan?” I asked.

As if in answer, the tall, stooped figure of Anselm Thune came into the refectory and headed toward our table. We all fell silent. “The Committee wants to see you, Mick,” he said.

There are committees for every conceivable thing in Feynman, but when someone says “the Committee,” capital C, it means the governing committee. It’s elected, but the same people have dominated it for years, because no one wants to put up with the drama that would result from voting them out. Just the mention of it put me in a bad mood.

I followed Anselm into the meeting room where the five Committee members were sitting around a table. The only spare seat was opposite Chairman Colby, so I took it. He has the pale skin of a lifelong cave dweller, and thin white hair fringing his bald head.

“Did you find anything useful?” he asked as soon as I sat down. He’s always thought my roving is a waste of time because none of my samples have produced anything useful to the colony. All I ever brought back was more evidence of how unsuited this planet is for human habitation.

I shrugged. “We’ll have to see what the lab says about my biosamples. I found a real pretty geothermal region.”

He grimaced at the word “pretty,” which was why I’d used it. He was an orthodox rationalist, and considered aesthetics to be a gateway drug to superstition. “You’ll fit in well with these gullible young animists we’re raising,” he said. “You and your fairy-tales.”

I was too tired to argue. “You wanted something?” I said.

Anselm said, “Do you know how to get to Newton’s Eye?”

“Of course I do.”

“How long does it take?”

“On foot, about 200 hours. Allow a little more for the buggy, say 220.”

I could see them calculating: there and back, 440 hours, plus some time to unload the cargo capsule and pack, say 450. Was there enough time?

I knew myself how long the nights were getting. Dust is sharply tilted, and at our latitude, its slow days vary from ten hours of dark and ninety hours of light in the summer to the opposite in winter. We were past the equinox; the nights were over sixty hours long, what we call N60. Umber already rose about midnight; you could get a sunburn before dawn. But most of its radiation didn’t reach us yet because of the cloud of dust, gas, and ionized particles surrounding it. At least, that’s our theory about what is concealing the star.

“I don’t suppose the astronomers have any predictions when the shroud will part?” I said.

That set Colby off. “Shroud, my ass. That’s a backsliding anti-rationalist term. Pretty soon you’re going to have people talking about gods and visions, summoning spirits, and rejecting science.”

"It's just a metaphor, Colby," I said.

"I'm trying to prevent us from regressing into savagery! Half of these youngsters are already wearing amulets and praying to idols."

Once again, Anselm intervened. "There is inherent unpredictability about the star's planetary nebula," he said. "The first time, the gap appeared at N64." That is, when night was 64 hours long. "The second time it didn't come till N70."

"We're close to N64 now," I said.

"Thank you for telling us," Colby said with bitter sarcasm.

I shrugged and got up to leave. Before I reached the door Anselm said, "You'd better start getting your vehicle in order. If we do this, you'll be setting out in about 400 hours."

"Just me?" I said incredulously.

"You and whoever we decide to send."

"The suicide team?"

"You've always been a bad influence on morale," Colby said.

"I'm just calculating odds like a good rationalist," I replied. Since I really didn't want to hear his answer to that, I left. All I wanted then was a hot bath and about twenty hours of sleep.

That was my first mistake. I should have put my foot down right then. They probably wouldn't have tried it without me.

But the habitat was alive with enthusiasm for fetching the cargo. Already, more people had volunteered than we could send. The main reason was eagerness to find out what our ancestors had sent us. You could barely walk down the hall without someone stopping you to speculate about it. Some wanted seeds and frozen embryos, electronic components, or medical devices. Others wanted rare minerals, smelting equipment, better water filtration. Or something utterly unexpected, some miracle technology to ease our starved existence.

It was the third and last cargo capsule our ancestors had sent by solar sail when they themselves had set out for Dust in a faster ship. Without the first two capsules, the colony would have been wiped out during the first winter, when Umber revealed itself. As it was, only two thirds of them perished. The survivors moved to the cave habitat and set about rebuilding a semblance of civilization. We weathered the second winter better here at Feynman. Now that the third winter was upon us, people were hoping for some actual comfort, some margin between us and annihilation.

But the capsule was preprogrammed to drop at the original landing site, long since abandoned. It might have been possible to reprogram it, but no one wanted to try calculating a different landing trajectory and sending it by our glitch-prone communication system. The other option, the wise and cautious one, was to let the capsule land and just leave it sitting at Newton's Eye until spring. But we are the descendants of people who set out for a new planet without thoroughly checking it out. Wisdom? Caution? Not in our DNA.

All right, that's a little harsh. They said they underestimated the danger from Umber because it was hidden behind our sun as well as its shroud when they were making observations from the home planet. And they did pay for their mistake.

I spent the next ten hours unpacking, playing with the dogs, and hanging out in the kitchen. I didn't see much evidence of pagan drumming in the halls, so I asked Namja what bee had crawled up Colby's ass. Her eyes rolled eloquently in response. "Come here," she said.

She led me into the warren of bedrooms where married couples slept and pulled out a bin from under her bed—the only space any of us has for storing private belongings. She dug under a concealing pile of clothes and pulled out a broken tile with a colorful design on the back side—a landscape, I realized as I studied it. A painting of Dust.

"My granddaughter Marigold did it," Namja said in a whisper.

What the younger generation had discovered was not superstition, but art.

For two generations, all our effort, all our creativity, had gone into improving the odds of survival. Art took materials, energy, and time we didn't have to spare. But that, I learned, was not why Colby and the governing committee disapproved of it.

"They think it's a betrayal of our guiding principle," Namja said.

"Rationalism, you mean?"

She nodded. Rationalism—that universal ethic for which our parents came here, leaving behind a planet that had splintered into a thousand warring sects and belief systems. They were high-minded people, our settler ancestors. When they couldn't convince the world they were correct, they decided to leave it and found a new one based on science and reason. And it turned out to be Dust.

Now, two generations later, Colby and the governing committee were trying to beat back irrationality.

"They lectured us about wearing jewelry," Namja said.

"Why?"

"It might inflame sexual instincts," she said ironically.

"Having a body does that," I said.

"Not if you're Colby, I guess. They also passed a resolution against figurines."

"That was their idea of a problem?"

"They were afraid people would use them as fetishes."

It got worse. Music and dance were now deemed to have shamanistic origins. Even reciting poetry aloud could start people on the slippery slope to prayer groups and worship.

"No wonder everyone wants to go to Newton's Eye," I said.

We held a meeting to decide what to do. We always have meetings, because the essence of rationality is that it needs to be contested. Also because people don't want responsibility for making a decision.

About two hundred people crammed into the refectory—everyone old enough to understand the issue. We no longer had a room big enough for all, a sure sign we were outgrowing our habitat.

From the way the governing committee explained the options, it was clear that they favored the most cautious one—to do nothing at all, and leave the cargo to be fetched by whoever would be around in spring. I could sense disaffection from the left side of the room, where a cohort of young adults stood together. When Colby stopped talking, a lean, intellectual-looking young man named Anatoly spoke up for the youth party.

"What would our ancestors think of us if we let a chance like this slip by?"

Colby gave him a venomous look that told me this was not the first time Anatoly had stood up to authority. "They would think we were behaving rationally," he said.

"It's not rational to sit cowering in our cave, afraid of the planet we came to live on," Anatoly argued. "This cargo could revolutionize our lives. With new resources and technologies, we could expand in the spring, branch out and found satellite communities."

Watching the Committee, I could tell that this was precisely what they feared. New settlements meant new leaders—perhaps ones like Anatoly, willing to challenge what the old leaders stood for.

"Right now, it's a waste of our resources," Anselm said. "We need to focus everything we have on preparing for Umbernight."

"It's a waste of resources *not* to go," Anatoly countered. "You have a precious resource right here." He gestured at the group behind him. "People ready and willing to go now. By spring, we'll all be too old."

"Believe it or not, we don't want to waste you either," said Gwen, a third member of the Committee—although Colby looked like he would have gladly wasted Anatoly without a second thought.

"We're willing to take the chance," Anatoly said. "We *belong* here, on this planet. We need to embrace it, dangers and all. We are more prepared now than ever before. Our scientists have invented X-ray shielding fabric, and coldsuits for temperature extremes. We'll never be more ready."

"Well, thank you for your input," Anselm said. "Anyone else?"

The debate continued, but all the important arguments had been made. I slipped out the back and went to visit Bucky, as if he would have an opinion. "They may end up sending us after all," I told him in the quiet of his garage. "If only to be rid of the troublemakers."

The great announcement came about twenty hours later. The Committee had decided to roll the dice and authorize the expedition. They posted the list of six names on bulletin boards all over the habitat. I learned of it when I saw a cluster of people around one, reading. As I came up behind them, D'Sharma exclaimed emotionally, "Oh, this is just plain *cruel*." Someone saw me, and D'Sharma turned around. "Mick, you've got to bring them all back, you hear?" Then she burst into tears.

I read the list then, but it didn't explain D'Sharma's reaction. Anatoly was on it, not surprisingly—but in what seemed like a deliberate snub, he was not to be the leader. That distinction went to a young man named Amal. The rest were all younger generation; I'd known them in passing as kids and adolescents, but I had been gone too much to see them much as adults.

"It's a mix of expendables and rising stars," Namja explained to me later in private. "Anatoly, Seabird, and Davern are all people they're willing to sacrifice, for different reasons. Amal and Edie—well, choosing them shows that the Committee actually wants the expedition to succeed. But we'd all hate to lose them."

I didn't need to ask where I fit in. As far as the Committee was concerned, I was in the expendable category.

My first impression of the others came when I was flat on my back underneath Bucky, converting him to run on bottled propane. Brisk footsteps entered the garage and two practical boots came to a halt. "Mick?" a woman's voice said.

"Under here," I answered.

She got down on all fours to look under the vehicle. Sideways, I saw a sunny face with close-cropped, dark brown hair. "Hi," she said, "I'm Edie."

"I know," I said.

"I want to talk," she said.

"We're talking."

"I mean face to face."

We *were* face to face, more or less, but I supposed she meant upright, so I slid out from under, wiping my oily hands on a rag. We looked at each other across Bucky's back.

"We're going to have a meeting to plan out the trip to Newton's Eye," she said.

"Okay." I had already been planning out the trip for a couple work cycles. It's what I do, plan trips, but normally just for myself.

"Mick, we're going to be counting on you a lot," she said seriously. "You're the only one who's ever been to Newton's Eye, and the only one who's ever seen a winter. The rest of us have lots of enthusiasm, but you've got the experience."

I was impressed by her realism, and—I confess it—a little bit flattered. No one ever credits me with useful knowledge. I had been prepared to cope with a flock of arrogant, ignorant kids. Edie was none of those things.

"Can you bring a map to the meeting? It would help us to know where we're going."

My heart warmed. Finally, someone who saw the usefulness of my maps. "Sure," I said.

"I've already been thinking about the food, but camping equipment—we'll need your help on that."

"Okay."

Her face folded pleasantly around her smile. "The rest of us are a talky bunch, so don't let us drown you out."

"Okay."

After she told me the when and where of the meeting, she left, and I realized I hadn't said more than two syllables at a time. Still, she left me feeling she had understood.

When I arrived at the meeting, the effervescence of enthusiasm triggered my fight or flight reflex. I don't trust optimism. I stood apart, arms crossed, trying to size up my fellow travelers.

The first thing I realized was that Amal and Edie were an item; they had the kind of companionable, good-natured partnership you see in long-married couples. Amal was a big, relaxed young man who was always ready with a joke to put people at ease, while Edie was a little firecracker of an organizer. I had expected Anatoly to be resentful, challenging Amal for leadership, but he seemed thoroughly committed to the project, and I realized it hadn't just been a power play—he actually *wanted* to go. The other two were supposed to be "under-contributors," as we call them. Seabird—yes, her parents named her that on this planet without either birds or seas—was a plump young woman with unkempt hair who remained silent through most of the meeting. I couldn't tell if she was sulky, shy, or just scared out of her mind. Davern was clearly unnerved, and made up for it by being as friendly and anxious to ingratiate himself with the others as a lost puppy looking for a master. Neither Seabird nor Davern had volunteered. But then, neither had I, strictly speaking.

Amal called on me to show everyone the route. I had drawn it on a map—a physical map that didn't require electricity—and I spread it on the table for them to see. Newton's Eye was an ancient crater basin visible from space. To get to it, we would have to follow the Let's Go River down to the Mazy Lakes. We would then cross the Damn Right Barrens, climb down the Winding Wall to the Oh Well Valley, and cross it to reach the old landing site. Coming back, it would be uphill all the way.

"Who made up these names?" Anatoly said, studying the map with a frown.

"I did," I said. "Mostly for my mood on the day I discovered things."

"I thought the settlers wanted to name everything for famous scientists."

"Well, the settlers aren't around anymore," I said.

Anatoly looked as if he had never heard anything so heretical from one of my generation. He flashed me a sudden smile, then glanced over his shoulder to make sure no one from the governing committee was listening.

"What will it be like, traveling?" Edie asked me.

"Cold," I said. "Dark."

She was waiting for more, so I said, "We'll be traveling in the dark for three shifts to every two in the light. Halfway through night, Umber rises, so we'll have to wear protective gear. That's the coldest time, too; it can get cold enough for CO_2 to freeze this time of year. There won't be much temptation to take off your masks."

"We can do it," Anatoly said resolutely.

Davern gave a nervous giggle and edged closer to me. "You know how to do this, don't you, Mick?"

"Well, yes. Unless the shroud parts and Umbernight comes. Then all bets are off. Even I have never traveled through Umbernight."

"Well, we just won't let that happen," Edie said, and for a moment it seemed as if she could actually make the forces of Nature obey.

I stepped back and watched while Edie coaxed them all into making a series of sensible decisions: a normal work schedule of ten hours on, ten hours off; a division of labor; a schedule leading up to departure. Seabird and Davern never volunteered for anything, but Edie cajoled them into accepting assignments without complaint.

When it was over and I was rolling up my map, Edie came over and said to me quietly, "Don't let Davern latch onto you. He tries to find a protector—someone to adopt him. Don't fall for it."

"I don't have maternal instincts," I said.

She squeezed my arm. "Good for you."

If this mission were to succeed, I thought, it would be because of Edie.

Which is not to say that Amal wasn't a good leader. I got to know him when he came to me for advice on equipment. He didn't have Edie's extrovert flair, but his relaxed manner could put a person at ease, and he was methodical about thinking things through. Together, we compiled a daunting list of safety tents, heaters, coldsuits, goggles, face masks, first aid, and other gear; then when we realized that carrying all of it would leave Bucky with no room for the cargo we wanted to haul back, we set about ruthlessly cutting out everything that wasn't essential for survival.

He challenged me on some things. "Rope?" he said skeptically. "A shovel?"

"Rationality is about exploiting the predictable," I said. "Loose baggage and a mired-down vehicle are predictable."

He helped me load up Bucky for the trip out with a mathematical precision, eliminating every wasted centimeter. On the way back, we would have to carry much of it on our backs.

I did demand one commitment from Amal. "If Umbernight comes, we need to turn around and come back instantly, no matter what," I said.

At first he wouldn't commit himself.

"Have you ever heard what happened to the people caught outside during the first Umbernight?" I asked him. "The bodies were found in spring, carbonized like statues of charcoal. They say some of them shed tears of gasoline, and burst into flame as soon as a spark hit them."

He finally agreed.

You see, I wasn't reckless. I did some things right—as right as anyone could have done in my shoes.

When we set out just before dawn, the whole of Feynman Habitat turned out to see us off. There were hugs and tears, then waves and good wishes as I ordered Bucky to start down the trail. It took only five minutes for Feynman to drop behind us, and for the true immensity of Dust to open up ahead. I led the way down the banks of a frozen rivulet that eventually joined the Let's Go River; as the morning warmed it would begin to gurgle and splash.

"When are we stopping for lunch?" Seabird asked.

"You're not hungry already, are you?" Edie said, laughing.

"No, I just want to know what the plan is."

"The plan is to walk till we're tired and eat when we're hungry."

"I'd rather have a time," Seabird insisted. "I want to know what to expect."

No one answered her, so she glowered as she walked.

It did not take long for us to go farther from the habitat than any of them had ever been. At first they were elated at the views of the river valley ahead; but as their packs began to weigh heavier and their feet to hurt, the high spirits faded into dogged determination. After a couple of hours, Amal caught up with me at the front of the line.

"How far do we need to go this tenhour?"

"We need to get to the river valley. There's no good place to pitch the tent before that."

"Can we take a break and stay on schedule?"

I had already planned on frequent delays for the first few days, so I said, "There's a nice spot ahead."

As soon as we reached it, Amal called a halt, and everyone dropped their packs and kicked off their boots. I warned them not to take off their UV-filtering goggles. "You can't see it, but Umber hasn't set yet. You don't want to come back with crispy corneas."

I went apart to sit on a rock overlooking the valley, enjoying the isolation. Below me, a grove of lookthrough trees gestured gently in the wind, their leaves like transparent streamers. Like most plants on Dust, they are gray-blue, not green, because life here never evolved chloroplasts for photosynthesis. It is all widdershins life—its DNA twirls the opposite direction from ours. That makes it mostly incompatible with us.

Before long, Anatoly came to join me.

"That valley ahead looks like a good place for a satellite community in the spring," he said. "What do you think, could we grow maize there?"

The question was about more than agronomy. He wanted to recruit me into his expansion scheme. "You'd need a lot of shit," I said.

I wasn't being flippant. Dumping sewage was how we had created the soil for the outdoor gardens and fields around Feynman. Here on Dust, sewage is a precious, limited resource.

He took my remark at face value. "It's a long-range plan. We can live off hydroponics at first."

"There's a long winter ahead," I said.

"Too long," he said. "We're bursting at the seams now, and our leaders can only look backward. That's why the Committee has never supported your explorations. They think you're wasting time because you've never brought back anything but knowledge. That's how irrational they are."

He was a good persuader. "You know why I like being out here?" I said. "You have to forget all about the habitat, and just be part of Dust."

"That means you're one of us," Anatoly said seriously. "The governing committee, they are still fighting the battles of the homeworld. We're the first truly indigenous generation. We're part of *this* planet."

"Wait until you've seen more of it before you decide for sure."

I thought about Anatoly's farming scheme as we continued on past his chosen site. It would be hard to pull off, but not impossible. I would probably never live to see it thrive.

The sun was blazing from the southern sky by the time we made camp on the banks of the Let's Go. Edie recruited Davern to help her cook supper, though he seemed to be intentionally making a mess of things so that he could effusively praise her competence. She was having none of it. Amal and Anatoly worked on setting up the sleeping tent. It was made from a heavy, radiation-blocking material that was one of our lab's best inventions. I puttered around aiming Bucky's solar panels while there was light to collect, and Seabird lay on the ground, evidently too exhausted to move.

She sat up suddenly, staring at some nearby bushes. "There's something moving around over there."

"I don't think so," I said, since we are the only animal life on Dust.

"There is!" she said tensely.

"Well, check it out, then."

She gave me a resentful look, but heaved to her feet and went to look in the bushes. I heard her voice change to that cooing singsong we use with children and animals. "Come here, girl! What are you doing here? Did you follow us?"

With horror, I saw Sally, one of the dogs from Feynman, emerge from the bushes, wiggling in delight at Seabird's welcome.

"Oh my God!" I exclaimed. The dire profanity made everyone turn and stare. No one seemed to understand. In fact, Edie called out the dog's name and it trotted over to her and stuck its nose eagerly in the cooking pot. She laughed and pushed it away.

Amal had figured out the problem. "We can't take a dog; we don't have enough food. We'll have to send her back."

"How, exactly?" I asked bitterly.

"I can take her," Seabird volunteered.

If we allowed that, we would not see Seabird again till we got back.

"Don't feed her," Anatoly said.

Both Edie and Seabird objected to that. "We can't starve her!" Edie said.

I was fuming inside. I half suspected Seabird of letting the dog loose to give herself an excuse to go back. It would have been a cunning move. As soon as I caught myself thinking that way, I said loudly, "Stop!"

They all looked at me, since I was not in the habit of giving orders. "Eat first," I said. "No major decisions on an empty stomach."

While we ate our lentil stew, Sally demonstrated piteously how hungry she was. In the end, Edie and Seabird put down their bowls for Sally to finish off.

"Is there anything edible out here?" Edie asked me.

"There are things we can eat, but not for the long run," I said. "We can't absorb their proteins. And the dog won't eat them if she knows there is better food."

Anatoly had rethought the situation. "She might be useful. We may need a threat detector."

"Or camp cleanup services," Edie said, stroking Sally's back.

"And if we get hungry enough, she's food that won't spoil," Anatoly added.

Edie and Seabird objected strenuously.

I felt like I was reliving the Great Dog Debate. They weren't old enough to remember it. The arguments had been absurdly pseudo-rational, but in the end it had boiled down to sentiment. Pretty soon someone would say, "If the ancestors hadn't thought dogs would be useful they wouldn't have given us the embryos."

Then Seabird said it. I wanted to groan.

Amal was trying to be leaderly, and not take sides. He looked at Davern. "Don't ask me," Davern said. "It's not my responsibility."

He looked at me then. Of course, I didn't want to harm the dog; but keeping her alive would take a lot of resources. "You don't know yet what it will be like," I said.

Amal seized on my words. "That's right," he said, "we don't have enough information. Let's take another vote in thirty hours." It was the perfect compromise: the decision to make no decision.

Of course, the dog ended up in the tent with the rest of us as we slept.

Stupid! Stupid! Yes, I know. But also kind-hearted and humane in a way my hardened pioneer generation could not afford to be. It was as if my companions were recovering a buried memory of what it had once been like to be human.

The next tenhours' journey was a pleasant stroll down the river valley speckled with groves of lookthrough trees. Umber had set and the sun was still high, so we could safely go without goggles, the breeze blowing like freedom on our faces. Twenty hours of sunlight had warmed the air, and the river ran ice-free at our side. We threw sticks into it for Sally to dive in and fetch.

We slept away another tenhour, and rose as the sun was setting. From atop the hill on which we had camped, we could see far ahead where the Let's Go flowed into the Mazy Lakes, a labyrinth of convoluted inlets, peninsulas, and islands. In the fading light I carefully reviewed my maps, comparing them to what I could see. There was a way through it, but we would have to be careful not to get trapped.

As night deepened, we began to pick our way by lantern-light across spits of land between lakes. Anatoly kept thinking he saw faster routes, but Amal said, "No, we're following Mick." I wasn't sure I deserved his trust. A couple of times I took a wrong turn and had to lead the way back.

"This water looks strange," Amal said, shining his lantern on the inky surface. There was a wind blowing, but no waves. It looked like black gelatin.

The dog, thinking she saw something in his light, took a flying leap into the lake. When she broke the surface, it gave a pungent fart that made us groan and gag. Sally floundered around, trying to find her footing in a foul substance that was not quite water, not quite land. I was laughing and trying to hold my breath at the same time. We fled to escape the overpowering stench. Behind us, the dog found her way onto shore again, and got her revenge by shaking putrid water all over us.

"What the hell?" Amal said, covering his nose with his arm.

"Stromatolites," I explained. They looked at me as if I were speaking ancient Greek—which I was, in a way. "The lakes are full of bacterial colonies that form thick mats, decomposing as they grow." I looked at Edie. "They're one of the things on Dust we can actually eat. If you want to try a stromatolite steak, I can cut you one." She gave me the reaction I deserved.

After ten hours, we camped on a small rise surrounded by water on north and south, and by stars above. The mood was subdued. In the perpetual light, it had been easy to feel we were in command of our surroundings. Now, the opaque ceiling of the sky had dissolved, revealing the true immensity of space. I could tell they were feeling how distant was our refuge. They were dwarfed, small, and very far from home.

To my surprise, Amal reached into his backpack and produced, of all things, a folding aluminum mandolin. After all our efforts to reduce baggage, I could not believe he had wasted the space. But he assembled and tuned it, then proceeded to strum some tunes I had never heard. All the others seemed to know them, since they joined on the choruses. The music defied the darkness as our lantern could not.

"Are there any songs about Umbernight?" I asked when they paused.

Strumming softly, Amal shook his head. "We ought to make one."

"It would be about the struggle between light and unlight," Edie said.

"Or apocalypse," Anatoly said. "When Umber opens its eye and sees us, only the just survive."

Their minds moved differently than mine, or any of my generation's. They saw not just mechanisms of cause and effect, but symbolism and meaning. They were generating a literature, an indigenous mythology, before my eyes. It was dark, like Dust, but with threads of startling beauty.

We woke to darkness. The temperature had plummeted, so we pulled on our heavy coldsuits. They were made from the same radiation-blocking material as our tent, but with thermal lining and piezoelectric heating elements so that if we kept moving, we could keep warm. The visored hoods had vents with micro-louvers to let us breathe, hear, and speak without losing too much body heat.

"What about the dog?" Amal asked. "We don't have a coldsuit for her."

Edie immediately set to work cutting up some of the extra fabric we had brought for patching things. Amal tried to help her wrap it around Sally and secure it with tape, but the dog thought it was a game, and as their dog-wrestling grew desperate, they ended up collapsing in laughter. I left the tent to look after Bucky, and when I next saw Sally she looked like a dog mummy with only her eyes and nose poking through. "I'll do something better when we stop next," Edie pledged.

The next tenhour was a slow, dark trudge through icy stromatolite bogs. When the water froze solid enough to support the buggy, we cut across it to reach the edge of the Mazy Lakes, pushing on past our normal camping time. Once on solid land, we were quick to set up the tent and the propane stove to heat it. Everyone crowded inside, eager to shed their coldsuits. Taking off a coldsuit at the end of the day is like emerging from a stifling womb, ready to breathe free.

After lights out, I was already asleep when Seabird nudged me. "There's something moving outside," she whispered.

"No, there's not," I muttered. She was always worried that we were deviating from plan, or losing our way, or not keeping to schedule. I turned over to go back to sleep when Sally growled. Something hit the roof of the tent. It sounded like a small branch falling from a tree, but there were no trees where we had camped.

"Did you hear that?" Seabird hissed.

"Okay, I'll check it out." It was hard to leave my snug sleep cocoon and pull on the coldsuit again—but better me than her, since she would probably imagine things and wake everyone.

It was the coldest part of night, and there was a slight frost of dry ice on the rocks around us. Everything in the landscape was motionless. Above, the galaxy arched, a frozen cloud of light. I shone my lamp on the tent to see what had hit it, but there was nothing. All was still.

In the eastern sky, a dim, gray smudge of light was rising over the lakes. Umber. I didn't stare long, not quite trusting the UV shielding on my faceplate, but I didn't like the look of it. I had never read that the shroud began to glow before it parted, but the observations from the last Umbernight were not detailed, and there were none from the time before that. Still, I crawled back into the safety of the tent feeling troubled.

"What was it?" Seabird whispered.

"Nothing." She would think that was an evasion, so I added, "If anything was out there, I scared it off."

When we rose, I left the tent first with the UV detector. The night was still just as dark, but there was no longer a glow in the east, and the increase of radiation was not beyond the usual fluctuations. Nevertheless, I quietly mentioned what I had seen to Amal.

"Are you sure it's significant?" he said.

I wasn't sure of anything, so I shook my head.

"I'm not going to call off the mission unless we're sure."

I probably would have made the same decision. At the time, there was no telling whether it was wise or foolish.

Bucky was cold after sitting for ten hours, and we had barely started when a spring in his suspension broke. It took me an hour to fix it, working awkwardly in my bulky coldsuit, but we finally set off. We had come to the Damn Right Barrens, a rocky plateau full of the ejecta from the ancient meteor strike that had created Newton's Eye. The farther we walked, the more rugged it became, and in the dark it was impossible to see ahead and pick out the best course.

Davern gave a piteous howl of pain, and we all came to a stop. He had turned his ankle. There was no way to examine it without setting up the tent, so Amal took some of the load from the buggy and carried it so Davern could ride. After another six hours of struggling through the boulders, I suggested we camp and wait for daybreak. "We're ahead of schedule," I said. "It's wiser to wait than to risk breaking something important."

"My ankle's not important?" Davern protested.

"Your ankle will heal. Bucky's axle won't."

Sulkily, he said, "You ought to marry that machine. You care more for it than any person."

I would have answered, but I saw Edie looking at me in warning, and I knew she would give him a talking-to later on.

When we finally got a look at Davern's ankle inside the tent, it was barely swollen, and I suspected him of malingering for sympathy. But rather than have him slow us down, we all agreed to let him ride till it got better.

Day came soon after we had slept. We tackled the Damn Right again, moving much faster now that we could see the path. I made them push on till we came to the edge of the Winding Wall.

Coming on the Winding Wall is exhilarating or terrifying, depending on your personality. At the end of an upward slope the world drops suddenly away, leaving you on the edge of sky. Standing on the windy precipice, you have to lean forward to see the cliffs plunging nearly perpendicular to the basin of the crater three hundred meters below. To right and left, the cliff edge undulates in a snaky line that forms a huge arc vanishing into the distance—for the crater circle is far too wide to see across.

"I always wish for wings here," I said as we lined the edge, awestruck.

"How are we going to get down?" Edie asked.

"There's a way, but it's treacherous. Best to do it fresh."

"We've got thirty hours of light left," Amal said.

"Then let's rest up."

It was noon when we rose, and Umber had set. I led the way to the spot where a ravine pierced the wall. Unencumbered by coldsuits, we were far more agile, but Bucky still had only four wheels and no legs. We unloaded him in order to use the cart bed as a ramp, laying it over the rugged path so he could pass, and ferrying the baggage by hand, load after load. Davern was forced to go by foot when it got too precarious, using a tent pole for a cane.

It was hard, sweaty work, but twelve hours later we were at the bottom, feeling triumphant. We piled into the tent and slept until dark.

The next leg of the journey was an easy one over the sandy plain of the crater floor. Through the dark we walked then slept, walked then slept, until we started seeing steam venting from the ground as we reached the geothermically active region at the center of the crater. Here we came on the remains of an old road built by the original settlers when they expected to be staying at Newton's Eye. It led through the hills of the inner crater ring. When we paused at the top of the rise, I noticed the same smudge of light in the sky I had seen before. This time, I immediately took a UV reading, and the levels had spiked. I showed it to Amal.

"The shroud's thinning," I said.

I couldn't read his expression through the faceplate of his coldsuit, but his body language was all indecision. "Let's take another reading in a couple hours," he said.

We did, but there was no change.

We were moving fast by now, through a landscape formed by old eruptions. Misshapen claws of lava reached out of the darkness on either side, frozen in the act of menacing the road. At last, as we were thinking of stopping, we spied ahead the shape of towering ribs against the stars—the remains of the settlers' original landing craft, or the parts of it too big to cannibalize. With our goal so close, we pushed on till we came to the cleared plain where it lay, the fossil skeleton of a monster that once swam the stars.

We all stood gazing at it, reluctant to approach and shatter its isolation. "Why don't we camp here?" Edie said.

We had made better time than I had expected. The plan had been to arrive just as the cargo capsule did, pick up the payload, and head back immediately; but we were a full twenty hours early. We could afford to rest.

• • •

I woke before the others, pulled on my protective gear, and went outside to see the dawn. The eastern sky glowed a cold pink and azure. The landing site was a basin of black volcanic rock. Steaming pools of water made milky with dissolved silicates dappled the plain, smelling of sodium bicarbonate. As I watched the day come, the pools turned the same startling blue as the sky, set like turquoise in jet.

The towering ribs of the lander now stood out in the strange, desolate landscape. I thought of all the sunrises they had seen—each one a passing fragment of time, a shard of a millennium in which this one was just a nanosecond of nothing.

Behind me, boots crunched on cinders. I turned to see that Amal had joined me. He didn't greet me, just stood taking in the scene.

At last he said, "It's uplifting, isn't it?"

Startled, I said, "What is?"

"That they came all this way for the sake of reason."

Came all this way to a desolation of rock and erosion stretching to the vanishing point—no, uplifting was not a word I would use. But I didn't say so.

He went back to the tent to fetch the others, and soon I was surrounded by youthful energy that made me despise my own sclerotic disaffection. They all wanted to go explore the ruins, so I waved them on and returned to the tent to fix my breakfast.

After eating, I went to join them. I found Seabird and Davern bathing in one of the hot pools, shaded by an awning constructed from their coldsuits. "You're sure of the chemicals in that water, are you?" I asked.

"Oh stop worrying," Davern said. "You're just a walking death's-head, Mick. You see danger everywhere."

Ahead, the other three were clustered under the shadow of the soaring ship ribs. When I came up, I saw they had found a stone monument, and were standing silently before it, the hoods of their coldsuits thrown back. Sally sat at Edie's feet.

"It's a memorial to everyone who died in the first year," Edie told me in a hushed voice.

"But that's not the important part," Anatoly said intently. He pointed to a line of the inscription, a quotation from Theodore Cam, the legendary leader of the exiles. It said:

Gaze into the unknowable from a bridge of evidence.

"You see?" Anatoly said. "He knew there was something unknowable. Reason doesn't reach all the way. There are other truths. We were right, there is more to the universe than just the established facts."

I thought back to Feynman Habitat, and how the pursuit of knowledge had contracted into something rigid and dogmatic. No wonder my generation had failed to inspire. I looked up at the skeleton of the spacecraft making its grand, useless gesture to the sky. How could mere reason compete with that?

After satisfying my curiosity, I trudged back to the tent. From a distance I heard a whining sound, and when I drew close I realized it was coming from Bucky. Puzzled, I rummaged through his load to search for the source. When I realized what it was, my heart pulsed in panic. Instantly, I put up the hood on my coldsuit and ran to warn the others.

"Put on your coldsuits and get back to the tent!" I shouted at Seabird and Davern. "Our X-ray detector went off. The shroud has parted."

Umber was invisible in the bright daylight of the western sky, but a pulse of X-rays could only mean one thing.

When I had rounded them all up and gotten them back to the shielded safety of the tent, we held a council.

"We've got to turn around and go back, this instant," I said.

There was a long silence. I turned to Amal. "You promised."

"I promised we'd turn back if Umbernight came on our way out," he said. "We're not on the way out any longer. We're here, and it's only ten hours before the capsule arrives. We'd be giving up in sight of success."

"Ten hours for the capsule to come, another ten to get it unpacked and reloaded on Bucky," I pointed out. "If we're lucky."

"But Umber sets soon," Edie pointed out. "We'll be safe till it rises again."

I had worked it all out. "By that time, we'll barely be back to the Winding Wall. We have to go *up* that path this time, bathed in X-rays."

"Our coldsuits will shield us," Anatoly said. "It will be hard, but we can do it."

The trip up to now had been too easy; it had given them inflated confidence.

Anatoly looked around at the others, his face fierce and romantic with a shadow of black beard accentuating his jawline. "I've realized now, what we're doing really matters. We're not just fetching baggage. We're a link to the settlers. We have to live up to their standards, to their . . . heroism." He said the last word as if it were unfamiliar—as indeed it was, in the crabbed pragmatism of Feynman Habitat.

I could see a contagion of inspiration spreading through them. Only I was immune.

"They *died*," I said. "Two thirds of them. Didn't you read that monument?"

"They didn't know what we do," Amal argued. "They weren't expecting Umbernight."

Anatoly saw I was going to object, and spoke first. "Maybe some of us will die, too. Maybe that is the risk we need to take. They were willing, and so am I."

He was noble, committed, and utterly serious.

"No one wants you to die!" I couldn't keep the frustration from my voice. "Your dying would be totally useless. It would only harm the rest of us. You need to live. Sorry to break it to you."

They were all caught up in the kind of crazy courage that brought the settlers here. They all felt the same devotion to a cause, and they hadn't yet learned that the universe doesn't give a rip.

"Listen," I said, "you've got to ask yourself, what's a win here? Dying is not a win. Living is a win, even if it means living with failure."

As soon as I said the last word, I could see it was the wrong one.

"Let's vote," said Amal. "Davern, what about you? You haven't said anything."

Davern looked around at the others, and I could see he was sizing up who to side with. "I'm with Anatoly," he said. "He understands us."

Amal nodded as if this made sense. "How about you, Seabird?"

She looked up at Anatoly with what I first thought was admiration—then I realized it was infatuation. "I'll follow Anatoly," she said with feeling.

The followers in our group had chosen Anatoly as their leader.

"I vote with Anatoly, too," said Amal. "I think we've come this far, it would be crazy to give up now. Edie?"

"I respect Mick's advice," she said thoughtfully. "But our friends back home are counting on us, and in a way the settlers are counting on us, too. All those people died so we could be here, and to give up would be like letting them down."

I pulled up the hood of my coldsuit and headed out of the tent. Outside, the day was bright and poisonous. The coldsuit shielded me from the X-rays, but not from the feeling of impending disaster. I looked across to the skeletal shipwreck and wondered: what are we doing here on Dust? The settlers chose this, but none of us asked to be born here, exiled from the rest of humanity, like the scum on the sand left by the highest wave. We aren't noble pioneers. We're only different from the bacteria because we are able to ask what the hell this is all about. Not answer, just ask.

Someone came out of the tent behind me, and I looked to see who it was this time. Edie. She came to my side. "Mick, we are so thankful that you're with us," she said. "We do listen to you. We just agreed to go to a twelve-hour work shift on the way back, to speed things up. We'll get back."

I truly wished she weren't here. She was the kind of person who ought to be protected, so she could continue to bring cheer to the world. She was too valuable to be thrown away.

"It's not about me," I said. "I've got less life to lose than the rest of you."

"No one's going to lose their lives," she said. "I promise."

Why can't I quit asking what more I could have done? I'm tired of that question. I still don't know what else there was to do.

Ten hours later, there was no sign of the supply ship. Everyone was restless. We had slept and risen again, and now we scanned the skies every few minutes, hoping to see something.

Edie looked up from fashioning little dog goggles and said, "Do you suppose it's landed somewhere else?" Once she had voiced the idea, it became our greatest worry. What if our assumption about the landing spot was wrong? We told ourselves it was just that the calculations had been off, or the ship was making an extra orbit. Now that we had made the commitment to stay, no one wanted to give up; but how long were we prepared to wait?

In the end, we could not have missed the lander's descent. It showed up first as a bright spot in the western sky. Then it became a fiery streak, and we saw the parachutes bloom. Seconds later, landing rockets fired. We cheered as, with a roar that shook the ground, the craft set down in a cloud of dust barely a kilometer from us. As the warm wind buffeted us, even I felt that the sight had been worth the journey.

By the time we had taken down the tent, loaded everything on Bucky, and raced over to the landing site, the dust had settled and the metal cooled. It was almost sunset, so we worked fast in the remaining light. One team unloaded everything from Bucky while another team puzzled out how to open the cargo doors. The inside of the spacecraft was tightly packed with molded plastic cases we couldn't work out how to open, so we just piled them onto the buggy as they came out. We would leave the thrill of discovery to our friends back home.

Bucky was dangerously overloaded before we had emptied the pod, so we reluctantly secured the doors with some of the crates still inside to stay the winter at Newton's Eye. We could only hope that we had gotten the most important ones.

There was still a lot of work to do, sorting out our baggage and redistributing it, and we worked by lamplight into the night. By the time all was ready, we were exhausted. Umber had not yet risen, so there was no need to set up the tent, and we slept on the ground in the shadow of the lander. I was so close that I could reach out and touch something that had come all the way from the homeworld.

We set out into the night as soon as we woke. Bucky creaked and groaned, but I said encouraging words to him, and he seemed to get used to his new load. All of us were more heavily laden now, and the going would have been slower even if Bucky could have kept up his usual pace. When we reached the top of the inner crater ring we paused to look back at the plain where two spacecraft now stood. In the silence of our tribute, the X-ray alarm went off. Invisible through our UV-screening faceplates, Umber was rising in the east. Umbernight was ahead.

We walked in silence. Sally hung close to us in her improvised coldsuit, no longer roving and exploring. From time to time she froze in her tracks and gave a low growl. But nothing was there.

"What's she growling at, X-rays?" Anatoly said.

"She's just picking up tension from us," Edie said, reaching down to pat the dog's back.

Half a mile later, Sally lunged forward, snapping at the air as if to bite it. Through the cloth of her coldsuit, she could not have connected with anything, even if anything had been there.

"Now *I'm* picking up on *her* tension," Davern said.

"Ouch! Who did that?" Seabird cried out, clutching her arm. "Somebody hit me."

"Everyone calm down," Edie said. "Look around you. There's nothing wrong."

She shone her lamp all around, and she was right; the scene looked exactly as it had when we had traversed it before—a barren, volcanic plain pocked with steaming vents and the occasional grove of everlive trees. The deadly radiation was invisible.

Another mile farther on, Amal swore loudly and slapped his thigh as if bitten by a fly. He bent over to inspect his coldsuit and swore again. "Something pierced my suit," he said. "There's three pinholes in it."

Sally started barking. We shone our lights everywhere, but could see nothing.

It was like being surrounded by malicious poltergeists that had gathered to impede our journey. I quieted the dog and said, "Everyone stop and listen."

At first I heard nothing but my own heart. Then, as we kept still, it came: a rustling of unseen movement in the dark all around us.

"We've got company," Anatoly said grimly.

I wanted to deny my senses. For years I had been searching for animal life on Dust, and found none—not even an insect, other than the ones we brought. And how could anything be alive in this bath of radiation? It was scientifically impossible.

We continued on more carefully. After a while, I turned off my headlamp and went out in front to see if I could see anything without the glare of the light. At first there was nothing, but as my eyes adjusted, something snagged my attention out of the corner of my eye. It was a faint, gauzy curtain—a net hanging in the air, glowing a dim blue-gray. It was impossible to tell how close it was—just before my face, or over the next hill? I swept my arm out to disturb it, but touched nothing. So either it was far away, or it was inside my head.

Something slapped my faceplate, and I recoiled. There was a smear of goo across my visor. I tried to wipe it off, and an awful smell from my breathing vent nearly gagged me. Behind me, Amal gave an exclamation, and I thought he had smelled it too, but when I turned to see, he was looking at his foot.

"I stepped on something," he said. "I could feel it crunch."

"What's that disgusting smell?" Davern said.

"Something slimed me," I answered.

"Keep on going, everyone," Edie said. "We can't stop to figure it out."

We plodded on, a slow herd surrounded by invisible tormentors. We had not gotten far before Amal had to stop because his boot was coming apart. We waited while he wrapped mending tape around it, but that lasted only half an hour before the sole of his boot was flapping free again. "I've got to stop and fix this, or my foot will freeze," he said.

We were all a little grateful to have an excuse to set up the tent and stop our struggle to continue. Once inside, we found that all of our coldsuits were pierced with small cuts and pinholes. We spent some time repairing them, then looked at each other to see who wanted to continue.

"What happens if we camp while Umber is in the sky, and only travel by day?" Edie finally asked.

I did a quick calculation. "It would add another 300 hours. We don't have food to last."

"If we keep going, our coldsuits will be cut to ribbons," Davern said.

"If only we could see what's attacking us!" Edie exclaimed.

Softly, Seabird said, "It's ghosts." We all fell silent. I looked at her, expecting it was some sort of joke, but she was deadly serious. "All those people who died," she said.

At home, everyone would have laughed and mocked her. Out here, no one replied.

I pulled up the hood of my coldsuit and rose.

"Where are you going?" Davern said.

"I want to check out the lookthrough trees." In reality, I wanted some silence to think.

"What a time to be botanizing!" Davern exclaimed.

"Shut up, Davern," Amal said.

Outside, in the empty waste, I had a feeling of being watched. I shook it off. When we had camped, I had noticed that a nearby grove of lookthrough trees was glowing in the dark, shades of blue and green. I picked my way across the rocks toward them. I suspected that the fluorescence was an adaptation that allowed them to survive the hostile conditions of Umbernight, and I wanted some samples. When I reached the grove and examined one of the long, flat leaves under lamplight, it looked transparent, as usual. Shutting my lamp off, I held it up and looked through it. With a start, I pressed it to my visor so I could see through the leaf.

What looked like a rocky waste by the dim starlight was suddenly a brightly lit landscape. And everywhere I looked, the land bloomed with organic shapes unlike any I had ever seen. Under a rock by my feet was a low, domed mound pierced with holes like an overturned colander, glowing from within. Beneath the everlives were bread-loaf-shaped growths covered with plates that slid aside as I watched, to expose a hummocked mound inside. There were things with leathery rinds that folded out like petals to collect the unlight, which snapped shut the instant I turned on my lamp. In between the larger life-forms, the ground was crawling with smaller, insect-sized things, and in the distance I could see gauzy curtains held up by gas bladders floating on the wind.

An entire alternate biota had sprung to life in Umberlight. Dust was not just the barren place we saw by day, but a thriving dual ecosystem, half of which had been waiting as spores or seeds in the soil, to be awakened by Umber's radiation. I knelt down to see why they had been so invisible. By our light, some of them were transparent as glass. Others were so black they blended in with the rock. By Umberlight, they lit up in bright colors, reflecting a spectrum we could not see.

I looked down at the leaf that had given me new sight. It probably had a microstructure that converted high-energy radiation into the visible spectrum so the tree could continue to absorb the milder wavelengths. Quickly, I plucked a handful of the leaves. Holding one to my visor, I turned back toward the tent. The UV-reflecting fabric was a dull gray in our light, but Umberlight made it shine like a beacon, the brightest thing in the landscape. I looked down at my coldsuit, and it also glowed like a torch. The things of Umbernight might be invisible to us, but we were all too visible to them.

When I came back into the tent, my companions were still arguing. Silently, I handed each of them a strip of leaf. Davern threw his away in disgust. "What's this, some sort of peace offering?" he said.

"Put on your coldsuits and come outside," I said. "Hold the leaves up to your faceplates and look through them."

Their reactions, when they saw the reality around us, were as different as they were: astonished, uneasy, disbelieving. Seabird was terrified, and shrank back toward the tent. "It's like nightmares," she said.

Edie put an arm around her. "It's better than ghosts," she said.

"No, it's not. It's the shadow side of all the living beings. That's why we couldn't see them."

"We couldn't see them because they don't reflect the spectrum of light our eyes absorb," Amal said reasonably. Seabird did not look comforted.

I looked ahead, down the road we needed to take. Umber was bright as an anti-sun. In its light, the land was not empty, but full. There was a boil of emerging life in every crack of the landscape: just not our sort of life. We were the strangers here, the fruits that had fallen too far from the tree. We did not belong.

You would think that being able to see the obstacles would speed us up, but not so. We were skittish now. With strips of lookthrough leaves taped to our visors, we could see both worlds, which were the same world; but we could not tell the harmless from the harmful. So we treated it all as a threat—dodging, detouring, clearing the road with a shovel when we could. As we continued, the organisms changed and multiplied fast around us, as if their growth were in overdrive. It was spring for them, and they were sprouting and spawning. What would they look like fully grown? I hoped not to find out.

I can't describe the life-forms of Umbernight in biological language, because I couldn't tell if I was looking at a plant, animal, or something in between. We quickly discovered what had been piercing our coldsuits—a plantlike thing shaped like a scorpion with a spring-loaded tail lined with barbs. When triggered by our movement, it would release a shower of pin-sharp projectiles. Perhaps they were poison, and our incompatible proteins protected us.

The road had sprouted all manner of creatures covered with plates and shells—little ziggurats and stepped pyramids, spirals, and domes. In between them floated bulbs like amber, airborne eggplants. They spurted a mucus that ate away any plastic it touched.

We topped a rise to find the valley before us completely crusted over with life, and no trace of a path. No longer could we avoid trampling through it, crushing it underfoot. Ahead, a translucent curtain suspended from floating, gas-filled bladders hung across our path. It shimmered with iridescent unlight.

"It's rather beautiful, isn't it?" Edie said.

"Yes, but is it dangerous?" Amal said.

"We're not prey," Anatoly argued. "This life can't get any nutrients from us."

"I doubt it knows that," I said. "It might just act on instinct."

"We could send the dog to find out," Anatoly suggested.

Sally showed no inclination. Edie had put her on a leash, but it was hardly necessary; she was constantly alert now, on guard.

"Go around it," I advised.

So we left our path to detour across land where the boulders had become hard to spot amid the riot of life. As Bucky's wheels crushed the shell of one dome, I saw that inside it was a wriggling mass of larvae. It was not a single organism, but a colony. That would explain how such complex structures came about so fast; they were just hives of smaller organisms.

We cleared a place to camp by trampling down the undergrowth and shoveling it out of the way. Exhausted as we were, it was still hard to sleep through the sounds from outside: buzzing, whooshing, scratching, scrabbling. My brain kept coming back to one thought: at this rate, our return would take twice as long as the journey out.

The tent was cold when we woke; our heater had failed. When Amal unfastened the tent flap he gave an uncharacteristically profane exclamation. The opening was entirely blocked by undergrowth. No longer cautious, we set about hacking and smashing our way out, disturbing hordes of tiny crawling things. When we had cleared a path and turned back to look, we saw that the tent was surrounded by mounds of organisms attracted by its reflected light. The heater had failed because its air intake was blocked. Bucky, parked several yards away, had not attracted the Umberlife.

It was the coldest part of night, but Umber was high in the sky, and the life-forms had speeded up. We marched in formation now, with three fanned out in front to scan for obstructions, one in the center with Bucky, and two bringing up the rear. I was out in front with Seabird and Davern when we reached a hilltop and saw that the way ahead was blocked by a lake that had not been there on the way out. We gathered to survey it. It was white, like an ocean of milk.

"What is it?" Edie asked.

"Not water," Anatoly said. "It's too cold for that, too warm for methane."

I could not see any waves, but there was an ebb and flow around the edges. "Wait here. I want to get closer," I said.

Amal and Anatoly wouldn't let me go alone, so the three of us set out. We were nearly on the beach edge before we could see it clearly. Amal came to an abrupt halt. "Spiders!" he said, repulsed. "It's a sea of spiders."

They were not spiders, of course, but that is the closest analog: long-legged crawling things, entirely white in the Umberlight. At the edges of the sea they were tiny, but farther out we could see ones the size of Sally, all seemingly competing to get toward the center of the mass. There must have been a hatching while we had slept.

"That is truly disgusting," Anatoly said.

I gave a humorless laugh. "I've read about this on other planets—wildlife covering the land. The accounts always say it is a majestic, inspiring sight."

"Umber turns everything into its evil twin," Amal said.

As we stood there, a change was taking place. A wave was gathering far out. The small fry in front of us were scattering to get out of the way as it swept closer.

"They're coming toward us," Anatoly said.

We turned to run back toward the hill where we had left our friends. Anatoly and Amal reached the hilltop before I did. Edie shouted a warning, and I turned to see a knee-high spider on my heels, its pale body like a skull on legs. I had no weapon but my flashlight, so I nailed it with a light beam. To my surprise, it recoiled onto its hind legs, waving its front legs in the air. It gave me time to reach the others.

"They're repelled by light!" I shouted. "Form a line and shine them off."

The wave of spiders surged up the hill, but we kept them at bay with our lights. They circled us, and we ended up in a ring around Bucky, madly sweeping our flashlights to and fro to keep them off while Sally barked from behind us.

Far across the land, the horizon lit with a silent flash like purple lightning. The spiders paused, then turned mindlessly toward this new light source. As quickly as they had swarmed toward us, they were swarming away. We watched the entire lake of them drain, heading toward some signal we could not see.

"Quick, let's cross while they're gone," I said.

We dashed as fast as we could across the plain where they had gathered. From time to time we saw other flashes of unlight, always far away and never followed by thunder.

In our haste, we let our vigilance lapse, and one of Bucky's wheels thunked into a pothole. The other wheels spun, throwing up loose dirt and digging themselves in. I called out, "Bucky, stop!"—but he was already stuck fast.

"Let's push him out," Amal said, but I held up a hand. The buggy was already dangerously tilted.

"We're going to have to unload some crates to lighten him up, and dig that wheel out."

Everyone looked nervously in the direction where the spiders had gone, but Amal said, "Okay. You dig, we'll unload."

We all set to work. I was so absorbed in freeing Bucky's wheel that I did not see the danger approaching until Seabird gave a cry of warning. I looked up to see one of the gauzy curtains bearing down on us from windward. It was yards wide, big enough to envelop us all, and twinkling with a spiderweb of glowing threads.

"Run!" Amal shouted. I dropped my shovel and fled. Behind me, I heard Edie's voice crying, "Sally!" and Amal's saying, "No, Edie! Leave her be!"

I whirled around and saw that the dog had taken refuge under the buggy. Edie was running back to get her. Amal was about to head back after Edie, so I dived at his legs and brought him down with a thud. From the ground we both watched as Edie gave up and turned back toward us. Behind her, the curtain that had been sweeping toward Bucky changed direction, veering straight toward Edie.

"Edie!" Amal screamed. She turned, saw her danger, and froze.

The curtain enveloped her, wrapping her tight in an immobilizing net. There was a sudden, blinding flash of combustion. As I blinked the after-spots away, I saw the curtain float on, shredded now, leaving behind a charcoal pillar in the shape of a woman.

Motionless with shock, I gazed at that black statue standing out against the eastern sky. It was several seconds before I realized that the sky was growing bright. Beyond all of us, dawn was coming.

In the early morning light Anatoly and I dug a grave while Seabird and Davern set up the tent. We simply could not go on. Amal was shattered with grief, and could not stop sobbing.

"Why her?" he would say in the moments when he could speak at all. "She was the best person here, the best I've ever known. She shouldn't have been the one to die."

I couldn't wash those last few seconds out of my brain. Why had she stopped? How had that brainless, eyeless thing sensed her?

Later, Amal became angry at me for having prevented him from saving her. "Maybe I could have distracted it. It might have taken me instead of her."

I only shook my head. "We would have been burying both of you."

"That would have been better," he said.

Everyone gathered as we laid what was left of her in the ground, but no one had the heart to say anything over the grave. When we had filled it in, Sally crept forward to sniff at the overturned dirt. Amal said, "We need to mark it, so we can find it again." So we all fanned out to find rocks to heap in a cairn on the grave.

We no longer feared the return of the spiders, or anything else, because the Umberlife had gone dormant in the sun—our light being as toxic to them as theirs was to us. Everything had retreated into their shells and closed their sliding covers. When we viewed them in our own light they still blended in with the stones of the crater floor.

We ate and snatched some hours of sleep while nothing was threatening us. I was as exhausted as the others, but anxious that we were wasting so much daylight. I roused them all before they were ready. "We've got to keep moving," I said.

We resumed the work of freeing Bucky where we had left off. When all was ready, we gathered behind him to push. "Bucky, go!" I ordered. His wheels only spun in the sand. "Stop!" I ordered. Then, to the others, "We're going to rock him out. Push when I say go, and stop when I say stop." When we got a rhythm going, he rocked back and forth three times, then finally climbed out of the trench that had trapped him.

Amal helped us reload the buggy, but when it came time to move on, he hung back. "You go ahead," he said. "I'll catch up with you."

"No way," I said. "We all go or none of us."

He got angry at me again, but I would not let him pick a fight. We let him have some moments alone at the grave to say goodbye. At last I walked up to him and said, "Come on, Amal. We've got to keep moving."

"What's the point?" he said. "The future is gone."

But he followed me back to where the others were waiting.

He was right, in one way: nothing we could achieve now would make up for Edie's loss. How we were going to carry on without her, I could not guess.

When we camped, there was no music now, and little conversation. The Winding Wall was a blue line ahead in the distance, and as we continued, it rose, ever more impassable, blocking our way. We did not reach the spot where the gully path pierced it until we had been walking for thirteen hours. We were tired, but resting would waste the last of the precious sunlight. We gathered to make a decision.

"Let's just leave the buggy and the crates, and make a run for home," Amal said. He looked utterly dispirited.

Davern and Seabird turned to Anatoly. He was the only one of us who was still resolute. "If we do that, we will have wasted our time," he said. "We can't give up now."

"That's right," Davern said.

Amal looked at me. There was some sense in his suggestion, but also some impracticality. "If we leave the buggy we'll have to leave the tent," I said. "It's too heavy for us to carry." We had been spreading it as a tarpaulin over the crates when we were on the move.

"We knew from the beginning that the wall would be an obstacle," Anatoly said with determination. "We have to make the effort."

I think even Amal realized then that he was no longer our leader.

We unloaded the buggy, working till we were ready to drop, then ate and fell asleep on the ground. When we woke, the sun was setting. It seemed too soon.

Each crate took two people to carry up the steep path. We decided to do it in stages. Back and forth we shuttled, piling our cargo at a level spot a third of the way up. The path was treacherous in the dark, but at least the work was so strenuous we had no need of coldsuits until Umber should rise.

The life-forms around us started waking as soon as dark came. It was the predawn time for them, when they could open their shells and exhale like someone shedding a coldsuit. They were quiescent enough that we were able to avoid them.

Fifteen hours later, our cargo was three-quarters of the way up, and we gathered at the bottom again to set up the tent and rest before trying to get Bucky up the path. The X-ray alarm went off while we were asleep, but we were so tired we just shut it off and went on sleeping.

When we rose, an inhuman architecture had surrounded our tent on all sides. The Umberlife had self-organized into domes and spires that on close inspection turned out to be crawling hives. There was something deformed and abhorrent about them, and we were eager to escape our transformed campsite—until Seabird gave a whimper and pointed upward.

Three hundred meters above, the top of the Winding Wall was now a battlement of living towers that glowed darkly against the sky. Shapes we couldn't quite make out moved to and fro between the structures, as if patrolling the edge. One fat tower appeared to have a rotating top that emitted a searchlight beam of far-ultraviolet light. It scanned back and forth—whether for enemies or for prey we didn't know.

We realized how conspicuous we were in our glowing coldsuits. "I'd give up breakfast for a can of black paint," I said.

"Maybe we could cover ourselves with mud?" Davern ventured.

"Let's get out of here first," Anatoly said.

The feeling that the land was aware of us had become too strong.

Getting Bucky up the steep trail was backbreaking work, but whenever we paused to rest, Umberlife gathered around us. The gully was infested with the plant-creatures that had once launched pins at us; they had grown, and their darts were the size of pencils now. We learned to trigger them with a beam from our flashlights. Every step required a constant, enervating vigilance.

When we had reached the place where we left the crates and stopped to rest, I announced that I was going to scout the trail ahead. No one else volunteered, so I said, "Amal, come with me. Seabird, hold onto the dog."

Amal and I picked our way up the steep trail, shining away small attackers. I saw no indication that the Umberlife had blocked the path. When we reached the top and emerged onto the plateau, I stood looking around at the transformed landscape. At my side, Amal said, "Oh my God."

The Damn Right Barrens were now a teeming jungle. Everywhere stood towering, misshapen structures, competing to dominate the landscape. An undergrowth of smaller life clogged the spaces in between. Above, in the Umberlit sky, floated monstrous organisms like glowing jellyfish, trailing tentacles that sparked and sizzled when they touched the ground. Ten or twelve of the lighthouse towers swept their searching beams across the land. There was not a doubt in my mind that this landscape was brutally aware.

I spotted some motion out of the corner of my eye, but when I turned to see, nothing was there. I thought: only predators and prey need to move fast.

"Look," Amal said, pointing. "Weird."

It was a ball, perfectly round and perhaps a yard in diameter, rolling along the ground of its own accord. It disappeared behind a hive-mound and I lost track of it.

We had turned to go back down the ravine when one of the searchlight beams swept toward us, and we ducked to conceal ourselves behind a rock. Amal gave an exclamation, and I turned to see that we were surrounded by four of the rolling spheres. They seemed to be waiting for us to make a move, so I pointed my flashlight at one. Instantly, it dissolved into a million tiny crawlers that escaped into the undergrowth. The other spheres withdrew.

"They're coordinating with the beacons," I hissed at Amal. "Hunting cooperatively."

"This place is evil," he said.

We dashed toward the head of the gully. Too late, I spotted ahead the largest dart-thrower plant I had ever seen. The spring-loaded tail triggered, releasing its projectiles. I dove to one side. Amal was not quick enough, and a spine the size of an arrow caught him in the throat. He clutched at it and fell to his knees. Somehow, I managed to drag him forward till we were concealed in the gully.

The dart had pierced his neck through, and was protruding on the other side. There was no way to give him aid without taking off his coldsuit. He was struggling to breathe. I tried to lift his hood, but the dart was pinning it down. So I said, "Brace yourself," and yanked the shaft out. He gave a gurgling cry. When I got his hood off, I saw it was hopeless. The dart had pierced a vein, and his coldsuit was filling with dark blood. Still, I ripped at his shirt and tried to bind up the wound until he caught at my hand. His eyes were growing glassy, but his lips moved.

"Leave it," he said. He was ready to die.

I stayed there, kneeling over him as he stiffened and grew cold. My mind was a blank, until suddenly I began to cry. Not just for him—for Edie as well, and for their unborn children, and all the people who would never be gladdened by their presence. I cried for the fact that we had to bury them in this hostile waste, where love and comfort would never touch them again. And I cried for the rest of us as well, because the prospect of our reaching home now seemed so dim.

• • •

When Anatoly and I brought the shovel back to the place where I had left Amal, there was nothing to bury. Only an empty coldsuit and a handful of teeth were left on the ground; all other trace of him was gone. Anatoly nudged the coldsuit with his foot. "Should we bury this?"

Macabre as it sounded, I said, "We might need it."

So we brought it back to our camp. We let the others think we had buried him.

We convened another strategy session. I said, "Amal had it right. We need to make a run for it. To hell with the cargo and the buggy. Leave the tent here; it only draws attention to us. We need to travel fast and light."

But Anatoly was still animated by the inspiration of our mission. "We can still succeed," he said. "We're close; we don't need to give up. We just have to outthink this nightmare."

"Okay, how?"

"We bring everything to the head of the gully and build a fort out of the crates. Then we wait till day comes, and make a dash for it while the Umberlife is sleeping."

"We can only get as far as the Mazy Lakes before night," I said.

"We do the same thing over again—wait out Umbernight. Food's no longer such a problem, with two less people."

I saw true faith in Seabird's eyes, and calculated self-interest in Davern's. Anatoly was so decisive, they were clearly ready to follow him. Perhaps that was all we needed. Perhaps it would work.

"All right," I said. "Let's get going."

We chose a site for our fort in the gully not far from where Amal had died. When it was done, it was a square enclosure of stacked crates with the tent pitched inside. I felt mildly optimistic that it would work. We slept inside it before bringing Bucky up. Then we waited.

There were sounds outside. Sally's warning growls made us worry that something was surrounding us to make an attack, so we set four of our lanterns on the walls to repel intruders, even though it used up precious battery life.

Hours of uneasiness later, dawn came. We instantly broke down the fort and found that the lamps had done their job, since there was a bare circle all around us. We congratulated ourselves on having found a way to survive.

The daylight hours were a mad dash across the Damn Right. We had to clear the way ahead of Bucky, and we took out our anger on the hibernating Umberlife, leaving a trail of smashed shells and toppled towers. We reached the edge of the lakes at sunset, and instantly saw that our plan would not work.

Around the edge of the wetland stood a dense forest of the tallest spires we had yet seen, easily dominating any fort walls we could build. There would be no hope of staying hidden here.

At the edge of the lake, the blooming abundance of horrors stopped, as if water were as toxic to them as light. "If only we had a boat!" Anatoly exclaimed. But the life around us did not produce anything so durable as wood—even the shells were friable.

The light was fading fast. Soon, this crowded neighborhood would become animate. Ahead, a narrow causeway between two lakes looked invitingly empty. If only we could make it to a campsite far enough from shore, we could build our fort and wait out the night.

"Let me get out my maps and check our route first," I said.

Davern gave an exclamation of impatience, but Anatoly just said, "Hurry up."

We were on the side of the Mazy Lakes where my maps were less complete. On the outward journey, we had cut across the ice; but now, after forty hours of daylight, that was not an option. I was certain of only one route, and it seemed to take off from shore about five miles away. I showed it to the others.

Davern still wanted to follow the route ahead of us. "We can just go far enough to camp, then come back next day," he argued. "We've already been walking twelve hours."

"No. We're not going to make any stupid mistakes," I said.

Anatoly hesitated, then said, "It's only five miles. We can do that."

But five miles later, it was completely dark and almost impossible to tell the true path from a dozen false ones that took off into the swamp whenever I shone my lamp waterward. I began to think perhaps Davern had been right after all. But rather than risk demoralizing everyone, I chose a path and confidently declared it the right one.

It was a low and swampy route, ankle-deep in water at times. I went out ahead with a tent pole to test the footing and scout the way. The sound of Davern complaining came from behind.

As soon as we came to a relatively dry spot, we set up the tent, intending to continue searching for a fort site after a short rest. But when we rose, Bucky had sunk six inches into the mud, and we had to unload half the crates before we could push him out. By the time we set out again, we were covered with mud and water.

"Now we can try Davern's plan of covering our coldsuits with mud," I said.

"We don't have much choice," Davern muttered.

Umber rose before we found a place to stop. Then we discovered that the lakes were not lifeless at all. By Umberlight, the stromatolites fluoresced with orange and black stripes. In spots, the water glowed carmine and azure, lit from underneath. We came to a good camping spot by a place where the lake bubbled and steam rose in clouds. But when the wind shifted and blew the steam our way, we nearly choked on the ammonia fumes. We staggered on, dizzy and nauseous.

The fort, I realized, was a solution to yesterday's problem. Staying put was not a good idea here, where we could be gassed in our sleep. We needed to be ready to move at a moment's notice.

Geysers of glowing, sulphur-scented spray erupted on either side of our path. We headed for a hummock that looked like a dry spot, but found it covered by a stomach-turning layer of wormlike organisms. We were forced to march through them, slippery and wriggling underfoot. As we crushed them, they made a sound at a pitch we couldn't hear. We sensed it as an itchy vibration that made us tense and short-tempered, but Sally was tormented till Seabird tied a strip of cloth over the coldsuit around her ears, making her look like an old woman in a scarf.

I didn't say so, but I was completely lost, and had been for some time. It was deep night and the water was freezing by now, but I didn't trust ice that glowed, so I stayed on the dwindling, switchback path. We were staggeringly weary by the time we reached the end of the road: on the tip of a peninsula surrounded by water. We had taken a wrong turn.

We stood staring out into the dark. It was several minutes before I could bring myself to say, "We have to go back."

Seabird broke down in tears, and Davern erupted like a geyser. "You were supposed to be the great guide and tracker, and all you've done is lead us to a dead end. You're totally useless."

Somehow, Anatoly summoned the energy to keep us from falling on each others' throats. "Maybe there's another solution." He shone his light out onto the lake. The other shore was clearly visible. "See, there's an ice path across. The whole lake isn't infested. Where it's black, the water's frozen solid."

"That could be just an island," I said.

"Tell you what, I'll go ahead to test the ice and investigate. You follow only if it's safe."

I could tell he was going to try it no matter what I said, so I made him tie a long rope around his waist, and anchored it to Bucky. "If you fall through, we'll pull you out," I said.

He stepped out onto the ice, testing it first with a tent pole. The weakest spot of lake ice is generally near shore, so I expected it to crack there if it was going to. But he got past the danger zone and kept going. From far out on the ice, he flashed his light back at us. "The ice is holding!" he called. "Give me more rope!"

There wasn't any more rope. "Hold on!" I called, then untied the tether from Bucky and wrapped it around my waist. Taking a tent pole, I edged out onto the ice where he had already crossed it. I was about thirty meters out onto the lake when he called, "I made it! Wait there."

He untied his end of the rope to explore the other side. I could not see if he had secured it to anything in case I fell through, so I waited as motionlessly as I could. Before long, he returned. "I'm coming back," he yelled.

I was a few steps from shore when the rope pulled taut, yanking me off my feet. I scrambled up, but the rope had gone limp. "Anatoly!" I screamed. Seabird and Davern shone their lights out onto the ice, but Anatoly was nowhere to be seen. I pulled in the rope, but it came back with only a frayed end.

"Stay here," I said to the others, then edged gingerly onto the ice. If he was in the water, there was a short window of time to save him. But as I drew closer to the middle, the lake under me lit up with mesmerizing colors. They emanated from an open pool of water that churned and burped.

The lake under the black ice had not been lacking in life. It had just been hungry.

When I came back to where the others were waiting, I shook my head, and Seabird broke into hysterical sobs. Davern sat down with his head in his hands.

I felt strangely numb, frozen as the land around us. At last I said, "Come on, we've got to go back."

Davern looked at me angrily. "Who elected *you* leader?"

"The fact that I'm the only one who can save your sorry ass," I said.

Without Anatoly's animating force, they were a pitiful sight—demoralized, desperate, and way too young. Whatever their worth as individuals, I felt a strong compulsion to avenge Anatoly's death by getting them back alive. In this land, survival was defiance.

I ordered Bucky to reverse direction and head back up the path we had come by. Seabird and Davern didn't argue. They just followed.

We had been retracing our steps for half an hour when I noticed a branching path I hadn't seen on the way out. "Bucky, stop!" I ordered. "Wait here," I told the others. Only Sally disobeyed me, and followed.

The track headed uphill onto a ridge between lakes. It had a strangely familiar look. When I saw Sally smelling at a piece of discarded trash, I recognized the site of our campsite on the way out. I stood in silence, as if at a graveyard. Here, Amal had played his mandolin and Anatoly had imagined songs of Umbernight. Edie had made Sally's coldsuit.

If we had just gone back instead of trying to cross the ice, we would have found our way.

I returned to fetch my companions. When Seabird saw the place, memories overwhelmed her and she couldn't stop crying. Davern and I set up the tent and heater as best we could, and all of us went inside.

"It's not fair," Seabird kept saying between sobs. "Anatoly was trying to save us. He didn't do anything to deserve to die. None of them did."

"Right now," I told her, "your job isn't to make sense of it. Your job is to survive."

Inwardly, I seethed at all those who had led us to expect the world to make sense.

We were ten hours away from the edge of the lakes, thirty hours of walking from home. Much as I hated to continue on through Umbernight, I wanted to be able to make a dash for safety when day came. Even after sleeping, Seabird and Davern were still tired and wanted to stay. I went out and shut off the heater, then started dismantling the tent to force them out.

The lakes glowed like a lava field on either side of us. From time to time, billows of glowing, corrosive steam enveloped us, and we had to hold our breaths till the wind shifted. But at least I was sure of our path now.

The other shore of the Mazy Lakes, when we reached it, was not lined with the towers and spires we had left on the other side; but when we pointed our lights ahead, we could see things scattering for cover. I was about to suggest that we camp and wait for day when I felt a low pulse of vibration underfoot. It came again, rhythmic like the footsteps of a faraway giant. The lake organisms suddenly lost their luminescence. When I shone my light on the water, the dark surface shivered with each vibration. Behind us, out over the lake, the horizon glowed.

"I think we ought to run for it," I said.

The others took off for shore with Sally on their heels. "Bucky, follow!" I ordered, and sprinted after them. The organisms on shore had closed up tight in their shells. When I reached the sloping bank, I turned back to look. Out over the lake, visible against the glowing sky, was a churning, coal-black cloud spreading toward us. I turned to flee.

"Head uphill!" I shouted at Davern when I caught up with him. Seabird was ahead of us; I could see her headlamp bobbing as she ran. I called her name so we wouldn't get separated, then shoved Davern ahead of me up the steep slope.

We had reached a high bank when the cloud came ashore, a toxic tsunami engulfing the low spots. Bucky had fallen behind, and I watched as he disappeared under the wave of blackness. Then the chemical smell hit, and for a while I couldn't breathe or see. By the time I could draw a lungful of air down my burning throat, the sludgy wave was already receding below us. Blinking away tears, I saw Bucky emerge again from underneath, all of his metalwork polished bright and clean. The tent that had been stretched over the crates was in shreds, but the crates themselves looked intact.

Beside me, Davern was on his knees, coughing. "Are you okay?" I asked. He shook his head, croaking, "I'm going to be sick."

I looked around for Seabird. Her light wasn't visible anymore. "Seabird!" I yelled, desperate at the thought that we had lost her. To my immense relief, I heard her voice calling. "We're here!" I replied, and flashed my light.

Sounds of someone approaching came through the darkness, but it was only Sally. "Where is she, Sally? Go find her," I said, but the dog didn't understand. I swept my light over the landscape, and finally spotted Seabird stumbling toward us without any light. She must have broken hers in the flight. I set out toward her, trying to light her way.

The Umberlife around us was waking again. Half-seen things moved just outside the radius of my light. Ahead, one of the creature-balls Amal and I had seen on the other side was rolling across the ground, growing as it moved. It was heading toward Seabird.

"Seabird, watch out!" I yelled. She saw the danger and started running, slowed by the dark. I shone my light on the ball, but I was too far away to have an effect. The ball speeded up, huge now. It overtook her and dissolved into a wriggling, scrabbling, ravenous mass. She screamed as it covered her, a sound of sheer terror that rose into a higher pitch of pain, then cut off. The mound churned, quivered repulsively, grew smaller, lost its shape. By the time I reached the spot, all that was left was her coldsuit and some bits of bone.

I rolled some rocks on top of it by way of burial.

Davern was staring and trembling when I got back to him. He had seen the whole thing, but didn't say a word. He stuck close to me as I led the way back to Bucky.

"We're going to light every lamp we've got and wait here for day," I said.

He helped me set up the lights in a ring, squandering our last batteries. We sat in the buggy's Umbershadow and waited for dawn with Sally at our feet. We didn't say much. I knew he couldn't stand me, and I had only contempt for him; but we still huddled close together.

To my surprise, Bucky was still operable when the dawn light revived his batteries. He followed as we set off up the Let's Go Valley, once such a pleasant land, now disfigured with warts of Umberlife on its lovely face. We wasted no time on anything but putting the miles behind us.

The sun had just set when we saw the wholesome glow of Feynman Habitat's yard light ahead. We pounded on the door, then waited. When the door cracked open, Davern pushed past me to get inside first. They welcomed him with incredulous joy, until they saw that he and I were alone. Then the joy turned to shock and grief.

There. That is what happened. But of course, that's not what everyone wants to know. They want to know *why* it happened. They want an explanation—what we did wrong, how we could have succeeded.

That was what the governing committee was after when they called me in later. As I answered their questions, I began to see the narrative taking shape in their minds. At last Anselm said, "Clearly, there was no one fatal mistake. There was just a pattern of behavior: naïve, optimistic, impractical. They were simply too young and too confident."

I realized that I myself had helped create this easy explanation, and my remorse nearly choked me. I stood up and they all looked at me, expecting me to speak, but at first I couldn't say a word. Then, slowly, I started out, "Yes. They were all those things. Naïve. Impractical. Young." My voice failed, and I had to concentrate on controlling it. "That's why we needed them. Without their crazy commitment, we would have conceded defeat. We would have given up, and spent the winter hunkered down in our cave, gnawing our old grudges, never venturing or striving for anything beyond our reach. Nothing would move forward. We needed them, and now they are gone."

Later, I heard that the young people of Feynman took inspiration from what I said, and started retelling the story as one of doomed heroism. Young people like their heroes doomed.

Myself, I can't call it anything but failure. It's not because people blame me. I haven't had to justify myself to anyone but this voice in my head—always questioning, always nagging me. I can't convince it: everyone fails.

If I blame anyone, it's our ancestors, the original settlers. We thought their message to us was that we could always conquer irrationality, if we just stuck to science and reason.

Oh, yes—the settlers. When we finally opened the crates to find out what they had sent us, it turned out that the payload was books. Not data—paper books. Antique ones. Art, philosophy, literature. The books had weathered the interstellar trip remarkably well. Some were lovingly inscribed by the settlers to their unknown descendants. Anatoly would have been pleased to know that the people who sent these books were not really rationalists—they worried about our aspirational well-being. But the message came too late. Anatoly is dead.

I sit on my bed stroking Sally's head. What do you think, girl? Should I open the book from my great-grandmother?

ABOUT THE AUTHORS

A Que was born in 1990 in Hubei province, and now lives in Chengdu. His work is regularly published in top magazines like Science Fiction World. He has won both Chinese Nebula and Galaxy Awards for his short fiction. His collection *Travel With My Dear Android* was published in 2015.

Baoshu is a Chinese science fiction and fantasy writer. After receiving his Master of Philosophy in Peking University, Baoshu continued to study at Katholieke Universiteit Leuven and got a second masters there, and finally became a full-time science fiction writer in 2012. His previous books include *What Has Passed Shall in Kinder Light Appear, Garuda, Ruins of Time,* and *Maharoga.*

Bo Balder lives and works close to Amsterdam. Bo is the first Dutch author to have been published in *F&SF, Clarkesworld, Analog,* and other places. Her science fiction novel "The Wan" was published by Pink Narcissus Press. When not writing, she knits, reads and gardens, preferably all three at the same time. For more about her work, visit boukjebalder.nl.

Born in the Caribbean, **Tobias S. Buckell** is a New York Times Bestselling and World Fantasy Award winning author. His novels and almost one hundred stories have been translated into nineteen different languages. He has been nominated for the Hugo Award, Nebula Award, World Fantasy Award, and Astounding Award for Best New Science Fiction Author. He currently lives in Ohio.

Mike Buckley is a widely-published short story writer whose work has appeared in national journals such as *The Alaska Quarterly Review, The Southern California Review, and Clarkesworld, Daily Science Fiction,* and *Escape Pod.* His work has been anthologized numerous times, including in *The Best American Non-Required Reading, 2003,* and the *Red Hen LA Writers Anthology.* His debut collection of short fiction, *Miniature Men,* was released in 2011.

Sue Burke is the author of the novels *Semiosis, Interference,* and *Immunity Index,* as well as short fiction and translations. Learn more at sueburke.site.

Eleanna Castroianni is a writer, poet, and oral storyteller from Greece. A cultural geographer by training, Eleanna tells stories from the margins of history and the far futures of the Anthropocene. Their words have also appeared in *Fireside, Strange Horizons, Beneath Ceaseless Skies, PodCastle,* and elsewhere.

Carolyn Ives Gilman is the author of four novels and over thirty works of short science fiction and fantasy. She has been nominated for the Nebula Award three times, and for the Hugo Award twice. Her first novel, *Halfway Human* (Avon), was an exploration of gender and society. Her most recent, *Dark Orbit* (Tor), is a space adventure that raises questions about consciousness and perception. Her short fiction has appeared in places such as *Tor.com, Clarkesworld,* and *Lightspeed,* and numerous "Best of the Year" anthologies. Her work has been translated into a dozen languages.

Gilman is also a historian who writes nonfiction about North American frontier and Native history. She currently works as a museum consultant, with her main contract being at the United States Capitol. She lives in Washington, DC.

Osahon Ize-Iyamu is a Nigerian writer of speculative fiction. He is a graduate of the Alpha Writers Workshop and IWP summer institute and has been published in *Nightmare, Strange Horizons,* and *FIYAH.* You can find him online @osahon4545.

Kij Johnson writes speculative and experimental literatures, and has won the Hugo, Nebula, and World Fantasy Awards and the Grand prox de l'Imaginaire, among others. She teaches fantasy and creative writing at the University of Kansas.

Cassandra Khaw is an award-winning game writer, and former scriptwriter at Ubisoft Montreal. Khaw's work can be found in places like *Fantasy & Science Fiction, Lightspeed,* and *Tor.com.* Khaw's first original novella, *Hammers on Bone,* was a British Fantasy award and Locus award finalist, and their novella, *Nothing But Blackened Teeth,* is published by Nightfire.

Julie Nováková is a scientist, educator and award-winning Czech author, editor and translator of science fiction, fantasy and detective stories. She published seven novels, one anthology, one story collection and over thirty short pieces in Czech. Her work in English appeared in *Clarkesworld, Asimov's, Analog,* and elsewhere. Her works have been translated into eight languages so far, and she translates Czech stories into English (in *Tor.com, Strange Horizons, F&SF, Clarkesworld,* and *Welkin Magazine*). She edited or co-edited an anthology of Czech speculative fiction in translation, *Dreams From Beyond,* a book of European SF in Filipino translation, *Haka,* an outreach ebook of astrobiological SF, *Strangest of All,* and its more ambitious follow-up print and e-book anthology *Life Beyond Us* (Laksa Media, upcoming in late 2022). Julie's newest book is a story collection titled *The Ship Whisperer* (Arbiter Press, 2020). She is a recipient of the European fandom's Encouragement Award and multiple Czech genre awards. She's active in science outreach, education and nonfiction writing, and co-leads the outreach group of the European Astrobiology Institute. She's a member of the XPRIZE Sci-fi Advisory Council.

Finbarr O'Reilly is an Irish speculative fiction writer. He has previously been published in *Clarkesworld, The Best Science Fiction of the Year, The Year's Best Science Fiction,* and *The Best of British Science Fiction.*

Finbarr has worked as a journalist for more than two decades and, like many Irish writers, lives in self-imposed exile. He currently resides with his wife and two children in a small English town, too far from the sound of gulls and the smell of saltwater.

Josh Pearce has stories and poetry in *Analog, Asimov's, Beneath Ceaseless Skies, Cast of Wonders, Clarkesworld, IGMS,* and *Nature.* He currently lives in California with his wife and sons, and can be found on Twitter: @fictionaljosh or at fictionaljosh.com. One time, Ken Jennings signed his chest.

Lettie Prell's science fiction often explores the edge where humans and their technology are increasingly merging. Her short stories have appeared in *WIRED, Tor.com, Clarkesworld, Analog, Apex,* and *Martian Magazine,* and reprinted in a number of anthologies, including *The Best American Science Fiction* and Fantasy and *The New Voices of Science Fiction.* Her work has been translated into a number of languages including Chinese, Japanese and Vietnamese. She is a life-long Midwesterner, and currently lives in Des Moines.

Robert Reed is the author of hundreds of published stories, quite a heap of novels, and perhaps most importantly, he is the owner and soul pilot of the Great Ship stories. Reed won a Hugo in 2007, for his novella, "A Billion Eves."

Erin Roberts is a Black speculative fiction writer who tells stories across formats. Her short fiction has appeared in publications including *Clarkesworld, Asimov's Science Fiction, Podcastle, The Dark,* and *THEN AGAIN: Vintage Photography Reimagined by One Artist and Thirty-One Writers* and been selected for three Year's Best anthologies. Her interactive fiction and game writing has been published or is forthcoming in *Sub-Q Magazine, Strange Horizons, Pathfinder Lost Omens: The Grand Bazaar,* and *Zombies, Run!*

Erin is a graduate of the Odyssey Writers Workshop, holds an MFA from the Stonecoast program at the University of Southern Maine, and is currently a Provost's Early Career Fellow at The University of Texas at Austin. She has been the recipient of grants and awards from the Maryland State Arts Council, Arts and Humanities Council of Montgomery County, and Speculative Literature Foundation, and will be a Writer in Residence at Hedgebrook in 2022. You can follow her on Twitter at @nirele and read more about her work at writingwonder.com.

Jack Skillingstead's *Harbinger* was nominated for a Locus Award for best first novel. His second novel, *Life on the Preservation,* was a finalist for the Philip K. Dick Award. *The Chaos Function,* a science fiction thriller, appeared from Houghton Mifflin Harcourt in 2019. He has published more than forty short stories to critical acclaim and was short-listed for the Theodore Sturgeon Memorial Award. Jack's first twenty-six stories are collected in *Are You There and Other stories.* He lives in Seattle with his wife, writer Nancy Kress, and a puppy named Pippin.

D.A. Xiaolin Spires steps into portals and reappears in sites such as Hawai'i, NY, various parts of Asia and elsewhere, with her keyboard appendage attached. Her work appears in publications such as *Clarkesworld, Analog, Strange Horizons, Nature, Terraform, Uncanny, Fireside, Galaxy's Edge, StarShipSofa, Andromeda Spaceways* (Year's Best Issue), *Diabolical Plots, Factor Four, Lady Churchill's Rosebud Wristlet, Grievous Angel, Toasted Cake, Pantheon, Outlook Springs, ROBOT DINOSAURS, Shoreline of Infinity, LONTAR, Mithila Review, Reckoning, Issues in Earth Science, Liminality, Star*Line, Polu Texni, Argot, Eye to the Telescope, Liquid Imagination, Little Blue Marble, Story Seed Vault,* and anthologies of the strange and beautiful: *Deep Signal, Ride the Star Wind, Sharp and Sugar Tooth, Broad Knowledge, Make Shift,* and *Battling in All Her Finery.* Select stories can be read in German, Spanish, Vietnamese, Estonian, French and Japanese translation. She can be found on Twitter: @spireswriter and on her website: daxiaolinspires.wordpress.com.

Natalia Theodoridou is the World Fantasy Award-winning and Nebula-nominated author of over a hundred stories published in *Uncanny, Strange Horizons, F&SF, Nightmare, Choice of Games,* and elsewhere. Find him at www.natalia-theodoridou.com, or follow @natalia_theodor on Twitter.

Genevieve Valentine is a novelist, comic book writer, and critic. Her short stories have appeared in over a dozen Best of the Year anthologies, including *Best American Science Fiction and Fantasy.*

Nicoletta Vallorani made her debut with *Il cuore finto di DR,* which won the Urania Prize in 1993 and was published in France by Rivages under the title *Replicante.* She has published novels with Einaudi and Mondadori. Her most recent novel, *Avrai i miei occhi* (Zona 42), won the Premio Italia 2021, and was selected for the Premio Campiello and the Premio Napoli.

Juliette Wade is insatiably curious, especially about language and culture. She is the author of the Broken Trust series from DAW, and of short fiction which has appeared in *Clarkesworld, Analog,* and *F&SF* magazines. She lives in the San Francisco Bay Area with her Aussie husband and her two sons, who support and inspire her.

Suzanne Walker is a Chicago-based writer and editor. She is co-creator of the Hugo-nominated graphic novel Mooncakes (2019, Lion Forge/Oni Press). Her short fiction has been published in *Clarkesworld* and *Uncanny Magazine,* and she has published nonfiction articles with *Uncanny Magazine, StarTrek.com, Women Write About Comics,* and the anthology *Barriers and Belonging: Personal*

Narratives of Disability. She has spoken at numerous conventions on a variety of topics ranging from disability representation in sci-fi/fantasy to comics collaboration. You can find her posting pictures of her cat and chronicling her longsword adventures on Twitter: @suzusaur.

Izzy Wasserstein is a queer and trans writer of fiction and poetry. She teaches writing, literature, and film classes at a public university in the American Midwest and shares her life with her spouse—the writer Nora E. Derrington—and their animal companions. Her work has appeared in *Apex, Beneath Ceaseless Skies, Fantasy,* and many other magazines and anthologies. Her debut short story collection is forthcoming in 2022 from Neon Hemlock Press. Her website is izzywasserstein.com.

Xia Jia (aka Wang Yao) is Associate Professor of Chinese Literature at Xi'an Jiaotong University and has been publishing speculative fiction since college. She is a seven-time winner of the Galaxy Award, China's most prestigious science fiction award and has published three science fiction collections (in Chinese): *The Demon-Enslaving Flask* (2012), *A Time Beyond Your Reach* (2017), and *Xi'an City Is Falling Down* (2018). She's also engaged in other science fiction related works, including academic research, translation, screenwriting, and teaching creative writing.

Xiu Xinyu is a writer living in Beijing who enjoys collecting stones, swimming in the sea and gorging on chocolate. She mostly uses her master degree in Philosophy to make up tragic novels.

E. Lily Yu is the author of the novel *On Fragile Waves,* as well as a forthcoming collection of stories, and the librettist of *Between Stars.* She received the Artist Trust LaSalle Storyteller Award in 2017 and the Astounding Award for Best New Writer in 2012. She has published over thirty-five stories in venues from *McSweeney's* to *Tor.com,* as well as twelve best-of-the-year anthologies, and they have been finalists for the Hugo, Nebula, Locus, Sturgeon, and World Fantasy Awards.

CLARKESWORLD CITIZENS

OFFICIAL CENSUS

We would like to thank the following Clarkesworld Citizens for their support:

Citizens

Nat A, A Fettered Mind, C A Morris, A Strange Loop, Michael Adams, Magnus Adamsson, Warren Adler, Alan & Jeremy VS Science Fiction, Rowena Alberga, Pete Aldin, Jacob Aldrich, Marianne Aldrich, Alexander, Elye Alexander, William Alexander, Alexi, A. Alfred Ayache, Richard Alison, Ed Allen, Joshua Allen, Alllie, Imron Alston, TJ Alston, Amelia, Ancestors Guide Me, Ro Anders, Clifford Anderson, Kim Anderson, Tor Andre, Dan Andresen, Anon, Author Anonymous, Antariksa, Dennis Anthony, Joseph Anthony Dixon, Aragos, ArbysMom, Ari&Eric&Tim, Therese Arkenberg, Sharon Arnette, Randall Arnold, Catherine Asaro, Ash, Stephen Astels, A. Alfred Ayache, David Azzageddi, Alan B., Bill B., Paul B. Joiner, B.H., Ray Bair, Benjamin Baker, Kate Baker, M-Jo Baker, Great Barbarian, Jenny Barber, Barlennan, Jennifer Barnes, Laura Barnitz, Dion Barrier, Johanne Barron, Charles Basner, Jeff Bass, Meredith Battjer, Anna Bauer-Baxter, John Baughman, Moya Bawden, Cheryl Beauchamp, Paul Becker, Aaron Begg, Deborah Bell, Ben, Judy Beningson, Matthew Bennardo, Tom Benton, LaNeta Bergst, Julie Berg-Thompson, Leon Bernhardt, Clark Berry, TJ Berry, Kevin Besig, Lovelyn Bettison, Steve Bickle, Amy Billingham, Tracey Bjorksten, John Blackman, Brett Blaikie, John Bledsoe, Mike Blevins, Adam Blomquist, Bluebuel, Dominykas Blyžė, Allison Bocksruker, Kevin Bokelman, Clare Boothby, Michael Bowen, Brian Bowes, Winfield Brackeen, Michael Braun Hamilton, Commander Breetai, Nathan Breit, Allan Breitstein, Cristiano Malanga Breuel, Don Bright, Jennifer Brissett, Mary Brock, Britny Brooks, Jeremy Brown, Kit Brown, Mark Brown, Richard Brown, Laurence Browning, Mark Brumbill, Tobias S. Buckell, Jacki Buist, Thomas Bull, Michael Bunkahle, Karl Bunker, Alison Burke, Cory Burr, Jefferson Burson, Kristin Buxton, Graeme Byfield, Bryce C, c9lewis, Andrew J Cahill, Darrell Cain, Caitrin, C.G. Cameron, Jo Campbell, Isabel Cañas,

Ricardo Canizares, Paul Carignan, Yazburg Carlberg, Liam Carpenter-Urquhart, Michael Carr, Carrie, Cast of Wonders, Nance Cedar, Celtgreenman, Greg Chapman, Timothy Charlton, David Chasson, Steve Chatterton, Catherine Cheek, Zichen Chen, Paige Chicklo, Joe Chip, Maria Cichetti, Diane Claire, Lázaro Clapp, Jeremy Clark, Maggie Clark, Victoria Cleave, Heather Clitheroe, Blair Cochran, Alicia Cole, Elizabeth Coleman, Greg Coleson, Marian Collins-Steding, Ian Collishaw, Elisabeth Colter, Che Comrie, Johne Cook, Claire Cooney, Martin Cooper, Lisa Costello, Thomas Costick, Ashley Coulter, Charles Cox, Michael Cox, Matt Craig, Sonya Craig, K Crain, Yoshi Creelman, John W Crispin, Katherine Crispin, Tina Crone, Kaitlin Crowley, Alan Culpitt, Cathy Cunliffe, Curtis42, Gary Cusick, Shawn D'Alimonte, Lorraine Dahm, Steve Dahnke, Shawn D'Alimonte, Sarah Dalton, Ang Danieldeskbrain - Watercress Munster, Gillian Daniels, Chua Dave, Morgan Davey, Ed Davidoff, Chase Davies, Katrina Davies, Craig Davis, Lee Davis, Gustavo de Albuquerque, Alessia De Gaspari, Del DeHart, Maria-Isabel Deira, Daniel DeLano, Dennis DeMario, Frank Den den Hartog, Pieter Derdeyn, Patrick Derrickson, Michele Desautels, Paul DesCombaz, Allison M. Dickson, Geri Diorio, Mark Dobson, Tsana Dolichva, Giu Domingues, Robert Dowrick, Aidan Doyle, dsbjr, DT, Alex Dunbar, Albert Dunberg, Susan Duncan, Andrew Eason, Roger East, Barbara Eastman, The Eaton Law Firm, Mela Eckenfels, David Eggli, Eileen, Jesse Eisenhower, Alamon Elf Defield, Sarah Elkins, Brad Elliott, Warren Ellis, Dale Eltoft, Steve Emery, Rick English, Douglas Engstrom, Lyle Enright, Peter Enyeart, Nancy Epperly, Eric, Erik, Collin Evans, Yvonne Ewing, EXO Books, Extranet Vendors Association, Edward Fagan, Feather, Denis Ferentinos, Ferretofmerit, Josiah Ferrin, Melina Filomia, Stephen Finch, Fixit, Jenna Fizel, Joseph Flotta, Rick Floyd, Ethan Fode, Dense Fog, Frank Fogarty, Vanessa Fogg, Chelsea Foreman, Francesca Forrest, Jason Frank, Carol Franko, Michael Fratus, Zachry Frazee, William Fred, Amy Fredericks, Amit Fridman, Michael Frighetto, Andrew Frigyik, Sarah Frost, Froxis, Fyrbaul, Max G, Jennifer Gagliardi, Paul Gainford, Robert Garbacz, Eleanor Gausden, Leslie Gelwicks, Mark Gerrits, Susan Gibbs, Phil Giles, Kate Gillogly, Rebecca Girash, Holly Glaser, Susanne Glaser, Sangay Glass, Globular, Tom Gocken, Eric Gomez, Martin Gonzalez, Laura Goodin, Don Grayson, Marc Grella, Grendel, Besha Grey, Valerie Grimm, Damien Grintalis, Janet Groenert, Tom Groff, Michael Grosberg, Nikki Guerlain, Xavier Guillemane, Shannon Guillory, Gaurav Gupta, Geoffrey Guthrie, Richard Guttormson, Jim Hagel, James Hall, Lee Hallison, Douglas Hamilton, AMD Hamm, Janus Hansen, Happybunnyatthezoo, Roy Hardin, Jonathan Harnum, Harpoon, Dan Harrington, Jubal Harshaw, Lou Hartman, Sarah Hartman, Ben Haskett, Pat Hauldren, Darren Hawbrook, Emily Hebert, Dean Heiford, Theresa A Hemminger, Leon Hendee, Jamie Henderson, Philip Henderson, Samantha Henderson, Dave Hendrickson, Steven Hennig, JC Henry, Steve Herman, Ann Hess, Karen Heuler, Dan Hiestand, John Higham, Renata Hill, Björn Hillreiner, Tim Hills, Mark Hinchman, Peter Hogberg, Peter Hollmer, Jesse Holmes, Melanie Hopes, Andrea Horbinski, Clarence Horne III, Brian Horner, Chris Horton, Richard Horton, Jon Hoskins, Bill Howell, Margaret Howie, Fiona Howland-Rose, Alexander Huberty, Roger Hudman, Matthew

Hudson, Pete Huerta, Rex Hughes II, Jeremy Hull, John Humpton, M. L. Hunt, Iain Hunter, Gene Hyers, Dwight Illk, Skye Im, John Imhoff, Inc, GRO Industries, Elisabeth M. H. Infield, Iridum Sound Envoy, Isbell, J.B. & Co., Joseph Jacir, Jack, Jack Myers Photography, Marie Jackson, Danya Jacob, Stephen Jacob, Sarah James, Michael Jarcho, Cristal Java, Jayarava, Joseph A Jechenthal III, Ciel Jennings, Jimbo, Jimi, JJ, Elizabeth Jo Otto, Dick Johnson, H Lynnea Johnson, Steve Johnson, Patrick Johnston, Laura Jolley, Garry Jolley-Rogers, Benjamin G. Jones, Judith Jones, Paul Jones, jschekker, Ryan H. Kacani, C. L. Kagmi, Gereon Kaiping, Gabriel Kaknes, Philip Kaldon, Alina Kanaski, KarlTheGood, Conner Kasten, Sara Kathryn, Chris Kattner, L Katz, Leah Katz, Cagatay Kavukcuoglu, Jonathan Kay, KC, Keenan, Jason Keeton, Kel.shire, Robert Keller, Mary Kellerman, Betty Kelly, Jared Kelsey, Kelson, Chris Kern, Shawn Keslar, John Kilgallon, KillZoneOZ, Dana Kincaid, Kisaki, Phil Klay, Kate Kligman, Kloster, Peter Knörrich, Bryan Knower, Seymour Knowles-Barley, Matthew Koch, Will Koenig, Marlon Koenigsberg, Peter Kolis, Konstantinos Kontos, Sean CW Korsgaard, Travis Kowalchuk, Frances KR, Lutz Krebs, John Krewson, Deb Krol, Heiti Kulmar, Derek Kunsken, Dale Kuykendall, MJ LA QUOC, Lacuna, Cam Laforest, Michele Laframboise, Jason Lai, Jan Lajka, Paul Lamarre, Brian Lambert, Dylan Lane, Gina Langridge, Scotty Larsen, Darren Ledgerwood, Brittany Lehman, Robert Lehman, Terra Lemay, Annaliese Lemmon, Lena, Wayne Lester, Andrew Levin, Philip Levin, Brian Lewis, Iver Lewis, Ao-Hui Lin, Steve Lindauer, Danielle Linder, Matthew Line, Simon Litten, Jerry Little, Susan Llewellyn, Renata M Lloyd, Jay Lofstead, Lornak, Thomas Loyal, Luke, Sharon Lunde, Donald Lutz, James Lyle, Alex M, Tim M, Christopher M McKeever, Robert Mac, Meredyth Mackay, Peter MacMillin, Sven-Hendrik Magotsch, Ilia Malkovitch, Raegan Mann, Cat Manning, Dan Manning, Margaret, Ann Margulies, Marius the Mage, Mariusmule, Mark, R. Mark Jones, Ivan Markos, Marlene, Eric Marsh, Jacque Marshall, John Marshall, Ray Marshall, Tony Marsico, Dominique Martel, Janet Martin, Fernando Martinez, Cethar Mascaw, Daniel Mathews, Daniel Maticzka, Matthew, Delvon Mattingly, David Mayes, William Mayson, Derek W McAleer, Mike McBride, Robert J. McCarter, T.C. McCarthy, Andrew Mcculloch, Jeffrey McDonald, Susan McDonough-Wachtman, Holly McEntee, Josh McGraw, Demitrius McHugh, Roland McIntosh, Mary Means, Steve Medina, Brent Mendelsohn, Kristen Menichelli, Regan Mercer, Seth Merlo, Sol Meyer, Michelle, Stephen Middleton, John Midgley, Matthew Miller, Stephan Miller, Terry Miller, Claire Miller Skriletz, Alan Mimms, Serene Mirkis, Dale Mitchell, mjpearce, Moritz Moeller-Herrmann, Aidan Moher, David Moore, Marian Moore, Tim Moore, Sunny Moraine, Griffin Morgan, Jamie Morgan, DJ Morrison, Jon Moss, Lynette Moss, Robina Moyer, Tomasz Mrozewski, Patricia Murphy, Lori Murray, Karl Myers, Mike Myers, Nadine, Derek Nason, Keegan Neave, Leona Nette, Glenn Nevill, Jeffrey Newman, Stella Nickerson, Matthew Nielsen, Robyn Nielsen, Richard Nishimura, Elaine Nobbs, Val Nolan, Christopher Norberg, Norm, Tom Nosack, Robert Nowak, Zam Nuclear Wesell, Nicholas Nykamp, Hugh J. O'Donnell, Brett O'Meara, Ruth O'Neill, David Oakley, Jennifer OBoyle, Jon O'Brien, Oddscribe, Scott Oesterling, Christopher Ogilvie, Daniel Ohanian, James Oliver,

Lydia Ondrusek, Reed O'Neal, Erik Ordway, Dan Osborne, Aaron Osgood-Zimmerman, Felicia Osullivan, Nancy Owens, Moe P, P.C., Thomas Pace, Simon Page, Norman Paley, Mieneke Pallada, Amparo Palma Reig, Clifford Parrish, Thomas Parrish, Paula, Andrea M. Pawley, PD, Sidsel Pedersen, Edgar Penderghast, Tzum Pepah, Chris Perkins, Sara Pfaff, Nikki Philley, Jeremy Phillips, Aimee Picchi, Adrian-Teodor Pienaru, Rebecca Pierce, Jeff Pink, Jamison Pinkert, Adam Piper, Beth Plutchak, Merja Polvinen, Andy Pond, David Potter, Prettydragoon, Ed Prior, Jon Pruett, David Raco, Žarko Radulović, Mahesh Raj Mohan, Adam Rakunas, Ralan, Steve Ramey, Diego Ramos, Dale Randolph Bivins, Madeline Ray, Tansy Rayner Roberts, Robert Redick, George Reilly, Steven Reneau, Renmeleon, Joshua Reynolds, Julia Reynolds, Rick of the North, Zach Ricks, Carl Rigney, Jorge A. Rivera, Ashley Rivers, Robert, Hank Roberts, Tansy Roberts, Kenneth Robkin, Ronald Rogers, Chris Ronderos, James Rowh, RPietila, Sarah Rudek, Oliver Rupp, Paul Rush, Caitlin Russell, Abigail Rustad, Ryan, Michael Ryan, Stephen Ryner Jr., Clayton Sallade, S2 Sally, Tim Sally, Sam, Samantha, Samuel, Sanders, Larry Sandhaas, Nadia Sandren, Jason Sanford, Juan Sanmiguel, Saskia, Maria Pia Sass, Erica L. Satifka, Steven Saus, SausageMix, MJ Scafati, David Schaller, Gregory Scheckler, Chris Schierer, Gabe Schirvar, Ken Schneyer, Nancy Schrock, Jason Schroeder, Don Schwartz, Gerald Schwartz, Graham Scott, Seeds in the Wind, Maral Seyed Ali Agha, Richard Shapiro, Kieran Sheldon, Espana Sheriff, T. L. Sherwood, Udayan Shevade, Josh Shiben, Heather Shipman, Kel Shire, Robert Shuster, Tom Sidebottom, Josh Simons, Aileen Simpson, Taylor Simpson, Siyi, Claire Miller Skriletz, John Skylar, Kate Small, Josh Smift, Brilee Smith, Rebecca Smith, Karen Snyder, Allison Sommers, Morgan Songi, Søren, Michelle Souliere, Álex Souza, Jozef Sovcik, Dr SP Conboy-Hil, Elisabeth Spalding, Mat Spalding, Gary Spears, Elwood Spencer, Julian Spergel, Carl Spicer, Stephen Sprusansky, Zachary Stansell, Chris Stave, Keith Stebor, Claire Stevenson, Lisa Stone, Stone, Blake Stone-Banks, Jennifer Stufflebeam, Julia Sullivan, Scott Sullivan, Jennifer Sutton, Fredrik Svensson, Jherek Swanger, John Swartzentruber, Swole Little My, Kenneth Takigawa, Charles Tan, William Tank, Beth Tanner, Jesse Tauriainen, David Taylor, Paul Taylor, Teck, Tessler, The Unsettled Foundation, TheBigWeeHag, Colin Theys, James Thomas, Brent Thompson, Peter D. Tillman, Brett Tofel, Jaye Tomas, Sharon Tomasulo, Felix Troendle, Steven Tu, Diane Turnshek, Chris Urie, Talie Van Groeningen, Julia Varga, John Vassar, Adam Vaughan, Nuno Veloso, William Vennell, Kenneth VenOsdel, David Versace, Vettac, Theodore Vician, Ortija Vitola, Derek W McAleer, Alan Walker, Walker, Matthew C Walker, Shiloh Walker, Diane Walton, Jo Lindsay Walton, K.E. Walton, Stefan Walzer, Robert Wamble, Bobbi Warburton, John Watrous, Matthew J Weaver, Nat Weinham, Robert Werner, Neil Weston, Peter Wetherall, Adam White, Mr. Robin White, Spencer Wightman, Dan Wilburn, Jeff Williamson, Neil Williamson, Nicola Willis, Willoughby, Willowcabins, Kristyn Willson, A.C. Wise, Devon Wong, Woodworking Running Dog, Mr J R Woroniecki, Chalmer Wren, Dan Wright, Kevin Wynn, Anna Y. Baskina, Isabel Yap, Joe Yaremchuk, Lachlan Yeates, Catherine York, Zackie, Barbara Zagajšek, Rena Zayit, Peter Zeller, Frederick Zorn, Stephanie Zvan

Burgermeisters

7ony, Daniel A Kaplan, Rob Abram, Paula Acton, Adam, Andy Affleck, Donald Ahalt, Rowena Alberga, Frederick Amerman, Carl Anderson, Mel Anderson, Randall Andrews, Daniel Andrlik, Andy90, Marie Angell, John Appel, Misha Argall, Karl Armstrong, Jon Arnold, Bruce Arthurs, Catherine Asaro, Mike R D Ashley, Robert Avie, Chris Aylott, Joe B., Mr. B., Erika Bailey, Michael W. Baily, Brian Baker, Jim Baker, Nathan Bamberg, Michael Banker, Jay Barnes, Laura Barnitz, Patricia Barrett, Jennifer Bartolowits, Andrew and Kate Barton, Kate Barton, Anna Y. Baskina, Deborah Beale, Jeffrey Allan Beeler, Lenni Benson, Kerry Benton, Leon Bernhardt, TJ Berry, Matt Bewley, Bill Bibo Jr, Steve Bickle, Edward Blake, Samuel Blinn, Jeff Boardman, Johanna Bobrow, Kaye Bohemier, David Boldt, Greg Bossert, Joan Boyle, Big Brain, Brakeparts1234, Patricia Bray, Tim Brenner, Brodonalds, Arrie Brown, Ken Brown, BruceC, Brian Brunswick, Carl Brusse, Sharat Buddhavarapu, Garret Buell, Max Buffington, Adam Bursey, Jeremy Butler, Robyn Butler, Roland Byrd, Jarrett Byrnes, Janice Calm, Brad Campbell, Paul Cancellieri, Anthony R. Cardno, Carleton45, James Carlino, Nicholas Carney, Ted Carr, Benjamin Cartwright, LeRoy Cassidey, Evan Cassity, Sean Cassity, Lee Cavanaugh, Eleanor Cawte, Peter Charron, Randall Chertkow, Farai Chideya, Michael Chorman, Maria Cichetti, cin3ma, Patrick Ciriello, Maggie Clark, Matthew Claxton, Cary Cohan, Marian Collins-Steding, Theodore Conti, George Cook, Brian Cooksey, Brenda Cooper, Lorraine Cooper, Lisa Cox, Matt Craig, James S Cullen, Lucy Cummin, Cezar Damian, Gillian Daniels, Dasroot, David, Nicholas V David, James Davies, Pamela J. Davis, Tessa Day, De, Jetse de Vries, Brian Deacon, Bartley Deason, Benjamin Deering, Ricado Delacruz, Keith DePew, John Devenny, Peter Dibble, Lindsey Dillon, Dino, Fran Ditzel-Friel, Gary Dockter, Nicholas Doran, Christopher Doty, Nicholas Dowbiggin, Robert Drabek, Sage Draculea, Paul Dzus, Mela Eckenfels, Eileen, Steve Emery, Sagi Eppel, Thomas Ericsson, Christine Ertell, Joanna Evans, Patricia Evans, B D Fagan, Matthew Farrer, Dietrich Faust, Rare Feathers, David Finkelstein, Tea Fish, Rosemary Fisher, Tony Fisk, FlatFootedRat, Bruce Fleischer, Lynn Flewelling, Adrienne Foster, Keith M Frampton, James Frederick Leach, Matthew Fredrickson, Alina Fridberg, John Fritsche, Eric Fritz, Jerry Gaiser, Elia Gar, Christopher Garry, Pierre Gauthier, Drue Gawel, Gerhen, Mark Gerrits, Bita Ghaffari, Caroline Gillam, Tanya Glaser, Lorelei Goelz, Ed Goforth, Melanie Goldmund, Martin Gonzalez, Inga Gorslar, Peter Goyen, Tony Graham, Jaq Greenspon, Eric Gregory, Marc Grella, Jessica Griffith, Ryan Grigor, Stephanie Gunn, Russell Guppy, Jim H, Zachary Haddenham, Laura Hake, AMD Hamm, Skeptyk/JeanneE Hand-Boniakowski, Mark S Haney, Jordan Hanie, John Hanley, Alan Hazelden, Joseph Heizman, Helixa 12, Normandy Helmer, Theresa A Hemminger, Daniel Herman, Buddy Hernandez, Corydon Hinton, Jon Hite, Elizabeth Hocking, Sheridan Hodges, Beth Hoffman, Ronald Hordijk, Fawn M Horvath, Justin Howe, Bobby Hoyt, David Hudson, Benito Huerta, Huginn and Muninn, Chris Hurst, Brit Hvide, Kevin Ikenberry, Joseph Ilardi, Joe Iriarte, Adam Israel, Jalal, Patty Jansen, Michael Jarcho, Jason, Cristal Java, JC, Toni Jerrman, David John Sewell, Audra Johnson, Erin Johnson, Russell Johnson, Robert Jones, Virginia Jud, Kai Juedemann, Andy Kaden, C. L. Kagmi, Jeff Kapustka, David Kelleher, James Kelly, Jim Kelly, Kennedy, Barbara Kerr, Brian Keves, K. L. Keyserling, Joshua Kidd, Alistair Kimble, Harvey King, Eben Kirksey, Erin Kissane, John Klima, Cecil Knight,

Michelle Knowlton, KP-ShadowSquirrel, Frances KR, Eric Kramer, JR Krebs, Chris Kreuter, Neal Kushner, Darren Laberee, Stephane Lacoste, Jan Lajka, Brian Lambert, Andrew Lanker, Kevin Lauderdale, Krista Leahy, Kate Lechler, Robert Lehman, Alan Lehotsky, Leland, Annaliese Lemmon, Walter Leroy Perkins, L Leslie, Edit Leventon, Philip Levin, Kirby Li, Kevin Liebkemann, Ao-Hui Lin, Mike Lindsey, Grá Linnaea, Jerry Little, Joyce E Lively, James Lloyd, Gavin Lobo, Travis Love, Susan Loyal, Kristi Lozano, Dimitri Lundquist, LUX4489, Alicia Lynch, Cory Lyon, Peter Mackey, Bob Magruder, Erin M Maloney, Adam Mancilla, Brit Mandelo, Cat Manning, Mark Maris, Marlene, Matthew Marovich, Marqman, Andrew Marsh, Eric Marsh, Aaron Marshall, Samuel Marzioli, Luke Mattheis, Jason Maurer, Rosaleen McCarthy, Peter McClean, Michael McCormack, Barrett L McCormick, Sean McFall, Tony McFee, Mark McGarry, Ace McInturff, Robyn McIntyre, Doug McLaughlin, Andrew McLeod, Craig McMurtry, Oscar McNary, Margery Meadow, Jim Mehnert, J Meijer, Geoffrey Meissner, Barry Melius, Kristen Menichelli, Sarfo Mensah, Alan Merriam, David Michalak, Mike, James Miles, Dave Miller, Scott Miller, Robert Milson, Dale Mitchell, Sharon Mock, Eric Mohring, Jacob Molaro, Samuel Montgomery-Blinn, Lyda Morehouse, Griffin Morgan, Rebekah Murphy, John Murray, N M Wells Foundry Creative Media, Margaret N. Oliver, S. Kay Nash, Will Nash, Patrick Neary, Dan Newland, Alan Newman, Barrett Nichols, Tishangela Nierman, Jennifer Noga, Val Nolan, Jenn Sam Norberg, Peter Northup, Sean O'Brien, Vince O'Connor, Vince O'Connor, Jason Ogdahl, Am Onymous, Stian Ovesen, David Packer, Simon Page, Justin Palk, Norman Papernick, Richard Parks, Paivi Pasi, Paula, MJ Paxton, PBC Productions Inc., Katherine Pendill, Henry Vizurraga Peteet, Matt Peterson, Mark Phagan, Eric Pierson, Janayna Pin, E. PLS, Lolt Proegler, Jonathan Pruett, QLM Aria X-Perienced, Robert Quinlivan, Thomas Rado, Parker Ragland, Rainspan, Lori Ramey, D Randall Kerr, Joel Rankin, Sherry Rehm, Erin Reilley, Dixon Reuel, Paul Rice, Zack Richardson, James Rickard, Karsten Rink, Richard Roberts, Anthony Rogers, Emily Rohrig, Chip Roland, Erik Rolstad, Joseph Romel, Leena Romppainen, Tim Rose, Sophia Ross, Lisa Rubio, Michael Russo, Miranda Rydell, Jenn Sam Norberg, Mike Sanders, Larry Sandhaas, Juan Sanmiguel, Matthew Saunders, Patrick Savage, J Scott Scheeler, Stefan Scheib, Alan Scheiner, Ken Schneyer, Eric Schreiber, Patricia G Scott, Terriell Scrimager II, Seeds in the Wind, Bluezoo Seven, Cosma Shalizi, George Shea, Mike Sherling, Jeremy Showers, Lisa Shumaker, Eric Simmons, Siznax, John Skillingstead, Patrick Joseph Sklar, Josh Smift, JR Smith, Rue Smith, Allen Snyder, David Sobyra, Daniel Solis, Caitlin Sticco, Lisa Stone, Jason Strawsburg, Stuart, Keffington Studios, Jerome Stueart, Robert Stutts, Fredrik Svensson, Patrick Sweetman, Portia X.Y. Tang, Gregory Taylor, Margaret Taylor, W. Taylor, Maurice Termeer, Tero, Chantal Thomas, Daniel Thomas, John Thomas, Brent Thompson, Gavin Thomson, Chuck Tindle, Raymond Tobaygo, Tradeblanket.com, Kima Traynham, Heather Tumey, Mary A. Turzillo, Aaron Umetani, Jitendra Vaidya, Ann VanderMeer, Matthew Varga, Andrew Vega, Sam Veltre, Nick Ventricelli, Emil Volcheck, Andrew Volpe, Margaret Wack, Wendy Wagner, Ralph Wahlstrom, Alan Walker, Jonathan Wallace, Mark Walsh, Jennifer Walter, Rob Ward, Tom Waters, Tehani Wessely, Liz Westbrook-Trenholm, John Whitaker, Chris White, Shannon White, Dan Wick, John Wienstroer, Kristine Wildman, David Williams, Seth Williams, Kristyn Willson, Paul Wilson, Dawn Wolfe, Wombat, Sarah Wright, Isabel Yap, Zackie, Peter Zeller, Zig111, Slobodan Zivkovic

Royalty

Pandora A Young, Paul Abbamondi, Eric Agnew, Jonathan Alden, Albert Alfiler, Dan Allen, Rose Andrew, Anonymous, Karl Armstrong, Bruce Arthurs, Rush Austin, Randy Avis, Raymond Bair, Jim Baker, Kathryn Baker, Lukas Karl Barnes, Anne Barringer, Zach Bartlett, Catherine Beach, David Beaudoin, Randall Beeman, Nathan Beittenmiller, Ralf Belling, Kevin Best, Brian Bilbrey, Nicolas Billon, Nathan Blumenfeld, BoloMKXXVIII, Marty Bonus, David Borcherding, Robert Bose, brakeparts1234, Palanda Brownlow, Brian Brunswick, Nancy Buford, John Burkitt, Karen Burnham, Anders Cahill, Heather Cailaoife, Robert Callahan, Carrie, Mackenzie Case, Lady Cate, Brad Cavallo, A Chambers, Richard Chappell, Joseph M Christopher, John Chu, Heather Clitheroe, Tania Clucas, Chad Colopy, Carolyn Cooper, Darcy Cox, Tom Crosshill, Michael Cullinan, Andrew Curry, Kathy Cygnarowicz, Darren Davidson, David Demers, James Denman, Cory Doctorow, Brian Dolton, JS Draper, Dayne Encarnacion, Marcello Fabrizi, Matthew Farrer, Kathy Farretta, Stephen Finch, Sean Flanagan, Greg Frank, William Frankenhoff, David Furniss, Jennifer Gagliardi, John Garberson, Brian Gardner, Kate Gillogly, Alexis Goble, Hilary Goldstein, Nithia Govender, Adam Haapala, Michael Habif, David Hall, Jonathan Harvey, Carl Hazen, Andy Herrman, Brendan Hickey, Robin Hill, Kristin Hirst, Colin Hitch, Ian Hobson, Victoria Hoke, Marolynn Holloway, Jeppe V Holm, Todd Honeycutt, Jason House, Morgan Howell, David Hoyt, Nancy Huntingford, ianwillc, inane raving, Christopher Irwin, James Jackson, Willie Jackson, Marcus Jager, Erskine James, Justin James, Stephen Jenkins, Linda Jenner, Mary Jo Rabe, Janna Jones, Jennifer Joseph, Virginia Jud, Gereon Kaiping, Youriy Karadjov, Robert Kennedy, Fred Kiesche, Kenji Klein, Corey Knadler, Matthew Kressel, G.J. Kressley, Ugur Kutay, Jamie Lackey, Jonathan Laden, M. Lane, Abby Larkin, Abigail Larkin, Katherine Lee, Ilia Levin, Jeffrey Lewis, Marta Lillo, Dave Lister, Warren Litwin, Justin Livernois, Vincent P Loeffler III, Jack Londen, Kevin Lyda, Osborne Lytle, Robert MacAnthony, Pete Macfarlane, Edward MacGregor, Ross MacLean, Bob Magruder, Phil Margolies, Sean Markey, Andrew Marsh, Carroll Mary, Arun Mascarenhas, Marcella Massa, Daniel Maticzka, Gabriel Mayland, Wes McConnell, Barrett McCormick, Matthew McKay, Kevin McKean, Margaret McNally, Glori Medina, Michelle Broadribb MEG, Dave Miller, Lucy Mitchell, Carlos Mondragón, Nayad Monroe, James Moore, Kat Morgan, Jennifer Morrow, James Morton, Ellen Moskowitz, Anne Murphy, Jennifer Navarrete, Patrick Neary, Stephen Nelson, Persona Non-Grata, Charles Norton, David M Oswin, H. Lincoln Parish, Marie Parsons, Rational Path, Lars Pedersen, David Personette, George Peter Gatsis, Matt Peterson, Joshua Pevner, Matt Phelps, Karsten Philip Aichholz, Jeremy Phillips, Gary Piserchio, Merja Polvinen, Lord Pontus, Mr. Potato, Ian Powell, Kevin Quagliano, Rossen Raykov, Andrew Read, James Red, Captain Red Boots, Corey Redlien, Wesley Reeves, Patrick Reitz, Rik, RL, Rob, Kelly Robson, Jenny Ross, Peter Roy, DF Ryan, John Scalzi, Anthony Schleizer, Scroggie, Stu Segal, Carol Seger, Maurice Shaw, Ross Shaw, Jan Shawyer, Bill Shields, Madeleine Shopoff, Gabrielle Silverman, Angela Slatter, Saskia Slottje,

Carrie Smith, Paul Smith, Samuel Smith, Nicholas Sokeland, Richard Sorden, Cheryl Souza, Kevin Standlee, Neal Stanifer, Chris Stave, Bobbie Steinkraus, Naru Sundar, Jonathon Sutton, SuzB, John Swartzentruber, Jeremy Tabor, S. Rheannon Terran, Colin Theys, Bailey Thomas, Kim Thomas, Josh Thomson, TK, Terhi Tormanen, Andre Twupack, Marc Tyler, Sam van Rood, Az Vedye, David Versace, Saoirse Victeoiria, Natalie Vincent, Suzanne Vowles, Daniel Waldman, Jonathan Wallace, Jasen Ward, Izzy Wasserstein, Ian Watson, Taema Weiss, Bradley Wells, Weyla & Gos, Graeme Williams, Jessica Wolf, Zac Wong, Matt Wyndowe, Jeff Xilon, Bob Z, Zola

Overlords

Aarnold Aardvark, Renan Adams, Thomas Ball, Michael Blackmore, Adina Bogert-O Brien, Adina Bogert-O'Brien, Nathalie Boisard-Beudin, Greg Bossert, Shawn Boyd, Mark Bradford Sr., Jennifer Brozek, Vicki Bryan, Karen Burnham, George C Mable, M C VanderSchaaf, Barbara Capoferri, Paul Chadwick, Clarke Chapman, Gio Clairval, Tania Clucas, Gregory Copenhaver, Andrew Curry, Dolohov, ebooks-worldwide, Sairuh Emilius, Lynne Everett, Joshua Faulkenberry, Fabio Fernandes, Benjamin Figueroa, Tony Fisk, Thomas Fleck, Eric Francis, Overperson Franklin, Brian Gardner, L A George, Michael Glyde, Alex Gragg, Bryan Green, Hank Green, Michael Habif, Andrew Hatchell, Berthiaume Heidi, Melissa House, Bill Hughes, Chris Hyde, Jacel the Thing, Marcus Jager, Justin James, Jericho, jfly, jkapoetry, Larry Johnson, James Joyce, Lucas Jung, Gayathri Kamath, Alina Kanaski, Youriy Karadjov, James Kinateder, Jay Kominek, Alice Kottmyer, Sarah L., Daniel LaPonsie, Susan Lewis, Sarah Liberman, Edward MacGregor, Philip Maloney, Paul Marston, Gabriel Mayland, Patrick McCann, Joe McTee, MJ Mercer, Achilleas Michailides, Adrian Mihaila, Adrien Mitchell, Overlord Mondragon, Cheryl Morgan, James Morton, MrMovieZombie, Jose Muinos, Stephen Nelson, Joshua Newth, Frederick Norwood, Dlanod Nosreetp, Richard Ohnemus, Andrea Pawley, Mike Perricone, Jody Plank, Clarissa R., Rick Ramsey, Thomas Reed, Jo Rhett, Rik, Jason Sank, Laura Schmidt, Lorenz Schwarz, Joseph Sconfitto, Marie Shcherbatskaya, SK, Sky, Tara Smith, Theodore J. Stanulis, David Steffen, Naru Sundar, Matthew the Greying, Robert Urell, Thad Wilkinson, Elaine Williams, James Williams, Richard Wyatt, Doug Young

Deities

Claire Alcock, Bruce, Kenneth Burk, Daniel Clanton, Eric Hunt, Gary Hunter, Robert Munsch, Rajeev Prasad, Kelvin Tse

ABOUT CLARKESWORLD

Clarkesworld Magazine (clarkesworldmagazine.com) is a monthly science fiction and fantasy magazine first published in October 2006. They have received three Hugo Awards, one World Fantasy Award, and a British Fantasy Award. Their fiction has been nominated for or won the Hugo, Nebula, World Fantasy, Sturgeon, Locus, Shirley Jackson, WSFA Small Press and Stoker Awards. For information on how to subscribe to our electronic edition on your Kindle, Nook, iPad or other ereader/Android device, please visit: clarkesworldmagazine.com/subscribe/

The stories in this anthology were edited by:

Neil Clarke (neil-clarke.com) is the editor of *Clarkesworld Magazine* and *Forever Magazine*, owner of Wyrm Publishing, and a nine-time Hugo Award Nominee for Best Editor (short form). His anthologies include *Upgraded, Galactic Empires, Touchable Unreality, More Human Than Human, The Final Frontier, The Eagle Has Landed,* and Best Science Fiction of the Year series. He currently lives in NJ with his wife and two sons.

Sean Wallace is a founding editor at *Clarkesworld Magazine*, owner of Prime Books, and winner of the World Fantasy Award. He currently lives in Maryland with his wife and two daughters.

Made in the USA
Columbia, SC
17 July 2022

63589619R00250